COLD HARD CASH

TRAIN RIDIN'

V. J. NICHOLAS

1

The alarm woke Jaeger up at six in the morning. As he rolled out of bed and went downstairs it gradually hit him that this could be the last morning of his life. The coffee was already in the process of its drip as he turned on the TV and poured his cereal and watched the events of the day drone on.

He was to meet with Ortega later on in the day to complete the transaction. So far as he could determine he was still in the driver's seat, but at any moment Dame Fortune could switch sides in an instant. Given what he'd learned of Ortega in the last six months, Ortega would see to it that Jaeger played ball in Ortega's Ball Park, using his bat, ball, gloves and rules, which was a fluid thing at best.

Ortega would promise anything to retrieve the plans for the Embraer commercial aircraft and the money, but Jaeger had worked for the man long enough to know that Ortega never kept a promise he didn't want to keep. No compromise was ever possible with the man, because in his world, everything was a zero sum game. For every winner gave birth to a loser.

No forgiveness was ever possible for perceived betrayal and Ortega had no intentions that Jaeger would see another sunrise. This had little to do with the business at hand it was purely personal. Never mind that Ortega's attempt at killing Jaeger in Sao Paulo was completely reversed and it was Jaeger who came back from Brazil alone and in possession of the stolen aircraft plans. That didn't matter, for Ortega would never allow himself to be bested in anything.

As Jaeger sat there on his barstool drinking his coffee, he thought about his life thus far. Joining the Marines early on to escape an overbearing father, he lived several lifetimes compressed in his brief career. Followed by his year at the University of Texas and his walk on role with the football program ending with fame and glory only to be overshadowed by the execution of his family. His conviction for their murder. His years in Huntsville Prison, yet another lifetime of experiences. His unexpected release. His years as a bounty hunter working for Rafferty. Then the gift of those who murdered his family finding a bitter end on a mountaintop overlooking the Rio Grande River. Finally his brief relationship with Melanie O'Bannon. The only woman he would ever love. He'd left her to shield her and her son from Ortega. Had he known of their relationship it would have eventually meant their death at some point. Should he ever emerge from all of this he had to make things right.

He went back upstairs with a refill of his coffee and went to his clothes closet, separated the clothes and opened the interior sliding door, built long ago, revealing his mini armory. Scanning his array of weaponry, he selected two .25 caliber automatics as backup pieces to be worn in ankle holsters. Then he selected a box of explosive shells of the same caliber, guaranteed to penetrate a Kevlar vest then explode. Good for the close up work that was certain to be at hand.

The time for words was long past, and Ortega was a man of few words anyway. He next extracted his "Old Equalizers", from the inner sanctum, one for each forearm. His one off specially crafted forearm shot guns, chambered for the .12 gauge shell, with four barrels per arm. He connected a fresh 9 volt battery to each one strapped to his forearms unloaded, setting the trigger mechanism to the firing position. Then he went to the bathroom and stood in front of the mirror and stood in front of the mirror. He practiced over and over the slow move of shaking hands as Ortega approached. Curl the wrist inward, pressing the first of the four slender firing rods connected to the electronic firing device and the outer barrel would fire. Curl the wrist outward and the inner barrel would fire. The two barrels flanking them would be similarly engaged by the opposite firing motions. He went through three test runs on each arm and after hearing the desired click of the firing pin each time was satisfied of their function ability. The devil was always in the details. He'd but only one occasion to use it in the past, when he was bringing back a runner from Villa Acuna just across the Rio Grande. In a crowded alleyway surrounded by six men all intent on keeping him from bringing back his prisoner, they received the surprise of their soon to be over lives as his forearms erupted in flames and in the space of less than five seconds, all lay dying in that dirty alley as Jaeger rushed to extinguish his burning shirtsleeves. Leaving a muted testament of the perils of .12 gauge double ought buckshot.

God only knows how many of Ortega's men he would bring to the party, but at least Ortega would be the first to check out.

Next he reached for the maroon colored Kevlar shirt specially tailored to have larger than average sleeves to accommodate the forearm weapons. The Kevlar ended at the elbow with normal cloth of a similar hue stitched to the main body of sleeve meant for destruction. Learning from his previous experience he had the sleeves coated with a fire retardant. The shirt was to be loose fitting and tucked inside his trousers waist band as was his custom, to visibly indicate that he was carrying no hidden weapons.

He then took his morning shower and shaved. After he emerged he went to the four large briefcases and examined them. Inside were copies of the original Embraer plans, copied by his friend Rae on paper specially designed to disintegrate forty eight hours after printing. Since they were printed fifteen hours ago they would shortly be of little use to anyone. Finally inside of each briefcase was a pound of carefully fitted Semtex explosive into each briefcase, triggered by a dual trigger mechanism attached to the locking mechanism. Any attempt to open any of the cases would be met with a rather nasty surprise. Only Jaeger knew the bypass combination. They were Ortega's briefcases, so he knew the original combination. Three briefcases with soon to be useless plans and one with the payoff money that was conveniently not paid to the agent on the hotel in Sao Paulo, but resting with Rae at his office in town, along with the real Embraer plans, substituted with mediocre counterfeit currency.

The circle of fate was soon to close by the end of the day. Even if Jaeger didn't survive, neither would Ortega, nor any of the others. What concerned Jaeger was why Ortega wanted him dead? In the time that Jaeger worked for him he'd done well. They never exchanged hostile words. A mystery he would never know the answer to. 'Very well, it was beyond mattering', he thought as he got dressed.

He carried everything down into his garage of his town house and opened the trunk of his fully restored 1963 Grey Ford Galaxy. Salvaged from a junkyard in San Antonio, he had it towed back to Houston, placed in the capable hands of an auto restoration mechanical master and helped completely tear down the vehicle and rid every usable part of rust and corrosion and then the long laborious task of restoration. Two and a half years later and thousands of dollars along with hundreds of man hours expended a vehicle emerged that was far better than the one that originally came off the assembly line. Almost five thousand pounds in weight it was not only fast in the extreme but could handle almost as well as any car on the street.

Into the trunk he placed the brief cases, securing them via several bungee cords to specially installed inside hooks. That completed he opened the front hood and inspected the entire engine compartment as well as the undercarriage looking for any surprises as a precaution. He already knew that Ortega had his men scouring the entire northwest part of town desperately looking for him. Finding nothing out of the ordinary he went back inside his town home and checked the security system, disengaging it then reengaging it and locking the entrance to the garage as he went. His external video feed revealed nothing out of place on the back street where he lived as he started the big Ford and pressed the visor button that opened the garage door. The Ford rumbled its throaty response as its sequential idle loped as he slowly backed into the street scanning carefully in all directions for unwanted guests. As he placed the gearshift lever into first gear, then punched the visor button lowering the garage door. Once the door came to rest, the blinking red light in the remote mechanism went out and he let out the clutch, driving slowly down the street.

A state of the art security system he had in place courtesy of a bank robber he once knew. An electronic wizard he was wiring his entire town home against any successful intrusion. Should the municipal power source be interrupted, the Lithium battery backup would be engaged, with the security system. Buffered against any external power surges and penetration techniques known at the time every window and door opening that was penetrated or breached would trigger an electronic timing device built into the home's interior, shielded from detection. After a full five minutes had passed, allowing any intruder to gain entry, the system would trigger the explosives built into every wall surrounding the home. No one inside would survive the explosion, the entire place having been rendered in to matchstick sized wooden splinters. Of course, the neighbors would suffer, but that was the price one paid for living in close proximity to a careful man.

Jaeger slowly made his way out of the subdivision in the west side of Houston, snaking his way through the streets until he came to Eldridge Parkway and turned south towards Interstate 10. He drove at the speed limit for some fifteen minutes in the post early morning rush hour traffic. Coming to a stop at the I-10 underpass he caught sight of a Grey BMW 750 series sedan with several people in the car about four cars behind him in the lane next to his. The vehicle was too far back for Jaeger to recognize any of the occupants. Ortega would have all of his people out on the street, as well as any others willing to pick up any bounty offered for Jaeger. He rarely paid the bounty offered to outsiders, deciding to kill them instead, either at the time of exchange or days later. He turned on his left hand turn signal and within seconds so did the Grey BMW, which told Jaeger this was beyond coincidence. Everyone in Ortega's crew knew what kind of car he drove. How many slick looking vintage 63 Fords can there be in greater Houston? His first mistake of the day? He should've driven to the secondary small apartment he kept and switched cars to the old Ford Bronco 4x4, but they had all seen him drive that too. Still it was old and raggedy looking and might've blended in better while in traffic. But for sheer speed and maneuverability, the big Ford was the best wheels he had.

As he turned left into the traffic of the access road flanking the freeway, he was joined by a County Constables cruiser that came from the opposite direction. Driving along parallel to each other Jaeger and the Constables cruiser kept pace with each other as Jaeger noticed the Grey BMW slowly closing the gap between them being just three cars behind the Constables cruiser, well within rapid closing distance were it not for the traffic that surrounded them all. If Ortega was playing the stupid card he would have issued orders to shoot on sight, rather than shadow. If that happened, the commotion it would cause would diminish their chances to retrieve whatever Jaeger was carrying. Just then as he glanced in his side mirror he caught sight of the driver talking into his cell phone to someone. That sealed it as far as he was concerned. They were calling Ortega. Then the Constable speeded up and allowed Jaeger to slide in right behind him as within a block he quickly pulled into a Shell Service Station with Jaeger close behind pulling up to a pump to refuel. The Beemer pulled up to the traffic light with both of those in the back seat paying close attention to Jaeger and the Constable. As the Constable got out of his cruiser, he went inside and then remerged with a key in his hand as the light changed forcing the Beemer into the intersection. Jaeger seeing they were through the intersection as the Constable was quickly making a bee line to the men's room, decided to top off his fuel tank and see everything unfold. Ortega got the call from one of his auxiliaries while in his high rise condo not five miles away, yelling at them to keep him occupied until he got there and ran out of his place with two others and waited for the elevator's arrival to his floor.

The Grey BMW dropped off one of the rear seat riders at the opposite corner and made its way into the large Mall parking lot on the opposite corner racing to the nearest exit and stopped with an eye on the Shell station a hundred yards away across the esplanade. The driver wasn't certain that Jaeger had spotted them or not, but since Ortega was on the way all he needed to keep close. Then there was the proximity of the Constable, in the Men's Room of the service station unaware of what was about to unfold around him. Ortega expected the matter to be handled with complete delicacy.

Jaeger kept an eye on the spotter across the street as well as the idling BMW in the Mall parking lot exit signaling others to drive around as they sat there waiting. He prepaid the pump with his credit card and took his time with the fuel up, trying to time it with the emergence of the Constable. Eventually the Constable emerged with a relieved look on his returning to the office to return the key and coming back outside with a canned drink in his hand as he approached the patrol car. Just before the Constable reached for the door handle, he heard a car honking its horn repeatedly across the street in the Mall exit. A Grey BMW was apparently blocking the other cars right of way, refusing to move. The Constable waited and watched for a moment as the driver of the BMW, eventually tired of hearing the commotion, emerged from his car with a drawn weapon and threatened the driver behind him.

The Constable immediately dropped his soft drink, jumped into his cruiser and peeled out of the Service Station driveway, with his lights flashing and the siren engaged. Within seconds he came upon the BMW and emerged with his weapon drawn, yelling at the BMW driver to drop his weapon.

Seeing all this unfold, Jaeger started his car and pulled into the freeway access roadway and waited for the light to change.

Ortega was but a mile back on the very same Freeway access road and coming fast, weaving his way in between cars and lusting for his confrontation with Jaeger. The light in front of Jaeger changed to green as Jaeger slowly kept pace with the car in front of him as the first shots rang out.

The driver of the BMW wasn't about to comply with anything the Constable said as he pumped a round into the driver of the other car and swiftly turned and started shooting at the Constable some twenty yards away. The front seat passenger jumped out and joined in at firing at the Constable as the first volley of the Constables returning fire found their mark on the driver, with all of his rounds impacting on the open driver's door of the patrol car. The Constable then turned his fire in the direction of the front seat passenger who was standing apart from the BMW sedan firing round after round at the Constable.

As Jaeger started across the intersection, one of the rear seat passengers seeing this quickly jumped into the front driver's seat, slammed the car in reverse gear and slammed into the car behind him, then put the car into drive gear quickly turning the BMW around, tires screaming and burning rubber and drove across the parking lot towards the exit it first entered into after the escaping Jaeger.

Seeing that both of his original assailants were down from his gunfire, the Constable carefully led the escaping vehicle and squeezed off a 'double tap', two shots in quick succession in hope of one of them finding its mark. One of them luckily did as it impacted upon the drivers left temple, killing him instantly as his right foot was pressed against the accelerator. Now the BMW was careening obliquely in the general direction of Jaeger across the Mall parking lot with the driver dead at its helm. It took several seconds for the rear seat passenger to realize the driver was dead as the BMW quickly gained speed, but there was nothing to be done as a few seconds later, the BMW exited the parking lot at speed, slamming into the cars of two hapless citizens late for work, thus causing them to crash into several others.

Jaeger glanced into his rearview mirror briefly, seeing the BMW slam into the other cars, deciding to slow down as he made his way into town. No point in him becoming a statistic, when Ortega's men were doing a great job all on their own.

The Constable couldn't concern himself with the BMW any longer as the other two shooters were still taking shots at him, as he quickly went around to the rear of his patrol unit, grabbing for his shoulder mike and yelling, "Unit six, Unit six, Patrolman under fire at the intersection of Gessner Road and I-10. Need help quick"!

Traffic was slowing to a crawl as Ortega's car pulled into the Shell Stations parking lot as everyone was crouching down behind anything that would stop bullets, watching the final stages of the gunfight on Gessner Road.

He saw the Constable approach two bodies in the Mall parking lot and kick away their weapons then his eyes were drawn to a burning vehicle on the access road on the other side of the intersection. The vehicle that was ablaze resembled one of his associates Grey BMW's. Then his eyes came back to the Constable standing by his patrol car talking into his shoulder microphone with an animated motion. As his eyes scanned the service station surroundings repeatedly he could see no evidence that Jaeger was here, except for the mute testimony of the aftermath.

The traffic was still moving although slowly now with on lookers preening to gain a view of the aftermath of the Great Gessner Road shootout they would no doubt learn more about during the evening local television news reports.

Ortega hearing the sirens signaling their approach got back into his car and said to the driver, "Vamanos. We catch up with dat Cabrone' later on inna day. I know where he gonna be. We show up early an give him a beeg surprise"!

Jaegers heart rate started to slow as he turned right, onto a side street that led to a residential area. He scanned his rearview mirror as he slowly drove through the neighborhood, going several blocks and turning right, then several blocks more and turning right once again, then several blocks and turned left. It was now midmorning and he could still hear the distant wail of both police and fire department sirens a mile away rushing to the scene of an urban tragedy.

He was going to go for breakfast at a restaurant but somehow his appetite had fled him, opting straight away to head for the seashore house on Jamaica Beach on the Gulf of Mexico. Jaegers father always told him not to eat before a big tussle because it always slowed you down. Instead he dropped another stick of chewing gum in his mouth. The sugar in the gum would provide sufficient fuel for the day. He could always eat afterward. If he made it the food would taste better, if he didn't it wouldn't matter anyway. He opted to snake his way through the city rather than take the quicker Loop or the Freeways, where he knew Ortega's eyes and ears would be positioned.

Jaeger assiduously avoided the Latino parts of town as he snaked his way across the city. Eventually emerging from the main entrails of the city after working his way in a southeasterly direction and crossing under the South Loop 610, that encircled the city eventually coming onto I-45 south, the main route to Galveston. As he drove his eyes darted everywhere, and as luck would hold, no one apparently noticed his big Ford as it turned south onto the Interstate. Now as traffic started to thin out he wondered how he could remain unnoticed as he worked his way towards the target location. The lone house almost to the very end of Jamaica Beach. The shoreline home that proved to be Ortega's favorite meeting place for all transactions. Since the locals were in his hip pocket financially, anything went.

As he hugged the right hand lane traveling the posted speed limit he was passed by four tractor trailer trucks gaining speed for the fifty mile haul towards Galveston Island. Turning on his CB Radio, he pressed the transmit button on his mike saying, "Yo, breaker one nine, the Conga Line headin' towards Galveston, you got the One Cincinnati Kid. Comeback"!

"Moon Doggie here. Come back Kid"!

"Where ya headed, Doggie? Come back"?

"Last exit before we hit Galveston City Limits and we're runnin' late. Come back"!

"Well, I'm in a hurry too. Mind if I park my Ford into your rockin' chair. I'm comin up hard on your six, drivin' a white 63 Ford Galaxy. Come back"!

"The pedals to the metal and we're drivin' hard to make time pilgrim and we don't need any amateur in our innards. We'll be hittin' the Century and above. But what's in that Ford? Comeback"!

"A 427, factory balanced mill, full race cam, with dual quads up top, straight pipes and a 270 positrac rear axle for starters. So can I come and play"?

The CB was quiet for the better part of thirty seconds, then it came alive, "Hey, the boys say OK, so come on in and tuck yourself in right behind me. I'm drivin' the lead vee hickle and we'll give ya some snuggle room, come back"!

"Thanks Doggie, here I come", said Jaeger as he touched the accelerator and the big Ford leapt forward and he tucked right behind Moon Doggies tractor trailer truck.

As soon as he slid in place the wind noise died down to a whisper as the speedometer raced past ninety miles per hour eventually settling in at slightly over a hundred. He was drafting for certain carefully paying attention to everything in front of him with great care. He calculated in his mind that in a little over forty minutes he'd be crossing the Galveston Island causeway, as he listened to the chatter between the others in the convoy back and forth.

The truckers timing was exquisite for their trip south whereas the law was usually on their early lunch break, passing Webster, Dickinson and points south this time in the late morning. No cops on the road meant the pedal was to be put on the metal. Besides stopping a lone truck was one thing, but a convoy? Who needed the aggravation?

As the forty minute marker came up, Moon Doggie crackled on the CB, "Hey Kid our exit is just up ahead a mile, so get ready to make tracks.

Boomers in the rear and he'll sing out when your lane is clear. Come back"!

"Ten four Moon Doggie. Got my ears on and much grass for the ride"! Some seconds later the CB came alive again. "Hey Kid, Boomer here. Your lane is clear. Show us what ya got"!

Jaeger drifted out from behind Moon Doggie's truck and pressed the accelerator down about a half inch as the big Ford sped ahead passing the lead truck swiftly at speed, the convoy growing smaller in his rear view mirror, without a further word. He gradually started to diminish his speed to under a hundred, then eighty. Finally back to the posted speed as his radar detector remained mute as he crossed the causeway onto Galveston Island. He took the 45th Street exit and turned right, driving the ten blocks towards Sea Wall Boulevard which fronted the sea shore. Other than I-45 South, it was the Islands main drag housing several tourist hotels and most of the tourist attractions and vendors. At the boulevard he turned right again and headed south out of Galveston proper towards the hamlet of Jamaica Beach.

The boulevard eventually petered out into a two lane blacktop road as Jaeger drove on, revealing a host of beach house residences, which gradually thinned out in number the farther on he drove. Twenty minutes later he came upon the shuttered house on the left, not fifty yards above the high tide mark of the shore line of the Gulf of Mexico. All senses on high alert, Jaeger slowly turned the big Ford onto the blacktop driveway circular driveway that surrounded the house, to the overly large carport that covered the rear of the home facing the Gulf's shore.

He turned off the ignition and reached into the glove box retrieving his Ruger .357 Magnum revolver. Then he went to the car's trunk, opened it and retrieved from his small tool bag an electronic lock picking device. Within a minutes time he picked both locks securing the rear door and entered into the kitchen, turning on the lights and carefully searched the house, for any sensing devices or preset explosives and finding nothing, went back to the kitchen and opened the refrigerator, full of food and beer and withdrew a cold brew to slake his growing thirst.

He went back outside and returned his lock picking tool back into his bag. Leaning on the rear fender of his car Jaeger looked out towards the wide expanse of the Gulf of Mexico.

For the moment he enjoyed the endless series of gentle waves that came lapping onto the shore. Seagulls endlessly searching for their next meal. The occasional fish or porpoise that jumped out of the water. All of nature's bountiful gifts might soon be taken away. He wondered how much longer he would be permitted to indulge his senses?

After this day was done, an ending of sorts was about to occur. Either his, or Ortega and however many of his pals he brought to the party. He'd come to grips with his fears. Fear of failure. Fear of not being able to complete the restoration of all that was taken from him long ago and most important the fear of death itself. Only one single thing lay in his path. The death of Ortega.

No telling when Ortega would arrive with his friends. They agreed to meet here, the previous evening around seven in the evening. He knew that Ortega would be combing the town for him. That manifested itself several hours ago. One thing was certain. It would be over quickly one way or the other. Other than a brief perfunctory smiling greeting, things would happen at light speed. Jaegers early arrival could be easily trumped by an overwhelming number of Ortega's men arriving with him. Yet none of that mattered now. The only thing he prayed for was Ortega's overconfidence and that he could get within arm's length of the man. That accomplished, everything else was in the hands of fate.

For the first time in days, he allowed part of his mind to wander into the recent past.

As Jaeger thought back to the time, some six months ago when he first encountered Ortega, he wondered what exactly drew him to this guy. It was late in the afternoon at the Balls Health club in Northwest Houston. Jaeger was in the upstairs mezzanine section of the club, working out with the free weights in front of the long mirror wall that paralleled and separated the free weight section from the jogging track that encompassed the facility. He was just completing his fourth set of curl exercises with one hundred twenty pounds on the short curl bar, surrounded by several others of both genders. All going through their respective exertions, peering intently into the mélange of full length mirrors, concentrating on the correct form, for the most part, while some others, no doubt, were engaging in either self- adulation, or self-loathing.

The facility was starting to fill up with the 'After Work' crowd comprising a wide spectrum of individuals, ranging from the serious body builders, to the 'Teletubbies', then to the few of the morbidly obese, intent as best they could of giving it a go. Poor souls as they were, clad in the offerings of the mythical, 'Omar the tent Maker', clothier of the fatties, replete with rivulets of sweat pouring forth from their ample bodies.

The joke around the club was that there were two types of muscle. The 'real muscle', the dedicated were intent of either building or at least maintaining and the 'table muscle', that many were intent on shedding.

"Sure I got a six pack", he overheard one guy telling a girl nearby. "It's just covered by insulation for the coming winter"! Clearly he was there to justify an hour at the local, "Meet and Grunt", sufficient to justify that mega caloric meal that just lay ahead, after his exertions. A quick glance around was sufficient to determine who was serious about personal fitness and who was there to socialize.

As Jaeger started on his fifth set of curls focused on his image in the mirror wall, he noticed a short well-muscled Latino come into view, of around sub medium height, entering the free weight section of the mezzanine. Following closely in his wake came a small trio, no doubt his entourage, garishly attired, covered with the tattoos that signaled previous prison time. He'd seen this before but never in his current surroundings.

The group approached two benches close by to where Jaeger stood, and picked up the towels left by others, who went briefly to the water fountain, a signal to all that this spot was occupied and tossed them away, thus taking over that spot. When the former owners of the towels came back to reclaim their workout spot, finding their spot now, 'Occupado', a quick assessment of the situation suggested they move elsewhere as they gathered their towels and moved away, grumbling silently about Ballys policy of non- confrontation.

The lower portion of the long mirror wall was replete with barbells neatly stacked and sorted by weight as the Latinos gathered just two seats away from Jaeger. He finished his set and rested a bit, going over to where the weight plates were stacked and then coming back to his spot, adding two plates for the final twenty pounds of his session. With over sixty feet of barbells neatly arrayed in front of the mirror wall, two of the smaller, tattoo laden Latinos stood right in front of Jaeger carrying on a conversation in Spanish. Jaeger waited several minutes for them to conclude, but when they showed no sign of moving, he noticed the curl bar stanchion just to his left open up, the former user moving on, so Jaeger simply moved his weight laden curl bar over to the newly vacated stanchion to prepare for his final set. All the while he kept an eye on the well-built leader of the intruders and picked up a single, two and a half pound circular plate and placed it on the stanchions rest.

Then as he was about to start his final set the two Latinos, once again drifted to a spot between Jaeger and the mirror, pretending to look for a certain set of barbells. Jaeger then said to the two "Hey comprende' Englese"? Pointing to a sign on the mirror asking all members to be respectful of others.

Then one of them slowly turned towards Jaeger saying, "Joo talkin' to me Vato"? Jaeger then made a sweeping sign with his arm directing them to move elsewhere. "No sabe Englese Cabrone'," said the Latino, anger growing in his eyes as he refused to move, standing just ten feet away.

Thinking then about simply walking away from it all, Jaegers mind was changed when his newly found antagonist said, "Joo say another word to me, we fock you up"! Then he made a quick step towards Jaeger, who quickly picked up the small circular weight plate and flipped it towards the man as one would hurl a Frisbee. The weight hit the man just above the eye, felling him instantly as both fell to the well-padded floor silently. Quickly he went and got two more of the small weight plates and assumed a defensive position as the leader of the group went over and glanced at his fallen comrade, then at Jaeger saying, in heavily accented English, "You must forgib my brash young friend, we will take care of everything", as he directed the other two to hoist up their friend and carry him down the stairs and out the front door as onlookers gawked and out to a large Black Mercedes Benz driving away into the burgeoning rush hour traffic. Jaeger, picked up the weight plate that hit the Latino, briefly examined it and put it back walked over to the other side of the facility and watched them depart.

Big Randy, the manager of the facility came quickly up the stairs as he saw someone being carried out of the club. At six foot seven and bristling with muscles, he was every bit a walking advertisement for the Bally Brand of health club. After briefly chatting with a few of the members regarding the commotion he walked around the track to where Jaeger was standing and asked, "What happened"?

"Randy. You guys just have to tighten up your membership criteria. It's getting so that you let anyone in here who has the price of admission"!

"That doesn't tell me what happened pal"!

Looking out of the huge bank of windows that flanked the parking lot as the Mercedes slowly drove away Jaeger said, "Four Mexicans came upstairs and started messing with the members, chasing them away in mid routine. One of them decided to mess with me. He fell down injuring himself. One of them apologized and the two others carried him away quickly. No blood was spilled. No need for anything else, much less bad publicity for your company. End of story"!

"Any idea what their names were"?

"No names were exchanged. But since they terrorized several of your long standing members, you might want to think about canceling their memberships, for the common good"!

"Good idea. Don't need corporate climbing down my back"!

"They came in about fifteen minutes ago as a group of four as far as I can tell Randy, so you might want to get into that computer at the main desk and track four male Mexicans that came in together"! "You OK, Jaeger"?

"Heart rate a bit on the high side but other than that, everything's cool"!

As Ortega's Mercedes drove around the block he directed one of his men to quickly change into his street clothes as the car stopped and he let his man out saying, "You know what he look like. Stay low and be cool. All I need is the make of his car and his license plate nomber. That is all you hab to do. Then I can find out all I need to know about this Cabrone', what make trouble. Joo think joo can do that"?

"Si Padrone", said the man as he exited the car.

Jaeger went downstairs and into the locker room, changing into his swim trunks and took a brief shower then went into the steam room, where once settled, he deeply inhaled and exhaled into a deep rhythm that started to relax him all over. Slowly closing his eyes, he allowed thoughts to drift into his mind of this woman he'd just started seeing about a month ago.

In the years since his release from Huntsville Prison, he'd been a Manager of one of Buffy's Gentlemen's Clubs, in Houston along with his two former inmates, Roy Seltzer and Duke Vultee. The trio entered the club business at the very same time working for Buffy. Tiring of that, he'd quietly severed his relationship with Buffy, after a time and was in search of a more suitable way of making a living. After an encounter with Rafferty, owner of Houston's largest Bail Bonding company, while still in the Club business, he decided to become a 'Chaser', aka a Bail Enforcement Agent, aka, Bounty Hunter.

Refereeing the seemingly endless cat fights between the dancers and the endless forays of the local vice squad, better known as the 'Pussy Posse', along with the occasional removal of a drunk from the premises, began to slowly bore Jaeger, who wondered whether or not this was to be his life's work. He never thought he'd see the day when the sheer sight of mostly unclad and often totally naked women would leave him unmoved, but there it was. Every day, naked women. No romance. No mystery. This must be what gynecologists eventually came to after years of looking deeply into the deep abyss. All was not necessarily pink on the inside.

Thus after connecting with Rafferty, in a counterintuitive way, Jaeger saw a purpose in his life being a 'Chaser'. It was always a nonstop battle of wits, to see who could outwit the other. After all, wasn't his very name 'Jaeger', which in German meant 'Hunter' well suited for his new occupation? Didn't the hoard of bail jumpers need to be brought back? The answers all came back in the affirmative. Thus after he learned the ropes under Rafferty the master, he teamed up with a man named 'Hondo'. Together they proved to be a force to be reckoned with in Texas and the surrounding areas, always bringing back wanted criminals who fled their bail often at the expense of family and loved ones. In short order they'd swept clean the backlog of cases Rafferty had and were being farmed out to other bail bonding agencies at a premium. As they took great care with Rafferty so was the reciprocation back financially with both Jaeger and Hondo, the men with only one cognomen.

Yet after some four years as a Chaser, something greater beckoned. Of what he didn't know, feeling that another phase of transition was just around the corner, since his relationship with Melanie was starting to take root. She was a delightful breath of fresh air, with an inner beauty that completely matched her visual accoutrements that Jaeger never thought possible in a human being considering his exposure to the seedier aspects of humanity. Taking constant stock of the progression of his life thus far, since his release from prison, with a full pardon he was probably where he should be, given the hand he'd been dealt in life. His years in stir had yielded a Master's Degree in Business via a special state funded program at the local University, but no matter what he try his hand at a serious background check would always reveal the mysterious gap in his work history. Of course he could probably sell used cars, wait tables, drive a truck, or be a day laborer, but a rational use of his education in the mainstream of society was out of the question. Yet bail bonding companies didn't usually ask the hard questions, taking in their employ people on face value, only concerned with the ability of one to deliver the goods consistently. In that environment, Jaeger had thrived economically.

As his relationship with Melanie O'Bannon and her young son began to solidify, he'd started to consider whether or not to take this relationship to the next level, unless he could achieve some normalcy career wise and this meant a breakthrough of sorts. A stable home environment was the only viable option for Mel and her young son. Given Jaegers past the probability was bleak.

Over the recent years, he'd been tempted to take the low road many times, turning down high risk ventures repeatedly, staying with what he knew, earning a very good living as a Chaser, making few friends and a slew of enemies along the way. It came with the territory. But now his concerns shifted from himself to the well-being of Mel and her son. It was abundantly clear that she'd be in danger as long as she was part of his life, which lead to vulnerability of both parties. A hard decision had to be made and sooner rather than later. Yet Jaeger, normally a very decisive sort held back, for he just couldn't bear to separate from happiness long denied him by circumstance.

From the very first moment they met, all she knew about Jaeger was that he was a private investor, nothing more. She made no further inquiries into his personal or professional life, taking him at face value in all things, since he conducted himself in such a manner that was consistent with his story.

As he dressed in the locker room and went to his car, his thoughts were on the recent encounter, having a feeling and nothing more about this group of Latinos and their leader. Somehow he felt he'd not be seeing the last of this guy so as he emerged from Ballys and into the afternoon sun his every sense was on full alert. Seeing nothing that came to his attention as he walked through the parking lot towards his old Ford Bronco, he unlocked the vehicle and tossed in his gym bag, then just before he got in gave the entire undercarriage the once over.

Pulling out of the parking lot into the late afternoon rush hour traffic, Jaeger didn't notice a lone man crouching between parked cars, writing his license plate number on the back of an IHOP restaurant napkin. He then went back into the IHOP restaurant and called Ortega's cell phone number from the pay phone inside, giving him the make and model of Jaegers vehicle as well as his license plate number.

"Bueno, muchas Bueno. Joo done good. Now grab a cab and get back to the restaurant on Hillcroft, to help with the evening dinner rush. I be dere later on"!

"Jefe, how is the new man"!

"Oh him? Muerte'! The big man, he dent his skull with that plate, he threw! We tried to find a pulse as we drove to the nurses place, but there was none! Tomorrow I want you to call Davalantes in Monterrey and tell him what happened and to send me another shooter, only this time not a Loco Grande"!

"What's to be done with the new guy"?

"Not your business, but I hear the menudo at a certain Carnacia in town will be magnificent tomorrow"!

That weekend, since Mel and her son were to be out of town visiting her parents, Jaeger decided to join Rafferty and Hondo for the grand opening of "Hellzapoppin", Houston's newest and gaudiest night club. The owner had fled from Lebanon during the bloody civil war in the eighties, taking millions of dollars with him. Settling first in Miami, then drifting to Houston Texas, he first invested in the down real estate market at that time, then eager for further profits and excitement, bought an entire retail shopping center for a song. Only half full of rent paying businesses due to the shuttering of the large Kmart anchor location, it seemed a prime location to open the biggest, baddest nightclub in Texas. Live bands of every kind were his theme along with the craziest of operational modalities. The rules of civility were to vary from night to night.

Abdullah el Ibrahim was a very clever bunny. He always made money no matter what he was involved in. His very name drew silent partners from all over the globe, certain that he was their guiding light towards silent profits in excess of the norm. He'd never failed them yet even under the most onerous of circumstances. His salesmanship knew no equals and he always kept the balls in the air often defying the laws of gravity. He had the gift. Always operating from the shadows, except for the select few. Thus was born "Hellzapoppin".

Of course, Ortega had a piece of the action, which is why he, Ottavio and Davlantes were in attendance for the Grand Opening. They saw to it that Rafferty and Company received a personally mailed invitation for the Grand Opening. Everyone who was any importance in town was there, for it was guaranteed to be The Event of the year. The night was clear with Klieg Lights in the parking lot and a live band outside to greet everyone who entered along with a small army of 'off duty' policemen to direct traffic, on a Friday night. Every single thing was in place to ensure an unforgettable evening.

Rafferty gave his car to the valet service as he Jaeger and Hondo entered Hellzapoppin at the stroke of ten PM, followed by a long line of 'Invitation Only' vehicles in their wake. The former Kmart Store was completely redone, from stem to stern, unrecognizable as to its former purpose. With multiple levels of seating and dance floors, flashing lights and as a surprise, every hour on the hour no matter what, a Dwarf in clown costume would emerge from a small door near the roof and hook himself on to a high tension wire and slide across the entire club laden with sparklers and screaming obscenities in a variety of foreign languages from a bull horn for the shock value.

Jaeger had kept busy during the week returning several skips back into the arms of justice, while keeping an eye out for the unseen ever since his confrontation at Ballys. Tonight, he decided to relax and enjoy the evening, as they ordered their drinks and wandered around the club drinking in all of the sights and sounds. The place was filling up quickly and by eleven in the evening the Dwarf made his appearance to the utter astonishment and delight of all.

Of course Jaegers appearance didn't go unnoticed as Ottavio pointed out Jaeger to Davlantes and went back to alert Ortega of his arrival, while Davalantes kept a discrete distance hiding in plain sight amidst the crowd.

"Convince the waitress that covers their section to stay busy, when they call for drink refills" said Ortega sliding a C note into Ottavio's hand, saying "For the waitress"! A half hour later, joined by several women who appeared eager to gain a good seat near the dance floor, they tried in vain to summon their waitress so Jaeger decided to take matters into his own hands and get their drinks at one of the bars some distance across the club.

He returned later with an arm full of drinks for the table. In spite of a few things recently he began to feel at ease with himself, mixing easily with each of the women he came in contact with. He drank, flirted, laughed and danced with a bevy of very attractive women, growing more at ease with every passing moment.

Amidst the delightful chaos that surrounded him, an errant thought forced its way into his mind. The ghost of his long ago mentor and former cellmate, Roy Seltzer, spoke to him. 'Stupid Clot' the thought intoned. 'Always keep everything in front of you. Can't respond to what you cannot see. Far too many people about'!

Later, Jaeger drifted back through the crowd to the bar coming upon the full length horizontal mirror that stood as a backstop to the plethora of bottles that lay before it. He ordered his drink saying, "Vodka tonic bit of lime"! The thought continued, 'Sure mate, you gotta big mirror ahead of you, but anyone could suddenly appear from this crowd and do you before you could blink you stupid arse. All the bloody Sheila's about make for a great distraction, leading to your destruction, especially the Norwegian milkmaid over there with the low slung peasant blouse, barely covering those pendulous Golden Bozo's, standing close at hand. So heads up mate', the thought concluded.

Jaeger lit a cigarette just as his drink arrived and at that very moment, as predicted, the face of Ortega appeared from the depths of the crowd and put his arm across Jaegers broad shoulders as Jaeger was about to pay for his drink saying to the bartender, "Yo Hank, joo put dees man's drink as well as his table in my tab, cause he a frien ob mine"!

"As you wish Mister Ortega"!

"This your place", asked Jaeger trying to mask his surprise, feeling the spiritual wrath of his mentor ringing in his ears?

"My place? Oh no. Just gotta a piece ob da action". Just then he felt Jaeger stiffen slightly saying, "Relax Hombre'! If I wanted you dead, you'd be Vamanos before you even saw me. I am a man of impression and joo make a very big impression on me Mister Jaeger, bounty hunter who work for Rafferty"!

"So how come you know so much about me Ortega"!

"Like I say, joo impress me at the gym the odder day, Mister Jaeger who live on Jones Road in a small apartment and drive an old truck"!

The Milk maid next to Jaeger was about to ask him for a light when Jaeger turned his back on her and faced Ortega directly saying, "How many pairs of eyes you got watching us right now"?

"Enough hombre"!

"And the reason you went to all of this trouble is? Certainly it can't be because of that little spat at the gym. By the way how is the little fella"?

Ortega's drink arrived unbidden as he picked it up saying, "Oh him. He dead. But not to worry. He was new and stupid deserving of death. It should not bother you at all. I take care of everything"! It was the matter of fact way Ortega put it that sold Jaeger that this guy was very bad news indeed as he said, "So let's get down to it my friend, what do you want"?

"I like that in a man, straight talk and I think we both could be ob service for each other. I check joo out. Joo spend time up Norte' in Huntsville Prison. You get pardoned all of a sudden like. People disappear completely. You manage Clubs for a few years then throw in with Rafferty. You even bring back a few ob my people from Mexico, the hard way. All of which tell me that we were meant for each other and I could make things very worth while for joo, since I hab several projects in mind that could prove worthy of you talents. Then I see how you handle yourself at the club and I say to myself, I need to talk with this man and introduce him to some of my people. You already have Davalantes vote and he's standing behind you"!

Jaeger looked into the mirror and saw a man with black hair tied into a pony tail slowly nod his head as he looked back at Ortega and said, "OK sport, I'll bite, what's next"!

"I will be outta town all next week", he said reaching for a cocktail napkin, writing an address on the napkin as he continued, "But if joo will be kind enough to meet me at one of my restaurants next Monday a week from now, there's some people I want joo to meet. Then we can discuss future plans and money and see if we all fit. About one thirty after the lunch rush and we can exchange ideas". He shoved the napkin over to Jaeger and said, "Enjoy the evening, my friend", as he disappeared into the crowd. As he turned back to his drink the milk maid leaned over saying, "Can I have a light"?

He pulled out his lighter and obliged, seeing that she was a willing bunny, but thoughts of Melanie flooded his mind at that very moment, as he whispered in her ear, "Sorry babe, but I prefer virgins", disappearing into the crowd back to his table, to see the waitress had miraculously returned to their table eager to serve, announcing that everything was on the house.

Just then Jaeger felt the spiritual wrath of Seltzer intoning, 'You were lucky this time mate. Can't count on luck, you see. Keep that up mate and before too long you'll be served up as lunch for the ants. Sloppy mate, rather sloppy all around', came the disdainful voice without sound in his head.

At midnight and again at one in the morning, the sparkler laden Dwarf came bursting forth from the now unlit door high on the wall of the club, slowly sliding down the steel cable that ran the length of the club screaming obscenities through his bull horn that no one understood, to the utter surprise and delight of the crowd. In the coming days of Hellzapoppin's existence, a new ethos would emerge, with the patrons screaming back at the flaming Captain Midget, obscenities that could easily be understood.

Rafferty looked at Jaeger as the clock approached the two AM closing hour, yelling above the crowd and music noise, "The word is the club has a special wink from the County Government to stay open till four in the morning, for the time being. Seems the right reelection campaigns got contributed to. I'm starting to crap out being the old geezer that I am, how about you Jaeger"? "You're the one driving"! "Good lets fold tents and boogie"! "Hondo what about you sport"? With his arms around two seemingly randy blondes, Hondo sang out, "Me boss, no you two go ahead, I'm in the process of doin' a little social work amongst the rich for the evening", as his two willing blondes, then stood up in unison giggling and badly belted out the song, "Double your pleasure, double your fun. Two blondes in bed are better than one", as all doubled up in laughter.

"Lets cut trail", said Rafferty as he and Jaeger made their way through the swirling crowd and out to the parking lot. As the valet delivered Rafferty's car he said, "Sure hope Hondo's got the sense to examine their VD control cards. No telling' where they been"!

"No tellin' where Hondo's been either" said Jaeger with a wry smile. The following morning Jaeger with nothing scheduled awoke at ten, made coffee, grabbed some aspirin for his hangover while he was waiting and started to think, while the coffee dripped.

Apparently Ortega watched Jaegers car leave the lot at Ballys. He circled around the block and let out one of his boys to watch out for Jaeger as he left. Taking the plate number from the Bronco, which with the help from someone downtown yielded his name and address for his back up apartment on Jones Road.

'The guy only has a partial picture of me, thought Jaeger. Yet a little further digging yielded up his employer Rafferty. Which explained the from out of the blue specially engraved on parchment invitation for the Hellzapoppin's grand opening for Rafferty's entire company. Jaeger walks in with Rafferty and Hondo, he is seen, marked, the waitress is slipped some travelin' money to be elsewhere, ergo Jaeger goes to the bar and up pops Ortega, all smiles and forgiveness with a job offer of sorts.

He had to give it to the guy, he was slick. Therefore he must be of some importance. His coffee made, he sat down and turned on the telly for the news. The voice of reason that sometimes invaded his thought process was this time silent, which meant, 'Sport yer on yer own. Rotsa ruck'!

On the appointed day, Jaeger woke up late in the morning, made his coffee, showered, shaved, put on his light weight Kevlar vest, then covered that with his collarless Kevlar shirt, then had to decide what to bring with him. No doubt he'd be completely searched soon after he arrived, so the magic belt was just what the doctor ordered. The belt within a belt, which could be quickly withdrawn from his waistband, separated in an eye blink and divided into two weighted whips that were designed to maim or kill. By casual scrutiny it looked like just any other belt, sold in the stores, with no remarkable characteristics. With that he departed for his meeting.

Several days before, he'd made a recon visit to the shopping center that housed Ortega's restaurant. He went completely around the place trying to find avenues of exit, just in case, things turned to shit. Later on, he'd gotten into every computer data file he could, to find out something, anything, about Ortega. The real Ortega. Many of them in the data files but all low level operatives. Cannon fodder. Nobody with any real juice. The guy was visibly clean. Then he searched the immigration data bases, laden with pictures and again came up croppers. Clearly the guy was in country illegally but apparently no one was aware of it. Then he searched the data base of Harris County Restaurant licensures, plugging in the name and address of the restaurant, he was to meet Ortega and once again another name, other than Ortega, came up as the owner. Then he plugged in the name of 'Hellzapoppin' into the database and examined the list of names, hoping to see Ortega's name, yet once again, nothing. There was one name he remembered that Ortega mentioned that appeared as one of the owners. 'Davalantes'. No doubt a well trusted Captain in his organization.

'A very smart bunny', thought Jaeger. 'Put everything in the name of trusted associates'! The man on paper owned nothing, yet in reality he owned much. Beyond any formal adjudication. Everything on an informal hand shake basis. Yet break just one of the unofficial rules and one ended up as Mexican Stew. The guy knew the right people and information about anything of interest would be his stock and trade. Anything that would soon turn a buck. He drove from his town house, to the secondary apartment he kept on Jones Road, traded vehicles and drove off in his old Ford Bronco. No use tipping his hand until he knew a whole lot about the guy. The guy had checked him out and had discovered everything Jaeger wanted anyone to know. As far as the world was concerned, he lived in a small apartment in the northwest part of town and drove the old Bronco. Of course before he left he gave the undercarriage of the Bronco the once over, just in case. Just the way Jaeger wanted to keep things. He drove across town in no particular hurry, since the noon traffic rush was on with seemingly every one in their cars going from one place to another within the allotted time span for lunch.

Jaeger gave special attention to his rearview mirror, as he drove. On several occasions, he made the classic, four right hand turns, just to see if the same vehicle was in his rearview mirror at the fourth turn. Universally basic stuff. Seeing he wasn't being followed, he motored south on Hillcroft eventually coming across the sign of the "El Mariachi Cantina" across the esplanade on the opposite side as he made the left hand turn pulling into the parking lot.

He wondered as he approached El Mariachi jus why he agreed to break bread with this guy. He had this look of someone well heeled, connected and of the old school. The very old school of the streets and barrios, who made his living and his way in the world by any way that was profitable. Soon Jaeger would find out if he had any profitable work coming his way, or was this an elaborate ruse to take him out for the absence of a few of his guys.

As he entered the place, he was somewhat impressed by the surroundings Early whorehouse, with bright red velvet everywhere, but the music that played softly in the background was Brazilian Samba. A contradiction of tastes. The hostess approached and Jaeger said, "Ortega. He's expecting me"! She nodded her head and turned, motioning for Jaeger to follow her to the rear of the restaurant to a semi curtained off area, where half dozen tough looking men stood, listening to someone yet unseen. Just before they arrived, the men disbursed back to their tables and their cooling meals, as the hostess and Jaeger arrived.

Ortega had an angry look on his face. But that changed as soon as Jaeger arrived, as he said, "Ah, Mister Jaeger, so good of you to come. Please take a seat. As Jaeger sat down he recognized the pony tailed one known as Davalantes as he nodded to him.

"I believe you've met Davalantes last week in the club. Ottavio you've already met at Ballys and he's in the restaurant taking his meal. But the sullen one across the table is Nestor Magellan.

Just then completely unbidden, a waiter appeared with Jaegers drink, "Vodka with tonic Senor, a slice of lime over ice", he said then left without further word. Jaeger tasted his drink with a smile saying, "You've a very good memory Senor"!

"De nada", he answered.

"Senor Ortega makes it a point of being observant, almost to a fault", explained Magellan!

"Today, we relax, not worry about nossing, eat, drink, exchange ideas and talk about making money", said Ortega lifting his glass in toast. "Hombre's. Buena Fortuna"!

As they put their glasses down, three waiters appeared with a bevy of trays laden with a variety of selected dishes, which were quickly arrayed in the center of the large table in a circular buffet fashion.

Magellan said as he started to select his meal, "I hope you don't mind that 'El Jefe' has taken the liberty to order for us all. The cuisine here, is a departure from the typical Tex Mex food usually found in this area. The type of fare served here is more commonly found in the interior of Mexico"!

"I thank the Senor for his cordiality", said Jaeger "And I'm quite at home with the type of fare arrayed before us all"! "That is quite right Nestor. For Senor Jaeger hab been to Mexico a number of occasions for business and should be right at home with our food"!

"Over the course of the dinner Magellan took over the bulk of the conversation, given his flawless command of the American idiom and the various nuances native to the local dialect.

Jaeger clearly saw that Magellan was Ortega's 'Segundo', as he was trying to take the man's measure. Where Ortega was clearly of Mestizo, or mixed Central American ancestry, Magellan had the clearly Euro or Castilian look about him, with flawless table manners, quite unlike

Ortega and Davalantes, who attacked their meal with the gusto of a starving Gaucho.

Yet Magellan was clearly not a dandy, despite his gracious manners and style. The weathered look on his face, his hands and sinewy forearms, were the only visible betrayal of hard times past. Then there were the eyes. The one visible thing he had in common with Ortega and Davalantes. Magellan had the hard eyes of one who terminated life quickly and efficiently, without a trace of hesitation or remorse.

As Magellan droned on repeating what was known of Jaegers past, his time as a Marine, his brief College football career, the murder of his parents, the loss of his family estates, his incarceration in Huntsville prison for their murder, his rapid and complete pardon from The Texas Department of Corrections, along with several others and finally the mysterious disappearance of the trio of characters about to be indicted, including the Governor, Magellan said, "You Senor, have survived an interesting life, seemingly against all odds and are the kind of man Senor Ortega would like to bring into our family"!

As Jaeger concluded his meal, another Vodka Tonic was placed before him, again unbidden and the empty glass removed he replied, "Seems you guys have done your homework well, so what particularly do you have in mind"?

"I like that in a man Nestor", said Ortega continuing, "Tell him what we need"!

"You will be paid two thousand dollars a week, for starters. You'll be on constant call at all times as it were. We call and you stop what you're doing and respond to our needs whatever they may be at the moment, immediately and without question. There may be weeks at a time when you hear nothing from us. There may be times when you are away for weeks at a time. Regardless, you will be paid well for your availability. In short order we will pay you more as you indicate your value to the family. We expect complete honesty, loyalty and will tolerate nothing else"!

"When do you want me to come on board"?

Magellan and Ortega looked at each other, then glanced over at Davalantes, who gave an imperceptible nod, as Ortega reached into his open briefcase and removed a bulging large envelope, tossing it across the table to Jaeger saying, "In this envelope is a signing bonus of ten thousand dollars senor Jaeger. Congratulations, you've just joined the family"! At that point Ortega raised his glass in salute of Jaegers arrival.

In the coming months ahead, Jaeger was eased into the organization as either Magellan or Davalantes, would certainly call upon him at any time of the day or night, to provide security for meetings. Collect a variety of debts owed Ortega, by any means necessary. Meet incoming people at either of Houston's airports and getting them to Ortega, Magellan, or Davalantes in one piece then putting them back on the plane from where ever they came. After about a month and a half of relatively benign work, Magellan suggested that Jaeger commence courier work around town, intrastate, interstate and finally internationally.

Jaeger was kept moderately busy during this period, with each assignment going off without a hitch, when he was invited by Davalantes to join them for a swim. Which meant wet work. A trip down to Panama, to meet with a local banker, who was contracted long ago to massage and wash their cash flow through his bank, for a hefty fee. Only thing was the banker's lifestyle had expanded past that of the norm and was very noticeable. This prompted a second look at the subject and it was discovered the banker had developed sticky fingers far in excess of his very generous fees, along with a noticeable change of behavior, indicative that he was deep in the throes of chemical dependency. Something had to be done and soon.

Both Davalantes and Jaeger flew down to Panama, spent a week reconnoitering, and then abducted the banker. After a weekend session away from his family, they cleaned the banker up and all drove to his office, the following Monday morning where he wire transferred all of Ortega's remaining funds in the bank to a variety of other offshore banks, then all walked out smiling ostensibly for a golfing outing. Davalantes wanted to siphon off all of the bankers ill-gotten gains also from his personal accounts, but listened to Jaegers sage counsel that indicated it was certain to raise the attention of the locals as to what was happening prior to their departure. Besides, if the subject was to remain cooperative, he must have hope of survival and the safety of his family.

Davalantes considered the suggestion briefly and concluded that Jaeger made sense. Just to be chalked up as the cost of doing business. Since the abduction and the funds transfer went off without a hitch and they all left the bank for apparently a round of golf and the waiting helicopter exfiltrated them successfully into Columbia in the dark of night, all went well. They returned back to Houston several days later carrying a newspaper with an article reporting on the abduction of a Panamanian banker and the discovery of his half eaten body on one of the local golf courses presumably by one of local gators. Only thing was the banker had a single bullet wound in the back of his head.

Normally when a banker turns 'Sportin' Man' with the funds of a crime family his entire family is left to pay the price with their lives. Since the local banker was a well-known local womanizer, the subsequent investigation by the locals, stayed local and eventually came to naught.

Jaeger had entered a world, where he had his choice from a small fleet of vehicles all of which were the results of acquisition of debts by many to Ortega, along with a fluid number of safe houses around the immediate area. There was a round robin number of circulating cell phones, along with the temporary, use them then lose them, cell phones. Multiple identities and pass ports were designed to be used only once then discarded and were available of such a quality that never once was there a question raised.

As far as Ortega knew, Jaeger was what he seemed. A capable soldier, who used his brain. Never once questioning, always making recommendations that worked effectively. Ortega never became aware of Jaegers primary residence not twenty minutes away. Yet both men worked in similar ways to protect themselves from the unexpected.

Ortega had two primary residences, one of which was in the spacious condo high up in the Tealstone Towers, that occupied a third of the floor, on Houston's far west side. His other primary residence was a sprawling two level gated affair, that consumed over six thousand square feet, replete with a four car garage, tiled roofs, and surrounded by an eight foot wall with embedded with rusty nails around the entire perimeter. He could look out of his second floor bedroom window and see directly into the bowels of NASA, as the rear of this residence fronted a large boat dock housing a state of the art, fifty foot 'Scrub', twin engine cigarette boat, along with an equally imposing, seventy five foot Chris Craft, cabin cruiser, tethered to the northern most part of the Clear Lake estuary. For any given reason one could jump into one of his boats, motor on down the estuary, then out onto Galveston Bay, then out into the Gulf of Mexico within the hour, or less.

Of the two, Jaeger led the more sedate aesthetic life style, while Ortega's social life was more 'of the moment', bedding the finest women the club community and money could provide. Drinking the finest most expensive wines and liquor and eating at only the finest establishments wherever he went.

Ortega was chameleon, fluid, unpredictable and most of all deadly. A man of his word, up to a point, from his point of view, as long as his word cost him nothing. The only thing that mattered was his point of view, unless that changed for some reason or whim, then the 'Nuevo' point of view was the only thing that mattered.

The very thing that fueled the absolute loyalty and obedience to Ortega was his generosity. His people would and often did, give their very lives for him, for while they were in his employ, they wanted for nothing.

Several years earlier he'd brought into his family Nestor Magellan, of European descent, unlike the rest of the Mestizo's he'd employed. Magellan, a linguistic expert, amongst a host of other talents, could speak a host of languages fluently and move in circles Ortega could not and like Magellan before him, Jaegers acquisition began to bear fruit even faster than he anticipated.

Of Ortega's many legitimate business interests, was a meat market and Cantina on Canal Street, on the eastern edge of down town Houston, amidst a solidly Latino working class section of town. Jugos and his wife immigrated to Houston illegally over a dozen years ago. Through hard work and diligence they kept a low profile opened their market and expanded it into an establishment that was famous for offering the finest Chorizo sausage and Menudo soup, a staple for the locals that was a delicacy reminiscent of home.

This was where the individual that accosted Jaeger ended up. Rendered in the dark of night into the variety of sausages and food stuffs labeled 'Specially Imported Meat', with his bones and gristle cooked for hours until only the bones were left, making the resultant Menudo Soup for the following days menu. What Jugos was unable to turn into a salable product, such as skin, rendered bones, hair and the head, ended up as food for the fishes, in the dark of night some sixty miles out into the Gulf of Mexico.

Whenever one of Ortega's operatives or victims met their end, they were always taken to Jugos, to be rendered into one of his 'Specialty' products. Jugos made it a point to specially label the 'Specialty' products and fully cleanse the implements used in their manufacture. It was a win, win proposition for Jugos and served a purpose for Ortega who depended upon him for this important service. People disappeared completely and Jugos food costs were significantly diminished in the process. Everything else entered a series of commercial trash dumpsters far across town.

Eventually Ortega required that some of the Menudo Soup that came from the departed, be delivered to him for his personal consumption having developed a craving for the soup. Nothing was wasted, everything had a purpose, for one side of Ortega's persona was a variety of compulsions amongst which was a drive for detail and neatness. Hold up your end and live well. Fail in any way and cease to exist. Life was cheap, Ortega reasoned. For every winner there had to be a loser. Serve him well and live well, get careless and disappear completely. Either way one served his interests.

He came into town and started to grow from almost nothing to a dozen years later having a variety of interests, loan sharking, book-making, strip clubs, restaurants, smuggling, but his first love was the importation and distribution of illegal drugs, both organic and man-made.

Life in America was berry berry good to him, for he was awash in money.

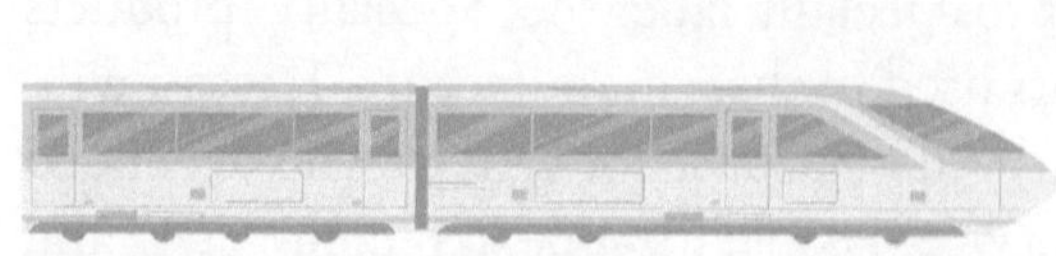

3

Ortega and Jaeger kept their communications completely superficial and businesslike. Jaeger was paid reasonably well and had the freedom to pursue other endeavors, as long as they didn't conflict with anything Ortega needed. "He's my bitch now", Ortega privately confided!

Jaeger made it a point to never to question and Ortega was never one to explain a plan or directive. One either figured it out, or didn't. Ability to deliver was the only criterion acceptable. In Ortega's world there were no second chances. Failure was usually met by ones quiet and complete disappearance, followed the next day by a 'Special' at a certain Cantina in the barrio.

The man was always in complete control of himself. One never saw him drunk or high on the drugs he so successfully provided the community at large. His forays with women, while legendary in scope, were always short term and discrete. Never over committing to anything, if he said something was going to be done, it was done exactly as he ordered.

He kept himself physically fit, always practicing a variety of martial arts at a high level of proficiency and was considered exceptionally adept at a Brazilian form of knife fighting. His competence with firearms was quietly considered marginally acceptable, however his first love, ever since his early days while making his reputation, was killing up close and personal, was the blade. Now, as Jefe of his own organization he employed a host of others to take care of those mundane tasks.

Ortega's wide circle of partnerships were so well crafted, that he never had to do business with an unknown, thus as far as Jaeger could determine from his position on the fringes, he had no Achilles Heel to exploit. Ortega had so insulated himself with competent people that the average soldier on the street had no idea who they worked for.

Seeking to expand his interests, Ortega entertained a conversation with some agents from a consortium of Argentine Bankers and Industrialists brought to him by Nestor Magellan. The purpose was International Industrial Espionage of the burgeoning Brazilian commercial aircraft industry. The target was a company called 'Embraer Aircraft', a successful and rapidly growing aircraft manufacturer, nursed along in its infancy by the Brazilian government and currently on the verge of an explosive growth, courtesy of a recent contract for the purchase of their aircraft at prices significantly lower than those of American manufacture. Of course with the large order of commercial aircraft came an agreement favoring the buyer with a more favorable access to the Brazilian market, in key cities. In time Continental Airlines would be able to replace their aging fleet with a quality aircraft at a considerable savings.

The countries of Argentina and Brazil were always an abrasive element towards each other since their inceptions for a myriad of reasons. If the Argentine Industrialists could find a way to get hold of the entire manufacturing plans and testing criteria of the Embraer fleet, they could reverse engineer everything, and start their own Aircraft Industry at a fraction of the startup costs and time constraints required.

The catalyst that made things gel was the discovery and exploitation of the dissatisfaction of Embraer's Director of Operations, with his own Board of Directors and elements of the Brazilian Government. His expectation of being appointed as President of the Company was overshadowed by not only his own Board of Directors, but the very elements of the Government he'd worked so long to cultivate.

Known as a hardworking and intelligent aeronautical engineer and designer, he'd sacrificed all for his first love, the Embraer family of aircraft products. His family social and private life everything. Working often far into the night to get things right. The only social life he embraced was the occasional gatherings where he could discretely impress those whose favor he needed to advance the company and make known his efforts and success's. Yet knowing precisely the political environment he was dealing with, he'd taken the liberty to make a copy of every single plan and detail of his company's family of products.

When the announcement was made of another to assume the Presidency of the company, an obscure accounting type who knew naught about aeronautical engineering, a political hack appointed by those in Brasilia, the nation's Capital. He took the news with a quiet aplomb and dignity as was his custom all the while internally seething with rage at the indignity. A month later, while attending an engineering seminar in Montevideo Uruguay, he was introduced to a man who identified himself as Carlos Meyers. During the several days of the conference, they discovered they had much in common and of course Myers was ever the consoling sort decrying the corporate slap in the face endured by his new friend. Over the course of the conference, The Director, began to gradually express his dissatisfaction with his lot, to the completely empathetic attention of Carlos Meyers. After the conference, the two men stayed in touch with each other, with Meyers traveling to Sao Paulo several times to cement his new bonds of friendship, with the disgruntled director. Upon one of his trips, Meyers discretely sounded out the Director, with the possibility of starting up his own aircraft company in Buenos Aires, quietly subsidized by the Argentine government and a consortium of bankers and industrialists.

"I've sounded out all the right people and they are intrigued at the possibilities. All I've talked to agree that you have been wronged. Everyone I've talked to has agreed that you've been the single irreplaceable component to your enterprises success", said Meyers casually while turning his snifter of Napoleon Brandy. "With what you must have in your head, from all the years, as Operations Director, the startup costs would be minimal for such and enterprise"!

"Carlos my friend, what if I told you that I could have the Company up and running within the year"! "A year, impossible", said Meyers.

"With the right backing and complete carte' blanch and a guarantee of total control, I could guarantee that production could commence within nine months of inception"!

"Three years perhaps, but a year? Why the logistics alone would be monumental. You'd have to recreate all of the engineering plans and documents, then testing. Perhaps three years, but not one"!

"The Argentine Government would have to run interference for a plant location and along with the banking and industrialists provide a facility for production along with runways and electrical access. Etcetera"!

"That's already been discussed and it's a given the government would act to clear the way of any impediments. But the manpower requirements alone would be monumental.

"Carlos you have a sea of unemployed in Argentina that can serve as the rank and file workers, as for the key engineers, I can get all I want. The key element I have safely locked away, to guarantee success"!

"And that would be my friend", asked Meyers?

"The entire set of plans. Engineering drawings, testing data everything. Tooling specifications, vendors and alternate sources. Everything required for an almost instantaneous startup"! Meyers eyes opened wide as he said, "I see what you're driving at now"!

"Has anyone ever given thought of a suitable name for the enterprise Carlos"?

"Nothing concrete as of yet, but the name 'Aero Argente' has been discussed"!

"Seems a suitable name"!

"So what guarantees will you require to give birth and nurture this enterprise? Two things seem essential my friend, first of which is your expertise and continual service guiding the enterprise for an extended period of time and of course the entire plans for the Embraer fleet of aircraft, everything", said Meyers!

"In that we are in complete agreement my friend, so here is what I will require. In advance of everything, complete Argentine citizenship papers for me and my entire family, signed by the President. Guarantee of a suitable residence, in proximity of the manufacturing facility, along with transport and bodyguards for myself and my family. Next a contract guaranteed, by both the Government and all of the entities involved in the new company as Senior Managing Director. I will have complete veto power on anyone appointed on the board of directors. I will be in charge of everything. Production, sales, everything. My annual remuneration will be at one hundred thousand pounds British Sterling, or its equivalent in Argentine currency, guaranteed by the Argentine Government. Next, upon delivery of the entire plans, a payment of Four Million pounds in British Sterling banknotes, wire transferred to several foreign banks of my choosing. Finally, at the signature of the very first sale of the new aircraft, a bonus of a million pounds in British Sterling banknotes or its Argentine equivalent will be wire transferred to my offshore banking facilities and each and every year thereafter for the duration of my non-cancelable contract. Of course all will be guaranteed by the Argentine Government. These are my terms Carlos and they are non-negotiable"!

"Other than the up-front monetary requirements of yours that appear to be rather steep I'd think everything you require is completely possible for a man of your stature. I know how keep all of the parties involved in Argentina of acquiring your knowledge and expertise and indeed it would be a boon to our economy, so given that, I think I can sell your requirements to the interested parties. Of course you've surmised the much needed boost it will provide for the Argentine economy. Thus if all goes well and I suspect it will, statues will be erected in your name and the recognition of your hard work and talents over the years will finally be accorded to you, many times over my friend"!

Meyers quickly made his way back to Buenos Aires the following day, to set up meetings with the necessary ministers in government and in the private sector to bring together all of the vital elements of the plans to launch "Aero Argente". Of course nothing in the transfer could be traced back to Industrial, Banking, or Governmental partners, so Meyers suggested that he visit an old and reliable friend of his in Houston Texas. Nestor Magellan had the talents sufficient to bring everything to fruition. He was well placed in an organization well versed in the arts of smuggling and after all this was an enterprise tailor made for smuggling.

Thus the trip to America, specifically Houston Texas and a meeting with Magellan and his employer the nonentity Ortega, to work out the details.

The meeting was held in a secluded section in the restaurant of the Weston Galleria Hotel where Meyers stayed. After the appropriate introductions by Magellan and the meal, Meyers went to work outlining the plan. After he concluded he asked, "So Mister Ortega can you help us"?

"Can we help you? Of course! The question is will we help you bring home your bacon"?

"Then I shall rephrase my question. Will you help us"?

"Yes, but for a price. Our price Senor, non-negotiable"!

"And that is Senor", asked Meyers waiting for the first shoe to drop?

"A quarter of a million dollars working capital up front wired into an account of our selection. That will put everything in motion. Next, I will send a team of men, to wherever the transfer is to happen. I will know the exact location a week in advance so I can have my people in place. Your government will furnish us complete and unquestioned Argentine identity documents, two weeks in advance of the transaction for each member of the team. Upon agreement, pictures and vital descriptions will be sent to you, of the selected team members, for you to work with"!

As Ortega spoke, Meyers nodded his head as he went to each aspect of the agreement. "Finally Senor, to the transaction. To guarantee our end you will be the one that accepts delivery, but the delivery point will be in Houston Texas at a place of my choice. You will arrive alone and with an amount of two million dollars in American currency. You will bring with you, in addition, corporate preferred share documents that indicative of my ownership in a company name I furnish upon receipt of the advance working capital, in the amount of five percent of the ownership of 'Aero Argente'. Of course it will be a shell company that I control via an offshore banking entity. Of course while in Houston we will guarantee your security and that of your plans back to Argentina"!

Meyers leaned back in his chair and made a perfunctory show of thought before saying, "I'm certain I can sell my people on your terms Mister Ortega. Tomorrow morning I will fly back to Buenos Aires. Give me a few days to get everyone to agree then I'll call you with a request of your banking instructions. Is that acceptable"?

"I will await your call Senor Meyers, with great interest"!

Two days later, Meyers was back in Buenos Aires, making the rounds of the various Industrialists, Bankers and Governmental Ministers trying to tie up all the loose ends. It was agreed for all of the interested parties to meet at a resort down the River Plata. During the course of their very private meeting, there was a point where the entire process started to unravel where it came down to the various upfront costs involved. It seemed that Meyers must insert some sanity back into the process.

"Gentlemen, while we seem to be at an impasse regarding the initial outlay of funds involved for this enterprise, I can't stress enough how much it will mean to this nation. If you'll all recall the disastrous war we engaged in some years ago trying to wrest the Malvinas Islands from the British for the possibility that oil existed just offshore. Here, we risk no war as such with our neighbor, Brazil, if we but keep our wits about us. First, our friend in Brazil must be taken care of initially, completely. His plans are vital to the enterprise as well as his expertise in getting the enterprise up and running to the point of profitability. He will, of course reengineer all of the aircraft quickly to make it unrecognizable from the product he gave birth to. The Brazilians then can protest all they want but proof of our involvement will be impossible to obtain once State Secrets sanctions are imposed.

After the first contracts are fully executed and delivered to willing buyers, any number of things are likely to happen to the man and his family, our country still being rife with counter revolutionaries, going back to the days of the Generals. Kidnappings gone awry of entire prominent families still are an occasional occurrence with the bodies later discovered up river in Paraguay. The country mourns, statues are erected, perhaps even a street or two is named and life goes on. People are employed in a viable enterprise that makes money for all involved. The man dies along with the estate and the recipients of our further largesse cease to exist"!

Meyers then paused a moment and then continued, "As far as those that will affect the transfer in America, their price is non-negotiable. My contact has an unblemished record of always delivering what he says he will. If two million dollars is too high a price to pay initially so be it. A lesser sum will have to suffice. Perhaps a half million can be the amount are we all agreed"?

Meyers looked around the room as he saw each and every head nod their acceptance of his modest proposal, with one exception. A Brigadier General who asked, "Since we are dealing with scum and outlaws, what will keep them from betraying us all? How will they accept a lesser sum of money"?

"First my General as to ownership of the enterprise, should everything go awry in the first case and the Company never form the shares will be worthless. Next, when the company grows to what we all think it will become the board of directors at that moment in time can vote to declare all preferred shares of stock into common stock, diminishing their value. Finally my good General, since your brother in law is the Director of the National Police, I'm certain he can tell us the identity of a master forger adept in making what appears to be well used counterfeit currency in one hundred dollar denominations that can be successfully included with the real currency of a lesser amount. But the forger must be a master of his craft. The right banknote paper, the right ink and the right engravings. It must look real as real as the genuine currency, for I will be the delivery agent on the ground. So General is this possible"?

"Senor, it is possible. I will see my brother in law tomorrow"!

Ortega had Jaeger in mind rather than Nestor Magellan, to lead the operation in Brazil. He had other plans for Magellan on the front burner. And why not? He'd performed well in the past and the event with the Panamanian Banker went smoothly. This would appear to be a step up for him and the carrot of a six figure reward at the end would be certain to be of interest. But in case of anything going awry, then he was expendable, not yet a member of Ortega's inner circle and simply a Gringo, worthy of sacrifice.

Ortega had received the funds transfer of the quarter million working capital he'd required to get things in motion from Meyers in Argentina, so he summoned both Jaeger and Magellan to meet with him at one of his restaurants. Magellan was there just to be made aware of what was in the works, the real purpose was to inform Jaeger of his next assignment and let him know of the six figure bonus at the end of the rainbow. Jaeger would head up the operation along with three others he'd never met, two of which were fluent in Portuguese, to meet with Carlos Meyers and the Director of Operations of Embraer, to effect the exchange of the documents with the exchange of funds that would be essential for the Aero Argente' startup. New identities and documents were to be provided for everyone prior to departure and each would make their way separately to the Excelsior Hotel in Sao Paulo Brazil.

Each one would be in a previously booked room at the Hotel. The director was to be there as well as Carlos Meyer. Since the 'Director' was to be in Sao Paulo on corporate business anyway it provided great cover for the transaction. After the transaction, came the question of how to get the purloined papers back to America?

"Mail them back", said Jaeger!

"What", exclaimed Magellan?

"Yeah Nestor. The principle of Occam's razor. Keep things simple. It goes like this. There's gonna be a lag of a few days between the time I get down there and meet up with the others and the time in which this guy Meyers and the Director arrives to make their exchange. Isn't Sao Paulo the largest city in South America and pretty much the epicenter of Brazilian capitalism? Well then the city will have any number of private air freight carriers throughout the city and like right here in America, a number of retail outlets in which to place packages to anywhere on the planet. Now all you're shipping is paper right? The trick is to break down the packages to those small enough not to attract attention. I've used these in the past often enough that I can say that most of them can deliver most places on the earth within twenty four hours. So here's the deal. I go all over Houston and rent about three or four private post office boxes. Not the ones like the US Post office, but private postal stations. There are a lot of them all over town. Before I leave for Brazil, I tell you where they're at and give you the combination numbers of the boxes. Of course the boxes will be too big to accept the packages. But they will leave you a note inside the box when they arrive. All one has to do is present the note left in the box, sign my name and they will surrender the package or packages to the one who presents the note. Simple isn't it"?

"Oh, one thing more. Since everything is shipped via aircraft, you can buy insurance on every package, just in case a plane crashes somewhere between point 'A' and point 'B'! This method is not very good at moving anything else other than paper; the trick is to reduce the packages to a small enough size to not attract attention"!

'Won't the number of packages heading towards Houston attract attention", asked Magellan?

"Yeah it would if you shipped them all at the same place, with the same company. But with Federal Express, UPS, and other Airfreight companies all eager for business, it gets down to a clerical thing. It'll probably take the better part of a day to package everything then another day to send everything out. Then when the last package has been delivered, I ring you guys up long distance; let you know the, "Package has been sent", then head for the airport and home. Twenty four hours later or so, you send some of your people around to collect the packages"!

"How much joo going to need for carrying cash", asked Ortega? "Don't know the quantity to be shipped, and the going rates are not in my Cabeza, but say ten large for walking around money and since two of your guys will be fluent in the language and have to do the most of the talking once we're down there, give them five grand each for walking around money. You want insurance on the packages"?

Magellan and Ortega looked at each other with Ortega nodding his head as Magellan said, "You'll get twelve and the others six each"!

"How will I know what the other three look like", asked Jaeger?

"Everyone will have rooms at the Excelsior pre-booked on separate floors. Everyone will have a picture of you. You will be the boss of the operation", said Magellan calmly. "They will take their orders from you. You will be paid a hundred thousand dollars for your efforts upon the successful conclusion of the transaction back here in Houston. Are we agreed"?

"A hundred large, for a few days of paper shuffling? We are agreed Nestor"!

"There is one other that you will meet in Sao Paulo. He will be an MIT trained aeronautical engineer, who currently works at NASA in Clear Lake. He will examine the documents to be exchanged, between the director and Meyers. The engineer is a Brazilian National with permanent resident status in the States, fluent in his native Portuguese and English. He will be the one who will verify that the documents are genuine and viable. You then will be furnished with the banking access codes for the funds transfer. Once the engineer documents the authenticity of what he has examined and this may take a few days, then Carlos Meyers is to transfer the funds to our various accounts that you will provide him with"!

"Once he has access to your account information aren't you concerned that he'll raid your accounts at a later date", asked Jaeger?

"I've known Carlos for some time and we've done business together. The accounts the fund are to be wired to are for transitory purposes only. Within a half hour, a secondary transfer will be affected thus draining the account of the bulk of the assets. Even if he wanted to fuck us, he couldn't", said Magellan!

"Once everything has authenticated, you will direct one of your men to escort our man back to the airport and put him on a jet back to Houston. The Director will return to his work and Meyers will no doubt fly back to Buenos Aires and wait for our call. You and the rest will package and ship the documents to Houston. When completed each of you will fly back to America by a different carrier and routing. Are we understood", asked Magellan?

"Completely", said Jaeger! "But what happens later", asked Jaeger?

"You get paid and enjoy your money. The rest is none of your business", said Ortega testily!

As Jaeger drove back from his meeting with Ortega and Magellan he began to feel ill at ease from his meeting. His last question had apparently stepped over that imaginary line that Ortega drew in the sands. Somehow he'd no concerns about Magellan, but of Ortega, there was always that aura of shifting sands, that indicated a lack of moral scruples. Reminding him of what he'd read about Ludovico Svorza, the historical Duke of Milan. The subject of Shakespeare's 'Othello'. Somehow he equated Magellan with Nicolo Machaivelli his foreign minister, mouthpiece and fixer, who did the dirty work while Othello pulled the strings. Machiavelli ended up in a dungeon for a number of years, all because of an errant statement. Because of his last question and the reptilian response from 'El Jefe', Jaeger had every reason to believe he'd crossed the line of no return and wondered how long it would take before Magellan had traversed that chasm himself.

As he drove on, he wondered about the convolution of the big picture. So many unknowns to consider. If all went well the Argentines would get a fast track into the aircraft production business. The Brazilian aircraft industry would receive unwanted competition from an unexpected source, utilizing their own documents. Ortega's reputation certainly would benefit far beyond whatever he was receiving in compensation, in certain circles. Yet should news leak out somehow of the Argentine connection in the stolen State owned documents of Brazils, Argentine and Brazilian diplomats and international lawyers were assured of work for months, if not years to come.

T he group Ortega assembled, met at one of his homes on the Clear
Lake estuary, a thirty minute drive south of Houston. The house
mirrored Ortega's visible persona, consisting of mostly metal and
glass construction, anchored by kiln dried red brick at all the load bearing
junctures. The property surrounded by the tall stucco wall, just a scant
mile from NASA's main entrance. Birds never landed upon the wall for
a good reason. Rusty nails and shards of glass lay hidden by a seven inch
metal reveal that shielded their presence from the street.

It occurred to Jaeger, as he toured the property with the others, that
Ortega had more money tied up in his two boats docked in the rear,
than most people would ever see in a lifetime, much less his digs in Clear
Lake.

Once everyone arrived and the introductions were made, Ortega made
it clear to all that Jaeger was in charge and responsible, thus turning over
the meeting to Jaeger, who went over each ones responsibility and role
at every juncture of the event. Eventually each man knew not only his
role, but that of all the others from beginning to the time they boarded
the planes back to the states. Travel documents were issued, comprised of
forged passports and visa's authentic looking local drivers licenses, credit
cards and the agreed amount of traveling currency.

Each man fixed the image and the name of the other in his head
before the meeting broke up. As usual, Ortega tossed a small party before
they departed, sparing no expense for the cuisine. By Ten PM, they all
departed with their marching orders well fixed in their heads. As Jaeger
left, he paid little attention to Santos, his appointed Segundo, who hung
back claiming that he had to go to the bathroom. Santos was the other
Brazilian national, raised on the streets of Sao Paulo, immigrating to
Mexico as a teen, then to The States. Fluent in his native Portuguese
and Spanish, with a working knowledge of colloquial English, he'd been
with Ortega almost since the beginning. He was out of the country, more

often than not working on deals with the shadow community of South American society. He'd contacts in most of the major cities in Central and South America. Usually a reliable man he always saw to it that things got done, being the natural selection to act as guide and provider for the group. He knew the local people to go to for whatever was needed and the lay of the land, in Sao Paulo. His prime function was to provide for vehicles, lodging and a local source of weaponry.

Of course DeCunha was the Aeronautical engineer, recruited from NASA whose sole function was to examine and certify all of the engineering drawings, while Obregon and Bujo's sole purpose was to provide muscle and security. Both Obregon and Bujo were of Central American origin; spoke little English and no Portuguese. Both were solidly built men, of slightly less than medium height, proven reliable in the past, who said little and sported a menacing appearance.

Shortly after the teams arrival and check into the Excelsior Hotel, both Jaeger and Santos were to visit a local friend of Santos to obtain vehicles and weaponry, all of which were to be discarded prior to leaving the country.

The following day, each man left from either Intercontinental or Hobby Airports at different times, on different carriers, in different directions all programmed to land in Sao Paulo Brazil, within a six hour window. Each man was check into the Excelsior Hotel in separate rooms, where Jaeger booked a separate suite of rooms reserved as the site of the transfer.

DeCunha checked into a hotel a short walk from the Excelsior as a precaution to separate him from the others. The following morning Santos and Obregon took a taxi to meet with one of Santos local contacts, obtaining two cars and handguns for each of them including Jaeger, while Jaeger met with DeCunha at his Hotel for breakfast, after which they strolled over to the Excelsior. DeCunha was visibly nervous all the while, never having been involved with anything like industrial espionage. Jaeger spent most of his time mapping out the activities of the next hours ahead of them all, carefully compartmentalizing all of the players and the roles to be played.

"Just concentrate on verifying the plans laid before you as genuine and workable. We will see to all the rest. When you've finally put your blessing on all of the plans, another gentleman will see to it that the funds agreed to are immediately wired to your offshore account in your presence. Then I'll personally drive you to the airport and put you on a flight back to Houston"!

They rode the elevator in silence up to the fifteenth floor and made their way to the room where the transfer was to take place. The door opened up and a well-dressed man in a business suit greeted them in slightly accented English saying, "Good Morning gentlemen, I'm Carlos Meyer", shaking hands with each in turn as they entered, "And this gentleman is Senhor Eduardo Dos Palmas. If you Senor DeCunha will make yourself comfortable with Mr. Dos Palmas, here are the keys to his Grey BMW parked on the roof of the hotels car park. In it you will find the documents we are interested in all sealed in boxes", he said to Jaeger who took the keys and signaled Santos, Obregon and Bujo to follow him to the car park, a separate building attached to the hotel.

As they all rode the elevator up to the top of the car park Santos said, "We have the vehicles and the weapons, here is yours just as you've asked, a Brazilian made Taurus .357 Magnum short barrel, along with a box of ammo, just in case there's an unforeseen event"!

"Thanks, but you know your boss Santos. He just doesn't tolerate problems", said Jaeger.

They found the BMW and opened the trunk and pulled out the sealed boxes of documents from both the trunk and the rear seat of the car, without a word and carried them back to the Dos Palmas suite downstairs.

Once they arrives back at the suite both Dos Palmas and Decoma set to the long and laborious process of document verification of the Embraer fleet of seven commercial aircraft, four of which were short, medium and long range commercial jet aircraft, a military VTOL propjet, similar to the type the US Navy was currently testing as well as two prototypes of turbo helicopters. Now all anyone could do was wait, while Dos Palmas and Decoma huddled over the documents. Dos Palmas leading DeCunha over every engineering drawing step by laborious step working in two hour shifts, then taking a break, then back huddling over the drawings.

As soon as a section of drawings was verified, they were handed to Jaeger and Santos who quickly packed them separately into smaller sealed boxes, for later disbursal via International UPS and Federal Express. Bujo took up his position by the entrance door to the suite, while Meyers sat watching the TV with Obregon. The work droned on steadily throughout the rest of the day and far into the night, interrupted only by the periodic arrival of room service in the adjoining suite. At midnight both Dos Palmas and DeCunha were at the limits of their endurance, begging off and in need of sleep. It was agreed to let them sleep in the adjoining suite with Meyers going back to his suite down the hall and Obregon and Bujo going back to theirs, all to meet back at Dos Palmas suite at six in the morning for breakfast while Jaeger and Santos baby sat the documents.

As Jaeger started to relax in his easy chair, he had an uneasy feeling that he just couldn't wrap his arms around about the entire affair. He cast an eye upon Santos curled up on the couch, his arms wrapped tightly around his front apparently sound asleep. He replayed everything in his mind, from the night of the meeting at Ortega's digs in Clear Lake to the plane trip down to Brazil, to every moment that passed between them. Something about this Carlos Meyers, the Argentine agent just didn't sit well with him. Furtive glances between him and Santos. Passing comments between them when they thought Jaeger wasn't looking indicated that something was up. But what? Jaeger closed his eyes, and kept a hand on the revolver. The five thirty wakeup call from the desk was just around the corner.

He woke with a start looking at his watch, which indicated a few minutes before four in the morning. He glanced over at Santos, who had turned over on the couch facing the other way, still with his arms folded across his chest, snoring peacefully. Still with that nagging feeling surrounding him, he pulled out the revolver, from his waist band, looked at it turning it over and over, unloaded the cylinder and carefully examined the firing pin, with one eye on Santos. Finding the firing pin in good working order, he glanced at the bullets, lifting them up one by one. They looked OK, but somehow didn't feel right. He reloaded the weapon and stood up. Only one way to find out if something was up.

He walked to the door, certain that Santos was deep asleep and let himself out, taking the elevator to the top of the car park; he made his way to Santos vehicle and got inside. He tore thin strips off the linen napkin he lifted from the buffet table on his way out and stuffed them into his ears, lifting the passenger side floor mat and pulled the revolver from his waist band pointing it towards the floor and pulled the trigger.

All that happened was the sound of "Click". He pulled the trigger again and with the same result. He opened the trunk and rummaged through the tool kit finding a set of pliers. He then unloaded the revolver and wedged the bullet under the tire tread and prized the lead bullet away from the casing. As he suspected, the round had not one bit of powder in the shell. He did the same with each of the rounds in the revolver and came up with the very same result.

He was being set up. Give him a serviceable weapon, but if the bullets won't work, the gun won't fire. A nasty surprise, at the worst possible time. No doubt they would wait until after all of the documents were safely mailed back to the three private postal boxes he'd set up back in Houston, prior to their departure. Ortega had the locations and the lock box keys.

Within twenty four hours after they left Jaegers hands, the documents would be safely in Ortega's hands and Jaeger was to be just another dead American on the streets of a foreign land. He took a deep breath wondering just how he could brazen things through. He got out of the car, locked the door, gathering up the bullets and the shells and flung them towards the far reaches of the top floor of the car park. He reached into his pocket and reloaded the revolver with six more of the bogus shells and made his way to the hotel lobby to get another pack of cigarettes. Should anyone be awake when he returned, he had a simple excuse for his absence.

He let himself back into the suite quietly and as he tiptoed back towards his couch, he noticed a gift from the gods lying on the floor in front of Santos's couch. Santos's revolver had somehow slipped from his waistband while he was asleep and had fallen silently on the plush carpeting of the floor. He was still peacefully asleep on the couch, snoring softly facing the wall just as Jaeger had left him, with his arms folded in front of him, the single lamp light still on in the far corner of the suite casting a modest shadow.

Jaeger picked up Santos's weapon and walked back to his oversized lounge chair and sat down examining Santos's revolver. He unloaded it discovering that the shells were of .38 caliber. He compared the heft of Santo's shells with the bogus .357 shells he had as reloads. Of course they were slightly heavier, because they had the propellant in them. The .38 shells would work just fine in Jaegers revolver, so he loaded Santo's shells into his revolver and put in the bogus shells into Santos's revolver, rising silently from his chair and softly walking over to the couch, carefully placing Santo's revolver between one of the cushions and his rear, instead of the floor. With any luck Santos would wake up, find the revolver in the recesses of the couch, feel sheepish that it had slipped out, put it back in his waistband and think nothing more of it.

As Jaeger settled back into his chair he glanced at his watch, which indicated 4:35 in the morning. He was feeling slightly better about things, but not by a lot. They were still going to come for him in the aftermath. Perhaps just another forty five minutes of shut eye, before the fools parade began again. As he drifted off, he smiled slightly wondering about old George Carlin's favorite saying that always made Jaeger chuckle, given the truth it told, "Paranoia, is simply the flip side of complete awareness"!

Yet sleep wouldn't come, as he reclined still with one eye on his luminescent watch and the other on the sleeping Santos. At 5:15 he picked up the phone and called the desk informing them that the 5:30 wakeup call would not be needed. At 5:35 he walked into the other bedroom and woke up both DeCunha and Dos Palmas suggesting they both shower and dress, that room service and breakfast would arrive in a half an hour. Then he casually padded back into the main room and gently awoke Santos, telling him that the others had been awakened and that room service was a half hour away. He walked back to his chair, made a show of looking for his shoes, finding them and slowly putting them on while keeping an eye upon Santos who was slowly waking up, then reaching for his waistband and in a small panic looking for his revolver, then finding it, quickly placing it in his waistband, with a look of sleepy relief.

Santos cast a quick glance at Jaeger, who appeared to be fixed upon tying his shoe laces. Six AM had come and gone, with room service arriving with the buffet in the adjoining bedroom, then quickly leaving, the Brazilian duo of Dos Palmas and DeCunha busy eating breakfast and talking shop, while Santos disappeared for his shower in the other bedroom, emerging still half asleep, while Jaeger handed the responsibility of keeping an eye on their guests, while he took a quick shower.

By Seven Thirty, Carlos Meyers entered bringing with him a small electronic machine, that he quickly hooked up to the phone system in the room, saying when completed, "This will affect the transfer of funds as agreed to the appropriate offshore accounts, instantly when our business is concluded, with paper printouts of the transaction, for each party"!

At Eight AM both Obrigon and Bujo appeared at the door saying they opted to eat downstairs at the hotel's restaurant rather than in the room, as Dos Palmas and DeCunha, were hard at work verifying the engineering documents. As usual, as soon as they completed a section of verification, they turned them over to Jaeger and Santos who quickly boxed and sealed them in cardboard boxes setting them aside. Every two hours, they took a break to replenish themselves with food and coffee, before plunging back into the morass of verification. By afternoon with both engineers still hard at work, and the downside of the work now ahead of them, Obregon and Bubo were starting to grumble impatiently about shortcuts. It took Jaeger speaking to them through Santos to bring them back into line, reminding them about how everything must be right, or else Ortega would not be a happy man should things go wrong. The very mention of Ortega's name, brought the grumbling to an immediate halt, while Meyers sat by patiently smiling, knowing full well that a dead man was doing his work for him. Or so he concluded.

By five that afternoon, the engineers had passed the point of diminishing returns and were exhausted. As usual, everything took longer than originally expected, thus it was concluded that all verification would stop for the evening. Everybody would rest for the following morning, as it was estimated that by noon the next day verification should be completed.

Santos had spent most of the day, identifying the various Federal Express and United Parcel drop off locations, in greater Sao Paulo, where each box could be taken and addressed to the private postal locations Jaeger had set up back in Houston.

By 10:30 the following morning, DeCunha and Dos Palmas had concluded their work, both looking as Carlos Meyers for approval, since he was the money man. He reached into his briefcase and pulled out the partially executed corporate papers guaranteeing Eduardo Dos Palmas, as the Head of the newly incorporated Argentine Aircraft Company and spent the next hour going over the papers with him and gaining his approval via signature on each page of the document. That concluded he got to work transferring funds as agreed to both DeCunha's and Dos Palmas offshore accounts, providing each of them with the telexed copies of account receipts. Whereas the newly funded accounts were funded by other offshore Swiss accounts, everything was washed and untraceable.

That concluded Jaeger and Santos left with DeCunha to dive him to the airport and place him on the first flight back to Houston. While they were gone Carlos Meyers placed a brief call to Ortega, to tell him that all was concluded successfully. Then he disconnected his telex and departed, eager to check out and depart on the first flight back to Argentina to report to his people that all was on schedule.

By a little past one in the afternoon Jaeger and Santos returned to the roof top of the hotels car park and met with Obregon and Bujo who loaded the boxes into the Jaegers vehicle. All had forgotten Eduardo Dos Palmas, who had by now had checked out of the Excelsior and was on the first flight back to Rio De Janeiro, certain of the newly enriched life ahead of him.

As DeCunha's jet gained altitude, he reflected upon his previous activity with Senhor Das Palmas. While hectic and grueling, they both chatted with each other regarding aeronautical engineering theory and practice and struck up a bond between them with Dos Palmas giving him his personal card after their work was concluded and offering him a senior engineering position in the very near future, with the fledgling Aero Argente', in Argentina. His contract with NASA was to conclude within the next nine months and here was a way out from under the grinding thumb of that pig Ortega and a new and rewarding life. In his wildest dreams DeCunha could never conceive of working for someone like Dos Palmas.

Forced into the relationship with the man as a result of Ortega's discovery of his deviant sexual proclivities about six months ago at one of the many Oriental owned massage parlors that dotted the Houston landscape. Of course he was grateful by the intercession by his man Magellan and his local lawyer who miraculously made the charges by the Houston Police disappear completely, thus saving his job at NASA and certain deportation. From time to time he was required to retrieve classified information from NASA's files at great danger of discovery. But as they had him in a box, he also was able to satisfy his deviant urges, which long ago he'd grown to embrace in one of Ortega's several bordello's in town, in complete secrecy and safety. His certainly was an onerous paradox. Freedom to pursue his deviant urges, while held virtual prisoner in that velvet prison provided by Ortega. For the first time in a long time DeCunha could now start to relax and enjoy his first class ride back to Houston, for he had a good feeling his fortunes were about to change.

Immediately upon Santos and Jaegers arrival back at the Excelsior Hotel car park, they joined up with Obregon and Bujo, driving the other car full of the packaged Embraer engineering documents. Santos signaled the others to follow him as they all made their way around the city to the various UPS and Federal Express offices, for air trans-shipment back to Houston.

As Santos drove to the first stop Jaeger asked, "Did you tell Obregon and Bujo to wipe down everything in the suite as well as theirs"!

"I tole them before we left"!

"How do you know it got done"?

"They do what I tell them to do"!

"But how do you know, so you can guarantee Ortega if the question ever gets asked"?

"When we get back, you can do it yourself, or we can all play hotel maids", Santos shot back testily.

As they pulled up to the first stop, Jaeger got out of Santos car and went back to Obregon's, as Bujo retrieved the first package and followed Jaeger into the Federal Express office as Jaeger addressed and paid for the package. His sole function was to guard and monitor the transaction. As Jaeger filled out the addressing documents to Houston, Bujo paid scant attention. It would serve little purpose even if he did, for he was barely literate in Spanish and not at all in English, as Jaeger addressed the documents to his own two Private Post office boxes. Regardless of whether or not Jaeger returned, Ortega was not going to gain access to the documents.

After the forth stop, Bujo already tiring of such a mundane task, simply left Jaeger in the office to his own devices and returned to Obregon's car. A brief argument occurred between Santos and Bujo as to why he was not staying with Jaeger, with Bujo responding in Spanish that Jaeger was filling out everything correctly and paying the clerk all along so he didn't see why he should hang around for the silly girls work.

By six in the evening the last stop had been made and they found themselves on the outer edges of the city. Since Santos was the only one who knew his way around the City of Sao Paulo, he designed the route to leave them in the Favela's, the slums on the edges of the city.

As Jaeger approached the cars, he saw Obregon double up in apparent pain, "What's the matter", asked Jaeger? "His stomach, it musta been he something he ate! He be complaining for the last two stops. I know where there a clinic open late not too far away up in the hills we can take him."!

"You take his car and follow us. I know the way", said Santos. Bujo helped the visibly ailing Obregon into the passenger seat of the second car then flipped the car keys to Jaeger and joined Santos as the two cars took off in search of a clinic.

The word 'Bullshit' had immediately flashed into Jaegers head. The job was ended, Jaegers role completed and now he disappears, deep into the Brazilian slums. With one exception, the previous day, they had all eaten the same food from the Hotels room service buffet and no one else had gotten ill.

As Jaeger followed Santos car through the winding streets up and up through the hills of the metropolis, he wondered where they would stop? Somewhere remote no doubt, for that's what he would do, but he wasn't Santos. Before Jaeger had left Houston, he went to the downtown Public Library and poured over a Michelin map of Sao Paulo, mostly to fix the positions of the airport and the Excelsior Hotel in his mind, but while there he spent several hours going over the entire map of Sao Paulo for reasons of mainly general interest, with no apparent purpose in mind. Now as he drove, he was glad he did. This city of seventeen million disparate souls was far larger than Houston and New York City combined and far more complex. Easy for a native to get lost, much less than some Norte' Americano. As he followed Santos, up into the foothills, he noticed the change in the neighborhoods of the poorer section. Shabbily erected residences and buildings, many no doubt without electricity, plumbing or sanitation.

He kept a wary eye on Obregon as he drove, seeing that he'd not fastened his seat belt like Jaeger. Obregon had briefly looked up at the road ahead, mumbling something incomprehensible in Spanish as he shifted his weight in the seat, maintaining the appropriate groan in the process.

Jaeger sensed that a major move would occur soon, but when, where? Clearly they all knew that his weapon was useless, so any move on their part was? He stopped second guessing, realizing that he must be prepared for everything, for the road was now working its way down a long gradual decline that snaked its way in a lateral fashion down a several mile long hillside, with Favela's dotting the hillside on his left and a sharp heavily wooded hillside of approximately several hundred feet came after a brief shoulder in the roadway, with no protective railings to his right, above a small shanty town below.

As Obregon made his move withdrawing his automatic from his waistband, it snagged briefly, just as Santos's car ahead suddenly swerved to avoid one of the many potholes that dotted the roadway. Jaeger seeing up ahead suddenly turned the steering wheel to avoid the pothole, as he saw the gun try to emerge from Obregon's waist-band. He hit the brakes hard briefly, causing Obregon to lurch into the dashboard, then floored the accelerator, causing Obregon to lurch back in his seat, as Jaegers revolver came swiftly out, meeting the side of Obregon's head with a tremendous force.

As both vehicles approached a sharp curve ahead, Jaegers car smashed into the side of Santos's car, as Jaeger frantically jammed his feet onto the brakes. The force of the collision was sufficient to cause Santos's car to lose adhesion on the partially gravelly road surface as both vehicles careened towards the edge of the roadway. With no road railings to stop Santos's car, it slid right up to the edge of the road way as Jaeger's was stopped just scant feet away, as his pistol whipped Obregon once again.

Santos's car was teetering on the edge of the roadway as he screamed and looked back at Jaeger briefly. The look of sheer terror was in Santos eyes as his car finally surrendered to the law of gravity and disappeared over the edge, tumbling hundreds of feet down the slopes of the hill into the small community of the dirt poor down below, exploding upon final impact, with a fiery crescendo.

Seeing no other vehicles on the hillside road, Jaeger slowly backed up and then drove away. On a hunch he found a road that led further up into the hills as he gave a quick glance at Obregon who while unconscious still had his gun in his hand. As Jaeger drove he reached over and removed the gun. 'Multi-tasking does indeed have its limits', he thought. As he drove further up into the hills, he briefly considered the lot of those below, no doubt having the indignity to have their evening meal interrupted by a fiery death. He hadn't meant for that to happen, but it did, as he intoned a brief prayer for the souls of the unknown. Victims of random circumstance.

While following a twisting and turning gravel roadway, up to the summit, he remembered what an old Texican cowboy once said, when the radio announced a massive earthquake halfway around the world, killing untold thousands in its aftermath. "Why son, that's just the Almighty's way of thinin' out the herd"! A rather crass way of putting it, but there it was, the luck of the draw.

The road ended at the summit of the hill and up ahead was a small copse of trees Jaeger drove into. He turned off the ignition, then felt Obregon neck for a pulse. Finding a pulse he got out of the car and went around to the passenger side and dragged Obregon out and pulled him up to the side of a tree, propped him up then fished around for a well needed cigarette.

When it was finished, he removed Obregon's shoes and clothes, for naked men have a propensity to talk when they're starker's. He ripped off long strips of Obregon's shirt and tied his hands behind his back and his ankles tightly together. Then waited for him to regain consciousness.

It was summer south of the equator and by Jaegers reckoning, there was an hour's worth of sunlight still remaining in the day. After a half hour, with the sun racing towards sunset, Obregon regained his senses, seeing that he was in a rather difficult spot, naked and completely bound.

Jaeger lit another cigarette as he said, "Sport, you have just one chance of staying alive. Tell me everything and start with telling me the whereabouts of Magellan"!

"I no speak English", yelped Obregon with terror in his eyes!

"Yeah, I know what you're thinking. If Ortega ever found out that you ratted him out, your fate would be worse than death. But you have my promise I'll never say a word"!

Jaeger was met with silence for the next few seconds. Then he reached for Obregon's sock and several strips of his trousers he ripped up and went towards him and stuffed the sock into Obregon's mouth and wound the strips of cloth around his wriggling head and Jaeger hit him in the jaw to settle him down.

He waited for a minute then hearing nothing, took Obregon's automatic, and reached for his jacket folding it several times the fired a bullet into his foot, through the folded jacket, which suppressed the gunshot into a cough, quickly stamping out the fire it caused on the jacket.

Obregon writhed in muted pain as Jaeger said, "Now see what you made me do? I ruined a perfectly good jacket and then your left foot. Gee, I'll bet that hurt, but it's your call sport"! He waited another minute, then grabbed the jacket and said, "Where's Magellan"?

Met by more stubborn silence, he placed another silenced round into his left knee.

He stood up as he witnessed a man in the extremis of pain, allowing him to roll around on the ground for several minutes, before he again spoke. "Now amigo, the suns goin' down muy pronto and when it's down if you're still determined to remain silent then I'll have to kill ya. Now if ya cooperate, I'll leave you alive. A tad shattered, but alive and far away from Ortega, the decision is yours. So one last time where's Magellan and what is he up to?

This time Jaeger left Obregon several minutes to think things over and mull over his situation. He paid special attention to the man's eyes which were darting back and forth a sure sign that the fear of certain death was soon at hand if he remained silent. Jaeger lit another cigarette saying, "When this cigarette is finished and if you haven't talked and told me what I need to know, then say a prayer sport for then, 'Muerte' you will be"!

They locked eyes with each other, a test of wills, as Jaeger slowly puffed away. Obregon paid keen attention to the cigarette, fight the massive pain that racked his body. Just as Jaeger was about to take his last drag, Obregon struggled to say through the gag in his mouth, "I calk, I calk"!

Jaeger replied, "Buenos. Now I'm going to remove your gag, be a good boy and yam might survive the night"! After he removed the gag, he offered Obregon a cigarette which was greedily accepted. "Now once again, where's Magellan and what's he up to"?

Through the cigarette smoke from the parched lips of Obregon came, "Magellan, he on a special trip for Ortega. He in Soviet Union. Somethin' to do with a submarine then down to Chile for some new kind 'Jejo', we get"!

"What else"?

"Nossing, that all I know"!

"So what about this plot to kill me? Why"?

"I dunno senor. Ortega say do something. We do what he say. Nossing personal"!

"I understand. Say are you thirsty"?

Obrigon nodded his head. "Stay put and I'll be right back", as he made his way back to the car for the rest of a quart bottle of cheap local high test beer that Bujo was drinking. He quickly returned with a smile on his face and opened the cap and lifted the bottle to Obregon's lips as he greedily drank the rest of the now warm brew. When completed Jaeger asked, "How're ya feelin' now sport"? "My leg"!

"I got an idea that'll take the pain away," said Jaeger casually!

A look of relief flashed briefly across Obregon's face as if he was to survive his ordeal.

"Tiempo Muerte", said Jaeger looking sad! "You say, if I talk I live"!

"I lied", said Jaeger as he quickly lifted Obregon's gun up to his head and covered it with his coat firing it but once. Obregon went immediately limp, a single bullet hole in his head. Jaeger then placed the gun in Obregon's hand covering it with the coat again to muffle the sound and fired it into the ground near Obregon's slumped body. He then positioned the body over the hole in the ground he made with the gunshot. He stood up and stepped back admiring his work then with the last vestiges went back to the car to examine himself for any signs of blood splatter. Finding none, he then went back to the slumped Obregon and removed the restraints. He remembered the local weather report indicating that a cool front was to drift over Sao Paulo from the Argentine in the south, bringing rain during the evening. With any luck it would rain shortly as he felt the cool humidity of a weather front soon to arrive. Having cleaned up the area, of the remnants of Obregon's clothing he got back into the car and slowly backed out of the copse of trees and slowly made his way back down the gravel roadway. A half hour later, when he came back to the roadway that laterally ran across the hillside, he saw about a mile away, the flashing lights of the local authorities, to his right from which he came. Of course he turned left deciding to take the long way back to civilization. As he drove, during the night he wished he'd had the Michelin guide with him, since he's but a scant idea as to where he was. He'd sufficient gas in the tank and was in no great hurry to get back to the Excelsior. Eventually he'd sort things out location wise. An hour later, after wandering about the outskirts of Sao Paulo, and trying to read the street signs in a language that was almost completely a mystery to him he caught sight of something that indicated a direction to downtown Sao Paulo. He drove past a taxi stand and pulled the car over to a shaded area, near a petrol station. He removed the clothes from the car and dropped them into some nearby trash cans and walked into the filling station and bought a pack of cigarettes, then went into the Men's Room to relieve himself and again examine himself for any telltale signs of blood splatter. Finding none he left and walked back the car leaving the keys in the ignition and wiping the car clean with some paper hand towels he's secreted from the filling station. He then rolled down the window half way and walked to the taxi stand and told the driver to drive him to a location five blocks from the Excelsior Hotel. With any luck, someone would steal the car in this crime ridden city the following day.

As the taxi drove back to the center of the city, it started to rain. Jaeger feigned falling asleep as not to engage in any conversation with the driver. When they arrived, he paid the driver and gave the appropriate tip shielding his face from clear view and walked across the street as the taxi drove off without even a backward glance looking for its next fare.

By eleven in the evening Jaeger entered his hotel room tired and in need of food, but decided not to call room service. He'd not eaten since early morning, but he didn't want to draw any attention to himself in any way. He would shower and go to bed hungry. In the morning he would call the desk, tell them he was checking out, gather his passport and other papers, grab a taxi and head for the airport. He still had sufficient funds to get back in a circuitous way. He could always eat at the airport while he was waiting for his flight.

As his jet gained altitude on a clear and sunny day, he reflected on recent events, his overt hunger satiated. He'd been lucky for certain. But he was certain he'd covered his tracks sufficiently as he read of the tragedy in the English edition of the local newspaper. There it was, a report of an automobile driving off a mountain road, falling to the ground below, killing its two occupants in the explosive aftermath. The real tragedy was the death and injury of five closely packed families in the Favelas of Sao Paulo. The charred wreckage of the car was later examined and two charred firearms were recovered, leading the local authorities to conclude a dispute had occurred between two local gangsters who were burned beyond recognition.

From Sao Paulo, to Santiago Chili, then to Lima Peru, then to Bogota Columbia, then to Mexico City, then to Los Angeles, then to Dallas, finally landing back at Intercontinental in Houston. Each leg of the odyssey, with a different air carrier, each trip paid in cash, with a single carryon bag carried by a weary pilgrim. He was happy that no one ever noticed.

As he picked up his car at the airport parking facility, he thought it funny that Ortega's anticipated schedule didn't have him arriving at all. They made their living smuggling illegal drugs and were doing really well. Now they wanted to elevate themselves to the big time, but clearly didn't think things through. Place too much trust and responsibility in someone that you're going to betray? Put in place those to carry out the act of betrayal, Who clearly not ready for prime time? Ortega was clearly guilty of over reaching his abilities. Like many tyrants, his was an overarching ego, oblivious of the details.

He still wondered where Magellan was. If his reckoning was correct, the packages should start arriving sometime later in the day or early tomorrow at his private postal boxes. Ortega should start to worry starting sometime tomorrow. Jaeger wished he could be a fly on the wall, when he came to the realization that not only did Jaeger not appear to have returned, but no one else did, with the exception of 53 DeCunha, the NASA engineer. He would have someone visit the private postal boxes for several days with no results. He would have a lot of explaining to do to this Carlos Meyers, the Argentine operative. DeCunha and Dos Palmas already had their money. Santos and Obregon were replaceable, but the Embraer documents were the key to Ortega's future.

Jaeger wondered if the Argentines had access to a competent kill team they could send after Ortega. Only time would tell. One thing was certain. Jaeger was sitting in the catbirds seat as long as he had control of the documents. If he played his cards very skillfully he just might come out of this in good shape. One misstep and he was history. Yet things had been set in motion. For the common good, Ortega must die. All else was a distant second.

5

J aeger was up at the crack of dawn the following day. After coffee, vitamins and an energy milk shake, he was one of the first to hit the gym and put in two solid hours with the weights, then a steam bath, another shower and then visit his two postal boxes by midmorning. He wasn't disappointed, for every single parcel had arrived as scheduled, as he gave a silent salute to both UPS and Federal Express for their existence. Then he drove straight to the Montrose section of Houston, the heart of the community's counter culture, to visit his old friend Rae.

Rae owned a successful printing establishment, housed in an old two story brick house, built back in the 1920's. After gaining his release from Huntsville Prison on an illegal currency printing conviction and a very profitable five year run at it, he made for his stash, purchasing and renovating the home into a legitimate commercial printing establishment. Interestingly enough, the time he spent as a guest of the State of Texas, was teaching the legitimate skills of printing to selected inmates of the prison, of course under the closest of supervision, as well as running the prisons print shop that churned out all of the forms used by the Texas Department of Corrections.

During the course of the renovation of the Montrose home into a business, he'd met, courted and married 'Bunny', who was the general contractor of his home. An attraction of opposites, one might say, with Bunny being a tall and somewhat generously apportioned woman, with a take charge attitude, uniting with Rae, smaller in stature, highly detailed, soft spoken and reflective.

The marriage took place immediately after the completion of the renovation, with the print shop occupying the entire first floor of the structure and the second floor comprising their living quarters.

While in Huntsville Prison, Jaeger met Rae, through his cellmate, Roy Seltzer and his friend the master bank robber, Duke Vultee and all four became inseparable and protective of the smallish built Rae, lest he become someone's girlfriend, or 'Punky' against his will.

As Jaeger entered Rae's Print Shop, Rae had just completed a project for a local Real Estate Developer and peered over his half-moon shaped reading glasses screeching, "Ya old sumbitch! Where ya been"? "Been away sport, been away awhile. Can ya use some additional business"?

"Never been one to turn away business"!

"How's about you take a lunch break and we take a walk up to the Silver Dollar to feed our faces and listen to the floor show"?

"Who's buyin'"?

"We flip a coin as usual, but this time no two headed quarters"! "Oh that", said Rae continuing, "No heads I win, tails you lose"?

"Forget it, I'll pick up the tab, to keep things simple", Jaeger replied!

Both men ambled the city block up to the Silver Dollar Café, famous for two things, a world class greasy spoon diner replete with the best apple and cherry pie in the western hemisphere and the non-stop floorshow by both patrons and the staff, driven by the homosexual counter culture that permeated the locale. "Like listening to a room full of escaping steam", said Rae!

"Or a den of snakes, suddenly riled", Jaeger shot back!

Settling into a booth, just ahead of the lunch rush, Jaeger was always put off and somewhat ill at ease at first, every time he entered the place, feeling the eyes of every artsy type giving him the once over, deciding whether he was worth the effort, yet it was nearby and the service and the food demanded a larger than normal tip. Then there was the nonstop floorshow, between the patrons and the staff that either brought a smile or summoned disgust, depending on one's point of view.

After they both ordered, Jaeger began a modified monolog, of his recent experiences with Ortega's group in Sao Paulo and what was in the trunk of his car. After the food arrived, both ate in relative silence, giving occasional note to the nonstop floor show that flowed around them. When they cleaned their plates and the heavily made up waitress, brought their hot apple pies and the coffee refills, Jaeger broke the silence saying, "Sorry to bring you into this old buddy, but this is a bit more than I can handle"!

"Yeah, I been thinking about it while we ate and decided that what's needed is a biblical solution as I wondered, 'What would Roy do'?"

"A biblical solution", repeated Jaeger?

"Straight outta the old testament pal. Get the check and lets blow this place and drive your car to the back of my building and I'll show ya what I have in mind"!

"I'll pick up the check, but as far as blowin' the place, I'll have at pass on that", said Jaeger rising, check in hand. Jaeger drove his car to the rear of the building as Rae unlocked the rear metal door allowing Jaeger to bring in all of the boxes of documents, to the rear storage room.

"Unload the boxes, and arrange them into the appropriate groups, by aircraft design. I've this rush order to get out and it should only take a few hours to button up. Then I'll send everyone home early with pay and we can then get to work.

Two hours later Rae appeared in the storage room saying, "Everyone gone", as he went straight away to his small glass enclosed office, opening the door and went to a large metal cabinet moving it easily out of the way as it was on rollers, to reveal a small door as he said, "Jaeger my boy do you believe in ghosts"?

"Hell I don't know. Ghosts. What do ghosts have to do with anything"? "Ghosts. Those who occupy that other dimension remaining unseen to us mere mortals. You know, they see you when you're sleeping, they know when you're awake, they know when you've been bad or good, they see you when your choke your chicken or poking' your old lady, etcetera, etcetera"!

"Rae, what the hell are ya babbling about"? Just then Rae looked up at the ceiling saying, "He doesn't know Roy. He hasn't a clue. What you say Roy? OK I'll tell him"! Turning back to a bewildered Jaeger Rae said, "Remember back at the Silver Dollar when we brought up the subject of, 'What would Roy do'? Our dear departed pal Roy Seltzer who we shared time with back in stir. Well he heard us. He's been talkin' to us all along, watching and listening, except I'm the only one who is listening. If ya listen you can hear him screaming to us the way out of this"!

"Rae, the only thing I'm hearing is you"!

"That's because you're not tuned in. He used to say that about you all the time if you'll remember, 'That bloke just won't tune into the entire reality', he used to say about you all the time"!

"Yeah, I remember all that far eastern hocus pocus bullshit", Jaeger replied sardonically.

"Then, if you'll recall, Roy always seemed to know what was bothering all of us. You me and Duke Vultee. He always seemed to know what we was bothering any of us. Then sport, ask yourself how many times he save our bacon by being tuned in to the yard scuttlebutt about something going down? And remember that closet fight with Elsasser? He told ya exactly how to beat him, exactly. You did what he said; exactly what he said and ya beat him. Cost most of the prison guards and those who bet against you a bundle, but Elsasser never bothered you or anyone else ever again.

Remember? Tell me was there ever a time he was wrong, even once"? "Ok, OK ya made your point Rae"!

"From what you've told me at lunch, seems like this Ortega will be coming at you from every direction, starting as soon as he discovers he's been had and if ever there was a time for you to tune into the celestial forces, now's the time so pay close attention to the magic because now, it's show time"!

Then he went into one of the cabinets and extracted a number of boxes and instructed Jaeger to carry them into the print shop, while he carried all of the segmented Embraer documents and arrayed them, in sequence on one of his long tables. Pointing to the various sizes of boxed printing paper he said, "Say hello to Methuselah Paper". Came by it quite dishonestly before I was sent up to Huntsville, as a favor for services rendered and been hanging on to it ever since. The CIA uses it all the time"!

"So that's how a federal beef for counterfeiting got smacked down to State level", said Jaeger! "Quid Pro Quo my friend. The Old boy school in action. Besides, the guy what saved my ass died last year from a heart attack. Had me do some work for him that was not designed to last and there was all this wonderful paper left over. So pay attention. This paper is impregnated at the paper mill that is responsible for the paper stock for Federal Currency. A chemical is incorporated into the paper that is activated by the harsh light of any photocopier. "When a copy is reproduced, regardless of color or black and white the printing is produced as well as any other paper. Then you store the printing at room temperature. Just before you are about to transact, you must place all that has been reproduced in a cold place, for at least twelve hours, outside during the winter, or a refrigerator, a cold storage facility, thus effecting a chemical change in the reproduced paper, which will start a gradual irreversible disintegrating process, that will be complete within the next forty eight hours. By seventy hours the paper is all dust.

"So why is it called Methuselah paper"?

"A play on words. The biblical Methuselah lived a long time; this print media once activated does not. So we print a copy of everything here. I've a friend who has a restaurant two blocks from here, who owes me favors for free, printing of fliers I've printed for him. You're intending to connect with Ortega to return his stuff for a price. Once you know where and when your meet will occur within twenty four hours, you come by; we go over to the restaurant load the cold and now activated printing into your car and off you go. Hopefully you'll return in one piece and with gelt in hand. But if you don't make it, by the time he can put the drawings to good use the paper will have disintegrated completely. Which is why the spooks, have been using this paper for years in special circumstances. A wonderfully untrustworthy institution, don't ya think"!

A broad smile gradually appeared on Jaegers face as Rae went through his explanation. When Rae was finished Jaeger said, thinking out loud, "There's this Argentine paymaster, Meyers is his name. He's apparently well connected in the Argentine Government somehow. He's the one who controlled all the action in Sao Paulo. He's also the one who will fly up to Houston and transact with Ortega. I'll wait a few days then call Ortega to set up a meet with my terms at a place of my choosing. After the printing is completed I'll store the originals in a storage facility and give you the location. In case I don't make it out of the meeting, you're to get Rafferty and Hondo involved, contact the media then send the originals to the Brazilian Consulate. Make certain your exposure is limited, which is why I want you to let Rafferty to handle things. Ortega's name is to be mentioned liberally to the authorities. Before I get out of here, I'll write out just what he's involved with and where he can be located. Everything he owns is in someone else's name"!

"So warrants will be hard to come by right", asked Rae?

"Unless someone has some unusual pull with a friendly judge"! "One thing though, just passed through my mind"!

"What's that"?

"How well does this Ortega know this Argentine guy Meyers"?

"Superficially is my guess. They were introduced by Nestor Magellan, who I gather is off on something else for Ortega.

"So this Magellan is the one who knows Meyers from awhile back and now Ortega and Meyers are doing business together"!

"That's about it Rae"! "Can't ya hear him"? "Hear who"?

"Our old pal, Roy Seltzer. He's screaming at the both of us, at this very moment"!

"Aw Christ, what now"?

"Open your ears and your mind pal. Seltzer knows that when ya meet Ortega, wherever ya meet him, he has no intention of having you walk out alive. The man has made a living by trusting no one, which is why he cranked out this elaborate long range exchange, on his turf, playing by his rules, except you fucked things up. You weren't supposed to survive Sao Paulo and now he's really pissed. Oh, by the way, Roy says your welcome"!

"For what"?

"Listening to him in that hotel room in Sao Paulo early in the morning when you checked your weapon"!

"Wait a minute. I never told you anything about that"! Rae smiled as he said, "Of course you didn't pal. Roy did"! Jaeger was perplexed. He was speechless as a gradual understanding of the unseen gradually began to unfold.

"Jimmy Stewart had his guardian angel in that movie long ago and so do you sport. He's never far away. You've had one for a very long time he says. Just that when he went up he traded places with someone else. You had one when you were in the Marines, especially on your last rescue mission in the desert. He hung around on that very last play during the Cotton Bowl long ago and all through your time in the Ellis Unit in Huntsville. When Roy passed, it was time to trade places and who better than Roy Seltzer, if you'll only stop and try and tune in"!

The truth of it all gradually began to take hold in Jaegers head. For he'd told no one of that last mission in the Sahel, not even Seltzer. Only Colonel Bollinger knew of it and Bollinger was not a man with loose lips.

"And No, Bollinger said nothing to me about that at the little party we had at Buffy's house the day of our release", said Rae!

"Ok, Ok ya made your point. Does this mean that every time I take a crap, Roy's there checking me out"!

"How many years did the both of you share a cell in Huntsville"? Jaeger remained silent.

"He sees you when you're sleeping he knows when you're awake. Just stay tuned is all he's saying and right now he saying that when you meet Ortega, Meyers is likely to be with him for the exchange. Soon as the money comes out, question the quality of the money. Meyers is likely to have skimmed a bunch of it off the top and replaced it with quality funny money which a suspicious man like Ortega will have to consider. Ortega will bring along this NASA engineer to reexamine the documents, before money changes hands, for Meyers will insist upon it. If the documents arrive back in Buenos Aires and are bogus Meyers will be toast. So everyone will be as nervous as a whore in church. Ortega will insist on cash money, so your assertion that something might be wrong with the money will place doubt. For that's what Ortega would do if given half a chance"!

"And Roy just told you all of this just now", said Jaeger! "How else would I know"?

"There are times when you absolutely amaze me Rae", mused Jaeger! "Times awaistin' sport so let's get to work", said Rae turning to the documents!

6

Every day for the last three days, Ortega had his men visit the private postal facilities Jaeger had set up for him and every day they reported that nothing had arrived. Santos, Obregon and Bujo went missing, for they had not returned from Sao Paulo. Jaeger was not expected to return, which went as no surprise, but Santos, Obregon and Bujo had never failed him before. Carlos Meyers had just called several hours ago regarding the packages and Ortega had to tell them they hadn't arrived yet and that he was back tracking via the shippers, which of course was a lie. Neither Meyers, nor Ortega had expected Jaegers return and fortunately Meyers had not asked about Ortega's men. This was something that need not have the light of day shown on it. If Meyers called again, he'd simply say that engine problems developed on both aircraft and that the shipments should arrive the day after next. Everyone knew of the reliability of Federal Express and UPS, so the plausibility of the lie should hold. He knew that Meyers would arrive via private jet and since he was carrying a large amount of money along with legal papers to be executed, he would be accompanied by one or more bodyguards. So during the interim Ortega would have to simply brazen things out. He was very good at that. If worst came to worst, he would simply have them killed and take the money. He'd done that before.

Magellan was out of pocket working on getting the Crystalline concentrate into the US, which would prove far more lucrative for his purposes in the long run.

The following day Meyers called again, telling him of his travel plans to Houston and again asked about the shipment. Ortega casually told him the prepared lie about the dual engine problems with the carriers and assured Meyers the shipment would be in hand within forty eight hours, which apparently assured a concerned Meyers.

Of course the down side of all of this was as Magellan had indicated prior to his departure. Certain well connected industrialists in Argentina had expectations and in any way should those expectations not bet completely met as they were given to understand, one had every reason to expect one or more kill teams to arrive in Houston to extract revenge. The Argentine military had shown a great deal of expertise not too many years ago, during the days of the military dictators in making people disappear.

Ortega was eager for a good relationship with the Argentines, but should worst come to worst, he vowed to be ready.

While deep in thought, the cell phone rang. He picked it up saying, "Pronto"!

"Jaeger", said the voice on the other end. "Que Paso Hombre'?" Then came the pregnant pause from Ortega before he said, "Santos an Obregon, dey neber make it back. Jus da engineer DeCunha"! He listened for a response, then hearing none continued, "The packages, they never arrive at where you say"!

"There's a reason for that sport"!

"An da reason is"?

"The reason is Santos, Obregon and Bujo are dead"!

"Why are they dead"?

"Because they tried to kill me", said Jaeger stringing things out!

"Why would they do that"?

"Because you told them to"!

"An you believe them"?

"Him", Jaeger corrected. "Obrigon ratted you out and told me everything, just before he died. He was the last to go"!

"You kill him Jaeger"?

"Now what do you think? I gotta give the guy credit though. He hung in there through it all, but I guess the pain just was too great"!

"So you got the packages"?

"That's right Ortega, I have the packages"! There was another pause on the other end as Ortega was trying to compose himself, before he said, "What I gotta do to make this right"?

"It'll cost ya a smooth million large in Cold, Hard, Train Ridin' Cash money sport and that figure is non-negotiable"!

"I can't get my hands on dat much money right now, it's all tied up elsewhere"!

"Sure you can. You got way more than that stashed all over town and elsewhere. Now if I've connected the dots right, Carlos Meyers should appear at the Weston Galleria Hotel, in a day or two with that amount and more, expecting you to turn over the Argentine documents. Only problem is you don't have em, I do"!

"I work hard to put dat deal together Jaeger"!

"No ya didn't, Néstor did. He's the one that put you together with Meyers a while back, because Meyers was the one that brought Magellan to you"!

"Jaeger"!

"Shut up and listen. I'm only gonna say this once. You're in a box of your own making pal. If Meyers doesn't get what he wants, highly probable that a few kill teams will pay you a visit from Argentina. That's the bad news. The good news is that I'm in a position to have your name plastered all over the newspapers, inviting a Federal Investigation. You've been flying under their radar for way too long. The even better news is that you cool your jets, pay me, get your documents and we all part company. I'll have your money and you'll still be alive to prosper"!

"I'll have to have the Engineer examine the packages", said Ortega weakly!

"Non-negotiable, so forget it. It was done in Sao Paulo"!

"How I know I can trust you"?

"You got no other choice. I'm starting to get weary of this whole thing. I'm about to hang up and say Fuck It. Next move is to either set fire to all of the documents or take em down to the local FBI office for their annual Christmas present. You got ten seconds to make up your mind"!

"OK, OK, we do things your way"!

"Good. Hears the way it's gonna go down. I'll call you only once tomorrow and the following day to see if Carlos Meyers has arrived at the Weston Galleria. The following day after he's arrived, I'll let you know where and when we meet"!

The line suddenly went dead as Ortega slowly put his cell phone down in his desk, suddenly bellowing "Fock", jumping out of his chair behind his massive desk. "Dat cock sucking Maricon. Dat scumbag Heche. He cost me three of my men and the packages. To get em back he want me to pay him a million. The money I'm gonna get from Meyers"!

"Jefe", said Davalantes wanting to get his attention.

"Shaddap joo fock. I'm tryin' ta think"!

"Jefe, please hear me out"!

"So talk"!

"Muy permisso. We pull everybody offa everything and scour da city for him. I gotta few ideas where he might be.

Remember he work with us for six months and I watch him alla time. He got certain habits I see and if he keeps with those habits we can get him. We get him then we sweat him good and make him talk. We get the packages then we kill Jaeger and turn him over to Jugos for his Menudo. Now in case we no get him in time for Meyers, No hey Problima. We meet wid him, we give him Meyers dinero, we get the packages, then we kill him anyway. Meyers go home with what he wants, you get Meyers dinero and Jugos gets what he need for Menudo"! "Best idea joo got"?

"Best idea I got Jefe"!

"Your idea. Make it happen"!

For the next two days, Davalantes rounded up everyone he could gather, numbering almost a hundred men, giving them photocopied pictures of Jaeger and a description of the Ford Galaxie he drove. They had an idea that he lived somewhere in Northwest Houston, but where? He worked out regularly at the Ballys, in Houston's Northwest side, but a dawn to well past dusk surveillance of the parking lot revealed nothing.

Later in the day Davalantes placed a call to Jugos at his restaurant on Canal Street. "Hola Jugos, is Davalantes calling for Ortega. Sometime in the next few days there gonna be a night shipment of Carne' for your Menudo. So I jus wanna let you know so you can be prepared"!

"How big the shipment Davalantes"?

"Minimum about two hundred fifty pounds, maybe up to a thousand pounds, so be prepared. You serve the best Menudo in town, so the meat she gotta be fresh, No"?

"I unnerstand. I be ready"! After Jugos hung up he took a deep breath, the Roman Catholic guilt already building as he said a brief prayer to his patron Saint. His sins were about to grow and the only one who knew the depths of his sins was his wife. This sin was so collective in his mind that even his priest was unaware of the coercive nature of the sin. An emotional burden he simply had to bare.

The conversation with Davalantes ended, Jugos gathered his thoughts, took a deep breath and thought about the task ahead of him, spending the next several hours cleaning the kitchen and the meat preparation area. As his wife joined in with the preparation tasks, she asked as to the quantity of the meat to be delivered and made notes for the following days supplies to be garnered. They'd done this many times before and by noon the following day she'd make certain that Jugo's had all that he'd need to accomplish their tasks for their patron, Ortega. They worked together in silence, each silently intoning the seemingly endless Mantra of Hail Mary's for the nameless ones Jugos was about to embrace. A time was reserved for the coming evening of "Muerte"!

The following morning Jugos wife got into their old Dodge pickup truck and began driving around to the several grocery supply and hardware stores, making a variety of small purchases, such as large rolls of black plastic garbage bags, several large rolls of construction grade, heavy mill thickness Visquene plastic wrap, colored black, then a variety of vegetables and special spices, two jars of mentholated petroleum jelly and a pack of painters face masks.

"Gonna make your world famous soup", asked Paco?

"Si. Maybe sometime tomorrow or the next day, depending on when the hunters arrive from the valley. Just watch for the sign out front of our place"!

As Paco tallied up her purchases he said, 'You know I always look forward to your Menudo, soup cause it always has that special something that make me come back for more.

Not even anywhere in Mexico and especially for my Madre', god rest her soul, make such good Menudo. I know you do something special to your soup, for it never taste the same two times inna row. Is it the meat, the spices, or do you pees inna soup"?

In a hurry to depart, Jugos wife simply said, "Paco, what kinda question you ask me? The recipe, she older than Moctezuma and I'm sworn to secrecy. But I can tell joo thees, no one pees inna soup. You come by when the sign outside say it's ready inna few days and I promise I save a special bowl for you"!

As far as anyone knew, the neighborhood word of mouth circulated that every so often, unknown friends of Jugos went hunting either in the piney woods of east Texas, or down in the Rio Grande valley, usually bagging some deer, but sometimes a wild boar, a javelina, or perhaps the odd Armadillo or two. So there was no telling what kind of meat was ever in Jugos Menudo. All his repeat patrons knew was that the very taste of the soup reminded them of home. Far better off they were in the States than in Mexico, but still the memory of earlier days brought a certain longing that Jugos offerings periodically rekindled.

Back with the supplies by late in the morning, she joined her husband in preparing for the lunch rush buffet of Central Mexican offerings. After Jugos brought the last tray of tamales to the steam table, he started to reflect back on how he'd ever allowed himself to ever become so indebted to Ortega.

Many years ago, Ortega, a daily patron to their small Canal street Carnacia, rescued their only daughter from an East Houston street gang of "Pachuco's", of which she was a fledgling member at the age of thirteen. Their one and only "Precioso", the light of their life. How strange, he thought, 'How love can blind people to reality'. We see what we want to see and hear what we want to hear. Both Jugos and his wife worked all day long at their struggling family business, the small eatery on Canal street, with precious little time to afford their daughter and thus were blind at the onset to the reality of her drug addiction. Eventually they noticed a gradual personality change, but chalked it up to the fact that she was slowly becoming a woman What once was a sweet young child, evolved into a sullen, brooding, highly mercurial teen ager. Both had turned a blind eye to their daughter's behavior, until the night gone wrong when she was peripherally involved in a drive by shooting that had gone terribly wrong.

The shooters, high on Crack Cocaine, got the wrong address of a rival street level drug dealer they were about to put out of business permanently. Instead, they sprayed the house across the street where a house party was in full swing. Standard operating procedure, four guys drive by in a stolen sedan, comprised of a driver and three shooters. The shooters are sporting the latest version of stolen TEC 9's each one emptying two clips of 9mm rounds into a given house then speeding off into the night. The beginning of a turf war between different minorities. The house in question was of clapboard design, cheaply built of a pre World War Two vintage.

The only bullets that didn't completely penetrate the thinly clad house, ended up embedded in the bodies of many of the occupants within. A dozen occupants ended up in the County Morgue that very night and another eight ended up in the Emergency Room at Herman Hospital. Three of the bullets magically missed Jugos daughter by the slimmest of margins, only to find a home in her boyfriend of the moment. Having already snorted two lines of Columbia's finest product, the terror of what had happened overcame her and she fled in an instant, along with all that were not stricken. Running through yards, eluding neighbors dogs, jumping fences, running the three miles all the way back to her family.

Tragic as things were, the city at large was immune to the news of a street fight in the ghetto. It was too bad that the nineteen year old wife of a US Navy Corpsman, away on a six month deployment was a victim of such mindless destruction, but that incident, a mere ripple in the affairs of a major city in many cases washed over the cynical populace, that this was the Almighty's way of just 'Thinnin' out the herd.

What got the attention of most people was the news of the Naval Corpsman's wife, who was residing with the Corpsman's parents, while she was just weeks away from delivering twins. None of them survived the evenings activities.

The whole affair mattered not a bit to those occupying the house across the street. For the following evening they visited another neighborhood, for a fist class "Airing Out", which included four convenience stores where their antagonists were known to hang out. At the end of the following evening, fifteen others were to meet a violent and bloody end with another two dozen ending up in various emergency rooms. It didn't matter whether or not you were connected, with either a Black or Latino gang. If you were in close proximity you were fair game.

The Police were at first baffled, because they were unable to tie any of the victims to the various phantom shooters, who always arrived in stolen cars, with stolen plates, clad in either bandana's over their faces or black balaclava head coverings. Eventually the odds caught up with the shooters, who never seemed to learn the lessons of getting rid of their firearms in the aftermath and getting new ones, or at least wiping their weapons clean of prints, or wearing rubber gloves so no gunpowder residue would show up on their hands, or tossing their garments away. They always used auto and semiautomatic weapons, thus leaving a hoard of shell casings for the police to process and trace. Eventually the carnage diminished as the various body counts escalated. Some said because they all just ran out of bullets, while others chalked it up to mere battle fatigue.

The local police eventually caught up with many of the perpetrators who ended up in the Texas Penal System, while others still plied their wares in the street, till fate caught up with them.

In time the various gangs got smart, kept their mouths shut and laid low for a period of time. For now with night time street patrols seemingly everywhere, it seemed the prudent thing to do.

Unknown to everyone, Ortega's people were the very ones who sold the bulk of South American 'Jejo', to the street gangs on both sides of the street. All any of the locals knew of Ortega was that he was a businessman of unknown origins, with his fingers into a number of profitable enterprises. A week after the original shooting he was seated in Jugos place eating a wonderful 'Barbacoa' when he caught wind of Jugos predicament with his daughter.

After discovering the depths to which she'd sunk do to his product, he had a long talk with Jugos and his wife. With their agreement, he and Davalantes spirited her away to an expensive Institution on the Cayman Islands that dried her out and provided an environment where she could acquire the right habits that would serve her educationally very well in life.

While there she completed three years, worth of education in the space of two years and when she returned to her home in Houston she appeared to be a completely changed person in every way. Ortega had personally gone to the Caymans to retrieve their daughter and bring her home. She was home. She was cured of the devilish influence. She was calm and respectful. Their prodigal daughter again was what they envisioned the moment she was born and now a visible example of rebirth. Her bona fides established, she was re enrolled at her local high school at the grade level she would normally have achieved.

There was a God in heaven and to the Jugos family; Ortega was their guardian angle on earth. A tearful and joyous Jugos was overwhelmed by how well his daughter had turned out and one day when Ortega was in his restaurant enjoying his Mexican Buffet, he offered to loan Jugos the money at a zero interest rate in which to modernize and expand his current facility. "Just one thing senor", said Ortega casually. From time to time I will need a man of your skills to provide two services for me", he said very slowly. "I see how clean you keep your kitchen and watch how you go about things. I see how you personally prepare and butcher your meat with the skill of a master of your craft. From time to time, it is unfortunate that some I have to do business with have and continue to try and harm me and those who I employ. Of course they will always meet with an accident and they will have to be disposed of. I will need you to do this service for me, when the occasion permits"!

Ortega then proceeded to outline precisely what he required to Jugos. Those few who knew Ortega intimately knew that he was a man one never refused. Given what he'd done for Jugos, it was impossible to deny Ortega anything he desired.

The next few years went very well for Jugos and his family. His daughter had graduated her high school with honors and received an academic scholarship to the local St. Thomas University. Business was very good and their daughter's future looked bright indeed. In addition Ortega had become a godfather of sorts for their daughter, picking up the tab for all of the various incidental expenses not covered by the terms of her scholarship, so she could focus he time on her studies. By the end of her freshman year, she was at the top of her class, with a new set of friends from all over the city. Her difficult years were but a rapidly diminishing memory, with Ortega achieving the title of Uncle.

But tragedy was to visit the Jugos family yet again via a phone call from the Houston Police Department. Normally when classes for the day were completed Jugos daughter immediately drove home to help her father in the family restaurant, now trebled in size and volume. The time of her normal arrival had come and gone by several hours and her parents began to worry that she'd perhaps she'd relapsed back into her old ways. Calls to her cell phone that Ortega had gotten her went unanswered and messages were left. Then at Nine in the evening, the phone call arrived that changed their lives forever.

When Jugos hung up he had that ashen look in his face. His wife came into the room as he desperately grabbed for the nearest chair and sank into it.

"Was that Encarnacion", she asked? "Is she alright"? Hearing no reply and seeing the look of utter desolation in his face as he looked at her with pleading eyes already tearing up. He tried to speak then uttered, "That was the Houston Policia. They say that Encarnacion is dead. They ask that we come down to the Morgue to identify her"!

His wife screamed at the news then fainted crashing to the floor.

Summoning up the strength, Jugos rose from his chair and went to his wife, to comfort her. Amidst their worst possible nightmare, there was only one person to turn to. Ortega. As soon as Jugos was able to revive his wife, he placed a call to Jugos at his private number and told him of the call he'd received. Jugos told him to go to the Harris County morgue and that Davalantes would meet him there with his lawyer.

For the obvious reasons Ortega made it a point to never enter a governmental office of any kind, going back to his days of his youth in Central America. He had a host of well paid people that could do this for him. Several hours later after the identification had been accomplished. Everyone met back at the restaurant on Canal Street. Jugos, his wife, Ortega, his lawyer, Davalantes and a nurse that always did patch up work on any of his pistoleros that were wounded by gun fire. She was there to administer sedation to both Jugos and his wife and stay with them for a few days to tend to their needs. The following day the parish priest would be summoned to tend to their spiritual needs in their moment of grief.

Jugos gathered the strength to address Ortega saying, "Jefe, I cannot thank you enough for what you do"!

"Calma Jugos. I will handle everything. You will close your restaurant for a week or more until you are better. The Priest will be here tomorrow for you and to meet with me so we can make the arrangements for the funeral. I will see to it that a tasteful sign is prepared to put in front of your business to tell the neighborhood of your daughter's death and announce the funeral. I have taken the liberty through my lawyer who is acting in your behalf to have her body taken to the finest funeral home for preparation for the funeral. She is in God's hands from now on. No expense will be too much and I will take care of everything. Now since Davalantes and the lawyer were present and talked with the police at length about the manner in which she died, I will let him describe what happened"!

"Senor Jugos, apparently sometime around 4:30 your daughter, while on her way home from class, stopped by a convenience store on Gulfton to get a pack of cigarettes. As she was leaving with the cigarettes in hand several cars with gang members drove through the parking lot and machine gunned a rival gang. As you know this happens from time to time. Your daughter was in her car and the key was in the ignition as she was in the process of leaving. The police were convinced that she was not targeted in any way, but simply a victim of the incident. Of the gang members that were just hanging out in front of the store, five were killed and four others seriously wounded", as Davalantes concluded.

"Will the Policia do anything", asked Jugos wife? Ortega's lawyer then took the lead saying, "They say they will investigate the matter but in reality your daughter's death will no doubt be shuffled aside with a host of others in this city. Probably little will be done, I'm sorry to say"!

Then Ortega rose and said, "Muy Gracias gentlemen"! Then he addressed the Jugos's saying, "The Policia have little interest in finding who killed your daughter, but I do and I will bring these Maricon's to justice. I swear by the Virgin, that I will find them and bring them before you Jugos, so that you alone will decide their fate", he said calmly!

As Jugos looked into the eyes of Ortega, he knew with certainty that it would be done, as Ortega continued, "They will never be in a court room and the very last thing they see, is you looking into their eyes as they are sent to Hell"!

Jugos father always told him, "Beware of the one who speaks softly and with certainty"!

As they all walked out of the restaurant on Canal Street, Ortega drew Davalantes aside saying, "So tell me what you know or suspect"!

I have Obregon running things down and will join him shortly but putting together what the Policia told the lawyer, it looks like it was one of the Negrito gangs we sell to was trying to eliminate street completion of a Latino gang that we also sell to. A simple yet unfortunate turf war. We have a description of both cars involved and apparently the stupido's used their own cars in the shooting, rather than using stolen ones. There were six involved, two cars, two drivers and four shooters using Mac-10's by the look of it. We have a good idea where their crib might be, so we will gather some men to find out exactly where they'll be holed up, make certain that they are the exact ones then capture them silently and alive so they can be brought to you and Jugos for disposal. It may take a few days Jefe, for in this no mistakes can be made, so I ask for your patience"!

As they approached Ortega's car, he put his arm around Davalantes saying, "I know that you will deliver, because you always have. But what about Encarnacion's car"?

"It is in the HPD's impound lot. I took the liberty to have the Lawyer get it back early tomorrow since the policia are finished with it. There are a few bullet holes in it along with Encarnacions blood. It will be taken to a body shop for repairs and restoration and be returned to the Jugos family when completed".

"Mucho Bueno Davalantes. Keep me aware of all that develops", said Ortega as he got into his car and was driven off into the night.

For the next several days, business took a back seat to the affairs at hand, as Ortega made the rounds to the mortuary, the sign company and the church, always with more than sufficient cash to insure that his directives were carried out to the last jot and dot. Several time a day he received calls on his cell phone from Davalantes to keep him aware of progress in the hunt for Encarnacions killers.

The following day, the restaurant draped in black and a large sign erected announcing the death of Encarnacion and the forthcoming funeral, greeted Ortega as he was driven to the front entrance to see a crowd of onlookers intently reading the overly large sign out front, printed in Spanish. This was part of Ortega's daily routine as on the second day he suggested that Jugos come with him so they could visit the site of their beloved ones death.

The bullet riddled plate glass windows had been replaced, the appropriate interior repairs had been quickly done and most of the blood had been washed from the sidewalk, except for the occasional and random droplets here and there. The business of life must forge ahead. They talked together in fits and starts, with words coming with difficulty from each of them. For Ortega death of others made little difference in his emotions, for no one had ever seen him cry, but for Jugos, a simple man, the death of his loved one placed a heavy burden on his spirit. Life had blessed him, then placed him in that whirlpool of despair, then blessed him once again, ever so briefly during the span of time, then once again placed him on that event horizon of the whirlpool of despair. Had it not been for Ortega, serving as his guardian angel on earth, Jugos had no idea how he could've survived. Even now several days later he struggled every day with the challenge with his emotions, going to a far corner of the house next door to his business and crying in silence. Yet he resolved that he must be strong for his wife was lying in bed each day unable to eat, staring at the ceiling muttering, "Muerte, Muerte", every so often.

The nurse Ortega had contracted visited her each day for an afternoon seeing to her needs cautioning, "She must be given time to hear her heart.

You must be strong for the both of you"! That along with the daily visits in the morning from the parish priest, ministering to her spiritual needs, served to bridge the divide between celestial blessing and an earthly curse.

As Ortega's driver drove them back to Canal Street Ortega said, "I know this occasional service that you perform for me from time to time has been distasteful to you. But as you know it was part of the bargain that had served you very well and you've never complained. For that I am grateful. But our agreement still stands. I say this because if all goes well as I expect it will, sometime after Encarnacions funeral tomorrow you will be visited to perform your greatest task yet. We think we know where the Vato's are that murdered your daughter. We are taking great care to bring them all to you alive, so they can be sent to hell in front of you and disappear from the earth. There may be a half dozen or so of them, so I ask that you be prepared. My men will be at your service for anything you need"!

Jugos looked back at Ortega, fighting back the tears and said, "Jefe, I will not disappoint you"! Then he looked back out of the back seat of the car window wondering once again, 'How could God allow mankind to treat each other so cruelly? When would the despair that he and his wife leave them? The despair of his daughters decent into the earthly hell and her ascent back to the land of the living then the sudden and tragic death seemed too cruel to grasp. In the blink of an eye she was gone. He tried to see in his mind's eye and recall how his daughter looked, healthy, vital and alive, with that flashing smile and wonderful giggle that was her unique trademark. But no matter how hard he tried the image of her cold gray bloodless face on the City Morgue slab would not subside. The senseless death of his daughter rolled over continuously in his mind every waking hour of the day and far into the night.

'When', he wondered, 'would it end'?

"As they drove up to the sidewalk in front of his home, a crowd of neighbors, patrons and well-wishers were being led in prayer by the parish priest who was earning the overly generous offering presented to him by Ortega in Jugos behalf.

"I will let you join your friends and neighbors in prayer for the soul of Encarnacion. I have our business to attend to. Remember what I have said to you Jugos. Steel yourself for what is about to happen"!

As Jugos emerged from the rear of Ortegas car into the crowd, the priest along with several others nodded in his direction, clutching their rosary beads, to join them while continuing without pause, their mantra of the Holy Rosary. "Ave Maria, Ileno de gracia, el dios esta con tu. Bendecir estar tu entre Muher. Bendecir esta los fruta utero Jesus. Sagrado Maria Madre de Dios, orar para nos picadors, ahora y en los hora de nuestro Muerte'. Amen"!

Jugos silently joined them, picking his way through those assembled, kneeling next to the priest and continued the benediction. Perhaps the Lord would visit him once again, bringing peace to his heart.

When the ritual was finished, he rose and accepted the sympathy of well-meaning friends, neighbors and patrons. He'd been a long standing fixture in local community. Yet as he tried to display a brave face, inside he was crumbling. Soon he would have to go into the house and face his wife, lying in bed in a semi-comatose posture. It almost seemed as if there was a dark and ominous presence that had settled over her as she lay in bed staring at the ceiling. When he tried to join her in bed, she seemed to radiate such heat while in a supine position that never changed, that he had to try and sleep on the living room couch.

Tomorrow was the Funeral Mass at the local church and the funeral thereafter. All of the rituals would be observed, his only hope was that she'd be able to carry things off with some dignity.

The following day he was grateful of the support from friends and neighbors who helped his wife bathe, dress and stayed with her during the Mass and all through the funeral, never leaving her side and partially absorbing some of the grief she experienced publicly.

Hovering over the entire day was Ortega, working in the background, who choreographed every aspect of the funerary ritual down to the second, with his men standing on the periphery to insure that nothing went amiss.

As the funeral drew to a close and all of the attendees faded into the overcast afternoon, one by one, Ortega was the last to join Jugos as they walked to the black Limousine.

"Muy Gracias Patron, for all that you have done", said a somber Jugos! "De Nada. But now we have to consider what we discussed the other day. Have you made the preparations in the kitchen for your delivery this evening"?

"You've caught them", asked Jugos his eyes opening wide?

"Not yet, but things are in the works. Sometime before midnight, I anticipate results. Have your cell phone at your side at all times and be ready to work all night. I will provide any additional people you need to help you with your task. Have your knives sharpened and your pots ready"!

While his wife slept the sedated sleep of the deeply distraught, Jugos left her minders to go to the restaurant next door and made the kitchen ready. By eight PM, his cell phone rang and it was Ortega. "Are you ready for company compadre"?

"Si"!

"In about twenty minutes, listen for a knock at the rear door of your kitchen. It will be the delivery"!

Ten minutes later, a knock came at the door with Jugos eagerly opening it, to see Davalantes and several other of Ortega's men, hoisting six black plastic bags, each containing an inert form.

When everything was inside the restaurant, in came Ortega bringing up the rear saying, "Mejo, you have much work ahead of you. Two of your daughter's killers are dead for they chose to put up a fight. But four of the others are alive but sedated. They are all bound and gagged. I suggest that you process the dead ones first, so as the sedated ones wake up they will see what fate awaits them. Fortunately their leader is alive and Davalantes knows who he is. He will be the last one to greet the ferryman. Are we agreed"?

"Si patron", said Jugos

"Bueno. Perhaps this one time you can find it in you to find joy in what you do. Now I have to leave, my business needs attention"! With that Ortega turned and left without further word.

Jugos went to work as he was told, taking charge of Ortega's men telling them what he wanted done as he cleaned and started to dismember each of the relatively fresh cadavers. Ortega's men took turns every hour, rotating out one of the men to guard the four men still alive, as the other took up his duties with the rest. The clothing and shoes were placed in an industrial grade trash bag that would find its way into a dumpster in a far off section of town before too long. Each man working with rubber gloves and a surgeons mask did precisely what he was directed to do by Jugos as the first and second cadavers were completely rendered and the muscle tissue was made into sausage encased by each of their cleansed intestinal tissue, the head and flesh were all placed in a separate industrial grade plastic bag for disposal later on in the evening far out in the Gulf of Mexico. The bones, sinew and other detria were placed in boiling chili ten gallon chili pots for Menudo soup the following day. By ten PM, the first two cadavers were completed, just in time as the others were awakening from their sedation, naked, bound and gagged.

"Muy permisso Jugos, this is thirsty work for my men", sad Davalantes! "The Cerveza is in the cooler up front. Please forgive me and help yourself, as your thirst permits"! When each rack of sausages was completed, they were places into the walk in freezer.

As they waited for their beers to return Davalantes said to Jugos, "El Jefe, suggests that all of the Negrito sausages be gathered and distributed into their neighborhoods before dawn. They are to be wrapped in Kraft paper as one normally would and the words 'Southern Style Sausage' written on the paper. We will handle it as we have a few of their neighborhood restaurants in mind for unexpected gifts"!

"As you wish, Davalantes"!

After a brief break since the work was going well, they extracted their first of the still living prisoners and laid him on the meat working table that was some seven feet in length and made from galvanized steel. It was exactly like what a coroners table or that of a commercial butcher, with a swing arm overhead water supply and two drains on each end to carry off dirt, blood and assorted material, surrounded by a three inch lip of metal to contain everything.

The Prisoner's blind fold was removed as he was now fully awake, naked, tattoo ridden and still fully bound and gagged. As the others held him down on the table as he tried to struggle free, his muted cries falling on deaf ears, everyone beheld his eyes, as wide as afternoon tea saucers with fear.

Davalantes summoned Jugos to join him in leaning over the prisoner as he said, "Soon my friend it will be lights out for you and you will join the fishes in the Gulf as their breakfast. Now you see the man next to me? The reason why you're here is the shootout a few days ago your boss orders you to do. This man's daughter you kill and she was buried this very afternoon. A petty disagreement with others led to all of this. Now the next stop for all of you will be in Hell, where you can argue with your boss for all eternity. One thing more. Your flesh will be eaten by those in your old neighborhood, the very same time the fishes in the Gulf eat what's left. Consider this your funeral"!

The subject tried to fight all of those who held him fast, as his breathing and heart rate reached their maximum volume. Slowly Davalantes placed the razor sharp paring knife point at the man's throat and slowly pressed it forward towards the man's spinal column. The body jerked and sputtered for a few seconds violently, then as Davalantes made two quick motions with his knife, all movement ceased as the man's spinal column was severed at the neck.

"You see", said Davalantes, "The Maricon is still alive for the moment. He cannot move, he cannot breathe too good and he will soon choke on his own blood for his heart still beats. But for the moment he hears and he sees and he is helpless completely for what is to happen next"!

He then waited for several seconds then withdrew the thin blade from the man's neck and slowly placed it over his heart and pressed forward until he met metal some eight inches away. Feeling all movement come to halt. He then sliced open the man's jugular and was met with a slow stream of blood, rather than the spurting that indicated a heartbeat.

"Caballeros, you may begin", said Davalantes. As he stepped back from the table allowing Jugos and two others to proceed, Davalantes said, "You may think my performance a bit odd, but it was done for a purpose. To place the maximum of terror in the minds and hearts of those others. It will serve as no example to others, for they are less than animals, filled with 'La Droga' and have been long past any redemption for their sins. Yet it will serve them well, for the journey they will begin, for all eternity. Me and Ortega have discussed the miraculous journey of your daughter often and he was very proud of her. Her death affected him deeply, for the investment that was made in her precious life was lost forever. His grief and disappointment will have to take second place behind yours. The ferryman must be paid"!

By One AM the very last of the murderers was placed at the table. Davalantes dispensed with the ritual for the previous two deciding that an example had been made for the others.

The chili pots boiling with the remains of the previous five others, with room for the sinew of just one more, Davalantes said, "Here is the one who ordered the death of your daughter. Do you wish to do the honors, Senor"? Offering the paring knife to Jugos.

He looked at the knife for a time then turned to Davalantes saying, "No Senor. I do what I am good at and I leave it to you, to do the same"!

"Very well", as he turned the knife around in his hand with the flick of his wrist and plunged it into the man's throat making the swift two strokes with his blade and then withdrawing it, the man's spinal column severed. The man's eyes moved and his hearing registered sound to the brain as the last thing that registered in his mind, amidst his coughing and choking was Davalantes saying, "Bujos, Cervezas for everyone"!

An hour later, the last of the murderers was completely rendered and everyone was in cleanup mode in the kitchen area. Obrigon and Bujos were off to deliver the garbage bag containing the deceased clothing to a commercial shopping center dumpster some ten miles away in the near the murders neighborhood, then off to Ortega's home in Clear Lake to take his Cigarette Boat out into the Gulf some twenty miles off shore to dispose of the heads and the skin belonging to the former gang members. Santos was to drive into the old neighborhoods, to deliver the frozen sausages links to various Soul Food restaurants. This unknown gift was a random occurrence from time to time and the proprietors never once gave it a second thought, featuring it in their menus the following day.

By four in the morning, the last of Ortega's men had departed, leaving the kitchen and the entire prep area spotless. The whole kitchen had a faint odor of Chlorine Bleach that would disburse by noon the following day. As he reached into the beer cooler for his final Cerveza of the morning, he noticed that some three cases of beer had been consumed. A small price to pay for every ones help. He would place an order the following day for resupply with his distributor.

The kitchen side door opened and his wife shuffled into the kitchen in her bedclothes, rubbing her eyes as if she'd just awakened. She stopped, sniffed the air, looked around, saw the boiling Menudo pots and said, "Ortega was here this morning wasn't he"? Jugos nodded wearily as he struggled to stand, looking at his apparently alert wife in amazement. "We're going to serve Menudo to everyone are we not"?

Again Jugos nodded his head. She then went to the walk in freezer opened the door and went in, coming back out some ten seconds later and slammed the door shut. Her eyes once again bright and alive. A far cry from these last days of sorrow. She walked around the metal prep table and quietly embraced her husband saying, "Maybe we could begin again. The sun will shine tomorrow and we still have each other"!

"How are you feeling me amor", asked Jugos feeling great concern?

"Encarnacion is but a memory now. We should cherish our time with her. In time the wound will heal, but until then we have to continue in her memory. All too soon we will join her in heaven where there is no pain or suffering, but until then we have to cherish the life we have together and be each other's strength"!

Jugos softly tightened his embrace with his wife and said, "I'm very happy that you agreed to become my wife, for nowhere in the world could a man have a better woman", as tears of joy returned to his face. While in their embrace he heard her say, "Tomorrow you call Ortega and tell him to have the sign taken down, so the following day when the Menudo is ready we can open for business. Now let's turn down the fire on the Menudo, turn out the lights and go to bed"!

Several days later, Ortega summoned Garcia by cell phone. When he hung up Garcia looked at Davalantes saying, Ortega wants us to come to a party at his Condo at the Teal Stone. Just one thing, we gonna to stop by 'Rosa's Casa' in the Heights and the 'Nueva Costa' titty bar out on I-10 West. He's already called the Managers and told them to expect us. We gonna have our pick of his best dancers, no less than six or eight and bring them to a party that's gonna start in an hour"!

"I better call my woman and tell her I'm working late cause something come up an not to expect me before morning", mused Davalantes!

"Yeah and better take a change of clothes and shower before you come back to your woman tomorrow. A woman can smell strange pussy on her man a mile away and Mexican women got no sensahumor about their man cattin' around on em"!

s Father Kennedy left the Jugos residence the following day, he was happy to see Senora Jugos up and around working at reopening their restaurant. Although not the usual cheerful person she normally was, she appeared to maintain a semblance of normalcy. Her husband was somewhat better in his apparent road to emotional recovery after the death of their daughter, but only by the slimmest of margins. Better to stay busy than to do nothing and permit Satan to work his will.

Still he felt that something was very wrong. Perhaps it was an overreaction on his part, but never, as long as he'd known them had they refused the Confessional. Even in the previous dark days of their daughter's addiction, they welcomed the Confessional with open arms. But now after their terrible and senseless loss, they chose to keep their own counsel an uncharacteristic behavior pattern.

Walking down the street on a bright sunlit morning, he felt an ominous chill suddenly surround him. No apparent reason for it, for the weather was such that everyone he saw on the street was attired in summer clothing, with the weather forecast indicating temps in the low seventies for the next several days. He had grown a special attachment to this family quite apart from his weekly visit to their establishment to partake of the Menudo soup he's grown to enjoy. Along with others, there were days when the soup had that little something extra, that compelled not only him, but everyone else, to sip it ever so slowly and savior the special taste. When asked what was different, Jugos would always smile and say, "The hunters. I get deer meat when they go hunting. When that gone I have to rely on my meat wholesaler"!

He especially was gratified whenever their daughter Encarnacion was there to serve him. Since her recovery from drug addiction, she had an especially gratifying demeanor that could only be brought to mind of the eternals lasting grace. Now she was with the angels. Even Father Kennedy struggled with that logic. How was he to explain why bad things happen to inherently good people, when the tired and down trodden came to him for spiritual comfort? The old saw that, God's wisdom and reasoning was beyond mortal understanding, just didn't come up to muster.

His recent sessions with the Jugos family placed an additional burden on his being, with long sessions of prayer for not only Encarnacion's salvation, but the remnants of what she left behind, in the form of her father and mother. His inability to provide comfort in their time of need sorely tested his faith, in his creator and himself. He was the one who represented the 'Eternal' and 'Great Comforter' to his flock and he was apparently striking out. In his experience, he noted that the onset of true spiritual comfort was a gradual thing that grew with time and patience. This sudden and apparent healing was unknown to his experience and he didn't trust current appearances not one little bit. He sensed the apparent forces of evil and darkness had again descended on his poor neighborhood. Feeling a sense of loss and frustration he recalled the baptism of their daughter, her first communion, watching helplessly as she descended into the deep abyss of addiction, exulting at her recovery after some few years away at a clinic, provided by an unknown benefactor.

As he entered the parish residence, he recalled the admonition from his seminary rector as he studied for the priesthood, many years ago. "Boyo", the rector began, "You're calling for the priesthood for the rest of your life, will consist of a never ending series of absorptions. You will become a sponge for the evils of the Universe, which are considerable, absorbing all the pain and suffering of your flock.

Expect constant disappointment as the normal course of events, with the occasional victory, for through you, is the spiritual fountain that provides sustenance on this earth and their salvation in the eternal afterlife. Expect no vain glory for yourself, because you are merely God's instrument for all mankind"!

One of the many reasons Father Kennedy's parishioners adored the man was that he was seemingly everywhere, exactly when needed, tending to his flock in both spiritual and temporal ways. Then there was his deliverance of the Mass. Unlike many other parishes in the city, he maintained the daily ritual of afternoon Vespers. Always at the stroke of five in the afternoon, he would conduct Mass at Vespers. With rarely more than a few dozen people in attendance, his resonant tones would echo throughout the miniature neighborhood Cathedral. Behind his back, many of his flock nicknamed him 'Machinegun Kennedy', for the rapid, yet distinct method in which he conducted the Mass. Quite unlike other priests who slowly droned through the ritual of the Mass, Father Kelly's style and manner of booming delivery of the Homily kept all in attendance quite awake. "Better than two cups of espresso coffee", one of the parishioners was overheard to say upon exiting!

Yet this very afternoon Father Kelly was greeted at the beginning of Vespers by several hundred people in attendance for the late afternoon service, which he dutifully dedicated to the Resurrection of the Jugos family. They were surprised by the tears that were in Father Kennedy's eyes as he repeated much of the litany he'd preached the previous day during Encarnacion's funeral. His normal Homily which took no more than ten minutes to deliver was extended past the thirty minute mark as his voice broke from time to time as he stopped to compose himself, resuming his bellowing message of a vague warning that shook the rafters. As he left the podium, he walked amongst his flock while addressing his them, something not commonly done. As he moved amongst them he felt a welling up of inner strength, the message of what unseen evil was to soon visit them all and providing a roadmap and a way ahead, that welled up from that unknown place.

"Why in the name of heaven are we all here at Vespers that few find time to attend? Could it be that at some spiritual level of humanity, we all have a sense of evil that has invaded our existence? An evil that takes many forms and serves many masters, all except the Eternal. We all sense it do we not? A seemingly random act to all, I suggest may have been targeted by the overarching Lucifer, who comes to us bearing a smile and an outstretched hand, yet brings pain and suffering. This evil takes many forms. Some easily identifiable, some not. So loved ones, I beseech all of you to be on guard in all that you say or do. At this very moment I feel that I have let all of you down in some manner"!

As he said that a resounding, "No", came forth from the congregation. He waited for the silence once again, as he continued, "From this moment onward I vow to replenish my spirit with the Holy Spirit through prayer, to ward off the evil that I fear has visited our community and welcome all of you to do the same. From this moment onward, the doors to this sanctuary will not be locked and during the night times the lights will be lit for anyone who seeks God's blessings and comfort"!

"But Father Kennedy", came a voice from those assembled, "What about the robbers and thieves that will visit when no one is here"?

"You are afraid and perhaps justly so, that this Holy Sanctuary will be ravaged by the forces of evil while we sleep, are you not"? At that juncture the congregation was silent, as he repeated his question, "Well are you not afraid"?

The entire congregation bellowed back, "Yes, or Si"!

"Then my children I recommend that we all say the "Lord's Prayer" and work to that end by temporal means. Then he began to bellow, "The Lord is my Shepard, I shall not want". The congregation fell in with him as he continued, "He makes me to lie down in green pastures, he leads me beside still waters, he restores my soul", then he remained silent as the rest of the congregation continued.

When the David's Psalm had concluded, he again strode up to the podium and bid them all to rise as he began the ritual of the Profession of the Faith. "We believe in one God, the Father, the Almighty, maker of heaven and earth, of all that is seen and unseen"!

After that concluded, Father Kennedy walked behind the altar to prepare for the communion. As he went through his ritual, one of the parishioners whispered to another, "The Padre. He sure in the zone tonight"!

He then summoned one of the altar boys to bring the large chalice of holy water, with a small pine branch to his side. On the other was another altar boy holding the holy cup of wine in one hand and the blessed wafers, representing the body and the blood of the savior. As each approached for communion he bid them towards the communion with his left hand, and dipped the small pine branch into the Chalice of the holy water, taking care to shake its laden branch on each and every one that came before him.

As the Mass came to a close, with everyone experiencing the "Big Sprinkle", the congregation rose in silence as he boomed out, "The Mass is ended, go in peace one and all", then he slowly made his way towards the main entrance to greet the parishioners as they filed out. He then went to the rectory and removed his vestments, pouring himself a stiff drink and looked for that pack of cigarettes he'd secreted some months ago trying to quit.

He pondered over the fact that perhaps he'd gone too far in keeping the sanctuary open and accessible at all times and the lights on at night. He decided that he'd made the commitment and that it was up to him to provide the vigilance. A half an hour had passed as he finished his drink and stubbed out the remainder of his cigarette. He went to the bedroom for a pillow and then back into the sanctuary thinking about where in the world was he going to get the money to pay for the higher utility bill that keeping the lights to the sanctuary lit at all times.

As he entered the sanctuary he encountered a rather rough looking man who was sitting in one of the rear pews. The man stood as he approached, making the sign of the cross. He recognized the man's face as being an occasional attendee, clearly one who made his living by the sweat of his brow, rather than his wits or intellectual skill and asked as he approached, "Can I help you my son"?

"No Padre. It is I who can help you", he said reaching into his jacket pocket and removing some cash and coins and placing it into Father Kennedy's hand. In the process Kennedy caught a brief glimpse of a pistol in the man's waist band.

"You can go back to the rectory Padre and get a good night's sleep. We will need you at your best in the days to come. After Mass we meet inna parking lot and a dozen of us have decided that we will all take turns protecting the sanctuary. You doan have ta worry about any Vatos coming in an stealing or tearing up things, cause this is the Lords house an we watch over it. As for the money we take up a collection, to keep the lights on at night. We hope you like it"!

As he put the offering in his pocket he put one of his hands on the man's head and said, "Thank you my son and may the Lord watch over you at all times of the day and the night"!

"Oh he will Padre. El Dios will be with us. Every one of us that was here tonight, for sure"!

"Just as a point of curiosity how do you know this for sure? Is it your faith my son, asked Father Kennedy?

"I dunno Padre. I work for the City digging ditches. All time I pray for things. Things importante' to me and never get em. I have faith in only what I feel, touch, see, taste and smell. All's I know is that Jugos little mejo, she get killed by da Negritos and he a good man. I go to the funeral yesterday an listen to you and see the Jugos. I hear the Vespers bells ringing on my way back from the store and I gotta walk in. We listen to you and all agree that somethin' bad has come. We hear what you want to do. You are only one man, to serve all of us. We are many to serve God. We gotta help out and you show us the way. So accept our help as long as you need it. You take care of us and we take care of you"!

"Thank you my son and I accept"!

"So good night Padre. Go get your rest. We got your back. I gotta mug of coffee from the convenience store down the block"!

As father Kennedy went back to the rectory he stopped to look at the remnants of the sunset and started to regain his faith. God was indeed residing in his fellow man. More often than not the Holy Spirit was covered up by the machinations of the temporal world, but every once in a while the memory of what his only begotten son was all about, surfaced with all of the authority of an Oil Well gusher. He'd spent ten years as the keeper of the flame in this small and struggling parish, ministering to the poor, secretly envying other priests who were in much wealthier parishes, who lead dull mundane existences. As of this very moment, he envied them no longer. He was exactly where he was supposed to be. Right in the middle of Satan's domain, amongst the poor. He was exultant.

The Lord was indeed his Shepard. All he had to do was tune in. He shall not be left wanting.

8

Many years ago Ortega made his bones while still in his early teens, with the Cali drug Cartel, first as a lookout, then elevated to that of a runner, then finally as a shooter. An assassin for the Cartel, he never missed, always working from in close. As a skinny kid, who would suspect someone so young of having the skill, much less the cold blooded efficiency to stalk and eliminate a target, much less the 'Cojones' to operate in such a manner? Ortega was absolutely incapable of fear. His only concern was doing the job then scurrying away. No one knew where he came from or who his parents might be. He simply showed up at the doorstep of one of the Cali Cartel's lieutenants one day, with the dirty appearance of another street urchin, begging for work. Any work. And thus a career began.

Rapidly moving up the ladder of the organization, via a combination of luck and acquired skill, he learned early on never to trust anyone at any time. Eventually the time came when he was called upon to eliminate the very lieutenant that brought him into the organization and acted as his mentor as he progressed. Without batting an eye he saw to it, poisoning one of his mixed drinks with a slow acting potion during one of his parties, his padron' passing out on a couch never awakening the following morning. Over time he mastered the art of the double cross, that mystical sleight of hand that always put money in your pocket and the blame on the other guy.

While visibly affable, with a growing chorus of associates, contacts and acquaintances, he had not one person that he could or would call a friend. Friends eventually betrayed you and that could get you dead very quickly in his line of work.

One of the many unwritten rules he was required to live by in his line of work was that everything was short term. Cash on the barrel head, and no credit extended and no excuses offered or accepted. On the way up act with moderation and look to the long term. Live for the moment if you must, but the high rollers that made a practice of that always went up then out, with the out indicative of their death.

Rarely if ever did one strike out on his own, unless he was very lucky and selectively ruthless. Ortega had an abundance of both. A Leprechaun couldn't be luckier and Ortega would kill another on the spot, without a second thought, if he thought things were going awry.

One evening while at a cocktail party hosted by a Panamanian Banker his group was parking their money with he was introduced to an Argentine named Carlos Meyers. The meeting eventually proved beneficial to them both, with Meyers having deep connections with key elements with the Argentine Military Junta, that was in political control of the country at the time. In addition to his key political contacts, he was connected with to various elements of the Argentine Banking and Industrial establishment, as well as a host of other international entities.

As a result of vast incompetence, mismanagement and pure greed by the Argentine political and later military rulers, many important people needed to find other sources of revenue that circumvented the inflationary policies destined to drive the entire country into bankruptcy. Thus for those who mattered, Carlos Meyers was the perfect man. Smooth, polished and with the manners of an aristocrat, his outward appearance covered a Machiavellian ability to obfuscate and deliver profits. Their eventual union would soon prove beneficial to both, with Ortega's skills and contacts, providing the exact synergy required function as a key element, for a massive plan that he'd been crafting for some time. Fronting for a select consortium of Argentine business and governmental interests, Meyers discovered the timing was right to put his plans in motion.

Quite unlike many of the other various members of "La Droga", the various Columbian cartels that purveyed illicit drugs to the world, eventually with the key members becoming known, Ortega had been sliding under the radar for years. The authorities knew nothing of him or how he worked. On only two occasions that never came to light, Ortega acted simply on instinct, eliminating a potential rat. Eventually various parts of the body surfaced around a given rural area, but never enough to identify with precision.

He moved about the entire Western Hemisphere, taking care of business, often by private aircraft, with skillfully forged documents of identification, using well-chosen others as go be tweens never once being discovered by any police agency anywhere. Neither his prints nor photos were on file anywhere in the world.

After several more meetings to solidify their relationship and several trial, ad hoc, sorties that proved mutually profitable they decided to join forces, with Ortega breaking away from the Cartel in such a way to eliminate him from scrutiny.

One sunny day while driving through the mountains returning from a meeting, the brakes failed on the vehicle carrying Ortega and his current boss, the car careening through a road barrier and falling off of a steep precipice into the valley below bursting into flames. Both occupants burned beyond recognition. Dental records revealed that Ortega's boss was one of the occupants, but dental records were not available for the driver. Only a partially melted signet ring know by a select few indicated that Ortega was probably the driver. Only the driver was not Ortega, but just someone that had the same height and build as Ortega.

Months later after a brief stop at a clinic in Costa Rica known for its reconstructive surgery, Ortega surfaced in Houston Texas, starting completely over. Within six months, he purchased a local Gentlemen's Club and gradually hand-picked several associates, before contacting Carlos Meyers. Within a year, they developed a carefully growing coterie of local business's that shielded their import organization from scrutiny, providing a gateway into the largest seaport on the Gulf Coast and the largest city in Texas, with a heavily populated Latino community.

With the help of self-help tapes, he developed a workable command of the colloquial English language, sufficient to conduct business on any level without interpretation. In time, much of his dialect would disappear, with one exception, when he was excited or disturbed.

For years Carlos Meyers had been gradually cultivating a relationship with a number of important people in Asuncion Paraguay and La Paz Bolivia, to gradually become a presence in the international narcotics business. The idea was a dangerous one initially. To bypass the middle men of the established Cartels in Columbia given the hard line the held on the acquired price of product and the international attention to their affairs. He reasoned correctly that if the growers discovered a source that would pay them more for their products they would be happy to gradually shift more and more of their harvests to that new benefactor in secret, for the growers were becoming additionally disenchanted with their Columbian middlemen who in their minds were "Suffering from Prosperity".

Meyers and his people showed the growers that gradually shifted their attention his way a way to somewhat gain better control of their destiny and eventually expand their business creating their own processing plants, deep in the jungles and secluded mountainsides. As time went on the growers opened new areas of growth and processing in the wilds of far western Brazil and Bolivia on the eastern side of the Andes Mountains ceding the northern territories to the established Cartels. The Southern growers still did business with the Columbians but at a lesser rate, gaining the bulk of their newfound wealth by their covert expansion into Western Brazil. In addition Meyers assisted them in shielding his newfound partners from scrutiny by helping them form apparently legitimate front companies, impenetrable by any local governmental scrutiny.

This gradual growth of a secret confederation of growers and processors of Cocaine simply branched out in other directions, diminishing their risks and increasing their profits. Deeply ingrained in each was the fact that their current direction was in the best interests of all involved and the Columbian Cartels remain ignorant of their other activities.

Avoidance of the Columbian and Mexican middlemen remained the keystone of their future collective success and for the better part of eight years their good fortune held. While the Columbian and Mexican middlemen went to war with the local police and military, having to pay extraordinary amounts of money in bribes and do battle with the various judiciaries, Carlos Meyers, Ortega and their southern associates went about their business relatively unscathed.

Meyers Argentine partners couldn't have been more pleased, for their original investments grew exponentially beyond their most liberal of expectations without a single hitch. Better even was their tax free offshore accounts, growing at an ever increasing rate, in spite of a poorly managed Argentine economy that was sliding into international bankruptcy, run by corrupt and incompetent politicians and bureaucrats.

But eventually the slumbering giant began to sense that something was amiss quite apart from the increased rate of governmental incursions and secret American military intervention, proving very bad for business, their sources of supply were gradually shrinking. They sensed a competitive element somewhere. But where? By whom?

The Cartels did not like or tolerate competition and would do anything to eliminate the intrusion of others. This was resolved in part by a series of carefully orchestrated kidnappings, revealing a host of smaller entities in the southern part of the continent, each one smaller in stature, yet each apparently acting on their own behalf. Thus for the next two years a cleansing of sorts occurred between parties, resulting with the established Columbian Cartels making a comeback of sorts. The Cartels were all out looking for a phantom organizer. The mysterious individual responsible for the loose confederation that had been eroding their profits for years.

A secret source of information had been providing the Columbian authorities with information about the Cartels for years. No picture existed regarding the source. Only a rough description gleaned by excruciating torture in secret jungle camps, at the point of death, revealed the existence of relatively young, late thirties to mid-forties, well-bred and educated man, who spoke Spanish in an aristocratic Argentine dialect. Some said his hair was blonde, while others said he was a redhead. Thus came the million dollar bounty placed on the head of the Argentine, placed by the Cartels collectively.

Three North American entities became involved as steady buyers for the narcotics that flowed unabated through the Port of Houston during the interim. Ortega acting in his own behalf, as well as Meyers and his Argentine partners did business with people he knew very well. The Chicago partners, consisting of the remnants of the Giancana crime family, somewhat diminished over time thanks to the efforts by the Federal Government, yet still active and viable.

The Los Angeles contingent were "The Crips" street gang, now all grown up and somewhat sophisticated, gradually shedding themselves from their long time connections with the Mendaca crime family based out of Tia Juana Mexico. "Da Crips", as they had become to be known, were the fastest growing crime organization in the nation, spreading their narcotic grip through almost every black neighborhood in the west and heading eastward at a dizzying pace.

Finally the Seattle partners were the "Lao Tang Tong", which monopolized the distribution of all drugs in the Seattle, Vancouver

British Columbia areas all the way down to the greater San Francisco Bay area and all of the Pacific Islands, back to their roots in Shanghai, Hong Cong and Macao.

Even through the time of troubles with the Columbian Cartels, the Ortega connection, shipments continued unabated to his North American partners. The many headed hydra was proving to be far too numerous for the Cartels to eliminate.

Nestor Magellan waited patiently for Carlos Meyer's flight into Houston Intercontinental Airport to be driven into town and for a stay at the Weston Galleria Hotel. The room was booked in the name of Carmine Fiore', the former Western Hemisphere Vice President of the Fiat Motor Car Company, long into retirement, in questionable health and not going anywhere in Montevideo. Meyers traveling papers were in the name of Carmine Fiore, since both bore a remarkable resemblance to each other in appearance and stature, with the modest exception of a twenty year difference in their ages.

As Meyers cleared Customs, he looked for the tall man holding the hand written sign saying, "Mr. Fiore". catching sight of Magellan, Meyers approached smiling and said, "So good to see you my friend as they shook hands and started to walk out of the airport. "It's been about three years since you've come to America and I'm hearing nothing but good things about you"!

"Really", said Magellan looking straight ahead not breaking his stride.

"Of course, your Jeff' would be the last one to ever tell you"!

"In that we'd agree"!

"Are you prospering financially"?

"I've no complaints. El Jefe' is a generous man for those who prove useful. For those who do not," his voice trailed away the statement standing on its own.

"I wouldn't concern myself if I were you since about relationships, seeing that you've been elevated to 'Segundo' long ago. Everyone knows that when you speak, it's as if your Padrone' had spoken"!

"As the Corsicans are so fond of saying, "Every day above ground is a good day" and in that regard, I suppose I've as good a relationship with him as anyone"!

"I'm glad you've still a sense of sardonic humor", said Meyers as they stepped on the down escalator to the ground level baggage area.

"So, just what brings you to Houston? Is the competition in your part of the world getting a bit frisky"?

"In our line of work things are always, 'Frisky', as you say. Fortunes ebb and flow. The Columbians are busy fighting the politicians and the American advisors, given their propensity for hubris. Their recent emergence from their slumber as of late was inevitable.

We've had a very long run of good fortune at their expense, with this Ad Hoc Confederation of growers and processors eventually drifting away from the base, which never treated them well anyway.

The concept of their Confederation gave each of the growers the freedom they wanted, under the umbrella of unity and the illusion of security. The recent incursions by the Columbians, does not require that we respond in kind to every incident, inflicted upon us. Given the multitude of associates we're allied with allow for the sufferance of minor setbacks from time to time. Let's wait until were driving into town then I can be more expansive"!

Once the car was underway Meyers said, "The reason I'm here Nestor my friend, is to finalize plans with our friend Ortega for the final stages of the Embraer scenario in behalf of our Argentine partners and in addition to whet his appetite for a completely new venture that I've been working on for several years, quite apart from our normal involvements. All I'm prepared to say is that if Nestor will come on board and serve as our North American conduit, then we can remove ourselves from the rest of the South American operations completely should we so choose"!

"So why don't I remain patient and wait until you reveal your plan to Ortega, when we're all together"?

"Precisely, because you will a key element to the latter aspect I've just discussed. By the way, have your linguistic abilities been kept up to date"?

"It all depends on what language", said Magellan!

"Principally Russian and the Ukrainian dialect"!

"I'm certain I can translate effectively"!

"You'll have to be able to pass as a native"!

"A few days to brush up on the local colloquialisms and I'll be fine"?

"Oh, by the way Nestor, has that package I sent a week ago to Ortega been delivered"?

"It's in Ortega's safe. Arrived several days ago, awaiting your arrival"!

"Good, for that package represents a newfound freedom and overwhelming prosperity for all of us"!

Upon arrival at the hotel, Meyers was checked into his suite and showered away the remnants of his long flight from Santiago Chile, in preparation for his meeting with Ortega. As he left, Magellan called Ortega to inform him of Meyers arrival and to confirm, their meeting later on in the evening at the 'Colorado Club' for dinner and drinks at the Southwest's premier Gentlemen's Club.

At seven in the evening Magellan and Davalantes car arrived at the Weston Galleria's front entrance and picked up Meyers as he emerged from the hotel for the ten minute drive to the Colorado. Upon their arrival the trio were escorted through the main salon by Konrad, the large Swiss born manager who guided the fortunes of Ortega's trio of clubs locally. It was the weekend and the upscale crowd of late happy hour businessmen were forgoing the joys of rush hour traffic, ostensibly working late on budgetary concerns or contractual involvements that were vital to their ongoing business interests. At least that's what their wives and girlfriends were told.

The Colorado was humming with a full room of eager clientele, surrounded by a swirl of scantily clad Puellae, of such magnificent quality to guarantee adornment in a Sultans Seraglio. The girls alternated between working the room and taking their turns on the strategically positioned podiums writhing and moving to the rhythms, of the programmed music, displaying their wares often just an arms-length from eager patrons intent on engorgement of every one of the seven sins, often carrying on not so innocent conversation with the objects of their unbridled attention.

As Konrad led the trio through the large salon, they had to work their way around a podium upon which a tall, lean and heavily breasted blonde was in a supine position, resting on her elbows, her hands on her hips, legs spread wide, slowly opening and closing to reveal the insufficiency of the micro G-string in covering her gateway to paradise.

As Meyers passed her, their eyes met as she cooed sweetly, "Dinner Anyone"? As they passed, Konrad mildly admonished her saying, "Brigitte, behave with the guests"! "Oh Konrad, you know I always do", she replied following the quartet around the four foot tall podium, her legs still far apart propelled by the continually alternate flexing of exquisite gluteal cheeks and a clitoral rhythm hitherto unknown on the face of the earth.

They climbed the stairs to the ring of enclosed VIP suites that encompassed the main salon, with Konrad escorting them into one of the rooms, where there Ortega greeted them.

"Senor Ortega your guests have arrived", said Konrad as everyone entered the room.

"Ah Carlos, how good of you to come", said Ortega embracing his partner!

"Ortega I salute you", said Meyers. "But tell me, how is it possible for a pussy to wink"?

"Ortega looked at Konrad as they both smiled. "Oh you must have met Brigitte. She is Konrad's star attraction. Tonight we're all in for a special treat, Konrad tells me. For she has added a magic act of sorts in addition to her already, uh, Konrad help me. What is the word you used earlier to describe her act"?

"Superlative, Senor Ortega, Superlative"!

"That's it. Superlative. Konrad, will you see to the refreshments"? "Right away Senor", he said turning on a dime and closing the door. "So Carlos how was your trip and how are your quarters at the Weston"?

"The flight was long and yet manageable and the quarters are what one would come to expect"!

After several minutes of banal small talk the red light on the table blinked repeatedly indicating the drinks were but seconds away. One of the many unspoken requirements of someone in Konrad's position was to know just what every repeat customer's favorite drinks were without asking and Konrad had an excellent memory.

After the drinks arrived, and the scantily clad waitress left Ortega said, "This room is secure so we can speak freely"!

Magellan interjected, Other than various devices we've installed in selected locations the entire place is swept electronically on a random basis, no less than weekly. This room was swept by me personally late this afternoon after I dropped you off at the Weston"!

"And the possibility of directional detection", asked Meyers?

"Unless science has progressed within the last week impossible. The equipment required to penetrate double pane glass that surrounds us is far too large to escape detection here, besides, we're surrounded by a barrier of 'White Noise' installed a last year", answered Magellan. "If your reach over and touch the glass enclosure you'll feel a slight vibration, that will block any possibility of audio penetration. Besides once the loud music down below starts, it's impossible to differentiate one recorded sound from the next"!

"Good Nestor and now to the business at hand. Senor Ortega have you the package I've sent you"?

Ortega reached over to his briefcase and extracted a small package and opened it revealing a small three ounce container similar to that of an eye drop dispenser. "The principal reason that I'm here is to introduce you to what our South American partners have been working very hard to develop. In that small bottle is the world's first true 'Syncotic'. Of course within that container is something so new it has no chemical cognomen to describe it so let's just call it, 'Crystalline'. Within a month there will be ten tons of highly concentrated product that needs no refrigeration and has an indefinite shelf life"!

Meyers paused for a moment to allow the effect to set in before continuing. "Crystalline is a synthetically manufactured chemical, that dependent on what and how it is combined with as a ingestible medium, can completely mimic the effects of any narcotic, stimulant, depressant, hallucinogenic, or most poisons known to man. It is an easily transportable concentrate as it resembles clear corn syrup in appearance and consistency. It gives out no discernible odor to man or beast and thus is undetectable. Best of all, our organization controls its manufacture and soon its distribution worldwide"!

Once again Meyers paused, taking a drink before continuing. "It will be completely legal everywhere on the planet because of its newness. Or course eventually the world's political entities will catch up with science, but I'll give them at least ten years until they catch on effectively. Best of all its newness and variability of its chemical composition has one important advantage. Once orally ingested by the host, it works its will, dependent on the liquid medium it's combined with, then within twenty four hours leaves no trace of its composition, once the selected effects have run their course. Thus, let us assume someone has overdosed or experienced physical complications after initial ingestion? An autopsy of the body, no matter how through, will reveal not a trace of its presence"!

"So how much is in this little eye dropper bottle", asked Ortega holding up the bottle.

"What you hold in its highly diluted form of three ounces, is more than enough to keep someone happy, pumped or delusional for almost a year. A single drop in a glass of moderately chlorinated sugar water will render a football lineman Muerte' within the hour. He'll simply fall asleep and within thirty minutes all bodily functions will shut down"!

"If I may ask Senor Meyers", said Magellan. "Perhaps we want to stimulate, or subjugate someone"?

"Then all you need to accomplish this is under this very roof Nestor", said Meyers continuing. "The rocket science has already been done and is soon to be available to the world at large for a price, which you will determine at the wholesale level since everything will flow through our organization here in Houston"!

"We will need a different way of getting the product in port Carlos", said Ortega!

"This is why we will need the linguistic services of Nestor, for the initial event. I have taken the liberties to bring in some additional very silent European partners that will provide us with the ability to bring in the product undetected and in quantity. The logistics are almost complete. All you must provide Ortega is a remote and discrete place in Texas in which to store the initial shipment and annual shipments thereafter. Then a remote location where transfer can be effected"!

"You mean where the buy, she go down"!

"Precisely Ortega", said Meyers continuing. "Should anything go awry after the buy, the transporter will be transporting a case of Retail Corn Syrup. At least that is what the packaging will indicate"!

"Now when our business is concluded a few days from now, I'll be making the rounds of our current customers and our new Euro partners to demonstrate the varied effects of our product"

"So next we get a demonstration, eh Carlos", mused Ortega?

"The sample in front of you is in the right place for a proper demonstration, with several of your dancers to serve as unwitting examples"! Ortega and Magellan exchanged glances, with Magellan getting up, motioning to Davalantes to join him and leaving the room to seek out Konrad in the main salon below.

While Magellan was gone Meyers said, "We will leave it to you

Ortega, to determine the wholesale price to your customers, my only task as I make the rounds is to demonstrate and get their attention. To make the initial sale, get their whistles whetted, and then direct them to you. You will determine price per quantity and conduct business as before. You will take your standard cut off the top; incur what expenses you normally incur, rendering the rest of the money to us as usual. Are we in agreement"?

"If these shit works like you say, then we be in agreement Carlos as before. Nothing change an we all make plenty more money"!

"As time goes on and the Crystalline increases in sales as I know it will, then we will charge whatever the traffic will bear. Should the situation with the Columbians prove untenable, which is always a possibility, and then we simply abandon the field to the Columbians and focus on the Crystalline, which may prove all that we can handle in any event. This will wholly depend upon the quality of our people. The political and military spotlight is currently on the Columbian families as well as a host of others world- wide and I suggest we keep it that way. Thus we benefit in both the short and long run. I'd appreciate your thoughts on the matter"!

"My thoughts are simple Carlos. I will insist that you completely know the Europeans that you bring to the table as so called partners. Anything go wrong with them and it's your ass, just so we unnerstan each other. My customers are golden an we been doin' business for years"!

"Those I'm bringing in are Corsicans, who have their connections with certain Russian elements newly liberated from the collapse of the Soviet Union. The Russians will never know of any of us. As far as they know it will be a Corsican operation. We will sell to the Corsicans and they will sell to the Russians. The Corsicans territory will consist of Western Europe and the entire Mediterranean basin and the Russians of course control Eastern Europe and all of Mother Russia"!

"What if the Russians want to expand, Carlos"?

"It will be the Corsicans concern not ours"!

"It just come into my mind Carlos"!

"What is that"? He could see that Ortega was really interested, because the quality of his English always went south when excited or angry.

"Bookies. Sports Bookies. Crooked Sports Agents, Trainers. Boxers.

Slow a key player or a fighter down a jus the right time you can make a killing"!

"Far too risky right now Ortega. Let's us all make our mega millions at least for the next five years or so. Best we remain invisible for the time being. Involvements in sports are just too visible. Things that shouldn't happen occur. The authorities smell a rat. Someone gets a case of the runny mouth. They have to be silenced. Investigations get started"!

"But you say that the Crystalline fade away an is undetectable in about a day after"!

"Yes Ortega. I've seen the statistics. I've witnessed the tests and autopsies myself and followed the science. But once the light of day is shined on the events due to pure unrestrained greed and hubris and governments get wind of things, current science can quickly catch up and our gift is revealed to the world. Pressures will be brought to bear, people will start to talk. Once that ball gets rolling then all is lost. The gift ceases to bear fruit. Best we stay in the shadow's, make our millions out of sight and enjoy our wealth without the unnecessary risks. This we will need to impress upon our buyers selectively. We do this right, and then we will enjoy our wealth far into our old age. If not, Muerte'"!

"So, how much you say of this Crystalline, will be ready to ship", asked Ortega?

"Ten tons of concentrate will be ready to head towards us within the month. What you have in front of you is a highly diluted form of Crystalline"!

"So this stuff been stepped on"!

"A great deal, but it's still a potent concoction"!

A long slow and barely audible whistle came from Ortega and Meyers knew he had Ortega interested. He could almost see his mind calculating the unimaginable profits that lay ahead.

"Just one thing Meyers. I still not comfortable with the Corsicans and the Russians as partners and why you need Magellan for what you say a month or more"?

Meyers every so often wondered about his partner and his agrarian attitudes about things. Then he took a deep breath and said, "The Russians are not our partners but our customers, paying cash on the barrelhead for the product and the Corsicans are seemed to be our partners but will be in fact just another customer. Nestor is needed for both his linguistic abilities and his former military acumen. For the mode of transport will be a former Soviet Diesel Submarine that we will obtain in secrecy from the Black Sea fleet while on maneuvers. Of course a significant amount of money will have to change hands, half of which will be from our Argentine partners and the other half from the Corsicans. The Russian Navy is but a shadow of its former self. Many of the officers and crews haven't been paid on a regular basis and are ripe for the picking. Every one of the ships in the Russian Navy are operating on a skeleton crew basis. As the Russian Flotilla approaches Istanbul, a single submarine will disappear and that will be ours. It will rendezvous with a refueling ship in the middle of the South Atlantic and end up in a Southern Chilean fjord for a week of refueling and refitting. Then it will make for another rendezvous just off the Port of Valparaiso Chile to receive the Crystalline. By that time I expect that you will have provided the coordinates for its final resting place somewhere safe in Texas"!

"Now I unnerstan. I get Davalantes to work on a place I got in mind to store the stuff. Have it for you inna few days. So we gonna steal a Russian Submarine eh"?

"In a manner of speaking Ortega, yes"! What Meyers carefully avoided telling Ortega was of the long standing connection that Magellan had with the Unione' Corse', based out of Marseilles, dating back to his days in The Legion. Through their contacts with elements of the Russian Mafia, in the Caspian seaport of Baku, the plan to obtain the submarine was developed. Large amounts of cash have been known to unite people into a common cause. His meeting with the Russians and the Corsicans had already taken place over a month ago. The demonstration of the product had already taken place, and things were already taking place at a rapid clip. Of course they were unaware of Ortega's existence.

The Russian connection, was headed by a former Colonel in the old Soviet KGB, who still kept tabs on key individuals in the current Russian and Ukrainian military, with whom he'd done business with periodically. Given their miserable pay structure, it posed little problem to gain access to vast quantities of military stores when the occasion warranted. Everyone knew the risk one took, of discovery. Thus fear of discovery, along with an eternity in the wilds of Siberia, versus the reward of a substantial Swiss Bank account, made decisions relatively simple.

The already compromised Admiral of the Russian Navy's Black

Sea Fleet, was offered a hundred thousand Swiss Franc's to be placed in an account set up in his wife's maiden name, at the Banc de Securite', in Berne Switzerland. Once the vessel completed passage through the Bosporus and into the Aegean Sea, a coded radio signal would be sent and funds would be transferred into the newly created account and his family would be allowed to return from their vacation.

Plans were in motion for one last training exercise for a small flotilla to make a swing around the entire Black Sea. Obtaining the services of a skeleton crew of eighteen experienced submariner's, wasn't difficult. All were single with few familial ties to the motherland. Each was given an account in the same Swiss Bank, in the amount of ten thousand Swiss Franc's with the same terms and conditions of their Commander. Far more than they ever hoped to see in a lifetime. Plus permanent residency papers in Argentina.

Then Magellan reentered the room saying, "Pardon me gentlemen, Konrad is ready downstairs with three of the dancers, ready to join us individually, for our little experiment, upon your signal"!

"Please go back to him and have him bring the appropriate mixing mediums as I've written down on this paper and set up the bar prior to the subjects arrival", said Meyers handing Magellan a slip of paper.

Minutes later Konrad arrived leading a member of his kitchen staff with a small portable bar that was wheeled into the room. "Good", said Meyers. Konrad please introduce us to your first subject.

As was previously arranged, each dancer's mixed drink of choice was prepared in advance of her performance. Five hundred dollars was advanced to each dancer, with the instructions to say nothing to the men in the room. Simply enter, consume the proffered drink entirely them perform their normal couch dance routine, to the rhythm of the music piped into the room then depart.

Meyers then told Ortega what to expect from each dancer, while they were waiting for the first one to arrive, fresh from her exertions on one of the small podiums in the main salon, slightly glistening with perspiration from her exertions. As she entered, she was handed a small fresh bar towel to pat dry the sweat from her glistening body, then handing the towel back to Konrad with a flourish, she was handed the proffered drink by Konrad and downed it in a single gulp, placing the empty glass on the table. Then she looked at Ortega, Meyers and Magellan, one by one seductively and started to slowly walk around the room in concentric circles, pausing at each one's chair and letting her musk permeate their senses as she slowly blended with rhythmic lilt of the sultry music. As the Crystalline was absorbed by her body quickly, the symptoms of the narcotic was quickly evident as she slowly worked her well-practiced magic on each man. In minutes what little covering that adorned her body, lay on the floor, as she mounted each of her subjects in turn and compelled their complete attention.

During the course of her exhibition, any semblance of caution she may have had, lay on the floor with the rest of her ever so brief coverings, with her repeated silent exhortations to each of her subjects of her urgent need of immediate gratification. As the last of the music faded from the room, she found herself astride of Ortega, her pendulous breasts slowly swaying in front of him as Konrad assisted her back to a standing position. He handed her the scanty coverings that were on the floor and gently ushered her out of the suite.

Still under the influence of the Crystalline she calmly walked across the main floor of the salon below with her coverings in her hand, to the joy of the customers she passed along the way.

Half way across the room she was intercepted by Davalantes, who insisted that she cover herself up. Facing a brief resistance, he quickly, but gently ushered her from the salon to recover.

The second dancer entered, took her proffered drink then slowly promenaded around the room, for everyone's personal and extensive inspection of her feminine bona fides. Five minutes later as the piped in music grew in tempo, so did her exertions, her coverings quickly finding their way to the floor. For the next twenty minutes, she did her very best to spread her extensive and personal musk on the trio each in turn to cover up that of their previous visitor. Not quite as generously blessed as her predecessor with protuberances, she none the less, performed in a yeoman like fashion, leaving none in the room with a single complaint or criticism regarding her performance or her physical appearance.

As the tempo of the music faded from the room she was reluctant to depart, eyes wide open and pupils dilated with the effects similar in scope with that of a full on rush of Cocaine. Once again the dancer returned to the main salon, coverings in hand, not adorning her body as normally expected, only to be intercepted by Davalantes in mid room with a mild admonition saying, "Be too bad if the Vice Squad were in the house this evening, wouldn't it"!

That said, she turned to one of the nearby tables, interrupting a conversation and asked for assistance in putting on her ever so brief attire. There are times in men's lives, when interruptions are a welcome respite. This was one of them.

As she mounted a nearby podium, having the complete and undivided attention of the party of four just scant feet away she swayed to the music in the main salon and proceeded to completely undo what had previously been done, eventually displaying completely, all of her considerable external as well as internal charms, to the extensive monetary delight of those nearby.

The party of four were all doctors in some need for feminine resuscitation after a long day at a nearby hospital. One of them turned to another saying, "Harvey, as a gynecologist, wouldn't you get weary looking at pussies all day long"? The others laughed as Harvey replied with a smile on his face, "Normally Herb, you'd be correct, but after looking at that exquisite entrance to Heaven, my faith in femininity is completely renewed", he paused then continued, "At least until next Monday"!

Konrad was standing by the window of the VIP Suite ready to summon the final example for everyone's scrutiny when he overheard an apparently excited Ortega say, "That stuff, she go to work fast. Don't she Carlos"?

"It mimics a composition similar to that of the sports drinks that athletes use. Gets into the bloodstream triple quick. Works its magic for its normal duration, eventually disappearing without a trace"!

"Gentlemen", said Konrad. "Our last subject for the evening I thought proper to save for last. You made her acquaintance on the way in. It is our star performer of the evening, Brigitte. She is scheduled to perform on the main stage in ten minutes for our patrons below. Her new act is such that it is guaranteed to leave all breathless in wonderment. She is down below with Davalantes awaiting our invitation, so may I suggest that we invite her up for the introductions and ingestion, then release her to the main stage and watch and wonder"!

Meyers and Ortega looked at each other and nodded in agreement. Then Konrad signaled Davalantes below to bring their guest Brigitte, standing proudly on one of the podiums for all to see and lust for. At Davalantes nod, she followed him slowly up the stairs to the VIP suites that ringed the lower salon. Striding into the room she stood proudly in front of them all as Konrad said, "Gentlemen this is Brigitte. Standing almost six feet in height cast your eyes upon her and wonder. Perfect symmetry in every way"!

"Brigitte may I introduce you to"!

"Never mind Konrad", she chuckled in a slightly Euro accent, "We've met as they arrived and from what I've displayed, that is all they need to know. Is it not"?

At that very moment each of them had only one thought in mind. Even Konrad, who one would think had grown accustomed to the presence of barely clad women in his every day working environment, found himself growing large.

Meyers recovered his composure quickly enough to pick up the cocktail he'd prepared and offer it to his guest saying, "Konrad has been singing your praises and we eagerly anticipate your new show, that he assures will leave us breathless"!

As she drained the proffered drink in one lusty gulp, she replied, "Merely breathless? Konrad understates as usual. Boys, when I'm finished all of you will be completely drained. Then you can ponder what can be done, should any of you have the chance to ride the pony bareback".

She then flipped the drained glass back at Meyers with a slow wink, and said "Konrad, its show time"!

Konrad followed her out and down the stairs escorting her through the main salon to the dressing rooms in back of the main stage, while Davalantes stayed in the VIP suite with the rest. It wasn't so much her raw boned beauty that held men in awe, but the simple panache' in which she displayed a supreme example of feminine beauty. In the back of men's minds was the simple fact that here was a woman that required no obvious adornments, to enhance what already was evident in overwhelming abundance. A celestial gift for whoever had the price and the price was steep.

For several minutes all was silent in their private salon, the room awash in estrogenic pheromones, before Meyers said hoarsely, "Maybe we should get back to business, while we wait for this Brigitte, to knock us on our asses again. Are we all clear on the Crystalline transfer and the need for Nestor. In a few days he and I will depart for the Mediterranean in I'll hand him off to my connection and he'll be in charge of everything thereafter. Then I'll fly back to Buenos Aires to set everything up for the meeting germane to the Embraer transfer in Sao Paulo. We are in agreement Ortega"?

"We are in agreement Carlos"!

"Good. Now tell me about this Jaeger that is to be in charge of the Embraer affair"!

"He been wid us for about six months. He done time in prison. He's an ex-Marine.

I meet him in a gym one afternoon and was impressed. He was maybe looking to jump to something other than be a local bounty hunter. I put him wid Magellan soon as we bring him in and Magellan, he OK wid him. He done very good work since he with us"!

"But a common bounty hunter", exclaimed Meyers?

"Far from a common bounty hunter Carlos", said Magellan! "Oh he is, is he"?

"The US Marshall's Service both loves and hates him, depending on who you talk to. Apparently in the last few years, his local and state recaptures, to venturing forth into Mexico and as far as Costa Rica to bring back felons for their worth. Seems he's never failed yet. Seems he's been doing well financially"!

"Then what magic did Ortega have to bring him with us. He's doing so good then why get with us"?

"Carlos, who knows ones motivations? Who can look into ones soul? Why did I allow you to talk me into leaving the 'Legion' and seek adventure elsewhere"?

"Because you've made a lot of money since then. More than you would have made in the French Foreign Legion"!

"And so has our hunter Jaeger. He's done everything asked of him without fault and Ortega has handsomely compensated him. The man is a pro. Besides Ortega and I can't be everywhere at once. You set the agenda Carlos. Someone has to run the Sao Paulo meeting and see it through"!

"Is that right Ortega"?

"I got no complaints Carlos. If I did, he'd be Jugos Menudo soup and Chorizo the very next day. He's downstairs right now"! Just then

Konrad appeared to tell them of Brigitte's show which was to start in five minutes.

"I change my mind", said Ortega. "Konrad find Davalantes and have him bring Jaeger here and make sure he got a drink in his hand. Not the same as the girls, at least not yet"!

Several minutes later Davalantes appeared with Jaeger in his wake, a drink in hand. As the introduction to Meyers took place, the house lights below dimmed, signaling the start of the evening's premier act"!

"Everyone shoosh", said Ortega. We talk after the show"! The lights sufficiently dimmed the stage lights flashed, but once and then the music drifted into a sultry Latin rhythm as the DJ smoothly announced, "You've seen her once, you've seen her twice and all that you've seen is far beyond nice. You've seen everything she has to display and every time you were glad to pay. We don't know where you come from we don't know where you've been, but pay close attention to the Queen of Sin. Here she is, the incomparable Brigitte"!

The spot light focused on the Ferrari red curtain as it slowly opened for a quick wink, allowing the statuesque Nordic beauty to appear, then quickly closed. As the entire audience stood in abject attention and a round of applause crested like a wave, then slowly faded away, as the DJ mildly admonished them to pay close attention to every little thing and nuance saying in his finest, sotto voce stage whisper, "Think you've been everywhere, or seen everything, had all that life has to offer? Been from Maine to Spain, even seen goats fuck in the marketplace in Marrakech? Cast your eyes upon the ultimate desire, the ultimate wonder and remember this night"!

Emerging slowly onto the main stage, seeming to float rather than stride, enveloped in a diaphanous cladding that revealed as well as concealed with no apparent beginning or end, she moved about the stage effortlessly, her half lidded eyes casting appealing glances at everyone and no one. Her expression shifting life the sands of time from listless boredom, occasionally focusing upon a visible target and drifting into a pleading look of helplessness, a signal of a deep seated need for eternal unity, lingering ever so briefly, then fading away into the deep abyss of one's memory.

As Brigitte seemingly floated around the stage and out on the three runways, her covering gradually began to unravel ever so slowly as every eye held her in rapt attention. Even the other dancers and staff had to stop and gaze upon her, the supreme compliment as all commerce ground to a halt for the duration.

The music drifted gradually into a carefully crafted amalgam of Mozart, overlaying a gradual up tempo Euro/Electro multi layered beat as she lithely moved about the stage, her covering falling from her form as if by unseen hands with the tempo of the music. Once again making the circuit, she left in her wake and was greeted again, with every jaw agape in wonder as well as a seemingly endless length of diaphanous nothingness that crumbled at the touch. After what seemed like an eternity yet was only ten minutes in duration, she stood onstage proudly and completely unadorned, save for the briefest of micro, flesh colored G-strings that might as well not have been there for all of the covering it rendered.

Her audience now completely gripped in the throes of rapture, Brigitte moved towards the centerpiece of every dancer's appearance, the gleaming stainless steel pole that demanded her attentions. Wrapping her long legs around the pole without any assistance from her upper extremities, she seemed to slowly climb the pole to a height of well over eight feet, the muscles in her legs alternately contracting much like a centipede, hanging effortlessly and somehow started to turn ever so slowly, again casting her glances upon first one then another of the patrons, as the DJ, once again softly whispered, "As each of you gaze at Brigitte, note the pole. It's not moving but she is. How in the world does she do it"?

Then after some time, she slowly allowed the laws of gravity to take hold and ever so slowly drifted back to the main stage, sticking out slowly one of her legs to the hardwood floor, then the other to regain her standing position, to the applause of the ever excited room. The DJ quickly brought the applause to and end saying, "People, please? She's not done with you yet. Not by a long shot. Try and restrain yourselves, until she's completed with you"!

There she stood, in all her proud glory, making a small sad face for all to see, and then apparently with great effort shaking her head and continuing as she walked slowly out towards the end of the runway, then stopping as she slowly allowed gravity to overwhelm her as she slowly descended into the forward splits as she leaned forward in front of a group of slack jawed men, her hands on her hips, allowing her ample breasts to lean forward in invitation as all focused on her body and every scintilla, not seeing her reach toward her nearest patron and apparently pluck a large shiny silver dollar from behind his ear and slowly withdraw holding the silver dollar up in the air clasping the coin with both fingertips as she slowly started to rise.

Once again, a few over eager patrons started to applaud but were quickly stopped by those around them, as Brigitte carefully walked back down the runway towards center stage, sensing the desire and her mastery of the moment from all in attendance. As she made her way back, the music gradually morphed into an up tempo classical aria, from the Opera 'Othello' called 'Pace de Meo', or 'Peace for Me', as she slowly made her way around the stage holding the Silver Dollar on high for all to see. Many had seen coins appear from people's heads by magicians from time to time, by fully clothed magicians, figuring correctly that it was well practiced sleight of hand, yet here in front of everyone was a woman, devoid of almost every article of concealment, producing a Silver Dollar out of seemingly thin air. The only possibility of concealment for such a large coin might emanate from an area covering her pubic region only slightly larger than the coin itself, yet at all times her hands never descended lower than her ribcage.

She finally stopped at center stage, slowly bending over at the waist and stood the Silver Dollar on its end, for all to see and then arose, gradually lifting her right leg to a complete vertical position while standing on her left, once again her inner charms on complete display, her arms overhead pleading with some unseen entity, then her leg descended back to the stage, as she slowly curtsied to the audience. Then as the sad music droned on she slowly stepped around the Silver Dollar, mouthing the words of the aria in silence as if it were her very last act on this mortal coil, she stopped astride the vertical coin and ever so slowly descended upon it, again her hands uplifted towards the heavens as if pleading. Lower and lower she went. Her ankles signaling the only movement as her right and left legs spread wider and wider into, what is called the 'Russian Splits' as she completely enveloped the coin, her pubic arch, eventually kissing the hardwood floor of the stage.

Suddenly her expression gradually changed from sadness, to a smile as she slowly started to rise, with every patron standing to see that the Silver Dollar completely disappeared.

By the time she came completely erect, the entire room was in a state of bedlam, of shouts and applause, with people approaching the stage showering it with wadded up currency of every denomination.

Nothing else needed to be said, for everyone in attendance would remember this night for the rest of their lives. Brigitte had worked long and hard on perfecting her new act and stood still, in appreciation of the audience reaction, before she turned and slowly walked to the rear curtain. As the curtain opened, she stopped looked back over her shoulder and winked before disappearing. Meyers and Ortega watched the busboys that were quickly summoned to the stage to gather up Brigitte's well-earned gifts as he said, "It seems that you've selected your talent well Ortega. Should guarantee a standing room only patronage for foreseeable future"!

"It is Konrad who is responsible for the selection of our performers, but I will be happy to take credit", said Ortega beaming.

"So Senor Jaeger", said Meyers, "What did you think of the performance you've just witnessed"!

"Very impressive, Senor Meyers"!

"A man with an economy of words I see. Very good. Now tell me of what you know of the plans regarding the Embraer transfer"? Jaeger glanced at Ortega, who nodded his head for him to speak. For the next few minutes Jaeger repeated Ortega's plans to Meyers as he knew them to be.

"Very Good Senor", said Meyers upon his completion! "Have you any suggestions for improvement"? Again Ortega nodded his head, as Jaeger said, "Just a few minor things," and proceeded to comment.

"Makes good sense to me", said Meyers! "Ortega what are your thoughts"?

"I agree, with his suggestions"? As Meyers turned to Magellan, he saw Magellan nodding his head as well as Davalantes, standing by the door. "Well then, it appears we're all in agreement, with Senor Jaeger being in charge of the Embraer transfer. I'm happy to meet you Senor and when next we meet, it will be in Sao Paulo", he said shaking hands with Jaeger nodding his head to Davalantes to escort him out.

Meyers then turned to Ortega saying, "The man seems capable enough and if he has Magellan's approval that should be sufficient".

Konrad then called them on the clubs interphone. Ortega picking it up an after a few seconds hung up. "Any problems", asked Meyers?

"Brigitte our star performer. It appears she had a bad reaction to our drink and is now backstage with Konrad and Obrigon, trying to hold her down. I told Konrad to give her a sedative"!

"Keep in mind, that she cannot be seen by any medical people for at least twenty four hours, to allow all traces of the Crystalline to disappear", said Meyers!

"I hate to lose the Chiquita, for after tonight she be a real moneymaker", said Ortega wistfully!

"Hopefully she'll survive and shower you with good fortune, but if not, then there's always Jugos", said Meyers as Ortega grudgingly shrugged his shoulders in agreement.

"Tell me now, this Jaeger. He knows only about the Embraer transfer and nothing about the Crystalline and Magellan's work"!

"Nossing, Nada", answered Ortega. None of his business until maybe later. We see how he do in Sao Paulo, then if we need his help on the other thing, then OK"!

"It's late and I'd like you to have Davalantes drive me back to the Weston", said Meyers. "Tomorrow, we meet with your other partners to talk over our potential investments down the road". Ortega nodded his head as Meyers departed, passing Magellan as he left. As they both stood in the VIP suite watching the crowd down below, still abuzz over Brigitte's performance, barely paying any attention to the dancers all around them, Magellan handed Ortega a drink as Ortega said, "Tell me what you think about Meyers Nestor. Tell me true"!

"What I think? I don't understand"? "You an me, we tight, right Nestor"?

"No daylight between us as far as I can see, Jefe. Is there a problem"? "You been to Dr. Kominski's lab in the Andes right, with Meyers months ago with Meyers an you tell me, how he show you completely around, right"? Magellan nodded his head in agreement, as he sipped his drink.

"Over time, many little things Meyers said and done, not sit right with me. So far he be right every time, but I think with all the different things he getting' us into he may be, how you put it"?

"Over reaching"?

"That's right, spreadin' us too thin. There's somethin' you always say about this"?

"Oh, you mean the point of diminishing returns"?

"That's it Nestor, diminishing returns. I think we almost there with Meyers"!

"So what do you propose"?

"This Crystalline thing is gonna be a moneymaker for us all in the long run, yet the control will be in the hands of Meyers. This Embraer thing be too iffy an I worry about Meyers Argentine military and industrial partners and government involvement. I see it through, but only as a means to an end for the Crystalline business. That we can control. Then the other thing about the Corsicans and the Russians. I doan know them, an I doan trust em"!

"We need them as an intro to the Russians. Meyers people and the Corsicans are fronting all the money for this enterprise."!

"I hear that the Argentines are getting most of their money through certain people in Peru. Any currency and the printers there they do real good work, American Dollars, Russian Rubles, Swiss Francs, anything you want. Almost as good as the real thing. Interpol is keeping it quiet so far, but the Peruvian Government is so far holdin' them off. News of this gets out and if we be in the middle of things, then we get a lot of angry visitors we don't need Nestor and wee been doin' real good stayin' invisible"!

"I see what you mean. If we're paying with bad currency to the Russians and the Corsicans, only bad things can be happening. So what do you have in mind Jefe"?

"Through this DeCunha, I meet and have my arms around a brilliant chemist, a real genius. graduate from Rice University, with a Doctor Degree. He work in town but he got the same tastes as DeCunha, if ya know what I mean. We got him under wraps. So you do what ya gotta do with the submarine, but after you leave Valparaiso with the Crystalline, if the entire factory, she blow up and Dr. Lothar Kaminski he don't make it, then we control the manufacture of the Crystalline through the genius Chemist. I set him up somewhere in west Texas, he crank out the stuff as we need it. He, how you say it"?

"He reverse engineers the formula"?

"That's it. We control everything"?

"What if things go wrong"?

"All you gotta worry about is getting the stuff back to Texas. Davalantes has a place in mind where we can stash the shit. Then you gotta make sure that place in the Andes Mountains she disappear along with Kaminski"?

"What if the chemist turns out to be a bust or proves to be a problem at some point"?

"Then we take our time and find another chemist and introduce the old one to Jugos"?

"What'll Meyers and his people say when their plant explodes"? "That is why it must happen a few days after you take delivery Nestor. You be at sea and clearly it be an accident. Not the first time chemists have had explosions, is it"?

Magellan took another drink thinking, and then said, "Yes, I'll find a way to make it work Jefe. What about the Russian Submariners and the submarine"?

"Before you leave Davalantes will give you the coordinates of where the helicopters are to land as well as where the refueling points in Mexico and Arizona are to be for the helicopters. If the submarine meets with an explosion on its return trip and disappears in the pacific"?

"I see what you mean", said Magellan with a sly nod!

"Good Nestor. I leave everything up to you"!

The suites phone rang and Ortega picked it up listening then a minute later put it down saying, "Good news Nestor. That was Konrad and it looks like our Brigitte is resting comfortably back stage. There were some doctors in the house this evening and they were eager to attend our star performer. In appreciation Konrad extends, gratis services for the foreseeable future. Brigitte will recover to dance again and fill the club to overflowing. Konrad will be happy. The doctors will no doubt be happy and no doubt Brigitte will show her gratitude to each and every one of them at some point in the future. A good omen for what lay ahead don't you think? Upon our return perhaps Brigitte will visit our tents also"!

The following day after their meetings with Ortega's local partners, as they were driving back to the Weston Hotel, Ortega said, "I think the meeting went well Carlos, don't you think"? "Very impressed with your partners. I like their plans to shelter our money in the US, especially the way they can get use it to gain control of companies that we can use as collateral, bleed of tangible assets, then allow to go bankrupt and we get away clean, all without touching our own funds"!

"I been thinking about one of your concerns yesterday, Carlos"!

"Oh really"?

"Yes. Your concern about this Jaeger"?

"Having second thoughts? I thought that you were the one who brought him on board and that Nestor has placed his blessing on him"?

"Yes that's true, but your concern rang a bell in my head and a number of things he's said and did, none of which appear important at the time, when added all up, gave me a reason to consider your concern and I've made a decision, that I wanted you to know about"!

"And that is"?

"Jaeger will still head up the Embraer transfer, but he'll never make it back. He will stay in Brazil forever. Santos will be his Segundo and I've instructed him to see to it, after everything is completed and the plans are on their way back to Houston"!

"As you wish Ortega. This Jaeger means nothing to me"! "There is another thing Carlos that you must know"! "And that is"?

"The original agreed upon price for the transfer of the Embraer documents is not enough. We will need Ten Million"!

"Carlos, we had an agreement"!

"Things change Carlos. My partners up here need cash, not documents of ownership too complicated to turn into cash in which to accomplish their ends. They have no interest in ownership of a company far away. So what has been proposed is that you keep your interests in Argentina and we all wish you every success, but in exchange, we will need Cold, Hard Cash, in order to effectively complete the transaction when next you come to Houston"!

"Why didn't they express this when we met"?

"It is not their way. They elected me to give you the news"!

"Give me a moment Ortega"!

Several minutes later Meyers said, "I'll call them tonight and have an answer tomorrow"!

"Will this affect our future relationship Carlos"?

"No, it shouldn't. An unforeseen bump in the road. It's up to me to sell your partners point of view and neither of us has failed the other yet have we"?

"Not yet Carlos"!

"So let us consider it done shall we"?

"Done and done again", said Ortega spitting in his hand and offering it to Meyers who took it and sealed the bargain.

9

As Carlos Meyers sat in his hotel room, sipping his drink, he couldn't say this recent change of events was completely unexpected. In the years that he'd been affiliated with Ortega, all had gone without a hitch, but given the origins of the man and the way he came up in the world, why should he expect anything different. It was the nature of the world they all lived in and the path they'd all chosen. A deal never was done, until all of the money had changed hands and parties to the transaction were miles away from each other. Of course he could not go back to his partners in Buenos Aires and give them the news. He'd most likely not survive that. So he took another path. The printers in Peru were always in search of new business and it wasn't as if they hadn't done business before. So he placed a call to a private number in Lima and left a callback message with the code word used several times before. Within the hour he received the call back, placed his order and wire transferred the agreed half in advance when placing an order and the final half upon pickup.

It would simply mean a small detour to the counterfeit printers in Lima Peru, after the Embraer exchange, to examine and pick up the additional currency and add it to that he gleaned from the Argentines. No hey problema.

This could still work out to his advantage. After getting the corporate papers prior to his trip to Sao Paulo, he'd simply take them to a master forger he knew in Montevideo, have some names changed to a corporate structure he'd long had in place and now he'd own a bit of history. The peasants in Houston be damned. Given the quality of product he'd previous seen in Peru, with any luck, everything would pass scrutiny. If not, well he'd have the Embraer documents, Argentina would have an economic boost and should anyone try and end things for him, there was always the Argentine military to stand in the way. He'd spent a life time doing favors for important people in important places. He knew things. Many things. He'd money in offshore accounts and a host of different identities if needed, a secure place to steal away in the suburbs of Montevideo that no one knew about, then there was always this clinic in Costa Rica that could change his appearance. He had a multiplicity of fall back options should the need arise. He was still young enough to be able to enjoy all that life had to offer and the intellectual skills to repel those who wanted to best him. Things would work out. They always had in the past.

The world can be a very small place indeed more often than not. Magellan discovered this as he was met in Marseilles, by an old friend of his earliest days in the Legion. He was supposed to be introduced by Carlos Meyers to Gianni Scaramanga after their aircraft landed in Marseilles. Instead no introduction was needed, for long ago Gianni and Nestor went through the grueling sixteen weeks of Legionnaire basic training.

"Carlos. Had I known that you would be accompanied by Nestor, I could have saved you a trip", said Scaramanga, as he embraced Magellan.

"So the both of you know each other"?

"Once one has served in the Legion, one is a brother in arms for life", said Gianni beaming as they all walked into his villa up in the hills.

"Gianni was a week ahead of me in basic training, not far away in Arles, north of here", said Magellan. Scaramanga motioned for several of his men to take the visitors bags upstairs, then to leave them alone until the dinner hour. Whereupon they discussed the matters at hand. But first some fond memories had to be resurrected.

"The thing I remember most was that Alsatian Sergeant", said Scaramanga continuing. "What was his name? Anyway, the man was a brute of the first class. He adored one thing and that was striking the recruits, for sins both real and imagined. Now Carlos, you see that small scar just above Nestor's lower lip? Once upon a time it was a much larger scar and it was given to Nestor by the Alsatian, who hit him without provocation. I also felt his anger physically and vowed if there ever came an opportunity, I would kill that cretin. But Nestor saved me the trouble. The Alsatian Sergeant pulled out his blade, never knowing that Nestor was a master at close quarter knife fighting, compelling Nestor to reach for his blade. The Alsatian was much larger than the rest of us, and was well trained, but against Nestor, he was outmatched in the art of the blade. Of course Nestor killed the brute, right there on the parade ground in front of everyone. The only thing that saved him from a full courts martial and prison or possibly execution, is that everyone, including the entire senior staff, saw that the Alsatian had acted without provocation and that Magellan was acting defensively. The following day he was transferred to French Guyana for jungle survival school ahead of schedule, or that was what everyone was told"!

"What happened to the Alsatian Sergeant", asked Meyers?

"We all supposed that he was buried in an unmarked grave, wrapped in simple canvass. That was what the Legion normally does to those who disgrace the service. Not worth the expense of a simple wooden casket or grave stone. The French Foreign Legion is at the bottom of the food chain when it comes to expenditures by the government. All are considered cannon fodder"!

"Interesting Gianni. Now perhaps you can enlighten us to our latest acquisition"!

"Ah yes, the Russian Submarine. Nestor should know that it is your idea that made this all come together Carlos"!

"Carlos is famous for seeing what others cannot", said Magellan in agreement!

"The boat is an older model Romeo class, diesel electric, vessel. One of the last built of its type in 1961. Since its inception, it has been assigned to the Black Sea fleet and has never been anywhere else. This is to be the boats last voyage. As you know the old Soviet Union is no more and Russia has fallen on hard economic times which allows us to take advantage of the current affairs. The boat in question was to be scrapped after this final voyage. Its normal crew is 58 sailors, but for the purposes of this exercise, only a skeleton crew of 15 will be assigned. The food and fuel assigned for this mission is just enough to get around the perimeter of the Black Sea and back to port in Sevastopol. Thus the necessity for a resupply of both in the Mid Atlantic. The Romeo class boat has six torpedo tubes fore and two aft with a total compliment of 14 torpedoes. But given the current economics only the existing torpedo tubes will be armed with no spares available. This allows us sufficient space in which to transport the Crystalline, at the appropriate time"!

"This evening we will all dine together and tomorrow you will go back to Argentina, while Nestor and I will fly to Istanbul and then to

Sevastopol in the Crimea, where we will be met by our associates. By nightfall of the following day, both of us will join the Captain and crew. We will be wearing the uniforms of Russian naval officers, with the appropriate assignment orders in hand. Now the Captain will be fully aware of our presence and he has carefully selected the entire crew, for their competence and their silence. The Captain and crew will be fully rewarded with Argentine papers and significant money after the mission is completed. All are understanding that any breach of security will be rewarded by a death sentence. Everyone selected wants a better life away from their native land and none have family left behind that be exploited by the Russian Government. If all goes well, the Russian authorities will simply cover the missing boat up with a veil of silence. They are very good at that. The anticipated explanation should be the boat had an unfortunate accident resulting in the sinking of the craft with all aboard lost at sea. Given the quality of the Russian workmanship at that time, of its building, the age of the boat and the quality, or lack thereof of the ongoing maintenance, given the times, all are reasonable to assume. Besides, this is one of their older boats, destined for the scrap yard"!

"Yet I've been assured, this boat is capable of good service for some time to come, as long as it operates within its design capabilities and enjoys a reasonable maintenance schedule. Once the boat reaches its first mooring in Tierra del Fuego, it will undergo a refitting and refueling for a ten day duration before moving on to Puerto Valparaiso. It also will have an additional twenty, carefully selected seamen from the Argentine Navy on "Secret Assignment", to augment the existing Russian crew"!

"Now, the part where things get very tricky. The boat is of an earlier generation and by current standards, is like a car without a muffler, leaving a sound signature when underwater or at snorkeling depth that is relatively easy to detect. Yet our selected Captain of the craft, has become quite expert in eluding the Turkish Navy for years, in spite of his naval impediment. To counter this somewhat, Russian engineers, have taken to sealing the front flooding ports, to reduce the sound signature the boat makes as it moves through the sea. The tradeoff is that it will take twice as long to dive underwater if necessary"!

"Sounds reasonable", said Meyers as he took a sip of his Brandy. "Two chokepoints that have to be traversed", said Scaramanga continuing. "First the Bosporus and the trip down the Dardanelle's and finally the

British Naval Station at Gibraltar. Now our Captain has studied old Nazi reports of how they accomplished this and feels that it can be done. Once out in the Atlantic, a night rendezvous will accomplished with an Argentine freighter for refueling and resupply for the rest of the trip around the Straits of Magellan and to the mooring in Southern Chile. I will leave the boat after the mid-Atlantic resupply and Nestor will be in charge the rest of the way"!

"And you will handle the funding of the Admiral, the Captain and the crew, while on the boat", stated Meyers!

"Once we have cleared Gibraltar and are well out into the Atlantic, I'll send a coded message to my people, to release the Admirals family and the funds agreed upon to the appropriate banks. Once I have reached the supply ship I will send you a coded message of my arrival. Once Nestor reaches the Chilean mooring he will send you a coded message of his arrival. When he departs, you will receive yet another message of his departure. When he then departs Puerto Valparaiso, he is to send a message to your American contact. Other than that electronic transmission silence will be maintained. Two months later Nestor will make another trip to Valparaiso, pick up a shipment of Crystalline, then traverse the southern tip of South America, to a night rendezvous in the Southern Atlantic, where we will be there to receive our first shipment of the product at the agreed upon price"! "That is our agreement Gianni and let us toast a long and mutually rewarding enterprise", said Meyers lifting his glass as the others did the same.

"By the way, how is your father Malatesta", asked Meyers?

"Greedy and intractable as ever. Soon he will be the whore master of all of France and soon enough the rest of Europe. He bests the Italians and the Sicilians almost at every turn in La Droga. We lose a few men, they lose more. Yet we all make money. Whenever I talk to him and ask him how he is, "Every day above ground is a good day", he always replies, yet he is in great anticipation of our enterprise, seeing virtue in the profits"!

The following day they all went their separate ways. Scaramanga and Magellan to Istanbul and beyond and Carlos Meyers back to Buenos Aires.

Two days later, Nestor and Gianni having been outfitted with Russian Naval officer uniforms, traversed the checkpoint with ease, orders in hand,

Nestor doing all the talking in perfect Russian and Gianni following in silence, having orders in hand showing him recently released from the base hospital after throat surgery, sporting the appropriate bandages, boarded the Romeo class Russian boat without a problem and met the boats commander, Oleg Rasmonovitch.

"Shall we conduct our business in English", asked Rasmonovitch?

"That would seem appropriate Commander", said Nestor, "Since it is a language we apparently have in common"!

"Your orders state that you are both Political Officers attached for the purpose of the trip. Now under the old regime, every vessel has a Political Officer attached to watch over us. Political Officers, usually no nothing of seamanship and the workings of a boat. Like teats on a boar hog. So I suggest both of you keep a low profile for at least the first few days, until the crew grows accustomed to your presence. As you know we are vastly undermanned and a simple way to get the crews confidence is to say little, be extremely careful, touch nothing, give way to others at all times and be ready to offer another set of hands whenever asked in silence. Tread lightly and whisper at all times, especially when we traverse the two chokepoints and are running as silently as possible. Once we are at least a day out in the Atlantic we can surface during the night and run on the surface. Once we go under, it will be either running on the electric under sea during the day, or to snorkel depth for extended periods running on diesel power to charge the batteries for night running. From time to time you can occupy the conning tower and be of help watching, the surface radar. You are to stay close to me and watch what I do and say at all times. Are we in understanding with each other"?

Both Nestor and Gianni nodded their heads in agreement, as the Commander added, "In one hour we will leave port at high tide and join the battle group for our proscribed exercises. Within two days we will slip away from the flotilla and then the fun will begin. Should all go well it will take a day to traverse the Bosporus and Istanbul, under the very noses of the Turks at night. This will be a nervous time for all on board. It should take the better part of a week to cross the Mediterranean. We have the schedules of several freighters in mind so we can follow in their wake. The final hurdle will be Gibraltar. Everything must go to perfection to elude detection by the British. All of us will be on station most all of the time. Be ready, stay alert and keep a level head and all of us will get through this"!

Even though Russia was now viewed as mostly a benign threat in the area, far less lethal than its old former Soviet self, the neighboring Turkish Government still kept a wary eye upon their ancient enemy. Having received in advance notice of the Russian Naval exercises in the Black Sea, they were none the less wary as the remnants of the once formidable Black Sea Fleet approached their shores. The few submarines available were responsible for acting as picket ships for the flotilla's perimeter and their sailing orders placed Commander Rasmonovitch's boat in a trailing position protecting the aft portion of the flotilla. Operating at snorkel depth with only the top of the conning tower exposed, at a speed of ten knots, the sub quietly slid under the surface just after sundown as the Russian Squadron made the wide turn eastward, a hundred miles from the Turkish coast. Magellan had just come down from the conning tower to join the Commander and Scaramanga, as the Captain gave the order to head for the Bosporus and Istanbul. Turning to both of them he said, "We've just reported in with the fleet with our position and situation report. It is now 2000 hours. Our next check in time will be midnight. Your visual report of the Bulgarian freighter on our Starboard, checks with our information of the freighter destined for Alexandria Egypt. We will join the freighter and move forward in its wake, through the Bosporus and all the way down through the Dardanelle's, throughout the long night. We've current charts of these waters and will follow the freighter into the Aegean Sea. If all goes well we will pass through these waters and separate into the busy waters of the Aegean shortly after dawn. The passage will a slow one since the freighter will only be traveling at eight knots"!

At midnight the sub rose to snorkel depth just prior to entering the Bosporus and was greeted by a rainstorm, sending its final coded message to the fleet. The clouds overhead shielded the view of the brief surfacing from anyone as the sub again slipped under the surface, trailing the freighter by a scant hundred yards. Its batteries charged and moving slowly through the waters in the dark at night it moved undetected, by even the most alert of watchers, by its electric motors.

"We're in luck", said Commander Rasmonovitch. The same weather conditions that greeted us passing Istanbul will be with us at dawn when we separate from the Bulgarian. We'll wait until the freighter is on the far horizon and subject to visibility conditions on the surface, which should not be good, we'll surface to snorkel depth and make our way into the Aegean in good time. The Greek and Turkish fisherman should be sitting ashore"!

It wasn't until noon the following day when someone in the Russian squadron noticed that one of their picket submarines had not checked in for the last twelve hours. By that time the errant Romeo class boat was far into the Aegean running at snorkel depth at a speed of twelve knots, putting distance between them and any possibility of pursuit. The storm persisted for the entirety of the next day and into the evening before the Russian boat cleared Greek waters and out into the Mediterranean and clear sailing. For the next three days and nights, the Russian boat ran both submerged and at snorkel depth, trailing in the wake a combination of freighters and pleasure boats, for periods of time. A hundred miles out from the British Naval Base at Gibraltar, the Commander gave the orders for the engines to go full stop, as the boat awaited night fall and yet another weather front to descend upon the area.

Sitting in the small eating quarters, Commander Rasmonovitch said to Magellan and Scaramanga, "This is the tricky part of the entire affair. We must wait for several things, an Egyptian freighter outbound from Tunisia and they're rarely punctual, nightfall, for this is a new moon with less reflective light and the weather front to arrive all at the same time.

We were blessed by the less than attentive efforts of the Turkish government as we passed through the Bosporus. We can expect a higher level of scrutiny from the British. We will carefully monitor all of the radio traffic as it occurs. The Egyptian freighter will announce their approach to the British. The British will confirm. Once we hear the confirmation we will surface to snorkel depth. Once we catch sight of the Egyptian vessel we will submerge and follow the freighter through the straits and out into the open Atlantic. The entire boat is in shut down gentlemen so I suggest we all get some sleep"!

By night fall, the Russian boat rose to snorkel depth fifty miles from Gibraltar to gauge current weather conditions, then quietly submerged once again to a depth of fifty feet. Weather conditions were starting to worsen and the Egyptian freighter, if running on time should appear on the horizon within a half an hour. Everything was in place for a successful traverse of Gibraltar, with the exception of the human element. The freighter. With each passing hour the radio traffic was monitored awaiting the arrival of the freighter. Everything depended upon the freighter. The Admirals family held hostage in their Dasha, the money to be transferred to private accounts and the freedom of every man jack aboard the boat and a new life.

Suddenly at 0100 in the morning the radio operator summoned the Commander Rasmonovitch, as they both listened in to the radio traffic up top. It was the Egyptian boat announcing its approach to Gibraltar and the British announcement of approaching traffic and the approved travel coordinates for passage. The additional news of current bleak weather conditions in the straits and a warning to the Egyptian freighter to have hands on the forward decks along with full radar, came as further good news to Rasmonovitch as he knew that everyone would have their attention to what was ahead of them, paying no attention to what was trailing in its wake.

By 0200 hours, the Russian boat quietly rose to snorkel depth, after the freighter passed on its port side and followed in its wake closing to a distance of seventy yards astern. The weather on the surface was delightfully horrible with visibility close to zero. As the British had state of art sonar detection electronics, only scant visibility from the con and chart recognition of the sub sea surface directed the slow path of the sub as it moved slowly through the straits of Gibraltar under the very noses of the British.

By 0600 hours, both boats emerged into the open Atlantic, the Egyptian craft heading northwards towards Rotterdam and the submerged Russian boat slowly heading in a southwesterly direction towards its rendezvous in the South Atlantic. By nightfall, several hundred miles off the Coast of Morocco the Russian boat finally surfaced with everyone coming on deck to breath the fresh salty air, under the sparse reflective moonlight.

"We are miles away from the normal trade routes, so we can travel on the surface all night long to recharge our batteries. My only concern now is fuel. To conserve fuel we can only travel a maximum of ten knots on the surface to the rendezvous position, two days sail away", said Rasmonovitch! "This will leave us with but three more days' worth of diesel fuel in the tanks"!

"That's cutting things a bit slim isn't it", said Scaramanga?

"It all depends upon the refueling ship you've contracted with. If it arrives on time then no problem. If it in any way is impeded then we will have a significant problem. So the question is, how reliable are your connections with the refueling ship", he asked looking at Scaramanga?

"The freighter in question is of Liberian registry, owned by a company my father has controlling interests in. My father has made all of the arrangements and has assured me that those involved have a long record of reliability. If not, they wouldn't be with the living, plus my presence on board should be sufficient to allay all concerns Commander"!

"Then I will not be concerned, until or unless it is time for concern. Let us breath the night air and rejoice and allow me to apologize for my previous expression"!

"Nothing to worry about Commander. I might add that I commend you on your skill and seamanship and attention to detail Commander. Thus far, this has proved to be an extraordinary adventure worthy of a novel. Your skill combined with some good fortune has gotten us through some interesting moments, that someday in the distant future, I'll pass on to my grandchildren"! "But Gianni, you're not married", smirked Nestor!

"True enough, but I must have some children somewhere and eventually I'll have to settle down with some woman or another and grow old and fat. She'll probably be Italian and we will argue and shout at each other"!

"And you Magellan", asked Rasmonovitch. "Have you a woman in some far away port, that pines for your return"?

"I'm afraid not Commander. Far too busy making my way through the world, involved in a series of never ending adventures. Perhaps, some day if I live long enough"!

"That's our Nestor", mused Scaramanga. The eternal mercenary. Loved by no one, in love with no one. He cares for no one and is cared for by no one"!

"And you Mon Capitan", asked Magellan! "What's on the horizon for you"?

Oleg Rasmonovitch looked westward out onto the unseen horizon and said haltingly, "I as well as the entire crew have nothing behind us. There is only the future and what we can make of it. When this initial task is concluded, all of us will have to become quickly conversant in

Spanish if we are to settle and become productive citizens of Argentina. We will have a stipend of money offshore in our accounts, but as agreed, we are to continue to provide service to your organization from time to time. That is what we all agreed to and we are honor bound to continue. So while the future ahead is cloudy, we all have our collective skills to rely on. Perhaps, I'll meet some beautiful Argentine and she will teach me how to Tango"!

"Commander, with the skill and courage you've displayed these past days, I've no doubt, you will live a long and productive life and we Corsicans welcome you and your crew into our family as brothers", said Scaramanga as he embraced the Commander. As they joined the others on the main deck below, Magellan stayed behind in the conning tower, lost in thought.

Here he was, after concluding a perilous adventure. Of itself, just one of a host of involvements he'd chosen in his life. He'd schemed and taken lives of others without a single thought. As far as he knew, those lives he'd ended, were not worthy of existence in the world we live in. This was the way he had chosen, his eyes wide open to any and every consequence. Yet in some respects he felt that Ortega was correct in his assumption that Carlos Meyers was in things only for himself and that should the occasion arise, Magellan would end up as Mexican Stew. A victim of circumstance. On the other hand, Ortega was a brute, untrustworthy to the core. Caught in between two commanding entities, each driven by relentless greed and each capable of the guile worthy of Machiavellian salutation, it would be only a matter of time until that day when Magellan's number came up.

What concerned him the most was that he grown fond of Oleg Rasmonovitch and his selected crew, seemingly honorable men to a man. These men were worthy of longevity and some measure of prosperity. They mattered not a bit to Ortega, who wanted Magellan to make certain the boat would sink, only after the initial ten ton delivery of Crystalline was secured. With the familiarity he'd established with the boat and the crew, this was easily possible. He knew where all the nooks and cranny's were on board. Plant a timer and some Plastique on board and out in the Pacific a day away, an explosion and one more boat to join the depths of Davy Jones locker. 'Was there no honor in this world', he thought? This would weigh upon him from time to time. If he didn't do this thing, then Ortega would have him killed. If he did as Ortega had bidden, his very soul would remain lost forever.

Two days later, the rendezvous had gone off without a problem as, Scaramanga sent a coded message back to his people to release the Admirals family and the funds to all parties as agreed. A second coded radiogram was sent to Meyers in Buenos Aires, confirming that "Uncle Sasha was well and enjoying his vacation".

Scaramanga then departed from the company of seaman saying to Magellan, "We should meet again after this business is finished so we can enjoy Paris and sip from the cup of life"!

"Until then Gianni", said Magellan as they embraced and Magellan rejoined the refueled and refurbished boat.

While under way, as they submerged to snorkel depth, Oleg Rasmonovitch said, "Once we arrive at Tierra del Fuego for refitting, the first thing we do is remove all the markings and repaint the boat. The boat now was running at near flank speed just a hundred nautical miles outside of the internationally recognized shipping lanes, still observing its normal operating discipline as it traversed the Brazilian then the Argentine coast, constantly monitoring the Marine radio channels. They decided to round Cape Horn and the southern tip of the continent submerged, thus avoiding the severe ocean at sea level. Taking several days longer than normal the boat gradually came to the surface in stages as it emerged into the expanse of the Southern Pacific. Now tracking with both normal radar and sonar soundings, the craft made its way to its new home, nestled deep in one of the Southern Chilean fjords, a long abandoned and forgotten oil exploration mooring, replete with still workable docking and working facilities as well as living quarters. Upon arrival Meyers was contacted. After several days of rest, the crew met their Argentine counterparts, who were flown in secretly to augment the crew for the trip north. On loan from the Argentine Navy, all of them had shipboard experience and several of the new arrivals had even experience on the two ancient French diesel submarines fielded by the Argentine Navy. All those on board were adept with firearms and were equipped should the need arise. The ship was refitted with additional fuel tanks so it could complete the round trip to the Gulf of California and back without refueling. Its boats stores completely replenished, Meyers was again contacted by radiophone and they departed for a location fifty miles south of Puerto Valparaiso where they briefly surfaced at night, fifteen miles offshore of the Chilean coastline, just long enough for Magellan to be hoisted aboard and flown by helicopter to the laboratory of Doctor Lothar Kaminski, high in the Andes Mountains at nine thousand feet in elevation. Alerted of his arrival Dr. Kaminski personally went to meet the arriving aircraft and greeted Magellan.

"We are quite alone up here", said Kaminski in his thick eastern European accent! "The nearest roads are at the four thousand feet level far below. Please come with me so we can together contact Carlos Meyers to alert him of your arrival. You will be our guest for the evening. Meyers will make the necessary arrangements for the helicopters to transport the Crystalline to your boat tomorrow after sundown"!

"That sounds fine to me Doctor Kaminski", said Magellan. "Shall one of my men carry your back pack Mister Magellan"?

"No Doctor, it's not heavy at all just some personal belongings. Please lead the way"!

As they walked towards the main plant an eager Kaminski said, "After we make contact with Senor Meyers I'll show you to your quarters then we can dine together. Tomorrow, I'll show you the entire facility. I'm rather proud of it. Here we are, high up in the mountains, away from prying eyes, a model of ingenuity if I may say. Compact and efficient, completely self- sustaining energy wise with solar collectors and wind power and all of the water needed to produce our product. Only mountain goats and helicopters can gain access"!

After they contacted Meyers and coordinated the following evening's activities and Meyers briefly chatted with Magellan did they take a late dinner together making small talk. The following morning Kaminski, true to his word, gave Magellan the grand tour of the facilities. Half way through the tour Magellan asked "I noticed Doctor that I haven't seen one security camera on the premises. Can you tell me why"?

"It's simply not needed. Our remoteness is our security. The staff we have are all blood relatives and compensated very well. Only a well chosen few know of our existence and they are compensated handsomely for their silence. We are family here and since Senor Meyers is one of the principles responsible for our existence and he is well connected politically to the Argentines as well as a chosen few here in Chile, we have no reason to fear intruders. Hardly anyone knows of our existence. We are self-sustaining"!

As they made the rounds Magellan could see the genius of the man's engineering, surrounded by snow the year round, the array of solar collectors and wind driven generators guaranteed self-sufficient power and water. Almost all of his equipment was computer driven and virtually automatic, with only periodic maintenance and final packaging equipment necessary for the human touch.

"I will tell you this Senor Magellan" said Kaminski. "The secret formula is safely locked into my Cabeza", pointing to his head. "Yet the original catalyst is self-replicating and only requiring simple water for reproduction, with the final product arriving in a highly concentrated Gel form and thus more easily transportable"!

Duly impressed by Doctor Kaminski's achievement, Magellan made certain that his jaw remained agape as they walked as a visible guarantee of his impression. "I must say Doctor Kaminski, this entire complex is a marvel of engineering. As we walk around, it's almost as if the entire facility had a mind of its own. One can almost feel the pulse of this creature"!

"Mister Magellan, I'm quite surprised that a man of your endeavor's, was able to foster such insight into my efforts. Other than Senor Meyers, you've been the only one to have a feeling for my work. Sometime in the near future you must visit again. Once cash is flowing from our products in abundance, I've plans to make small upgrades to the facility in the form of Robotry to make it completely automatic"!

"There's much to be done in the meantime Doctor, but I'd be flattered to return should circumstances permit"!

As they stood together surveying the plant Doctor Kaminski mused, "In over forty years of scientific research, the Nobel Prize committee has ignored my accomplishments, on three different occasions, awarding their precious prize to lesser men. Here and now, in the twilight of my life is my greatest accomplishment. If I can't have recognition, then retribution upon mankind will have to suffice"! Magellan put his arm around Kaminski saying, "There are those who matter, who appreciate your accomplishments Doctor. Let us pray for a long and productive life, so you enjoy the fruits of your labors"!

"I appreciate your comments more than you know Senor Magellan.

Now let us take an early lunch and then I must have a nap this afternoon, so I can be alert this evening when the inaugural delivery occurs"!

After lunch both men retired to their quarters, as Magellan reviewed the layout of the facility in his mind. He just couldn't imagine that a facility as important would have not one single security detector. No sensors, no cameras, nothing. In his backpack were three pounds of Plastique and four detonators, along with a like number of miniature electronic timers. In an hour when he was certain the doctor was napping, he'd make the rounds again and set the timers to make contact by dawn the following day. Sufficient time, to offload the product on the series of helicopters and be far away. He'd be with the very last helicopter, returning to the boat, to insure things went well. Of course, the quarters of Dr. Kaminski would have to be exploded, but with luck the good Doctor would be asleep and greet his maker without a bother.

By 0100 hours early the following morning, Magellan bid goodbye to the Doctor and his small staff and boarded the last helicopter along with the last plastic barrels of the product. The chopper lifted off heavily from the small helipad and made its way down the mountain side. After a thirty minute trip, hugging the mountainside they came out on the lowlands, skimming the earth towards the boat fifteen miles out in the Pacific. As Magellan looked out the starboard side of the chopper, he could barely make out the lights of Puerto Valparaiso far to the north. He briefly glanced at his watch, noting the time, the briefly thought of Dr. Kaminski. In their brief time together, he'd grown to like the man. His craggy face, no doubt well earned by countless hours of scientific research in pursuit of his accomplishments, diminished by the lack of recognition of those who apparently mattered. It came as no surprise to Nestor, that it most likely was the single factor that drove him into the arms of someone like Carlos Meyers. In several hours Dr. Kaminski would be no more along with all he'd striven for.

Magellan wondered how he'd end up for the first time in a long time. Carrying out Ortega's orders, to garner the Crystalline and monopolize distribution. He could only imagine what story Ortega would have for Meyers when they next met. Yet still another conundrum confronted him. The fate of the Romeo class submarine, along with its entire crew. In their adventures, he'd earned the confidence of Commander Rasmonovitch and his crew and in turn grew to like and respect them.

He could easily sabotage the boat upon its departure in the contact zone after the last shipment, heading towards South Texas. Ortega would be pleased, but could Nestor Magellan have it in him to betray two fine people in such a short period of time.

As the pilot approached the boat riding calmly in the Pacific waters, he briefly radioed the coded message of his approach without the normal running lights. The boat acknowledged and briefly flashed a light some three miles to the port side of the chopper. The chopper pilot slowly approached the boat, now barely visible on the ocean. Loading the helicopter on land was relatively easy. It was the unloading of the heavy product, each plastic barrel weighing approximately three hundred pounds that proved a dangerous task as the chopped had land on the boat yet keep the engines revs up to lessen the weight on the boat. To complicate things further, while the chopper was being unloaded, the chopper had to be refueled simultaneously. A clear safety violation in every part of the world. Yet apparently three other choppers had done the very thing several times during the nights work and all apparently had gone off without a problem. A fitting testament to the skill of the Chilean pilots and the now international crew of the Russian boat. The last of the Crystalline offloaded and making its way into the innards of the sub. Magellan waved the chopper away into the night, as it skimmed the ocean at a height of ten feet heading in a southerly direction.

The crew worked fast securing the last of their load, as all of the hatches were secured and the boat slowly submerged, its electric motors slowly driving it northward. As Magellan slept in his bunk, he suddenly awoke, glanced at his watch which read, 0615 hundred hours in the morning. A half an hour ago, the explosives went off. He felt a sadness that was inexplicable somehow. Later on in the morning as the sub made its way northward across the Pacific, a seismologist in Santiago, examined his geological seismographic charts, noting an ever so small blip registering up in the Andes. He figured that it was a landslide of sorts and didn't give it another thought.

Now in the Pacific, the very same operational orders were in play. Travel submerged during the day on the electrics. Travel northward well outside of the normal shipping lanes. Intermittent use of radar for a brief glance of any surface traffic. Surface travel only during inclement weather at night and only for short periods not exceeding an hour in duration to allow the crew on deck access, then back to snorkel depth. On two occasions, they fell in behind several pods of Whales and Orcas traveling north as the submarine detected their sonar signature. They were in no particular rush to arrive at the rendezvous point in the Gulf of California, separating Baja California from the Mexican mainland. Magellan and the boat commander knew that Ortega would be monitoring the short wave radio traffic at certain hours and upon receipt of a brief seemingly innocuous message, would then put into play, the logistics of the transfer.

As the sub entered the Gulf of California, moving silently at snorkel depth at night it found itself surrounded by another pod of Orcas circling the mostly submerged boat with great curiosity, no doubt wondering what manner of creature this was. The sonar operator delighted in receiving the array of sonic messages from the Orcas, yet was constrained from response. Arriving at their designated rendezvous coordinates the Commander and Magellan sent their message of arrival to Ortega. Within a half hour Ortega had returned his acknowledged response. Now all they could do was wait.

Magellan knew that Davalantes and some of his people would be heading towards Val Verde county and the old farm house nestled deep in an arroyo, awaiting the shipment. As that was developing he knew that Ortega would contact an associate in El Centro California, to alert him to send four older Huey helicopters normally used to ferry supplies to off shore oil platforms. The operator as well as the pilots were being well paid for their efforts. In addition, an errant fuel tanker truck was alerted to position itself at a location on a high mesa atop the Sierra del Diablo. There, the helicopters bound for Val Verde County would briefly land to refuel before making their way northward. The original flight southward by the choppers was accomplished by virtue of additional fuel tanks for long distance flight. But after their pickup of the Crystalline from the boat, the extra weight of their cargo, would rule out any possibility of extra fuel. Thus the necessity of refueling stops on the submarine, the Sierra del Diablo, the location in Val Verde County and one final stop south of Lordsburg New Mexico, prior to their return to El Centro.

Both Magellan and Commander Rasmonovitch had an additional unforeseen concern, because of the arrival of a group of Great White Sharks in these waters. Clearly they were after a pod of whales lounging and feeding nearby. Looking for an easy meal in several of the younger members in the pod.

The sub was located in the middle of the Gulf's waters, east of Punta Pulpito, when the first shark struck the pod late in the afternoon. It was riding at snorkel depth as the sharks struck the pod. Looking out from inside of the conning tower, the Commander witnessed the suddenness of the carnage that surrounded his boat. Fortunately there were no other vessels on the horizon. The very last thing that was needed after all they'd gone through was ocean scientists and other onlookers viewing the attack of the Great Whites.

Forgotten was a pod of Orca, Killer Whales, tending to their own feeding some few miles distant, apparently alerted by the underwater pleas from the cousins. The sonar operator was listening in to the entire thing, when suddenly he announced the arrival of others which proved to be the pod of Orcas coming to the rescue. The water was fairly clear from the view ports of the conning tower as Magellan and Rasmonovitch witnessed a male Orca ram a Great White, not twenty yards from the starboard side of the boat, stunning the shark then grabbing the stunned shark by its teeth and turning it on its back and holding it on its back for some minutes, then releasing it briefly as it floated helplessly in the waters as the other Great Whites circled around the boat as if not knowing what to do. Then suddenly the Alpha Orca swiftly rammed its helpless prey as it floated listlessly in the water, biting it almost in half as the water immediately turned red. Then several other Orcas took their turn in as the other Great Whites, suddenly disappeared from view.

The sonar operator then patched the subsea microphones into the ships public address system so everyone could hear the underwater victory soundings of the Orcas. Several minutes later the Commander admonished the sonar operator for breaking operational discipline and the sonar was turned off as well as the ships PA system.

"You might as well know Commander, the Great Whites are all fleeing back south as fast as they can", said the sonar operator. "A great victory has been achieved. A victory of mammals over fish. One predator over another"!

"I suggest you control your passions comrade, or else you may never live to enjoy what you have helped to achieve. We need your skills to complete our journey. But should another breach of discipline occur,

I will personally cut your throat and feed your putrid remains to the sharks. Do we understand each other comrade"?

"Yes Commander", said the sailor meekly!

Rasmonovitch returned to the Conning tower as he said to Magellan, "Sorry, but I had to discipline one of our overzealous men"!

"You have to admit Commander, we just observed something that probably no one has ever seen" offered Nestor.

"I'd say Nestor; this just might settle any argument as who the greatest predator in the sea is"!

"I agree Commander. Now all we can do is watch, wait and listen"!

The entire evening passed without incident as the sub descended to a depth of seventy feet for a period of two hours, then ascended back to snorkel depth, to observe any surface activity, then back to resume the cycle. Everything was dependant upon the arrival or the old post Korean War vintage Sikorsky guppy choppers. Old and relatively slow they were, but well maintained and reliable. Just the thing for hauling heavy loads. As dawn broke upon the waters of the Gulf of California, the sub broke the surface at snorkel depth and looked for any pleasure boat traffic that may have been drawn to the location as a result of the previous afternoon's activity amongst the Great Whites and the Orcas. As time went on Magellan and the boats commander were relieved the confrontation drew no notice above those on the boat. Nature's way of self-correction of an aggrieved imbalance.

As dusk again descended upon the waters, the boat again resurfaced to snorkel depth and sent out a brief radio direction beacon on an obscure VHF channel, for a fifteen second duration. Then descended back down to its stand by depth and waited, repeating this cycle now on an alternately hourly and semi hourly basis. At midnight it surfaced once again and sent the radio beacon, this time it received a response and the signal that the initial Sikorsky chopper was but minutes away.

The Commander then went up top of the conning tower and flashed northward his hand held, thousand candlepower spotlight and flashed it twice in recognition of its position. In the far off distance a single flash of the Sikorsky's front lights, signaled its arrival. Rasmonovitch plugged in his hand held mike and ordered the boat to surface and for all hands to be ready to commence reloading and refueling.

The boat was riding now upon the surface of the Gulf waters quite near to the absolute middle of the water way, neither of the land masses being visible, quite similar to the earlier down loading in the Pacific weeks ago. The forward hatch's ramp was employed, normally for the use of loading of torpedoes and other supplies swiftly, was busy with activity in uploading the plastic barrels of Crystalline concentrate. The Sikorsky was precariously perched on the forward deck, its engines still engaged to strike a balance on the deck, as the refueling and the loading of the product occurred. Its normal tanks now full, it waited for the final barrels to be loaded without a word.

Then as the final barrel was loaded Magellan tapped the shoulder of the pilot twice and exited the craft slamming the door shut and the Sikorky's engines revved up and the craft lifted off of the deck, turning to the north east skimming the waters, without lights eventually disappearing into the night.

Everything was buttoned up and the sub again descended back to snorkel depth to await the arrival of the second chopper, presumably an hour away. Every hour the sub repeated the cycle and every hour a Sikorsky appeared from the north to resume the loading and departure.

As the third chopper lifted off and disappeared into the night, Magellan joined the Commander on the internal portion of the conning tower as the sub went back to snorkel depth for the final time. As he joined the Commander he was offered a fresh cup of coffee laced with Vodka.

Wincing as he took the first sip Magellan said, "That's quite a cup you brew Oleg"!

"A man's brew for a man's work, my friend. Shortly we will be losing you Nestor and I must say that having you along on this adventure has been an interesting experience. I hope to renew our acquaintance sometime in the future"!

"My sentiments are the same Oleg! From what I've observed, I can't imagine a better submariner anywhere in the entire world, driven by a man of skill and honor. I trust that all will go well for you and your crew, in the days to come"!

"Soon the final craft will land upon the boat and now that we have said our good byes, I trust your bag is packed and at the ready"!

"It's been packed since nightfall and is standing by the forward loading hatch", said Magellan. Neither man given to extended conversation parted their ways, the Commander standing at the Con and Magellan rejoining the others near the forward loading hatch, bag packed and ready to depart with the final Sikorsky.

By 0300 hours the final Sikorsky lifted off of the deck and followed the others towards the western Mexican coast just over wave top level. As Magellan cast a final glance at the Russian sub now descending into the deep, he'd no doubt the Commander would bring everyone back to Tierra del Fuego safely and wished them well. He was happy that he'd listened to his better angels and not left any Plastique on the boat to explode. Eventually Ortega would find out and be angry but that could simply be explained away by saying the Commander or one of his crew probably discovered the package. It wasn't important anyway. He'd accompanied the boat away from the Russians, eliminated the source of the Crystalline, and guided the precious cargo to its resting place. That should be more than sufficient. In the event it wasn't, he'd watch Ortega's eyes, for they always signaled his irreversible anger. Should it come to it, he'd make it a point to kill Ortega on the spot regardless of the circumstances. Although it had never been discussed, there were a few that would sleep more comfortably in the group, starting with Davalantes. Yet one could never be certain.

At just after eight in the morning Magellan's chopper, landed on the high mesa in the Sierra del Diablo Mountains. Magellan talked to the driver of the tanker and verified the arrival and departure of the other helicopters. When the chopper's refueling was completed, Magellan paid the tanker driver the ten thousand dollars in American currency as agreed and lifted off of the mesa for the final leg of the journey. Davalantes in Val Verde was responsible for the complete refueling of the helicopters and the payment of thirty thousand dollars each, for the chopper pilots services, as each helicopter lifted off and headed westward back to their point of origin.

On the old property was a barn, replete with a large underground storage bunker, laboriously dug out by hand a few years ago for just such an occasion, the storage of either hostages or product. The product went into the bunker as Scylla was removed still in chains, partially drugged and a far cry from her former self having been held hostage for the last several months. She was fed daily and relieved herself into a bucket and was hosed off completely every day, to keep her in some semblance of good condition. As the bunkers heavy metal doors were shut and locked, the men shoveled dirt and loose hay over the area, then those who could, urinated over the area and placed several bales of hay over the bunker door. With silent Scylla well secured atop the hay bales. Magellan and Davalantes went inside the old house to call Ortega on the cell phone to tell him of Magellan's arrival with the Crystalline. It was late in the morning when Ortega answered the call from Davalantes. He quickly turned the phone over to Magellan who assured Ortega of the safe delivery of the product. All ten tons of it. He then was instructed to contact the prospective customers and inform them of the date time and location of the delivery of their product and the amount each barrel would cost in cash. Then Ortega began to get excited and related that there was a little problem with the Embraer transfer regarding Jaeger. When Magellan tried to press Ortega for details he was rebuffed by Ortega who shouted that Davalantes and his crew were to depart for Houston immediately and that Magellan was to stay put until further notice.

"Padron, your orders are understood. But please leave me a few people here to be able to guard your hostage effectively", pleaded Magellan! As he hung up the phone he looked at Davalantes saying, "Apparently something has gone wrong with the Embraer situation and Ortega wants you back in Houston right away. You are to leave me with two of your men to help guard our guest"!

"But who's gonna contact the buyers"?

"I am to make all arrangements. Just get done whatever needs doing quickly and get back here soonest, for your crew will provide security just in case"!

After Davalantes had left with the remnants of his crew, Magellan sat down on the front porch and reflected upon the last action of Jaeger that caught the eye of Ortega.

10

After returning Magellan's page, a call to action, Jaeger showered, shaved and prepared for his trip to town. Donning a specially tailored Kevlar vest, underneath a loose fitting, collarless Kevlar shirt and tailored Kevlar slacks, an exact replica of the Louis Raphael slacks he grown accustomed to. He then reached for the dual shoulder rig that housed two Ruger .357 Magnum Police Six revolvers, with a three inch barrel. Finally he attached four six round speed loaders, containing alternately preloaded Glaser Safety slugs, for guaranteed one shot stopping power at close range and Teflon shrouded Talon, penetration rounds, which rendered most Kevlar body protection ineffective. Finally he attached to his right ankle his back up piece, a Biretta .25 automatic, which contained seven rounds of specially prepared shells. Hollow points, of expanded capacity containing a mini encapsulated Sodium Cyanide gel, covered with a high density waxen plug. If all went south, at least any round that found a home warranted eventual death within minutes. A double breasted Kevlar sport coat rounded out his sporting attire.

Giving himself a quick once over prior to leaving, Jaeger went into his attached garage and made the rounds of his vehicle prior to getting into the old Ford Bronco. Old habits die hard, especially when one's life depended on security. The luxury of serendipity was not an effective alternative in his line of work, if longevity was ones goal in life. More often than not, even the most assiduous care of one's surroundings was insufficient given the circumstances.

As he made his way through the subdivision he scanned his surroundings, carefully shifting up through the gears as he made his way towards the inner city. It was late in the morning and he surmised that a drug deal was about to go down, somewhere on the outskirts of town. Rumors were that a new source of revenue was about to surface, in the form of the Rasta's that were gaining ground in the southwest. He'd just have to wait until the event and see just what was what. This day he was simply a Shepard, concerned with providing security.

As he blended into the aftermath of the Northwest Freeway rush hour traffic, he turned on his tape deck, listening to 'Miles Davis's' rendition of 'Killer Joe'. Somehow the clear crisp tones of the man's trumpet set the stage for what was ahead. Ten minutes later he blended into the Loop 610 traffic heading south, skirting by the vast Galleria business, entertainment and upscale shopping district. Houston's new uptown. Still heading south on the Loop he made the big turn towards the Astrodome complex, taking the Kirby Drive exit and looping under the freeway, finally spotting the Sheraton Astrodome Hotel. As he drove through the parking lot, he spotted the trio of cars in the lot, attended to by Ortega, Magellan, Davalantes and Nacho Quintanilla.

He parked his old Bronco in the space next to Davalantes car, nodding his head to all in recognition and joined the group. "Hola Hombre", said Davalantes as Jaeger approached. As he approached Ortega said, "Eh Vato, you ready to rumble"?

"When am I not", answered Jaeger as he opened his sport coat revealing his twin sisters nestled in their respective shoulder rigs.

"Still with the pistols and not the automatics? You stay low tech, eh hombre", commented Ortega at the sight of Jaegers hardware!

"You pay me for being able to deliver what you want don't you? Pistols never jam at the wrong moment and automatics have been known to jam at the worst possible moment. So what's up Jefe"?

"You gonna ride with Davalantes. Me an Magellan gonna ride together. Quintanilla gonna transport a trunk full of 'Jejo'. We gonna go way out on South Main and meet with some new people to us. The Negrito's that call themselves the 'Crips'. They from LA and they in a spat wit their supplier in Tijuana, OK? Me an Nestor we lead the way, Quintanilla drive the middle car wid the 'Jejo' and you and Davalantes follow. You, Davalantes an Quintanilla will stay roun da edges, to make sure nobody fock op. Me an Nestor, we do all the dealin', Que Sabe"?

"Si Jefe", said Jaeger with a nod!

"Good. Now we go", said Ortega as everyone went to their separate cars, filing out of the hotels parking lot. Soon enough they were driving down South Main Street, out past the Loop, passing a string of No Tell Motels that covered a mile of the street who's only reason for existence was to provide a brief sanctuary for the areas 'Working Girls', who blanketed that part of town. Then passing through an area of industrial parks that lined both sides of the road, the traffic started to thin out considerably as the convoy made its way to the far southwest suburbs.

As the Taurus containing both Jaeger and Davalantes continued on, Davalantes turned on the radio and inserted a Cassette saying, "Hope you like Cubano music mejo, cause it's the latest thing. The Buena Vista Social Club. The Fidelistas are getting soft in their old age and letting the old men play the old music before they all die"!

"You Cubano", asked Jaeger?

"Came in the boat lift years ago, when I was a little skinny one. We all hit Miami at the same time. Think I was about nine at the time. Didn't know shit about English, but I learn soon enough. Shine shoes for the tourista's on Collins Avenue, on my way up, but I never forget the Cubano music"!

"So what are we in for", asked Jaeger?

"Jus like the man say, gonna try an move some high quality Jejo, to these west coast Negrito's, called the Crips. We hear they bad Mojo all the way around, but Jefe he working on something' special and wanna clear out a lot of his inventory. One thing she worry me"!

"What's that" asked Jaeger as the lilting guitar strains of old Havana, worked their magic?

"We hear rumor's, they throw in with the Jamaican Posse, rather than fight em. Eh, hombre', you oughtta know. Last month in South Padre Island. You and Nestor working that offshore deal. I heard about how you gutted three of the Hoo Doo Chile's Dreadlocks, with your knife inside that boat's cabin offshore. Nestor, he tell me all about it. The reason he say is because, he think you pretty good with a blade in close. He impressed. The reason I mention this is because I know Nestor and be with him when he cut up a circle of men in less than a dozen seconds. He raised with a blade since he was a gnat"!

"If we see Negrito's sportin' dreadlocks and wearing a long leather car coat in this warm weather, make certain your gun hand isn't cramped. As Nestor probably told you, they had no intention of buying our stuff. The money they were using was bogus. Just for show till they could get the drop on us"!

"I keep that in mind", said Davalantes as the music played by men in their nineties summoned memories of their glorious youths. Of dreams realized and dashed, of triumphs and failures. Hopes and expectations. Of glorious sultry nights, dancing with a willing woman, sweat pouring from their bodies, knowing full well how the evening would end. Laying on the beach, in the aftermath locked in an embrazio, professing endless love and devotion, uncertain as to what the future may bring, yet devoted just to the moment. "That music she pretty good, no"?

"Sounds great", said Jaeger. Then to make conversation Davalantes said, "That Lincoln of Ortega's, he spend a fortune on that car. A company in San Antonio, she work on it, Trick it out with everything. Bullet proof glass all around, armor plating, a beefed up six liter V-8 supercharged engine, Kevlar interior, self-sealing run flat tires and you push a fuckin' button and five gallons of oil is sprayed out the back of the car, to ruin the day for anyone chasin' you. Push another button and one by one fragment grenades come rollin' out from under the car. Every time you push the button another grenade come rollin' out from under the car with a three second delay. After he take delivery, we drive it down to Brownsville to have a meet with some of the Mexicans that come over. We gonna go for dinner and they follow us all inna same car. I'm driving and Ortega lean over a push the button three times. They drive over the first one and just as the car passes over the first grenade, it go off. Musta hit the gas tank. Didn't really need the two others, still they finished things. Ortega, he say they shorted him on a deal a while back. He say nothing. But he remember. He got a long memory. I'm fifty yards ahead of em and got my foot on the pedal goin' muy rapido"!

"Looks like a wise investment", said Jaeger!

"One thing about that man", said Davalantes. "With him, ya never see it comin'"!

As Magellan drove Ortega southward, he glanced briefly in his rearview mirror seeing Ortega deep in thought. He was thinking about the other meetings with the Chicago Italians and the Chinese out of Seattle. The demonstrations went well and they were extremely interested, in the undetectable quality, the short duration of residual existence and the varieties of effects it was able to affect on the human body. Shipped in half pint bottles similar to one labeled "Karo Corn Syrup", the concentrate could be stepped on a hundred times by the suppliers in anyone's kitchen. He could see their minds working and the look on their face when he announced the finest scientific minds in the world couldn't duplicate the product. Which gave him all the leverage he needed in setting the price.

Just a few more deals like the one this day to winnow down his supply of Jejo and he would be the seller of a not illegal product, serving the needs of a certain part of humanity. If this went well, then he would look to the Negrito's to be another buyer. He'd thirty kilos in the trunk of the car behind him and looked to make a bang, bang transaction. In a month Magellan would deliver ten tons of Crystalline, to the hide out in Val Verde County and thanks to Davalantes, the point of transfer would be in the middle of nowhere, in Menard County Texas, visited by them both along with Quintanilla over a month ago. It was perfect, several hundred yards off a rural road, on a long abandoned property fronting one of central Texas's rivers. A horseshoe shaped clearing surrounded by a hill that wrapped around the clearing. The nearest dwelling being well over a mile away on the rural road. He recalled that when they inspected the site, there were no signs that anyone had traveled down the old gravel driveway, long overgrown with weeds. It was perfect.

The only thing in question were the, Ortega wondered what the word was that Jaeger called the Negrito's? Then he recalled the word, "The Schwartzers", he said! "The Dark ones"!

For the next five miles, the trio of cars droned southwards towards the bedroom community of Richmond, a sleepy little community southwest of the Houston city limits, with nothing going for it other than being the next stop after Sugar Land, the ancient home of Imperial Sugar and the Texas Department of Corrections work farm.

Hardly a day went by when one didn't see a phalanx men in prison whites, toiling in the fields, tending to their veggies, from sun up to sun down, ringed by TDC guards astride their horses with shotguns at the ready. On the other side of the roadway was the modern and affluent Sugar Land, replete with a state of the art shopping mall and upscale homes of the affluent.

As Davalantes drove, he glanced at Jaeger, who was watching the prisoners in the fields and asked, "The time you spend up in Huntsville. You ever work in the field"?

"Nope. Worked in the prison infirmary"! "What you do there"?

"Just about everything, from cleaning at first, then after a while, they taught me how to use the machines, do testing, take blood, then after a while I assisted the doctor in minor surgery. Even performed a number of circumcisions on the inmates, subject to the doctor's approval"!

"Circumcisions? I thought only the little ones got that", exclaimed Davalantes surprised!

"You'd be surprised at how many men aren't circumcised. Especially the Schwartzer's and the Mexican's. Pretty simple really, just cut and snip around the edges really. Lotta guys had it done to get a vacation from work for ten days. Really funny watching them hobble bowlegged back and forth from meals in the chow line. Everyone had a chuckle. But even that had its downside other than the hectoring from the other convicts"!

"Yeah, what's that"!

"Your lack of mobility. During the time I was there, three inmates got the shiv from other inmates and died as a result. One ratted out several inmates and got the horns and the other two were gang boss's who were overthrown"!

"Ay Bendito", exclaimed Davalantes. "So you were like a doctor"? "Hardly that. Just another convict"!

"You were there a few years ago when they had that big riot weren't you"?

"In the yard but not part of the riot luckily. Was between several of the prison gangs. Things were said and done that apparently couldn't or wouldn't be forgiven or forgotten. Time passes, pressure build the one day BOOM. Luckily one of the guards on the wall knew me and saw that me and the group I was with weren't part of what was going on and pointed his shotgun elsewhere. Saw him bring down a dozen guys at least. Was busy for the entire day and far into the night helping the doctor and the nurse, with those who weren't too badly injured"!

"Heard that a lotta guys got killed that day", said Davalantes! "They all brought it on themselves. From what I know all of them deserved what they got. After that, things settled down for awhile. Just Gods way of thinin' out the herd"!

"Funny thing you being such a good soldier for Ortega, yet you do good things in prison", said Davalantes!

"We do what we have to", replied Jaeger!

"OK, heads up. The place we go is a mile away"! The Han Cheng Mall, as it was once called was ground zero for the moment. Long abandoned and never occupied after it was built, as legend had it, by a group of local Vietnamese businessmen, pooling their financial resources, during the heady days of the early eighties, when the Savings and Loans could operate as banks in commercial ventures. They got the land for next to nothing and decided to be the very first to build way out in the boonies, as a testament to the statement, "If you build it, they will come"! They build the small mall yet nobody came. The Mall was a replica of Oriental architecture, with a plan to occupy it with mostly Oriental owned businesses. Yet not one tenant could be convinced to sign a lease so far away from the activity of the city. A victim of unrestrained overbuilding by commercial enterprise. Now fenced in by the Resolution Trust governmental entity and overgrown with chest high weeds, the vast structure sat there, still in the middle of nowhere. The Oriental partners made out, having no personal liability, on the construction loan, simply declared their shell corporation bankrupt and went their merry way.

The Mall was a perfect place for Ortega to conduct his affairs in broad daylight, since an eight foot high chain linked fence surrounded the entire property, which was penetrated repeatedly by the locals. The local cops had little interest in the property since it was technically federal government property.

Each time one of Ortega's men visited the property to conduct business; they simply removed the long broken padlock from the chained gate and went right in, careful to replace the padlock as if it were still operational. Every hundred feet or so, surrounding the entire premises was a sign attached to the fence which read; "No Entry. Property of the FDIC. Violators will be prosecuted". A sign which few paid any attention to.

South Main street had long since merged with Highway 90 A, as just ahead lay a gravel turnaround in the middle of the sixty yard wide grassy esplanade separating the north, south traffic as the cars all slowed, made the left hand turn heading back a quarter mile in the opposite direction, then turning right on another gravel road which surrounded the abandoned malls perimeter. They all drove to the rear of the property coming up on the rear entrance gate. Magellan jumped out and undid the padlock allowing the cars to enter then carefully replaced the padlock and chain as it was before.

The cars slowly drove into the rear shipping docks of the area, well out of view of anyone, working their way around abandoned constriction debris, until they discovered four vehicles parked beside a long abandoned and never used loading dock. The giant roll up door was partially elevated to shoulder level no doubt to allow air and a source of light to flow into the interior of the building. A standard metal entrance door lay wide open next to the loading dock.

A light brown haired, dreadlocked lightly tanned Negro, appeared in the doorway as Ortega stepped out of his Lincoln, and yelled, "You Ortega"?

Ortega nodded his head. Then the Mulatto said, "You come on in mon, we been expecting you. You bring da shit"?

"You bring the money", answered Ortega?

"The High Yellow nodded his head slowly, his hazel colored eyes narrowing.

"Then we can do business", said Ortega, quickly turning to his men saying softly, "Quintanilla, You stay here with the Jejo an make sure you got the Mac-10 ready to rock an roll if you hear any shooting. The rest of you follow me inside"!

The Rastaman disappeared into the doorway after motioning to them to enter as he grabbed his long black leather coat moving away from sight. As the four of them moved towards the building Magellan quickly said, "If they are wearing black leather coats in this weather, its certain the coats will be bullet proofed and they will have automatic weapons. Anything wrong happen shoot first for the legs or the head, anything else will be wasted"!

Ortega had heard rumors of a possible truce between the Jamaican Posse and the Crips, enemies for so long, as each member of the opposing group had standing orders to kill the opposite member on sight. Such was their mutual enmity towards each other as each organization butted heads with the other, in their expansion struggle for the American marketplace.

Throughout the drug world, most had heard of the Jamaican Posse. On a par, if not exceeding the Columbians in treachery in any of their dealings. Wanting to expand their enterprise from wholesale into retail, all members of the Posse, were at least initiates into the Voo Doo rites of Santeria, combining the worship of the dead, and an amalgam of Christianity and West African spiritual rituals, blended into the

Rastafarian belief as they were God's truly chosen people. Through drugs and hallucinogens, the worshipers of the dead, revered the 'Baron Samedie' as their Voo Doo supreme entity. The king of the dead, leader of the underworld. The supreme Prince of Darkness.

Central to their hybrid beliefs, was the ingrained certainty of all initiates, that they could never be killed, for they were already dead. Thus if one was already dead, how could they be killed? So fear of the unknown never was permitted a place in their mind, as true believers of the 'Baron', adding to their fearless demeanor. Each Rasta was deemed a shooter, as that was their adopted style. There wasn't a true marksman in the lot, but one didn't have to be armed with either the compact Mac-10 for the close in work, or the short barreled Uzi machine pistol.

In the temporal world, things were very simple for them. "When in doubt, pull da trigger", or "Git da money mon, den pull da trigger"! Or, "You want somthin' bad enough, pull da trigger"! Anyone coming away from an encounter with a Rasta Man was indeed fortunate, for the time being. Given the vast quantities of hallucinogens they ritualistically consumed on a daily basis and the twisted values of their beliefs, your average Posse was at least marginally insane. The error that others continually made when dealing with the Posse, was a continued effort of the relatively sane people to anticipate the motivations of the insane. To a Rasta Man, there where no 'Why's", just a host of 'Because's'. Coupled with the fact that the Posse had a burning hatred of all who wasn't one of them.

Moving forward into the depths of the vast badly lit warehouse, with the only light coming through some skylights in the roof that cast large shadows everywhere, Ortega wondered about the improbable set of unholy circumstances that could possibly join the Crips and the Posse at the hip. He shifted the aluminum briefcase, that held a sample kilo of his Jejo and a jar of his Crystalline concentrate, to his other hand, to ready his gun hand just in case the need arise. Then he stopped, turned to Magellan saying, "I want you to go back to the car and tell Quintanilla to join us. You stay with the car, OK"?

Magellan nodded his head and went back to the car, as the trio moved slowly allowing for their eyes to adjust to the dark interior. The trio walked forward joining the High Yellow, hazel eyed Rasta, who by now had donned his long leather coat. His arms folded across his chest as he drawled, "Come on in mon, Scylla, she be waitin' for ya"! Ortega waited until Quintanilla joined them.

"Lead the way", said Ortega, as the Rasta at first made no move to move ahead of the quartet, then after some moments of eye contact with Ortega, unfolded his arms and led the way. Rounding a corner, the trio could see as they approached, a small group of four people sitting around a small table some thirty yards away, the area illuminated by three, equally spaced battery powered lamps on metal tripods, elevated to shoulder height all pointed towards a central point, the table.

As Ortega approached the table, without having to be told, Jaeger moved to his left some ten yards away from the table and Quintanilla moved to a sport equally distant to his right, while Davalantes stood his ground ten yards behind Ortega. All of them peered into the shadows and refrained from looking into the well lit portion near the table.

As Jaegers eyes gradually adjusted to the interior, he made a mental note of just where someone might hide. Corners, alcoves, sheet rocked roof support columns, anywhere wide enough to shield an average body from view. One thing that bothered him were the four cars were outside and just four of the others were inside. Assuming what he heard about the Rasta's were correct, that they never went anywhere alone, always traveling in two's and three's, there could be anywhere from four to eight more folks out in the shadows ready to jump at the first sign of trouble. His sport coat was unbuttoned and he felt the weight of the twin magnums slung under his armpits, unclasped and ready. His peripheral vision indicated what Ortega was facing. Two Rasta's flanking a black man of medium height and a striking Negro woman with her hair cut short, a statuesque figure, clad in almost knee high brown leather high heel boots, contrasted with white shorts and tank top shirt. A small leather jacket lay on the table. As she stood, she towered over the shorter Ortega, clearly a woman of considerable attraction, exceeding the six foot mark by a few inches.

As he peered into the shadows trying to see something, anything. His thoughts carried him back to that first meeting with Ortega and Magellan. He remembered Ortega's words. "I pay you a thousand dollars a day, to take care of my business. Cash money. Don't need to see you every day. You can do what you want when I don't need you. But when I call, better bet it's important and I need you pronto, so you gonna need a cell phone on you all times"!

He would later learn of Ortega's generosity upon occasion. A far better amount than the government paid for combat pay, as he squinted his eyes in order to see the unseen he sensed was out there. He could just feel their presence as every hair on his head started to tingle.

As Ortega came upon those gathered, he placed his aluminum briefcase on the table saying, "Hola Chulita"!

"Back at ya Ortega. You bring the shit and the sample"?

"The Jejo is safe in the trunk of my car outside, with a sample test kilo in the briefcase, along with a sample jar of the Crystalline. You bring the money we agreed on"?

"Sitting here beside me in three separate briefcases all in hundreds like you said"!

"Then we get down to business", said Ortega as he opened up his briefcase producing the kilo of coke in a plastic bag and the pint bottle with the Karo Corn Syrup label.

"This the Crystalline we talk about. Hola, looks like corn syrup"! We set it aside after your man test the Jejo, OK"?

Scylla motioned to one of the Rasta's who stepped forward and made a small slit in the plastic bag and extracted a small amount of coke with his fingernail and deposited it into a small vial mixing it with a clear medium. He shook it and held it to the light for a moment saying, "Shits good, over ninety percent"!

"Bueno", said Ortega. "Now did you bring the women to test the Crystalline with and the mixing product"?

"Three street whore's outta sight and the mixers are in the cooler underneath the table"! She then turned her head and motioned to one of the Rasta's to get the women, as another reached slowly under the table and pulled out the Igloo Cooler, carefully turning it around to face Ortega. Then a metal door opened up on the far end of the space and three blindfolded and gagged women came through the doorway, escorted by the Rasta that went after them and one other. As the women struggled against their bindings being pushed and prodded forward, Ortega gradually began to see they were indeed common street whores that lurked around bus stops during the day on South Main Street, and offered themselves around the black clubs of the area after dark.

As they approached, Ortega had prepared three plastic cups and opened the container of Crystalline, while Davalantes was motioned forward to perform a cursory examination of the three large brief cases full of money. As the whores approached, He signaled Ortega with a nod that all the money was there, closing the briefcases and moving them to the side, stepping back to his position behind Ortega.

The others now having relinquished the three chairs to the new arrivals stood behind them as they were seated and the gags and blindfolds removed. As they started to complain, Scylla bellowed, "Shut up bitches. No you're here for an experiment. You be real good and soon you'll feel real good"! She then reached inside her bra and extracted six hundred dollar bills saying, "Now ya do what we tell ya and stay quiet and after it's all over each of you'll get two, hundred dollar bills for your time and a ride back to town, just in time for the night shift if ya want"!

She then got a brief nod from each of the working girls, saying "Good"! "Ortega, pour the drinks.

Ortega poured and added several drops of Crystalline concentrate in each if the plastic cups and handed it the one of the nearby Rasta's who served the cups to the women. When through, he stepped back into the shadows as Ortega said, "Now we wait", as he looked at his watch. "Should take about fifteen to twenty minutes for the stuff to do its work. Coke, Heroin, or Crystal Meth. We all know what to look for. Of course all of this is highly concentrated and has many other uses, depending what it's mixed with. You'll be able to step of this over a dozen times, before you sell it to others. Complete directions come with the beginning shipment. So now we look and wait"!

"What guarantee we got if the shit we buy later don't work and you be scammin' us"?

"Scylla. We never do business before, but you know how things work. We sell you bad shit, then you not like us anymore and come looking for us. Now that be bad for, how you say, uh, future business for both of us. Now we gonna have a lotta Crystalline on our hands very soon and we be the only ones in the world that got it. We gonna have a steady supply of the stuff, for a long time and it's not on anybody's list of illegal drugs. So from now on you can still deal in Horse, or Coke, or anything else if you want, but you don't have to, Que sabe"?

Scylla nodded her head then shifted her gaze to the three women sitting erect and afraid in their chairs.

Little by little, by incremental inches at a time, Jaeger shifted his position silently to his left, towards a sheet rocked roof support column just ten yards away, moving nothing but his feet. While the activity was happening at the table, no one took notice. The vacant structure was silent, except for the occasional muted rumble of a tractor trailer truck making its way along the old Highway 90 roadway.

While everyone was waiting for the effects of the Crystalline to make itself known, Scylla broke the silence by bringing up the terms of and conditions of the anticipated sale. Everyone seemed to know about the Crystalline except Jaeger, who yards away from where they were ironing out the terms should acceptance occur. As far as he knew, he was securing just another cocaine transaction. He wondered why three raggedy looking South Main hookers were trotted out blindfolded, gagged and secured, then offered drinks, but that was overshadowed for the moment by his instincts of something terribly wrong. As he inched towards the buildings support column silently, he thought he saw the image of the toe of a shoe, behind the nearest column. Again, glancing back at everyone around the table, seeing their interests focused on the three women, who by now were starting to act erratically, he chanced one last step backwards and the faint image of the shoe grew to include that of a leg and what seemed to be the hem of a dark coat. Now the question was answered as to where the rest of the Rasta's were. Behind the wide three foot support columns they were, all awaiting a signal.

Ortega had walked into a trap unknowingly. Quite uncharacteristic of the man, from what Jaeger knew of him, for it was usually Ortega that set the trap. Jaeger had to warn Ortega, but how? The best way, he figured was to get in the first shot. No time to put the cotton in his ears, for the cacophony he knew was soon to happen, would cause his ears to be ringing for a long time to come, that of course if he was still alive. The Ruger in his hand was brought up quickly as he fired a round at the man's ankle and closed the distance to the support column, catching the Rasta as he fell writhing in agony. Jaeger ripped the Mac-10 machine pistol from the man's grasp before he could fire it and clubbed his head once as he felt a sickening crunch as the skull caved in on itself.

There was no time to warn anyone as the Rasta's appeared from behind the support columns and started firing everywhere their automatic machine pistols. Grabbing the dead Rasta, Jaeger propped him up to a sitting position and used the body as a shield, far better than hiding behind a sheet rocked clad building column that provided zero protection from bullets. He spotted a Rasta some thirty yards away who just appeared and started to fire his weapon and took the Rasta's Mac-10 and fired a short volley towards the man's feet, many of which ricocheted off the cement floor, slamming into his legs, knocking him to the ground. Then further away, Jaeger took yet another long shot and repeated his short burst firing at yet another dark form clad in long leather firing away and once again the bullets bounced off the cement and their now misshapen jagged edges slammed into the legs of the Rasta, as he too fell to the floor grabbing his legs in pain.

Then Jaeger noticed the previous Rasta reaching for his weapon that had fallen away and fired a burst in the direction of his head, just as the far metal fire door opened and two more Rasta, burst into vacant area that had by now turned into a meat grinder. Once again just as they both came through the door. Jaeger ripped off a short volley of fire at their lower extremities, one of which found its mark falling one of them. The other in his haste tripped over his comrade, falling to the floor.

Jaeger pressed the trigger and found the weapon empty, tossing it aside and reached for his Ruger and took careful aim and fired twice at both of the new arrivals one of the rounds finding its mark, in the man's neck. Then he took a chance, quickly rising and ran towards the second man he shot, firing off two quick shots as he ran with zero hope of any of them finding a home, quickly covering the yardage and performed a perfect hook slide on the concrete, grabbing the unused Mac-10 from the dead man and quickly firing off a burst in the direction of the remaining man. Then he ran in their direction, the Mac-10 in one hand and the Ruger in the other, firing two short bursts as he ran, sliding once again into the duo grabbing their weapons and firing off one round each into each of their heads for insurance. As he holstered his Ruger and reloaded the Mac-10's quickly, he could hear the cross firing from the other locations. He quickly wondered whether or not Magellan would join the party and then heard the unmistakable rip from the Uzi he was carrying.

Now armed with three fully functioning Mac-10's Jaeger took careful aim at the third Rasta, trying to rise and fire his weapon and ripped off a half clip volley at the man cutting him down.

He quickly glanced at the partially opened metal door behind him concluding that if there were others on the back side of the door, they would already have joined the party. Then he quickly rose and ran to the position of the third man he'd just shot and again slid in behind him, as he felt a hail of bullets pass over him.

Now he had the remainder of the Rasta's in a cross fire and the only way he could see them was by following the sight of the gunfire coming from their direction. He then started to fire in their direction and one by one they emerged from their locations only to be cut down by Davalantes, Magellan and Quintanilla.

Then everything was quiet, except for the ringing in everyone's ears. Jaeger called out their names as they all responded. Then he heard from Davalantes, "Quintanilla, he's hit". As Jaeger closed the distance between them, he could barely hear the passing freight trucks passing by over the ringing in his ears. Approaching a prostrate Quintanilla, he said to Davalantes, "Go to Ortega, I'll take a look at him"!

After some minutes Davalantes came running back saying, "Ortega's OK and Magellan just ran outside to see if anyone heard the gunfire. How's Quintanilla"?

"He caught a stray round, glanced off his right hand collarbone, so his gun hand is useless and it hurts like hell. Too bad we don't have any anesthetic to give him. Need to get him to the nurses in the heights, soon as possible.

"You go outside and join Magellan", said Davalantes. "I'll call the nurses and Jugos"! As Jaeger walked away Davalantes yelled, "Hey Vato, Muy Gracias for the heads up, or we all might be goner's"!

As Magellan saw Jaeger join him, he said, "We certainly walked into that one and you deserve a huge thanks. It never hit me until I came outside, that four cars and four people were not the Rasta's way of travel. Then the gunfire. Davalantes said you were the one that started the shooting. What tipped you off"?

"Hell Nestor, I don't know. Maybe that little Angel that sits on my shoulder"?

"So you believe in Angels, do you"? "How else do you explain it, pal"? "How's Quintanilla"?

"Bullet broke his collarbone. I stabilized his bleeding, so he'll keep until Davalantes or someone can alert the nurses in the Heights. He's getting them on the phone right now along with Jugos, the cleaner.

Jaeger then fished out a crumpled box of cigarettes and offered one to Magellan, who lit one and got on his cell phone spoke gruffly, then hung up saying, "Jugos is going to need some help and afterwards we'll need some help to dispose of these cars. Looking around it was apparent that the vacant shopping center had done its job well, being in the middle of nowhere and contained the noisy onslaught that had just occurred.

As they went back inside, and approached Ortega, they caught sight of Quintanilla being helped to a seat at the far end of the table. On the floor was the prostrate Scylla, who lay unconscious as Davalantes said, "Ortega is walking around", just then a gunshot rang out, as he continued, "Inspecting the dead. He's just making certain their dead"! As he said that, yet another gunshot rang out, as he continued, "That's just Jefe doin his body count"!

"Why waist the bullets" said Jaeger. "My guys are dead for sure"! "The only ones who didn't get shot were, this Scylla and that other nappy headed Negrito", said Davalantes. He catch a scratch on his head but he be OK. We see what Ortega wanna do with him when he get back". Then yet another gunshot rang out as Ortega made the rounds.

As he made the rounds, Jaeger looked at Quintanilla and asked, "How ya doin' sport"?

"They gimme a pain killer and it doan feel so bad anymore". Just then Davalantes cell phone rang and he spoke a short while then said, "That's the nurses in the heights, they get off shift at the hospital inna half hour and will be ready for Quintanilla", as Ortega finally approached.

He looked at Jaeger a long while, then spoke to Magellan for a bit before returning his gaze to Jaeger saying, "We gonna say thanks to you for all of this. By my count, there was a dozen of the Rasta's and you get seven of em, all by yourself. We were out gunned an you even things up. Good work. Gonna earn you a big bonus. Now Jugos and others are on the way, I want you to take Quintanilla to the nurses in the Heights, so they can fix him up, good as new. Then he reached inside one of Scylla's bags of money saying, here, take ten thousand and give it to the nurses for their trouble. They'll know what to do. We'll sit here and wait for Jugos and the others an take care of business here. When you get done with Quintanilla, go get cleaned up and eat something then join us at Jugos to help out"!

Then as an afterthought he said, "Wait a minute", reaching back into the bag and pulled out four stacks of hundred dollar bills, tossing them one by one to Jaeger saying, "Almost forgot your bonus"!

After Jaeger left with Quintanilla, Ortega then turned his attention to the remaining Negrito saying, "We gonna let you live. You go back to your people and tell em what happened. We still willing to do business with em. But not with the Hoo Doo Chile? We see any Rasta's we kill em and feed em to da fishes. You know the terms, nod your head"!

"Bueno. Tell em we got their money an we got Scylla. She be our guest an we take good care of her. You know our terms and we tell you later on when and where we meet up. To guarantee everything we have this Scylla. To cover her expenses, we gonna need an extra half million in cash when we next meet, then we return her in good shape. You make a mistake and we kill her. Unnerstan"?

The Crip, Scylla's second in command, nodded his head, then Ortega said to Magellan, when we get done here, take him to his car and cut him loose.

An hour later four additional cars arrived at the rear gate, followed a half an hour later by Jugos in his old pickup truck. From that point onward he was put in charge, directing the others to strip the bodies and bag the up in the black Visquene plastic bags and all of the clothing was placed in several other bags, to find a home in a dumpster somewhere across town in the early morning hours. Blood was disposed of with mops, rags and liberal amounts of chlorine bleach and water.

Jugos personally inspected the work of everyone an hour later and pronounced the area clean, as Ortega reached into the large briefcase full of hundred dollar bills and tossed two stacks towards Jugos, and gave the others each a stack of someone else's money. As he walked out of the warehouse he gave a stack of bills to Davalantes and Magellan saying, "The day after all, she didn't turn out too bad. We still got the Jejo and the Negrito's money after they try an screw us, and there be more to come.

Everybody get paid and the only one who get hurt is Quintanilla"! "So what's your opinion of Jaeger Jefe" asked Magellan?

"That man he a shooter all right. We gotta watch him"! Then he turned back to Davalantes and said, "I want you to take this Scylla out to our Place in Val Verde after we get done to night. No one but us knows about that place. Take three men with you and make sure they good. You secure the woman good cause we gonna have her as our guest for a little while. Then come back in town. You gonna be goin back and forth for awhile"! Then he reached back into the briefcase and tossed another stack of bills to Davalantes saying, "For expenses"! Then he drew back before they reached the cars and said to Magellan, Before we go, leave the Negrito wid a broken jaw so he remember we give him life, but not so bad he can't drive.

One by one the cars left the scene, one every two minutes as not to draw attention. The bodies in the black plastic bags divided amongst several vehicles all headed toward Jugos place for their final rendering.

The three whores never made it back to South Main Street for unfortunately they were all inadvertently gunned down by the Rasta's in the early part of the melee. Of course their pimp was livid with rage because three of his earners were among the missing, even going as far as filing a missing persons report several days later with the HPD. Of course, the reports never gained anyone's attention and soon were filed away.

By nine in the evening Jaeger arrived at Jugos restaurant which had closed for business early as everyone in the kitchen was hard at work in the process of rendering the bodies of their flesh and grinding the remnants into chorizo sausage and five chili pots were hard at work rendering the bones and sinew into Menudo soup, as the pots were stirred and various spices and condiments were added.

Around ten in the evening, an older couple was walking back to their home from evening Mass as they smelled the odors wafting through the air as the passed by Jugos restaurant. The wife commented, "Can you smell that Jorge', it's Jugos and he's making the Menudo"!

"Ay Caramba. Now I will not get any sleep tonight thinking about his wonderful Menudo"!

"Just be patient Jorge. He always have plenty"!

By four in the morning, Davalantes had long since departed for Val Verde, with Scylla, his special cargo and the others had departed in every direction, while Jaeger and Magellan had loaded the host of the heads, bones and skin of the departed into one of the cars and headed south towards Ortega's place in Clear Lake. An hour later they went through the gates of Ortega's home, unloaded the plastic bags onto the big Chris Craft cruiser and headed out of the Clear Lake estuary and out onto Galveston Bay. By seven in the morning they reached the Gulf of Mexico. It had been a long day and a gunfight will take a lot of energy out of anyone, so they had little to say to each other as they traveled and worked. Especially since neither one was prone to idle chit chat. Magellan driving the boat would give an order or direction with Jaeger complying and vice versa. Traveling at twenty knots for an hour then turning thirty degrees to starboard, they traveled another half hour before Magellan turned the engines to idle. Then one by one, they punctured the plastic bags all over and tossed them over the side until all were overboard. Then sat and drank a beer until they all sank beneath the surface, falling into the briny deep. All the while Magellan was thinking. Reevaluating this strange one that he was slowly growing to like. This Jaeger was a real warrior and seemingly a man of honor as far as that went.

He said little and did a lot. Competent and highly dangerous. A man he'd value at his side rather than be his enemy. He wondered what he would do should the mercurial Ortega should tell him to kill Jaeger? But from his recent reactions to Jaegers accomplishments, that possibility seemed unlikely.

After everyone had departed, Jugos still had a half an hour of further cleaning to do. Using the last of his chlorine bleach he took a final glance a pronounced the kitchen clean. He made a final check of the Menudo slowly simmering away on his five, natural gas fed floor burners. Three ten gallon chili pots and two additional, newly purchased galvanized garbage cans were put into service, in order to accommodate Ortega's needs. He checked the kitchen exhaust vent to make certain it was fully open. His walk in freezer and cooler were full of recently made Chorizo sausage, as he gave it a final glance.

He locked the rear door and went to his house next door and after a shower he silently slid into bed, for a few hours' sleep. His wife's eyes came open briefly as she felt the familiar form of her husband join her. She smiled and drifted back to sleep, knowing that all apparently went well and life as they grew to accept, would continue a little longer.

D avalantes sudden departure for Houston, left Magellan high and dry in the wilds of Val Verde county, Texas. His guest/hostage Scylla was well enough he supposed, given the treatment she'd received by Davalantes and the others. The last time he's laid eyes upon her was during the incident at the abandoned oriental shopping center and that was well over a month ago. A great deal had occurred during the interim. Clearly she had an appeal that was considerable, but that was then. Fed only one meal a day and chained constantly to the barn's floor, she was permitted to bathe once a week in full view of her captors. Thus, they jokingly concluded, that even her considerable charms had eroded. By the end of the sixth day of each week, she started to smell like dead fish. Only Ortega's verbal threat of death kept them away from sampling her considerable charms. Purely a business move to be sure. For there was business to be done with her brother, the 'Zulu Man' on the horizon and nothing could intrude upon Ortega's business.

During Davalantes absence, Magellan decided that Scylla had lost too much weight and started to feed her twice a day, to put some meat back on her bones. Not out of compassion, but purely in the interests of furthering business interests. All other constraints stayed in place as he checked on the teenaged Panamanian man child, Davalantes had taken under his wing. Left with only the teenaged Panamanian and one other that had no name, who spoke no English, said little and answered to "Hey you", It was late in the morning and the kid was sitting under a tree thirty yards from the front of the open barn with Scylla in full view as he said, "I'll be on the front porch in the rocker, catching a nap for the next few hours, so don't fall asleep"! He made a mental note of Davalantes message that Ortega had contacted the buyers including the Zulu Man, informing them each of the date and time and location of the transfer.

Yet he was particularly disturbed by two items of interest. Davalantes recent departure for Houston with the other's, indicated that something had gone wrong with the Embraer affair, involving Jaeger. Their departure indicated a full on alert. Next, the news that Quintanilla had gone missing. The only one wounded in the shopping center gun battle with the Rasta's, taken to the nurses in Houston's heights by Jaeger. Ortega had his people check on him every other day during his convalescence and several days ago he'd suddenly disappeared one afternoon. His wife leaving during an afternoon nap to go shopping and when she came back, he was gone with no apparent sign of struggle. In his condition any struggle was out of the question. He briefly wondered whether or not this had something to do with Jaeger and concluded that it probably didn't.

He leaned back in the old wicker chair and soon drifted off for a much needed nap. Much lay ahead, for tomorrow he would have the nameless one drive him down to Del Rio and rent a U Haul truck for the transfer a few days away. Then his eyes became heavy as his bodily needs for rest guided him to slumber.

Normally Nestor didn't dream much, or if he did he rarely remembered what he'd dreamt. But as he slid into the realm of unconsciousness, allowing his body to rest, events of long ago charged back into his mind, as his eyeballs rolled back and forth under his eyelids.

Carlos sat on his heels staring at what he'd just done. Before him lay the body of his beloved Joselita. 'Mi amore', he thought. 'My wonderful Joselita', as her name rolled lovingly from his lips, he whispered, "Why, why"?

Carlos and Joselita were teenage lovers, secretly engaged to be married to each other, when Carlos completed his primary schooling five short months from now. From time to time Joselita would elude the clutches of her 'Duenna' to secretly rendezvous with Carlos in several places known only to them. Once there, in their private Seraglio, desperate bouts of extended love making would occur, then Carlos would escort her back before dawn, with Joselita always successful in slipping back into the family encomienda prior to the servants awakening, with none the wiser. The appropriate precautions to avoid pregnancy were usually taken by Joselita, given her conservative Catholic upbringing. In addition she always abstained from normal intercourse with Carlos, during the periods of her prime fertility.

For the better part of a year their dalliances took place, with each occasion bonding them closer and closer to such a degree that time passed slowly when they were apart and raced by at light speed when they were together. In the afterglow of their lovemaking, each would gaze wordlessly into the others eyes, thinking that in the entire history of human existence, no two people were ever so deeply in love with each other and perfectly bonded.

Only one problem existed, how to tell her father, they were in love? A major obstacle, considering his status in Spanish society. Of course they concluded that they would both think on the matter, but never did always kicking the can down the road for another day. But eventually Carlos sensed a gradual change in his lover's demeanor. Their meetings becoming less and less frequent and when they did rendezvous, her ardor gradually diminished incrementally. Their last two meetings resulted in no lovemaking, with long periods of silence between them with Carlos pleading with her to discover what was bothering her. At their last meeting Joselita could no longer with hold her passion, a flood of tears bursting forth, followed by the usual recriminations of how they both have sinned against God and the Holy Mother Church, by having sex out of wedlock with each other, over- whelming her with the guilt of her sin. At first he wondered why this came up especially since she never seemed overwhelmingly religious, attending Mass out of duty rather than absolute conviction.

Carlos tried repeatedly to calm and sooth her, yet no matter how many times he tried to calm her with professions of eternal love, she rebuffed his advances by pulling away from his embrace as if he were a Leper, with a look of utter distain on her face. Then as a flood of words burst forth blaming Carlos for the loss of her virginity, (never mind that she was Carlos first experience) she sobbed continually explaining that under no circumstances would her family approve of a marriage between her and Carlos, given societies class difference between their families. He from a family of middling origins and Joselita of a family of Hidalgo's, prosperous, aristocratic, with a lineage tracing back to the era of Conquistadors.

The moon in its final phase of the evening was gradually falling to the earth, soon to force the ascendant glow of the rising sun, signaling time for Joselita's departure. As he tried to join her to escort he home, she again rebuffed him saying that she knew the way. As she departed in tears, she grudgingly agreed to meet again in four days.

Both were in their seventeenth year of life, with an entire lifetime ahead of them, yet neither able to peer into the mists of the future, with any degree of accuracy, having to trust their respective fates to the fickle hands of the unseen.

The ensuing days were the worst of Carlos's young life to date. His normally robust appetite falling to nil, worrying his parents. His normally cheerful self now reversed for reasons that no one could fathom. He lay awake at night unable to sleep, tossing and turning completely unable to sleep and greeting the following day with the zeal of a tree sloth, shoulders bent as he walked seemingly with the weight of the world crushing the very spirit from his body. Each night he would recite his rosary repeatedly in spite of the sorrow that surrounded him, imploring the Blessed Virgin to allow this cup to pass him by and to intercede in his behalf by speaking to Joselita's heart. After he concluded that that wasn't working, he went outside got on his knees, looked to the starry heavens and implored all the Angels and Saints, the Cherubim and the Seraphim he knew of to speak to her heart. Yet the heavens remained silent save for the occasional shooting star falling from the heavens and the moon that was almost to its complete fullness. For most of each night he would pour out his heart to the celestial orbs in hope that some entity was listening and yet with each coming dawn his hopes were dashed by silence. By all the church had taught him, prayer should bring peace and contentment, yet his efforts at celestial communion appeared to be met by complete apathy. He didn't matter, no one that mattered cared. His parents, aware of his angst, tried to ask him repeatedly what was bothering him, but he gently put them off by saying it was a private matter and went about his daily routine as best he could, the weight of his gloom and despair drawing them forward for all to see. The love of his life was slipping away from his grasp and he was powerless, sensing that her heart was already gone. He could see it in her eyes, hear the truth of it in her voice, sense it from her mannerisms and judge it from the cutting words she used at their last meeting. Yet he had eyes that could not see, ears that would not hear and a brain that would not process the truth of it.

On the night of their rendezvous, when she didn't arrive on time, his mind processed that perhaps something bad had happened to her. After an hour passed, he decided to search for her. Perhaps if he saved her from a horrible fate, her attitude towards him would change. Then again possibly she had become confused as to the exact location of their meeting, as he visited each of their secluded spots, finding her not there. Then he thought of the location of their first ever meeting, a secluded grotto up in the hills above Ciudad de Zaragoza, reachable only by a little used goat path.

As he climbed the goat path he could see the distant city lights below and had no problem following the goat path, by the light of the full moon above. As he walked, looking down he could make out some freshly laid footprints on the path. One clearly male and a smaller set of footprints that sent his mind reeling. As he approached the entrance to the grotto, following the fresh pair of footprints, he thought he heard the sounds of a woman groaning.

Standing by the entrance he glanced up to the heavens one last time only to see the fullness of the moon, pregnant with the reflective light from an unseen sun, riding high in the night sky. He returned his glance to the grotto and slowly advanced stopping and listening, allowing his eyes to adjust to the darkness within. As his eyes adjusted, he gradually heard the sounds and made out the unmistakable form of a naked woman astride an almost naked man oblivious to their surroundings. Squatting astride his midsection, riding the bull, with vertical bucks, while the bull in question, in a supine position held her heaving hips, his pants down around his ankles and shoes, the occasional grunt issuing forth, both intent on doing whatever possible to extract his precious spermatozoa deeply into the eternal crevasse.

Neither of the partners of betrayal was aware of Carlos's presence just yards away standing frozen in shock at the sight of their exertions. Stunned as he was, he stood for several long minutes, cemented in place by this voyeuristic apparition in front of him. Her grunts of animalistic of pleasure, once only for his ears alone were now the property of another. He would know of Joselita's sounds, imprinted in his mind over many sessions of chasing Eros and here she was right in front of him, doing for another what she did for him. Gradually the sounds of her pleasure, gave way to a gradual roaring in his head, similar to that of a volcano on the verge of eruption as their gradual rhythm of intercourse increased in intensity and speed, signaling an eruption of its own.

Carlos could feel the presence of a hoard of unseen demons swirling about as his rage built up to the point of no return, he heard the caterwauling of thousands of the eternally damned and felt the demons grasping for his very soul. At that moment he crossed the threshold of sanity transported to the place of the Reptilian Response. His reason for life vanishing before his very eyes, his eardrums about to burst he bellowed, "PUTA", rushing forward grabbing Joselita by her hair and flinging her off her lover right as he erupted, with her landing roughly on the jagged grotto wall, falling to the ground stunned.

Her lover still in the process of eruption, not a scintilla of which made it towards its intended target was defenseless as Carlos grabbed him by the shirt he was still wearing beating him senseless, his pants still gathered about his ankles. His heart still racing and his chest still heaving as Joselita was coming to her senses, Carlos reached into his jacket pocket and pulled out his flick knife and with a simple twist of his wrist brought forth the blade, grabbing the now flaccid member of the unconscious lover, looking at Joselita as her senses returned and whispered hoarsely, "This is what you want over me? Well now you can have it forever" and with one swipe from his razor sharp blade separated it from its master right at the base, flinging it at her striking her in the face.

As her lovers member struck her falling to the ground, she recoiled in horror screaming, scrambling to her feet and rushed headlong into Carlos in a rage. As he turned to meet her advance, he forgot to lower his blade as instincts took over and she ran straight into the blade, severing an artery deep within. Her eyes widened as she felt the sharpness of the blade and she pushed herself away from Carlos falling to the ground.

In his rage Carlos might have taken her life anyway, but he didn't. Her reception of his blade was purely an accident of fate, or perhaps, by design of the scores of unseen apparitions hovering around the grotto, their work here concluded, retiring to parts unknown for their next assignment.

The roaring in his ears gone and sanity returned, Carlos said, "What have I done" as he rushed to Joselita's side, blood starting to ooze from her mortal wound. Still in command of her senses she gasped, "Stay away from me Carlos", as she lay there naked and mortally wounded trying to stop the blood that was now starting to leave her body, her stomach starting to well up as she struggled to breathe. Carlos started to speak, but she said to him, gasping for breath, "Don't speak to me. I'm dying and when I'm gone don't ever think about me. Ever"!

The rage Carlos felt was replaced by the sorrow that surrounded him. How he wanted this thing between them to be otherwise, he stared at his lovely Joselita, not so lovely anymore, her face contorted by pain and death scant minutes away. He would learn in the not so distant future, that a man's measure could be reckoned in the way he left this mortal coil. Some left it bravely, while others whimpered and still others cursed others for their own malfeasance. As the spirit left Joselita's body and she lay crumpled and naked in a pool of her own blood, it appeared she chose to take the latter path. Cursing her former lover for what she had brought on herself. Of course there was more than enough blame to go around as passion replaced reason on the Via Vita, "The road of Life". In the days ahead Carlos Vega, would need to learn the lesson of life in order to survive in this world,.

"To control ones passions and not allow ones passions to control you"! He sank to his knees and cried and asked her lifeless body to forgive him, yet she failed to respond, her lifeless eyes staring into the vast emptiness of death. After several minutes, he turned to look at his antagonist. His closed eyes and the large pool of blood gathered around his midsection indicating the man had bled out from his scrotal wound, his heart having nothing more to pump simply stopped and Carlos felt for a pulse, as he'd seen in many movies and felt none, concluding that both of them were to cross into whatever eternity that awaited together. He wondered if they would get along in that other dimension and concluded nothing. He picked up his knife and wiped the residue upon the dead man's trousers that lay at his feet. Then he walked over to Joselita's body and found the dead mans severed member and walked to the grotto entrance and flung it far down the hill for the carrion he knew would consume it soon after. He looked up into the night sky and whispered, "Now are you happy"!

Several minutes later he went back into the grotto to say his final goodbyes. As he stood over Joselita, his mind was overwhelmed by his circumstances. In spite of everything, he just couldn't leave her there looking like this. He looked around and quickly found her clothes and as carefully as possible as not to get her blood on him he dressed her, where she lay. As he worked on her, his mind, now back to a semblance of normalcy, wondered what to do next. By sunrise when she wasn't at her home, her parents would call the local police and file a missing persons report. He couldn't be certain that she hadn't at least one confidant she'd told of her affair with Carlos, so the local police would eventually pay him a visit and connect the dots together. The other one was that he certain to be eventually reported missing at some point. If they were seen together? His mind went blank. The only answer was for him to get as far away as possible as fast as possible. How would he live? How would he survive? All he had were several pesetas in his pocket and his flick knife. His mind raced into survival mode as he went outside. He looked at the ground, illuminated by the moonlight and saw a hoard of footprints, mostly his. Then remembering an American western movie he'd seen long ago, he looked for a branch of a bush then finding one suitable cut it from its base with his knife and went back into the grotto and working his way back towards the entrance brushed away all evidence of footprints from the dry ground, then he did the same around the entrance of the grotto and retraced his steps all the way down the pathway to a rocky area he noticed on his way up the hill. Suddenly he stopped. Something was tugging at him. He turned and went up back the pathway towards the grotto. In the darkness of the grotto he never got a good look at Joselita's new lover, but there was something familiar about him.

As he entered the grotto, he went up to the dead man, pulled out his cigarette lighter and illuminated the face. There amidst all the puffed up and bruised flesh was the face of Jose Quiniones, his eternal antagonist. The bully son of his father's Patron and employer. The son of the richest landowner of the region around Zaragoza. The son of a Spanish Don and his mortal enemy from childhood, no doubt returned from his studies at the University in Madrid. He removed the wallet, extracted most of the cash and threw it down the hill.

Now the picture became a bit clearer. Somehow Jose and Joselita had crossed paths. His were Hidalgos as well as that of Joselita's. Here he was Carlos caught in the middle with no chance. Of course she would catch the eye of that bandit Jose, who was a son of a bitch of the first order. Didn't matter who initiated things, the fat was in the fire now.

That was the truth of it. Carlos wasn't good enough by accident of birth he would never be good enough. His time with Joselita was simply an illusion until something better came along.

Carlos then got up went back out of the grotto not giving Joselita another thought, wiping away his foot prints as he went and worked his way back down the pathway to the rocky area, the stepping away from the path and admiring his work. Now it was the hares and the hound's time to put as much distance between him and Zaragoza. He remembered the roadway over the far hill on the other side. If he could get to it quickly as possible perhaps he could hitch a ride with a long distance Lorry driver.

As he walked, his mind fumed at the thought of Joselita being married to Jose Quiniones of all people. His father has worked for that family for well over thirty years at the vast rancho raising and nurturing the finest bulls in the entire Iberian Peninsula for the corridas in Madrid and elsewhere. His father and mother had worked for Don Quiniones for as long as he could remember. Carlos had known no other life other than that of the Quiniones family and rancho for as long as he could remember. As soon as he was old enough, his father had allowed him to work at his side, assuming his formal studies were completed for the day. Not only with the bulls, but with all of the other livestock at the rancho. Later he was given a small stipend each week by the elder Quiniones, which proved to be that of a weekly allowance, given his age at the time. Carlos grew to have a certain affection for the elder Quiniones whereas his mother worked at the main house in the kitchen as his father served as his ranch foreman, having come from the Pamplona area of Northern Spain where the finest bulls were bred and raised. Once the elder Vega came onboard, the quality of the Elder Quiniones herd began to improve and within five years Pamplona was challenged by the Quiniones in Zaragoza as producing the finest bulls in the world.

Being the only son issuing forth from the loins of Don Quiniones and surrounded by sisters, Jose was pampered and spoiled from the moment he emerged from his mother's birth canal.

From the very moment of their first meeting Jose, being several years older and larger than Carlos, bullied him at every opportunity, during their formative years, turning him into his very own private 'Lickspittle'. As they grew into their teens, the inevitable class friction developed between both of them, both being prideful and a bit cocky, short of common sense. After several brief clashes between them when Carlos refused to turn the other cheek, Carlos was informed of the facts of life by his father, in a painful manner, which he adored. The family fortunes depended on the good will of the Quiniones family. The roof over their heads, the clothes on their backs, the shoes on their feet and the food in their bellies, all courtesy of the extensive largesse of the Quiniones family. Each and every one. From that very moment on Carlos made it a point to avoid any contact with Jose Quiniones. When Joselita came into his young life, Carlos began to dream and plan for a better life, than that experienced by his father and mother. He dreamed for a day when he would be beholding to no man when he would. He would endeavor to study harder, work more efficiently and towards the goal of never having to become subservient to another as his father and mother was. He would close his eyes and envision a marriage between him and Joselita in the Main Cathedral in Zaragoza. Make a good living, having and raising a slew of fine children, to maturity and have a good life together, growing old with grandchildren in abundance. For Joselita was his joy and inspiration, he would endure any privation, any pain for her, or so he thought. All good and proper reminisces to have, now destroyed in an instant. A grand illusion, that was never to be.

As he climbed, he came upon a small stream and took off all his clothes, examining every inch and after finding a few small blood splatters washed the spots off in the cool water of the stream, then washed himself and put his cloths back on, resuming his journey. From now on he would be constantly on the move towards the French frontier. He glanced at his watch which read two thirty in the morning. A half an hour later he came upon the roadway he'd been seeking.

Traffic was sparse this time of morning, but with luck he might catch a ride with a lorry on its way towards Barcelona, his goal being the French frontier as soon as possible. As he walked along the Strada, he thought, 'Never again will I see my family, my mother, my father'. Then he wondered what would be their fate, once the Guardia's investigation tried to join the pieces of the puzzle. Suddenly a chill swept over Carlos. The chill had nothing to do with the night air, but entirely to do with the elder Quiniones.

Once one was perceived an enemy of the family, whether right or wrong, Don Quiniones, would do anything, spend any amount, and go anywhere to wreak his vengeance. He'd longstanding personal contacts in the Guardia that would do his bidding. Should they somehow connect Carlos's disappearance, with the death of his son, things would no doubt go extremely hard on his parents. His upbringing by his parents and Holy Mother Church compelled him to recite the rosary repeatedly as he walked eastward on the side of the roadway.

After some minutes, he recalled the rosary had done nothing to prevent his current situation and he stopped the ritual. He wasn't exactly on speaking terms with the creator. As he walked, he felt abandoned and cast adrift. God was probably in some far away Galaxy light years away busy creating other worlds, or fighting the forces of evil, but he wasn't here.

After about twenty minutes of walking, Carlos could see a pair of headlights approaching. As the lights grew nearer, he could tell from a distance the lights belonged to a long distance freight Lorry. As it grew closer, Carlos stuck out his thumb in the classic manner of the hitch hiker. From a kilometer away, the Lorry's high beam illuminated Carlos as he back pedaled and he was relieved when the Lorry gradually slowed down, its massive air brakes hissing and snorting as the big Volvo diesel came to a stop fifty yards ahead of him.

Hauling himself up into the cab, he settled into cabs passenger seat as the driver, a burly set man, spoke in French, "Good evening traveler. Where are you going"? Responding in halting French, a language he'd just completed a year of study in, Carlos said, "Bon Jour, Mon Ami. Does this road take one to Barcelona"?

"That it does and beyond"! "Then that is where I'm headed"!

Shifting up through the gears, the lorry straining to regain its road speed as it climbed up a long hill, the driver remarked, "Merde', I've got to get to Marseilles by early afternoon, drop this load off, then trot over to the Elf refinery and pick up a load of petrol and go straight back to Lisbon this very day, without any time to eat or shit"!

"Seems unfair", said Carlos absently!

"But that's the way things work my friend. Life's unfair. The suits have fucked up their petrol consumption projections once again and are scurrying about like the fine little rats they are, dropping us long haul lorry drivers in the grease"!

The driver talked up a blue streak all the way into Barcelona, which Carlos occasionally chimed in with a comment, saying little in the process. As they approached the outskirts of Barcelona and a sign pointed to the roundabout that would carry lorry north along the Riviera the driver asked, "Have to drop you off soon Mon Ami, for the roundabout is about a kilometer away"!

"Could you take me as far as the French frontier", asked Carlos continuing, "I didn't think you'd be going any farther than Barcelona, but I really need to get to the French frontier.

The veteran driver, being a man of the world, quickly glanced at Carlos as if appraising him for the very first time, as the lorry slowed for its exit to the roundabout taking it around Barcelona and northward.

As the lorry driver found the right gear, the driver said, "The French frontier eh? And a bit beyond I'll wager, No"?

Carlos sheepishly nodded his head and responded "Yes, a bit beyond"!

For the next miles ahead both remained silent, then the roadway sign flashed by indicating, "Perpignan, 264 km". A half kilometer ahead the driver took the exit which carried them north towards the E-15 and the French Frontier. Clearly the driver without a word was taking Carlos towards his destiny and a new life as he said, "Too old to be a run away, so you must be on the run eh"?

Clearly Carlos was frozen in place, unable to speak, like a deer caught in the headlights. Another Kilometer ran by before the driver spoke again, "No matter son, put yourself at ease. I've been on the scatter a time or two myself over the years, for one thing or another".

As the sun began to peek above the eastern horizon, the driver glanced at the dashboards chronometer saying, "In about ninety minutes, I'm going to put into a rest stop about a kilometer from the French Frontier customs check point. Clearly you have no papers allowing cross transit. So I'll drop you off at the rest stop, go inside take a quick piss, grab some coffee and return. When I return you'll have disappeared. Are we in agreement"?

Carlos nodded his head saying "Yes and I'm grateful for your help"!

"Before I leave you, I'll draw you a small map indicating a path where you can work your way around the check point on foot if you're careful. It'll take a few hours to do and I'd wait for you on the other side, except my first loyalty is to my schedule, you understand. I suggest you keep on foot as much as possible, sleep during the day and travel during the evening. Follow the E-15 as much as possible and you'll be able to get by to whatever destination you're going. Avoid heavily populated areas. You're lucky for the Town of Perpignan is only a day's walk once you cross into France"!

The driver was silent again for several minutes as he again spoke, "Any idea where you're going"?

Again Carols nodded his head saying, "Yes, I've a destination in mind"! "Good, then keep it to yourself, for its none of my business"!

For several more kilometers the large Volvo diesel droned northward, its headlights piercing through the intermittent shrouds of early morning fog, blanketing the E-15 roadway. The audible singing of the massive tires, gave harmony to the droning of the diesel engine interrupted as the burly driver offered, "I've an idea for you to consider. You seem to speak French pretty good for a Spaniard. Can you write in French as well"?

"I've studied French and English in school and received high marks"!

"Then reach over into the glove box and remove the small pad of paper and the ball point pen. I'm going to dictate a note for you to write, to some very important people, who just might be of help to you"! Carlos did as he was asked as he readied the pen as the driver again asked, "Just a couple more things, before we do this. Are you in serious trouble"? "Yes, I think so"!

"The kind of trouble where you can never go home again"? "Uh, yes", answered Carlos haltingly!

"How tough do you think you are"?

"I really don't know, but I have heavy calluses on my hands and have used my fists and feet successfully"!

"Reach over here so I can feel your hands", said the driver, as Carlos complied, the driver felt of his hands with his eyes leaving the road and smiled. Carlos wondered what all the questions were about.

Part of him wanted to tell the driver to mind his own business, yet something told him the driver could be trusted, so he went with his instincts.

Carlos then added, "I really don't know how tough I am, but I've a feeling I'm going to find out"! The driver again smiled, thinking, 'Good, he doesn't answer too quickly. He's a thinker, careful and just maybe he'll do'.

"Then take the pen in hand and write exactly what I tell you in French", as he continued his dictation. As the driver's dictation slowly progressed, Carlos began to understand the reasons for the drivers concern. It started with the usual, "Two whom it may concern, and then identified the driver by a serial number and a series of dates of service, rank achieved and locations around the world, in the service of the French Foreign Legion. The main text recommended the bearer of this letter to be considered for service in the Legion. In the end he added a post script to a sergeant presumably still on active service with the Legion.

"Here boy, hand it over so I can sign it"! As the driver handed back the notepad, he said, "The Legions main recruitment center is in Arles, north of Marseilles. As of a year ago the Sergeant indicated on the post script used to work for me when I was a Legionnaire some time ago. I retired from the Legion after twenty plus years of service and the Sergeant knows me well, since we correspond from time to time"!

"Now you've a place to go if you're up to it. A place to disappear completely and emerge with a completely new identity, surrounded by a fraternity of men, all former thieves, robbers, spurned lovers, canards and usually men on the run like yourself. All with one thing in common. Either they are wanted by others or by no one. Should they measure up to the Legions standards, La Belle France will embrace them all into a fraternity of men"!

For the time left to them, the driver kept up a nonstop litany of what to expect if he kept on the run by himself, as opposed to immersing himself in the service of the Legion, a new name and identity, with the old falling off the face of the earth. French citizenship granted after completion of his first enlistment. He was told of what to expect and how to respond to orders, during his initial sixteen weeks of training and beyond.

"Yeah, it's a real ball breaker alright initially. The instructors are all brutes at first, relentless in their zeal to hone the blade, at least until you graduate from your basic course of instruction. Even afterward, depending on where you go to receive additional training, things sometimes don't get much better. But eventually things even out. As one demonstrates proficiency, then one slowly gains the respect of the old hands, the Sergeants that run things. The sooner this happens, the better off one is and you progress in rank and stature. Now you might ask yourself why it is so difficult. Why are they so brutish? Well they are brutish because they are supposed to be and because they can be.

Almost everyone is there because they have to be, there is no other alternative other than perhaps death or imprisonment, the Legion being their saving grace. Accepting the dregs of society and turning them into vintage Champaign more often than not. Remember this, discipline is to be imposed upon you initially to break your spirit and shed you of your old habits, replaced by new habits and a sense of worth.

This never happens easily. Like steel, that must be repeatedly thrust back into the fire and pounded into the desired shape, one goes in as raw iron and if one is successful emerges as steel"! "And this you have done", said Carlos!

"Twenty five years ago I was on the run, went to Marseilles and disappeared into the belly of the beast. Served all over the world, mostly in Africa though and retired five years ago. Met a Portuguese woman in Lyon, married her just six months short of my retirement. I have dual French and Portuguese citizenship, three little Nino's and a pension from the French Government. A nice house in Torres Vedras, north of Lisbon and a good living driving the company lorry. All thanks to my time and efforts as a Legionnaire. Once I was summoned to march with the Legion down the entire length of the Champs de Elyse, during Bastille Day years ago with my unit, years ago. A grand memory. One could do much worse"!

As the weather started to clear and the fog now a memory the driver gave Carlos a brief glance and saw that his message had struck home. The boy had nowhere to go and if he had the juice, if he could endure what lay ahead, the Legion would be the right ticket for him.

If not, then it was only a matter of time before the exigencies of life, chewed him up and spit him out as it had many others.

For the next few minutes he dictated the exact directions as to the Legions headquarters in Arles. When finished he said to Carlos, "Keep the note pad and the pen on you, I have others, as the Volvo lorry began to ascend up a grade, the driver shifting into a lower gear to maintain his momentum, the diesels supercharger springing to life as the lorry worked its way up one side of the Pyrenees's having just passed through the town of Gerona.

"Look at it this way boy. As you trudge your way north, Hannibal and his Legions, came this very same way some two thousand years ago. We should be at the rest stop in the next half hour, so why don't you try and get a bit of shut eye, for you've a long journey ahead of you. I'll wake you up as we approach your rest stop"!

Carlos nodded his head and looked out of the passengers window, the passing landscape, now brightly visible as his eyes slowly closed, signaling the arrival of a new day.

"Drop your cock and grab your socks", bellowed the driver, emphasizing it with a blast of the Volvos klaxon horns. Carlos quickly bolted upright and rubbed his eyes, just in time to see the lorry exiting the E-15 and onto the rest area with a slew of other lorry's in for food, a quick relief and some petrol. Pulling the lorry to a stop in a designated area, the driver turned off his engine, removed the keys from the ignition and turned to Carlos saying, "Well my young friend it's time we parted company and I wish you well in all that you do, but remember when I return to this cab you will be somewhere else"!

Then as an afterthought he said, "Remember this one thing above all else, the discipline you receive from the Legion, should you choose that path, is nothing compared to the self-imposed discipline you must always impose that comes from within. Vaya con Dios my son"! Then he turned, opened the cab door, jumped to the ground, closing the door and walked away without a backward glance.

After the driver disappeared, Carlos left the cab and walked across the roadway and into a small bakery. He purchased a small bag of fresh croissants and a cup of coffee, finding a window seat and sat down, where he could observe everything coming and going. He had not eaten anything since noon the previous day. Minutes later a newspaper vendor came into the shop and Carlos purchased a copy of the areas paper, He scanned the paper to see if any mention of the previous evenings activities were mentioned. Finding nothing, he concluded that it was still early days, as he'd expected. Then he looked up just in time to see the lorry driver that had proven a life saver and partial mentor, approach his Volvo laden with his breakfast that he'd consume as he drove, climb into the cab, fire up the big diesel and slowly pull away. As the lorry climbed through the gears disappearing from sight, Carlos realized he was truly at the crossroads of his young life. Having acted stupidly and impetuously, he'd ended two lives unnecessarily and placed his family in jeopardy. He tried to feel some semblance of remorse for the deaths of Joselita and her lover Jose, but couldn't.

He was surprisingly calm. Two lived ended in less than a minute.

One on purpose and the other by accident. The lorry long gone and the deaths behind him, his youth had ended and the chapter regarding his manhood was just beginning. He spent the next few minutes slathering butter and marmalade on the freshly baked croissants, savoring every bite. Then finishing his coffee he rose and left the bakery walking along the roadway until he spotted a path that took him away from the roadway, some hundred yards or so just as the driver had indicated. It then straightened out and paralleled the roadway for as far as he could see, hidden from view by an endless series of trees and bushes.

As he pressed on at a steady pace, the rising sun on his right indicating his northerly direction, Carlos recalled a message from the bible, the Jesuit priests had drummed into his head. Something to the effect, that in every man's life comes a time when he has to leave his childhood behind and cease doing childish things and as a man start doing manly things. He recalled talking about that very thing with his father one evening several years ago, while they both tended to Don Quiniones prize bulls. His father explaining at some length, the concepts of, responsibility, loyalty, the obligations to one's family, dedication to a task, or goal, the bond of affection one had towards his loved ones and how they all blended together. He wished he'd now paid greater attention, to what was said. If so, perhaps he'd not be in the fix he was currently in. He was grateful that his father was a patient teacher, for it was Carlos that had little patience or tolerance. Something he vowed to develop in the coming days.

He wished he'd taken the time to discuss the situation with Joselita with his father, rather than, insulate himself from embarrassment thinking foolishly that he could resolve things himself. His father would've given wise counsel and direction. His heart would have been shattered, but in time that would've healed. Instead, he was on the run and his family's fortunes were certain to experience eventual reversal. Once again as he trudged northward, he silently broke in to the familiar mantra of the Holy Rosary, almost without knowing. His way of summoning assistance in his time of need except he pleaded with the almighty to shield his family from any results coming from his actions in the coming days.

Later he recalled reading the novel Les Miserables in school, the saga of a police inspectors dogged determination in tracking down Jean Val jean during the post Napoleonic era, over something rather trivial.

'Well I'm guilty of murder, plain and simple', thought Carlos. He was certain that he'd never find peace in his heart. He resolved to harden his heart in all things pertaining to man and women and in all things act as a man, never allowing a woman's actions to summon the inopportune response. He must survive. For what purpose was unclear, yet he must survive and eventually prosper.

Putting one foot ahead of the other, trudging along the seldom used pathway he thought, 'Marseilles that is where I must go. The school of my youth is now out of session. Welcome to the real world'.

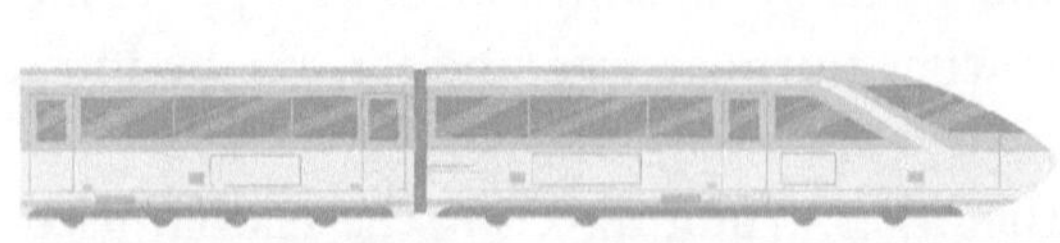

12

While Carlos was working his way across the French frontier, Joselita's mother had gone to her bedroom to awaken her. The family was downstairs and she had missed breakfast. Seeing that she was not there and her bed lay undisturbed, she summoned her husband, the banker 'Pregoso' who was just leaving for the office.

After personally inspecting his daughter's room with his wife, Don Pregoso quickly summoned the entire family and servants for an intensive inquiry. A quick assessment of her known friends was made, with the appropriate phone calls to them all as to her whereabouts.

When the last of her known friends had no information to give, panic began to set in, with her mother collapsing in a heap. While the family retainers tended to his wife, the father made a decision to call his friend at the local headquarters of the 'Guardia Civil', Teniente' Cardoso.

An hour later as Teniente Cardoso, arrived at the Pregoso home, located in the deeply affluent suburbs of Zaragoza, yet another cursory inspection of the premises revealed nothing out of the ordinary. Yet another cursory interrogation of the Pregoso household staff, revealed nothing not already known, which nothing was. He then took down all of the names and information of Joselita's friends, acquaintances and teachers at her school promising to quickly interview each and every one, complaining that the Don's request that the investigation was to be conducted in complete secrecy in respect for the family's station.

"But Senor Pregoso", pleaded Cardoso, "With the deepest respect, time is of the essence here. Should she be kidnapped and held for ransom, or be laying wounded in some dark place, every moment we waste in secrecy may be important to her survival. To do a thorough investigation I will need to bring in additional people to assist"!

"Teniente', I will not allow my misfortune to be grist amongst the little people once the press catch wind of her absence. The family's reputation must be protected at all costs and that is my final word sir", blustered the banker!

"As you wish Senor. I will work diligently and through the day and night to get to the bottom of this. But I must tell you that if the newspapers ever discover this, it will be front page headlines, then my superiors will over rule me and others will be brought in"!

"Just you see to it that everything is kept, under the tongue Teniente. I expect this investigation will receive your undivided attention"!

When he returned to his office, he was given a message to call Don Quiniones immediately upon his return. Upon their connection, he apologized for the tardiness of his call, explaining that he was called away for another investigation. The rancher quickly explained that his son, Jose, just recently returned from his studies at the University in Madrid, was missing and had not slept in his bed. The Teniente' said that he'd immediately leave the office and to expect him shortly. The call concluded, he rushed out of the station to his official car and drove to the Quiniones rancho, past the city limits. As he drove, his mind was wondering about the confluence of events. Both residences were but a fifteen minute drive from each other and a young man and a young woman, both being high spirited and of the same class, somehow had probably sown some wild oats and would come wandering in later on in the day with some cock and bull story, and a lot of explaining to do. Either that or perhaps they'd eloped and gotten married by some secular magistrate. He immediately eliminated the latter theory as being so unlikely given the status of both families in the local society and staunchly Catholic.

Upon his arrival, he immediately performed the requisite inspection of the premises along with the entire family and staff, with the exception of the Vega family. Senor Vega was in the far northern reaches of the ranch along with the rancho's veterinarian tending to several bulls, while his wife was at the market purchasing victuals for the family's dining. No mention was made of their son Carlos, for it slipped everyone's minds.

As the entire family was assembled Teniente' Cardoso said, "An interesting thing has occurred this morning. I was at the residence of the banker Pregoso and their eldest daughter was also missing during the night. They have held me to the promise of the strictest secrecy, yet I tell you this because I'm not a great believer in coincidences. With your permission Don Quiniones, I'm going to summon them to join us here immediately so perhaps we may get to the bottom of this. I'm also going to summon my superior Capitan Garza to join us; Of course I'm assuming that just like the Pregoso family you'll want this investigation to be conducted discretely as possible Senor"!

The elder Quiniones nodded his head, as Cardoso made for the nearest phone asking the family to make a list of Jose's friends so he could quickly contact them while they waited for the others.

Upon his arrival an hour and a half later Capitan Garza was shown into the large Quiniones family study and was greeted by the sounds of argument between them as Cardoso was valiantly trying to bring peace between them and losing the battle as both families shouted at each other one blaming the other, both jumping to unfounded conclusions. As he stood at the entrance, both families gradually took notice and the argument subsided. As he entered the study, Garza was met but polite yet constrained greetings, the air thick with incriminations.

"Have you discovered anything yet Capitan", asked Pregoso angrily? "Don Pregoso, I've just arrived. You're in the very capable hands of Teniente Cardoso, yet I understand you've placed certain constraints upon him"!

"Teniente' Cardoso, tell me what you've learned thus far"!

What was discovered recently from one of Jose's friends was of recent secret liaisons between Jose Quiniones and Joselita Pregoso without the benefit of chaperone. This had been going on for several weeks upon his return from Madrid. There was talk of marriage between the two and most probably an elopement. Both parents of course were completely ignorant of these developments. Had they known of the interest between the two children, both would've immediately approved the union.

For the next two hours, the Guardia Capitan one by one, carefully brought forth all of the brothers and sisters of both families, this time going over the same ground previously examined by his subordinate earlier, yet this time he burrowed into each of them not too gently, bringing protestations from both family elders.

"May I respectfully remind both of you that this is now an affair of the Guardia Civil, which the both of you have summoned us to perform. I will get to the truth no matter where it may lead. Regardless of your political connections, I will not condone one iota of interference in the conduct of this investigation. Plainly spoken, you will all submit to my governmental authority immediately without another word, or you will be arrested for interference in governmental affairs"!

The very last family member to be interrogated was the youngest daughter of the Pregoso family. As Garza burrowed into her, he sensed she was holding something back, as she finally broke down crying. She indicated that she was snooping through her older sisters belongings about a month ago, finding a pregnancy test that was positive. As she read the report she was discovered by her sister she was sworn to secrecy upon the pain of eternal damnation.

"And how far along was she my child", asked Garza? "About a month I think", quivered the sibling!

"But it couldn't have been Jose", interrupted Don Quiniones. "He was in Madrid attending to his studies a month ago"!

"Was it a doctor's report my child" asked Garza? "Yes Capitan"!

"Then after we're through here, we will return to the Pregoso residence and try and recover that report and determine the doctor involved then talk to the doctor tomorrow. But that doesn't help us find her at this moment"!

Just then Senora Vega returned from her shopping as well as her husband from his work on the rancho and entered the room. As they entered the room they were greeted by Don Quiniones who introduced them to the Guardia commander who then explained why everyone was assembled.

"Senor Garza can you be of any assistance to us", asked Garza?

"Jose missing? The daughter of the Pregoso family missing? Why? How? Just then his wife said, "Our son Carlos wasn't there for breakfast this morning and I'm worried too. He's always at breakfast. Before I left this morning I checked his bedroom and he slept in the bed, he never makes the bed and I was too busy to make up his bed. When I returned I went to see if Carlos had returned, so I could prepare supper. He still hasn't returned"!

"And Senor Vega, where have you been for the last twenty four hours", asked Garza.

"Since noon yesterday, with Don Quiniones veterinarian helping cure his bulls. We worked all night and all day today"!

"Before I leave I will be furnished contact information and the name of the ranches veterinarian. Please everyone stay here upon my return. Senora Vega take me to your sons quarters"!

A half hour later Garza and the mother returned as he reported, "As she indicated, her son's bed shows signs of having been slept in, unlike that of either of your children. Senor Pregoso you will accompany me back to your home, so I can retrieve your daughter's doctor's report. I warn everyone not to enter either of the bedrooms for tomorrow I will return with several trusted officers and we will examine all three bedrooms. Consider them as potential crime scenes. In the interim should any or all of them return you will contact either me or Teniente Cardoso personally, so we can minimize this whole affair, in the mean time I intend to quietly issue an all-points bulletin for our officers on all three of your children"!

Not accustomed to be spoken to in the way that Garza had, Don Quiniones addressed Garza saying, "And that is it for the evening. You will simply depart and wait until morning? If both of you wish to remain in your posts, I insist you do what you can throughout the rest of the day and far into the night to find my son"! "And my daughter also", claimed the elder Pregoso"!

"Senor's", said Garza, the day is far from over and we do intend to work far into the night regardless of what you think"!

"Garza, I am not satisfied with your response", said Quiniones in anger. I'm going to call your Commandante"

"As you wish Senor Quiniones, but you will find discover that the Commandante' is in is in Lisbon for an Interpol conference for the rest of the week and has left instructions not to be disturbed during the conference for any reason"! With that, he summoned the Pregoso family and departed.

Discovery of Joselita's doctor's report that she was a month pregnant as of the writing of that report two weeks ago added some flesh to the evidence of their affair together. But just where did the missing son of the Quiniones ranch foremen enter into things? Was he part if this, or was it random coincidence? As drove back to headquarters Garza knew what no one but he knew. True enough the Commandante' was in Lisbon attending the Interpol Conference. But should Senor Quiniones decide to contact his superior, the Provincial Governor, he would also discover that he too was unavailable, supposedly attending a conference somewhere on the continent, but in reality having a week's dalliance with his Parisian mistress, somewhere in the Swiss Alps. All the while his young thirty five year old wife was not really in Deauville visiting her parents, but ensconced at the Hotel Metropol, in Lisbon exchanging bodily fluids with the Commandante'. He'd met the woman and she was striking to say the least, which made one wonder why a successful politician, married to a much younger woman of significant beauty and prominence, found it necessary to carry around the baggage of a mistress?

Of course he could carry on without Commandante' Reyna and wait until his return and then inform him of the missing people. Should he contact the Commandante' and make him aware of the sad turn of events and particularly whom was involved, against his explicit orders not to be disturbed for any reason, he risked his mercurial wrath. As he got out of the car, he reached into his pocket and extracted a coin, flipping it in the air. As it landed in his palm, he saw his decision before him. Early in the morning he would contact the Commandante' and make him aware of developments. Might as well allow him one additional night of bliss, for it just might take the edge off his anger.

Early the following morning he hung up the phone after his contacting Reyna, who thanked him for informing him of the events at hand. He then informed him that he would be in his office the following day to take full command of the investigation. After all politics being what it was it was a good thing to cover ones superiors hind side, especially when dealing with people of prominence. During the interim, Capitan Garza had initiated several teams of detectives, to re interview, each of the family members including the Vega's and all of their employees. No ransom notes arrived and no letters were written, in the aftermath. At days end nothing of additional value was achieved. No leads as to any of their whereabouts and no one was talking. The following day when the Commandante' returned, the entire morning was spent going over the testimony of everyone interviewed. "You say, the Doctor that examined Pregoso's daughter Joselita, indicated that she was over a month pregnant and that she had just recently gotten involved with Quiniones son Jose not two weeks ago"?

"Si Commandante", said Garza?

"Then clearly someone else is involved in this affair! Return to the doctor and reexamine him and review his records regarding the daughter.

Bring him with you to the Quiniones rancho within the hour along with the entire Pregoso household where ever they may be. I will be there to personally take charge of this investigation", bellowed Commandante' Reyna!

By early afternoon Reyna and everyone else was gathered in the Quinones household as he took the lead, as he'd seen innumerable times in the television detective programs convinced in his bones, the guilty was in this very room. Yet as every question brought him back to the same place, he along with everyone else began to get frustrated with his questioning. All the while the Vega family remained silent, yet feeling all of the frustration everyone else was. For their son was also among the missing and no one seemed to question or care. Yet it wasn't their place being that they were mere employees.

"I will require the most recent pictures of each family of the missing in my office by tomorrow morning", said Reyna. This will have to become public knowledge. The media will have to become involved to help us. It is the only way"!

"I will commence a mobilization of my resources to conduct a province wide search for your children and heaven help us all if we discover them, laid up in a hotel somewhere doing what comes naturally to the young and foolish"! With that Reyna grabbed his hat gave a salute and summoned his men to leave.

The following evening the newspapers had a front page story regarding all of the missing family members, as well as the local television news casts and the radio. The entire province was cordoned off as various elements of the local militia and concerned citizens joined in along with police K-9 dog units. Various elements of the local underworld were caught unawares by the Guardia's intensive efforts as large quantities of illegal drugs; weapons and contraband were discovered at the various Guardia checkpoints. Various homes and businesses were entered and searched at will as the numbers of leads flooded the Guardia's headquarters, as a result of the media's announcement of a large cash reward.

Public areas were posted with fliers regarding the disappearance without a trace of the three individuals involved. Yet after the first week of intense round the clock searches, the jails were full to bursting from all of the criminals caught by sheer happenstance and not one lead panned out as to any of the trio's whereabouts. The authorities were in a quandary, for the national media had caught wind of the disappearance and by now everyone on the Iberian Peninsula was aware. Three young people had disappeared. No evidence of foul play was discovered. No note of ransom has appeared, ruling out eventual kidnapping.

Towards the end of the second week, as activities began to wind down, a gradual picture began to emerge as several people, reluctant and not wanting to get involved, were shown pictures of the trio and faintly recalled seeing two young people, generally fitting the pictures shown to them of Joselita and Jose, walking hand in hand in the general direction of the wooded area in the northern section of the city. They were taken to Guardia headquarters and repeatedly examined by Cardoso and Garza until the time and approximate date of the sighting was agreed upon.

Both family members and retainers were again brought to Guardia headquarters and repeatedly questioned with increased intensity and it was discovered that no one had seen Carlos Vega since the evening of their joint disappearance along with the other two. The two Vega parents were brought in for additional questioning, and could add little to what was already known except to verify that prior to his disappearance Carlos, for some unknown reason was apparently out of sorts and appeared dejected somehow. He clearly was not his usual cheerful self, which was verified by his parents.

Yet without a shred of proof and operating on instinct, the authorities gradually came to the conclusion that the coincidence of Carlos's disappearance coinciding with that of the others was too great to ignore. "There is a weak link somewhere" said Capitan Garza, "and I think I know where it is"! "Then speak your mind at once Garza", said Reyna!

"The daughter of Pregoso that revealed her sisters pregnancy. I feel she is holding back something else"! "What do you think it may be", asked Reyna?

"She's the younger daughter and it appeared to me some element of sibling jealousy might be involved. Clearly she's a snoop and has admitted to searching through her sisters belongings. We are fairly certain someone else was involved with Joselita, someone who got her pregnant. But who"? Garza stopped moment thinking, and then was bidden to continue by Reyna.

"We know that the young Vega was clearly out of sorts, for several weeks prior to his disappearance. Than much was verified by his parents.

So the only logical conclusion is somehow a lovers triangle is in the offing"!

"But where's the proof", asked Reyna?

"This may be nothing, Commandante', but in talking with the all of the family retainers a picture of Carlos and Jose emerges. Although no one will say this, Jose Quiniones, son of a prominent and wealthy rancher was a spoiled bully. He clearly had his way with Vegas son as they grew to maturity, yet the Vegas had to remain silent given their circumstances of employment with Don Quiniones, over the years. Carlos, rather than fight Jose, is counseled to avoid him at every opportunity. To complain would fall on deaf ears anyway. Jose goes off to college for the next two years in Madrid and is seldom seen at the rancho. Now everyone says that Carlos was a hard working studious young man and probably destined for a University somewhere. Plus he was well regarded by everyone"! Then Garza stopped to gather his thoughts, as Reyna said, "Continue Garza, please"!

"What if that other someone was Carlos Vega? What if he somehow made Joselita's acquaintance and they became lovers? What if he was spurned by Joselita? After all she is quite a looker? I should have seen this before. Then after I recalled talking to the retainers at the Quiniones rancho and later the Vegas, I recalled my youth when I was smitten beyond reason with this young girl. We were each other's very first encounters. She gave me her virginity, then months later met someone else dropped me like a hot rock. Took me months to recover and what made things worse was every so often I would encounter them walking arm in arm like young lovers do and she would glance over her shoulders and give me this, 'Eat your heart out', look. This would drive me into a silent rage every time she did this, the Puta"!

"Well what did you do", asked Reyna?

"What could I do? The other one was a football player and much larger than me. He would have beaten me to a pulp. All I could do was stick my tail between my legs"!

"So what became of them", asked Reyna his interest piqued by his subordinates revealing admission?

"He got her pregnant and abandoned her". He eventually went to Mexico and became a football star. As for her, who knows? All I know is that I'm better off"!

"So Garza you think that Carlos Vega was the other lover"? "Commandante'. Place yourself in the shoes of Carlos Vega. A hard working young man smitten with Joselita. Capable of University admission. He's in love with the daughter of a wealthy banker. A leg up is all he needs. Of course this will never be. She becomes pregnant with his child. Serendipity brings her together with Jose Quiniones, a suitable match and if she corralled him quickly enough; they can elope somewhere and return as man and wife. It's been done before. Then her problem is solved more or less. Of course there are those that will count the months of gestation, but the announcement of a premature birth can easily explain that away and her initial problem is solved as to her sanctity"!

"For the short term perhaps Garza, but if Jose Quiniones is as you say then perhaps her long range problems would have just begun. It makes sense Garza, so bring the other Pregoso daughter in and let's see what develops. For there is nothing else. Still doesn't tell us where any of them are but perhaps we'll get lucky"!

The following day the Pregoso's younger daughter was brought into the Guardia's headquarters by her parents, this time accompanied by the family lawyer. Within the space of a half an hour she caved in admitting to knowledge of a long affair with Carlos Vega. Of course Joselita didn't know of this, since all the younger daughters knowledge was gleaned by her incessant snooping. Even to the point of following her sister to several of their rendezvous locations.

Immediately Reyna formed a small task force and escorted the daughter who showed them two of the locations of their meetings, none of which were the grotto up in the hills. A K-9 unit accompanied them yet to no avail and a full search of the location revealed nothing useful. The Vega family was again summoned to the Guardia's headquarters and was confronted by the news of their son's long standing affair with Joselita Pregoso. Of course they were shocked by the news since they had no knowledge of the affair, as his mother whispered absently, "So that's what the matter with him was"!

In the next room was the Quiniones and Pregoso family observing their response through the one way mirror, as the Vegas felt the cloud of doom close in upon them. Normally anyone questioned by Capitan Garza would experience a very difficult time in his presence. Falling to the floor was common place at the very least, but since the eyes of both families and lawyers as well as his boss and the provincial prosecutor were all upon him he continued his interrogation on the Vegas limiting his repertoire to verbal shouts only.

Commander Reyna then turned to both families and related what they suspected. "We know and can probably prove that Carlos Vega and Joselita Pregoso were lovers for some time and that from time to time she stole away in the dead of night for their rendezvous in several locations. We know where two of them are. We suspect that she became pregnant by someone other than Jose Quiniones and are reasonably certain that someone was Carlos Vega. How they initially met is unknown as of the moment. We can infer that Joselita most likely broke off her relationship with her lover for the obvious reasons. He was Basque to begin with and not at all suitable for the daughter of a prominent banker. Prior to that she meets Jose Quiniones somewhere and sets her cap for him. He's a good looking young man and from a suitable family and should all go well, she can quickly marry him and her little secret will remain under the tongue. Further we suspect that young Carlos was greatly heart broken by Joselita's action. What he did about it we don't know. Whether he had anything to do with their disappearance is unknown. Where any of them are is still unknown, in spite of all our collective efforts. The only thing that can be done is have the remaining Pregoso daughter and both Vegas parents undergo polygraph testing to verify what they've thus far said to us. I'm fairly certain the two Vega's will agree, yet Senor Pregoso, since your daughter is legally a minor, you will have to give your permission to us as your lawyer and the provincial prosecutor will attest. Are we all in agreement"? The elder Pregoso looked at his lawyer who nodded and then at Don Quiniones whose face remained expressionless then said, "Prepare whatever you need to and I'll approve it"!

As the long afternoon wound to a close, the polygraph examiner brought in all of his papers into the room saying, "The Pregoso daughter knows nothing more and has told you everything. As for the Vega family, I'm convinced of several things. First they had no knowledge of any of their son's private activities and were completely unaware of the existence of Joselita Pregoso until recent events took hold. Next they cherish their service to the Quiniones family and business and are saddened and embarrassed by the recent turn of affairs. They appear to be simple hard working and loyal Christian people, who are sincere in their humility. I rarely say this, but they are completely innocent of any complicity in this affair. I believe them to be not culpable in any of this and their individual responses to my questions will bear this out, empirically"!

The elder Quiniones stood up and summoned Commandante' Reyna to join him at the one way mirror that separated the soundproof observation room from the interrogation room where both Vega parents sat huddled in a corner in apparent prayer. "Look at them", said Don Quiniones. "Surely they know something. Anything about my son's disappearance"!

"Senor. I understand your anguish, but all evidence indicates to the contrary", said Reyna! "Well over a week my son has been gone and all we have is nothing? This I cannot accept", he raged then stormed out of the room without another word.

Reyna then turned and looked at the Prosecutor, then at Capitan Garza and said "Release the child to the Pregoso family and release the Vega's. They're all free to go. These cases is still open and active but as of now let's all go home and pray. Tomorrow we will renew our efforts"! After everyone had left Reyna turned to Garza and Cardoso saying, "How well do the both of you know Senor Quiniones"?

Cardoso replied, "Well enough to not want to be a member of the Vega family"!

Two days later Teniente' Cardoso came rushing into his bosses office and said, "We've a break in the case of the disappeared lovers, Quiniones and Pregoso"!

"How so Cardoso", asked Garza glancing up from his paperwork? "Apparently a vagrant trying to find shelter from the rain up in the hills, stumbled upon a cave and in the cave he claimed were two dead bodies. He spent the night in the small cave, then came down into town on a mission of begging, then when he was chased away by one of our local Guardia he said something about the two bodies in the cave, pointed out the location then ran away. The Guardia investigates, knowing of the two missing people and there they are. He came back down and called it in. We have people on the way to the location and I think we should join them"!

An hour later Cardoso, Garza and Commandante' Reyna, made their way into the grotto and saw what two weeks decomposition could do to the dead, their bodies bloated with the gaseous buildup of a decomposing corpse and stiffened by rigor mortis.

"Look at this Commandante", said Cardoso! "His is missing his male member. It's been cleanly severed from his body"!

"We've already searched the entire cave and the surrounding area Teniente' and have found nothing", said the Sergeant attending!

"Something a jilted lover might do", said Garza! "Come over here Commandante", said Cardoso, pointing to the corpse of Joselita, barely recognizable in her bloated state.

"One knife wound near the heart. Apparently she bled out, by the pool of dried blood underneath her body, yet she is clothed with little sign of blood on her clothes"!

"Look at the male victim", said Garza. "There he laid, his pants around his ankles, his member missing and there she is dressed to a degree, with little sign of blood. They were discovered 'Flagrante Delicto'. He is stabbed, she is stabbed, they both bleed out together then she is dressed. Gentlemen what does that tell us"?

"Carlos Vega", answered Cardoso and Reyna together. "There was testimony that he was as good with a flick knife as his father and as everyone knows, Basques are good with knives and Carlos was known to keep a keen edge on his blade at all times", offered Cardoso!

"That's it then. Have the body bags arrived", asked Reyna? "Si Commandante", said one of the Sergeants!

"Then get them in here and to the morgue for autopsy, when the bodies have departed, bring additional lights in and scour the cave for everything and anything. Not a word of our discovery to anyone and I mean anyone, until the autopsy is completed and we have the official cause of death"!

As they all walked down the path from the grotto after the others carrying the bloated cadavers in the body bags, Garza said, "It could've been worse"!

"Worse you say Garza", asked Reyna? "How much worse than that could it be"?

"With respect Commandante. At least the carrion miraculously had not gotten to them. Neither of them have been chewed on by the birds or the foxes. A skilled mortician can insure the probability of an open casket funeral. Although I wouldn't suggest it. Commandante', I would suggest we say nothing regarding the missing member from Jose Quiniones body, to his father for the time being. He's at the point of rage. Should we capture Carlos Vega, then it would be more appropriate"!

"Point well taken Garza", said Reyna wondering what he would say to the elder Quiniones tomorrow. "In the meantime, issue an all-points bulletin to the Guardia Nationale' to apprehend Carlos Vega for the murder of the Quiniones and Pregoso children. For the moment that is all we can do"!

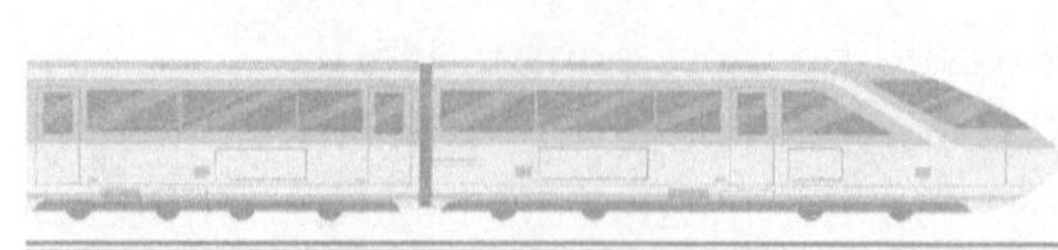

13

The entire Quiniones rancho had been in a foul mood, for the last several weeks ever since the disappearance of Jose. Not so much as for affection for the Quiniones eldest child and heir to the family estate by birthright. It was that the elder Quiniones during the interim, inserted himself personally in every aspect of the ranch, mostly to keep his mind busy, but in doing so disrupted the normal ebb and flow of daily business. No one dared tell a joke, much less laugh at anything lest the Don be close at hand and take it as a sign of disrespect. If the Quiniones family was going through their misery, then all of the family retainers would suffer as well. Such was the understood price of their periodic wage.

Appolonia Vega tended to her duties each day at the main house, much as she always had for years, talking little and exhibiting even a greater than normal attitude of humility. She could grieve for her son at the conclusion of each day's work. Her husband Motale' was only slightly more fortunate, whereas he was usually in one of the barns, or in a corral, or out in the fields tending to his Jefe's affairs which were his livestock. On two occasions, the elder Quiniones joined him making the rounds. Their normal level of communication descended to simple monosyllabic utterances. Motale' spoke only when spoken to not initiating any conversation, as if a cloud of guilt surrounded him for some reason.

The matriarch of the family, usually a rather cheery woman, grew appropriately emotional, regardless of her present company, drifting into prolonged bouts of despair, attended to by the family priest, friends and the family doctor.

Two days after the discovery of the misbegotten lovers, the final verdict of the autopsy was in. Pregnancy in the first trimester and murder of both parties by the same weapon. As Guardia Commander was reading the final draft of the autopsy report with the Provincial prosecutor, Capitan Garza burst into the office with the morning newspaper in his hand saying, "The fats in the fire now gentlemen. Someone leaked the news of the discovery of the bodies to the newspapers, before we had a chance to notify the families of the deceased. The Quiniones and Pregoso families will be outraged"!

Everyone in that room knew what that meant. Everyone in that room held their job as a function of patronage, not merit. That was the way things were done. The way things always had been done. One did the bidding of one's betters. One paid strict attention to tradition and custom. The so called 'rule of law', was for the common people, to keep the masses in line. One phone call from someone as influential as Quiniones, an old line Hidalgo, to his friend the Provincial Governor, could ruin careers in a host of ways.

"Quiniones will complain that we should've notified him of our discovery at the very instant we knew", said a concerned Garza!

"Police policy and procedure will shield us from any untoward criticism", mused Reyna! "Were we so unfeeling as to allow the grieving to witness their loved ones in such a bloated state? Of course not! You will immediately contact both families and tell them of our discovery and ask them to meet us at the Morgue for identification. That accomplished with all the dignity we could muster, we can then release the bodies to them for burial"!

Upon hearing of the formal death of her son, Quiniones wife fainted dead away. As she was being attended to by her family physician he noticed something strange and ordered that she be sent to the hospital immediately. It was later discovered that she had suffered a stroke of undetermined severity, as everyone surmised was because of her family ordeal.

The Pregoso family didn't fare much better at the news of their daughter's death.

Both parents casting blame on their youngest daughter for not revealing to them what Joselita was involved with, so all of this could've been avoided. Whereas Joselita was a strong willed young woman, her younger sister had none of her qualities, succumbing to the sense of personal guilt and familial ostracism the day of her sister's funeral. As the limousine carrying the family back home after the services, was passing through the center of Zaragoza, she flung open the rear door and leapt to her death in front of another vehicle, without a word.

The Quiniones family buried their son without his mother in attendance, for she had slipped into a coma as a result of her stroke. Some said it was because she'd lost her desire to continue in this world, as her devotion to her son above all others was well known to all that knew the family. Of all of the friends, family and family retainers that attended the Quiniones funeral, Motale' and Appolonia Vega were not invited to attend or even pay their respects. Yet both still continued at the ranch and household as before, grieving for their son Carlos in silence.

As the other Quiniones retainers worked about the ranch, they gossiped in hushed tones, uncomfortable with the atmosphere of never ending gloom that seemed to persist every single day, without abatement. In one thing they were in agreement. At least the Quiniones and Pregoso families, suffering as they were in the face of tragedy, had most of that behind them, but the Vega family was another matter. Their only son missing and the chief suspect in the murder of both young people, while his parents still worked for the family that all agreed suffered at the hands of their son. Don Quiniones refused to speak to Motale' or Appolonia, relegating any and all communication between them to others, even if they were but scant feet away. Many said at the time, that if it wasn't for the fact that Don Quiniones father made the Don, promise on his death bed, lifelong employment for Motale' and his family and for the fact that in all Spain no one could match his skills in producing prize winning champion bulls for the worlds corridas, the Vega family would vanish tomorrow.

For over four decades, Motale' Vega had served the Quiniones family, ever since the day the grandfather visited Pamplona to purchase some prize bulls and took an interest in a nine year old parentless street urchin, and brought him back to Zaragoza to help work the bulls.

Motale' in time learned to read, write and cipher well enough under the tutelage of the grandmother. Although he slept in the bunk house with the others, he was included in all of the family's activities almost as an auxiliary family member. Years later, now as a full grown man, assuming increased responsibility and duty's at the ranch, he was introduced to Appolonia and it was love at first sight between them. Of course the Quiniones took care of the wedding, a modest affair, and Appolonia, was welcomed into the fold, and given duties in the family kitchen. She as well as Motale' worked ten to twelve hour days, six days a week or until they were given permission to leave for the day. They both lived in a small cottage some distance from the main house. Both had a roof over their head and never wanted for a meal, along with the monthly stipend, or wage commensurate with their status. When they were ill, all medical expenses were taken care of.

As the grandparents passed from existence and the status of Motale' and Appolonia became a fixture of the family retinue, so did their status in the family as Appolonia, in addition to her kitchen duties helped raise each of the next generation of Quiniones as soon as they came into the world, with the same care as if they were her own. Her husband Motale' by now had worked long and hard in helping the Quiniones family develop the finest herd of cattle and horses second to none on the entire Iberian peninsula. His bulls were valued above all as the finest in the land. All had acknowledged that Motale' was an invaluable resource in advancing the family fortunes. By the time Carlos was born Motale' was given complete charge of the ranch operations, regarding the buying, raising and selling of all livestock and providing a meticulous accounting of all transactions. He had no enemies and was respected by all.

Yet in the aftermath of the murders, all that had gone before was apparently forgotten. No one in the family directly communicated with Appolonia or Motale' as they performed their daily tasks.

While the relationship with the current masters of the Quiniones family was not as they were for their father and mother before they passed away, they were always polite and cordial. But to see the look distaste on the face of the family Patron and Patrona, whenever their name was mentioned, indicated that all was on the downward slope.

Neither Motale' nor Appolonia could get their arms around the fact that their son was a murderer. There had to be a rational explanation for this. Of course there had been ill feelings between Carlos and Jose, subject to his incessant bullying, but Carlos was instructed to always turn the other cheek whenever possible and avoid Jose at all costs. As far as they knew, Carlos had done just that. For that was their place. Their fortunes were tied inextricably to that of the Quiniones. After all, hard work and obedience to the Quiniones masters had provided for the Vegas well enough over the years. For they wanted for nothing and were grateful for their lot in life. Motale' Vega never gave it one moment of thought of leaving the service of the Quiniones. He had little sense of his worth regarding the possibility of working for anyone else. Had he made a few discrete inquiries, he would have discovered his true worth. Then one day all of it went away.

The elder Quiniones gradually began having problems with insomnia. With his wife hospitalized and his increasing irrationality in all things becoming a problem, his doctor proscribed sleeping pills to help him get his allotted rest. At first this worked well enough until the dreams came and with the dreams came his principal visitor, his son Jose, speaking to him at length from the deep abyss, of that unknown dimension, that straddled his final destination. Of this he could speak to no one. One day while visiting his wife he tried to talk to her privately about it in the privacy of her hospital room, knowing full well she could not respond, except by the movement of her eyes. Now normally unfocused most of the time, yet when a significant stimulus occurred she was capable of sluggish eye movements.

Now as he talked about his dream visitations by his son Jose, he was looking not at his wife, but at the floor. Thus he failed to see her wildly rapid eye movements, every time he mentioned Jose's name, until he heard the heart monitor sounding off at her bedside. Then he looked up and saw her eyes moving back and forth wildly as several members of the hospital staff rushed into the room. Stepping away from her bed, he saw her slump helplessly as the heart monitor hit the constant tone and flat lined.

He was hurriedly escorted from the room by an orderly as he saw them valiantly try and revive her for the next twenty minutes, before finally pronouncing her demise. From the sweat on their collective brows, he could see they did all they could to bring her back to life, yet they had failed. Yet another tragedy visited his family. Another funeral to attend. As he glanced out of the hospital window, it was very late in the day. The death certificate was fully executed; the mortician had come and gone as well as his parish priest who gave her the last rites. He saw the sun setting in the west and wondered was it setting on all that he had inherited and worked hard to build. He resolved to see that it did not. Days later, in advance of the funeral, he would see what influence he could bring to bear on the authorities to see justice served. He'd done this before and he'd do it again.

That night he was visited in his dreams, once again by his son. Only this time he wasn't alone. Coming into view was the image of his wife standing next to her son. She appeared exactly as he'd last seen her hours ago, aged by her condition, with the scowl of death around her, attired in the hospital gown. Usually the Don's image of his son was from the chest up, yet no words were spoken as both his wife and Jose kept looking down ward. As if on que, the image of both withdrew to reveal that Jose's pants were down around his ankles and his male member was missing.

He awoke in a start and fell from his bed tumbling to the floor, screaming uncontrollably as one word screamed even louder in his head with deafening clarity. "REVENGE"! As he scrambled to a corner of his bedroom crouching in horror, sanity and some semblance of reason gradually returned as he wondered why no one responded. He certainly made enough noise?

Taking Don Pregoso with him, the following day, they both barged into the Provincial Governor's office, making him keenly aware of their collective displeasure in the manner Commandante' Reyna and his staff were conducting the investigation. Taken aback by the sheer aggression of two of Zaragoza's most influential citizens, he immediately contacted Commander Reyna, while both were in his office and insisted that he do whatever was necessary to Motale' Vega to get him to confess where his son was located.

Reyna, could've argued with his governor, but decided to follow his verbal instructions to the letter. After he hung up, he summoned Garza and Cardoso into his office saying, "The Provincial Governor just excoriated me for dragging my feet in the death of the Quiniones and Pregoso children. He insists upon quick results. Further, he insist that we immediately take Motale' Vega into custody and do whatever is necessary to get him to reveal the location of his son"!

"I can imagine that Don Quiniones is behind this", said Garza! "Along with Don Pregoso", replied Reyna. "Apparently they've united with a purpose"!

"And your instructions are", asked Garza?

"To follow the directive of our Provincial Governor, of course"!

As both men walked out of the office Reyna, called after them saying, "Leave no marks upon the man above the chest and below the knees. Short of that you both know what to do. I'm counting on you both to obtain the desired results"!

As Vega was brought before them and seated in the closed room for questioning. He looked around and saw that he was in a different room. Nowhere was mirror to shield him from seeing anyone, and no one could observe what was about to happen. Just a table and three chairs, one of which he occupied. Confronted with Capitan Garza and his subordinate Cardoso, he endured their hectoring and repetitive questions for the first hours, always bringing them back to the fact that they themselves told him that he and his wife had passed the lie detector examination. They always answered that those tests can be beaten and were not recognized in any court in the land. Then Garza leaned in and said, "Motale', you will start telling us the truth about the location of your son. Or else we will be compelled to take other measures. Measures you will not like. Measures that will be very painful"!

The fully enclosed room away from the others in a far corner of the building's basement was the site of inquisition. No one could hear the sound of the chair as Motale' fell to the floor. Slowly with great skill and care Garza and Cardoso, took turns beating Motale'. Rolled up magazines punched into some ones ribs repeatedly can inflict great damage. The heel of one's hand, the odd elbow or so to ones kidney's, left no marks upon the inquisitors. And so things went for hours.

Question and answer, or silence, was met by pain, and then the cycle would start all over. Oh there were other implements here in the headquarters that could've been employed, but that would've made others aware. His shoes and his belt removed, they left him by himself to germinate for an hour while they caught their wind. When they returned, they would work on the man's toes, one by one. But they must break the man's spirit one way or another. That was the only task before them.

Struggling to rise and regain his seat, Motale's throat almost closed shut from thirst, began to close as he painfully righted the chair and sat down. His first thoughts went to his wife, wondering what lay ahead. Then he thought about Carlos. Was he safe? Was he even alive? Then his thoughts drifted to Don Quiniones. Clearly it had to come to this, for that was the way the man's mind worked, at least in part. His son was dead and someone had to pay. Then his thoughts drifted to that of the Christ in his final hours, after having been turned over to the Legion to flog in the secluded courtyard. The Christ clearly knew that his time was near, suffering the pain and humiliation, his body repeatedly crisscrossed by the sting of "The Cat", what pain he must have endured on his way to his destiny. At that very moment Motale' knew that he would never cast his eyes ever again of his precious Appolonia. His prayers drifted to her as he asked the Blessed Virgin to help him face what lay ahead with a clear mind and a brave heart and that she look after his wife, steeling her for what was about to happen.

His mind clear, he stared at the door to the room awaiting their return. Despair had now disappeared, for he now knew his fate. The Holy Spirit now took over.

One by one Garza and Cardoso took turns slamming their heels upon his unshod toes, breaking each one in turn, to compel Motale' to answer their questions. As each of his bones broke, they became infuriated that he didn't cry out in pain like others, just staring silently ahead. His hands bound behind him tightly. After the last of his toes met their fate, Cardoso, jumped upon his instep breaking every bone. At least that brought forth a grunt and nothing more. As the second instep's bones made that crunching sound, Garza said, "Now you've done it Cardoso. The man will be unable to walk. They both left him sitting there, in the chair still as they left the room and made their way towards the office of Commandante' Reyna. The empty room confronted Vega, as his mind began to clear somewhat from the pain. Oddly enough the pain began to abate, several broken ribs, every toe on both feet crushed and his feet crushed beyond repair. His mind was unable to process the signals effectively from the various areas of his body, now in ruins. A gradual smile came across his face as he knew with certainty that his end was near. His silence was his only weapon, his only defense, as the Lord was certainly with his as he made his way into the valley of death.

Minutes later Commander Reyna, entered the room with Garza and Cardoso, immediately confronting Motale' Vega saying, "You've been a very bad man concealing the whereabouts of Your son who is a murderer. You will immediately tell us where he is", he bellowed. Motale' simply looked at him with glazed, half lidded eyes and made no response.

"Work on his fingers, one by one Garza. Make him talk"! His hand cuffs were immediately removed as Reyna and Garza held him firm as Cardoso went to work.

One by one every finger was broken after each question placed before him and after each finger ceased to be of any future use Motale', simply grunted and smiled. This caused them all to be reenergized as after the last digit cracked. Motale's hands now unusable met the heel of Garza's shoe as all of the carpal bones were crushed, while all Motale' could do was let them.

At Reyna's behest, Garza punched his now frail body just above his rib, driving the already fractured rib deeply into his chest cavity severing his aorta. The overtaxed heart still kept beating, yet the blood had nowhere to go but in his chest. As Garza stepped back, they all knew they'd gone too far as Vegas eyes grew wide as he struggled to breathe his last, his lungs burst forth a volley of blood, as he gurgled, "Appollonia" and collapsed to the floor in a heap.

Reyna felt for a pulse at his wrist and his neck and feeling none said, 'Well gentlemen, we're in it now. He's dead. Get him over to the morgue. You know what to do with the Doctor in Charge. Process the papers yourself. He is to be buried quietly in the potter's field, under a pseudonym. Are we all in agreement"?

They left him there on the floor as Cardoso went to gather some other to help with Motale's transport to the morgue. The heart was not pumping any longer and his body incapable of feeling or movement, yet his mind still was capable of partial functioning, much like a motor vehicle, running out of fuel, lurching forward in fits and starts finally depending on inertia to propel it onward at a slower and slower pace until it finally stops. Lying there on the cold floor, sightless eyes staring at an unseen floor, his final thought was of Appalonia and Carlos. And then darkness.

Reyna personally placed the calls to both Quiniones and Pregoso, giving his effusive apologies regarding the demise under the duress of questioning of their prisoner. Before either of them could protest, he reminded them of their overt complicity that should it become known, would certainly bring down all of them. "Senor, this is the end of things. We can only hope that Carlos Vegas is lying in a ditch somewhere or will meet an untimely and painful end sooner rather than later"!

"But what about Vega's wife", asked Quiniones?

"That Senor, is your affair"!

As Quiniones hung up the phone, he struggled to clear his mind and called Pregoso, who refused to take his call. Struggling to maintain some semblance his mind could not, as the overwhelming message kept repeating "Revenge, Revenge". He'd bullied his influence to have others do his dirty work and extract revenge on Motale' Vega. They'd botched their work and now he was dead. Soon to disappear completely. His son Carlos, the root of this evil that had descended of his family was nowhere to be found, thus the only one left was his mother Appolonia. Legally he couldn't kill her, but he could excise this last remaining pustule from his life.

Rising from his desk he grabbed his leather riding crop and stormed into the kitchen area, where she was working diligently and without warning started to rain blows upon her repeatedly until she fell. Then he grabbed her by the hair and dragged her from the kitchen, unconscious and threw her into the back seat of one of the rancho's utility vehicles, driving off in a cloud of dust. As he stormed out of the rancho, his thoughts drifted to the fact that anyone could run the family kitchen and that from now on it would be he, rather than Motale' Vega who would run the ranch. Less mouths to feed and clothe.

As night fell he found himself out in the country side, pulling to a stop beside the gravel road. He got out of the vehicle, looked around, finding the deserted location suitable and pulled the disheveled Appolonia out of the vehicle, just as she was coming awake and hit her, knocking her into a ditch that lay by the roadside.

Quiniones looked at her as she lay in tatters, clearly unconscious. It had been quite some time since he felt it necessary to lay hands upon anyone, yet the feeling was good. A sense of calm descended upon him for the first time, since his ordeal began. His last act was to spit upon her body in disgust as he turned on his heel, getting into the idling vehicle and drove off in a cloud of dust. As he drove, Quiniones made plans to have the ranch hands dispose of the Vega belongings, and then burn their cottage to the ground. He would talk to the kitchen staff, to promote their silence of what they had witnessed. Perhaps tonight he could finally get some restful sleep.

An hour later, Appolonia gradually came back to consciousness. As her senses returned, so did the pain from the blows inflicted by Don Quiniones. Part of her felt grateful that she was alive and part of her fell into misery because then she knew that Motale' was somehow dead. The Guardia had taken him, probably for interrogation, the others had said. In spite of, or perhaps because of his ordeal, she said nothing but kept at her daily tasks, trusting all of the Angels and Saints to provide for them all. Appolonia never complained. For it was not in her nature to complain, only to serve. Perhaps it was that fact that had endeared her to Motale' for so long, she reasoned. She loved Motale' from the first moments that she laid eyes upon him, somehow instinctively knowing that he was a good, loving and hardworking man. Never once through all the years of their marriage did a harsh word pass between them. Through him came Carlos, their mutual joy. Then this.

She rolled over in the ditch, feeling the pain and looked up into the night sky for answers, as she had done many times in the past, when crisis came upon them. Always God or one of his Angels had spoken to her clearly, providing comfort and direction, in that silent transference of consciousness. Usually under a starry canopy, yet this time the night sky was clear, the moon, nowhere in sight, with but a precious few stars visible to the naked eye. Appolonia was clearly alone. For the first time in her memory, she could not feel her husband's presence. Since she had known him, no matter where he was, whether away on the Don's business, or in another room close at hand, she could always close her eyes and feel his energy. Now as she closed her eyes once again, she could feel nothing. The love of her life, the only man she'd ever known, was gone forever. Of that she was certain.

Yet his memory was forever in her heart, as she struggled to say, "Me Amore', I love you. I have always loved you. Your memory will ever be in my heart", as the message went out into the universe.

Then her thoughts went to Carlos. A survivor he was. Clearly a fugitive on the run. Somehow she felt a faint presence that provided a little comfort that he was still alive and that was a cause for hope. Had she only known the cause of his distress, perhaps she and Motale' might have been able to reason with him. Then again, as she'd seen countless times, when it comes to matters of the human heart, all logic and reason falls on deaf ears.

Then she recalled something she'd read long ago, in a romance magazine, about love gone awry. It said, "All the logic in the world cannot overturn a simple feeling, once taken root"!

No doubt that was how she felt about Motale' and must have been how Carlos felt about that Joselita.

She decided that it was time she emerged from her misery and out of the ditch she lay in and made several efforts to stand upright. On the third attempt she was successful, making her way out of the ditch painfully on her hands and knees. Then she began to walk without knowing where she was going, trusting the universe to guide her to some safe haven. She gave thanks that she was able to walk somehow and that for all the pain there were no broken bones.

After several hours, her dwindling energy finally gave out as she sank to her knees and fainted, as she saw two headlights coming her way.

Father Anselmo had been to the Quiniones ranch on many occasions and knew of Appolonia and her husband as one of the family retainers. On many occasions he heard the Vegas family confessions and knew of their ordeal as well as that of the Quiniones family. Therefore it came as quite a surprise as he stopped his car in the early morning hours, to discover Appolonia lying in the middle of the road. He could tell that she had been beaten severely as she lay in the headlights, her clothes in tatters, battered and bruised. The priest quickly gathered her up and placed her gently in the passenger's seat and drove off.

Knowing of Don Quiniones propensities for violence and of the situation he quickly surmised that somewhere else was she to be for medical assistance. His visit to another chapel in the country for an early morning breakfast would have to wait as he decided the only place for Appolonia was Archdiocese and sanctuary. For this he would have to drive into town.

Once inside the grounds of the Chancellery, Father Anselmo quickly summoned a small band of helpers to bathe her, administer to her wounds and provide clean clothes and finally feed her. Slowly Appolonia began to emerge from her stupor and take over the task of feeding herself, amidst a small band of concerned onlookers.

As she finished her soup, the onlookers made way for the Archbishop, who quietly sat across the table from her without a word. Upon seeing the Archbishop across from her, she started to rise in his presence, as he bade her to remain seated saying, "Please finish your meal my child. Father Anselmo is the one who discovered you and brought you to us. We are all aware of the current situation and of your ordeal in particular. As of the moment you entered the Chancellory, you are granted sanctuary by the Holy Mother Church for as long as you desire. Father Anselmo suspect's that this is the work of your former employer. After you finish your meal you may rest for a time, then later we can talk if you so desire. We've the entire day ahead of us for Father Anselmo and I have cancelled all of our appointments for the rest of the day"!

As the Archbishop began to rise, all in the room genuflected, as he made the sign of the cross over Appolonia and left, bidding Father Anselmo to stay with her as everyone else departed. As he approached Father Anselmo asked, "May I join you my child"?

"Please father, please do and thank you for rescuing me"!

"Please Appolonia, finish your meal as best you can. There is time for conversation later as the Archbishop has said"!

"I'm afraid this much food will go to waste on me", said Appolonia meekly!

"Consume as much as you can for now. You must regain your strength, for clearly you have suffered a great deal. I suggest a sampling of the wine in front of you. I grow the grapes myself for the Chancellery. You would be doing me a favor my child since I've nurtured the plants from seedlings to their maturity. What is in front of you is from the very first pressing of the grapes and has emerged from the caskets in the basement only this week"!

She then gingerly lifted the glass to her lips, took a sip and then another and tried to smile saying, "Thank you father, the wine is wonderful"! Appolonia then tried to gather her thoughts, before continuing, finally saying, ""Oh father my husband is dead and my son is on the run from the Guardia accused of murder. Everything I've cherished is lost forever. I'm an old woman with no one left"!

Father Anselmo then reached across the table taking both of her hands in his, saying gently, "Senora, please look at me and hear my words. As the Archbishop has stated, you are now under the protection of Holy Mother Church for as long as you wish. All is not lost. You must retain your faith. Everything happens for a purpose. Gods will is often a mystery, not revealed until the day of final judgment. Of what happened to your husband, we will discover. The Archbishop is a man of considerable resources and does not suffer fools gladly. While he serves our spiritual master, he is very much a man of the temporal world. By God's holy writ, no further harm will come to you. Now please follow me to a place of rest. You have been assigned quarters within these walls. After you've rested we will be granted an audience with the Archbishop.

You will talk together. After that inquiries will be made. Answers will be gotten. Truth will be revealed and the culpable punished"!

Several hours later, as they were walking across the Chancellery grounds for the audience with the Archbishop, Father Anselmo said, "It has been my joy and pleasure to serve both God and the Archbishop for many years and you will find him truly God's servant. Speak only the truth to him as you know it and you will discover that all the celestial forces of heaven will be at hand"!

As they came to the door of the Archbishops office, Father Anselmo asked, "Are you ready to be received by the Archbishop, Senora"? Appolonia nodded her head meekly as Father Anselmo knocked on the ornate door.

"Come", bellowed a voice from within!

As the priest opened the door, he whispered in Appolonia's ear, "I'll be waiting outside when you're finished and we'll get you settled when you through"! He closed the door after her, crossing the foyer and settling into an oversized leather chair and pulled from his vestments his reading glasses and the latest issue of Paris Match, to read as he passed the time awaiting her.

Appolonia crossed the large heavily ornate room that served as the office of the Archbishop. The walls were festooned with a mixture of almost a thousand years' worth of pictures of prior prelates and various artifacts combining the ancient cultures of Castile and Navarre.

The Archbishop arose from his desk and came around to greet Appolonia, proffering his hand as she genuflected to one knee and kissed his ring. "Please rise my child and let us go over to the chairs in the corner where we can converse on a less formal basis. With some careful prodding the prelate, started Appolonia down the path of recollection of recent events as she knew them to be, omitting nothing. As she spoke, he made note of her visible welt's and bruises, recently administered and readily visible. From time to time the Archbishop carefully interrupted her with selective questions, to flesh out what he'd already been aware of, from the media reportage that saturated the area, for the better part of the last month. He went back over her story several times, carefully stressing her son's affair with the bankers daughter, finally certain that neither she nor her husband had any knowledge of their sons affair and was at last content that he had the entire story or at least what was possible to be known. Without a further word, he rose from his seat and commenced to slowly walk about the cavernous room that served as his office. His mind raced through and collated what he'd known about the Quiniones and Pregoso families. Their old moneyed ways and Castilian traditions. He should know them all too well, for he'd heard enough of their private confessions for several decades. They'd had much to confess and answer for repeatedly as he'd no doubt that he'd not heard it all. As he continued on his trek around his office, he searched his memory to recall what was known about the senior officers of the local Guardia Civil. He reasoned that Commander Reyna, their local Commander was the key to everything and the weak link along with the banker Pregoso. As he completed his final circuit around the office, he noticed the look of concern on Appolonia's face saying, "I'm so sorry my dear. It seems that my habit of pacing about when I'm trying to allocate my thoughts, might be off putting to some, but I'm almost completed in putting the final pieces of the puzzle in place."!

"I too share your concern about your husband. In a few hours there will be a call to Vespers and he will be mentioned in the homily, I sincerely hope you will attend. This evening I shall meet with the Archdioceses legal counsel to chart a secular course of action against the Guardia and the Province, to discover the whereabouts of your husband. As for your son Carlos, there is nothing I can think of to solve his situation except to pray that our Lord and Savior will forgive him of his sins and watch over him"! As he bid her to rise, she again genuflected on one knee and kissed his ring and as she rose, he said, "Now join Father Anselmo in the rectory so he can introduce you to your new home. Remind him that you will need clothes and effects fitting for your stay"!

As the door to his office closed, He went over to his desk and flipped the switch to the tape recorder secretly enclosed in his desk. The tape would prove an apt roadmap for the archdioceses legal counsel for their meeting later on in the evening and his subsequent meeting with the Provincial Prosecutor and the Guardia the following day.

Walking through the lush vineyard of the Archbishops rectory grounds with Pedro the Archbishops private secretary, they passed the time in silence contemplating the eternals wisdom, when Pedro suddenly blurted out, "Your excellency, I think it is a wonderful thing you do, for Senora Vega"!

"Yes, yes it is the right thing that we do", said the Prelate absently. "Do you remember Pedro, the last time we involved ourselves with the underbelly of the temporal world"? After a brief pause Pedro answered, "Quite well your eminence. "It caused quite a stir in Madrid, with several senior governmental ministers, finding it suddenly necessary to abruptly resign without a word, or face criminal prosecution by the state. The press was quite angry as I recall, for it left a host of unanswered questions regarding governmental malfeasance"!

Climbing the pathway towards the Archbishop's office the prelate added sorrowfully, "The suicides that followed were indeed unfortunate"!

"They met their fates without a final confession", added the secretary!

"Given their final actions, the final confession wouldn't have made any difference as to their eternal disposition. They made their choice of their own free will"!

"But your eminence, don't you think considering the length, breadth and depth of their considerable wrong doing, their actions were for the common good"?

"Perhaps Pedro, perhaps! Now let us prepare for Anatole and the Provincial Prosecutor, for they will attend us within the hour. Oh, and you met with your friend at Guardia's headquarters, the Sergeant"?

"Yes your eminence. He has furnished us with a complete set of secret taped cassettes that chronicle every moment of the interrogation of Senor Vega, several evenings ago. Plus the coerced signature of the Morgue's superintendent and where the body is, of Senor Vega. The tapes clearly implicate, Reyna and his subordinates, Garza and Cardoso"!

"Any mention of the Provincial Prosecutor or Governor"? Pedro shook his head.

"Good. It just wouldn't do for any additional culpability to reach the upper levels of government", he said wryly. "You will be kind enough to attend our meeting and take the required notes of all that is said, to back up the recording devise"!

"As you wish your eminence"!

An hour later, the Archbishop received the Provincial prosecutor as well as the Archdioceses legal counsel, the diminutive Anatole Vargas. The prosecutor was confronted with the tapes of the killing of Motale' Vega, in an interrogation that had gone wrong, by the prelate and Vargas.

Further he was furnished with proof of the assault of Senora Vega, via pictures taken the previous day.

"And where is Senora Vega", asked the Prosecutor?

"She is granted sanctuary, by the Holy See and is safe", said the Archbishop!

"I must confer with the Provincial Governor, your eminence"!

"You can do this now from our phone, where the light of day can shine on everything that is said"!

"Your eminence, I must protest your attitude and the inference of impropriety"!

"Impropriety you say? Merde'! Your entire life has been one of impropriety. That is why you have the job that you do! You will get the Provincial Governor on the phone immediately or else, the entire media will have the story by nightfall, with you, the Governor, Commander Reyna, the entire Pregoso and Quiniones families falling under the public's scrutiny and wrath. Are you prepared to unleash hell"?

"I would suggest you do as his eminence wishes", said Anatole Vargas. "For I shall be the instrument of his wrath and I relish the task. I believe you are in checkmate Senor"!

Within the space of an hour's time, a deal was negotiated, if one could call a one sided Imprimatur, a negotiation. The uncovering of the remains of Motale' Vega with the transport and reburial of him on the grounds of the Chancellery at the States expense. Next, the prosecution of those immediately involved with the death of Motale' Vega, for manslaughter to be concluded successfully in six months' time from the current date. Then upon initiation of their internment, the resignation of the current governor for personal reasons. The deal was quickly concluded over the phone.

As all rose to leave, the prosecutor said "Congratulations your eminence. Niccolo Machiavelli in his prime couldn't have engineered such a successful coupe'. I trust the Holy See will appreciate your temporal skills"!

"I detect an element of sarcasm in your statement Senor Prosecutor and you must know that you came perilously close to joining the others in this affair. As it is, you will act as an instrument of Gods will and press for swift justice. Anything less than you best efforts will be dealt with in a manner that will not meet with your approval. I trust we are together on this, are we not"?

As he knelt to kiss the ring of the Archbishop, the prosecutor said, "We are in complete accord your eminence"! Turning to leave, the Archbishop said, "One thing more. You will get together with my secretary Pedro a select a suitable time in which to bring before me Senor's, Pregoso and Quiniones for an audience.

We shall call it an audience of eternal souls"! "As you wish your eminence"! Over the course of days, the Archbishop kept in close contact with his superior, the Cardinal in Madrid filling him in on the minutiae of the events at hand and was pleasantly surprised, when he was in complete agreement with a further course of action regarding the elders of the Pregoso and the Quiniones families regarding their part confirmed by the Governor, admittedly of weak moral character, in the death of Motale' Vega. Normally, church affairs move at a glacial pace, regarding the dealings with the flock, but since the Vatican had given its quiet assent; the Archbishop now possessed all he required to bring celestial justice.

It came as quite a surprise, when the front page of the daily newspaper announced the prosecution of the Guardia officers in the death of Motale' Vega while under interrogation and further, under the front page fold was the secondary headline of the Official Pronouncement of "Official Papal Sanctuary of Appolonia Vega", under the auspices of the Archbishop of Zaragoza.

Like any good secretary, one anticipates ones employer's needs. Pedro was a very good secretary, after hearing conversation between the Archbishop and the Cardinal, he went to the archives to retrieve the exact copy of the "Rites of Excommunication" and prepare a brief for the Archbishop, just in case it was required as extra leverage against the Pregoso and Quiniones elders. In his long service for the Church, he could not recall a time when the ancient ritual was exercised. Yet here it was, still a viable alternative according to Canon law. Before he left for the day, the informative brief was placed in a leather folder and placed square in the midst of the Archbishops desk for his attention the following day.

As he left for the day, Pedro almost felt sorry for both families, having suffered back to back losses of precious loved ones. Clearly Satan and a contingent of demons were hard at work locally wreaking havoc and sorrow amongst a selected few. He knew from the newspapers that Reyna, Garza and Cardoso had been imprisoned by the Prosecutor and a contingent of the Guardia sent up from Madrid to take charge. For the first few days of their imprisonment and interrogation all subject to videotape recording, they all held firm even in the face of solid evidence to the contrary. It was only when the local Prosecutor, mindful of the Archbishops desire for his best efforts, threatened to change the charges to Murder that they started to all crack.

Although he wasn't an immediate target, all of the accused pointed to the Provincial Governor as the one who used his influence to start the ball rolling. A single self-inflicted gunshot to his head was all it took to end his life and simplify the prosecution's case as the wheels of justice moved quickly towards a conviction of unintentional manslaughter, for all three of the Guardia officers.

Motale' Vega's remains were buried on the grounds of the Chancellery after the usual Rites of the departed ritual was performed, in a quiet ceremony, by the Archbishop personally, signifying that a member of his flock was brutally separated from life before his allotted time.

The ceremony was interrupted as Appolonia was escorted to the casket and opened so she could cast one final glance of her beloved. The body so carefully prepared lay in quiet repose, as Appolonia knelt and said her goodbyes, hands clasped together in supplication, with tears in her eyes, as the Archbishop commenced to drone on with his ritual.

When completed, the prelate turned towards Appolonia and offered his hand saying, "It is time my child", as she rose up on unsteady legs, she bent over the casket, putting forth her hand for one final touch of his peaceful face in recognition of a life together.

She stroked his lifeless head gently for several moments whispering, "Vaya co Dios, me amor! Me esperar"!

Several evenings later, the Provincial prosecutor, escorted Don Quiniones onto the grounds of the Archbishops Chancellery and into the presence of the Archbishop apologizing for the non-presence of Don Pregoso, in the hospital in serious condition due to his heart attack.

As Don Quiniones approached the Archbishop in his office, he neither kneeled nor offered to kiss the ring of the prelate offered as was formal custom, instead standing ramrod straight and matching the prelates gaze with a stare.

"As you wish Don Quiniones", said the prelate as he turned and went behind his desk taking a seat. As he opened the folio prepared for him by his secretary he started, "This meeting is prompted by the unfortunate chain of events that have befallen three families in our midst. Setting the unfortunate deaths of Joselita Pregoso and Jose Quiniones, by the hand of by all accounts Carlos Vega aside for the moment, I wish to address the death of Motale' Vega and the egregious assault of Appolonia Vega. According to the evidence provided by the office of the Prosecutor, neither Senor nor Senora Vega had anything to do with the death of either party or any knowledge of the whereabouts of their accused son. By what has been surmised, the unfortunate deaths were an unfortunate act of untimely passion. Again that said and placed aside for the moment I wish to address the culpability of both elders of the Pregoso and the Quiniones family in exerting undue influence upon the Vega family in spite of evidence to the contrary. Since Don Pregoso cannot be here to answer I will address Don Quiniones to answer. Senor. What have you to say in your behalf"?

Quiniones slowly rose to his full height and said as the room fell silent, "My son is dead by the hand of a viper that lay in my midst for many years". His voice trembled as he continued, "A viper that drew sustenance from my family table, only to end the life of my son. The fruit of my loins. The one who would carry on, after I'm gone, the honor of the Quiniones name"!

"Yes, yes", interrupted the prelate "And evidence exists that your grandfather gained prominence and enhanced the Quiniones family fortunes as a result of the Spanish Civil War back in the thirties, working for the Generalissimo Franco and gained mightily as a result of his beneficence. Then later as your father had the good sense, to bring Motale' Vega to your household, he trebled your family's fortunes and reputation during his tenure, only to be rewarded by a murder at your behest. Your personal reputation has been in question for a number of years and Senor, Motale' Vega's blood is on your hands. It is time for your repentance and restitution to Appolonia Vega"!

"Is the Church threatening me? Haven't I given significantly to the Church these many years, of my family's fortune"!

"Far less than a fraction of your family's wealth Senor and at every turn expected a certain Quid pro Quo for you're over stated largesse, rather than giving of yourself out of the goodness of your heart. No, the question that must be answered is why you worked your wrath on innocent people in such a mindless fashion? I warn you sir; your answer may determine the future of your very soul"!

"That Puta knows where her son is and would say anything or do anything to protect him", replied the elder Quiniones in disgust! "Nothing of the Vega name has any meaning to me, or any value except the death of her son. All I care to know is that her son is responsible for the death of my son.

This I vow. I will move heaven and earth spend any amount to find that son of a whore and see him dead. His death a hundred times over would not balance the scales"!

"And that is your final word Senor", asked the prelate? Don Quiniones sank back down into his chair and remained silent, his blazing eyes guaranteeing that he was beyond reason.

"Apparently that threat of violence in front of witnesses is your final word on the matter Senor, is it not"? There he sat with nothing else to say choosing to remain silent and defiant in the face of both spiritual and temporal authority. After a slight period of silence, the prelate asked, "Has anyone else anything to say"? After an uncomfortable period of silence the Archbishop said, "Well, the Church has much to say"!

"Appolonia Vega has been formally granted Sanctuary and has become a ward of Holy Mother Church for the rest of her life. No harm will befall her from any quarter, either from the government or either the Pregoso or Quiniones families or their agents. The Pregoso and Quiniones families will see to it that an appropriate financial compensation of a quarter million Swiss Francs be tendered into an account administered by this office in her name and in her behalf at a bank of our choosing within the next forty eight hours. Finally, an open letter approved by this office will be written and executed by the heads of both Pregoso and Quiniones families, apologizing for the death of Motale Vega' and admitting culpability. This letter will be read aloud during the homily in the coming weeks in every Cathedral on the Iberian Peninsula"!

"No, No, a thousand time no", yelled Don Quiniones as he jumped up from his chair. 'Fuck all, never. I will go to my grave and never agree to pay that whore one single peseta or make any apology. Our families are the ones that suffered at the hands of those miserable Basque gypsies"!

"You dare to defy the findings of Holy Mother Church? You dare to question our authority"? He again was met with defiant silence, by the elder Quiniones.

"So I take it that is your final word on the matter"?

Again the prelate was met with defiant silence, as he finally said, "So be it"! "As of last evening, a Dictatum has been approved by not only Madrid, but the Papal offices at the Vatican and will be sent at my behest to be read aloud during every Mass for one week in every Cathedral, in Spain and Portugal. The Dictatum will require every Priest scheduled to deliver at every Mass to the faithful to perform the seldom used Rites of Excommunication, declaring both you Senor and Don Pregoso as "Anathema and Excommunicate', from the Holy Mother Church. While the both of you are free to attend Mass if you wish, neither of you will be permitted to receive any and all of the sacraments of Holy Mother Church. In addition, both of you specifically will be erased from the records of your parish of birth or current attendance. No holy communion, No last rites, not to be buried in sanctified ground, all of it gone forever. Catholics are encouraged not to communicate with you and to end any business dealings with you as soon as practicable. This will last for the rest of your natural lives. Of course, this Dictatum applies only to the both of you and does not affect the lives of the surviving family members. This will be delivered under the Imprimatur of the Vatican"!

"Your ostracism from society is to be complete for anyone choosing to do business, or socialize with you will do so at the displeasure of the church. As of this very moment this Dictatum is to be considered complete, binding and cannot be rescinded or compromised in any manner or form according to Canon Law. So it is written, so it is done. May God have mercy on your souls"!

Then to a quiet room the Archbishop concluded, "A terrible thing to have been brought upon yourselves by your own free will and to be formally disgraced in the eyes of God for all mortals to see. To know with certainty that at the moment of departure from this mortal coil, that you will be absolutely alone and that no one is to mourn your time spent on earth. Yes a terrible thing"!

The entire room remained silent, for a death had just occurred. Oh, all in attendance would rise and make their way in the world and in the morning the sun would still rise and the earth would rotate as it always had, but still a death had occurred none the less. The Archbishop finally broke the silence saying, "We are truly sad upon this occasion and will pray that your journey through life will not end prematurely"! He then arose from his chair, made the sign of the cross and went out a side door without a backward glance.

As the others rose to leave, they all looked at a defeated Don Quiniones. Yet as he slowly rose from his chair, he seemed to gain some semblance of resolve as he bellowed, "Fuck all. The Archbishop, the Cardinal, the Pope, and God and I place a curse on all in this room and especially that son of bull shit in Rome", as he stormed out.

True to his word, the following Sunday, each priest, at every Mass, in every Roman Catholic Church throughout the entire countries of Spain and Portugal, performed the almost forgotten "Rites of Excommunication", upon the heads of the Pregoso and Quiniones families.

Both names were read aloud for all to hear, along with the litany of sins committed against God and man. The explanations for their refusal to accept culpability, to make restitution and repent their sins were slowly stated for all to hear and understand. Two large candles were placed at the forefront of the congregation. As each man's name was read out loud at the conclusion, one of the candles was extinguished, followed by a single gong from the church bell.

That accomplished, each priest read aloud from a copy of the Church's formal declaration of Sanctuary, for Senora Appolonia Vega, formally declared as a ward of the Holy See. Each priest declared at the end of the ceremony, "So it is written, so it shall be done", as one final tone came from the bell.

In the following days, news editorials were written, regarding the sanctity of Excommunication by the Church and predictably responses came down along familiar lines of thought. Those of a more progressive and liberal point of view, thought the pronouncement as barbaric and draconian in nature. Conversely, those of a more conservative point of view, considered the ritual just, fitting and entirely appropriate considering the circumstances. Interestingly enough, attendance at Mass, that had gradually began to wane over the years, gradually began their ascendancy, an unintended consequence of events.

A scant month later, formal charges against Reyna, Garza and

Cardoso, of the Guardia Civil were brought. The resultant trial found each man culpable of unintended manslaughter. Their terms of incarceration varied, from six, to twelve years in duration.

Of course, the entire Iberian media had complete coverage of the trial from beginning to end, reporting of the various twists and turns the trial had taken, with even the most liberal of citizens agreeing with the verdict.

The subsequent pronouncements proved to be a body blow to the business and social fortunes of both families. The elder Pregoso, now out of the hospital, and on the slow road to recovery, was severed from the banking house by his board of directors. The elder Quiniones, now in complete charge of the rancho's operations, found his skills, such as they were, a far cry from that of Motale' Vega. The market for his prize bulls in the Corrida's of the world gradually began to wane. One by one, longstanding members of the ranch staff, began to depart, eagerly welcomed by others.

The Pregoso family, now living on a stipend, voted on by the banks board members, withdrew from normal society, as Don Pregoso spent each day passing the time, tending to his gardens, alone.

Raised since childhood in a world of wealth and privilege, they all were accustomed to being attended to by others. Now all of this was gone for what remained of their lives. Justice was done. The sun still rose every morning and the world still turned as before.

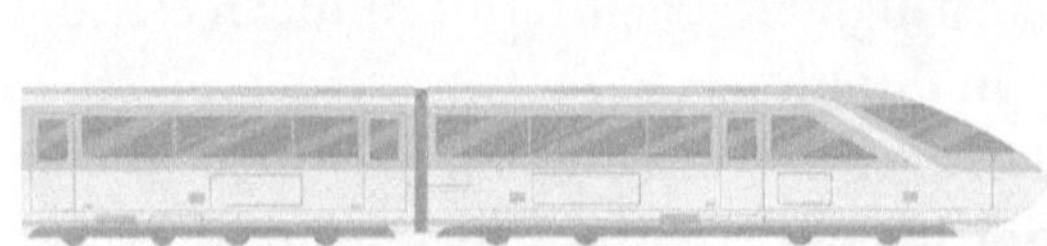

14

Carlos Vega had been on the dodge for the last month, working his way along the Cariberes range of Mountains; now well inside 'La Belle France', paralleling the roadway that skirted the French Riviera. Staying away from the beaten path, he touched the outskirts of each town and city that lay in his path, traveling while others slept and resting during the day. He depended upon dead reckoning and, pressed on along the well-worn animal trails, thousands of years old, with a single purpose, the City of Marseilles and the possibility of a new life.

Early in the morning of his final day of transit, he reached his goal. The address on the crumpled note pad read; "Bas-fort Saint Nicolas-2, Bd Charles-Livon". The headquarters of the French Foreign Legion, in Marseilles.

He walked into the building, made his purpose known to a clerk and was given a portfolio containing a host of forms to be filled out. After that was completed, he returned the form to the clerk and was directed to join several others in line and were eventually herded into a military truck, where they were driven thirty kilometers to the recruitment and selection centre, of the 'Le ler Regiment Etranger' at Abagne, a suburb of Marseilles. Once there, all were directed into the entrance of the primary assemblage building. As he entered with the others, Carlos noted the Legionnaires motto inscribed in stone overhead, 'Legio Patria Nostra', "The Legion is our Fatherland"!

Seeing that gave Carlos a new sense of hope and purpose as if he'd come home at long last. He thought to himself, 'So far so good'. For no indications as to his identity by anyone has surfaced. He wondered if his lack of papers would have any bearing on his acceptance. No one had recognized his face, which had appeared on a number of newspapers he'd had the occasion to read during his journey.

Remembering what, the Lorry driver had said to him, his first night on the run, that the Legion asked few questions of one's past and with but a few egregious exception's, once one was accepted by the Legion for training, one's past ceased to exist. Serve the Legion well and it will become your family. He thought silently to him-self, 'The Legion will become my family come what may. They will train me and I will become proficient in all things that I am ignorant. I will exist from this time on only in the service for the Legion. The Legion is my only option'. From that day on and for each day of his training, that was his daily mantra.

As he and the others followed the corporal down several hallways to a staging area, Carlos reflected upon his journey. Traveling at night, paralleling the roadway north, stealing food from stores, and carefully husbanding what money he had and stealthily removing a few articles of clothing from clotheslines, he cautiously made his way northward. Of course, while the Cote' de Azure and the vaunted Riviera, the worlds playground of the rich was just a few mile east of him, he had to ignore its presence and press on. From time to time he would follow the course of the investigation by the Guardia, in the local press as he traveled onward. As he discovered what had happened to his father and subsequently his mother, it further steeled his resolve to do what he could and return one day and make things right.

As the group made their way down yet another long hallway, after pausing for several minutes, he viewed the framed portraits and photos of famous Legionnaires that had preceded them. As they were gathered into yet another assembly room, they were all allocated into three different queues. As the queue inched forward, he waited until he came before a clerk finishing up the previous recruits folder and hand it off to another.

"Sign your name to the register", pointing at the clip board to his left, "and hand me your dossier prepared earlier", reaching his hand towards Carlos.

"Good, now go join the queue of those seated along the wall over there and wait until your summoned"! After twenty minutes, his name was called and a Sergeant summoned him to rise and follow him into another room, where he was met with a stiff greeting by another Sergeant, who was scanning his papers, without looking up. Carlos immediately came to attention and looked straight ahead, just as the Lorry driver had instructed him. The Sergeant's name badge indicated Didier Lambrage. Then the Sergeant looked up witnessing the young man in front of him and making a note of his apparent military bearing. A look of recognition came across his face as he said, "Most fortunate for you that you are not a French citizen my friend, or else I'd have to make a present of you to the local Gendarmes for possible extradition"!

At that very moment, Carlos's heart stopped. Seeing his angst, Sergeant Lambrage said, "Relax Mon Ami, you've been expected. I trust you have a message for me"?

Just then Carlos remembered his note pad in his pocket and asked permission to retrieve it, handing it over to Lambrage. After reading it he looked up handing it back to Carlos saying, "Got a call from our mutual friend almost a month ago. Seems you've made the journey as he predicted you would. Once a Legionnaire always a Legionnaire. So well done"!

As he looked back at Carlos's dossier he said, "Says here you're conversant in French"!

"Oui mon Sergeant. Enough to get by on"!

"Basque lineage from the Pamplona region is my guess, eh"?

"My father was born there", said Carlos as he stared at the wall ahead of him.

"Well it seems you've apparently led the Spanish Guardia and The French Flicks a merry chase, for all of Europe is alerted to apprehend you on sight"! Then he got up and went to another retrieving a batch of telex's and as he rumbled through them, retrieved one saying, "Every other day another telex from Interpol about you, complete with a photo of you clearly taken some years ago, before you fleshed out some. It barely resembles your current likeness. You can thank heaven for little mercies"!

"Yet you spotted me right off", said Carlos!

"Yes I did young man, but I cheated. I knew you were coming thanks to our friend and that you had no other alternative that made sense! If the local flicks had any sense, they would've had several of their men surveil our headquarters and snatch you the moment you appeared. The clerks at Interpol always send their reports to us as if we were common flics, which we are not. We are Legionnaires, period"!

Continuing, Lambrage added, 'You've successfully eluded police agencies all over southern Europe, which says something about your resourcefulness. Shortly you will endure a battery of tests, educational, psychological and physical. After which you will be evaluated and perhaps a place can be found for you in the Legion. Now, given your delicate situation, I should mention that among those who routinely are not admitted to the Legion are, convicted rapists, child molesters and murders. However since you were never convicted and by all reports a crime of passion occurred, with no premeditation, according to the press reports and no previous criminal record exists, prior to your appearance on our doorstep, indicates talents that can be expanded on and put to good use over time. So test well mon ami"!

Carlos was then handed off to a corporal and then joined a host of others who were herded into the unit mess hall where they joined others for the noon meal. After which the entire afternoon was spent testing, their body, mind and psyche. As he ate, he remembered the caution placed by the Sergeant that ran counter to the hunger pangs that were starting to bubble up from deep within, "I suggest you don't fill your belly too full of food. For a full belly doesn't bode well for proper thinking"!

As they ate together, Lambrage took full measure of the lad that sat across from him. Well mannered, reasonably polite, takes direction well enough and as he noticed, apparently hungry enough, yet finishing only half of the food placed before him. When they had both finished, Lambrage said, "Cigarette", shaking a Dunhill from his pack?

"No thank you Sergeant", said Carlos, his eyes sweeping the area ahead of him as others came and went.

"Did you do it", asked Lambrage? "I mean did you do all the things the press said you did". curiosity getting the better of him. Carlos turned and looked at the Sergeant for a moment realizing that the Sergeant held all the cards. He must answer with great care as he asked back, "Why do you ask Sergeant? Would it make any difference one way or another"?

"No my friend, just idle curiosity. It is rare that we get such a sub rosa celebrity, to offer up for training. In my opinion, you probably did what was indicated in the press, but it was a momentary crime of passion. My guess is that both probably deserved what they got. I came to that conclusion even prior to your arrival. Of course, it helped somewhat that my old boss and friend paved the way. Plus your general demeanor reinforces that view. So put your mind at ease and test well"! As he lit another Dunhill he continued, "Now listen very carefully to what I have to say. The Legion is comprised of mostly outcasts from society. Former thieves, con men, jilted lovers, refugees that bring skills that can be used. In fact we're it not for the Legion most of us would be languishing in a prison somewhere. Each of us has or acquires a skill of sorts that fits nicely with the whole. We pass on knowledge to each other continually for the benefit of the Legion. Should you be accepted, you will be provided with a completely new identity and history along with the appropriate papers for fool proof verification. For as long as you serve the Legion and La Belle France well, precisely in that order, the Legion will be your shield and protector. The brotherhood of outcasts is lifelong. Now young man, are you ready for testing"!

"Oui Sergeant", said Carlos as they both rose to depart.

For the next four hours, Carlos along with the others endured the rigorous testing and at 1600 hours, Carlos stood with the others awaiting the results. One by ones the names were called out as potential recruits left for an unknown fate. Then Sergeant Lambrage entered the room with a single file in his hand, motioning to Carlos to follow him. As they went outside to another building Lambrage said, "You've done quite well in your testing young man, now the final hurdle. You are to interview with Major Thierry St. Nathalie, for final determination. The hardest man I've ever known. He's been a Commander in the Legion his entire career, educated at the Lycee Academie Militaire at St. Cyr, just outside Paris. The man is a highly decorated, no nonsense career soldier, that doesn't suffer fools gladly, with a direct military lineage that traces back to Napoleon.

They entered the building and soon Carlos found himself standing behind Lambrage. Lambrage gave two sharp raps on the closed door before entering leaving Carlos behind him standing alone. Lambrage entered and approached the Majors desk giving a sharp salute as he stood silent while the Major finished writing a letter. Then he looked up seeing the Sergeant and returned the salute asking, "And what is your business Sergeant"?

"Sir, a recruits special dossier that will require your approval Major", as he handed Carlos's file to the Major. "And why will it require my approval"?

"It is the file of the Spanish fugitive, Carlos Vega, just recently arrived. A special case that will require your approval. He's tested extremely well and I've talked to him at some length. In addition he comes to us by way of someone you know, who has served with the both of us"!

"Talked to him at some length have you Sergeant"? "Oui Major"!

"And your impression is"? "He'll do Major"!

"He will do Sergeant"? "Rather nicely Major"!

"High praise. High praise indeed. Interesting. Have him come before me Sergeant"!

Labrange, smartly turned opened the door and motioned for Carlos to enter. Carlos quickly walked into the office, took two quick steps stopping in front of the Majors desk, standing at attention his arms at his side and looked at a spot on the wall above the Majors head, as St. Nathalie sat silent scanning the results of the testing.

Several minutes of silence passed before the Major closed the file and placed it on his desk. He looked up and said, "Seems you've led the police of two countries on a merry chase young man"; as he stood up to take the full measure of the young recruit. He slowly walked around Carlos, to see if he followed him with his eyes and finding that his gazed remained fixed at the wall behind the Majors desk as he made his circuit, came back to his chair and sat back down. He began saying, "The training you are to receive will be hard and oft times brutal, in order to weed out the undesirables and churn out men of extraordinary abilities. I liken it to development of silk purses, from sow's ears. Each of you will enter training as common ore, to emerge as finely honed steel. You will find the life of a Legionnaire, is often brutally hard, with tours of service in the most inhospitable of climates, either physically or politically. The Legion develops hard men, who often do the dirty work for their new father land that others either will or cannot. Should you decide to make a career of the Legion understand that you will never achieve any rank above Sergeant Major, for all Commissioned Officers are of the regular army and Graduates of St. Cyr. Once out in the world, your officers will quite literally have the power of your life or death at their disposal. Should you fail or refuse to carry out lawful orders once in the field, an officer may at his discretion, shoot you out of hand immediately without further need for explanation. That will be your due process. Should that ever occur, no questions will ever be asked, you will never be missed, for you never existed in the first place. Do you understand and accept this"!

"Oui Major", answered Carlos sharply! He quickly signed the proffered form saying, "Carry on Sergeant", said the Major. "Dismissed"!

As both men slowly walked back, Lambrage said, "There is a man that we should all emulate. Aways returning to the Legion as his permanent assignment. No doubt he'd be a General by now had he taken other opportunities to return to the regular army, but his constant return to the Legion assignments betray his interests. Normally career officers are rotated for command duty in and back out of Legion assignments as career builders. The theory is that if one can command scum effectively, then one can command anyone effectively. Twenty two years he's been at it, with eighteen of which directly assigned to the Legion. He's like the Pope, married to the church and the almighty, forsaking all earthly pleasures, so our Major is likewise linked to the Legion. Those of us who have served with him over the years, are loyal"!

"Even over the Legion", asked Carlos?

"Never contemplate that question too long. Consider that a metaphor"! As they entered the main building, they went to another assembly area, where all those that has passed the tests were assembled. Lambrage then turned to Carlos saying, "You will now join the others, for the propaganda and further processing. Perhaps our paths will cross again, or not"! Then he turned and departed as the rest of the group were herded into a small auditorium where for the next thirty minutes were spent viewing a film on the history of the French Foreign Legion. The film covered the entire history of the Legion from its inception in March of 1831, at the hands of King Louis Philippe, through its darker moments in French Indo China in 1954, when the Viet Minh, lay siege to elements of the Legion at Diem Bien Phu forcing their surrender. The overarching message was that whenever the Legion was left to themselves, they prospered quietly and achieved the desired ends, but whenever the Legion suffered defeat, it was usually at the hands of inept and bungling leadership, always resulting in the unnecessary loss of lives. Of course, never were those inept Senior Commanders ever sacked as a result of their incompetence, because the Legionnaires were considered cannon fodder.

At the end of the film the message received by Carlos was somewhat disturbing. Here were highly trained men, trained to a razors edge, who from time to time were used badly by their masters. 'But a place where I can begin anew', he thought.

The lights came on and Sergeant Lambrage entered along with a coterie of other noncommissioned officers. As he brought up his clipboard, he bellowed, "As I call out your names, you will assemble in the outer hallway for further processing"!

As Carlos's name was called he joined the others in the hallway passing Sergeant Lambrage without a glace by either of them. It suddenly hit him that the group that was assembled was significantly less than those he'd originally started with. The Legions way of thinning out the unsuitable.

"You will all follow me", bellowed another Sergeant as they all filed out of the building and out onto the parade grounds. As Sergeant Lambrage watched the group march in route step across the parade grounds, he was joined by Major St. Nathalie.

"Calling it a day Major", asked Lambrage saluting?

"Yes Sergeant. Its seventeen hundred hours and my day is concluded. Oh by the way, keep me informed on the progress of that one you brought before me. The Basque called Vega. He has the look, does he not Sergeant"! "Oui Major. The man has the look and now we will see if he has the ability to endure!

As the Major made his way across the Quadrangle, Carlos's group was marched by a thin corporal with a high pitched voice, who hardly looked the type of the robust Legionnaire, he'd seen marching during Bastille Day on the television news programmes. Yet he got them through the fifteen minutes of the evening meal, then he hustled them quickly through their inoculation procedures, by the base's medics and following that a scant thirty seconds in the barber chair, to rid themselves of the outside world and finally into the realm of the quartermaster, where they were directed to rid themselves of everything, everything, was thrown into a bag, clothing, shoes, everything and they were issued standard Legionnaire uniforms from the shoes to the Kepi that was their cover.

Once it was determined that everyone was dressed and shod properly they were trotted to their assigned barracks, in some semblance of formation and everyone assigned a bunk and area to share.

That done they were ordered to undress and lineup for their nightly shower. In groups of six, they were hustled into the shower room and allotted five minutes to thoroughly clean and rinse themselves, relinquishing their spots to six more before the entire group was dried and dressed only in their skivvies and ordered to stand at attention by the slightly built Corporal, who announced, "Shortly you will meet your training instructor for the next sixteen weeks. You will get to know each other very well. I can assure you that none of you will like him, while just a few may grow to appreciate him. That is all. Stand at ease, until ordered to do otherwise"!

Several minutes later, the door to the barracks was flung open, by the Corporal who as he entered shouted, "You will all come to attention, for I introduce, "The Alsatian"! In lumbered a hulking man. Tall and solidly built with a craggy face, square cut jaw line and a jagged scar that visibly ran from just above his eyebrow and down the entire left side of his face, ending at the jaw line. His Kepi sat squarely upon his head, with the standard scarf wrapped Legionnaire style around his neck, with a leather lanyard that housed a police whistle that rested in his blouses front pocket. His khaki trousers appeared freshly pressed and we're neatly tucked into his gleaming black boots.

As Carlos stood rigidly at attention, staring intently at a point on the wall across from him, the Alsatian passed him with little notice, slowly walking down the aisle that separated the men on both sides, taking the full measure of each in turn. As he passed one man down the line, he suddenly turned and bellowed, "What are you looking at Scum"?

"Why you Sergeant", said the unfortunate.

"Take one step forward and turn left", bellowed the Alsatian! After the man complied, he bellowed, "Do you know how to do a push up"?

"Yes Sergeant"!

"Then assume the position and do not start until I tell you"! As the man dropped down and assumed an elevated prone position. The Alsatian ran down the line and yelled, "You, you and you. Do you think I'm pretty? Do you want to fuck me? Step out of line each of you and join your Comrade on the floor. After that he went back along the line to ferret out the curious and finding no additional takers went back to the original quartet and bellowed, "At my command each of you will give us twenty perfect pushups. Then he took several steps forward and slowly knelt down as to get a better observation point as each of them was in position, he said "I will administer the cadence". Now I must tell you that should any of you fail to conduct your demonstration in an unsatisfactory manner, all will repeat the effort"!

Yet another minute passed the mark before he commenced. As the men all reached the twentieth repetition they all came to rest, with the arms pressing the floor beneath them as the Alsatian said softly, "No, no, no that will not do gentlemen. Three of you made mistakes. You will rest in place, for one minute then we shall start again"! Of course with each successive session rather than improve, the men, quickly tiring, did worse and worse. By the end of the fifth session one of the men fell to the floor exhausted.

The Alsatian quickly gave him the boot to his ribs bellowing, "Did I say for you to rest Scum? I did not. Rise and we shall all repeat. After the eighth session all lay on the floor exhausted and all had felt the repeated sting of his boot, as he finally relented saying, "Seems this class is in serious need for discipline and I am the man that will give it"!

He then summoned the Corporal and whispered into his ear as the Corporal shouted for everyone to stand at ease and for the next hour went over the basic rudiments of what was expected each morning when they were awakened and how clothes were to be rolled, how boots were to be displayed and the bunk to appear. Then as the Corporal concluded, he caught the eye of the Alsatian who stepped forward saying, "For the next sixteen weeks, each of you belongs to me body and soul. For the time being I own each of you completely, until either you wash out or are accepted by La Belle France. Consider yourselves the sole property of the Legion and the French government for as long as you prove yourselves worthy. Each of you are here because there is nothing to go back to. Your past will be expunged; there is only the present and what is to come. Consider yourselves as dead men and as dead men each of you is an empty vessel, currently worthless. Less than zero. From now on each of you will speak to either me or the Corporal only when spoken to and only in response to what is asked or directed. You will neither add nor subtract anything. Each of you will begin a response by stating the superiors rank and ending with the superiors rank. At no time will you address either of us by name"! "That time will arrive for those chosen to wear the Kepi upon graduation, until then none of you has any rights or privileges. There is much to teach, or pour into your empty vessels and not enough time in which to do it. Your complete attention will be required during every waking moment. My cognomen is Altesse and my rank is Sergeant and heaven help any of you who forget it. Now everyone, come to attention", he bellowed. Then as he looked at his new charges he bellowed, "Dismissed"!

The lights immediately went out and the men climbed into their bunk bed emplacements and immediately fell asleep. For just four and a half hours away was the start of a new day.

The following day at 0430 hours in the morning, the bugle blew, the flag was raised and Altesse turned on the barracks lights as he strode slowly down the center of the barracks bellowing repeatedly, "Drop your cocks and grab your socks", wake up you scum". The few unfortunates that were not out of their bunks by the time he passed them found the bunk tipped over and the unfortunate that still clung to his bed linens soon kissed the floor, very hard.

They all had five short minutes to get dressed and make their bunk and attend to their area, before falling out side and performing a half hour of calisthenics followed by a three mile run. Before their training was completed all would be running five miles.

Then back to the barracks, to shit, piss, shower shave, brush their teeth and further prepare your area for the Sergeants scrutiny prior to assembling for breakfast formation at 0630 hours. After thirty minutes had passed yet another formation to separate and allocate the training assignments for each day's regimen. By 1800 hours the recruits reassembled and marched off to their evening meal, allotted just one half hour, then back to the barracks to view further training either by film or video tape and then by 2030 hours, to tend to their boots and clothing and prepare for the following days exertions.

Altesse was right, for there was much to learn and precious little time to learn it sufficiently. Starting with breaking their spirit and reshaping it back into something far better than had previously existed. In time the "I", would be replaced with "We". Soon all would understand that even above ones country one served, or one's personal needs, or the needs of the Legion, everyone grew to depend upon their comrade in arms above all else. What was understood by all was the unspoken understanding that, "Should worst come to worst, would the comrade next to you hold up their end"? Nothing else mattered other than that singular value. Nothing.

Every day, six days a week all endured this routine. Discipline, in formation marching, weapons training, the basics of personal hand to hand self-defense, with a slant towards the French techniques of Savatte and knife fighting techniques with a smattering of Judo carried the day.

In time medium and long distance marches were performed with night cold camp bivouacs attended to. In time, injuries weeded out those who were not up to muster and by days end a bunk would be empty from time to time and the others would wonder, but not for too long for time was precious.

Altesse had proved to be up to his billing as a particularly harsh and often cruel taskmaster. While there was no particular prohibition in the Legion against repeated striking of a recruit while in training in order to gain his complete attention, Altesse constantly struck his men regardless of whether or not the deserved it and his rate of injuries were amongst the highest of all the instructors. Yet who would dare but endure such treatment? Never complain, nor explain, for no one was predisposed to listen. Either one endured or washed out.

Although he tried to cover it up, the faint odor of alcohol was ever present on Altesse at almost every occasion. Since the officers rarely had any contact with the recruits during training, Altesse's problem with alcohol went largely unnoticed, except for the recruits and the other Sergeants. The recruits aside, the other noncoms remained silent for the reasons of never ratting out a comrade for any reason and for the fact that Altesse was a proven killer of men. His sheer size, strength, speed and skill with the blade commanded respect by all, if not fear.

One of the inconsistencies in their training was that most of the Non-French speaking trainees were at first lost linguistically given that their instructors were forbidden to speak any other language but French. Forcing the desperate trainees to grasp even the basic rudimentary aspects of the French language as they went along. Those that didn't quickly grasp the language repeatedly felt the sting of Sergeant Altesse's boot. To accelerate things, all trainees were compelled to never speak in their native language and only in the French they gleaned along the way. The wisdom was simply that in the Legion, French was the Lingua Franca, and communication would suffer if a polyglot of linguistics were permitted to occur. Surprisingly enough the trainees quickly learned enough rudimentary French during this period in order to be assimilated into the whole. During the tenth week of training, Major St. Nathalie stood with Sergeant Lambrage on a balcony overlooking the parade ground late in the afternoon watching several units practicing their marching drills. When the Major asked, "By the way Lambrage, how is our Basque performing under the tutelage of Sergeant Altesse"?

"Better than expected Major, but not surprising"! "How so Didier"?

"Further testing indicates a remarkable aptitude for linguistics. His marksmanship abilities at the firing range, equals or betters top marks for any of the instructors, but not surprising since his distant vision acuity tests out at 20/15 and thus is able to hit targets at a distance of 400 meters repeatedly unaided. In his self-defense instruction he repeatedly has bested some our best instructors, leading to some rather spirited confrontations. His ability with the manual of arms is again flawless. Sergeant Altesse has already turned over the drilling of his troops to Vega, so he can steal away for a bit of the nip during parade ground exercises, along with his Corporal"!

"I thought that Altesse had successfully gone on the wagon Sergeant, after that last unfortunate beating he administered to one of the recruits almost a year ago, wasn't it"?

"Apparently Major, he had for a while, but it appears that lately he's fallen off, being far more careful in his forays with the golden flask"!

"Please continue with your critique of Vega, Sergeant"! "Nothing to critique worth mentioning. He gets top marks in comportment, military skills, endurance, and adaptability. Like the others he's felt the sting of Altesse's boot although far less than others and gives no response. If I was pressed to evaluate him right now, I'd consider him ready for further training. In fact regarding his recent instructions in Savatte and in the arts of the blade, I'd say he's as good as any of the instructors if not better"!

"Ready for advancement is he Sergeant. I'll have to keep that in mind"! "Major, if I may", asked Lambrage?

"Continue Sergeant"!

"Since the subject of Sergeant Altesse has arisen, I feel it necessary to bring several things to your attention, long overdue"!

"Continue"!

"His rate of unnecessary attrition due to casualties' has climbed far above what is acceptable. Of course, an audit of their progress reveals that along with the few marginal and subpar performers washing out due to injuries, rendering them, Hors de Combat, there are those with acceptable and even above acceptable marks on the training dossiers that have been injured in such a way that is beyond accidental. Coupled with his past performances, there is only but one logical explanation for this"!

"Are you asking that the Alsatian be transferred elsewhere"?

"We have needs in Mali, Cameroon and Niger that can use a man of his skills, for the good of the Legion. Further may I point out, the last thing we need is the Inspector General to drop down out of the skies, and stick his beak into the Majors affairs"!

"Merde', that pig in Paris. A political appointee under Mitterrand sits behind his Socialist desk and knows nothing of military affairs. You make your point well Lambrage. After this graduation I'll see to it that Sergeant Altesse gets to know the African continent better"!

What Lambrage knew of the Alsatians training methods was only the tip of the iceberg. Altesse was quite correct when he told his charges; the each of them would grow to hate him during their sixteen weeks. By the end of the first week each of the men dreamed of having the good Sergeant in their sights and the fire selector of their weapon on "full auto" and a full magazine inserted. Of course the man was a brute, for he drove them unmercifully causing event many of the fittest to drop from exhaustion. During full field pack runs, he drove his men with his leather riding crop always at hand and earning its merit.

Even the other instructors, every one considered, "hard men", by their contemporaries, had cause to question the methods and tactics of the 'Alsatians' brutality. Of course the officers often turned a blind eye to any excesses of their sergeant's tactics, considering only results as valid criteria. The training guidelines written into the Legions operational manual were simply that. Guidelines, always given the widest latitude of interpretation set forth by superiors. Normally the only thing that would get an instructor replaced was a lack of results.

In spite of the obvious fatigue and in many cases pain, all the trainees endured, all had no choice but to tough things out till the bitter end whatever may come, many masking injuries that often stay with them for some time to come. There were no malingerers in this unit even though their numbers had been whittled down by over a dozen. The survivors of the Alsatians attentions had come too far to quit.

Without the Legion, where would they go? What could they do other than limp back into their previous lives and look what that brought them? More often than not a Legion enlistee brought a lifetime of chronic failure, as part of his personal baggage. Here was their last stop. Those left would stick things out to the bitter end, or die.

Carlos was fortunate since he'd chosen to keep as low a profile as possible. Saying little, volunteering for nothing, constantly studying. His mind constantly absorbing all that came his way. More important was his constant state of alertness, which served him well in anticipating the occasional punch or kick courtesy of the Alsatian, with his ability to roll with the blow preventing serious injury.

The training in various skill sets would often rotate amongst the training Sergeants and the following week, the rotation came to the Alsatian to conduct the self-defense training on his own unit out on the parade grounds. Both Sergeant Lambrage and Major St. Nathalie took a mid-afternoon break on their quarterly evaluations of their instructors and walked out on the balcony to observe the various unit groupings that covered the parade grounds. Every thirty meters, was a unit gathered around an instructor and a different trainee focusing on a different move. The instructors were all trained, to break every aspect of a move down and demonstrate to their charges. Then all would break into pairs and repeat and repeat until everything became an automatic response.

As the Alsatians group was just starting their instruction, Major St. Nathalie commented, "Ah Lambrage, there is Sergeant Altesse's group almost below us. Isn't this one of the days that combat bayonette training is called for"?

"Yes major it is, with hard rubber blades! If you'll recall, when we were coming up, the practice knives were made of wood"! "Indeed Lambrage, an improvement lessening the injuries. Let us observe Altesse first hand and see how his training measures up", as he offered a cigarette to Lambrage from his pack of Dunhills.

"Gentlemen", said Altesse sarcastically as he strutted around those assembled around him. "Today is my turn to train you in the niceties of bayonette self-defense. As you have previously learned, the Corsican manner of knife fighting has served the Legion rather well over the years. You've been trained by others, but it seems time you've learned how it's really done, for none of the other instructors has ever been able to best me. In fact, no one has ever bested me in any armed or hand to hand contact. No it would seem unfair if I were to choose someone at random, so I've combed the training records and have come up with someone that has scored the highest marks, in fact someone that has bested all of the other instructors, right here in our midst"! All eyes suddenly turned on Carlos. As the Alsatian went to the box on the ground that contained all of the rubber knives for the group, he picked up two and tossed one of them in the center of the circle saying, "Forty One. You will stand and pick up the knife"!

All were quiet as Carlos stood and approached the center of the circle warily, as suddenly he feinted to his left and dove to his right scooping up the blade and rolling quickly to his feet. He'd seen the Alsatian before during instruction of others and every time upon commencement he quickly jumped the student and skewered him before the blade came into his hands as he began to circle the large Alsatian. Suddenly the Alsatian lunged unexpectedly and the only thing that saved Carlos was that he'd seen that move before during training on others. For such a large man he moved quickly, as Carlos barely eluded the blade by a whisker, still circling as Altesse rolled to his feet, circling his prey saying, "Come little fish, swim into my net", as he took a deep breath.

For the next several minutes, Carlos and Altesse matched thrusts and parries, neither gaining the advantage as the Major asked, "That doesn't seem to be what we are teaching is it Lambrage"? "No sir, it is not. I believe the method Vega is employing is that commonly used by the Basques"!

"Seems quite effective since our Sergeant hasn't struck a point yet. Altesse has proven to be the training units' best knife fighter of all and here a simple recruit is matching him move for move"! No sooner than the words left his mouth, Carlos eluded a thrust, quickly stepping inside the thrust, as Altesse was starting to fatigue acting as the aggressor and as he pirouetted around him gave two lighting fast slashes to Altesse's throat and head, both leaving their crimson mark, as he danced away from Altesse's wild parry.

Both the Major and Sergeant held their breath as Altesse simply stood there realizing that finally someone has got the better of him, with Lambrage saying, "Thank God they weren't real knives or we'd have a dead instructor on our hands"!

Before another word could be said Altesse tossed aside his faux blade and withdrew a real Italian long handle switch blade said as he moved forward, "Now to bring about your end scum", as he charged wildly at

Carlos, who again eluded his grasp again leaving a mark on the Sergeants head and swiftly moving out of range. Now outmatched as he quickly moved around the circle now making it a point to elude every move by Altesse, in hope that someone would call attention to this madness, he quickly summoned the universe by thinking, 'I ask not for any tomorrows, only for this day', as he eluded a thrust that had nearly found home, the razor sharp blade opening his field training blouse. Suddenly he saw a glint of metal land in the midst of the grouping. He ran towards the metal on the ground quickly scooping it up with Altesse in quick pursuit and as he avoided the next charge leaving but a slight gash on his trailing arm, he discovered that what he had in his hand was a flick knife delivered no doubt by the gods, as he quickly flicked the knife to the front evening the odds a bit even through his blade was significantly smaller. At the sight of a real blade finally in the hands of Carlos, Altesse held up slightly from his previously unrelenting aggression, as he said, "That won't help you scum. Prepare to die"! His bloodlust replacing any semblance of common sense that may have remained.

Breathing heavily now, the alcohol ingested clearly having an effect, Altesse made a final ill-timed lunge, side stepped by Carlos as he slashed at the left hand side of Altesse's neck severing the vein that carried the blood from the brain cavity and back to the lungs for recirculation. As Altesse sunk to his knees, Carlos walked away slowly keeping Altesse in sight much like a matador as he withdrew from the bull after his final thrust.

Summoning all of his strength to rise Altesse felt the blood seep quickly from his hands as he tried in vain to stop the relentless seepage from his neck. Had Carlos severed the artery on the other side, large spurts of blood would've been shooting forth with every beat of his heart. As it was Altesse began to feel a rapidly expanding weakness in his extremities as all stood in place, stunned by the recent occurrence. He sank to one knee and looked around silently pleading his plight and discovering by the look in their eyes that no one cared. Then he took one last glance at the raw recruit that had bested him.

Carlos looked at Altesse and without a further word, saw the Alsatian keel over to the ground face first. Suddenly a cheer erupted from those assembled as they rushed forward. The constant cheer drew the attention of the other instructors, as they came running at the loud exhortation that, "The Alsatian is dead"!

As all other activity on the parade ground, gradually ceased and the training instructors ran to the area of Altesse's unit, Major St. Nathalie said to Sergeant Lambrage, "My apologies Lambrage for restraining you, when Altesse and the young man got serious in their little life and death dance. But as you can see from the result, our problem concerning the Alsatian, appears to have been solved. See to it that our Basque is advanced no later than tomorrow, I'll sign the orders first thing, then see to it that Altesse' is given a quiet burial in the usual place and of course, the cause of his demise will have been a training accident"!

"At your command Major", said Lambrage, snapping to attention and saluting. As he made to leave St. Nathalie said, "And one other thing Sergeant. Find out who belonged to the blade that suddenly appeared on the ground for our recruit. A serendipitous occurrence don't you think"?

As Lambrange forced his way through the crowd of recruits and trainers, he came upon Vega, being held by several of the training instructors and said, "Release this man at once"!

"But Sergeant Lambrage, a murder has just occurred", said one of the senior instructors"!

"Quite the opposite Sergeant, for you see, Major St. Nathalie and I saw the entire thing from the balcony of his office", pointing at the major still standing on the balcony. "We observed Sergeant Altesse; pull his own knife upon the trainee when he was being bested during training. Now where is the knife that the recruit used to defend himself"?

"Right here Sergeant, said another trainer that produced the blade and gave it to Lambrage. After examining it and finding that it was simply a common flick knife, he saw an inscription on the blade and said aloud, "Who in Altesse's unit answers to the name of "Le Bouche"? The crowd of trainees parted and several of them brought forth Altesse's Corporal and assistant training instructor, in front of Lambrage. As he stood meekly before the Senior Sergeant, his entire future passed before his very eyes as Lambrage said, "They tell me this belongs to you Corporal. Well does it", he asked as her held the blade in front of him?

"Yes Sergeant, said the Corporal meekly.

'Well then Corporal, in the future you will be more careful with your personal property, won't you", said Lambrage handing the knife back to him. Then turning around he looked at one he recognized as a Senior Instructor and said, "Two things Sergeant. Altesse's unit will be needing a new Sergeant to complete their training. See to it before nightfall if you please. Then direct our Corporal here, to select a burial detail from Altesse's former unit and see to it that a proper burial is carried out in the usual place, after the evening meal, without any undue attention"!

"Lambrage then turned to Vega and summoned him to follow him away from the others and said, "You are directed to accompany the burial detail and be involved. Since you are the aggrieved surviving party, it is only appropriate, don't you agree"?

"Yes Sergeant", replied Vega not knowing what was to come next? "When that is concluded, you will clean yourself up and then pack all of your belongings. It has been determined that you are ready for the next phase of training and you will report to my office, the first thing in the morning after you've eaten breakfast for your orders. Are we understood"?

Vega nodded his head saying, "At your command Sergeant"!

"Good. Now run along and join the others. I'll talk to the Corporal and let him know of your disposition"!

An hour later, as Lambrage was personally typing the orders for Vegas advancement and the death certificate for Altesse, Major St. Nathalie entered his cubicle. As Lambrage rose to stand to attention, St. Nathalie bid him to be seated saying, "As you were Sergeant"! "Is everything in order"?

"As you've directed, Sergeant Altesse is to be buried after the evening meal. I've directed one of the Senior instructors to find a suitable replacement for Altesse, starting tomorrow morning. Combing through Altesse's personnel dossier, have discovered no known next of kin, thus a letter of condolences will not be required. Currently I'm working on Altesse's death certificate and recruit Vegas paperwork for his next assignment personally. The recruit has been informed that he will take a personal part in Altesse's burial detail and have instructed one of the Senior Sergeants to supervise the units Corporal to select and Command the detail. And as to the knife involved that was used in Altesse's demise? It belonged to his subordinate, the Corporal"!

"Seems the Corporal, in addition to others, had quite enough of the Alsatian, luckily for him"! Is he suitable for the NCO training yet Lambrage"?

"He shows some promise sir. Has been in the Legion for four years, but in my opinion he may need some additional time in grade before further review. Perhaps if he reenlists, then we should consider him, Major"! 'Very well Sergeant. You will have the paperwork ready for my approval first thing in the morning after I arrive"? "At your command Major"!

"Very well and thank you Sergeant. You've handled this incident well", said the Major as he rose from his chair. "This day we have witnessed the lamb devour the Lion. An interesting turn of events, wouldn't you agree"? Slowly a small smile came across Lambrage's face as he nodded his head in agreement as the Major departed. As he started back on his paperwork he has to agree with the Major that a problem had been resolved this day. Not exactly as he would've done it and certainly not by the book but quickly and efficiently. He knew the Major well enough to conclude the future of the fugitive recruit Vega would be interesting to follow.

The following morning Vega appeared in front of Sergeant Lambrage in a vacant office, with his belongings neatly packed in his duffle. He was presented his Kepi and new identification papers. "From now on Carlos Vegas had ceased to exist and Nestor Magellan is born and on the desk are the papers to prove it along with your dog tag and orders for your next assignment. Normally a ceremony is conducted but given the circumstances, I'm sure you won't mind the process. In an hour you will join another group that are on their way for further training at various units"!

Magellan read his orders that read as of an hour ago, he was released from his basic training assignment at the "Le 4eme Regiment Etrangers" and hereby assigned to the Le 3eme Regiment Etrangere d'Infrantrie, based at Kourou, in French Guyana, in South America.

On the old noisy propeller driven transport aircraft that lifted off from the Aerodrome near Vichy he took the time to read his new dossier in detail, as he kept rolling around his new name Nestor Magellan over and over in his head. Not exactly a name he would've chosen, but something he could work with all things considered. Then it hit him. A complete departure from the past. Complete and absolute. Reading on he discovered that he'd aged approximately a year and a half and was in his nineteenth year of life.

He was born in Tangiers, or so said his new birth certificate, of an

Algerian French woman and a French father in the employ of a French Construction Company, both deceased. Going through his new papers, he discovered an old and weathered newspaper clipping, encased in plastic, dated five years ago, indicating that a certain Hercule Magellan and his common law wife had perished in an auto accident. All of the documents of his origin seemed genuine enough as he wondered about his future, recalling Sergeant Lambrage's final words. "Your next training assignment will be in French Guyana. You'll be transported there along with a number of others on a supply transport craft and flown non-stop across the Atlantic to Cayenne and then transported to the Euro Space Drome at Kourou, where you will undergo Jungle survival training. Once there you'll be processed and temporarily seconded to the school just up the Approuage River from Regina"!

"Should you survive the first phase, then expect to spend some thirty days, more or less, in the jungle learning to live off the fat of the land like a native. I can assure you that you will not spend one dry moment there.

Should you survive that and still be with us, then you'll either be assigned further training or be assigned guard duty at the Rocket base at Kourou, the heart and soul of France's 'Arianne' rocket programme. For that is the Legions primary function there, the guarding of the base and security there is as tight as a virgins twat. But never fear, from time to time, you'll have company other than the reptiles and things that will eat you. The British SAS and the American Naval SEALS join in from time to time for their advanced training and joint exercises. So young man if you think Altesse was as bad as it gets, think again

15

The overseas flight on the noisy French Army transport proved uneventful other than it being the first time Nestor Magellan had ever been on an aircraft. Crammed in with another contingent of Legion trainees who had achieved the prized 'Kepi', normal airfreight and a contingent of French Army regulars, they landed without a problem and were met at the Cayenne Aerodrome and transported to the Rocket Drome complex at Kourou. Upon his arrival Magellan and the others were segregated for processing and forwarded to the Jungle Training Center. The following day several Army helicopters flew him and the others to the small town of Regina, where boarded an old rickety riverboat for the upriver trek to the roughhewn Jungle Training Center, literally hacked and constructed out of the jungle.

True to its reputation, the Jungle training center proved to be one of the most humbling tasks any human could endure. The equatorial setting brought almost daily rain deluges, a mélange' of insects that would drive even Darwin to distraction, predators of every sort, coupled with inescapable humidity and a relentless smothering heat, proved a never ending problem to one's physical and emotional health. One often went to sleep, if that was what you called it, wet and awoke wet. Trench foot and crotch rot we're a constant companion visiting everyone to varying degrees, regardless of care and preparation.

The instructors, physically the elite' of the Legion were all hard men, used to the ravages of the jungle reasoning that if the upriver natives could survive and prosper then so could anyone given the proper motivation and training. All were provided an additional significant financial incentive for their service and rotated every sixty days back to the Rocket Drome for two weeks of R&R before returning. After twelve months of duty they were then assigned other training assignments. The training they could provide, but each man's motivation lay within, always close to the surface with a recollection of what awaited, on the outside world, should he ever fail. In the Legion a new start in life was just at their grasp, all one had to do was reach out and endure. What the instructors failed to tell was that the life of the average native in the bush was relatively short, given the predators that were always on the village's edge, awaiting the fires to extinguish in the night. Then there were the innumerable diseases one could easily contract and the lack of proper medical care available. Such was the life of a native, but regardless they been occupiers for thousands of years.

During the latter days of their training, the trainees were to endure a four day death trek on quarter rations, armed with only their assault weapon, two extra clips of ammunition, their service bayonet and a box of waterproof matches. Traversing swollen rivers and engaging with poisonous reptiles, for nutrition, they learned to master the natural elements for battle field objectives. The mere survival of each man instilled a grudging sense of pride and accomplishment as the instructors constantly repeated the mantra, "What one man can do, another man can do"! This would remain with each of them for the rest of their lives.

On the returning flight back to the Rocket Drome at Kourou, Magellan became seriously ill, diagnosed with Malaria and hospitalized, during which he slipped in and out of consciousness, in the grip of an intense fever. Suddenly after the fifth day his fever broke and upon awakening early in the morning, he tried to speak but could not, since his throat was parched having survived by constant intravenous flow of nutrition and medication, during the interim to his fever ravaged body.

That next day he was able to take his first oral nutrition, a calorie laden soup and several days later graduating to a calorie rich stew to replace some of the bulk of his body lost by the illness. The following week he was well enough to be released and ordered to a barracks where he spent the entire week resting and working out at the base gym in order to regain his stamina, reporting daily to the hospital for evaluation. When it was discovered that he'd sufficiently recovered, he was assigned perimeter guard duty at the Rocket Drome while the Legions wise men decided as to his next training assignment. Thirty days later, his orders directed him back across the Atlantic to the Vichy Aerodrome, where for the next three months he was assigned to a Recon and Anti-Tank unit at the Le ler Regiment Etrangere de Cavalerie, based at Orange.

Magellan was next ordered to report to the Le 2eme Regiment

Etrangere de Parachutistes, based near Calvi, on the French island of Corsica. There he trained in airborne assault and additional anti-tank combat. After his second month when he successfully completed ten static line jumps and another twenty free fall jumps, he was considered and accepted for instruction in the art of "HALO" jumps, or "High Altitude Low Opening" parachuting. Upon successful completion he could claim fifteen successful HALO jumps, the most notable being dropped from an altitude of twenty thousand feet, high above the Mediterranean and opening his chute at approximately one thousand feet while carrying a full field pack between his legs.

The final planned phase of his development occurred when he was sent for a year's tour in Africa, posted to the la 13eme Demi-Brigade de Legion, based near Djibouti on the horn of Africa. While there he became proficient in desert survival, not so much as following a proscribed course of training, but more of an 'on the job' training exercise. His unit placed on high alert during his entire tour, whereas the native Muslim tribesmen were in the midst of a nonstop sub rosa war in the region against heretics and various nonbelievers and anyone else they could kill of kidnap for ransom.

His unit would depart in the dead of night on search and destroy forays to either destroy bases of operation or rescue missions where actionable intelligence indicated probable success. While there he quickly became proficient in the local dialect, negating the need for a local translator of questionable reliability. After his ninth month, he suggested to his Commander that he be allowed to lead a small contingent of his men in a hammer and anvil exercise against a particular tribe that had been harassing and kidnapping civilian missionaries.

One evening five heavily armed men slipped through the barricades unnoticed, traveling all night to reach three prepositioned desert vehicles. Word was leaked out that a convoy containing doctors heading towards a certain village to heal the sick was to depart at a certain date. Within the day, the Berber tribes Headman received the news from one of the translators working for the French Military.

The convoy was to pass through a certain choke point on the desert road between a string of high walled ridges, perfect for an ambush. The convoy of three civilian trucks was fronted by a military escort consisting of a single squad of French Regular Army soldiers, in two jeeps preceding the convoy and a third bring up the rear.

Since Magellan's fire team had been prepositioned in the pass for two days, they saw the tribesmen preparing several roadside bombs along a two hundred meter slot on the roadway, then saw them take position and wait through the night.

As the sun rose the following day replacing the frigid night's cold for the blistering heat of the day, they all waited in anticipation. The Tribesmen in anticipation of another large payday and the five Legionnaires in anticipation of a trap soon to shut. Magellan's men had all the fifteen tribesmen located on both sides of the pass chokepoint. It wasn't difficult since the hunters had never been hunted and were unaware of the presence of others almost in their midst. In the desert morning before the winds start to gust, one can hear the sounds of machinery from quite a distance, so as it was for both the tribesmen and Magellan's men as the convoy approached.

Armed with two RPGs strategically placed the plan was to allow the convoy to pass through the first set of trailing roadside planted bombs that flanked the road blocking any possibility of retreat, then fire on the second set of roadside bombs that was intended to blow up as the first Military escort jeep passed through. Since they wouldn't have sufficient time to fire two rockets on planted bombs a decision was made to fire on the first as the jeep reached a point fifty meters behind the bomb igniting one of them signaling danger then fire on the rear most bomb knowing the trailing jeep would be a hundred meters behind the last truck of civilians.

The plan went off as predicted. Just before the first jeep reached the fifty meter mark one of Magellan's men fired the first rocket, then seconds later the other fired on the rear most planted bomb as both exploded halting the column with no casualties. From time to time Allah smiles on other than the intended as every one of the tribesmen rose from their positions and commenced firing on the convoy only to be cut down by the accurate fire of the Legionnaires who lay doggo in the rocks above, working their way from the highest emplacements downward. Within sixty seconds all firing stopped by the Legionnaires and the French Army squad escort. After the recognition signals were exchanged Magellan's men slowly filed down from their emplacements, and as they passed the dead tribesmen, they dragged the dead from their hides and flung them down the rocky hillside, to the dusty road below.

After a body count was concluded, an Irish Corporal approached Magellan saying, "Fifteen tribesmen arrived, me bucko and fifteen lay at our feet"! The Regular Army Sergeant that led the contingent then said, "Great work men. Had it not been for you we'd all have been goners"! Then another explosion was heard behind them as Nestor said to the civilian missionaries that surrounded them, "Nothing to be afraid of. Just taking care of unfinished business", as one of his men carrying an old Soviet RPG was seen trotting up towards their position.

"There are a lot of people that must be buried immediately", said the leader of the missionaries"!

"No one gets buried this day especially these people", said Magellan! "But their religion requires immediate burial. No sir, it demands it"!

"These are not people, but animals. I doubt if any of them has observed their Friday prayers in quite some time. Even if they had, those sessions would be filled with sermons firing up the faithful to kill all infidels. And that sir would include you. Those they didn't kill they would take hostage for ransom. Expect no civilized treatment from them for they would rape your women repeatedly right in front of your eyes an if you protested there would one less mouth to feed and your naked body would be thrust in the desert to be fed upon by the carrion. So there will be no burials this day. We will strip their bodies, burn all of their belongings on the roadside in a pile then line each of their naked bodies up in a row and remove their eyes, ears, noses, private parts and fingers and toes, so they may meet their ninety nine virgins, Hors de Combat"! The missionary leader the turned to the Sergeant in command of their escort saying, "Sergeant, you outrank this man. Order him to bury these tribesmen"! The Sergeant looked at the man quizzically, then at Magellan, then back at the missionary saying, "He's a Legionnaire", shrugging his shoulders!

"What's that got to do with anything, you out rank the man and he's about to do an uncivilized act that will no doubt inflame the rest making our work here more difficult"!

"Oh you mean the conversion of the WOGS into Christianity under the guise of good works. Just how many converts have you gleaned into your flock lately? No sir I will do no such thing as you ask nor will any of my men, nor will you. In fact my men and I will help the Legionnaires in any manner they ask and be grateful, for they just saved our bacon. So please either help us of return to your vehicles ready for departure. Anyone not in the vehicles when we depart will be left to their own devices. Now get in your fucking vehicles"!

He then motioned to his men and they set to stripping the tribesmen's bodies then removing their protuberances and tossing them by the wayside. The removal of each one eyes proved particularly disturbing, but necessary in order to send a message.

In the space of ten minutes their task completed and the naked tribesmen's bodies lay naked in the morning sun, the last explosion erupted in front of the column as the final roadside bomb was detonated. Gasoline was poured upon the pile of clothing and ignited as the Escort Units Sergeant said to Magellan, "Well, we're off and thank you. Can we give you a lift somewhere"?

"No Sergeant our transport is over the hill in a secluded spot. Maybe our paths will cross sometime down the road and we'll lift a draft to recall this moment"!

"I'll agree to that readily Legionnaire and at that time your money will be no good"!

Nestor nodded in agreement as both men gave a casual salute of departure, the Sergeant yelling, "Saddle up we're going"!

Upon returning to their outpost at night fall, Magellan and the group made a full report to their Commander who said, "Well done gentlemen, well done. Now get some food in you and a good night's rest. That is all", as he rose to receive their salute!

"Oh, Private Magellan remain behind for a moment! When all had departed he said, "I'm putting you in for promotion to Corporal, Magellan. The way you planned and executed this operation without a single casualty with a minimum of resources deserves advancement"!

"Now I don't know whether or not I would've conducted the aftermath in the manner that you have, or not. I'll not quibble with your tactics, but it will indeed send a message to the tribesmen that will not soon be forgotten. We shall all keep this little foray into the desert under the tongue, if you understand my meaning"!

"Magellan immediately came to attention, lifted his hand in salute saying, "As you command sir"! His salute returned, he turned about crisply and left.

As his time and supposed training in Djibouti came to an end, his dossier grew as did his rank as by now his training was considered completed as his next assignment was to the French Embassy in the Central African Republic of Chad, where he met up with several other selected Legionnaires to eventually become involved in a 'Coup de Etat', in the ousting of a long standing and corrupt Dictator, of that land locked nation. As their ambassador related to them, the powers that be in Paris were ready to replace him with yet another equally corrupt head of government who was more amenable to French mining interests, in Uranium and other valuable ores. Since the mining consortium provided the vast majority of the country's revenue in the form of legitimate taxes and various under the table bribes, the unwarranted increase in bribes were the final stroke signaling the Dictators demise. With the replacement of the current Dictator with one more friendly to French interests, especially since newly discovered diamond deposits signaled an increased greed quotient. The arbitrary demand by the current Dictator sent the Ambassador into a frenzy of diplomatic activity, especially since his threat to nationalize all of France's legitimate business interests. The appropriate palms were greased, a new head of state was selected and the military was now brought into play in order to effect a smooth transition of authority. The task was handed to the Legion to implement the solution.

"Just one thing more gentlemen", said the Ambassador. "It probably doesn't mean anything but the man that's being replaced, is a lifelong cannibal. An exclusive partaker of human flesh. He's been reported to have consumed both his father and mother and the rest of his family down past his cousins. Human flesh is the only staple of his diet. This may just account for his emotional instability. So when you do what is to be your task, I would not suggest that any exchange of words occur"!

Within the time frame of two hours, early on a Sunday morning, prior to sunrise, the entire body of senior governmental ministers, save only two that were friendly to French interests, disappeared into the vastness of the entire eastern Sahara desert, followed by the entire general staff of the Army. By dawn a puppet government was quietly installed.

During the early morning hours, the still of the night was disturbed by the rumble of trucks carrying bound and gagged old men in their bed clothes in many cases, through their various communities to preselected locations out in the desert. Once there they were loaded into helicopters and flown out into the desert and once at altitude were shoved out of the respective aircraft without a word, for that mile long flight back to earth still bound and gagged. Since the air drops occurred far away from normally known caravan routes it was a given that the desert would take care of any remnants of their remains sooner rather than later. An assumption that proved correct with the passage of time.

The Prime Minister of France, through a few key associates, directed that medals quietly be bestowed upon each and every Legionnaire involved along with an extra significant stipend for each funded by the consortium.

After which Magellan receiving his promotion orders to Corporal along with the medal and stipend in a private ceremony at the Ambassador's residence, he received his next assignment to be directed to the Le 5eme Regiment Etrangere, based at Murora Island, in Tahiti. The site of France's Nuclear Test facility in the south Pacific, where he spent a mostly uneventful, if not peaceful tour of duty. With an easy job helping provide security for the next several years for the entire facility, it left him with a great deal of time on his hands, sufficient enough to work on his tan and master the SCUBA skills as a diver and no longer under the pressures of training and combat he took advantage of the French Army's School of Linguistics' mastering the French language in all of its forms and acquired a working knowledge of English, Italian, German and Russian to accompany his knowledge of Spanish and Portuguese acquired as a schoolboy.

His two years in paradise concluded, he was promoted to Sergeant and transferred to Mayotte, near Mozambique as part of the Detachment De Legion Etrangere de Mayotte. His unit was to provide Security Services to the embassy as part of its public persona, but in fact, the bulk of their time was spent providing security for the various business interests, when not engaged in training that operated in the French Governments sphere of influence. In reality, this is where Sergeant Nestor Magellan rounded into form as the complete agent of destruction for the French Government. He was selected, along with others, to join an elite cadre of Legionnaires, many on their second or third tour of enlistment, who'd proven loyalties, beyond question to the Legion and La Belle France. A basic requirement was a high degree of ability in a given area of specialization. Along with various instructors from all over the world, each Legionnaire cross trained the others in their area of expertise and each in turn was cross trained by the others in their various areas of specialization, such as linguistics, poisons and their various modes of delivery, specialized munitions, an array of personal unarmed self-defense methods that were quite apart from conventional methods, long range shooting, as well as short range quick fire, which was where Nestor learned the value of the 'double tap', demolition fabrication, espionage and most important of all, escape and evasion methods in both rural and urban settings.

The training atmosphere, while interspersed with actual duty assignments, was far less formal, than he'd grown accustomed to where rank took a back seat to proven expertise, yet was certainly no less intense. For all there, were accomplished and decorated professionals in their own right, with all the attributes that years of self-discipline and motivation along with the paucity of personal comforts and liberties would bring. Egos were all pocketed for the duration for the time spent together was valuable in gleaning knowledge from each other that would either save or extinguish lives quickly.

From time to time, their training schedule as well as their scheduled minor duties at the Embassy, was interrupted by necessity, requiring their sub rosa intervention, in behalf of either the French Government or that of various interests friendly with the French business interests in order to silently remove impediments to progress. The occasional kidnapping and complete disappearance of someone, or a sudden and unexplained illness that defied current treatment resulting with a mysterious death, an automobile accident on a lonely road or in an urban area, or an aircraft in flight that suddenly and inexplicably lost power at altitude that crashed into the jungle, trains jumped their tracks and seeming random occurrences that left everyone baffled as to their cause.

Not all of which occurred in the host country. However neighboring countries, all experienced these occurrences, leaving indications more often than not as to culpable parties other than the Legion as having much to gain.

Each and every occurrence was at the behest of the Embassy and once their mission was made clear, the cadre had 'Carte' Blanche', in anything needed to accomplish their objective.

Just one rule was inflexible. Rush jobs brought with them an increased probability of failure and the cadre' refused to be put in that position. Too many things, too many imponderables, were likely to occur, thus summoning failure and revelation as to cause. Their collective mantra was simply to "not be seen". Meticulous planning placed the odds squarely in their favor and their track record bore witness to that.

From time to time, several operations were planned and executed almost simultaneously, with several groups involved, but at no time would a single rush job be tolerated. If something just had to be done within a few days, then have a cutout hire lesser lights for there were certainly enough locals around who claimed proficiency at wet work.

Whether or not the job was done properly, the cut out always disappeared completely. After two years in that environment, in which Magellan reenlisted for another tour of duty, he was shuttled around to various African Embassies around the Continent performing a range of security functions.

Then one day Magellan was directed to return to his point of origin long ago, where the destination on his orders read, 'Le 4eme Regiment Etrangere. This time he was to be a training instructor, for entrance level Legionnaires.

As he rode the aircraft back to France, his thoughts turned to his parents. He knew that his father had died as a result of the actions of the Spanish Guardia and he knew that his mother was a guardian of the former Archbishop of Zaragoza, now a Cardinal, and a Prince of the Church in Madrid. Try as he may to shed all thoughts of his former life, they clung to him like a lead weight, somewhere in the recesses of his mind. He vowed that someday he would return to set things right.

As he entered the Training Prefecture to offer his orders and be processed into the fold, the familiar faces he'd hoped to see were no longer there. Gone was Major St. Nathalie, recently promoted to General and Superintendent at the Lycee Militaire' at St. Cyr on the outskirts of Paris, now married into a wealthy and prominent Parisian family.

Gone was the Senior Sergeant Lambrage, retired from the Legion after thirty years of dedicated service, just a few months ago. Pensioned for life and recently married to a massively breasted widow. A former dancer at the Moulin Rouge years ago, who inherited a string of meat markets in greater Paris.

"Ah the good life for Lambrage", said Magellan quietly. "A shop keeper, with someone to keep him warm on a cold winter night"! He owed both men much, for were it not for them, he most likely wouldn't be standing here at this very moment.

While being processed, he inquired of the clerk, a Corporal, processing his paperwork, "Corporal, can you tell me, ah, there was a training instructor here long ago, a rather large man called "The Alsatian", I believe his cognomen was Altesse. Yes, it was Sergeant Altesse"!

The Corporal, a friendly sort who took notice of Magellan's decorations and knew how to read between the lines of a military dossier interrupted his typing and invited Magellan to disappear with him back into the inner sanctum world of personnel records. Here, complete records of every Legionnaire were kept going back to 1946, no thanks to the Nazi occupation of Paris where the records were kept at that time. "Everything is in the process of being computerized", said the Corporal while he scoured the files long since winnowed down to three by five filing cards.

"Altesse you say, Altesse, Altesse, ah here it is a micro card of one Altesse, Deter P. Private", announced the Corporal!

"Private Altesse", exclaimed a surprised Magellan. "He was a Sergeant and a training instructor, when I last saw him!

"That may be Sergeant", replied the clerk as he scanned the card for further data. "But according to the personnel card his death came as a result of attempting to destroy government property. He was reduced in rank to Private and buried in an unmarked grave"!

"Does his card indicate the manner in which he died", asked Magellan? "No it doesn't Sergeant. It only indicates that he was an instructor and that he succumbed to injuries. Did you know this man well"?

"No one knew that man well Corporal. Thank you for your kindness"! "Magellan passed the better part of a year at the Legions training facility being a stern task master, driving his charges towards a disciplined life and telling them why and serving as an example yet recalling the memories of what a brute the Alsatian was and alternating between 'Firme' and Delicatesse' in his discipline.

At the end of each class of sixteen weeks, when his charges received their 'Kepi' and were ordered for further training assignments, all remembered Magellan as the 'seeker' and one who was firm yet fair in his punishments.

Several uneventful years passed, and then one day prior to his next class he received orders, immediately transferring him to the Lycee de Militaire at St. Cyr. There his assignment was to instruct future French Military officers. As he read the orders, he noticed the name, 'Brigadier General', T..P. St. Nathalie, Commandant, as the requesting officer. So the rumors were true. 'But why did he request me', thought Nestor? But quickly that didn't matter. The orders arrived just in the nick of time, for life was becoming boring for Magellan, pressing discipline upon the dregs of the earth, attempting to develop them into a cohesive fighting machine, while an entire world of events was swirling about and here he was wet nursing the remnants of the "Great Unwashed". He immediately caught himself, lest he become another butcher like the Alsatian. Thanks to the General, he'd now be training future officers and gentlemen all. As had been the case whenever Magellan became too full of self-importance, something always dug into the depths of his memory, to bring him back to the former days of Carlos Vega. He'd come a very long way since then and a small voice deep within, would always remind him that he should remain grateful for the existence of the Legion, from whom all tangible benefits flowed.

By all that was holy he should have been either dead, or incarcerated for life in some tuberculosis infected prison. In the service of the Legion, he experienced many a close call. The wounds experienced were all superficial. In the Legion he was a valuable commodity, witness the orders he held in his hand.

The trip to Paris by train was uneventful except for the memories of his parents that came upon him at an ever increasing rate. He'd just entered his second reenlistment and was still less than thirty years old and to be summoned by the Lycee Militaire to train officers was indeed a feather in one's cap career wise and usually a promotion in rank was in the offing. It seemed indeed coincidental that General St. Nathalie, who approved his entrance into the Legion, would bring him closer to him at this time.

As he was processed in and billeted in the NCO quarters with an overly large quarters for his modest needs. The General was vacationing with his wife in their summer residence in the resort town of Deauville on the English Channel and he was assured that upon his return he would be summoned. In the meantime he was escorted by his new Commanding officer around the grounds and furnished with the curriculum that he was slated to instruct. Escape and evasion, military tactics in an urban setting, long range marksmanship and personal defense tactics.

The following week he was informed the General had returned and directed his presence at 0900 hours the following morning. At the proscribed time Magellan presented himself in full field uniform to the Generals adjutant and was shown into his office. As he entered the General rose to greet him as Magellan said, "Sergeant Magellan reporting as directed Mon General", and crisply saluted! St. Nathalie returned the salute, then motioned for the adjutant to depart saying, "As you were Lieutenant", then to Magellan, "Please Sergeant stand at ease, or better yet take a seat"!

As they settled in with each other St, Nathalie said, "You've come a long way from that time when Sergeant Lambrage first brought you before me. In fact you've exceeded any expectations either of us had by a wide margin. Your service dossier to date is thick with your accomplishments and I've told Lambrage how grateful I am for keeping me abreast of your progress"! "Sir, may I inquire as to the status of Sergeant Lambrage, sir"?

"That you may Sergeant, with one small correction. It is now Citizen Lambrage and he's taken a widow as his wife and is a shop keeper here in Paris, managing a string of butcher shops, she inherited upon her former husband's demise. Gossip had it, the man died with his boots on, but he was grossly overweight and had a heart condition. Shortly thereafter they met and their brief romance coincided with his scheduled retirement, so he became a merchant, with hardly another thought. We'll have to get the both of you together sometime to exchange war stories"!

"Sir that would be nice sir", answered Magellan.

"Sergeant, you can dispense with the overt formalities in my presence.

For the moment let us talk as men of accomplishment"! "Understood General"!

"I directed you here for two reasons. First of which is the training of our future officer corps. Those lives you touched in Marseilles have as a group fared rather well in their extended training and either you were extremely fortunate in those you've trained, or it was something about your style, the way you connected with the men, the way you led by personal example and from the front. I prefer to think it was latter, and so perhaps our future officers can benefit from your extended range of experiences. Now for the second and perhaps the more important reason you're here. Within months you will be introduced to several men. These are serious men all and all have examined your service dossier and agree that you will fit in with their purposes rather nicely. They all hold significant positions in various aspects of governmental service, as will you here at St, Cyr. The other functions they serve are extracurricular in description and once you've settled in completely they will make themselves known to you. All I can tell you for the moment is that your proven skill sets mesh well with those you've employed while in Mozambique"!

"At your command mon General", said Magellan!

"Good. Now before I forget", a little something extra", he said while reaching for a set of papers in front of him. "These are orders promoting you in rank with yet another stripe and the appropriate pay that accompanies it", said the General signing all of the copies, "Effective immediately. So take these to my adjutant for disbursal upon your departure and go by the Base Exchange and get the appropriate stripes and have them affixed to your uniform". The General then rose from his chair handing the folder, to Magellan and reached forward to shake his hand rather than exchange salutes saying, "Welcome to St. Cyr Sergeant"! Then with a wink added, "Now get out of here, I've work to do"!

Several months passed as Magellan quickly settled in with his duties which weren't much different from those he was involved with his basic training unit with the exception of barracks inspections and the daily drilling of the cadets. He soon discovered that he had a significant amount of free time on his hands, with the more mundane functions of daily life attended to by others. A cycle of a certain amount of classroom work and field training was his routine along with the attendant paper work any teacher would have.

16

The phone rang and Magellan picked up the receiver on the third ring answering in German, "Hallo"! Then he heard on the other end a gruff sounding voice saying, "It took me eighteen years to achieve the rank that you now have in far less time"! Magellan was taken aback as he said, "Who is this"? "A voice from the past that you should be grateful to hear"! Magellan's mind raced as he ventured, "The name of a certain Sergeant Lambrage comes to mind. Would that be correct"? "Congratulations on your promotion Mon Ami and welcome to the City of Lights"!

"Thank you Sergeant", said Nestor!

"Correction Sergeant. It is Citizen Lambrage from now on"!

"That may well be the case, but please allow me to privately consider you as Sergeant"!

"As you wish, but that is not necessarily why I contacted you, to discuss old times that never were, there will be time for that later. I was wondering if you had any plans for dinner this evening". "Other than St. Cyr's general mess offering nothing. I'm wondering whether or not this is a command invitation"?

"I remind you again that I am a citizen Sergeant. Let us just say that there are some interested people that would like to meet you"!

"And take my measure while we break bread together", said Magellan continuing. "Will you be there citizen"?

"Oh course Sergeant, for I'll be the one picking you up"! "Then of course citizen". When and where"?

"In an hour and in front of your quarters. And wear casual garb"!

True to his word Lambrage arrived in a well maintained, black, twenty year old Citroen Sedan and picked up Magellan in front of his quarters. Other than his gruff exterior exhibited over the phone, he appeared quite expansive and glad to see him upon his arrival. As he drove into the city he said, "I don't mind telling you that it's not often, that I roll the dice and you Mon Ami, were a bit of a gamble. But you endured and prospered. The General and I are quite pleased of your accomplishments"!

"Thank you. The General mentioned that you were keeping tabs on me from afar", said Magellan!

"It did me some good Magellan, for the General promoted me to Warrant Officer just before I retired, which made my pension somewhat better to carry me into my elder years"!

"The General tells me that you're quite the 'Feather Merchant' and that you've married well"!

"'Never a Feather Merchant Mon Ami, simply a shop keeper and I suppose that one could say I married well. She's a younger woman in her early-forties, still able to raise the wood with a simple glance, if you catch my drift. Was a whore in Hamburg years ago, with a private following that captured the heart much older man, a widower with a faulty heart valve. Legend has it that she could simply enter a room fully clothed and raise the dead. Catherine Deneuve with tits! They marry and take up residence and she enters retirement"!

"She goes easy on the old fart for a few years and he's constantly enthralled. He restructures his will without her knowledge, leaving everything to her. Several months later he talks her into some rather strenuous activities in their boudoir and his heart gives out in the glow of the aftermath. Of course an investigation occurs especially since his children are removed from their birthright.

The subsequent investigation reveals no untoward culpability other than a man trying to climb a mountain, beyond his capabilities"!

"So citizen, our hero dies with his boots on, but with a smile upon his face. Or at least that was how the General put it"!

"So he mentioned it to you"?

"In passing, but ever so briefly. Please continue"!

"So our heroine inherits a string of eight meat markets in the greater Paris area and five restaurants. She settles with his children giving them four of the lesser performing bistros and keeping one of them. A month later we meet rather by accident on the Champs de Elyse one memorable afternoon that extended for several days. She has little interest for business and asked me of all people to marry her a month later, and to take over the management of her business affairs. It coincides with my retirement and with nothing better to do we join hands"!

"I trust things have been going well"!

"She has but one skill and keeps me warm cold winter nights and is the object of my interest upon all occasions. Other than that, the businesses are making a continual profit and consume the bulk of my time. I keep the General's household in steaks and victuals at all times. Life is good. But what about you, Mon Ami? Nothing on the side"!

"Nothing currently Citizen. The life of a Legionnaire as you well know is a mostly Spartan existence. However hearing of your good fortune is enough to trust that better days are ahead"!

"Changing the subject, you were correct over the phone. Soon we will meet some serious men, most of which are former Legionnaires, all of which are formidable in their own rights. Each is employed by the government in a non-military activity and each is a member of the Special Action Group"!

"Didn't that group cease to exist after their attempted putch against DeGaulle many years ago"!

"A dark time for the Legion. Units disbanded, the perpetrators hunted down and some put on trial and others disappeared from view. Those days they tried to over throw the government. These days things are quite different. The Special Action Groups purpose is the establishment of peaceful means of governance, within the constraints of a representative form of democracy. Often a messy business with many competing entities, from Anarchists who desire complete and mindless destruction of all authority, to Communists dedicated to governmental overthrow from within, to radical Liberals who would spend us all into mindless bankruptcy and a seemingly endless fool's parade of others on the fringes of society. The legislature unable to find their own collective asses and the courts swirling in their ivory towers leaves but one avenue to thin out the herd of those that would cause society irreversible harm. The methods employed are similar to those you and others employed so successfully while stationed in Mozambique. Should a marriage of minds and purposes occur this evening, you will become the youngest member of and part of this long resurrected group that of course, operates in the shadows"!

"Does the General have anything to do with this undertaking"?

"Of course he does he is central to the entire activity. I reveal all of this to you in advance, because of your service records wide range of unquestioned loyalty and accomplishments. Of course should a meeting of the minds not take place this evening, then It is understood that all that has passed between us is driven from your mind, the consequences of disloyalty is understood"!

"That is an understanding I've always had since the very first day I took the oath, Citizen Lambrage"! Lambrage smiled as he said, "The place we shall dine is owned by me and I trust you brought along an appetite. Regardless, anytime you arrive, your money will be no good; simply a generous tip to the server will suffice"!

Neither Lambrage nor Magellan had anything needed to have anything to concern themselves about since the meeting and subsequent meal brought about a complete acceptance of Nestor Magellan into their midst. For copy of his entire dossier was furnished to the key members, was memorized and shredded prior to the meeting. His exploits and accomplishments had preceded him. All this was simply for the rubber stamp approval. All of them were based in the greater Paris area, employed in other governmental venues in the main, while several, such as Lambrage, were engaged in private enterprise. Of course few even knew of their existence. But from time to time an operation had to be engaged, affecting a variety of high risk tasks deemed necessary by those in authority. These tasks were certainly a contravention of French law. Yet one rule still remained, "No Rush Jobs"!

The woods were full of Cannon Fodder who would engage in such activities. Abductions, assassinations of all sorts, protections, accompaniments, special disposing and other things were all aspects of which were far too risky politically, for either the standard Gendarmerie, The Suriete', or other elements of the French military. Yet from time to time, a man of General St. Nathalie would meet one of his peers in the military and ask a favor. The Old Boy School at work. Favors granted, questions never asked, because the well planned event never happened.

Quick in and out work that could plausibly be denied by governmental officials, was the Special Actions Group stock and trade. While the bulk of their activities occurred in France and the European Continent, assignments often took them abroad, but never for more than a few days at most. Simple to explain in the course of their visible jobs, should the need ever arise. The need never arose.

All initiatives went through the office of General St. Nathalie. Such was the security, that even his adjutant was unaware of the traffic. All messages delivered to the General by Lambrage, via the dinner they had with each other twice a week. The unmentioned aspect of the Generals importance was that of his family's prominence in French business, political and civic affairs. A simple phone call opened every door. In addition the General was the effective leader of the Special Action Group and along with a selective few whose loyalty to the Legion and France was beyond question were responsible for personally staffing, planning and assembling the respective teams according to their specific skills.

Of course, there was always the elements of the unforeseen, given the high risk nature of their tasks at hand, regardless of planning, tossing a spanner into the mechanism. It was seen to that each member was provided with alternative papers and a private numbered account in a number of countries that embraced banking privacy above all else. In addition each member was afforded certain modest perquisites in addition to their task driven additional remuneration, while attached to the group. Plus a special fund was set up for the purpose for the rare payment of bribes, should the occasion ever arise. It never did.

Only once did a member ever succumb to injuries and be LIA, "Lost in Action". That member's remains were retrieved and quietly buried in the potter's field outside of Chantilly under the pseudonym of "Jacque Deaux", since he had no known descendants; it was as if he'd never existed.

Thus life was good for Sergeant Magellan as his status was assured. It was privately agreed that he serve for the duration of his enlistment at St. Cyr and for the SAG and should he then reenlist he's receive yet another promotion in addition to all the other perquisites.

During the day he taught weapons training and escape and evasion procedures to budding and eager cadets at the Lycee, giving them all of the benefits of his varied experience. From time to time, he carefully pointed out certain elements of the curricula that were badly outdated or simply ineffective, planned years earlier by bookish officer's, that commanded little more than a desk.

One of the many reasons his charges loved him was that while he was compelled to train them from the operative text, he always then whenever it was appropriate, repeated the mantra, which his cadets railed back, "What works is good. What doesn't work is not good", by yelling, 'What is best in life"? The skills imparted here, were designed to keep themselves and their men alive, while ending the lives of the enemy"!

After a series of relatively minor tasks accompanying certain important individuals to freedom from repressive regimes abroad, Magellan and others were engaged in a stakeout of a suspected Moroccan terrorist cell with ties to the Libyan government. The terrorist cells each acted independently of each other, having no knowledge of the existence of each other for security purposes. If captured a cell member could expect a high degree of torture to extract information. Each cell operated with but three members and we're funded via a series of cut outs, with no ties back to their point of origin.

Having picked up the other two members of the cell earlier in the day, Magellan's unit lay in wait for the last member of the cell to arrive at the sidewalk bistro just off the Champs de Elyse. A utility repair truck across the street from the bistro provided the communications link for the unit plus acted as an extra set of eyes. Three other vehicles were on a constant move passing the bistro at random intervals ready to act as blockers for any vehicles in pursuit. Four pairs were in stasis at the location, with two groups on the inside and the others seated on the sidewalk, all of which were in disguise to effect the deception. Playing chess and sipping Calvados, and engaged in an animated faux entre-chat, were three young homosexuals near the entrance. Then across from them were two young lovers, spending a leisurely afternoon apparently focused exclusively on each other, oblivious to the outside world, whispering to each other with muted laughter, the variety of things young lovers attend to.

At approximately the appointed time, swiftly gleaned from the others the third member of the cell approached the bistro taking up his station at the sidewalk seating with his back to the wall facing the boulevard, giving him a commanding view of all who approached. During the interrogation of the others, an unclear description was given as to the final member looked like. But as the man sat down, from his general appearance and the furtive manner that he scanned the street, it was concluded that he was their man.

A waiter approached the Moroccan and took his order, then returned with his drink taking the money from the customer. Within fifteen minutes later the Moroccan's head began to nod forward and as he tried to rise, fell back in his seat. Before he came completely to rest, A white panel Van slowly pulled to a stop and several friends mysteriously appeared and helped him into the Van. The former waiter returned his apron along with a thousand francs to the real waiter and followed the others as the operation came to a silent end.

The last of the radio controlled munitions were to have been installed in the Parisian Metro, the following day, thus the purpose of the meeting was to co-ordinate the timing of the explosions in the latter part of the day for maximum effect, and to affect the frequency settings, for the rush hour. Thus the following day six different explosions in the underground were to wreak terror throughout the city.

The body count would've been massive and politically what good would the government be if it couldn't protect its citizens?

The Libyan planning was masterful, getting the explosive material into Paris along with the high powered, miniaturized electronics, all having passed French governmental scrutiny.

The third Moroccan awoke an hour later after an antidote to his drug was administered by a member of the SAG. He lay quite naked upon a cold stainless steel table, with each of his limbs tightly secured. His head was immobilized while his mouth was propped open and another was peering into his mouth with dental implements, finally withdrawing saying, "His dental cavity is free of any cyanide implants"!

Magellan stood close by as a burly pockmarked man loomed over the prisoner saying, "How unfortunate for him"! As the oral restraints were removed, the prisoner became awake, his eyes reflecting the terror he felt. For all appeared to be lost. His Libyan masters assured him that security was as tight as a virgin's twat. Clearly it wasn't. "We have the others well in hand in the next room and we need to verify where the explosives are that you were to plant tomorrow. Of course they are doing their best to resist, telling us various locations where they may be kept. They had already given you up, so it's just a matter of time. Seems you're the key element, the missing link. No doubt you're wondering just where the plot went wrong. Eh, Mon Poule'?"

"Tell us where the explosives are and we promise a quick and painless death. Make us have to exert any effort and it will take days for all of you to die. It will be extremely painful and we promise, the virgins your masters promised in the afterlife will greet you minus your key body parts, Mon Cher"!

He waited for the splayed out man to respond for a minute and when he remained silent, the man continued, "Your operation is blown, your failure is clear. Tell us what we need to know and your death will be swift and painless. This is the last time I will make the offer. I will now light a cigarette, you have the span of time of the life of that cigarette, in which to tell us where the explosives are", whereupon he lit the cigarette and walked away conversing with another out of earshot.

As Lambrage entered the empty kitchen he looked at his watch which read 1900 hours. and asked Magellan, "The market is now closed and all have gone home. How goes it with the WOG"?

"He's being difficult, but your head butcher has lit a cigarette and given him an ultimatum for the life of the cigarette"!

"Gives them time to ponder their fate, watch and see what happens next"!

As the last puff of the cigarette was taken, the swarthy butcher reached for the slender sectioning knife and began sharpening it, in full view of the prisoner. Then putting it aside, he reached for a vial and a syringe. The prisoner's eyes, wide as saucers, followed his every move as he nervously asked, trying to retain some semblance of bravado, "What're you doing"? The butcher answered, "Oh you mean all of this? Well we made you an offer and your silence told us you've declined. So the razor sharp knife will be for dissecting your body parts. Now as to the syringe and the container of clear looking fluid? The syringe will be filled with five cc's of a mild acid and will be injected into your veins. At first you'll feel nothing, but the initial prick of the needle, but into your veins will go acid. The syringe container is plastic so we will have to work quickly as it will dissolve from the acid. But have no fear we will place the container in front of you so you can observe the event. Just imagine what that acid will do for your innards"!

As the syringe was carefully filled, it was quickly put down as the butchers attention was diverted by another for a minute or so as the plastic syringe slowly began to change form. Then the butcher returned his attention to the prisoner and seeing the syringe compromised exclaimed, "Merde, now I will have to try again. Good thing I have more syringes"!

His heart beating wildly the prisoner croaked, "I'll tell you everything", as he breathlessly told them exactly where the bombs and the detonators were stored. Before he released his men the butcher said softly, "Mon Ami, There will be no nasty surprises for those who go for the intercept will there"?

The prisoner's lack of a quick response told him otherwise, as the butcher held his hand out as a restraining gesture to the others, then swiftly brought an elbow to the prisoners ribs breaking one or more in the process. "Well will there"?

Struggling to breathe, the prisoner gasped, "The lock. It is a combination lock. You cannot cut it with a bolt cutter for it will explode. Only the exact combination can be done, one digit off and the lock will explode"!

"And the exact combination is"? The prisoner slowly said the combination. "Now you will repeat the combination please"! The prisoner did precisely as he was told, as the butcher nodded his head and lowered his arm, signaling the others to take off.

As hour later Lambrage picked up the phone on the first ring, listened, said "Bon" then hung up, and nodded his head to the swarthy butcher, then picked up the phone and made a brief call.

The butcher leaned over the Moroccan saying, "Good news Mon Poule'. Everything was as you've said, the bombs and implements have been recovered and apparently a change of heart has taken place much to my disappointment. Since your clothes have been discarded, you are all to be drugged, placed into separate body bags and taken to a facility where the politicians are to haggle as how to try you in court. So apparently the best of both worlds has occurred. We save lives and you get to live out yours in prison. So relax"!

In the space of five minutes, the three prisoners were all sedated loaded into three body bags bound, gagged and loaded into the white panel van. An hour later they arrived at a field far from the center of Paris and were met by an idling helicopter as three others took the body bags and loaded them onto the helicopter, without a word. As the helicopter gained altitude and disappeared into the night. Magellan and Lambrage got back into the Van and drove back into Paris. After they had driven awhile, Magellan looked away from the road briefly and asked, "What caused the change of heart"?

"What change of heart", asked Lambrage? "There was no change of heart, simply a change of method"! "Please explain", asked Magellan

"We provided one set of expectations with a choice of alternatives, for the WOGS, and then substituted another. A certainty of death is expected, either an easy path or a painful path. Only the committed true believers will resist this until the very end. The martyrs. Few of them exist since most everyone embraces life, believing in the vicissitudes of hope and the occasional celestial miracle. There they lay naked and alone in a state of stupor. It will take the helicopter some thirty minutes to reach the English Channel and it will fly out to a distance of some hundred kilometers, yet another thirty minutes. By then all should've recovered from their modest injections. The aircraft will slow to a modest forward speed and the body bags will be unzipped one by one and the WOGGIES will undergo their very first flight test from a modest height of five thousand feet without a word of goodbye. I reckon that by the time the first one reaches the height of a thousand feet, the last will have left the aircraft and the door will have shut, with the operative statement being that, "Elvis has left the building" and that will be the message sent by the chopper after everything is concluded! The laws of inertia will hold until they hit the water. No one survives that"!

"Interesting", concluded Magellan as he drove on in silence!

"Quite a paradox isn't it. We give our word and then we do otherwise. Such is the world we live in. Yet I assure you that nothing of this shall reach the ears of my priest when I go for monthly absolution"!

"We are born alone and we die alone", mused Magellan absently! "Usually Mon Ami, but not always. You seem melancholy, for the moment"!

"Not really, just brought back memories of events long past"!

"Have you ever considered returning to Spain to sort things out"? "From time to time, the thought has crossed my mind. I can't permit the luxury of dwelling on the issue, or else I'd go mad and be of no use to anyone. Revenge is a luxury that only the few can afford. Besides, my life has become rather full at the present time, with time for little else"!

"Even women"!

"Upon occasion when the gods permit. But usually short term liaisons dangereuse. Nothing of consequence. However it's good to know that the other aspect of my plumbing still is in working order. Plus I recall the words of a very wise man, we both know that the Legion can be a very demanding mistress. Any idea whom I'm talking about Citizen"?

"Two things, Sergeant Magellan", said Lambrage. "First is I suspect sooner rather than later one of your skill sets will be in the preparation of sausage. The next is that in the course of time, say several years from now an unrelenting desire to return to your homeland will be too much to resist. For there is still much accounting to be done. When that time arrives, you are to tell us so we may help you. You will be the instrument; all we will do is pave the way. When that time arrives you will let it be known. Are we in agreement"?

"Oui Mon Citizen", said Magellan looking straight ahead at the roadway. "When the time comes"! A month later Lambrage true to his word introduced Magellan into the newly acquired skill of butchery in the wee hours of the morning. Yet another terrorist cell was apprehended while still in their beds along with their entire compliments of explosives bound for another session in the Paris Metro. Since little else was determined to be gleaned from them, they were quickly dispatched and taken to Lambrage's central shop in the dead of night and rendered down to the bone. The rest was considered offal and bagged up and sent to a high speed Donzi motorboat and whisked down the Seine River out several miles into the Channel and dumped overboard. The usable meat was ground into a special sausage, specially prepared to the Moorish tastes to be delivered to the two shops that served the so called Moorish quarter of the city at bargain prices. Being relatively new to the world of commerce, he was none the less an intelligent man in a modern world, grasping rather quickly the concept of 'Loss Leader' marketing. In the morning the specially prepared 'Goat' sausage would be displayed at one quarter of the going rate, assuming a certain additional amount of purchases accrued at the cash register. By the close of business all of the sausage was sold along with a host of other food products. Consumed by the eager Muslim housewives eager for a bargain.

As Lambrage showered after he returned and slipped into bed, next to his buxom wife, he placed the small box on the adjoining night stand, the remnants of the day's exertions gone down the drain. He slipped an arm around her, gently caressing her ample breasts. As her languid eyes opened to greet her lover, Lambrage placed a kiss on her shoulder.

"You certainly know how to greet a girl early in the morning Mon

Cher", she said rolling over to greet him face to face. Did everything go well last night"?

"Blanche', everything went so well that I felt it necessary to visit that certain vendor, a favorite of yours on the Rue St. Charles, the proof of my ardor lay on the bed stand for your approval when you awake"!

Blanche rolled over and gave a cursory glance at the jewelry box and returned he languid gaze upon her husband saying, and what did I do to deserve this Didier"!

"Simply to be. Exist and be by my side", he said as his head slipped under the covers. From the very first moment Nestor Magellan laid eyes upon Madeleine DuVilliers, his heart was lost. As she was the niece, by marriage, of General St. Nathalie, her safety was a matter of great importance. A recent graduate of the College de Sorbonne, majoring in legal studies, she achieved her Doctorate by her twenty third year and was to return from a six month sabbatical in Switzerland by train. Given the fluidity of the times, and the security threat posed by Anarchists and others in France, it was left to the General to select a suitable escort for Madeleine for her trip back to Paris.

Magellan knocked on the door to her apartment and as she inquired as to whom he was, he gave his name and the password. As the door opened up, he was greeted with an arched eyebrow and with a measure of suspicion, as he entered quickly closing the door.

"You gave the pass word correctly, but how can I tell if you're from my father"?

"Mademoiselle DuVilliers, you can't! In certain events the General operates verbally and in person, so I possess no written directive from him other than his word"!

"Well Sergeant Magellan, he said over the phone that you were amongst the best at what you do. Precisely what do you do"?

"As to your first statement, that remains to be seen. As to the latter, I do many things, however I'm currently an instructor at the Lycee Militare' at St. Cyr and have been seconded for this event, by directive of your father"!

"Well then Sergeant that will have to do. I'm all packed and ready to depart. Is there suitable transportation downstairs"?

"A local taxi is at our disposal, with the motor and the meter running, Mademoiselle"!

"Then let us depart Sergeant"! As the elevator took them down to ground level and the doors opened, he wondered about this vision of loveliness that went before him out the lobby door. He knew that she was highly educated and quite accomplished academically at an early age, expecting some dowdy, bookish looking female, rather than what was in his full view. As the taxi made its way to the train terminal, they both remained silent, watching the snowy streets as the blocks rolled by.

As they settled into their private compartment, He had to constantly remind himself that this was a mission of delivery only and that she was nothing more than a package, not unlike the dozens he'd delivered before. He tried as best he could not to make eye contact with those opalescent eyes, for to do so would alter everything. Yet as the train left the station, here he was in the private compartment meant for more than two, with this unexpected gift from the gods.

After the train had reached speed and was leaving the local environs she said, "It's going to be a rather long trip Sergeant and I do not relish addressing you by your rank the entire journey, so let us start by formal introductions. My name is Madeleine Theresa DuVilliers. What name do you go by"?

"Nestor Magellan, Mademoiselle"?

"Please call me Madeleine. So what name do you answer to"? Magellan thought for a few seconds and then said, "Most refer to me by my cognomen Magellan and at work I'm referred to by my rank"!

"Doesn't anyone call you by your first name, or do you have a nickname"?

"No, uh, Ma, Madeleine"! "It's Madeleine. Please say it"! "Madeleine"!

"Good. We're making progress. So may I call you Nestor"! "If it suits you, yes"!

"So you're an instructor at St. Cyr, and are a Legionnaire and apparently my father takes great stock in your abilities. How have you earned his trust so readily Nestor"? He thought a moment before replying and said, "Your Uncle and I met a long time ago and one might say he was my savior by allowing me entrance in the Legion. Since then I've striven every day to reward his then blind trust, with tangible accomplishments"!

"Well said, Nestor. I must say that you come as a pleasant surprise and not at all what I expected"!

"Expecting a Neanderthal no doubt"!

"Well, yes a Neanderthal, from what is printed about the Legion by the media"!

"Are you familiar with the works of the American songwriter Cole Porter"?

"Why yes I am Nestor. Night and Day, Begin the Beguine, all classics that endure"!

"Well legend has it that back in the nineteen twenties, he enlisted in the Legion when they were headquartered in Algiers and served a single tour of duty in Africa"!

"Why on earth would a man with that talent do such a thing"?

"Again, legend has it that he suffered a broken heart by some highborn American heiress. Rather than commit suicide, he joined the Legion to allegedly recover his humanity, suffering the multitude of privations the Legion at that time offered. After his single enlistment he rejoined the rest of the world. If one listens very carefully to his lyrics, especially of the song "Night and Day" and one is aware of his life history at that time, it becomes clear, that he is still pining over a long lost love that caused him to join the Legion. Of course that is one of many exceptions, yet you are quite right in some aspects of the propaganda that has been written by the Legion. True, it takes in scoundrels, but more often than not the discipline required by the Legion and the seemingly draconian punishments, keep the men in line and serving well, La Belle France"!

The look of utter astonishment in Madeleine's expression took Magellan aback as he said, "Did I misspeak in some manner"? Then her expression changed into a dazzling smile as she said, "Au contraire', Mon Sergeant. Rather the opposite. Please continue, for I'm becoming intrigued by your presence. Can you tell me about your family"? She suddenly saw an immediate change of expression on his face as he tried to speak; she interjected, "Perhaps at some other time or occasion then"! Something then spoke to her from deep within that this man, this self-improved man, had suffered some grievous injury long past that still festered, under the surface.

She wanted to cross to his side and embrace him, yet something held her back. "Now it's time for you to ask me some questions about myself, Nestor if you please"? He regained his composure saying, "I'm trying to think of something to ask without seeming too personal, yet I cannot think of anything, appropriate"!

"Then allow me to tell you all about myself if you will"! The smile on his face bid her to continue as she spent the next hour giving him chapter and verse regarding her upbringing as well as some aspects of her family affairs. As she prattled on like a school girl she saw that his eyes never left hers. From time to time she coyly looked away, yet when her eyes came back to his, he barely blinked. Intent on drinking in every single word every movement, every scintilla of her face. When she finally concluded her personal journey he asked, "So when you complete your studies, what do you intend to do"?

"I can tell you this. I do not intend to become some house frau in the country growing old and fat, nor some kept woman in the city dependent upon the generosity of some pseudo intellect with a mistress in the Rive Gauche'. No, I think the world of politics beckons in the future. There is so much corruption that requires rooting out and I'm just the one to do it", she said proudly"!

"You have just earned your first vote", said Magellan in earnest! "Danke' mon frere", she said, her face beaming with a smile. Then changing the subject she said, "Rumor has it that you're self-trained and have a facility for linguistics", whereupon they both started to communicate in a variety of languages, ending with Madeleine calling it quits saying, "You've out done me, Mon Sergeant. How did you get so conversant in so many languages"?

One of the first things a soldier does in a foreign land is learn the pejorative aspects of any language. It gets the immediate attention of the locals and often with time on my hands, I've studied various languages via correspondence with the Army's linguistics offerings. Thus over time, 'Viola', I speak therefore I am"!

For the rest of the trip, they engaged in conversation of everything they could think of save for the occasional meal, in which the exchanges continued and the relief breaks, which were separate and apart, thus continuing after conclusion. Neither became tired or bored, their two souls growing ever closer with every passing hour.

The train slowed as it entered the greater Paris suburbs, they heard the resonance of the train conductor as he made his way from compartment to compartment knocking twice saying, "Gare du Nord, Fin de Ligne"!

"Seems our journey is coming to an end Nestor, commented Madeleine sadly"!

"Never has time passed passed so quickly", he replied trying to tear his eyes away from her and failing. I trust I haven't bored you, Madeleine"!

"Never boring, Mon Sergeant. Anything but boring. I suppose you will return to your cadets at the Lycee when this is concluded"!

"That is my duty Madeleine, und du"?

"You will deposit me at my residence safe and sound and my mother will report to the General how wonderful and what a gentleman you were and I suppose life will return to normal", she said with sadness. Then she continued asking haltingly, "Do you ever think our paths will cross again Mon Sergeant"?

"A high born woman to be seen in the company of a Legionnaire? Society as well as Paris Match and Le Monde', would have a field day with the gossip. Your life would become a misery from the paparazzi, and as a Legionnaire my situation would become eventually compromised. The General can attest to that. This time can only be a fond memory, for my part"!

"Does that mean I've captured your heart, Mon Sergeant Nestor"? He slowly nodded his head as they both remained silent until the train came to a complete stop. He then assumed his protective mode as they left the car and sought out the Sedan that waited.

Arriving at the modest estate in the suburbs, he escorted Madeleine into her home, greeted her mother and left after the normal appropriate greetings, between them. As he entered the car to drive him back to the Lycee, he turned and glanced back at the house, seeing Madeleine at the window waxing a farewell. As Madeleine's mother came up to her seeing tears in her eyes, she asked, "Daughter, what is the matter"? As the car drove off she turned and said, "There goes my heart Mother and burst into tears", comforted by her mother's embrace.

"Nothing untoward happened during the trip did it"?

"No of course not. He was ever the perfect gentleman. A model of sobriety and discipline. We simply talked"!

"About what"?

"About everything under the sun. My life. His life to a limited degree. What I want and what he wants. Shoes and ships and sealing wax, cabbages and kings and why the sea is boiling hot and whether pigs have wings. .or not. And during the process something both wonderful and terrible happened. We became as one. Yet he was the sensible one, telling me just why society would make my family's live miserable. He is a Legionnaire and a lifer and I am of the upper class"!

"Unfortunately he's right Madeleine, but nothing happened during the trip"?

"If you're referring to sex, no Mother. Oh that it would! But everything else did. He's intelligent, resourceful, self-educated, has impeccable manners and has been everywhere, done everything and has the complete confidence of my father, the General. Yet after him I fear that no one else will ever do"!

"Europe is full of suitable men my dear. Eventually one will cross your path"!

"Then why did you marry my step father after my natural one died"?

After thinking a moment and defeated by the question she reluctantly said, "Because he captured my heart and never for one moment have I regretted the decision"!

"We shall say nothing to the General when he returns this evening other than the trip was uneventful and that Sergeant Magellan was polite, pleasant and the model of efficiency. Are we agreed Madeleine"?

"Yes mother"!

"In a month there will be a private event we'll be required to attend that will require our personal security. One never knows who will be part of that security detail. Now dry your eyes and go upstairs and unpack. The Sergeant was good enough to take your luggage upstairs and he knows where you lay your head each night. I dare say that will stay solidly in his head for some time to come"!

For the next several weeks, Madeleine's mother was proven correct. At various times of the day and specifically at night, the name 'Madeleine' kept rolling over and over in his head. His normal ability to concentrate on any given task was deflected, as her image kept flooding into his memory. Dark blonde hair, cut in a pixyish fashion, high cheek bones, mounting highly animated, piercing opalescent light green eyes, tall, slender and well made with impeccable manners, well-spoken and highly educated, who carried herself with grace and dignity only acquired by an environment of the elite'. Several times he privately went out to the parade grounds, killing a bottle of cheap brandy to drive the demons from his mind. Only to wend his way back to his quarters fall into bed, worse for wear the following morning. He tried to bring simple logic to bear telling himself over and over the myriad reasons why things just wouldn't work, yet every time, the old adage countered back in his mind the inescapable truth, "All the logic in the world, cannot overturn a simple feeling, once taken root"! Of course it didn't help him escape the misery of her absence, but it explained the inexplicable.

He would simply have to deal with this, on a daily basis, until things eventually improved with time. The Legion had taught him discipline and by god he would employ it in his personal life and yet everywhere he went he saw and heard the name Madeleine, on billboards, in the newspapers, on the radio and the television. Everywhere. Of course they were all there a month ago, but he didn't need the daily reminder everywhere he went.

Not a month later, he was summoned to the General's office. As he entered he was bidden to be seated, the normal salutations dispensed with. "Good afternoon Sergeant. I want to thank you for the way you conducted yourself in the matter of escorting my daughter back from her sabbatical. It seems your services will again be required to accompany our family to the City Mayors residence this Friday evening for an unavoidable political soiree. Of course a tuxedo and the appropriate attire will be the uniform for the evening. Scour the rental agencies and make certain you get something that fits well yet will allow for a firearm sans bulge. Afterwards present your receipt to the quartermasters for inclusion in your next pay period. Any questions"?

"No Mon General"!

"Good and thank you Sergeant. That is all. Dismissed"!

As he left the Generals office, he was perplexed. What game was the god of the demons playing? Just as he was starting to get an emotional grip on his feelings, this unnecessary impediment reentered his life. Yet he was given a directive by his Commanding General to which he owed all. Of course he would comply and endure. He had his orders or as least a request, which always were orders from ones Commander. He wondered if he should've said Something, anything to dissuade the General. Then he recalled what he'd seen on the entrance to Sand Hurst a few years ago. It was drilled into every British officer's head repeatedly from day one to day last. "Never Complain, Never Explain". That coupled with the Legionnaires unofficial motto of, "March or Die", ended his angst.

The evening of the event, everything went off as planned. By invitation only, arrived the hundred guests, dressed to the hilt to celebrate the engagement of the Mayor's eldest daughter, to the son of one of France's wealthiest families. A command performance between politics and wealth.

The security contingent was comprised of an outer circle comprised of the local uniformed Gendarmerie and an inner circle within the Mayor's mansion comprised of Regular Army and Legionnaires, formally attired and selected for their expertise, but more so to appear to resemble the invitees. Yet try as they did to blend in, it wasn't difficult to pick out the security operatives from the narrow shouldered diplomats, politicians and industrialists, with paunches from the rich life.

As the General, his wife and Madeleine arrived and made their way through the receiving line, Madeleine searched the room for a glimpse of her Sergeant, eventually seeing him in a far corner near the catered buffet and the bar, standing silent.

Of course, the General and his family circulated through the guests, working the room, from group to group before Madeleine's mother, tugged at her husband's arm saying, "Oh, I see the good Sergeant Magellan. You remember him don't you? I must go over to him and thank him properly for the service he performed. I'll return shortly"!

Before General St. Nathalie could respond, his wife was away and his attention was diverted by the greeting of a banker eager to introduce his family especially his eldest son returned from his studies abroad, to the Generals daughter.

The Generals wife, experienced in the ways of the elite, worked her way across the room and approached Magellan saying, "Ah my good man it's good to see you again", as she offered her hand in greeting palm downward for the continental kiss. Magellan complied as he bent to kiss her hand saying, "Enchante' Madame"! He felt her press something into the palm of his hand, as his lips left her hand and he came upright with a quizzical look on his face, having neatly palmed whatever she passed to him without a second glance, as he heard her say, "I just wanted to come over and thank you again for the kindness you demonstrated"!

Then she leaned forward and bid him to bend forward, as she whispered into his ear, "The General and will be away at our summer home next weekend. Should you be at the location described on the message, one never knows whom you may encounter"! Then she pulled back saying cheerily. "Good to see you again. Well duty calls", as she turned on a dime and worked her way back across the room, stopping from time to time, to chat briefly with others.

As she returned to her husband and her daughter, she couldn't help notice her husband still deep in conversation with the banker, while his son was chatting with her daughter, as she was offered a glass of Champaign from a passing waiter, she said to her daughter and the bankers son, "Allow me to steal her away for a few moments, we simply must see an old friend. I promise I'll return her"!

As the two slowly walked away heads together Madeleine's mother said, "I've done all I can do my child. The rest is up to you", she whispered, "The rest of what is up to me"?

"A certain Legionnaire Sergeant should be at a certain sidewalk bistro this coming Saturday morning late, while the General and I are driving to our place in Deauville for the weekend"!

"What, how", asked Madeleine flabbergasted?

"Simply went over to greet him and thank him and pressed a message into his hand. He is a charming and well-mannered brute. I can now see why the attraction. Now before we depart for the weekend, I'll let you know where he will be. It will be at the very same place the General and I rendezvoused before we married. A respectable, yet rather cosmopolitan crowd, serving very good fare, where one can become lost in plain sight"!

"But Mother". "Hush now my child, while we pretend to circulate. Of course you will have to accept a few dances from that dandy of a banker's son. But never fear. He will make no advances and you are not to be concerned. He's doing his duty to his family as you are to yours for appearances"!

"But how"? "How do I know? Simple, you're the wrong gender for him! Just go with the flow"! At that Madeleine began to giggle slightly. Normally a serious woman she rarely giggled since her teen years.

During the course of the evening she and the banker's dandy danced chastely for public consumption while Madeleine searched for her Sergeants eyes. Of course he was working and seemed to look everywhere, but every so often their eyes met, for ever so briefly sending a silent message. Time passed so slowly for them both, yet as the morning arrived and she waived he parent's farewell as the BMW motored out of the garage towards Deauville, she prepared for her rendezvous with her

Sergeant. She'd considered a sundress whereas the week had been strewn with intermittent rain and was at last to experience sunshine at last. Something revealing perhaps? No, she was a sensible woman. She opted for stylish slacks, blouse and a short jacket in case it got cold, a beret for her head and some low heeled pumps. As she flew out the door to meet the taxi she grabbed her sunglasses. If it was good enough for Holly Go Lightly, it should be good enough for her. She arrived at Broussard's on the Rue Charmaine slightly after ten in the morning. Common sense told her that a woman must not seem too eager and always arrive suitably late, yet her heart would hear none of it as she took a seat outside to enjoy the sunshine too long denied the city. As the oriental waitress arrived she ordered espresso and a baguette since she could not eat breakfast in her excitement.

As she looked around, she wondered that this was where her mother and the General, a Colonel at the time, had met for their initial series of rendezvous', while she was away at the private Academy. As her café arrived with her breakfast, she looked at the patrons through her tinted lenses as they gradually arrived, some inside and others out, for their victuals. A suitable place as her mother had said, Cosmopolitan, yet staid, where people met and were entertained by the plethora of street life.

As the time passed slowly by she ordered yet another espresso and began to wonder as the hour passed eleven in the morning. Had he gotten cold feet, she wondered? Then as the clock reached the bottom of the hour, she heard the deceleration of a motorcycle and the vehicle came to a stop right in front of the Bistro. The rider placed the kickstand on the pavement and dismounted, wearing jeans, a military style jacket and boots. He removed his helmet, looked around and smiled seeing Madeleine sitting there in reservation with her overly large sunglasses.

As he approached he said, "Bonjour Madeleine. Forgive me for being slightly tardy. Something arose at the Lycee that had to be attended"!

"Bonjour Mon Sergeant. I quite understand. Duty before all else. Such is the life of Militaire', is it not"?

"May I be seated next to you to observe the street", he said grabbing one of the chairs without waiting for response adding, "I like to keep everything in front of me, for old habits die hard"!

The oriental waitress arrived as he looked at his watch face, located military style on the inside of his wrist and placed his order saying, "It must be after 1700 hours somewhere in the world"!

"I see that you enjoy the American Jack Daniels whiskey as a preference", said Madeleine! "Plus a Cola mixer, to keep the Wolves at bay.

"But one must wonder about your mother. I received mixed messages, with the deft way she slipped me this message and then seeing you with this dandy on the dance floor"!

"Allow me to put your mind at ease Mon Sergeant. The young man was the son of a banker, returned from his studies somewhere abroad and interested in connecting him with someone suitable. Of course he was not suitable, because I was not suitable"!

"Mon Due. You not suitable? Impossible"!

"Au Contrare' Mon Sergeant, is possible. For you see I am of the wrong gender for his preferences"!

"Wrong gender? Why he was a lefty, he said laughing heartily. "Poor sod"! As his order arrived adding, "Do you think his father knows"?

"Apparently not"!

"Soon the family name will expire unless some technical arrangement occurs. I will try and say a prayer for his family at Mass, but not too hard. Other matters require the eternals grace"!

"So you attend Mass regularly"?

"Essential in my line of work. A good habit to acquire. To thank God for one's existence, for the rare pleasure and the ever present pain that is with us. I pray for wisdom continually and for the eternal to control my passions"!

"A soldier that is religious? Ah the paradox"!

"With respect mademoiselle, many soldiers are religious. It gets us over the hump when all hope is lost. My presence at this table before you is a testament to a higher powers presence"!

"I quite agree, Mon Sergeant, but I must blame you for something"! "And that might be"?

"Since we last spoke on the train, you are responsible for my addiction to music by the American Cole Porter and I've researched his life as much as possible. One can feel the pain of his passion and subsequent rejection, by some foolish woman long ago. They say that artists must suffer for their art and one can feel his angst simply by listening carefully to his lyrics". She smilingly continued, "So it's all your fault that I'm, hooked"!

Then she leaned forward and whispered, "Night and day you are the one. Only you beneath the moon and under the sun"! As their eyes met, he responded, "Whether near to me or far, no matter darling where you are I think of you, night and day"!

Without missing a beat she added, "Day and night why is it so? That this longing for you just follows wherever I go"! "One wishes it were otherwise", he said adding, "But there it is. Ice baths, cold showers, liquor consumed in abundance will not diminish what exists and will not depart"! Then she reached over and took his hand saying, "Other than a few brief moments brushing together in the closed space of a train compartment, we've never touched"!

"Do you feel the same spark I feel at this moment", he asked? She nodded her head taking his other hand in hers and caressing the rough exterior saying, "I never have noticed a man's hands before, I mean the rough exterior, the calluses"! As she looked up she saw that his eyes were closed and she bent down and kissed both of his hands saying, "According to mother, this is where she and the General got to know each other"!

As he opened his eyes, he looked around and recognized that he'd been here before saying, "So that is why this place is so familiar"?

"You've been here before"?

"Yes, but not for pleasure as I am now but for work"? "Work"?

"Security affairs. It ended well enough. The complete opposite of current circumstances. Odd how serendipity can bring one back to certain places", he said with a faraway look in his eyes"!

"She then took his head gently in her hands and kissed him on the lips. A chaste kiss that imparted a tenderness he'd never thought possible, as she said softly, "Whether near to me or far, no matter darling where you are I've thought of you, night and day", as he returned the kiss driven by a primal longing reserved for only one"! As they slowly parted she said looking deeply into his eyes, "My eating habits have suffered since that time on the train. We have the entire weekend ahead of us and I trust your duty will not interfere. So feed me, Mon Cher, for my appetite has suddenly returned. Then later you can display your skills as a biker, with me behind you. I've never ridden a bike before"!

"Please allow me to correct you", said Magellan! "I am not your standard biker, for they usually are festooned with tattoos, of which I have not a one. As to my motorcycle, it is not a mere bike. It is an Italian motorcycle, rescued from a junkyard and with the assistance of a few others, returned to the land of the living to resume its predominance in the motoring world. It is extremely fast and wholly worthy of your presence"!

The oriental waitress was again summoned with a menu and they ordered their luncheon. As the waitress left, Madeleine said, "Since we have the entire weekend ahead of us, May I mention that I have a girlfriend that is involved with a rock and roller. She is accompanying him on an extended tour in Scandinavia and Britain. He resides in a houseboat on the Seine and I have a copy of the key to the boat in my purse. When we are finished we have the houseboat is at our disposal and once there, I intend to discover, whether or not you have any tattoos"!

"I am yours to command, Mon Cher", said Magellan!

Something had awakened Madeleine early the following morning and that something was a full bladder in desperate need of relief. She slowly removed the covers as not to awaken Magellan fast asleep from his heroic exertions. She made her way quickly but carefully across the floor of the cabin, knees together in the attempt to keep what was within from, from premature escapage, making it to the Loo in just the nick of time. Quiet relief washing all over her face. She quickly cleaned herself before returning. It simply would not do for her to return to her lover, appearing less than appropriate. As she made her way back to his side and a warm bed, she glanced out port side window, seeing a light festooned travel boat making its way slowly back to its mooring to disgorge early morning tourists and perhaps a pair of lovers or two back on solid ground. A deep fog shrouded the riverbanks, casting an eerie glow upon the replica Statue of Liberte' as she shivered, in her nakedness.

Comfort and warmth awaited in the bed across the cabin as she quietly slipped under the winter quilt that covered her lover. She gazed fondly at Nestor as he slept soundly, gently passing her fingertips through his hair and settled back in next to him. As she closed her eyes, her thoughts drifted back to earlier in the day as they ate their meal at Broussard's, each knowing full well the outcome. They ate in mostly silence, each continually taking the measure of the other wondering whether or not this was a dream or reality. Their eyes in almost constant contact, searching, wondering, wanting. Each time they touched it was almost electric, yet each maintained their composure.

As he settled the bill, they went to his Ducati parked just scant feet away, as she said, "I've never been in a motorcycle"!

"Then it's good that you had the sense to wear slacks. Just climb up behind me. You will wear the helmet and hold on tight. Become one with me and lean when I lean as we round the curves"!

They just drove around for an hour as she became one with him as instructed, eventually arriving at the vacant houseboat as she'd directed, at its mooring on the Seine. As she dismounted, and returned the helmet she said, "Chloe's lover bought and old motor driven river barge from his concert and record earnings and had it converted to living quarters. It's quite spacious with all the comforts of home", as she grabbed his hand and dragged down the gangplank.

Once inside it seemed as if the world exploded as each of them frantically began to disrobe the other, in a frenzied state of passion that was long overdue. In the midst of their first of many trips to the heavens she said, "It's true Mon Amor. You have no Tattoo's"!

After their second session as they lay in each other's arms, in silence he said, "Pinch me and do it hard"! "Why my love? I've no wish to hurt you"!

"That will tell me whether or not this is a dream. Please do as I ask"! She immediately complied, as he said "Harder"! She again complied as she noticed a slight grimace, followed by a simple, "Thank You"!

"So is this a dream my love"?

"No. Far better than any mere dream. Here I lay with the reincarnation of Aphrodite' come alive. At last it seems as if all of the angels and saints in heaven are rejoicing. As I take stock of all that has happened in my life, the question looms, Do I deserve you"?

"And the answer is"? "A resounding Yes"!

They fell fast asleep in each other's arms, awakened by the sound of one of the river barges passing by with its fog horn blaring, leaving a gentle wake, for their barge to rock gently back and forth to. As the silence re-enfolded them, their co joined scent summoned a reemergence of passion as this time they made love, slowly and tenderly, each exploring every nook and crevasse of the other as if mapping a new world, yet resulting in a blazing crescendo, leaving both spent and falling tightly into each other's arms in a lasting embrace.

Again they fell silent as sleep came to the weary travelers. Once again the passing of another river barge brought them both awake as she nestled closer into the folds of his body. As her fingertips explored his body, she felt his member once again rise to the occasion as she said, "My Legionnaire again salutes"?

"When my sacred appendage salutes, it is for you alone. The others can be serviced by my upper extremities"! "I want you all the more" she whispered.

"I'm concerned about your health my love. We've both experienced Eros to the limits of human endurance"!

"Are you saying Mon Sergeant, that the Legion doesn't demand peak physical endurance in their men"?

"It is you my love that concerns me. But if I must, I am willing to conduct a complete and thorough physical examination of you in order to see if you've suffered any damage", as he brought her back to a reclining position and his head slipped beneath the covers. When he reemerged several minutes later and finding her flushed in the aftermath of yet another trip to the heavens he said, your abilities for self-lubrication astound me, so once more into the breach"!

As her reverie evaporated, she glanced at the digital alarm radio across the cabin as it read, 0255 in the morning. She decided that her soldier had fought a valiant series of battles and that rest was what he need for the present. There was time enough for other sorties in the days, weeks, months and years ahead and her soldier would need his strength.

The following day was Sunday and since Notre' Dame Cathedral was not far off, they prepared themselves unabashedly and attended the late morning Mass. As they knelt together holding hands in supplication just prior to the Apostles Creed recitation, they both looked at each other again. The cement job had set into permanency. For the remainder of each other's lives, there could be no other.

For the coming months ahead, both discovered time to rendezvous, for an afternoon, a stolen weekend or an evening. Spending each moment as if it were to be their last, easily avoiding the malaise that eventually sets in as each partner starts to take the other for granted. One thing for certain was their joint attendance at weekly Mass, be it a Saturday or a

Sunday, the weekly celebration provided them, cherished time together. While each had thoughts of a more permanent arrangement, since every separation was a painful experience, it was never discussed. Each thinking they would bring up the subject at a more suitable time.

Then came the annual Bastille Day, in the summer, when all France celebrated their independence from the Bourbon Kings. Paris every year was festooned with celebrations, especially the Parade down the entire length of the Champs de Elyse by the French Military. The crowning point of every Bastille parade was the contingent of the Foreign Legion, signaling the conclusion as they slow marched in formation, eyes straight ahead, resplendent in their butcher aprons, and Kepi's mounted squarely on their heads.

Sergeant Magellan lead the contingent from the front guide on position, on special assignment from the Lycee, for the purpose of this single day only, he passed the reviewing stands, containing key politicians and military personages, along with their families bellowing out the orders, "Eyes right, Salute", as the Legionnaires marched slowly past.

"The best laid plans of mice and men oft, go awry", as the saying goes. The Generals wife, in on the deception from the onset, was none the less responsible for its revelation as she said, without thinking, "There he is Madeleine, your Sergeant Magellan leading the Legion", as she pointed him out. Of course this didn't escape the notice of the General, who gave no notice that he heard the exclamation.

Sergeant Magellan eventually broke his own rules regarding his sorties with Madeleine and that key rule was situational awareness of one's surroundings at all times. Yet in order to keep that level of deception going for an extended period bordered on paranoia. Love and secrecy make terrible bedfellows, for eventually the truth will out.

Two weeks later Magellan was summoned into the presence of his Commanding Officer as he entered his office saying, "Sergeant Magellan reporting as ordered Mon General, saluting crisply as he stood at attention in front of the Generals desk. St. Nathalie kept him waiting the better part of a minute as he eventually looked from a report on his desk, to see the Sergeant looking at a point on the wall above his head, holding a stiff salute. He said, "I'm reminded of someone I took into the Legion long ago", as he returned the salute saying, "Stand at ease Sergeant"!

"Lesson number one in the engagement of an ongoing deception, is that no one must discover it. Wouldn't you agree"?

"Yes General"!

"Then why have you been so careless, in the governance of your affairs Sergeant"?

Magellan at that point knew that he and Madeleine had been found out and quickly came to the conclusion that brazening it out just wasn't going to work as he said, "Sir. No excuse Sir", stiffly!

As he looked at the spot on the wall above the Generals head, the General rose to his feet and said, "I should've seen this sooner so I suppose I'm as much to blame as anyone, especially my wife. I was the one that ordered you to transport Madeleine back from Berne. She was the one that suggested you as being part of the security detail at the Mayors soiree' months ago and it was she that suggested your initial dalliance at the very place we met years ago"!

"The only thing that is saving you from disgrace, is that the both of you are seen together attending High Mass at a variety of locations around Paris. Very sloppy of you to not spot your trailers. So soldier, what am I to do with you"?

"Sir. Permission to answer the General"?

"You may speak freely Sergeant, but the truth. I demand it"!

Standing eye to eye, Magellan said, "It started when we made the journey back to Paris. Knowing that she was your daughter, I had no intention of allowing personal concerns to develop. Yet in the passing of time, we conversed at some length and that is all that occurred. We both sensed a connection, but given my status as well as hers, I decided that it was impossible and we departed in that manner. Our second meeting was at Broussard's and I suspect you know the manner of how that was arranged sir"!

"Continue Sergeant"!

"After that extended time talking we both concluded that nothing could be done about it!

I take the entire responsibility for what has occurred. A fatal flaw in my character. As a Legionnaire, I submit myself to whatever punishment you decide General"!

"And should I decide to release you from the Legion and send you back to Spain, then what"? Magellan felt his life ending at that very moment, as he said, "It will be the worst day in my life General. Proof that I've betrayed your trust in your eyes. Yet even worse, the prospect of never laying my eyes on Madeleine ever again would be more than I could endure. She has become my life, my purpose for living. I've never had anything but honorable intentions towards her"!

"Would you give your very life and soul for her"? "Without a single thought, General"!

"Well then that poses a dilemma. Come be seated and we shall talk as men", as the General pointed at two chairs away from his desk.

"For you see, Madeleine feels exactly the same way. She has blossomed into quite a woman Sergeant. Educated, polished, quite the beauty and a woman of extraordinary wit, charm and what some would say an abrasive nature at times. Her cap is set upon a career in politics at some time in the future. Now in any young encounter between people, the initial attraction is little more than mere infatuation, with the superficial aspects of certain others. It's not until the passage of time, with the ebbing and flowing of events and good or ill fortune, that real love takes hold, Do you not agree"? "May I speak freely General"? St. Nathalie's head nodded in assent as Magellan said, "Never in my life had I been so at peace with myself as a person as I have felt with your daughter, especially at Mass. There, we would hold each other's hands as if it were the very last time and experience God incarnate. Without her by my side, I am less than nothing. Everything you feel for her mother I feel for you daughter. That cannot ever change. I hold her in great respect as herself and that has nothing to do with my relationship with you or the Legion. I would ask for her hand in marriage if I thought it had a ghost of a chance in happening'! "Your final word on the subject Sergeant"?

"Yes General"!

"After discussing the matter with Madeleine and my wife, it seems that you will have to do that very thing Sergeant, or I shall have not a moment of peace"! Then he went to his desk and wrote something on a slip of paper and gave it to the Sergeant. This is her ring size. There is a jeweler in the city, a former Legionnaire who owes me several favors. You are to visit him this very day after your classes here. You will get something suitable yet within your means. The ring is to be ready prior to this Thursday evening, where you will arrive at our home for dinner at precisely 1900 hours. There, you will present her the ring and formally ask for her hand. Does this meet with your approval Sergeant"?

He almost felt like leaping with joy as he stood up saying, "Yes Mon General. At your Command"!

"Good Sergeant. Now go attend to your cadets. Of course your other commitments will remain in force, although given your current state of affairs, a certain redirection of your time will be necessary. I'll inform the ladies, so the sun can shine once again", as he waved Magellan away with a sloppy salute.

17

It was an interesting matching of souls that was occurring betwixt Nestor and Madeleine. The beauty and 'Le Beast', as she jokingly called him during private moments. It amazed them both, their penchant for completion of each other's thoughts. Socially she seemed ever the chameleon, being ever assertive and dominant in one venue and compliant in another as Magellan simply watched and wondered in the background. His lack of formal higher education compared to hers drove him to improve himself intellectually by delving into the writings of the great minds of antiquity. Of course a University Degree would be completely out of the question, what with his schedule at the Lycee Militare', his obligations to Madeleine and the occasional odd job for the SAG.

The wedding was quietly scheduled for five months away and to be conducted at the Lycee's chapel. Just a small quiet and unobtrusive affair, to be celebrated and attended by a select few. The General, aware of Magellan's fractured past, ran interference in explaining away his lack of family as they made their way around socially.

As they made their way across the city one evening destined to attend the Opera de Paris, at the Place de Opera, for its final offering of the season, Othello. An opera by Guiseppi Verdi, complete in four acts, Madeleine held their tickets firmly in her hand while Nestor drove. She then placed the tickets in his breast pocket saying, "I'm so excited. It's been a long time since I attended an Opera, with all of my studies taking up my time in the past, that if I hold onto them any longer, the ink on the tickets may disappear"!

"The General and your mother are attending as guests of the Premier in his private box are they not", asked Magellan?

"Yes, however we shall encounter them at the end of the first act along with the Premier and his entourage in the Loge. So remember what my father told you. If they ask what you do, simply say that you are an instructor at the Lycee, Militaire' and nothing else. You look as handsome as a male model in your tuxedo. I'm glad that I accompanied you to the tailors in order to supervise the fit although the jacket seems to fit you loosely in the chest area. Still you make a grand appearance", she said beaming with pride!

As they made their way into the opulent Concert Hall, she said, "Have you made yourself familiar with the Opera's libretto"?

"Read a synopsis of Shakespeare's play Othello and I trust the composer Verdi followed the same plot line. Then something further intrigued me and I further investigated the possible source of his inspiration. In every concocted tragedy lays an element of truth and so it apparently went with all of Shakespeare's offerings. Of course he had to change the names often enough, to protect his skin, quite necessary for his time. But when I engage in some modest investigation, it appears that he was telling the story of Ludovico Sforza, the Duke of Milan and a periodic patron of Leonardo da Vinci. In my mind the description between parties of being Moorish like or dark and swarthy in appearance, indicates they were both of Sicilian ancestry, and of extremely jealous character"

"Bravo, my lover. You have done your homework well"!

"One wonders how people can misunderstand the purposes and allow jealousy to capture them so completely", he mused aloud, knowing full well the answer to that enigma.

"Just so you know my love, that there can never, ever be another for me other than you"!

"Like Cyrano de Bergerac and his courtly love for his cousin Roxanne", said Magellan!

"That brave and wonderful fool. He should've made his intentions known earlier. Perhaps they could've had a rewarding life together, rather than him sinking ever deeper into degeneracy and Roxanne spending the rest of her days in a convent withering away for a phantasm that never existed"!

"You mean her infatuation for the bumbling Christian"?

"Precisely"!

"But Cyrano was never good with money. A Bravo, in behalf of the King, a swordsman extraordinaire' as well as an outstanding writer of prose, able to skewer his enemies with his words as well as his rapier. So one is driven to wonder whether or not his nature would have caused failure in their union"!

"I've never asked Nestor, but you are good with money are you not"?

"I've some modest savings that you will discover soon enough"!

"No matter. Whatever you might lack will be filled in by me. For I am a thrifty sort you might as well know"!

"I would've hated to live during the renaissance as a politician. Having to constantly wonder who is going to try and kill you next and by what manner"!

"Thank goodness my love we live in modern times", said Madeleine as she tickled his palm smiling.

As they took their seats some twenty rows back on the main floor right on the aisle, Magellan glanced up at the Premiers box and saw the General and Madeleine's mother were socializing as was their due. Then his eyes cast across the vast emporium at the upper box seating across from the General and caught a glimpse of the object of the evenings exercise. The Foreign Minister of France. A known Socialist and far to the left of his benefactor Mitterrand the President of the Republic. Friends since their childhood days, there existed recorded conversations between he and his Soviet counterpart that clearly indicated that he was a Soviet spy infiltrated in a high position. Since Mitterrand would stand staunchly behind him politically, should he be uncovered publicly, possibly causing the governing coalition to disintegrate, a determination was made, by those highly placed in the government to have him liquidated in a visible manner. This should send a subtle message for the French President to rein in his socialistic propensities and drift back to the political middle, as well as his political masters in the Kremlin, to keep hands off. Of course the services of the Special Action Group would have to be employed. Thus the instrument of action was to be Nestor Magellan. He's long since earned his spurs in Africa, liquidating men in authority high placed in their respective governments, so to him this was just another assignment. Yet one more obstacle to achieve the absolute trust of the General.

He would have to excuse himself from Madeleine, shortly after the commencement of the fourth and final act, in order to carry out his assignment. Although married, the Foreign Minister had a long standing affair with his lover, the Parisian man on the street simply winked at. Usually when the both of them attended an affair such as this, they would both be highly visible during the first two acts. During the final act they would then retreat into the last row of chairs deep within the confines of the private box and have their way with each other, somehow satisfying some dangerous primal urge.

Thus during the fourth act of Othello when the big buildup towards Othello's murder of his wife Desdemona, when the music would be playing to an earsplitting crescendo, was the suitable time for Magellan to do his work. As the music began, Magellan made as if his stomach was under attack and asked to be excused to find the nearest restroom and quickly climbed the stairs, two things crossed his mind; the unfortunate Gendarme he knew would be standing guard outside the Foreign Ministers box and the memory of Joselita long ago. Verdi's opera bore a somewhat resemblance to her passing and his role in her demise.

Fifteen minutes later he rejoined Madeleine, with a pained look upon his face, as she whispered, "Are you all right my love"? "Gastrique embarrassment. Must've been something I ate. It will pass"! As the final act played out and Othello discovers Iago's treachery, he was grateful for the Gendarme's being asleep on his feet in front of the Foreign Ministers door. He would've hated to have killed him an innocent victim defending the indefensible. Instead he simply snuck up on him and subdued him in a sleeper hold, guaranteeing his unconscious state for at least several minutes. As he entered the private box, he couldn't believe his luck for there just feet away was the Foreign Minister, deep in the throes of passion with his head buried in the lap of his lover.

His razor sharp stiletto was quickly engaged, as the first thrust entered the Minister neck severing his brain stem leaving him immediately limp and dead within minutes, while his left hand covered his lover's mouth. The second thrust, came a scant second later entering the lovers neck burying itself deep in his brain, again severing the brain stem leaving him to the same fate. He quickly cleaned the blade upon one of the red curtains as he quietly exited the boxed enclosure, the music hovering an earsplitting crescendo capturing everyone's attention as Desdemona meets her fateful end at the hands of Othello. He paused a moment and picked up the unconscious Gendarme and carried him to the opposite exit stairs and threw him down the stairs.

It just wouldn't do for him to awaken prematurely. Soon the Foreign Minister and his lover would join each other in Purgatory.

The Opera coming to its conclusion caused Magellan to contemplate the possibilities of the aftermath. Of course, the bodies would eventually be discovered. If all went well, the members of the Press would be 'Johnny on the Spot', in their coverage, before the authorities could cordon off the area as a crime scene. Then the morning headlines in Le Figaro and Paris Match would scream of their inopportune demise, in living color. The manner of their dispatch would suggest that a lover's quarrel be the cause, leading the investigators in another direction.

As Magellan drove them back to his quarters at the Lycee, he was quiet as Madeleine, prattled on about how a glorious evening it was. Then asked rhetorically, "How could a woman of her qualities give herself so to such a brute as Othello"?

"Simple I would think. Back in those days, amongst the elite, arranged marriages were the custom of the time. In fact in some parts of the world that custom still exists", wincing for effect.

"Is your stomach still bothering you", she asked?

"Not my stomach but the processing unit much lower"!

"Are you trying to tell me that you have, Le Jaillessement Hershey"?

"It comes and goes and I wonder if you wouldn't mind if I we made it an early evening, my love. I would hate it if you saw me "Hors de Combat"!

"Of course my love I quite understand", she giggled! As her car came to rest in front of his quarters at the Lycee, he relinquished the car back into her hands as they briefly kissed goodnight. As she drove away towards the main entrance, she couldn't help but giggle at him walking knock kneed quickly towards his quarters. It would be a shame if he were to soil his newly purchased Tuxedo upon its maiden voyage.

It came as little surprise, to the citizens of Paris the following morning when headlines all over the continent revealed the untimely death of the French Foreign Minister and his escort, Rupert Toureville. Of course it was a scandal indeed and no longer could people simply wink and touch their nose. Of course the media was covering the story like a blanket and would do so for some time to come. The Gendarmerie was making all of the moves they could in the coming days and weeks ahead, but with only the recent divorce filings of the long suffering wife of the Foreign Minister, their focus on her quickly came to nothing whereas her locus for the evening was unassailable, spending the evening in prayer in a

Priory outside of the city in full view of people of the church until the early hours of the morning.

Given her years, it was quickly determined that she was past any motive for revenge, simply wishing to be shed of any further embarrassment from her sometime husband of many years.

Later in the day, General St. Nathalie paid Magellan a visit out at the firing range where Magellan was overseeing his cadets. As one of his subordinates pointed out the Commandants approach, Magellan said, "Take over Sergeant" and went to greet his Commander.

"Stand at ease Sergeant", said St. Nathalie. "How are the cadets doing"?

"They're coming along sir. Some show an ability for the long shot, while others require work on their mechanics. But in time they all will be marksmen"!

"Did you enjoy the Opera, with my daughter"?

"Quite well General. Very enjoyable"!

"I understand that you experienced a gastronomical event, during the last act"! At that Magellan shifted his view from the range to the General and then back at the firing range saying, "Well sir, there is that"!

"A shame what occurred last evening with the Foreign Minister. It's all over the news Sergeant. Yet there are two people that must be relieved of a burden"!

"And that would be Mon General"?

"His wife and the President. His wife avoiding any possible sanctions from the Church and the President, no longer having to concern himself with a political albatross around his neck"!

"So your health is back to standards Sergeant"?

"Yes General. Back to standards"!

"Well then seems that you have things well in hand, Sergeant. Carry on", said St. Nathalie as he saluted and walked off.

As the General wandered off he vowed to insulate Sergeant Magellan from any further liquidations as part of the Special Action Group. In fact he was considering talking to the Premier and asking for a position for his daughter, after the wedding between her and Magellan for a position in the Foreign Service. He could follow her postings all over the world, in a security role while she gained experience in Foreign Service. They would be together. Of course his wife might have something to say about it, but he would approach the subject with 'Delicatesse'.

As the days of the wedding grew near both Nestor and Madeleine were never so happy. Both discovering a new aspect of the other almost on a weekly basis that cemented their souls into one. Where he was in abundance, she was lacking and vice versa, each ebb and flow fitting together and meshing like a Swiss watch, ticking in unison. The General checked Magellan's personnel dossier and discovered that he'd accumulated, some four years of unused annual leave, making a note in his file to bring that up to date, on his first payroll remittance after the wedding. Lacking only the status of the elite, Magellan was none the less the perfect candidate for his precious Madeleine. She would give him children and be a success professionally as the years went by. In time, his service for the Special Action Group would be but a dim memory.

Somewhere up above, or down below, decisions are made that affects all mortals. Some make sense eventually, some never do. The ancient sages tell us that mortal man has been blessed with free will. His ability to decide one thing or another to be wise, or foolhardy to risk, or not. To venture forth or hunker down. We are told that man controls his destiny, and that no one is an island unto himself. That each one of us has a certain value to greater or lesser degrees. Yet when the inexplicable occurs, no one has a rational answer. Those wise men revered for their wisdom, simply shrug their shoulders and mouth their duck billed platitudes saying, "It was never meant to be".

Such was the case with Nestor Magellan and Madeleine Du Villiers St. Nathalie. He worked his way back from the deep abyss the hard way, by becoming a Legionnaire. She worked her way through school, losing one parent and eventually gaining another even better one in the process, using logic and hard work in her schooling, with a bright future ahead of her. By the vicissitudes of serendipity both people met and became inextricably as one. Had they been left to their own devices, who knows what could've been achieved? What happiness could've been derived? Yet it was never meant to be.

It was late in the afternoon as the phone rang at Magellan's office. He was in the process of finishing up his progress reports on his Cadets, when he said, "Sergeant Magellan"!

"Sergeant it is Captain Morneau, General St. Nathalie's adjutant"!

"Yes sir, How may I help you"?

"I'm calling in behalf of the General who directs you to stop what you are doing and go outside immediately. He is on his way in the staff car to pick you up. You are to go now"! Then the line went dead.

Magellan grabbed his hat and as he emerged from his building the Generals staff car was pulling up to greet him and he jumped in the rear seat asking, "General, what is the matter"?

"It is Madeleine. She's been in an accident. On her return from the city. I just received a call from the Gendarmerie and we are on our way to pick up her mother then to the hospital where she is en route"!

"Oh my god", is all that Nestor could think to say his mind becoming numb"! He wanted to ask more questions, but realized the General knew no more than he did, as the car pulled alongside the curb and picked up Madeleine's grieving mother. As the staff car made its way through the late afternoon traffic, each one tried to summon the angels and pray for her safety. The General being the one, who received the first report from the authorities, knew it was serious, since she was being rushed to the nearest hospital's emergency room yet held back any further information.

At the hospital they were greeted by the watch commander, who gave them a preliminary report on the accident. "With respect General, Madam, it appears that a driver of a propane delivery lorry ran thru an intersection illegally and broad sided your daughters vehicle. What made the accident so bad was that the delivery vehicle was traveling at an excessive rate of speed at the time he entered the intersection and after hitting your daughter flipped over and several of the propane canisters exploded, one of which caromed off of your daughter's car crushing in the roof. She was extracted as quickly as possible, still somewhat in control of her faculties, telling us to call you and someone named Magellan"!

"He is here with us officer. Can you tell us what condition she is in"!

"She appears to be in serious condition General. Other than that I cannot say. The doctors are doing everything they can do at the present"!

"The other driver of the delivery lorry"?

"He went up when his lorry exploded. He's in bits and pieces"!

"Any others commander"?

"About nine others, experienced collateral damage. Most of which were superficial and a few fairly serious in other hospitals. Since this was the closest medical facility I directed the ambulance to come here"!

"So the lorry driver is dead", asked Magellan!

"Sergeant, he is as dead as one can be"!

Madeleine's mother went to the window, looking out yet seeing nothing in the fading light of the day. She was the wife of a General of France and would conduct herself accordingly, overcoming the impulse to shriek in grief, yet she could not hold back the tears and wept in silence. Her eyes blind and her mind numb with concern and grief.

St. Nathalie, ever the officer, was ramrod straight alongside Magellan, as both of them held back the tides of emotion. Then Magellan pointed out that his wife was on the verge of a break down and said haltingly, "General may I suggest that your wife needs you by her side? I will stand firm and wait here, if you will allow me"?

"Thank you Sergeant. I'll await developments with Madeleine's mother"!

Who was left to blame? The driver dead. Simple for the authorities. One less to prosecute. One less to exact revenge upon. No one to accept culpability. Perhaps this was the long arm of fate, come to rob Magellan of happiness for his rash behavior many years ago. Had he not been so hot headed, two others might still been alive, as well as his father and perhaps he would've recovered and fell in love with another and all would've eventually evened out in time. Then the plot line of Othello came back into his memory. Seems he was no better than Othello the Moor. Then his thoughts drifted to his mother. How he missed her presence at this of all times. He wondered how she was, and just knew that if he and Madeleine were married, that his mother would've doted over her with love and affection beyond description. Suddenly he felt a chill. A presence around him. He could feel in his mind's eye, the presence of the Ferry Man, with his hand held out for the coinage. He shrugged his shoulders as if to drive off the feeling and said to himself, 'leave us and go elsewhere'. The specter' departed shaking his head with his hand still outstretched.

There he stood in the waiting room, ramrod straight, hoping, praying in silence, his eyes fixated on the door to the emergency room hoping that God would just sacrifice him instead of his precious Madeleine. Then the door opened and a tired looking doctor came forth, approaching them all. He needed to say nothing for his face said it all. Madeleine was lost to them. She was with the Angles.

Yet the doctor sat with the General and his wife and patiently talked to them in hushed tones, telling them of the extent of her bodily injuries that were beyond repair. "Yet I can tell you this if you'll allow me"! The General and his wife nodded their heads in unison. "I've seen similar injuries occur to accident victims and they usually succumb a lot sooner than your daughter did. All through the procedures I kept talking to her and she responded valiantly as if there was a great deal at stake in her survival. Her will was as strong as any I've seen but in the end her body was just overwhelmed, by the extent of her injuries"!

At that moment both the General and his wife knew precisely what the doctor was talking about as they looked at what was to be their future son in law, standing ram rod straight, his arms folded behind him, just feet away looking out into the night, with unseeing eyes, starting to mist.

"I'm sorry we couldn't save her General"!

"Thank you Doctor. You did all you could. May we see our daughter"? "Yes, you may if you will follow me"?

"Sergeant, will you join us, in our farewell's", asked the General? Magellan looked at him and said, "Sir. You and the Madam deserve to have your moments alone with Madeleine. That holds precedence. If I may be permitted to follow you, I'd like my time alone with her if you please"!

"As you wish Sergeant"!

A half an hour later they emerged as Madeleine's mother said to Magellan, "Nestor we've talked with her and she is in God's hands. So please go in and say your goodbyes"!

As he entered the cold emergency room, he drew aside the curtains and saw his precious Madeleine peacefully at rest. The eyes were closed and she had been cleaned up by the doctors, but as he lifted her hospital gown he could see the extent of her injuries and he quickly replaced her gown to preserve her dignity. Then he felt a presence hovering over them both. It was her spirit saying one final goodbye in words that were felt rather than heard. Then he heard, in his mind's eye, 'Our very first night together and every moment after will live with me through eternity. Farewell my love'!

The tears were finally pouring forth as he summoned her not to leave him, but she had gone to her final rest. Eventually he gathered himself and kissed her cold lips for the last time, opened the curtains and joined the General and his wife saying, "Thank you. You were correct Madam. Madeleine is in the hand of the eternal"!

In the aftermath of the funeral, when Magellan was to ride back in the General's Limousine, he begged off by asking Madam St. Nathalie, "Would you mind it terribly if I walked back to the Lycee. I need to be alone with my thoughts"!

"But it is some ten kilometers, Nestor", she exclaimed!

"I've walked farther. Much farther. Please make the appropriate apologies to your husband and tell him that I will be back to work next Monday, if you will. At that he kissed his almost mother in law's hand and walked off.

As the General broke away from the other mourners, he approached his wife asking, "Where is Magellan going"?

"He wants to walk back and be by himself. I think we owe him that. Oh and he said that he would be back to duty Monday morning next"!

Magellan took a circuitous route towards the exit, not wanting to be with anyone. Then a Gray Peugeot Sedan slowly pulled up beside him and he heard a gruff voice from inside say, "I think you need a ride Sergeant"! Magellan stopped as well as the sedan and he looked to his left seeing the friendly face of Old Sergeant Lambrage, who opened the passenger door Saying, "Get in Sergeant! You need a friend and that's what Legionnaires do in perilous times, so get in god damn it, there is much to discuss"! Magellan removed his Kepi and entered the Peugeot. As Lambrage slowly drove off he said, "Nothing can cure your grief. It will hang about your neck like an anvil, for some time to come. You must have a steel backbone as I know you do and direct your activities towards some business long ago that remains unfinished. Its time you revisited the land of your origins and I can be of help"!

"The members of the Guardia that were responsible for the death of your father have served their terms of imprisonment and are out amongst the free, although severely diminished in standing. The Pregoso family is but a memory all residing in the Elysian Fields or some other celestial dimension. The Qiuniones family fortunes are but a fraction of what they once were, since the elder was excommunicated from Holy Mother Church. No one talks to him. Few do business with him reluctantly, but en camera"! "Your mother thrives and is in the service of the former Archbishop, now a Cardinal residing in Madrid. Your father's burial casket was transferred to a place in the Cardinals residential grounds and a special plot awaits your Mother next to him, when she is ready to be called to God"!

"You have a significant amount of leave time accrued and things can be arranged so you can attend to long overdue private affairs"!

"But my responsibilities to the cadets at the Lycee", said Magellan as he was interrupted by Lambrage who bellowed, "There are others that can continue your work at the Lycee. What is most important now is that you be made whole once again. Time has passed, others have forgotten about Carlos Vega. Happenstance has worked its magic, but not completely. Strings are loose that need to be secured. All you have to do is nod your head and information and papers will be provided for you to reenter Spain and finish things"!

"Is the General aware of this", asked Nestor?

"We've discussed the matter and he's placed everything in my hands, with but one caution"!

"And that is"?

"That you be successful. Failure is not an option. With but one exception, once you cross the Spanish frontier, you will be completely on your own. Provisions will provided for you in Barcelona. Someonee will provide you with anything need once in Spain. He's a former Legionnaire and of Basque descent. We've talked as of yesterday and you are expected"!

Magellan nodded his head saying, "I shall request a thirty days leave next Monday when I resume my duties"!

"Good. Call me when you do so I can start assembling your new identity and valid documents of transit and as for those demons that are circling about your head? Embrace them for they will serve you well in the coming days"!

Three weeks later Magellan decided to take the scenic route south in his hired Citroen to cross into Spain. He left the A7 InterStrada at Permignan and took the Mediterranean coastal road, crossing the French/ Spanish frontier checkpoint at the sleepy village of Cerebere.

The border inspector barely glanced at the papers of Virmuel De Hozel, as he passed through his hands without a second glance. Simply another French tourist on his way to the Spanish Riviera on holiday. This was the very first time he'd returned to Spanish soil since that fateful evening that changed everything. By midafternoon he drove into Barcelona and was busy navigating the streets while consulting his Michelin Guide, eventually coming up to the busy pawn shop in one of the lesser parts of the city. All of Magellan's papers indicated that he was a certain Virmuel De Hozel, Drivers certificate, Insurance, Passport, Visa, business cards, everything, on official French Government documents. Of course upon his return they would be incinerated, but until then they guaranteed his official identity.

He placed a call to the proprietor from a half block away, from his cell phone and confirmed an appointment with him an hour from now. Then he waited and watched. If there was anything awry, he would notice the arrival of several vehicles on the streets, containing several men in each ready for apprehension. The hour passed and he waited ten minutes more and seeing nothing out of the ordinary emerged from his car and went inside.

An hour later he drove his Citroen around to the rear of the establishment and loaded the munitions and weapons into the rear of his car. "How much do I owe you", asked Magellan?

"Owe me? You owe me nothing. You are a Legionnaire on assignment. It's been taken care of already. Of course you were never here and I never saw you. Agreed"?

"Agreed"! They shook hands and the last Magellan saw of him was in his rearview mirror as he went back inside without a backward glance.

One of the wonderful things about the passage of time is that people forget. Almost everybody does. With the exception of the precious few of us that are paranoid, fearful of everything under the sun. And then the old adage that, "Paranoia, is simply the reverse of complete awareness", was always a consideration. Carlos Vega had disappeared from the face of the earth as far as anyone knew. Some would have slept better over the years had they known with exactitude his status. However with the passage of time, more pressing considerations held their attentions, such as daily survival.

The three convicted members of the Guardia, Cardoso, Garza and the former Commandante' Reyna, had emerged from prison broken men. Careers finished and any possibility of a pension nonexistent, being relegated to the status of night watchmen for low level security firms.

After Magellan spent the better part of ten days in due diligence, locating their modest apartments and charting their daily routines, he went to work on a segmented plan for their appointment with justice.

The first to depart was Cardoso, having met his maker while asleep in his bed, his absence never discovered until a week later when he failed to appear at work. His body was discovered peacefully asleep, a month later after his rent came due by his landlord, in the process of eviction, discovering his remains in his bed. A cursory autopsy revealed that he'd suffered a heart attack while asleep. A more detailed examination would've discovered the remnants of an inoculation in the cavity between his toes. His parting met with almost no notice, being a four line mention buried in the back of the death announcements in the Cadiz newspaper.

Garza met his end the following day, as he was making his rounds in the early hours of the morning while at his security job in Lisbon. The security cameras, in a state of constant disrepair due to the negligence of the owners at the warehouse complex failed to detect a shadowy figure coming up from behind and breaking the man's neck in an instant then depositing him in a nearby dumpster. The trash truck however did its job by promptly arriving an hour later and transporting the former Guardia Capitan to his final resting place, in the land fill outside of the city limits. His body covered by tons of garbage, quietly decomposing over the course of time. His departure met with not one element of curiosity by anyone, simply an unverified police report that gathered dust as a missing person. Unresolved.

The former Commander Reyna however had secured a position as a low level security supervisor for a security firm in Barcelona. As luck would have it, he was on a month long holiday on the Spanish Island of Majorca. He never took notice of a man who constantly shadowed him during the course of several days and followed him and his paid female escort on a nightly tour boat cruise around island. Emerging from his cabin in the early hours of the morning after a round of sex with his companion of the moment. He stood by the boats upper deck railing at the stern of the vessel. Trying in vain to light a much needed cigarette, he looked up as a stranger approached saying, "Need a light Senor"?

Reyna said, "Gracias", as he bent his head to receive the offered light and that was the last thing that entered his mind as the stranger swiftly stepped around him and broke his neck. The stern of the boat offered a prime platform for Reyna's entrance into the waters of the Mediterranean, for the noise made by the propellers was such that no one heard the splash of his body as it hit the waters. Being approximately some ten nautical miles from the island offered every possibility of not being discovered for days if not for weeks as it succumbed to the forces of nature.

The boat entered port at nine in the morning and by ten the cabin pursers awakened Reyna's companion to depart the vessel. Finding him not there, she quickly went through his belongings and removed his wallet and of course the money it contained quickly leaving. A very profitable cruise it was. As it turned out Reyna was never discovered. His disappearance causing no one to take notice.

As Magellan drove back to Zaragoza, his tasks almost completed far ahead of schedule, he thought to himself on how easy it all had been and that now was not the time to be complaisant. Just one final thing to accomplish.

Two days later as the elder got into his car for his weekly trip into Zaragoza, he drove off and made his way along the semi mountainous roads that led towards town. His brakes seemed to be a bit mushy as he pressed further and further towards the floor of his car to get them to engage. He made a mental note to go to a garage first thing after arriving in Zaragoza and have a mechanic take a look. He never got the opportunity as his car gained speed down a long incline, his brakes now completely useless and before he could think to do anything else, the car crashed through a wooden railing meant to protect drivers from a sharp curve, careening down a steep hill, bouncing through trees and boulders, coming to a rest on the valley below, upside down, crushing the body of the driver.

Magellan following at a discrete distance drove slowly past the scene of the wreck, not stopping and continued until he reached a street side telephone kiosk some distance away.

He anonymously dialed the local police and reported the accident quickly hanging up.

That evening in his hotel room, he saw the evening news telecast report of the terrible accident that had taken the life of the eldest remaining member of the Quiniones family. The following week, a special report was telecast locally of the history of the Quiniones family and their fall from prominence. No mention of Carlos Vega, or the disintegration of his family was mentioned in the special report titled, "El Muerte' de un Familia"!

Just one final thing remained for Magellan. A trip to Madrid and an audience with the Cardinal. Before he departed, he disposed of everything he'd gotten from his connection in Barcelona. His tasks finished he simply didn't need it anymore. It would be foolhardy to be stopped by the Guardia at some roving checkpoint and have his car searched and everything be discovered after all he'd accomplished. Now just armed with his wits, he departed for Madrid.

The following day after he arrived in Madrid, he called the office of the Cardinal to inquire as to his schedule and told that he was in residence. He asked for an audience with His Eminence and told that his schedule was very busy said, "I'm aware of his eminence's busy schedule, but I'm here in town on business and I apologize for the short notice, but I promised a close friend that I would make an inquiry in his behalf regarding the health and welfare of Appolonia Vega, of which he's very concerned"!

"Did you say Appolonia Vega, Senor"?

"Yes", answered Magellan! The line went silent for a moment then the Secretary said, "No one has inquired about her for many years. If you come by midafternoon, I shall see what I can do to fit you into the Cardinals busy schedule"!

"Muy Gracias", said Magellan, "I promise to be as brief as possible", as he hung up the phone.

The Cardinals personal secretary had been with him for many years and was well aware of the constant burden of activity placed upon the Cardinal, usually acting as a bulwark to many protecting his time and schedule from the unnecessary intrusions. However the mention of Appolonia Vega's name got his immediate attention. Her presence in their midst ever since the 'Time of Troubles' many years ago proved in many ways to be a blessing rather than a burden.

The caller spoke immaculate Spanish although with a slightly French accent as the Secretary's mind raced. Suddenly he thought, 'Could this be the resurfacing of Carlos Vega'?

As Magellan approached the desk of the Cardinal's secretary, the secretary, a man of the secular world, appraised the demeanor of this tall one, concluding in a snap evaluation that under the guise of a well-dressed businessman, who's manner and style indicated an element of breeding and education, lay the virtues of a self-taught man, hardened by life.

Magellan introduced himself as Virmuel DeHozel, the man he'd talked to over the phone that made the inquiry as to Senora Vega. Slowly the secretary rose to greet the visitor acknowledging their conversation, with a look of astonishment upon his face as he continued to take the measure of this man before him. They shook hands as the secretary said, "If you will be seated Senor, I will see what I can do for you. His eminence should be concluding his conference shortly. Then he turned and disappeared behind a pair of ornately massive doors that appeared to be hundreds of years old. As he waited, Magellan took in the full view of the Cardinals residence and thought, 'What history must surround this holy place of business. Was this the very place that Torquemada implemented the Papal dictates of the Inquisition, some five hundred years ago in order to cleanse the faithful? A decidedly satanic set of circumstances, promulgated by the anointed representative of the Holy Mother Church at that time. He prayed that the same influences were long driven from this residence. Then his thoughts drifted to that of his mother in residence, apparently thriving. His concerns slowly began to evaporate'.

As the minutes slowly ticked away, he looked at his watch and began to have second thoughts. Was the look on the secretary's face a look of recognition? Was the Guardia en route? He decided that perhaps this was a fool's errand and that if the doors didn't open shortly then he would leave. As the seconds ticked away the doors suddenly opened and the Secretary emerged escorting several men in business attire out of the inner sanctum and thanking them for their time. As they departed he turned to Magellan saying, "Thank you for your patience Senor DeHozel. It would seem that a cancellation has occurred, offering you a brief window of opportunity for an audience with his eminence. If you will be kind enough to follow me I will introduce you to his eminence"!

As he followed the secretary into the Cardinals private office, Magellan focused on the man in front of him, standing in front of his desk. He was of medium height, with a medium cut to his graying hair, attired in the black full length cassock with red piping that signified his status. And then there were the eyes. They were kind eyes. The eyes that bore witness and had seen as much as anyone the pain and suffering that mankind could offer.

Eyes that had absorbed the pain and suffering of countless others through reconciliation and overt acts of kindness. Eyes that had repeatedly given repeatedly of himself time and again to the point of complete saturation, only to be mysteriously restored on the morrow, ready to give of themselves again and again. The wellspring never ran dry deep within this man, absorbing all of the pain and anguish that befell all that came before him, affecting the very soul of the one who gave comfort to the soul.

As Magellan approached, the secretary introduced him as the Cardinal offered his ring hand and Magellan genuflected, kissing the Cardinals ring then arose to his full height.

"We understand that you are making some inquiries regarding Senora Vega my son", said the Cardinal as he offered him a seat and joined him in adjoining leather appointed armchair.

"Yes your eminence. I'm a distant relative of the Vega family and wish to convey the concern of a certain party near Pamplona, in a small village called Aoiz. I'm in the city only until this evening and apologize for this intrusion, but would be grateful for any news that I could convey back to those concerned, about Senora Vega"!

The Cardinal was silent for some time, contemplating his mysterious visitor. He'd taken into consideration the suspicions of his secretary, along with the news of the accident that befell the elder Quiniones just the other day and concluded that with the passage of time; here he was out of the mists of a time long past was this polite young man making veiled inquiries about Appolonia Vega.

"We were informed that Senora Vega had no living relatives upon the untimely death of her husband and since we've granted her sanctuary years ago no one has made a single inquiry in her behalf"! He waited for a response from the visitor and after receiving none continued, "Well no matter. Our Senora Vega is very well, in good spirits and had resided under our protection ever since the day she was brought before us, many years ago in the Archbishops rectory in Zaragoza. Upon my elevation to Cardinal, we found it necessary to bring her with us since she's proven to be an indispensable member of our family. While her duties here are loosely defined, she tends to serve in our kitchens in the personal preparation and serving of my daily meals and that of my secretary. In addition she tends to my personal clothing on a daily basis, mending, cleaning and replacement when necessary. She wants for nothing temporal and she attends daily Mass as well as evening Vespers and her monthly confessions, although she has little to confess, being of such a giving and agreeable nature. I hear her confessions personally and she spends most of the time recanting her life before and is in constant prayer for her missing son Carlos. From time to time we talk about her time long past and she'll regale me at length about her marriage with her departed husband and her Son. Her health is very good considering her vintage and she is attended to by my personal physician as is needed. Her husband Motale' is interred here on the rectory grounds in consecrated ground and when her time comes to join him, I've seen to it that she will be buried beside him. She is held in high regard and loved by everyone and her very nature is remarkably cheery considering all that she's been through. She is a whirlwind of daily activity, arising early and retiring after most have gone to bed. I'm afraid that she gives us all far more than we give her. We try and slow her down but she will have none of it and is indeed quite irreplaceable"!

Continuing on he offered, with a sly wink, "If she has a fault and I'm not saying that it is mind you, her culinary efforts are quite inspirational and upon occasion come in conflict with my personal physician. Yet they come to an accord, for at least a little while, before she starts spoiling me once again. Yet I secretly side with her. Yet as happy as she appears to be, I'm certain that she still yearns for news of her son Carlos, for his disappearance was never resolved"! Then he paused for a moment and said, "You say that you are a distant member of the family and are asked to make an inquiry of her after all these years of silence, so tell me my son, have you any news of Carlos Vega that I can impart to her in confidence"?

"Nothing of significance your eminence, only that he is seen from time to time and I understand that he is reasonably well"!

"Perdonna me, but how, may we ask do you know this my son"? After a brief pause where Magellan was searching his mind for an appropriate response, he carefully began, "Your eminence, the person once known as Carlos Vega, can never come home again, for there is nothing to return to. All that he's cherished has been taken from him by circumstance.

True enough, his youthful passion and hubris caused a cascading effect of events that caused unforeseen pain and suffering in many quarters and for that he will forever regret. However, I'm certain you'll agree that when God, or perhaps circumstance, closes a door, another portal is always left slightly ajar for each of us to discover. Her son has discovered that portal and has a life that has taken him in a different direction of what may have been originally intended and he is well enough"!

"Are you a Catholic my son"?

"Yes your eminence. Ever since birth"!

"A practicing Catholic"?

"My attendance at Mass has been known to ebb and flow from time to time"!

"Would you like me to hear your confession my son"? Again Magellan thought for several moments before responding, "Your eminence, it would probably take weeks, perhaps months, to adequately do justice for a proper confession. Your schedule wouldn't permit it, I suspect. Besides, I'm not certain that many of my transgressions I've committed, I'm sorry for and to ask for God's forgiveness, doesn't one have to admit culpability, sorrow and promise to sin no more"?

Yet again a brief silence took hold between the two, with the Prelate not exactly agreeing with the visitors point of view, fully understood his mindset. For the reconciliation with the eternal to take hold, one must believe in his heart that wrongs had been committed, failing that, it was an exercise in futility. "Would you like to visit Senora Vega my son, so your report can be an example of an eyewitness"?

As he fought back against the presence of visible emotion, at the mention of his mother's name Magellan quickly answered, "No your eminence that will not be necessary, for your word and revelation is and should be more than sufficient. Then there's the question of balance. Appolonia Vega clearly has found a purpose here deep in Gods bosom and in your service. One can clearly see the love you have for her. Here she is needed. Her whole life has been in the service of others. Here she is in balance. I fear that any mention of her son may bring that balance off center"! He paused for an instant then said, "So I must politely decline. Your time is at a premium your eminence and by this evening I must depart"!

At that point the Prelate thought it time for revelation as he leaned over in his chair placing his hand over the hand of the visitor saying, "Before you depart will you receive benediction Carlos"? His eyes grown wide, Magellan looked uneasily at the Prelate, knowing full well that one never lied to a priest and any attempt to brazen things out would be met with scorn and derision. A point of dishonor as he said, "So you knew all along"!

"I had my suspicions, but knew with the remotest degree of certainty? No my son. But your mother and I talked for years about you and even though you had clearly changed over time, you did bear a resemblance. Then there was the fact of your hands. Not soft like the appearance of the businessman you represent so well, but hard and calloused. But what gave you away was something that only two people alive would know. On your right hand, your little finger, bent at the fist knuckle from a football that went awry. It never was set by a doctor wasn't it"?

"I was playing with some other children in the field, your eminence, rather than tending to the livestock. I was eleven at the time. Never did tell my parents. In time the pain eventually went away and the finger grew into its current configuration. Eventually in time mother made the discovery and I told her a lie to cover it up"!

"A venial sin of no consequence my son", said the Prelate as he started to rise as he directed Magellan to kneel before him as he placed his hand over his head in benediction saying, "God has brought you at long last into our midst carrying a heavy burden. I suspect you are on a long journey fraught with peril as you have been these many years. The Lord has been by your side, whether or not you've felt his presence. Put your mind at ease regarding your mother and concentrate on the road ahead, for it has a multitude of ambuscades that befall those that travel the road. Always listen very carefully to that voice deep within that whispers, for it will show you the way"! Your life has meaning and no matter what deep resentments that leaves a scar, remember that goodness and mercy are a virtue and that you shall remain in our prayers, for as long as we live"!

"In nomine patris, et filius, e Sanctus, Amen", said the Prelate as he made the sign of the cross over him, bidding him to rise as he offered his ring to kiss. As he slowly escorted Magellan out of his office, his secretary rose up as he said, "Pedro, perhaps you would be kind enough to show our visitor, the final resting place of Motale' Vega."!

"Si your eminence. Senor DeHozel if you would be kind enough to follow me"!

"Thank you again your eminence", said Magellan as he turned to follow the secretary.

"Via con Dios", whispered the Cardinal as he made the sign of the cross, thinking 'He will need it'.

"If you follow that gravel path down the hill, you will come upon a small copse of trees. Therein lays the final resting place of Senor Vega"!

"Gracias", said Magellan as he started down the path.

The Cardinal stood by the window in the hallway that gave full view of the pathway to the small copse of trees down below. As his secretary joined him they looked after their visitor as the bells started to chime signaling the hour of Vespers was near. Hurriedly Senora Vega emerged from the tree line making her way up the path towards the sanctuary passing the visitor her head down as she rushed. As she passed the visitor she briefly lifted her head as if to speak in passing, then continued up the path. As she got to the top of the path she slowly turned to look back, but by this time the path way empty. She took two more steps and turned a final time, this time for a longer look and then looked at the ground, shook her head and continued onward towards the evening Vespers.

Magellan's heart stopped, as he saw his mother hurry past. She briefly glanced at him then back to the path way and hurried on as she mumbled a hurried greeting. Part of him dearly wished to embrace her, yet he recalled what he told the Cardinal. Here she was secure and in balance. If he ever revered her memory he would allow that delicate state of balance to continue. Besides, his presence, brought death and misery to all he loved. Joselita, his mother Appolonia, and finally Madeleine and her parents. He would spend some time with his father then vanish into the night, secure in the memory of their presence.

"Do you think Senora Vega recognized her visitor", asked the Prelates secretary?

"So you also connected the dots eh, Pedro"?

"Eventually"!

"Then it shall remain our secret. Senora Vegas must never know. Her life is in balance. Her son is on a troubled journey. Let us pray that he eventually finds peace with himself and with God"!

"Of course you have heard of the accident of Senor Quiniones yesterday in Zaragoza" said Pedro the secretary!

"Yes, Pedro I read it in the papers this morning. A coincidence perhaps or perhaps a case of unfinished business. Either way prayers have been made to the eternal and forgiveness asked for their eternal souls"! "Shall we pray for Senora Vega's son, your eminence"?

"Especially for him, for his soul and his sanity are on the razors edge. Now hurry and help me prepare for Vespers"!

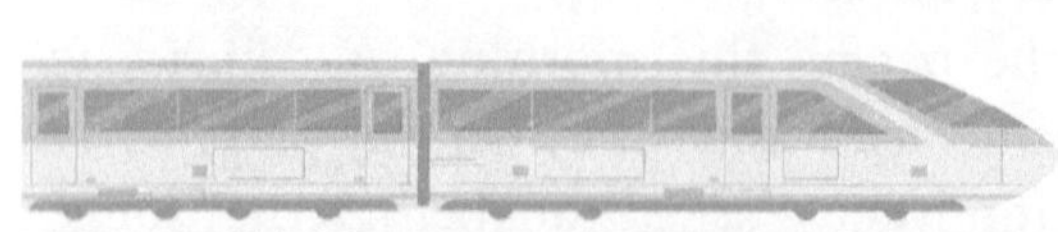

18

"**S**o good of you to attend us General St. Nathalie", said General Montfort as he rose to greet the General entering the meeting room in the Elyse Palace. May I offer my condolences for your terrible loss suffered by your family a few months ago. I trust your wife is holding up well"?

"Thank you General for your concern and as far as my wife, she is doing as well as can be expected", replied St. Nathalie solemnly.

"I believe you know everyone here with the possible exception of Hercule DesChamps of our Foreign Service Ministry"? General St. Nathalie walked over and shook hands with the civilian official offering, "So very good to meet you Monsieur"!

"Please everyone be seated so we can commence"!

"General St. Nathalie has been invited to join us for the purpose of assisting us in the evaluation a number of servicemen to be elevated to certain positions in the Foreign Service. We are tasked with the responsibility of selecting key personnel in certain areas within our sphere of political influence around the world. So gentlemen shall we begin"?

For the rest of the morning they went around the table exchanging viewpoints on various key positions in Embassies around the world. After a break for the noon luncheon, they resumed, with Montfort saying, "I'm grateful for your assistance St. Nathalie, for your presence has seemed to foster a certain consensus amongst the others I simply haven't been unable to bring about. We've been at it a week and have made more progress in a single morning than in the entire week. Your expertise is invaluable. If all goes well we should be finished by days end"!

"I'm happy to have been assistance General" said St. Nathalie as they joined the others. As it turned out Montfort was correct in his assessment of St. Nathalie's selection skills. He was able to spot certain personal traits of others and see what no one else could, the applicable skills of soldiers by a simple reading of their dossiers. Experience amongst men as an officer of the line, was of incalculable value, that staff officers generally lacked. St. Nathalie was able to glean and then sell his point of view to the others, demonstrating his swiftness in effective decision making, by seeing what others couldn't or wouldn't. As the middle of the afternoon beckoned Montfort announced," Gentlemen we've arrived at our final assignment and possibly our most important. The Embassy in Buenos Aires. We have special industrial needs that must be protected, if a continuum of orders are to continue courtesy of the Argentine Military. As we all know, their defeat in the Falklands War drained their military necessities as well as their ability to purchase additional replacements, thanks to their malfeasance in governance, resulting in an outrageous inflation rate and their default on their international debt. Now comes the International Monetary fund to their rescue and their ability to pay is restored for at least the foreseeable future"!

"The three dossiers in front of you are selected as the most likely to be a good fit for the position. I offer them for your perusal gentlemen if we shall take several minutes to read them"! The last dossier St. Nathalie read was that of Sergeant Nestor Magellan. He remained silent as he well knew his dossier by heart, as General Montfort resumed. "The individual chosen is to be assigned as an attaché', formally managing their linguistics' section at the Embassy. He will have several translators working for him and as many off you may have guessed, there is more to this than just a simple clerical function. This individual will be required to carry out, from time to time, a variety of, shall we say, onerous jobs, thus he should be able to employ a wide range of skills, in behalf of the French Government"! Continuing on Monfort said, "Of the trio of men presented, one stands out in my mind, a linguistics expert attached to General St. Nathalie at the Lycee at St. Cyr named Magellan. A Sergeant Nestor Magellan, I believe General"?

"Yes Magellan. A superior soldier"!

"General, if I may", asked DesChamps. "This Magellan, in addition to his duties at the Lycee, has other unofficial tasks assigned to him from time to time does he not"?

St. Nathalie, arched an eyebrow and glanced at Montfort briefly as if to say, 'What in the hell is a civilian to do with anything regarding the Special Action Group'? Montfort gauging his reticence said, "You may speak freely here General, for we all are of similar mind and sentiment.

As far as our civilian counterpart is concerned, he served as a Major in Military Intelligence and is a graduate of the Lycee. He's part of the decision making entity for your special undertakings. His position with the Foreign Service is invaluable and he has been vetted with the highest clearance"! "Mon General, if I may", asked St. Nathalie?

"Continue General"!

"I thought that only a chosen few at the Prime Minister's office were aware of the existence of the Special Action Group"!

"If I may respond to that General", asked DesChamps?

"The podium is yours DesChamps"!

"General. Over the years, the office of the Prime Minister is and always has been inextricably a creature of the Foreign Service. The General Assembly annually funds your activities without knowledge of your existence, because you're funding for extracurricular activities are always channeled through the Foreign Ministry in a host of rather creative ways. Thus each of us is aware to a certain degree of your activities and applauds the unfortunate necessary sub rosa service that you and your operatives provide. In addition, a select few of the members of the national assembly are aware of our existence. Without their splendid cooperation funding would be difficult to come by. They provide a certain lubrication when required and it is in our mutual benefit that we maintain our relationship, in an unspoken understanding. In addition should they ever experience a moment of sudden epiphany, they would do so certain of the knowledge the heavens would descend upon them as is with us all, effecting not only them but that of their immediate family. Thus our mutual interests of governance are in balance"!

"That said are we are of an understanding"?

"I believe we are Monsieur DesChamps", replied St. Nathalie!

"Good. This Sergeant Magellan is of interest, to me. Please tell us what you can to add some flesh to his dossier. Reading between the lines one suspects he's been a protégé of yours over the years, clearly a success story. You were the one who approved his entry into the Legion many years ago and somehow you've monitored his progress, to the degree of having his annual efficiency reports channeled to your office for scrutiny and when one reads his reports, one can see why. Even to the point of his escorting your daughter, may she rest in peace, back from her sabbatical. One thinks he is trustworthy and loyal above all else in addition to his proven abilities. His service at the Lycee is above reproach as well as his prior service and that of the Special Action Group. Thus the question is, in my mind, is there any impediments, blemishes, weakness' or encumbrances that you can recall that may perhaps prove as an impediment to our special needs for this assignment"?

St. Nathalie thought a moment then said, "Encumbrance I believe you said? Perhaps there was at one time, but I believe that has gone by the way side. For several months ago he was granted a long overdue leave. He was gone for less than thirty days. On his own time. Only later did I discover he returned to the land of his birth, Spain to correct some things. It seemed that the very reason for his entry into the Legion was still with us after all of these years. A once man of prominence in his community, had a fatal auto accident and three others who were convicted in the manslaughter of his father, simply disappeared. He returned to us a new man and freshly tanned by his vacation. In addition something else that has escaped your scrutiny. He was quietly engaged to my daughter and they were to have been married in a quiet ceremony just a few months from now. I suspect that my daughter's accidental death had something emotionally to do with his sudden interest of long overdue unfinished business in Spain, for they were deeply devoted to each other and I suppose he had to do something significant in which to channel his grief. We haven't spoken much since then only superficially in things germane to the Lycee and curriculum. But if you're asking whether or not he's the right man for your purposes? He is, in every way possible. I suggest a promotion to Warrant Officer status, should he be your selection and of course a certain fairly generous clothing allowance, if he is to be seconded to a civilian environment"!

"Will he be available for deployment within the next thirty days", asked DesChamps?

"It is the summer semester and his class schedule is minimal. He's trained an able replacement, since his rotation back to standard duty somewhere was inevitable at some time as is Lycee policy"!

Everyone around the table looked at each other and nodded their heads in agreement as General Monfort cast his eyes upon Hercule DesChamps who agreed with a nod of his head.

"Un Viola. Selection made and all are in agreement", said Monfort. "You will receive orders within the week seconding your Sergeant to the

Embassy in Buenos Aires and a promotion to Warrant Officer Status and a clothing allowance. You will be the one to deliver the news to Sergeant Magellan, General and after he receives his orders, you will forward him to Monsieur DesChamps at the Foreign Ministry. Of course he will have to be replaced at the Special Action Group and I trust that you will see to an appropriate replacement General. His unofficial status with the Special Action Group will be placed as "On loan, to the Corps Diplomatique". Gentlemen our work is done here. This meeting is adjourned"!

Less than a year later, found Magellan well settled into his new life as the Interim Director of Linguistics, of the French Embassy in Buenos Aires. His workload was more managerial in nature, having a staff of three graduate students doing the bulk of the work. He was provided with an automobile and an apartment not three blocks away. Life was good for Magellan for his normal workload wasn't onerous and from time to time, he was tasked with traveling to various parts of the country and the South American Continent on straight diplomatic assignments utilizing his linguistic skills.

Every much a cosmopolitan metropolis as Paris, Buenos Aires offered a rich urban life with all of the attractions and distractions one could imagine. Although in the prime of his physical life and still attractive to many women, he avoided the distraction afforded by a relationship for the simple reason of the ever present memory of his Madeleine, still lingering. The unspoken question lingered, 'How does one make love to another woman, when the image of a lost love still held sway in his mind'? Impossible'! Time would have to pass. His emotional recovery wasn't helped by the fact that he acquired several Cole Porter and Edith Piaf record albums, playing them in private moments repeatedly. The best emotional therapy for him was work and constant activity.

One fateful evening while attending a local Embassy affair, Magellan was introduced to Carlos Meyers, as economic attaché for the newly formed Argentine International Economic Development Ministry. His specific task was to act as an economic liaison between the Argentine Military and the French Aircraft Company, Dassault. With graduate degrees in Economics and International Law, from Cambridge University in England, Meyers was one of the rising stars in diplomatic circles. He was known as a "Closer", for he had the knack of finding just what buttons to push, to surmount the insurmountable. Sometimes, it was

'Mordida', (the bite) that proved a sufficient lubricant, while other times called for other tactics, such as kidnapping, of the complete disappearance of another.

"You come highly recommended for your position Senor Magellan", said Meyers sipping his Champaign!

"Really now. Anyone I know"?

"Perhaps. Does the name Hercule' DesChamps ring a bell"?

"Don't recall the name"!

"You must remember your old boss at the Lycee Militaire'. General St. Nathalie? For it was he through DesChamps in the Foreign Ministry that was responsible for your current posting"!

"So you know General St. Nathalie"?

"By reputation only which is impeccable. But I did meet him at an affair such as this in Paris about two years ago. A remarkable individual"!

"Seems to me that as I stand here talking to you, I'm waiting for the other shoe to drop. This is not a casual meeting is it"!

"They said you were capable of both tact and bluntness. No, this is not a casual meeting. It seems that your old skills are being required to be resurrected"!

"Old skills you say? What old skills"?

"The skills you often employed as a Legionnaire and at the Lycee, when not furthering the education of La Belle France's future officers"!

"Senor Meyers. We've just met and you claim to know much about me. Yet I know little about you except that you've the requisite charm of a diplomat. I'm merely an attaché and a translator. Should you require any of those services, in behalf of my government, I suggest you go through normal diplomatic channels and if directed, I'll be happy to be of any assistance"!

"As you wish Senor Magellan. Buena's Noches. We shall talk again", said Meyers as he turned and circulated throughout the room.

Two days later Magellan received an "Eyes Only", coded message from his old friend Lambrage, asking him to contact a certain Carlos Meyers and meet with him and be of assistance in any way possible. The postscript carried an oblique message that only Magellan and Lambrage knew about to verify its authenticity.

As the taxi drove down the narrow streets of Buenos Aries towards the Milonga La Ventura, on the Avenue San Juan, Magellan recalled his brief conversation with Meyers the previous day. He suggested they meet during the evening at the his favorite Tango Club saying, "I always like to mix business with pleasure whenever possible"!

He further suggested Magellan take a taxi whereas street parking in the narrow streets of this section of the city, would be impossible to come by.

Meyers proved correct, for once Magellan said to the driver, Milonga La Ventura, the driver took off, without further need of information. And there it was, a single nondescript building vintage building that had been combined with several others over the years to accommodate the audience that comprised the aficionados of the Tango.

Magellan paid the driver, plus a reasonable tip in order to comply with local custom as he made his way into the Tango club. He recalled what the driver told him as they made their way across the city that this was one of the more popular Milonga's in the city. Opening just before noon and closing well after midnight, with the afternoon crowds almost the size of that in the evening seven days a week nonstop.

As he entered, he remembered Meyer's instructions to immediately turn to the right upon entering then work his way around the crowd and ask any waiter he encountered for Senor Meyers reserved table. Easy to find since it would be on the men's side. He eventually made eye contact with Meyers who waved him over.

"Ah Magellan, so good of you to join me. Please be seated"! Then he motioned for a passing waiter to take Magellan's order. "One of my few vices Senor. The Milonga's of Buenos Aires. Are you familiar with the Tango"?

"I know the bare basics as it is performed in Europe"?

"Ah yes, the Euro style of Tango", he said disdainfully. Simply 'Merde', excreta. All this business of never making eye contact with one's partner. Just not the way the dance should be performed. An abortion"! Magellan could not help but chuckle at the man's passion, as he quipped, "Now you can tell me how you really feel about the subject"!

"As you wish. Allow me to explain. While no one really knows for certain, most feel the Tango gradually evolved over time, gradually paining popularity in the Bordellos of this city in the latter part of the last century. Women who immigrated into Buenos Aires with their husbands and others were left to fend for themselves and their men made their way into the country's interior, to find their fortune, or as the case may be simply find work. More often than not, not only did their men not return for a variety of reasons, death being only one of the possibilities, the women, usually having no marketable skills, save one, turned to prostitution to provide for their basic needs. Now as you can see as you look around, the Men take their stations on one side of the dance floor, while the women gather on the other. A simple custom that has endured over time for no good reason other than 'Because'. Now here's where the Euro style departs from the original. The dance, that has evolved over time, is the art of seduction, and they eyes are everything. In the bordellos, a glance simply held too long was an unspoken invitation to approach and the women who needed the work always were on the lookout. For the supine position was the one that relived the men not only of their hard earned cash, along with their bodily fluids, but proved profitable for the women"! As Magellan's drink arrived, Meyers continued. "Two sets eyes, searching across a crowded dance floor meet. Heads nod in mutual acceptance as the individuals make their way towards each other across a crowded dance floor, eventually coming together without a single word spoken. The woman, she seduces, while the man leads. He protects and supports, his love for the evening, while she elaborates and outlines the dance, her erotic eyes on her ad hoc paramour, her head resting upon his chest, her loins writhing and joining upon his lead leg spreading her moisture in order to see what arises"!

"Interesting concept on the evolution of a culture", offered Magellan "Which is why the Europeans, have it all wrong. To dance the Tango it is imperative that eye contact be maintained. The Euros have no sense of propriety"!

"Seems they find a way to maintain the population"!

"Ach a mechanical function that someday will be copied in a test tube artificially. Here, I will demonstrate", said Meyers as he stood up took two steps towards the edge of the dance floor casting his gaze upon the other side. Magellan watched, as Meyers eventually caught the glance of someone across the dance floor as the rhythmic lilt of the accordion and the violins made their way. Meyers head nodded as he stepped out onto the floor. Then Magellan saw two women emerge from the other side hurriedly making their way through the dancers arriving in front of Magellan at the same time. Before he could say anything, both women commenced to argue over which one he saw first, as Meyers took a step backwards. Both women fell to the dance floor grabbing and punching at each other with a fury as the other dancers made way for this interruption and the music never missed a beat. As Meyers carefully retreated several large men made their way onto the floor, each one grabbing one of the women by the waist and carrying them off to the other side in different directions disappearing into the crowd.

As Meyers approached his table, he saw Magellan doubling over in laughter. Taking his seat calmly he said, "Unfortunate miscalculation by the other side. A rare occurrence, but it happens"!

"I see what you mean by eye contact Meyers. I'll try and keep my eyes averted"!

"Is nothing. Now to why we're here. I trust my bona fides are in order Warrant Officer Magellan"?

"They are Senor Meyers. How may I be of assistance"? Meyers motioned for Magellan to lean forward so they could not be over heard in spite of the amplified music.

"From time to time your skills employed by the Special Action Group will be required to remove any impediments from our doing business with the companies of your mother country. At all times it will be in the mutual interests of our two political entities. At all times, all of the cards will be on the table. In order for you to function properly nothing is to be concealed from you. You will be given carte' blanche' for anything you may require from our government. Your Ambassador will be unaware of our special relationship since he is a creature of Mitterrand. Yet Monsieur DesChamps of your Corps Diplomatique', as well as General Monfort and General St. Nathalie are aware of our newly created special relationship as an extension of the work of the Special Action Group. Your current assignments will be maintained as they were at the Lycee and any assignments will be with the knowledge of the afore mentioned gentlemen. As it was before, your Ambassador will receive his directives from the Foreign Service office in Paris. They will of course be minor in nature and will be a cover for your normal functions at the Embassy. None of your assignments will require your absence from your Embassy for more than a few days. And there we have it, so what say you Senor Magellan"! "Anything on the horizon"?

"One of our leftist finance ministers is proving difficult in a business deal to supply your country with some much needed raw materials. Should this continue, his disappearance will prove quite beneficial providing Dassault Industries and others with much needed raw materials at bargain basement prices and our economy with much needed capital from abroad. The rub is he's trying to drive a better bargain for our raw materials, where they could be found elsewhere at a slightly higher price. We need the business and currently he's in the way. A decision has not been made yet, but I suspect it soon will be"!

"A private postal box has been provided across town", said Meyers and he slid a small envelope to Magellan under the table. Tomorrow afternoon there will be an envelope in your postal drop. In it will be a complete dossier on the object of your intentions. Should you not receive a green light, then you are to destroy the dossier. Should you receive a green light then the dossier will be invaluable and I will be available for anything you may require!"

"Just one thing. Perhaps I'm enquiring of the obvious however. Why the Special Action Group? Is there no talent for this sort of thing locally", asked Magellan?

Meyers leaned back for a moment then forward saying, "I think you have just answered your own question, but perhaps an elaboration is necessary. Our country is full of those who can extinguish a life. But when a microscope is placed upon our culture, seems that no one has the ability or desire to cultivate the range of skills to affect a disappearance, a complete disappearance without leaving a trail to follow. The Soviets, the Americans, the British, the Italians, the Corsicans and the French are the only ones. Something perhaps with the Spanish mindset demands publicity and of course that will not do. What is required in these instances is finesse' and your people have the resume'. Now let us relax and enjoy those around us, shall we"?

A week later the letter arrived at Magellan's new postal box. There was only one word written on the note inside. "Begin"!

Ten days later, the Argentine Minister of finance suddenly went missing. The last anyone had seen of the man, was on a Saturday morning as he kissed his wife goodbye, claiming that he had to go to the office, for additional work on the trade agreement he was working on in behalf of his government. He'd be working late into the night.

Instead he made straight for his mistress's house in a country casa on the northern side of the Rio de la Plata in Uruguay. He was never seen again. His body floated down the Rio de la Plata, the swift currents carrying his body out into the Atlantic Ocean eventually being consumed by the predators of the sea, while the unfortunate death his mistress was never connected with his disappearance. She simply died by an over consumption of proscribed barbiturates.

When the Minister never showed up for a scheduled meeting the following Monday morning, the subsequent investigation led nowhere, as the banner headlines in the local newspapers read, "Vanished into Thin Air"!

A week later, Magellan met with Meyers over lunch and was about to move a copy of the newspaper folded neatly near his plate, when Meyers suggested that he read it later adding, "I've already read the paper and in contains noting of consequence, but inside of that newspaper is an envelope and in it is a modest consideration you may consider as a little something extra for your services"! Magellan merely nodded his head in understanding as Meyers continued saying, our people are rather pleased, on both sides of the Atlantic. The new Minister of Finance has already announced that he is ready to approve the trade deal with Dassault and progress has been lubricated"!

As time progressed, Magellan was increasingly invited to a variety of social events and he always seemed to encounter Carlos Meyers at these events. In time their relationship, once one of fragile distance grew to that of a friendly acquaintance. Gradually Magellan grew uneasy with his life for no reason that could be pinpointed. Yet the overwhelming opulence of the ruling elite and his gradual emersion into their lifestyle began to take its toll little by little. The current battle with the plethora of Unions throughout the land seemed to Magellan to be a zero sum game. The Union's and the Owners both wanted the same thing. "More!" The Unions would strike, the owners would eventually exceed to their demands, simply raising prices sooner or later to maintain their profit margins. As prices rose, strikes would eventually rise from other quarters demanding that prices for certain goods or services return as they were. Thus, the cycle of democracy.

It seemed that the righteous on both sides of the political and economic fence always had something to hide. Overzealous gambling, homosexuality, women, drugs, etcetera, always provided Magellan with an easy path in which to quickly chart their demise.

An important "Unter" Minister in the Paraguayan Defense Ministry with a severe gambling problem found himself under a great deal of pressure to pay off his gambling debts and thus offered his disenchantment with the amount of "Mordida" he was receiving from the French owned construction company, contracted to construct a governmental project. The amount he attempted to extort quadrupled the original amount. The company appeared to relent to his demands at first, but it came as little surprise to those who knew him well, when his front tire separated from his car inexplicably as he drove away from the construction site at a high rate of speed as he was known to do quite often. The open topped convertible he was driving careened off a bridge abutment and into the upper reaches of the Rio de la Plata and into the river far below. His body was never discovered. Nine months later the project was completed, on time and on budget.

Some months later, when a French Mining concern was in the midst of contract renegotiations with the Brazilian Government in the northern port city of Reciefe', near the mouth of the Amazon, Magellan found himself right in the middle of things acting as interpreter in behalf of his French clients. As the negotiations were almost to the point of an impasse', due to the impossible financial conditions placed upon the French Company, it was discovered that their competition, a Brazilian concern, was tightly connected to the Chief Minister that was negotiating the terms. To publicly reveal the proof, would fall upon deaf ears whereas the Minister in question had friends highly placed in the government in Brasilia.

When one of the Senior Governmental Ministers suggested they travel up river to visit the proposed site near the foothills of the Andes Mountains, so the engineering problems could be better explained, a vote was taken and the trip was on. Traversing almost the entire length of the Amazon River was taken in several steps, the final of which was to be taken by a flat bottomed Riverboat, similar to that which traveled the Mississippi River. No expense was spared by the French Mining company in order to wine and dine their Brazilian governmental officials, especially keen was the attention paid upon the key Minister that had proven to be a stumbling block in the negotiations thus far.

Since the man was in his early fifties and had never taken a wife, questions abounded about his masculinity from time to time. Keen observations of his personal habits revealed the reason why. He had little interest in those of the opposite gender. His principle interest was his personal secretary, a tall willowy figure, contrasting to his shorter mesomorphic appearance, who traveled with the minister everywhere. While they always kept separate quarters when traveling, few were the nights that they spent apart. Close observers of the duo marveled at how their relationship was kept out of the view of the press. Key was the aspect that from time to time their quarrels were undertaken in private, rather than in the open, closeting their closeness from scrutiny.

As the stern wheeler was several days away from its destination, a party erupted in celebration of another minister's birthday, involving all of the governmental passengers on board on a moonless evening. Since before sundown the party kept going. As Magellan stood on the second level on the boats stern, he viewed and overheard, the impeding Minister engaged in a drunken quarrel with his assistant. Names were exchanged and the Minister called his assistant a name and slapped him. His injured assistant turned and fled in tears as his boss, turned and became sick over the stern, vomiting on the paddlewheels.

Amidst the noise from the music within, no one heard the screams of the minister as he suddenly flew into the paddlewheels. It was Magellan who rushed into the Salon and announced, "The Minister has fallen overboard. We must turn the ship around immediately". The boats pilot was immediately notified as the boat started its laborious turn in mid channel as the deck hands shined the rear mounted boat light on the churning waters in its wake, eventually falling upon the sight of a wildly thrashing form in the water, fighting for his life, some hundred meters astern of the boat.

Only a man with a death wish would dare to enter those waters infested with the deadly Piranha fish that could strip a grown man down to the bone in minutes. All on board gathered on the boats stern and port side, looking on in horror as the boat slowly turned.

"How did he fall overboard", asked one"?

"The Minister and his assistant were seen having a quarrel and he slapped his assistant", said Magellan!

"Where is he", asked another?

"In his cabin next to the Ministers, I might think", answered Magellan amidst the cries of the thrashing form in the water thrashing wildly at the attackers eager for a midnight meal.

And there he was, the long suffering assistant, administering to a large welt across his face, roughly resembling a hand print, as he was hustled by a number of the members to the boats stern. It seemed easy enough to Magellan, take advantage of a lovers quarrel, cast the blame elsewhere and allow the others to form their own opinion into fact. As the boat slowly came upon the Minister, he was yelling no more. He was thrashing about in the water no longer as the deck hands tried repeatedly to grab him with a boat hook amidst the swirling activity of the feasting fish. Eventually they were successful in retrieving his body from the swirling water, with wriggling fish still feasting upon the former minister. It might have been better if they left him sink to the bottom of the river. His remains, once the fish were removed and crushed by the deck hands caused everybody to become either instantly sober or physically ill or both were unrecognizable.

His assistant, for viewing the body of his former lover and most likely having a window into his now dimming future, made a dash towards the starboard side of the boat and leapt into the waters in a vain attempt at escape. With a great shout everyone went to where he leapt from the boat as the boat light followed his brief progress as he tried to reach the opposite shore. Within a minute, he was attacked by the razor sharp teeth of the Piranha and a grisly repeat of his demise was captured in the glare of the boats spotlight. This time it took the boat some ten minutes to turn again and reach the still churning waters around where he was last sighted, but by this time his body had submerged, the fish still feeding upon his sinking carcass as it descended to the river bottom, the echoes of his screaming still resonating in many of those present's ears for days and sometimes weeks to come.

As Magellan flew back to Buenos Aires, from Recife', he pondered on what had occurred. Two days river travel by everyone to a locale with an airstrip.

The trip in stages back to Reciefe' and several days of inquiry by the authorities while they sorted out the events at hand. Then the arrival of the departed Ministers replacement from the Nation's capital in Brasilia, then another two days while the Mining Company's contract was put to bed and codified and then here he was on the plane back to BA, with effusive thanks from the officials of the Mining Company. A simple task with some complications. Of course there was the media frenzy over the embarrassment and the revelation that one of Brazil's trusted governmental servants was "Oddly Suited"!

It had all seemed too easy to Magellan as he recalled the image of the drunken and retching minister, bent over the stern of the boat heaving his guts into the paddlewheels just a foot away from his head. He casually walked down the stairs, looked around and with a simple swipe of his foot, upended his target into the paddlewheels and into the water. How he'd survived the paddlewheels remained a mystery to Magellan? But there it was. The dirty laundry no more until the next time. His mind drifted to the protracted negotiating sessions, with the minister, his outbursts of emotive colloquialisms, his highly insulting and personal attacks upon his countrymen, left no one sorry that he was not a signatory to the negotiations. He would not be missed.

Some months later yet another task at hand. A construction contract by the same entity involved with in Paraguay was in the process of finalization in Montevideo Uruguay, for a sports stadium to be constructed. The key impediment was an influential governmental minister's insistence on certain union subcontractors to be employed. Of course this would drive up the costs of construction and eat into the budgeted profit structure, since the governmental minister in question as well as each of the Union Bosses involved would require significant kickbacks, (Mordida) before they signed off on the project. Of course the quality of the materials dictated as outlined in the contract, would never be adhered to because that was just the way the subcontractors made additional profit at the expense of those who funded the project, in this case the Government of Uruguay.

Once again a single impediment stood in the way of a business deal. An individual so invested in hubris and sheer greed at the expense of others, that reason and tact were never even attempted. As Magellan retrieved the envelope from his private postal box, he took it to his apartment and made himself familiar with the situation and the key individual that had to be rendered useless.

Two weeks later the Deputy Minister of Economics was found dead along with his mistress, in her apartment in one of Montevideo's upscale suburbs. They were discovered in her bed both completely naked, their bloated bodies the result of ten days of decomposition. It was the manner of discovery that disturbed most people when they read about it in the papers. The apparent recipients of a dual suicide, with each of them lying face up and each with their hand on a dagger sunk into the other up to the hilt, neatly in the others heart, as revealed in the blurred out photos of the crime scene. Of course a suicide note was left on the night stand next to the bodies. Graphic analysis soon after revealed the note was written in the mistress's hand. It revealed that "she", the mistress was so distraught and desirous of her paramour's leaving his current wife and family for a life with her. Her recognition that her paramour was not exactly of the same mind, since it would destroy a career of government service, his family unity as well as his place in the community of this very Catholic country made no difference to her. They would spend eternity together, or so she wrote.

The subsequent autopsy revealed some bruises on both bodies, initially viewed as a result of a lovers quarrel given the tone of her final epistle. Yet further examination found significant traces of the same narcotic in both bodies and an in depth inspection of both cadavers found evidence of a minute needle injection point on both bodies between the toes. Easy to normally overlook in most cases. Thus the obvious conclusion of third party involvement, but precisely who, was the question. Quickly a cloud of suspicion fell upon the grieving widow of the former deputy minister, when it was discovered that she visited a lawyer inquiring about the possibilities of divorce. Her marriage in shreds, because of his longstanding history of rampant philandering. Furthering the suspicions of the local authorities was the discovery of several insurance policies on her departed husband in case of his demise that paid handsomely. Their joint signatures on three of the earlier policies, guaranteed her a secure future, it was the policy purchased just eleven months earlier that called her motives into question.

Since the advanced stages of decomposition was so advanced, it was difficult to place a reliable time of death of the two paramours, yet the local officials chose to advance a case against the widow for murder. The case was tried in Montevideo and was overturned by a jury of her peers on the very week the construction of the sports stadium was completed on time and on budget by nonunion labor, utilizing quality materials as per the contact at hand. With nothing else to go by, the authorities had to declare the case finalized yet unresolved.

The very next month, the aging widow was seen performing a rather torrid Tango, with a much younger man at El Miramar, Montevideo's classiest nightspot.

Later in the City of Mendoza, located in one of the far western provinces of Argentina, in the shadows of the Andes Mountains, the relatively young Provincial Governor died suddenly of a heart attack while playing tennis with one of his aides. He'd just recently gotten a clean bill of health from his physician the previous week on his annual physical, the very day after his fiftieth birthday.

He was viewed by his contemporaries as being on the fast track for higher governmental positions. He had no known enemies, which was exceedingly rare for one who'd risen so fast in political circles. His roots were traditionally deep in the provinces, having originated from an old line patrician family that made their fortune in cattle ranching and mining, having settled the region over a hundred and fifty years earlier.

What was never brought to light, outside of a select few in the highest echelons of the federal civilian government, was the pivotal role the Governor played, in the attempted "Coup de Etat", of the current government, by dissonant elements of the Argentine Military eager to return to the draconian ways of previous military governments in order to smash the Unions control of society. The governor had gone to great lengths to insulate himself from the disgruntled military, while secretly offering aid and support far from the action developing in Buenos Aires, in the event things went wrong, which they ultimately did. The known ringleaders, of the "Coup", ten in number, were quietly rounded up in the dark of night, drugged and bound in their night clothes and flown to an airfield in the far southwestern part of the country. There the aircraft refueled and took off without a word spoken to any of those involved. Once the ancient C-47 reached an altitude over one of the many glaciers in that part of the country, the transports side door was opened and one by one their unconscious cargo was flung out the door, at altitude to find a final resting place, somewhere in the deep recesses of the glacier far below.

Time passed without any investigation of any sort, the offending officers simply replaced and the world moved on without revolution. For a few months, having heard nothing the Governor began to rest easy and was feeling more and more secure with each passing day, thinking that his role in the affair remained a secret, eventually dispensing with the services of the onerous body guards that were his constant companion. The fateful day of his tennis engagement at his club, he hardly felt the pinprick of the mini syringe, as he bumped into Magellan as they left the clubs locker room for the tennis court.

Magellan quickly dressed without showering, as he made his way out of the club and into his car. By his reckoning, the slow acting effects of the injection should, should be accelerated somewhat and take its effect within the hour given the strenuous nature of a standard tennis match.

Three hours later, as his plane was about to take off from the Mendoza Aerodrome, the first news of the Governors mysterious collapse was announced by the local media. The chemists in Paris apparently knew what they were doing, for the poison was designed to be slow acting with no known antidote. The best part was that in the event of an autopsy, that was sure to happen, the chemical makeup of the poison was diffused, accelerated by the body's process of decay, caused by the buildup of nitrogen in the cadaver. The fact that the subject was heated from his exertions on the court accelerated the process even more.

Later that evening back in Buenos Aires, Magellan sat alone in the Café Montage, steeped in thought, oblivious to the lilting music and the mélange of Adagio and Tango dancers that swirled about his table. From the moment he arrived, several women of whom he made acquaintance of approached him seeking a dance partner for the evening and perhaps a bit more, but he politely begged off.

"Merde", exclaimed one of the women in a huff. "If you wanted to be alone, you should've gone to the park. Normal people do not come here to be alone, they come to experience life to its fullest and perhaps if lucky, fall in love"! Seeing that he was just not going to respond, she turned her attentions to someone of lesser stature, guiding the fortunate soul to the dance floor. As Magellan's eyes followed them to the dance floor, he saw the woman perform the age old function of a woman scorned, as she glanced at him an overly long time as they commenced to dance, with the unspoken message, 'Eat your heart out'!

As he lit his tenth cigarette of the day, he peered into the half empty glass of Pernod that lay before him, mumbling to himself, "I am an automaton. A mess created by others and I am the cleaner. A mere janitor, soiling myself, so others can remain clean"! Of course, those he liquidated needed to be off the earth and in some other dimension and of course, his services were in demand because of his exactness. He didn't delude himself as to his particular skill level for the hard work had mostly been done before he arrived on scene. all he did was select the manner of their demise, taking advantage of their weakness' which were in abundance. As he looked up from his drink, he wondered whether or not to take advantage of some willing female for the evening. Then he thought better of it, for instead of making him feel better in the aftermath of erotic pleasure in the early hours of the morning, brief thoughts of Joselita and later, loving thoughts of Madeleine fought their way back into his consciousness, preventing sleep and guaranteeing that his paramour for the evening would awaken alone.

He was caught in a spiral of occurrence. For while his work both visible and otherwise was well regarded, by those who mattered, his current enlistment term was coming due within the coming months.

Further complicating things was the knowledge that his benefactor, General St. Nathalie was said to be scheduled for retirement at about the same time. Having a lifetime of service to La Belle France and having married well along the way, his future was assured well into his dotage. With Madeleine's demise, they apparently had no future use for each other.

Magellan's occasional bonus's for work done off the books, sat secure in a safe deposit box, paid always in Swiss Francs, since the Argentine currency was at best iffy, regarding value.

In another Milonga across town sat Carlos Meyers as he was entertaining an influential Air Force Colonel, dressed in civilian clothes, placed high up in the materiel's acquisition ministry as he said, "The French have been very helpful with our problems and we at the Air Ministry wish that relationship to continue"!

As he continued on, "Of course your services in acquisition of certain hard to obtain, products has been invaluable and we wish that continue, with the appropriate remunerative considerations as before"!

While the Colonel droned on, Meyers thought about the annual question, 'What is required to carry out our respective missions that our conventional sources of supply cannot provide? How it to be obtained and how much will it cost'? The Colonel continued on outlining his laundry list of munitions and aircraft parts he needed the plans for so they could readily be made in Argentina. Of course Meyers would have to milk his sources in the French Aircraft and Munitions manufacturer, 'Dassault', for copies of the various plans for specific upgraded aircraft parts and munitions. Of course all this was a result of the Falklands conflict some years back when the Argentine Military government tried to take the Falklands Islands back from Great Britain, claiming it for their own. While this was never reported in the press, the reason for this action was the rumor of secret reports that huge deposits of oil lay under the sea in close proximity of the islands. Britain won the conflict and Argentina lost, causing the United Nations to place an embargo on their economy. The Military Government was quickly overthrown and returned to civilian rule, but by then the damage had already been done internationally.

Yet Meyers had six well placed engineers in key positions throughout the Dassault organization, none of which knew of their counterpart's involvement with Meyers, who made it a point of paying them well and of keeping their involvements highly compartmentalized. Meyers made out well, for he was simply the paymaster and controller.

One went to the market, placed an order, received the goods, then an account in an offshore bank known for privacy grew. Of course, with every order, Meyers provided for himself with a secret carrying charge and everyone made out. Yes, industrial espionage could pay rather well if One knew how to go about it and for the last five years Carlos Meyers did very well operating right under the noses of the French Government. Suddenly the conversation changed course, when the Colonel mentioned, "Apparently one of the translators at the French Embassy has a multiplicity of talents"!

"Really? How so", asked Meyers suddenly alert?

"Carlos my friend, it's been all over the evening news. The Governor in Mendoza a man in the prime of his life, suddenly falls victim to a heart attack not a few days after receives an excellent report from his family physician. How could this be, since he has been reported to have a constitution of one twenty years younger"!

"So what does that have to do with some translator at the French Embassy", asked Meyers?

"Senor, think a moment. The old boy network at play. Diplomats ask another for a favor to eliminate a problem? People interested in maintaining a certain status quo, and what do we have? The reemergence of a mysterious person, 'Le Magiciane', or one who makes problems disappear"!

"So who is this mysterious person", asked Meyers directly?

"Perhaps I've misspoken, or then again perhaps not. Or perhaps I've already told you, either way, I'm certainly glad I was out of the loop when the rumors of a "Coup de Etat" were going around. Suddenly one day, a number of senior military officers, they were gone. Vanished into thin air and not a word of it in the media. Interesting is it not"?

"I don't know Colonel. I only know what is in the papers. But since you brought up the point. Whatever happened to the missing senior military officers"?

"Rumor has it they underwent flying lessons"!

"I take it from your analogy, the fact that they're missing indicates they failed"!

"Rather efficient when one thinks about it. The fiscal savings are quite significant. No show trials to be conducted, like it the old days. No formal executions as enemies of the state. No need for the added expense of incarceration"!

"So again Colonel I ask, what has this to do with anyone in the French Embassy", asked Meyers, gently pressing the issue"?

"Simply a vague rumor, that is making the rounds. Simple cocktail party discussions that go nowhere usually"!

"Interesting point Colonel, but one wonders about such rumors that are circulated. Let us take the case of the flying lessons, rumored to have been encountered by the military officers. Were their fate dictated by such rumors? Or our dearly departed Governor, assuming he was a victim of foul play. Was he also a victim of such rumors"?

"You make an interesting point Carlos" said the Colonel thoughtfully! Then Meyers injected. "As for me, I'll have nothing to do with any 'Coup de Etat'. Far too high risk. Too many things to go wrong. Too many people become involved for all the wrong reasons. Too many loose lips, my friend. If I hear any rumors and in my business as a diplomat I hear a great many things, I remain silent. I tend to my own business"!

As they parted for the evening, Meyers made a mental note that sooner rather than later, the Colonel had to disappear. Magellan was just too valuable to be revealed to the exigencies of politics.

Within the month his people in France would satisfy his requirements and then his business with the Colonel could be concluded permanently.

The following day, Meyers rang up Magellan at the Embassy and suggested he join him for dinner and drinks at his club that very evening.

The private club was strictly for Senior Embassy Officials of the various legations around the world that had diplomatic relations with Argentina. Elegant and replete with overwhelming ambiance, the entire atmosphere was conducive to the quiet discussions that often took place out of the eye of the public. As Magellan was guided to Meyers table, he heard the lilting strains of Vivaldi, playing sotto voce, by a string quartet on the mezzanine level. As he approached Meyer's table, Magellan saw Meyers rise as they shook hands. "So good of you to come. Please be seated. Your drink is on its way"!

True to his word, as Magellan took his seat a waiter brought his drink, while another announced his recommendation of fare for the evening. Both men agreed and the waiter departed, with Magellan asking, "It's been quite a while since we've laid eyes on each other Carlos. What is the occasion for our meeting"? "Several things my friend, several things. Commencing with the satisfaction with everyone on your private work done in our behalf. Your efforts have proved invaluable in removing obstructions", said Meyers as he lifted his glass in a modest toast.

"Everyone needs to be loved, so I thank you in behalf of others for their vote of confidence, yet I suspect another shoe to drop"!

"Direct and to the point as usual. Good. The other evening I had dinner and drinks with an Air Force Colonel that I'm doing some work for. He outlined some requirements, I duly took note, then he made mention of something rather disturbing. The unfortunate demise of the governor in Mendoza the other day. Then something about some senior military officers that had quietly gone missing. I believe he mentioned something about flying lessons. In addition, he mentioned something that had to do with an oblique reference to an apparent member of the Embassy staff working as a translator with shall we say, other talents"!

"It could be something, then again perhaps nothing", said Magellan lighting a cigarette!

"I hope you don't mind if I appear more concerned than you do. But when he further mentioned the fact that a cadre' of senior officers have quietly gone missing, after falling victim to mysterious flying lessons, I trust that you will share my concern"! Both men then leaned back as their dinner arrived and as the waiters left Meyers continued. "Our arrangements are predicated that I am your only contact. Now clearly the loose lips of this Colonel whose function is purely supplies and materiel, tells me that something is amiss and it sends my antennae up in every direction. Clearly this has the prints of someone I value greatly all over it and I have a plan to make things straight. Let us enjoy our meal and afterwards discuss what must happen"!

After dinner, Cuban cigars were offered and both men lit up in silence savoring the aroma, as Meyers continued, "So it's clear some other work was performed by you recently. While I'm not happy about it, I'll not put too fine a point to it except to say, Bravo your work went well, but in the process, your identity may well have been compromised and that fact alone acts as an abrasive, to some important things I've been working on involving you particularly"!

"I'm listening" said Magellan!

"In several months I believe your re-enlistment date comes up in the Legion. You are already a Warrant Officer in rank with zero chance for advancement any time in the future should you re-enlist and live out your twenty years. A lifelong pension and free medical care waits!

"Yet there are other alternatives available to a man of your proven abilities that can reward you financially far beyond anything you've realized and you are looking at the man that can make it all happen"!

"So the questions I have to ask myself are, can I trust you, how much can I realize and can we work well together"?

"My presence here right now, alerting you to what is at hand should answer that. Plus everything that has passed between us in the time we've been working together. Then I should think a look back at our history together should answer the last part of your inquiry, as to how much you could tend to make in future years, I cannot say for there is no pro forma for the ventures I'm putting in place, except to say that your presence and skills are needed and rather than working for me you would be working with me"!

"Let's assume I throw in with you, what do you have in mind", said Magellan! "I've known you for quite a while now Nestor and I've known about you for quite a bit longer, so I know that your word as a Legionnaire is everything. As a man of the world, I'm certain that you can appreciate, that I cannot, no will not, reveal anything of such a sensitive nature, until I receive a binding commitment. Your word as a Legionnaire means your commitment"!

"Sounds very high risk"!

"Very high risk. Also very high yield. You have to ask yourself, are you particular as to what you do and why"? Magellan looked away for several moments, reviewing his history, concluding that he'd done just about everything, risked all for others profit, now it was time he profited as he said, "Not particularly"!

"Then I assume we're together on this"!

"You can do more than assume. You have a commitment"! In the space of the next ten minutes, Meyers outlined three separate avenues of approach that completely fitted in to Magellan's abilities and capacity as he concluded; "Now I trust you can see why I cannot put an exact value on what can be gleaned, for there is no top"!

"I agree completely", said Magellan!

"So several things must fall into place before we begin. First, there is a Colonel and several senior officers in the Argentine military that must vanish from sight forever. This you are to do on your own. Of course you will be provided with their complete dossiers and anything you need as before. This you must do to maintain our joint security. Once that is completed, I will introduce you to a man that will arrive from Houston, Texas. He, as well you, does not make friends or acquaintances readily. The overarching plan is that you should you both be of a mind, you will eventually join him in Texas and become his Segundo. The depth of our relationship will be none of his affair"!

Two weeks later a Senior Adjutant, in the Naval Admiralty disappeared. Several years later what remained of his body would be discovered in the Buenos Aires sewer system and rendered as of an unknown origin, due to decomposition. The following week, a Major in the quartermaster corps would meet his end having mysteriously fallen under the wheels of a garbage truck as it was backing up. Two weeks after that Meyers gave the green light on the Air Force Colonel, with the loose lips and within days, he was gunned down at a service station as he was paying for a tank full of petrol, being right in the middle of an armed robbery that had gone wrong. The perpetrators of the robbery had the misfortune to emerge from the station just as a patrol car was pulling up to the entrance, with the loot in one hand and weapons in the other.

The following week, Magellan was introduced to a man from Texas, named Ortega, the week after that he announced that he was not re-enlisting in the Legion and leaving the Corps Diplomatique. Thirty days after that his plane landed at Houston's Intercontinental Airport as yet another chapter in his life unfolded. In the days and months ahead, memories of Madeleine and what might have been flashed through his mind. A normal life, a family, children, but none of that was to be, for as the Prophet was purported to have said, "Each man's fate is written in the sands at the moment of birth", or words to that effect!

19

Magellan awoke from his slumber with a start, glancing at his watch, through groggy eyes mumbling, "Twelve hours. Merde' I never sleep that long"! He went outside and went to the barn to check on his hostage. The guard was responsible for keeping watch and maintenance was asleep in his chair, his weapon having fallen to the ground, was upended by a furious Magellan, as he grabbed his weapon and clubbed him over the head, yelling, "Why are you asleep", at the cowering young Panamanian?

As he entered the barn he was confronted with a putrid stench resulting from his captive, Scylla, having soiled herself as she lay atop the hay bales in the barns center securely bound. He motioned for the young Panamanian to approach and undo her bindings, then marched her outside, to a water faucet and ordered her to disrobe as the Panamanian turned on the faucet, washing her off with a hose that was hooked up. "Make certain the clothes she wears are equally clean of refuse", he yelled at the Panamanian, as she offered her clothes to her young host to hose off.

As she put her wet clothes back on Magellan placed the outdoor chair in the middle of the barn yard and ordered her to sit, "The sun will dry you off soon enough", he said! As the Panamanian came back from shutting off the hose Magellan said, "I find you asleep anymore when you should be alert and your sleep will be permanent. Now go inside the barn and remove the soiled hay bales take them outside and replace them with fresh ones from the barns interior. Do it now to my satisfaction then come back to me"!

As the Panamanian toiled in the barns interior, Scylla sat still in the chair as ordered, with not a single word passing between her and Magellan as he held the Tec-9 machine pistol on her. When the Panamanian was finished, he approached Magellan, as Magellan asked, "Scylla. How long has it been since you've eaten"? When she failed to respond he then turned to the Panamanian saying, "Tell me that you've fed her since I've been asleep"! Meeting once again with silence, he said, "As I thought. Go inside and make her a few sandwiches, and bring a cold cola from the refrigerator. You can do that can't you"?

"Si Jefe" said the Panamanian as he turned a trotted off into the house. There was no need to tell Scylla not to try and make a break for it, for Magellan had the gun and she saw what he could do with an automatic, at the aborted attack back in Houston, as the muzzle of the weapon never left her presence. She then turned her head in Magellan's direction and spoke, "Kill the beaner, let me go and I'll make it worth the effort"!

Magellan thought for several seconds then he said, "What on earth make you think that I would ever agree to your offer? Here you are in the middle of nowhere, your considerable charms severely diminished, you have no money or weapons and if only half of what I've heard about you and your brother, the Zulu Man is true; neither of your words are worth zero"!

As the sun grew hotter overhead she asked, "Can I stand up, so I can dry out better"?

"As for your ability to stand I suppose so, but will I allow it? No. Remain seated till I tell you otherwise"! At that she stretched her arms, revealing the unadorned outline of her ample breasts pressing the limits of her still wet tank top for Magellan to consider saying, "It's yours for the taking any time you want"!

"True enough I suppose, but where's the wine, the violins? Without the ambiance, it is out of the question"! Just then, the Panamanian emerged from the house carrying a plastic plate in one hand and the drink in the other, placing in on the ground in front of Scylla, who still didn't make a move.

"I'm not going to beg you to eat what's before you nor will I compel you to eat. Whether or not you do, makes little difference. My offer is a standard one. For what you eat is what we consume"! Scylla then picked up the plate and started to reluctantly eat, the necessities of the body outweighing her will. As she chewed through her sandwich she appraised this Magellan character that held her captive, concluding that should their positions be reversed she would rot in hell before she wasted one morsel of food on him. However, given another look, his rugged looking appearance suggested that he was faceable. She'd gotten out of more than one tight spot in the past by merely spreading her legs. Perhaps a more subtle invitation could change a 'No' into a 'Yes', as she finished the last of her two sandwiches, wiped her hands upon her chest and spread her legs wide.

"One wonders why you remind me of Bourbon Street in New Orleans", mused Magellan continuing! "Now you're supposed to say something like, Hey sailor. Kitchee, Kitchee, Ya Ya Mamma. Kitchee, Kitchee, Ya Ya, right c'here, or words to that effect. Apparently that's worked for you before, in the barrios of greater Los Angeles, but not here, not today and not tomorrow"!

"Then that must make you some kinda Queer, or Faggot then", she shot back in anger! Magellan then turned to the young Panamanian saying, "A lesson in life young amigo. One just has to ask, how many others have given in to her charms? How many have lived to tell the tale? I'll wager no one! So stay alert and keep your hands off of her. Give in even once and your never see another sunrise, either from her, or from me! Enough sun for the present. Take her back into the barn and make fast her bindings"!

Once she was secured atop the hay bales in the center of the barn, Magellan inspected the bindings, stepped back and said, "Get a bucket for her to crap and piss in. She is to have two meals a day and two relief sessions a day. We will watch her in shifts and catch our sleep when we can. Stay alert and you can expect a very big payday. Get sloppy and expect death"!

Magellan then turned and walked out of the barn amidst a flurry of obscenities, thinking that she could scream her throat bloody, for they were all miles away from the nearest human being, here in the Southwest Texas wilderness.

For the first time in Scylla's adult life, she began to experience true fear. She was alone. Completely alone, without a single resource her whereabouts unknown and with time running out. Her best weapon had always been her sultry light brown beauty, with men of every race. For all of her young twenty seven years, she'd been successful at the side of her brother Antowan, who'd been known by the moniker, Zulu Man, since their early teens. From her earliest memory each had been highly dependent on each other and completely ruthless in their interaction with others. Starting with the murder of their father and mother, some ten years earlier, the deaths of Mack Daddy and Othella, set them out on a journey of death and destruction.

Mack Daddy earned his daily bread as a somewhat uncommon pimp, running a string of fifty some odd women along Los Angeles Sunset strip. His weekly payoffs to the local Police 'Pussy Posse', insured that only the girls he was ready to cycle out of his little family due to either attitude or normal wear and tear would make an appearance in night court. Any competition usually ended up in a trash dumpster as future food for the seagulls. As the very best of his girls warranted, he'd act as their agent working them through the local titty bars and taking his cut as well as the occasional porn movie.

His common law woman, Othella, a half white woman from the wilds of eastern Tennessee, graduated from common street walker, into his bed as his 'Main Squeeze', eventually becoming a street manager of the girls as their enterprise grew in volume, proving an even stricter enforcer than he was, when it came to keeping the bitches in line. Whenever she discovered that one her bitches held back from her, she proved far more ruthless than Mack Daddy ever was, operating by the 'One strike and you're out rule'. Othella would make certain that after she got done with a woman that no man would ever want her again and the sentence once passed always came without warning. On the other hand, she always had her girls medically inspected monthly and should they encounter any social disease, she saw to it that her girls received treatment until they were medically cleared to work again and become a producer. There was always a doctor that one could go to off the books and after all, money is only but one of many mediums of exchange. Then from time to time a client would become a bit too frisky with one of Mack Daddy's property and usually ended up with a decision. Either pay a significant sum of 'Cold, Hard, Train Ridin' Cash' for their hospitalization and assorted carrying charges, or end up in a land fill, unrecognizable and in pieces as food for the seagulls. Anyway one cut the cards, the customer always paid the freight for their playtime. Should any of his girls prove to be a declining earner, they would be put out to pasture without another thought, drugged to the gills and driven far out to the edges of the Mojave Desert. A shallow grave would be dug then a single bullet would be put in their head and buried, with Mack

Daddy returning at sunrise. Over the span of time, first Antowan, then Scylla, joined the family in quick succession, courtesy of the loins of Othella. Yet even while pregnant Othella never let up her supervision and running of the family enterprise. New talent recruited and turned out, then managed, medicated, bailed out, or released, she always something to do Having a fair amount of time on his hands, now that his 'Squeeze', Othella was now running the family business, Mack Daddy decided to branch out into the drug business, deciding that his network of girls, could "Move the Shit", in addition to their peddling of their "Cooze"! Gradually Mack Daddy and Othella, moved away from their network of sidewalk princess's. although not entirely, constantly upgrading their herd of 'Filly's', concentrating on working out of 'Men's Clubs', all over the Southern California area. Of course in order for their special type of Capitalism to work unhindered, many palms had to be greased, from the club managers to the local police, yet at the end of every month a number of people would exclaim, "Ain't America Great"?

Of course, none of this would be possible without the gradually growing relationship with the Mendaca Clan, the largest of the Tijuana Mexico crime families at that time. Over the span of five years, Mack Daddy's movement of product grew from less than one percent to slightly over a third of their variety of illegal drugs. Over that span of time, other players came and went through the Mendaca family as far as vendors went. Most of which were either killed by others or incarcerated by the authorities. Or killed outright and replaced by local competition. Yet through it all Mack Daddy and Othella seemed to soldier on, the chaos that surrounded them affecting others rather than them.

Eventually some female college students trying to find a way to better afford college tuition, opted to become 'working girls' and in the process of furthering their education, became movie stars of sorts and while they were there, move the product. Thus providing a whole new meaning to "Multiple Streams of Income"! Of course the same strict rules of accounting applied, along with similar Draconian measures for anyone who shorted the family. It usually only took one person inside the local Vice Squad, to work with him to quietly rid him of girls that came up short without having to make that trip way out into the desert.

A single phone call by Othella, was sufficient to guarantee the offender a one way ticket to a prison term out Lompoc way, of course without a warning. The Vice Squad officer would get yet another significant arrest, receiving an envelope at month's end, while Othella would be rid of a problem courtesy of the State.

Late into her eleventh year, Scylla began her trip into womanhood. Even prior to that people would comment all the time on what a looker she was going to be when she grew up. She was well aware of what her parents did to put a roof over her and her brother's heads prior to her, crossing over into woman hood, but never put too fine a point on things as she enjoyed her childhood. Her brother, Antowan, now known as Zulu Boy, a year older than she, dropped out of school, the previous year to join his father in the family business, via an on the job training program of the streets. Quickly he developed a feel for the streets, having earned his bones during his twelfth year of life by killing the very first guy he suspected of shorting him and dumping him into a trash dumpster, without a second thought.

Now, six months into her early menstrual cycle, as she was preparing for bed by taking a shower, Mack Daddy was waiting for her as she drew the shower curtains back.

Over the course of time, Mack Daddy himself has violated the cardinal rule, by a gradual ingestion of the very product he was selling, Cocaine. Of course, in his mind he reasoned that he been feedin' that little Hoe, long enough and it was time, he turned her out. "If'n she be old enough to bleed, she be old enough to earn"! Thus, he picked her up still wet from her shower and broke her in right on the bathroom floor, amidst the helpless flailing and the tears. In the aftermath as he rose up from her and turned around, there was Othella, standing in the doorway having observed the whole event. Seeing the product of her loins sacrificed to her common law husband, for the sake of commerce. Later, Scylla recalled having cried out to her mother, from the bathroom floor, to help her, because the severe pounding by her father hurt so much. But there she stood, leaning on the doorway repeating, "It's alright baby, everthang's gonna be alright"!

No one ever knew what Scylla felt that fateful evening, how she must have felt, or how much she must have cried, but the following day, instead of going to her classroom at her local school, she commenced another form of basic learning. The family business, in all of its many facets.

Every day Scylla went to work with Othella, becoming an advanced featured event in real time as well as film and the new videotaping, appealing initially to advanced pedophiles eager for a virgin to deflower. For such an event, even if it was contrived, pedophiles willingly paid at first triple, later quadruple the going rate. Of course it was all an act, but Scylla didn't have to go far with her motivation, simply relive, repeatedly the events of that first night on the bathroom floor. A Tour de Force performance every time. For the better part of a year this went on and as time went on Othella never ceased to be amazed, by her "baby fuckers". Regardless of how rich, or smart, or famous they were, they always seemed to believe they were scoring the very first squirt of her daughter's life. Hell, a Gypsy couldn't have sold it better, with a number of her regulars coming back for seconds and thirds, even with the full knowledge that she was being retailed on video tape. Dress her differently, put a wig on her, with glasses, "Un Viola". Scylla always sold the goods.

From time to time someone would try and short the Zulu Boy on a transaction and meet with immediate justice, with Mack Daddy's boy returning not only with all of his product, but all of the dealers money to boot placing it before Mack Daddy proudly. Better that than a beating. Of course, before his first year on the streets was up, he was now known as an "Ace", having luckily racked up five kills in broad daylight without a single witness to the event. Armed with only a .25 caliber Beretta automatic and a switchblade, he always did his work up close and personal, without a hint of what was coming. The Beretta armed with bullets that fragmented upon impact could bring a quick end to a much larger man in an enclosed space. Zulu Boys, instant justice, eventually proved to become a bit of a problem to his father, as one afternoon as he was wiping an excess of Coke from his nose, he exploded in rage screaming, "You dumb mutha fucka. Your shoot em up of alla da boys on the street'll get alla da cops all up inn air over a nuther dead nigger, plus the gangs he might be with. Jus who inna hell give ya permission to take someone out? No one. That's who! You ever go and take out somebody wid out my say so, again then you better get your black ass somewhere else, cause yo ass'll be mine. Of course, soon thereafter Zulu Boy was elevated from pure street work to more important things just as several of the gangs were getting wise to the way he worked and just who he might be.

Scylla had become a rapid learner of the oldest profession at the foot of her mother. By the end of her second year at the trade, she was long a seasoned professional, having experienced sexual practices every way possible as well as the hazards of the profession, having contracted and have being cured of Syphilis twice. Soon she became a seasoned practitioner of the art of Fellatio under the guidance of her mother, or as Othella often referred to it as, "The old easy", whereas it got the job done without all of the wear and tear. As Othella was often to say, "Child, you can get most folks off in less than fifteen minutes", she counseled. "Hell, some guys you can get off in under five and if they want you to swallow? No big deal, cause it'll just cost em another fifty or so. Besides a swallow a day'll get you all the protein you'll need for the day. Good as a steak dinner. Now the white guys, especially the Jocks, they'll let go if ya sixty nine em, within ten minutes, every time. Just make sure you're on top. Besides, being less wear and tear, give em a good Hummer, something most wives and girlfriends might not do, will get ya done quicker and guarantee repeat business"!

This came as good news to Scylla, ever since that very first night with Mack Daddy. Straight sex was just something she had to endure and at every opportunity she tried usually successfully to convert the "trick" to oral insertion. As she grew into womanhood, her act as a virgin faded into that of a well-seasoned courtesan as she entered her third year of the profession. Her demand placed a going rate that escalated to the five hundred dollar range, for private sessions and three thousand dollars for each film and video she featured in. Now fully grown and well fed, she filled out into a tallish five feet nine inches in height, with long, shapely legs and packing two solid "C" cups for headlights.

By her fifteenth year, she worked her first convention of Insurance Executives at the Beverly Wiltshire Hotel. At the end of a rather hectic day she placed slightly in excess of ten thousand dollars in the hands of well pleased Othella, not counting the three thousand in tips she'd learned to garner, well salted away for that rainy day, somewhere in the future. Intuitively she decided not to spend a dime of the tips on herself, for if it was ever discovered that she was holding out as she'd seen others do, she had little doubt what would become of her. As it was Othella peeled off a thousand dollars for her walking around money. Of course, Othella, being an old hand at the world's oldest profession knew her daughter as well as others, had that rainy day fund. Hell, she had done it herself. Just so it didn't become obvious to anyone. The moment it did, there always would be hell to pay and she was an excellent paymaster, even with her own flesh.

Eventually she was introduced to the joys of threesomes, by a wealthy bisexual couple at a Malibu beach house. From that afternoon on she herself became a bisexual, with a distinct preference for women. The men she encountered, had to pay through the nose, but it always troubled her to take money from a woman. For a woman she would have given it away, had it not been for the presence of Othella and Mack Daddy, expecting money with their hands always out. Yet unlike many of the other girls in the stable, Scylla was never in want of anything. She still slept at home as well as her brother. Her mother always selected her clothes, paying cash as always and saw that she was always properly coiffed. So she had zero expenses of her own. On her sixteenth birthday Mack Daddy bought her a top of the line Yellow Corvette. Never mind that it was stolen from someone in Milwaukee, but since the provenance was sufficiently secure, she was assured that it was relatively OK to drive, having passed muster by her insurance carrier.

Shortly after her sixteenth birthday, while Mack Daddy and Othella spent the entire weekend in Reno, engaged in gambling sex and drugs, Scylla stole away for a weekend with one of her steady "Johns", shooting two porno videos as well as servicing his needs, garnering five thousand dollars for her efforts for her rainy day fund. The seaside villa where the porno flicks were shot was rented for the weekend and awash with nonstop activity both day and night. The place, although three stories tall, with spacious grounds, heated pool and tennis courts, was crowded with a host of people involved with the production of no less than ten films involving a slew of actors and several selected guests, who bankrolled the project. The drugs flowed freely the entire weekend, with no one the slightest bit squeamish as to what was done. For that weekend, at that particular place there were no taboos. The expensive air conditioning system of the house was unable to remove much of the marijuana smoke that was constantly regenerated throughout the house, by the multiplicity of joints that constantly stayed lit. The following week when they tried to edit the video tape, it was discovered that very little of what was shot was of strict commercial use, given the overall level of intoxication present and the continual interruption by the invited onlookers, who were bankrolling the project.

But the director saw something of great use in the footage shot of Scylla, so he contacted her to invite her back for his next shoot several weeks later. She was so sensational, that she quickly became a regular performer whenever a shoot was scheduled in the area. At the end of each shooting she was handed two thousand dollars in cash for her efforts, a thousand of which she'd turn over to Othella to explain her absence.

The director of her films and videos became so taken with Scylla that he also became one of her regulars. On her periodic visits, after the video shoots were completed, she would linger behind, till everyone had left, always going through the same scenario. They would enter a bath room together and he would slowly undress her. She would then enter the shower stall, lathering up her body slowly revealing every orifice while writhing in ecstasy. The director would then undress and sit on the toilet and masturbate to completion. When he completed, he would always immediately leave her, while she rinsed and dried off, dressing before she joined him as he served her a fine dinner that either he'd personally prepared, of had catered. Sitting against the water crystal was always a sealed envelope, containing ten crisp one hundred dollar bills.

The following week things got out of hand. Othella, now operating a call service, received a request from an old client requesting the services of her daughter. He was an influential City Councilman from Modesto, in Los Angeles on business and was staying overnight. A few phone calls produced Scylla as his companion for the evening. They went out on the town, for dinner, drinks and dancing.

When Scylla awoke the following afternoon, in a cheap hotel just south of San Diego, after having been drugged, and beaten with just a faint recollection of the following evening, it took her several hours to clear her head sufficiently before she could place a call to Othella to come to her rescue. Three hours later, Othella arrived with Mack Daddy just minutes behind and were horrified at what they saw. Their very own daughter, their best earner, had been seriously beaten by her previous nights "John", to such a degree, that she was semi ambulatory. Of course, Scylla hadn't been paid for her evenings efforts and normally that would've infuriated her parents, but seeing her condition, they relented and not wanting this to become a police situation, placed a call to Mack Daddy's partner in TJ, Senor Mendaca.

Mack Daddy loaded his daughter in his car and drove across the border to Mendaca's personal physician for care and hospitalization. After she was examined, she was checked into one of the local hospitals under a pseudonym as the doctor explained that she would have to undergo extensive reconstructive surgery, to restore her to her previous form. "How much it gonna cost", growled Mack Daddy. Looking on Senor Mendaca drew Mack Daddy aside saying, "Your lovely daughter has been brutalized Senor and since we have done extensive business together for quite some time, allow me to bear the burden and expense for her care and restoration"!

"You tellen me your gonna pay for all this"?

"My gift to further show my gratitude to you over the years"! "Damn senor. Well OK then"!

Mendaca had seen the video byproduct of Scylla's pornographic efforts, wondering how such a lovely young woman could become a byproduct of such lowly creatures. Yet it wasn't entirely an altruistic motive lurking in the back of his mind when he committed to Scylla's care. Once her condition had stabilized, upon the recommendation of his personal physician, he had Scylla flown to a special clinic in Costa Rice that specialized in reconstructive surgery, with cost being of no object.

Thirty days later, the Modesto council member, who was known to spend an occasional afternoon at a certain seedy looking "Titty" bar in Modesto was about to summon one of the dancers to service him in his secluded booth, when a rather large Negro slid in next to him.

Normally management of these kinds of establishments are protective of the privacy of their regulars, especially when they are influential City Councilmen. But when Mack Daddy slid the envelope into the hands of the manager containing twenty crisp hundred dollar bills saying, "I need to spend some time this afternoon with one of your regulars. I know he's a spender, so accept this envelope as interruption pay"! The manager took one look at Mack Daddy, then peeked into the envelope, seeing the cash and said, "Go ahead on pal"!

"Do I know you", asked the councilman?

"Yeah", said a smiling Mack Daddy, flashing one of his gold teeth. "We used to go to different schools together, back in the day. Now lissen up and I'm going to tell yam how you can stay alive and go home to your family tonight and why. A while back you took a trip to LA and took to dinner one of my ladies. She woke up the next day all fucked up thanks to you and yam even ran out without paying' the freight. Now it's going to cost a lot to make her better so she can become an earner again. Now normally I'd be pissed and break you up or even kill yam after, but I hear you got a safety deposit box in town. Now don't tell me yam don't when I know yam do", said Mack Daddy when the Councilman started to object. "So I'm going to give yam a choice. Now if you're gonna look for the manager to help ya. Don't. He's been bought off and from what I hear the local fuzz, ain't too happy wid ya any old way, since you voted to cut their budget. So here's your choice. Either us walk out of here smiling' and we make a beeline to your bank before it closes and empty out your safety deposit box into my briefcase, or I shoot you right now with this little gun in your ribs with a silencer. It makes a little noise like a rat sneezin'. Say no and no one will approach your booth for a couple of hours and by that time, I can also run by your home and do the same to your wife and kids and be out of town headin' for parts unknown, so make your choice and do it now"!

The councilman glanced at the small automatic that was stuck into his ribs and asked, "How do I know you'll keep your word and not kill me anyway"!

"You don't. Now what's it gonna be"? The councilman nodded his head and they both rose up in silence and walked out of the bar smiling. The take down at the bank went smoothly with the councilman arriving with the conservatively dressed Mack Daddy as the both spent no more than five minutes in the booth emptying out the safe deposit box of all the money it contained, then walked out smiling together into the councilman's car and drove back to the club and around to the parking lot across the street. When the councilman turned off the ignition he said, "What happens next"?

"Time to pay the band", said Mack Daddy as he drove his fist repeatedly into the head of the councilman. Then suddenly he stopped saying to himself, "An eighty percenter is what he gets"! Then he reached into his briefcase and removed a syringe and injected his mark with a mild barbiturate, that should keep him under well after sunset. He then took the councilman's handkerchief out from his breast pocket and wiped the inside of the car clean of any prints. He wasn't worried about the security cameras at either the club or the bank if it came to that because of his snap brimmed hat and sunglasses, besides the light level and an envelope full of cash went a long way to dim a memory.

With any luck the councilman wouldn't wake up until he crossed the Nevada state line on his way toward Reno, with his recent haul. By his brief reckoning he was over fifty thousand or so dollars to the good. He should be pulling into Reno around ten in the evening, spend the night then head down to Vegas, spend the night and then back to La La land. With Mendaca picking up the freight for making Scylla an earner once again, he could pocket the councilman's money and have a real good time. Thanks to his stop over's in Reno and Vegas he was only Thirty Thousand dollars ahead of the game, but still a profitable venture.

True to his word, Mendaca and his physician kept Scylla in the local hospital till her immediate physical problems stabilized then they boarded Mendaca's private Lear Jet and flew down to Costa Rica, and checked her into the Private Clinic, in which they were partners. The clinics sole function was to provide Cosmetic Reconstruction Surgery, on a par with the finest clinics of its kind in the world at far less than half the price of their Brazilian or European counterparts. There Scylla was treated like a queen. Their standard top drawer medical practice was accentuated, by the appearance of the two owners of the clinic. Ninety days later when the final series of surgery's was completed and her bandages were removed, Mendaca and his partner made it a point to be there for the final unveiling, as the local doctor in charge as well as her two assistants gently removed the bandages. Everyone's eyes grew wide in wonderment, amazed by the transformation of Scylla, from the broken mass that arrived, to the world class beauty that confronted them.

Standing there in her green hospital gown, Scylla looked into the mirror at her image and slowly her face grew into a beaming smile, as her doctor asked, "Senorita, do you approve"?

She simply glanced at him and said, "I like", as she turned around to look at Mendaca and said, "Well"? Standing there in front of her, he looked at her and said, with a wistful grin, "Make me wish I were twenty years younger"!

Then his physician said, "We will need her to remain with us just a few more weeks, just to insure that all of the healing is going to plan, as well as her regimen of physical therapy before we release her to the world"!

Mendada nodded in agreement as he said, "Then we will return in two weeks"! Then turning to Scylla said, "You are to be my guest at our beach house, for a time to continue your convalescence. There we shall discuss your future"! The departure of Mendaca left the mountainside clinic in a state of relief. For the surgery far exceeded everyone's expectations, turning an attractive young woman, prior to her unfortunate incident into someone that brought out the finest attributes of her mixed blood ancestry.

For the next six months, Scylla was the guest of Mendaca at his high walled seaside villa just south of Ensenada in Baja California. During that period Mack Daddy and Othella drove down several times to conduct business and while they were there marveled at how well their daughter looked. Then Mack Daddy upon the occasion of his second visit commented on when Scylla would be ready to join them back in Los Angeles, claiming a back log in requests for her services.

Mendaca, seeing the look in his eyes, not as a loving father, but as a selfish pimp bent on the further exploitation of his own flesh and blood said calmly, "We are all making a great deal of money Senor at the present time and may I remind you that your daughter has been through a great deal. She will return to you when her convalescence is complete and when she is ready and not one second sooner. Now seeing as our business is concluded, I have another meeting to attend", as he rose up to shake hands.

Upon Mack Daddy's departure back to LA, Mendaca went out to the beach to join Scylla, as his body guards stood by at a discrete distance. Of course they didn't mind standing in the sun each day as she went into the surf for her daily swim and sun, for the mere sight of such a spectacular looking woman emerging from the surf, attired in the briefest of bikini's kept their loins at immediate attention. When there shift was over they would find relief with a lesser woman in Ensenada. There we're always an abundance of that sort eager for attention.

Helping her towel off as she emerged from the surf, she donned a shirt as they took their daily walk together up the beach. During her time with the Mendaca family she'd grown very close to the old man, with their long walks on the beach, discussing everything she could think of,

Mendaca took the measure of this young woman. As her knowledge of colloquial Spanish grew as well as her knowledge of her father's dealings with the Mendaca family, he gradually included her into his family dealings, being impressed with her quick grasp of his family's business. There came a time when she became to view him as the father figure she'd never known. As a result of their walks on the beach, he eventually discovered the depth of her father and mothers infamy as she calmly related how she came into her family's business.

Then came the point where Mendaca asked, "Do you wish to return to that life my dear"?

Scylla thought a second as they walked saying, "There's just gotta be something better out there for me"?

"Then I ask the question once again. Do you wish to return to that life"?

The both stopped walking as she turned to him and said, "No"! "Bueno my dear. Then return you shall not. You have become a member of our family since your arrival and I've been impressed at your rapid grasp of things, quite apart from your beauty. Should you wish I can find a significant place for you"!

"What about my brother", asked Scylla?

"Let us say that he remains a question mark for the present. He shows promise, not to your degree but potential none the less"!

"What about Mack Daddy and Othella"?

"They would have to be permanently dealt with"!

"Killed, uh, Asesino"? Mendaca nodded his head saying "Muerte"! "Good uh, Bueno Senor. But just as long as I get to do it"!

"Perhaps that can be arranged", said Mendaca casually as they walked.

Over the course of time she spent with Mendaca in Ensinada, she learned that Mack Daddy had grown sloppy and erratic in all of his business dealings, usually attributable to this instability, was the chronic sampling of his main product Cocaine. Little by little his girls were leaving him thus his ability to move product was eroded by the street gangs in greater Los Angeles and what was formerly an in excess of a third of Mendaca's business through Mack Daddy eroded to far less than ten percent of his monthly volume.

Several days later as they again strolled up the beach for their late afternoon walks, Scylla asked, "Before anything else happens, there is a little bit of unfinished business I have to handle on my own"!

"And what would that be my dear", asked Mendaca?

"That guy from Modesto, that drove me to you. He just gotta go. Zulu Man, my brother, overheard my Daddy braggin, about how he tracked him down, to his favorite titty bar in Modesto and stuck a gun in him and made him clean out his safety deposit box of over fifty thousand in cash. He says, the councilman just got elected to the California State Assembly in Sacramento and is livin large. Never killed anyone before, so if I'm gonna be with you, seems I gotta make my bones"!

"Or so it would seem my dear, but how do you intend to go about it", asked Mendaca?

"Zulu Man has found out where he hangs out in Sacramento to get his rocks off. Since I don't look exactly like I used to, I'm gonna get a job at the titty bar he hangs at. From there it'll be simple. We'll go to a hotel room and when I get done with him it'll be on the front pages of every paper in the state"?

"But what happens if he gets the better of you? Remember he drugged you before"!

"Simple. We'll be in adjoining rooms, with Zulu Man in the next room. Videotaped and recorded. He's gonna be the one what gets drugged and done in. Don't worry my brother's got my back. If ya want, I'll bring a copy of the video back to you as proof of what I can do, all by myself with a bit of help"!

A week later, Scylla and her brother drove up to Sacramento and took out two adjoining rooms in one of the local hotels. The following day he drove her to the Club where the State Assembly man frequented several times a week. By now he'd long since recovered from the beating administered by Mack Daddy the previous year and since his elevation to State elected office, his old habits resumed.

One look at Scylla, as she disrobed in his office, was all that the Club manager needed to hire her immediately. She was put out on the floor that evening. Of course, horned rimmed glasses and a blonde wig, went far to further alter her appearance. For three days she toiled at the club, dancing on the stage, couch dances at twenty bucks a pop and the occasional trip to the VIP rooms, always emerging many hundreds of dollars to the good, of course kicking back a few to the Club Manager.

On the fourth day she spotted her mark. Late in the afternoon, shortly after she arrived for her evening shift. In he drifted taking a seat in a booth by himself in the middle of the club in full view of the stage. She was the third girl to dance and as she started her routine, her brother sitting on the other side of the stage was alerted as she concentrated her efforts in the direction of her mark. Of course she caught his immediate attention as well as everyone else's, as she spread her ample limbs out for all to see what joys held forth deep within her inner sanctum. Just before she concluded, he caught her eye and motioned for her to join him after she was finished.

As she slid into his booth she heard him say, "Never seen you here before. You new in town"? As she acknowledged that she was, she made with all of the standard ploys a woman of her profession engages with, appealing eye contact, occasional licking of her lips and that killer move, her hand placed gently on his lap as their drinks arrived. Never making the same mistake twice, she pretended to sip her drink, spilling a bit on the floor every time his attention was diverted. After the second round of drinks and her second couch dance, comprised of her rubbing herself all over his midsection and licking his ear. He suggested they go someplace where he could make things well worth her time.

"I'll save you some money sport cause I got a room here in town we can go to. Pay your bill and I'll slip out the back door and meet you on the street"!

"But what will your shift manager say"?

"Him? I own him in a very special way that you'll soon discover. Never you mind about him"!

As Scylla disappeared into the back, her mark quickly settled his bill and in his rush to get outside, hardly felt the needle as he brushed past Scylla's brother. It would take about three quarters of an hour for the slow acting injection to settle him down, before her work could begin. Driven by his own lusts, the assemblyman followed Scylla's elevator up to the fifth floor, followed in turn by her brother, in the next elevator. As the elevator door opened, Zulu Man looked out the elevator in the direction of her room, just in time to see them both enter the room. He quickly went down the hall and entered the adjoining room and turned on the three, well placed mini video cams previously installed.

He was just in time for the big show, as he whispered into the microphone inserted into his neck tie saying, "Nod your head baby if everything's five by five"! As Scylla nodded her head, she spoke to her mark saying, "Now you just sit there in your chair baby cakes, while I give you the ride of your life", moving to the wall mounted radio unit and dialing up one of the local jazz stations, playing the muted strains of Miles Davis on the continuum. As he started to reach for her, Scylla deftly moved out of range saying, "Now you just calm down and let me tend to you proper", as she slowly removed the few articles of clothing she wore, ending up in just a garter belt tugging at her nylons and her stiletto heeled shoes.

"Ya evah been undressed by a woman before, slowly and with controlled anticipation?

Of course ya haven't. Now You just place yourself in my hands and you'll soon be in heaven"!

It took her ten minutes to get his clothes off as he sat there, compliantly on the hotel chair and another five minutes passed as she slithered all around him before she finally settled down, spreading his now limp legs on either side of the chair and slowly placed her lips upon his engorged member, in that well-worn ancient manner of the oldest profession guaranteed to summon an eruption. Her bother sat in wonder, in the adjoining room marveling at his sisters expertise thinking, 'My daddy sure musta taught her well', as he looked into the small five inch monitor.

No sooner the thought came into his mind, he saw the mark in the next room stiffen and his member erupt in completion, as Scylla deftly reach over and grabbed a hand towel placed nearby and slowly wipe up the remainder. As she looked up at her mark, she could see the injection had done its work as her mark lay in the chair completely inert. She quickly reached up and pinched his ear and got no response, turning to the nearest camera and making the slashing movement to stop taping and for her brother to come on in.

As he entered the room her quipped, "Ya get any on ya sis"!

"Not enough to matter Nigger. Now shut up and help me get this sucker on the bed. That was round one and we got nine or more to go"! Within the span of fifteen minutes, they completed their work securing the assemblyman, face up, on the bed, the bed covers on the floor. Each arm and leg was secured to a bedpost and a double wrap of nylon rope was placed around his ample waist.

"Did ya bring the medicine bag", asked Scylla? "It's in the next room. I'll get it"! When her brother returned he handed the bag to Scylla who placed the contents neatly arrayed on the adjoining lamp table. Then she whirled around smiling and said, "He's gonna be out for a spell, so I think I'll go take a shower"!

"How's about I join ya, so I can make sure you back is clean"!

"Do what ya want bro, but it ain't my back you're wantin' to clean", as she disappeared into the bathroom.

A half hour later as they were toweling off, both very clean and cleansed of a significant amount of their bodily fluids, Zulu Man looked at his sister and marveled, "Damn girl, you about the best trim a man could ever have", as he started to get hard once again.

"We got plenty of time for all that later. Now we gotta get to work. Our boy on the bed is sure to wake up soon and I gotta prepare. Just make sure the video is working' properly"!

All through the evening and far into the night, Scylla's ministrations assured repeated performance from her mark. His mouth properly gagged, the sounds he tried to muster were well muted, as pleasure evolved into a brutal ordeal. His well-worn male member being savaged by Scylla's mouth to the point that blood started to seep out of various parts of his flaccid member. This prompted her to inject his member with Novocain, to dull the pain, prior to the next session that arrived every hour on the hour.

After round ten just after midnight, his muffled screams fell mute as he screamed himself hoarse, yet still the gag in his mouth remained. Later she would tell her brother about the special medication Senor Mendaca had turned her on to that assured repeated erections, far past the point when the gas tank showed empty. After the tenth round Scylla found it necessary to take a shower after each session for the blood was now starting to seep out of his member with increasing regularity. After the fifteenth session, they checked his vital signs and discovered that he was non responsive. No pulse meant that their work for the evening was done. Within the hour they left the hotel separately, having cleaned up both rooms of any signs of their presence, leaving the "Do not disturb" sign hanging on the door, with only the assemblyman's prints on it. In the coming days ahead, his dead body would eventually be discovered by the hotels staff on the heels of several video tapes, delivered to the local media, of his initial session of oral bliss administered by a nearly naked blond woman wearing a floppy hat, sunglasses, garter belt, nylons and spiked heel shoes. The media just loves a juicy scandal especially when it involves a California politician.

Since the name of the registrant was false and both hotel rooms was paid for in cash for two weeks in advance, and no prints or evidence was left, the investigation went nowhere, for there was nowhere to go. However there were some blonde hairs left in the bathroom sink. Perhaps someday they could be evidence? Then again, perhaps not.

On the long drive back to southern California and points south, Zulu Man glanced at Scylla sound asleep in spite of the booming rhythms of the Gangsta Rap music that her brother played on the cars audio system. The sun was coming up in the east as he pushed the button and rolled down the driver and passenger windows airing out the tricked out Lincoln sedan. The first thing he would do after dropping off Scylla at Senor Mendaca's place would have his ride detailed to a tee. A car like this deserved to shine at all times. Then his thoughts turned to his sister and he marveled at what she'd just done. Sure it all was her idea, her plan and she pulled it off, with his help of course. The video recording equipment was neatly stored in the car's trunk, furnished by one of Mendaca's sons and they supplied them with the pharmaceuticals courtesy of Mendaca's personal doctor, but Scylla, she was the star of the show, methodically working the mark until he was no more.

As he drove on, the images of her last session with the mark stayed in his mind, for he never imagined that a man could be killed by a series of simple blow jobs. Too bad there was only the grainy image on the five inch screen of her naked body taking up her position at the foot of the bed. His eyes glancing back and forth between Scylla and the assemblyman laying all splayed out, on the bed. Would she be able to bring him out for the fifteenth round, even though his entire midsection was bathed in his own blood? He was betting with himself that she couldn't pull it off, as her head descended over his now limp and bloody hooter. The damn floppy hat she wore covered all of the action, but from time to time she would rise from her exertions, revealing the bloody flaccid penis, like a spent fighter, struggling to rise for one last time, as she then resumed her work, it finally rose to the occasion, thanks to her extended rhythmic manipulations, the blood seeping through the multitude of cracks formed previously in what was left of his skin. For a fat old white guy, he sure was a honker, his full extension covering the span of a hand. The terror in his eyes ran counterpoint to the fact that by all that was known, the man's dick should've been long retired, but here it was rising for one last time. Maybe it was true what women said about men, that our schlongs had a mind of its own. There it was, that bloody obelisk, now fully erect, leaking its precious blood with every heartbeat, a tribute to man's deeply ingrained desires overcoming common sense and perhaps even the laws of what was humanly possible.

As they cleaned up in preparation to leave, he just couldn't get out of his head her mark lying dead in the bed, his restraints long since removed, his hands placed by his side and his schlong still fully erect. Before they left the room, she picked up the single bed sheet and covered his body to his chest saying, "With all the blood he lost its gotta go down eventually"! But when the body was discovered, several days later, it didn't. Leaving the local authorities with even another conundrum. Of course scant mention of this ever reached the ears of the public at large, just to pass away as possibly another urban myth.

Then he recalled their trip up to Sacramento, her verbal feeling him out on whether or not he was happy with his lot in life under Daddy. As he gradually revealed the fact that business was suffering the encroachment of the other street gangs and that more and more coke was going up Daddy's nose rather than out on the street she said, "Good brother. We pull this off, and then we show Mendaca what we can do. He wants me to come work for him and I been telling him that I want to bring you in. The video, once we show him will be proof that we belong, cause he ain't exactly happy with the Mack Daddy either"!

Well, they pulled it off and now we would see what the future brings.

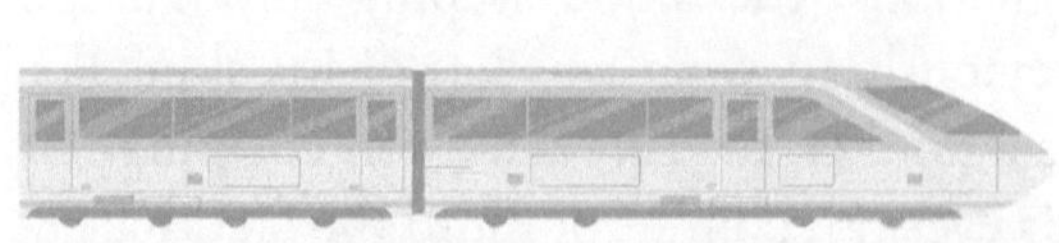

20

They were welcomed by the Mendaca family with open arms when they returned and a modest feast was prepared to celebrate what they'd accomplished in Sacramento. After their meal Scylla introduced the series of video tapes to be played during their after dinner drinks, as both entertainment and proof positive of what she could accomplish. Their hosts, being men of the world, were at odds and ends as they viewed Scylla's extended performance, never having been in the actual presence before, of a woman so completely devoid of modesty, as proof positive was before them of yet another way to take a life.

"Bravo my dear", said the elder Mendaca. "It appears that you and your brother have executed the plan correctly and in the coming weeks and months we should make a way to have you join our family as we've previously discussed. But before that happens the ground must be prepared. The fields will not produce a bountiful harvest until all of the rocks are removed. Accomplish this one last task and your membership into our family is assured"!

Scylla and her brother quickly exchanged glances and knew at once what the old man referred to, as Scylla said, "Senor, the next time you see us, the field will be ready for planting"!

Two days later, in the early hours of the morning, Zulu Man parked and locked his Lincoln two blocks away from the house as he and Scylla walked home as if they had not a care in the world.

It had been a long time since Scylla had been in this house and just less than three weeks since her brother had been at what was loosely called home. The rancid and musty smell they'd long ago became accustomed to was an unpleasant contrast compared to what they'd recently come from. As they both moved through the darkened house, in what used to be called a middle class community, long since over run by a mélange' of minorities, they came across a sleeping Othella. In a soiled nightgown, lying in a well- worn easy chair, her burnt out cigarette, just scant millimeters away from awakening her, in one hand and a warm can of Lucky Lager perched on the soiled cloth chair arm in the other. Across what passed for a living room sat Mack Daddy, in another cloth clad easy chair, simply in his boxer shorts and a tank top, the penile opening of his shorts bunched up to reveal the darkness that lay within. From the looks of the stains on his shorts, the presence of a syringe on the night table nearby and the apparent condition of Othella, it was clear they both had a party together. For a brief moment, it brought back horrible memories of her endless sessions with her father, as the fetid smell of whisky, drugs and bodily fluids hung in the air.

They'd both previously agreed, there would be no speeches, no final goodbyes, just the act itself as they glanced at each other, nodded and her brother reached into his pocket pulling out his .25 Caliber Beretta, checked the chamber and reached for one of the couch pillows and placed it by Mack Daddy's temple and squeezed the trigger. The muffled muzzle report replaced by a brief fire from gun barrel as the pillow was quickly turned as he fired a second round into Mack Daddy's head. The Glaser safety slugs he'd purchased had done their job penetrating the skull then rattling around in the brain staying well in the brain cavity, while not exiting the other side.

Scylla, grabbed another couch pillow as her brother turned and motioned towards the still sleeping Othella, as Zulu Man took several strides towards her, the pillow and the Biretta met at the very same time as he fired twice again in well muffled succession, quickly putting out the flames as they both stood back as if admiring their handiwork.

They both looked at each other and started to laugh. Both wondering why they hadn't done this earlier, for it had been almost too easy. For some inexplicable reason, Mack Daddy had been a lover of Country Western music and the radio was playing at a low level as Antowan, turned up the volume a bit in time to hear the beginning strains of his father's favorite song by Jerry Jeff Walker, "Up against the wall Red Necked Mother", "Sure does like his Falstaff beer and he chases it down with that Wild Turkey liquor. He drives a fifty seven GMC pickup truck, has a gun rack, goat ropen' is where it's at", as they both started to chuckle during the refrain, Antowan put his finger to his lips, as the song continued, "M is fer the mud flaps she gimme fer my pick-up truck, O is fer the oil I put in my hair, T is fer T-Bird, H is fer Haggard, E is fer aigs and R is fer

Redneck. Both Scylla and her brother let the song play out before she turned off the radio with both of them collapsing in each other's arms laughing with relief.

They both then got up and checked them both to see if they were still alive and nodded to each other when neither one felt a pulse. Scylla's brother said, "What do you say we celebrate sister"?

She said not a word as she went to the garage, seeing that her mother's car was in the garage and her fathers was in the driveway she said, "Go get your car and get it off the streets and into the garage. Afterwards we'll have the rest of this morning and all day tomorrow to do what we have to do and maybe what we want to do"!

Ten minutes later as Antowan pulled in his Lincoln into the garage for the night, they decided to start out by doing what they wanted to do, before concentrating on what they had to do.

Much later afterwards they lay together both in a state of exultation, or rather relief. They'd finally done it at long last. No more beatings, no more ropes, no more humiliations and all the crap that came from being the offspring of Mack Daddy and Othella. No longer would Antowan have to be bag man for the vice squad, at least for the time being. Both doubted the cops would mount any extended investigation of their deaths, if they worked it right, just two more problems off the streets, case closed. Of course things had to appear accidental. But all in all a huge weight was lifted from their young shoulders. The neighborhood was asleep and no one was aware of their return. As the early morning sunlight crept into the windows, they both set to work turning the entire house they'd lived in for years inside out, discovering an array of well crafted 'Hidey Holes', where everything from excess gold and silver jewelry and precious stones, money, drugs, guns and ammunition was secreted away between the walls. As noon approached, they went up into the attic and scoured it all finding still more valuables and money in twelve metal boxes, stashed at random under the insulation.

By mid-afternoon after assembling all of the discoveries on the kitchen table and in various piles on the floor, everything sorted out, Scylla's brother asked, "What's the final score babe"?

"Scylla, let out a long slow whistle saying, "Well de well. We have One hundred eighty nine thousand, six hundred dollars in cold hard cash, for starters, keys to three different safety deposit boxes, in Othella's name and all of their personal papers, we can visit them tomorrow. Then there's all of the jewelry and watches. God only knows what they'll bring"? We got enough guns and ammo to start a small war"!

"Sounds good to me", said her brother continuing. 'You get to pickin' all the stones out from the jewelry and I'll melt all of the gold and silver down into little bars in the garage. Daddy showed me how to do it a few years back"!

"What if there's something I want out of the stash", asked Scylla? "Everything gets melted down and turned into cash. That way there's no come backs to us. I know of a jeweler that we can fence the gold and silver to along with the stones with no questions asked. You want some jewelry later on, fine with me. We'll have the money to get it new if we want. Nothing, not one damn thing that reminds me of the past remains. We owe em nothing, no memories, everything starts new like Adam and Eve, unnerstand"?

Scylla nodded her head in agreement and set to separating the various stones from their settings and taking the gold and silver out to the garage, where her brother was hard at work meting them down into small gold and silver ingots, just as Mack Daddy had taught him awhile back.

As they walked back into the living room allowing the melted precious metals to cool down into their small ingots, Scylla went into one of the bathrooms and got a pair of beach towels to place over the corpses of the dearly departed. They were ugly even during the best of times, and in the rictus of death even more so grotesque. They took their time packing the bare essentials of what was needed, leaving much behind for the authorities to pick through if they wanted. As for the condition the house was in after they departed, it wouldn't matter, for the house was to explode in the early hours of the morning. It was simple really, the natural gas fire place, the gas fed water heater as well as the kitchen stove, all opened during the early morning hours. A mechanical timer set to go off one half hour after their departure that would produce a spark then a flame in a sealed home full of natural gas then "Boom". With any luck the timer set inside the oven would be blown apart as well as the rest of the house.

Scylla was the first to depart in Zulu Man's Lincoln and drove to the all night diner near the intersection of the 105 and the 710 Freeways in Southgate. Five minutes later Zulu Man backed up Mack Daddy's car and pushed the garage door button closing the garage door. When he arrived at the diner, his coffee was waiting for him as he slid into the booth and winked at his sister in silence. They didn't even hear the explosion of their former home some fifteen minutes later as their breakfast arrived, but as they were finishing up they saw the wall mounted television on one of the local all news channels come alive with a news bulletin of a residential explosion in Compton, just as they saw the glimmer of several fire trucks racing down the freeway.

"Damn shame the way some people live", said Zulu Man as he lit his usual after meal cigarette. The explosion wiped out any and every trace of their former lives and that of Othella and Mack Daddy. The collateral damage took out the home on either side of the house as well as the sleeping inhabitants as well as damaging two homes across the street and the house behind them in their closely packed neighborhood. By shortly before noon they both visited and cleaned out the safety deposit boxes at both banks. After lunch they paid a visit to Murray Guttman, their father's favorite jeweler, in Culver City.

Peering over his shoulder as he sorted through the stones, peering ever so carefully at each one through his jeweler's loupe he jotted down amounts on his pad as he went finally adding up the figures on his calculator saying, "Ok, this is what I can give ya. Four thousand for the mini gold ingots, a thousand for the silver, nine thousand for the stones and nine hundred for the Rolex watches"!

"You can keep the Rolex watches in exchange for this here single black pearl necklace", said Scylla who spotted the bauble on the ready table for display the following day. As Murray waddled over to where she was looking he said, "My dear, this is to retail for three thousand dollars tomorrow"!

"How do we know you gave us a fair price on all this stuff", asked Zulu Man? I come in with my Daddy a few times, which is why I'm here now and I know my Daddy give you a lotta business over the years", he said with an edge to his voice.

"How's about I throw in a world class hummer to round out the deal", offered Scylla?

"If I thought for a moment that anyone could raise the dead for this old man I'd agree with ya, but since I been the family jeweler of sorts over the years, let's say I agree to your deal. The Rolex's for the pearl straight up as well as the amount I previous quoted"!

Zulu Man glanced at Scylla and said, "Give the lady her necklace. We gotta deal"! Later on in the afternoon, they drove down to Ocean Side on their way to Tijuana and checked into a motel. As they further examined the haul from the safety deposit boxes, they counted an additional One hundred seventy five thousand dollars in cash, along with three small bags of uncut diamonds and assorted other precious gem stones, but the most important yield was the three different small note books chronicling Mack Daddy and Othella's activities over the years with the local Los Angeles authorities. A running chronicle of payments to whom and for what amount. Then in another note pad was a running tally of his dealings with the Mendaca family over the years, revealing names, dates, addresses and phone numbers. Then there were the micro cassette recording probably of transactions between Mack Daddy and God knows who"! A third note book revealed a complete list of all the key street pushers, that Mack Daddy had wholesaled his "Jejo" to, many of which Zulu Man already knew, chronicled with their approximate territories, their known and unknown alias's, and address's and contact numbers.

They spent the rest of the evening planning their next move. Tomorrow they would drive back to LA and scout out two different places to live in close proximity to each other, then find a bank and open a small account to start with then of course a safety deposit box of their own. Then Zulu Man would visit the various dealers his father had and reestablish relations and collect any overdue accounts. In a few days they would be ready to visit Senor Mendaca in Tijuana and offer him a deal they were certain he'd like. While Zulu Man revisited his street connections, offering them better terms than Mack Daddy did, Scylla made the rounds of Othella's former girls, having a fair idea as to whom she wanted to front for her. Since Othella always complained about one girl in particular who always seemed to be on the bubble, Scylla visited her first, telling her of Othella's passing and offering her Othella's place a far better terms, then said "We gonna be straight with each other, right"? Upon agreement they made the rounds of all their street hustlers, to let them know that "Mayflower was now in charge and that Othella was gone to that long, cold sleep"!

The following day they surfaced at Mendaca's place by the sea, after having consolidating their position and spent the entire morning with him, as they followed the happenings at Compton and the subsequent investigation in the aftermath.

"You did a good job as far as it went, but I forgive you, given your youth and lack of experience for completing your task", said the elder Mendaca!

"How you mean", asked Zulu Man?

"The both of you. Still alive. You have to die"! Scylla and her brother flashed a quick glance at each other, that didn't escape the attention of Mendaca, who quickly said, "Perhaps I should make myself better understood. You gotta think like the Policia, when doing such a thing. They gonna talk to the neighbors. They gonna know that the both of you still live with Mack Daddy and Othella. They gonna wonder what happened to you. They gonna wonder if the both of you had anything to do with this? Que sabe"?

"Now if two Negritos were found way out inna desert, similar to the both of you with your identification, in your brothers Lincoln burnt to a crisp. Inna few days the Policia find em, then they think that everybody get all tied up inna turf battle between gangs, and they close things up. They got plenty of other things on their mind.

"Loose ends, they get you every time. Now I get you with my oldest son Oscar, he knows of two people who owe us money they can't repay. They will become the both of you and end up in the desert. Oscar will work with the both of you on this. Then you both make the rounds of your pushers you recently visited with Oscar so they can disappear. All of em. When that's done, Oscar will the take you both into Tijuana and get you both completely new bona fide US identities, from 329 the birth certificates on up. Scylla and Antowan will be no more, to anyone else but us"!

By the end of the second day, Oscar and Zulu Man had just gotten back on Interstate 10, heading west, as the sun was just about to disappear, when Oscar counted down to zero and looked to his right. In the far distance he saw a brief flash visible from the interstate, saying, "Via Con Dios" Antowan and Scylla"! The Zulu Mans prized Lincoln had gone up in flames and inside we're two souls that wouldn't be missed. Far enough out in the hinterlands yet close enough to the well-traveled interstate that an explosion near sundown would be noticed by someone and reported.

By the end of the fourth day, poor Mayflower and two more of her associates ended their days in several dumpsters around town as well as four street pushers. The following day as Oscars younger brother was ferrying Scylla and Zulu Man around Tijuana to provide new identities, as Jorge Mendaca stood on the patio watching the boats out on the Pacific, he was at peace with himself, yet planning for the events that were about to surface when his thoughts were disturbed, by the sound of the sliding patio door, as his son Oscar came out with a couple of drinks in hand.

"Gracias Oscar, said the elder Mendaca. "You have a worried look on your face"!

"I'm wondering if the Negrito's can be trusted"?

"That is why we will keep an eye on them and allow them to earn our trust, Oscar my son. Scylla's brother we will send to our Clinic, to have some modest work done to change his appearance and as far as Scylla is concerned, I have a plan and a ready market for the seductive skills we've all seen with the man from Modesto. Of course they have a few rough edges, but they seem willing and know the ways of the street.

During the course of the next few years, The Zulu Man resurrected the surviving pushers he had around the greater LA area, always working the edges of the known Latino and Black gangs and their territories, even recruiting many of his ladies of the pavement as Mack Daddy had done as yet another outlet for Coke and Heroin. From time to time someone would try and make him go away, eventually disappearing from sight from one who lived in the shadows.

Jorge Mendaca's business thrived as the illegal drugs flowed almost unabated into the Southern California area. He was now selling to almost everyone in Southern California, and with help from Scylla, several of his competitors began to disappear one, by one. Then one Christmas eve, the elder Mendaca invited Scylla and her brother to his beach house for the annual Christmas Eve party. While there, they were surprised to find the leader of one of their arch competitors there enjoying himself with the entire Mendaca family. "What's he doin here", asked Zulu Man grabbing a drink from the bar?

"This is a night to celebrate the birth of Jesus el Christos, the son of

God", said Jorge Mendaca smiling. "Feliz Navidad"! This is also a night to celebrate a unity of purpose everyone and to formally introduce, the Boss Man of the Crips into our family"!

Scylla and her brother both glanced at Oscar the eldest son as if to question was it true? He nodded his head in direction of his father.

"We all know the Crips have been carrying on an extended street war their rivals the Bloods and we have kept out of things hoping not to take sides in their struggle selling our Jejo to both. But recent developments have convinced me that the time for neutrality is over. Zulu Man, I wish you to formally join your people to that of the Crips and declare yourself to be under the Boss Man directly as his number three man, in all things. Scylla, you are to become his personal bodyguard and chief enforcer, personally settling all disputes that arise. Now from time to time, the Boss Man has assured me that he will make certain that you're available to me on a contractual basis. Your earnings levels will continue as before. That will be your sole purpose and none other. As of this moment the Bloods will have to find someone else to supply their needs, for it will not be us. Perhaps they will, then again perhaps they will not. I'm certain some blood will be shed, just as long as it's' not ours. Are we in agreement"?

Scylla and her brother really had little choice in the matter as first she then her brother went over to the Boss Man to shake hands in agreement, with Scylla saying, "Just so's you know that I ain't gonna be one of yo Ho's at any time. You got plenty of that kind available", she said smiling.

The Zulu Man then shook the Boss Mans' hand saying, "Thas cool, but jus one little thing. None of the guys I bring over including me goes through any initiation, like ya normally do. We all made our bones. Ya know what I'm sayin'"?

The Boss Man gave an expansive smile and said, "No grabbin' the merch an no drop and grab! That's cool"!

21

I t took the better part of a year, for the Boss Man to finally persuade Scylla to submit to his advances. All part of her plan, to dangle the goods out there, do her job to his satisfaction and beyond, make herself indispensable in the only way a desirable woman could. Still in all, after their first night together, he awoke the following morning, expecting her to be asleep as all the others had, only to find himself alone as he'd done to many others. He examined his apartment expecting to find things missing as whores usually do, yet not a single thing was amiss. She'd spent the night, or at least part of one, and then left him cuddled up between the sheets holding on to his jewels. The first year of their experience with the Boss Man worked out very well with Scylla taking out a half dozen of the competition in ways that only she could, while Oscar and her brother engineered the tunnels under the border, between Mexico and California bypassing the border crossings continually insuring a full flow of Coke, Horse and Mary Jane into the States with no one the wiser. Over time they would catch wind of another group trying to run the border crossings with a sizeable load. Through well selected cut outs, they made sure the local authorities were informed with good information, thus making headlines in the papers days later.

One of the sidelines the Boss Man had was the retailing of Counterfeit US currency. Taking a portion of his sizeable profits, he engaged with a lone engraver and printer in Las Vegas, who printed the finest counterfeit currency anyone had seen to date. The finest paper, inks and engraving plates that printed out twenties, fifties and hundred dollar notes. He went to the extra step to age the bills prior to sale. Thus, to the average eye, they appeared to be genuine. Business was good, very, very good for in each part of his endeavors the Boss Man was gleaning an eight fold profit continually when all was said and done. Yet the better part of male hubris took hold of the Boss Man. Eventually visiting a Tattoo parlor in

San Diego and having two words tattooed on his palms. On his left was the word, "Gimme", while on the right was the word, "More".

Then on the date of the fullness of the moon, Mendaca agreed to an emergency meeting with Scylla and her brother at his beach house. They'd both motored down to Ensenada, in the new Donzi speed boat, recently purchased. They both appeared in a somber mood as they approached Oscar who asked, "So what's the problem you've both discovered", as they all trekked up to the beach house?

"It's the cash Oscar", said Scylla. "We all been getting paid with bogus cash by the Boss Man. Zulu Man has it all laid out, so hang on so's he only has to lay it all out once"! After their warm greeting with the Oscars father they all sat down on the patio as Oscar opened the briefcase they'd brought with them. He was greeted with a briefcase half occupied with one hundred dollar US banknotes, while the other half was occupied by fifties. "So is this a gift for me", asked Mendaca?

"Might as well be Senor Mendaca", said Zulu Man clearly angry. "I'll lay it out for ya"! In his explanation he revealed how several of his low level men had been recently been apprehended by the US Secret Service for the passing of counterfeit currency. Since all moneys for transactions between the Crips and the Mendaca family flowed through the Boss Man, they had every note they could find of recent transactions examined by some they knew and what was in the briefcase was all bogus bank notes. "At first we kinda thought it may have been you guys who were puttin' one over on us. Then we started to connect the dots. We heard that the Boss Man was now in the business of pushin' counterfeit dough all over the west coast. We got that info from the mouth of one of his crew leaders just before he checked out. He gets the bogus money from a printer in Henderson Nevada, just outside of Vegas. Pays ten or twenty cents on the dollar on average, then from there it's all gravy. He's been doin this for about a year. The money he gets from his drug business pays for it. Now we been getting our money from him, straight up ever since the beginning. Our friend took us to school on how you can tell the real bills from the bogus, so if you'll allow me, I'll compare real cash to the bogus and my guess is that he's been payin' y'all off in bogus at least in part"! Then he pulled out an envelope from his coat and extracted a hundred, a fifty and a twenty dollar bill and from the brief case pulled out a magnifying glass, taking Oscar and his father to school on how they could spot the bogus money, from the real currency.

"So what about the two that were apprehended, by the Secret Service", asked Mendaca? "We got em both out with a hefty bail. Neither one of em got a record and they got nothing' draggin' on em like family, said Scylla!

"Are they good men", asked Mendaca!

"They do what their told and keep their mouths shut"!

"Then you get them down to me in the next few days and I'll see to it they get new identity papers", said Mendaca. "It's that or they will have to disappear completely"!

"Oscar and I will have our people examine the recent monies received by the Crips. Next week there is a transaction that is to occur. That transaction will happen as if nothing is wrong. We both will examine the monies received from the Boss Man as a result of our suspicions. Soon thereafter we will meet to decide what course of action will take place", said Jorge Mendaca the elder crisply!

"Scylla, have you fully gained the trust and confidence of the Boss Man"?

"That fool just can't get enough of me", she answered.

"Good. I'm grateful that you've come to me with this information. Now enough of this unfortunate business for the moment and let us go inside and enjoy the luncheon that has been prepared for us"!

It was indeed fortunate for Scylla and her brother that they went to the elder Mendaca and share their proof with him when they did, for just two days before, one of his bankers in Panama, called him on a secure line to reveal the very same information regarding the bogus money he was receiving, for it removed them from any suspicion. He sent Oscar down to Panama to retrieve the bogus money that could be put to use elsewhere in Mexico. Upon further examination the money appeared to look good enough to pass amongst the population. Once each bill passed several transactions it was of a concern no longer.

A week later Scylla was summoned to the one of the Boss Man's houses, in greater Los Angeles, for it seemed that one of his several common law wives, had suspicions, that he was sleeping with Scylla and started a nasty fight. When Scylla arrived, his unfortunate was laying inert on the bed and the Boss Man had a series of very deep scratches on his face that matched his wife's ultra-long finger nails.

"Da bitch found out about us an look what she give me", he screamed at her arrival"!

"Oh, you poor baby", cooed Scylla, passing her fingers delicately upon his face. "That's gonna leave a mark, but let me clean out the wounds, so they can heal up proper"! When that was accomplished, she said, "Now what do ya want done with her"?

"I want ya to skin her alive and leave the body in a No tell Motel out in the valley, then bring the skin to me"! Scylla noted that when he was like this, all het up about anything, it was usually under the influence of drugs, which drove his thinking patterns into high orbit and decided not to question him saying instead, "Now that's a mighty tall order for this working girl. She's gonna die in the process ya unnerstand and there's a lotta work involved, so the price will be twenty large for the snuff, another ten for the skin job and yet another ten for the agida of bringing the skin back to ya"!

"Sure, sure, get it done", said the Boss Man!

"I'll need thirty of it up front right now", said Scylla.

"Thirty of it right now? What's the matter with the normal half and half, we normally do"?

"It's late at night. Ya wanted me here quick and there's extras involved, so thirty large in my hands before I leave, then you help me bundle her into the trunk of my car and leave me be until I come back for the last ten large, or ya can do her your own self", she stated matter of factly.

"Wait right here", said the Boss Man, disappearing into another section of the house. That alone told Scylla that he kept a sizeable portion of his money close at hand. Good thing to know in the coming days.

Several days later the cadaver of a female, was discovered by a horrified motel maid in one of the many motels that ran along Interstate ten. The body was completely skinned from head to toe. Eventually the FBI was brought into the case, only to conclude this was similar to a string of deaths that plagued the entire west coast.

This time in the aftermath she discovered that over thirty thousand dollars of her fee from the Boss Man for his dirty work was bogus and all of it was in hundred dollar notes, very difficult to pass, even though they were of good quality. She decided to keep this from her brother, since other things were in play in regards to the Boss Man.

Ten days later after the latest exchange of product and money with the Boss Man, Scylla and her brother were again invited to Ensenada for a luncheon with the Mendaca's.

"Your information was correct concerning your Boss Man's treachery. He mix in a little over half of the bad money with the good. But we are ok for the moment now that we know the game he's playing. We can find a market for most of the bad money in time and the product he received over all was of far less purity than normal since he quit checking the purity some time ago"!

"So what are we gonna do about this", asked Zulu Man?

"I make a decision two years ago that turn bad", said Mendaca continuing, steepling his fingertips in thought, then looking up he said to Scylla, "You and your brother think you're ready to run the Crips"? Without even blinking an eye Scylla said, "Yeah. Whattaya have in mind"?

"Bueno. Next week the Boss Man wanna take the biggest shipment yet up north from our warehouse in Calexico. He wants the shipment to be double the normal amount. He will get what he wants, except the Jejo will be stepped on so much by flamenco dancers. Everything will appear as it normally would. No doubt he will pay us with the bad dollars as he been doin'.

Now we both got contacts inside the Los Angeles Policia. It be up to you to find out just the exact route they take. To help out, I can get a special thing from my people in the Mexican Army that will send out little beeps that can be tracked electronically. Of course it'll be on a timing mechanism so it won't start until a half an hour after its leaves its starting point".

"So if all goes well and they get a lotta help from others and they know where the big shipment is going and can monitor its route, they can intercept, get their headlines. A big shootout will happen in the early hours, you will then let me know where the Boss man is, we grab him and you bring him here. Then we give him to Scylla, so she can make him tell us where all his money is. We split it up down the middle and you guys take over the Crips, so we continue to do business"!

Once again Scylla, nodded her head in agreement as well as her brother. She could feel the wheel of fortune spinning with half of the slots displaying the skull and cross bones, while the rest displayed the dollar sign. It didn't matter which way they landed, for now the game was rigged. "One last thing", mentioned Jorge Mendaca. 'When we get the Boss Man back here for you to work on him Scylla, we get a ringside seat"!

"You guys just wanna see me naked, now don't cha"?

"We already see you naked Scylla. We just wanna see you do your work. That and maybe a few other things", said Mendaca's eldest son Oscar. "Good now we eat"!

The following week, all the elements moved into place, like pieces on a chess board. Having received apparently through great reluctance information by two apparently different sources about a large convoy of illegal drugs heading north from the greater San Diego area. The point of origin was unknown and while one source emphatically stated that the route traveled was to be on the I-5 interstate north bound paralleling the ocean, while the second source stated with equal certainty that the route to be I-15 heading north, in a more mountainous terrain in the early hours of the morning. By now the Los Angeles PD's narcotics division had brought in the Federal DEA, to work with them on the case, yet faced with the apparent uncertainty of two different travel routes and manpower problems briefly toyed with the idea of bringing in another entity, yet this was quickly discarded in the interests of security. The knowledge that an electronic homing beacon was to be placed with the shipment and that the beacon was to be on a certain obscure radio frequency mostly erased that concern. This knowledge and the eventual revelation of the exact radio frequency the monitor would broadcast on was at first good news to all concerned, but when dealing with skilled smugglers anything and everything was possible, so the question was asked, "Why the monitoring beacon"? From both of the sources came the same logical answer. The Boss Man had two shipments hijacked in the last twelve months, by his very own people, one of which he got back eventually, but in each case the hijackers were eventually discovered and disposed of. He didn't want a third interruption in his business.

Thus a decision was made to split their forces with a contingent on both Interstate routes, with two choppers in the air with the electronics' to monitor the frequency to determine the exact route of travel.

As the final vehicle was loaded with the 'product', the monitor was skillfully placed inside the rear wheel well of the first vehicle to depart carrying the product. Inside the lead vehicle was the single sideband Citizens Band scanning monitor that also picked up standard police frequencies. In addition was yet another interesting element of electronics that would be able to change traffic lights from red to green at the discretion of the driver as they passed through urban areas. The very last thing they wanted was to be held stationary.

Some police forces had them, as well as the Secret Service, so why not the smugglers?

Oscar turned to his men as they bid farewell to the Boss Mans people in the warehouse in Mexicali. As he entered the warehouse, he saw three of his men going through the cash they received from the 'Crips'. The bills were placed in two separate piles as each of the men examined each item of currency. "So what does it look like", asked Oscar?

"It looks like every other bill is bogus so far Jefe", answered his man. "The bad money runs the gamut from very good printing on quality paper, then very good printing on less than quality paper. Right now we're separating the genuine currency from the counterfeit, and then afterwards we'll go back over the counterfeit and separate the reusable from that which only cigars can be lit from"!

"Bueno. Either way our problem will be eliminated before dawn"!

22

The rapidly assembled task force took up their positions along both interstate routes, just prior to midnight. They knew how the convoys usually operated, with a lead vehicle known as the 'Rammer', usually with specially welded and reinforced front bumpers whose sole purpose was to ram through any vehicular obstruction that was placed in the path of the convoy. The middle vehicles were usually those carrying the product, while the trailing vehicle was the 'Sweeper', to sweep up anyone who tried to intercept a shipment. With the exception of the Rammer, driving a specially reinforced ten year old Dodge pickup truck, its passenger was armed with an old Soviet styled RPM grenade launcher, while each of the other vehicles was manned by a driver and three others, each armed, with the short barreled AK-47 assault rifle. The three vehicles in the middle of the convoy were vintage Chevy and Dodge delivery vans, full of Cocaine packed in kilo sized clear plastic bags. The Boss Man had gone into hock for this shipment, taking almost every dollar he had, borrowing some from some partners he normally wouldn't do business with plus acquiring all of the bogus money he could add to the pot.

By his reckoning, if all went as planned, he could pay everyone off with interest, make a ton of cash to boot selling off his product then go find an island somewhere to buy and live the life of a king, telling everyone to kiss his black ass. If it didn't, there would be no place he could run or hide. Yet the idea of failure never even entered his mind. Unlike a few of the other times, he'd taken great care in selecting those that would transport him into the ranks of the superrich. He'd toss them enough money to further insure their loyalty, then at the right moment just before he was to disappear, he'd drop a dime on each and every one of them to John Law. He'd done it before and he'd do it again.

For better part of the last year, he'd been shorting the smart Mendaca Clan with bogus money and they apparently hadn't gotten wise, or else they'd have said or done something by now, was his reckoning. He'd foxed them for fair and they never had a clue. For the better part of the last eighteen months, Mendaca's people shuttled their illegal shipments via the tunnel dug underneath the border from Mexicali, in Mexico, to the sister City of Calexico, just across the border in California. The tunnel twenty feet underground was well lighted and had a track that ran for three quarters of a mile, from one old warehouse to another. The fun thing was that it was just a mile from the official border crossing manned by the US Border patrol and they hadn't a clue to its existence. No more need for the high risk mules to run the risk of capture.

Traveling north at normal speed, the convoy made its way through El Centro, Imperial and Brawley, before turning left and heading west on State Route 78. In about thirty miles, he Rammer had a choice to make, either continue on State Route 86, which ran concurrently with 78, which was a very good road and connect with Interstate 10 West at Indio heading towards Palm Springs and their eventual destination of Los Angeles, or take the 78 Junction into the Vallecito Mountains towards Escondido then turn right on Interstate 15 and head north. Had the convoy continued on its current northern direction they would've placed the task force awaiting them in a bad spot tactically for they would've forced them towards I-10 and completely upset all of their plans. Fortunately the timer on the locational beeper monitored by the two aerial helicopters engaged and started to reveal their location as heading due north towards Indio and Interstate 10. Then as the task force was scrambling to readjust, the Rammer driver of the convoy came upon the junction of the two roads, 78 and 86 and turned left heading for the mountains and the fog he knew would shield them from any aerial surveillance. He knew that everyone that trailed behind would be angry that he was taking the more difficult road through the mountains and the fog they knew would soon envelop them as they all flashed their head lights in his rear view mirror. The prime rule of the convoy was that no one talks on the Citizens Band radio unless there was a life or death emergency. There was a reason the diver of the Rammer was the leader of the convoy for he'd never failed, to deliver the goods. He'd some kind of sixth sense as to where the law was. Of course the single time someone called him to stop was when a driver was having an attack of diarrhea while enroute, stopping his vehicle to relieve himself off the main road. The Rammer turned around and joined the others watching the poor soul crapping in the bushes, a victim of the Hershey squirts. He asked who the one was that called him on the CB? They all pointed at the hapless driver grunting his guts out in the bushes. The Rammer, calmly pulled out his pistol and walked up behind the grunting driver pointing the weapon behind his ear and pulled the trigger just once and stepped away turning towards the others saying, "Now we can call it life or death"! Then he pointed to one of the others and said, "Now you're the driver and ya better keep up"!

That was the very last time that anyone failed to follow his directions as the convoy made its way westward and into the fog they knew was waiting for them in the mountains. As the convoy headed west, one of the chopper pilots said, "Hold on now people, they just turned west and are heading into the Vallecito Mountains. I'm at five thousand feet and the signal is strong. Twenty minutes later he broadcasted on the high band channel above that for normal police communication, "I'm above them for the signal is strong, but they're in the fog so I can't see them"!

Now all anyone could do was wait. The task force commander was sitting at a rest stop just west of Escondido on Interstate 15. He dropped down to another channel to talk to his counterpart awaiting developments on I-5. They both agreed to stand fast and await developments. Both had driven through the mountains many times and through the fog, knowing that anything faster than thirty miles an hour was an overly risky proposition. They were heading for them but it'd be awhile. There were a number of mountain roads they could take if the convoy was really trying to tie them up in fits given the limited manpower the task force could bring to bear. But every once in a while, one just had to SWAG it with a Scientific Wild Ass Guess. Thinking they would be tired of traveling at a snail's pace through the mountains in the fog, the task force commander discussed this with his counterpart.

"If when they get to Santa Isabel they continue on 78 then we'll know their headed for Escondido, but if at that junction they head north on 76, then it's a pretty good bet that their headed for I-15, heading north so we could pull the I-5 force off and send them north"!

"Their near Camp Pendleton now aren't they"? "Just North of Pendleton near San Clemente"!

"When's the next CHP chopper gonna come on duty"? "About a half hour from now they're do for the hand off"!

"We know they're coming yet we don't know what the convoy looks like", said the Commander!

"Boss, we do know one thing. Their movement discipline, once on the interstate. A rammer, the product carriers and the sweeper, all traveling at the posted speed limit and each one about a quarter mile distant from the next. Now there's a choke point just north of Temecula where I-15 splits off into 215. Once we know their heading north on 76, then I'll say it's a good bet that they'll surface on I-15 a few exits below the Fallbrook exit ramp. Then we hustle up everyone to deploy two roadblocks on 15 and 215 above both Murrieta's"!

Then they waited as the Commander asked, "How many units has CHP committed to"?

"They have five in the area, locally, five more at Oceanside and five more between Elsinore and Canyon Lake all working but with an ear to the ground that can be called in for support, after the fact. But it's gotta be after the fact because their radios don't have our special frequency and we just gotta know the runners have got to have a police scanner". Twenty minutes later, the eye in the sky came on saying, "Looks like they're moving north on seventy six. Fogs still too heavy to get a good eye on them but that's the direction they're heading"!

"No, no, no. The intercept point has to be moved up", said the task force commander to himself. "We let em get as far as the 15 and 215 split we won't have enough manpower to bottle em up. They're gonna emerge on the exit just south of Fallbrook, and then head north. We set up the intercept point at the Temecula exit"!

"But boss. What if they stay on the back roads and in the hills and go around us", asked his driver?

"Then you can say that I'm a complete fool. Look, they can't make any decent time driving up in the hills surrounded by fog that probably won't burn off till morning. They want the load delivered before sunrise and so they can go to breakfast and do their old ladies, to do that they have to make time and to do that, they have to get on the interstate. They'll be fog on the interstate but less of it"!

The orders were given over the high frequency channel and the units disbursed, as the Oceanside units made their way carefully northward on

State Route 13, to trail behind the convoy once it was fully committed to the Interstate. The rest of the units deployed just over a rise approximately a hundred yards past the Temecula exit, with four vehicles arranged in a dual chevron arrangement while a fifth vehicle pointing right back in a southerly direction. Two units were stationed at the top of the Temecula off ramp, to catch any stragglers, while two more were stationed on the southbound lanes of the I-15 interstate, in case any members of the convoy decided to elude the convoy and break across the wide, grassy esplanade and head north in the south bound lanes. Approximately one mile south of the Temecula exit, two of the task force were let out armed with their weapons and two sets of spike strips to lay out at the last moment to shred the tires of the trailing sweeper vehicle. Now everything was in readiness as the unit commander and his driver sat in their car hidden from view in a small copse of trees, at the intersection of 76 and I-15, listening for the overhead eye in the sky to tell them if they were right, or not.

Minutes later, the eye in the sky came alive, as the radio crackled alive saying," They just passed the R-3 cut off, if this transponder is working right and should be passing Dripping Springs any time now. The fog down there is like pea soup so they're not moving very fast. My guess is the lead car should come into view in about twenty minutes or so. I'll check back within ten"!

Fortunately in the early hours of the morning traffic was sparse, for the fog was heavy in many places, especially in the valleys and low spots, while on the Interstate, the fog was heavy only in spots, while lighter in others. Still in all, what little traffic there was moved slower than usual.

Twenty minutes later, the overhead choppers radio crackled alive saying, "Heads up, they should be upon your twenty in about five or so. I'll be quiet now and take up position north east of you. Let me know when breakfast is ready"! Eight minutes later, the Rammer emerged from the fog and stopped at the stop sign, turning right and made its way onto the Interstate. Seconds later a Van approached and did the very same thing as did another Van, followed close behind by yet another. Thirty seconds later the trailing Sweeper came into view and followed the others onto the entrance ramp, as the Unit Commander signaled the others, "Five vehicles heading North on I-15, everyone lock and load", then he slowly moved out to trail the action. A second CHP back up chopper was now enroute, to circle the area and was but ten minutes away. The units coming up from Oceanside were but five minutes away from the Interstate as they maintained radio silence. Minutes later the Rammer passed, the two task force operatives laying doggo in the tall grass beside the roadway as they had a partial view of the interstate noting that a mere hundred and fifty yards separated each vehicle as they passed. The fog in this spot was relatively light with about a hundred yards of visibility ahead of each vehicle and nothing like the pea soup they encountered in the mountains. It was still early in the morning and each of the smugglers felt that this was going to be yet another milk run.

After the fourth vehicle passed the spot of the two troopers, they quickly rose up and flung the four spike strips across both lanes of the interstate, and then hustled back out of sight as each of the vehicles was traveling at a sedate fifty miles an hour each in the far right hand lane. Each vehicle was barely able to make out the red tail lights of the vehicle in front of them.

The trailing Sweeper had lagged behind the last Van by yet another hundred yards as the driver was relaxed, then he thought he saw something moving in the far mists ahead. "D'you see that", he asked the shotgun rider in the seat next to him? "Yeah, musta been a rabbit of some kind, said the rider"! Seconds later he saw the two sets of spike strips in the roadway ahead of him. They were going too fast for him to stop or evade the strips as the vehicle passed right over both sets of strips as they motored on. Fearing a high jack from another gang, and not even considering that it was the law that was about to close in on them, the shot gun rider picked up the CB radio and summoned the Rammer up ahead saying, "Jackie, we just been spike stripped, so heads up"!

Since every vehicle in the convoy had their CB Radios turned on the same high end channel, everyone was brought out of their early morning reverie, coming instantly alert as the vehicles passed the Temecula exit ramp. Now they were committed to the path ahead as another half mile of the upward grade of roadway lay ahead. As the Rammer cleared the rise, his headlamps, on low beam, failed to see the roadblock ahead of them until five different high intensity, thousand candle power spotlights suddenly came alive, partially blinding him, as he instantly dropped down a gear and floored the accelerator.

The Unit Commander was startled as he slowly approached the interception lagging a mile behind the Sweeper. Unknown to everyone was the two drivers approaching from behind them on the Interstate at high speed. Weary from an all-night party in San Diego, each we're racing each other at high speed on the interstate with their lights off at speeds far in excess of a hundred miles an hour. The lead driver power shifted into fifth gear as his Supercharged Shelby Cobra nosed ahead of the red Ferrari V-12. The Ferrari briefly backed off barely missing the Command Vehicle then roared past in hot pursuit of the Shelby. Both of the drivers were young and successful actors that were racing to an early morning movie shoot in Palm Springs. Driven by success, money and a flood of testosterone, neither of them we're going to win the bet each made with the other.

In fact neither of them would be alive within the next minute or so. The game was Blind Man's Hare and Hound, run especially at night between two fast vehicles, an off shoot of the old "Chickie Runs" of the early fifties, where two stolen cars were run at each other at high speed, the first guy to bail out was "Chicken". In the 'Blind Man', the Hound chased the Hare to a certain destination, at night, without benefit of headlights. Especially endearing to certain aficionados of the sport was when the fog rolled in. The first to arrive at the designated location wins. The first to turn on his headlights loses.

The Command vehicle frantically accelerated as the Commander radioed ahead for all to be on the lookout for two civilian intruders, heading for the intercept point at high speed without headlights, as the Commander whispered to himself, "Murphy, oh Murphy, to you and your Ma. A pox upon you and your damnable Law"! He just had to let things play out, for the die was cast.

The distance between the racers, the convoy and the roadblock was rapidly closing as the fog cleared a bit and the two cars raced past the convoy in the left hand lane as the roadway was closing in on the Temecula exit. Just as the Rammer was cresting the long hill, the Shelby Cobra flew past, followed immediately by the Ferrari, with lights out, with the pedal to the metal, going full out. Just two more Macho's, doing the wrong thing at the wrong time, at play with their expensive toys, successful friends of long standing, each of which had performed this very insane adventure, dozens of times in the past, were soon to join their ancestors in a blaze of glory.

As both cars raced past the crest of the hill, the Ferrari began to pull aside the Cobra as both spotted something ahead. Suddenly their eyes were blinded by an array of high intensity spotlights, as in an instant they both noticed the funnel shape Vee of cars arrayed ahead of them in the roadway. They were moving far too fast for their brains to process the blur of men scurrying to get out of their paths, much less apply the brakes as both cars ploughed straight into the police vehicles that occupied their respective lanes, leaving no skid marks in their wake. The fuel tanks immediately ruptured upon impact, fuelling the dual explosions, destroying both drivers as well as several other members of the task force that couldn't move fast enough to escape.

The Rammer, wasn't all that concerned as both cars sped past for he was a veteran member of the California underworld since his teen years and had seen this before in the land of the crazies, for he was well known for engaging in things just as crazy over the years always coming out on top which was why he was known as Mr. Lucky. But as the cars exploded in front of him, the array of lights as well as the explosion a hundred or so yards ahead revealed the outline of a police roadblock, he hit the accelerator, as the powerful, reinforced Dodge truck leaped forward through the flames. Most of the vehicles in the convoy were equipped with the expensive self-sealing tires that were able to run awhile even through punctured, all except the Sweeper that trailed. There hadn't been enough time.

The Rammer began to catch rounds from the task force, as it aimed for a spot between two of the police roadblock vehicles as he approached the inferno at 80 mph and climbing as the accelerator was floored. Just then two other explosions occurred as his Dodge passed, the fuel tanks of two task force vehicles igniting. His last thoughts were, "Fuck em all but six and save em for pall bearers", as a fusillade of bullets and double ought buckshot slammed into his Dodge, as it ricocheted past two flaming vehicles at the very apex of the roadblock. The vehicle might have survived, had an unlucky bullet not buried itself into Jackie's head, signaling lights out as the speeding Dodge, flipped over, end over end, its fuel tank ruptured as several incendiary rounds found their mark in its fuel tank, the careening vehicle streaming fire and sparks for over a hundred yards or more as it slid down the other side of the interstate and into the center grassy area. The third Van in the convoy veered off into the grassy media area that lay between the northbound and southbound lanes, as the three men inside began returning fire from the Mac-10 machine pistols, in full automatic mode, as the driver pressed on, followed by the Sweeper, its punctured tires beginning to deflate rapidly. In short order it would be running flat out on its rims, still it motored onward after the third Van in which it was sworn to protect.

The two CHP choppers overhead were helpless in what they could do for the carnage below them and they never noticed a shadowing KNBC News chopper from LA, shadowing the entire entourage, having gotten wind of the affair from a reliable source. All was on instant video replay, telecast instantaneously back to the station by satellite as events unfolded, just in time for the morning newscasts. It hovered just above the two CHP choppers as they concentrated their video cameras upon the action that played out below them.

The first Van carrying product was trying to skid to a halt as the remaining members of the roadblock poured a barrage of weapons fire into it as the occupants of the Van fired wildly in every direction until their magazines ran out. The officers of the task force kept up their fire until they ran out, quickly reloading and charging the bullet and shot ridden vehicle.

The second Van veering off into the median and onto the south bound lane of the interstate, escaped most of the fire by the roadblock but came to an untimely end as one of the officers of the task force guarding the southbound lanes brought an unauthorized Korean War Vintage, Bazooka to the party and took careful aim at the speeding Van now fifty yards away and closing fast. He tried to lead the vehicle properly aiming for the front of the Van, but since he'd only dry fired the weapon, his lead wasn't fully on the mark hitting the left rear tire as it passed at a distance of thirty yards, exploding the entire tire assembly and the fuel tank, flipping the Van over on its side, as it slid to rest in the grassy median. Concentrating on his recent triumph, he barely had time to notice the third Van trailing after, as a barrage of Mac-10 rounds stitched across his chest, as they gained speed. The fog was now beginning to lift in spots as several of the task force vehicles gave pursuit in both the North and Southbound lanes of I-15, followed by the others that joined in from Oceanside and one of the CHP choppers overhead. The News chopper, decided to follow the pursuit at a discrete distance behind the other CHP chopper, getting a sometimes clear shot of events through the fog below that was thankfully starting to lift. By this time other members of the CHP ground units were racing to the scene ahead of the fleeing Van and the Sweeper behind that was having a difficult time keeping up since its tires were shredding off from their encounter with the road spikes.

What was in everyone's mind was that his had to end quickly, before the morning traffic started. Even if it ended right now, it would be afternoon until all of the investigations were concluded. Right now they all had a crime scene that was over a mile long and quickly growing.

The pursuing police vehicles with their lights flashing convinced the two remaining vehicles that it wasn't another gang hijacking, but John Law putting on the crunch. The Van was now traveling at speeds approaching a hundred miles an hour while the trailing sweeper, its tires shredded and running on its rims was going considerably slower, showering a slew of sparks on the roadway as it went. Given that its occupants were returning fire at a murderous rate, the pursuing units gave it some space. Making a PIT maneuver to roll over the vehicle completely out of the question. Just then the lead Van slowed down and foolishly crossed the grassy median ahead of the other pursuers in the northbound lane, hitting an unseen hole in the ground, which flipped the Van completely on its back. The Sweeper followed the Van off the roadway into the grassy median, grinding quickly to a halt, in the ground the flames now coming out from under the vehicle from the act of friction on the road, set alight the grass all around the vehicle as all of the remaining occupants emerged and started firing at the gathering of patrol cars on both side of the interstate. The officers held their fire and simply ducked behind their vehicles letting the bullets slam into the patrol cars instead of them.

Suddenly the Sweepers fuel tank erupted killing all but one of the occupants and knocking unconscious, the driver as the officers swept in from every direction to apprehend everyone. Of the four occupants of the Van that flipped over only the driver was killed from the impact, his neck broken from the impact.

Everyone agreed they were lucky for the crime scene was five miles long. It could've been worse, much worse. Four units of government property destroyed. Five officers slain with over another six seriously hospitalized. Well over several tons of cocaine confiscated or destroyed, nine assailants dead, with another four captured and by the by, two dead from unforeseen collateral damage as well as their vehicles that were obliterated. All in all not a bad day for Southern California. It wouldn't be until after midnight that day when everyone involved could go home for a nights rest.

It would be nine that morning when the KNBC News chopper came to rest in the parking lot quickly surrounded by the stations staff for the after action interviews. As the entire event was replayed again and again throughout the day, most everyone watching were touched by the epithets of the moment when mortal combat was revealed to the viewers, reminding some of the events of long ago when the Hindenburg Zeppelin came crashing to the ground in a field in New Jersey.

As expected, certain community activists in the minority community attempted to intervene via the media, injecting a racial element regarding the early morning I-15 event, since most of the criminal element that were dead, just happened to be of the black minority. Yet the subsequent, after action investigation revealed that each member of the convoy, possessed lengthy criminal records going back to their early teens, almost exclusively in the area of illegal drug related activities. When the public discovered this and in addition the fact that the casualty count of the law enforcement agencies involved in the interdiction, were divided almost equally between the whites and blacks, with repeated viewings of not only the media, but the police agencies video tapes, any criticism of the police fell upon deaf ears.

Yet from this point onward, the I-15 corridor would be known as the "Corridor of Death".

23

A s the interdiction of the 'Crips' convoy was unfolding, selected members of the Mencada family quietly entered the home in Garden Grove California, in the early hours of the morning. They were led through through the house by the Boss Man's chief bodyguard Scylla without a word, straight into the master bedroom. It made little difference to them of the garish style of décor in which the interior of the house was adorned, for each of their abodes we're of scant difference.

Upon entering, they discovered the Boss Man asleep in his bed flanked by a pair of part time lovers rented for the evening's entertainment, equally asleep and no doubt exhausted from their exertions. The musky smell of Eros, hung heavily in the room as Scylla discovered, a syringe propped gently upright on the nearby nightstand, clearly full of product.

The contents were injected in all three of the occupant's arms by Scylla, without a whimper. As she pumped the last of it into the Boss Mans arm, she withdrew it bending the needle around and inserting it into her pocket for later disposal. The Boss Man mumbled, "Whas dis", as she withdrew the needle from his vein and as he saw the blurred image of Scylla he mumbled, "Yeah, das cool", as the heroin coursed through his veins, dragging him back down into a deep slumber.

That his bed partners may or may not have received an overdose was of little interest to Scylla, for at worst they would be dead. At best they'd wake up sometime the following afternoon, wondering who was going to pay them. After securing the Boss man for transport, Mendaca's men was led through the entire house removing anything of possible value, ledgers, files, a computer, backup disks, money, tearing down sheetrock walls in places, looking for product, money and anything of value.

When the house had been determined to have been picked clean, some of Mendaca's men carried the naked Boss Man, zipped up neatly in a black medical body bag to the trunk of the waiting Cadillac in the driveway.

A minute later came the last of Mendaca's men, joining Scylla in her car slipping under the garage door as it closed. Both cars started, backing out onto the street and slowly drove away, into the early morning fog quietly. Scylla speaking in Spanish asked, "Where did you put the bomb"?

"In the cabinet next to the stove and oven since it's fed by natural gas. I hope you don't mind that I set the timer to ignite at two in the afternoon. Just to give the "Puta's" time to wake up and get out. It would be a shame to see such beauty go to waste for something they had nothing to do with"!

"Yeah, I suppose. They're working girls an they got a right to make a living. But if they don't wake up in time, that's tough shit"!

"Do you suppose, the Boss Man paid them in advance Scylla"?

"The Boss Man never paid anyone in advance for anything as long as I knew him"!

"Then I fear for them. They'll wake up, find the Boss Man gone, and no dinero anywhere, "They're gonna be pissed"! "Then they'll be dead Amigo. Too many whores running around anyway. Drive the value of their services down"! Within the hour, they all arrived at the Marina at Santa Monica, loading their cargo onto the Boss Man's own boat; a forty foot twin diesel powered cabin cruiser, with Boss Man emblazoned in large script letters on both sides of the bow and across the stern.

They slowly motored out onto the Pacific for the six hour trip south to the Mendaca enclave in Ensenada Mexico. Several hours after sunrise, the boat pulled slowly into the private quayside, adjacent to one of the homes in the Mendaca family compound. The blissful Boss Man was carried up and over to the main house on a stretcher and down into the specially constructed, water and sound proofed basement, as the Jorge Mendaca, the elder, watched.

During the early morning hours, the Zulu Man was busy consolidating his gains with several other chosen Crips, across town by stopping at several after-hours clubs, and seeking a number of crew leaders, killing them in full view of those assembled, then calmly waking out into the night. Of course in the aftermath those patrons, who viewed the carnage in horror, fled the club en masse. Of course in each establishment it was a dark and dimly lit atmosphere inside the clubs and those few who were tracked down by the police in the aftermath investigation were unable to provide a description of the assailants, leaving each club owner and manager to deal with the authorities relentless questions. Time and again the authorities hit stone walls, as a common theme by the owners was, "I dunno what happened. I was in my office counting the nights receipts, I hear gunfire and by the time I left my office, I see dead men and my customers falling over themselves gettin' hat and getting' gone, real quick"!

By the rising of the sun, Zulu Man was finished with his consolidation and was driving south to Tijuana, checking into a motel to await the summons from his sister to the Mendaca compound in Ensenada.

As they both watched Scylla, getting the sun in the briefest of bikini suits, the elder Mendaca said to his son, "Oscar, call Scylla's brother on his mobil phone. He should be at the motel and invite him for lunch"!

Shortly after one in the afternoon the Mendaca Limo pulled up and under the large portico of the Mendaca hacienda, disgorging a beaming Zulu Man into the arms of his sister, attired in the same bikini with only a brief diaphanous sari covering her subterranean charms. He gave her a brief wink as they walked into the house past the massive entrance door made of layered Mexican Mesquite wood, to be greeted by Jorge and Oscar Mendaca. "Good of you to come as our guest", said the elder Mendaca as everyone walked out onto the beach front patio. "I trust you've taken care of business on your side of the border"!

"All of the others are dead, and our people are in place. With everything else happening I guess the TV folks and the papers will find some time to squeeze them in to the news. Is the Boss Man in your hands"?

"Our guest is sleeping soundly in the basement below. Perhaps we can take our noon day meal out here in the patio where the ocean breeze is comfortable and watch the news from the San Diego station, in the states"! Then Jorge Mendaca turned to his son saying have the servants bring our lunch and roll the TV sets out onto the patio so we can see the news"! Within a minute, the patio area was a blur of activity, drinks were served, as the servants were busy setting and serving the table, while others rolled out three TV sets, connecting them to the satellite dish and tuning them into the San Diego and LA local stations. During the course of the morning and into the afternoon, most of the normal viewing programming was preempted in lieu of the saturated coverage of what had come to be called, "The gunfight on I-15", as one news reporter on the scene had coined it. On yet another, some wag attached the moniker, "The Mother of all Gunfights"! Almost as an afterthought, news coverage of the carnage at three after hour's night clubs in the greater Los Angeles area was almost overshadowed, by the I-15 event. The news reporters were not permitted to enter any of the clubs, and possibly contaminate a crime scene. Yet they could give out a body count from each club and partial identifications of the slain. In total nine men met their quick and grisly end in the early hours.

For the better part of the next two hours, everyone sat watching the TV sets almost in rapture while working their way through Caesar salads and a slew of Margaritas and the news reporters tried in vain to connect the dots between the I-15 event and the early morning after hour's massacres. Just then another news bulletin cut in from the Los Angeles station reporting an explosion at a private residence, in the suburb of Garden Grove, as Scylla looked at her watch saying, "Right on time. It was set to go off at the stroke of two. Sure hope the whores woke up in time"! Then she looked at Jorge Mendaca and said, "We decided to blow up his house, since he ain't gonna need it anymore"!

Mendaca lifted his Margarita and asked, "Did you bring all that you had gotten from his house, Scylla"?

"It's on the boat awaiting your attention Jefe"!

"Bueno", said Mendaca lifting his glass higher in a toast. This is turning our better than expected. All has gone well.

As the afternoon wore on Oscar and some others went to the boat and retrieved all of the papers and documents retrieved from the Boss Mans house bring them inside for later review, then rejoined the others as they eagerly reviewed the KNBC unedited tape and later the official CHP patrol helicopters video tapes of the I-15 event through the early morning fog as well as the running commentaries by various retired law enforcement officials.

"You know, it is a very good thing when one can get the Policia to do our work for us", said the elder Mendaca beaming from ear to ear.

As one reporter was interviewing a recently arrived FBI command supervisor from the local Los Angeles office, the agent was heard to say in officious well-rehearsed tones, "From all the we can gather, I think this event has broken the back of the 'Crips' gang as we know it, for its leaders were all destroyed in the early hours of the morning including the house of their leader, the infamous Boss Man who we think died in the explosion of his home in Garden Grove. It's a bit early as we've discovered the charred remains of what appears several female bodies in the rubble"!

"Let us all toast the FBI", said Mendaca as all joined in and another round of Margarita's was summoned. When the drinks arrived, he interrupted the telecasts by saying, "The DEA has their little pound of flesh they can bellow about for months to come, in their holy crusade against us"! Then turning to Scylla and her brother he added, "As of now the both of you are responsible for your affairs and we all have done well"! Continuing he added, "May the god of Buena Fortuna, smile on all of our fortunes far into the future", where upon all drank.

Then Oscar turned to the Zulu Man saying, "If things run true to form on your side of the border and no witness's turn up, the Policia will not waste their time chasing after the killers of other killers, since no 'Good Citizens' were involved"!

"It was early in the morning, the light levels in each place were low and nobody said a word. We were in and out in each place", said Zulu Man. "Naw man, there ain't gonna be no witness's"!

"I think we have seen all we can see from the American TV on the subject for now", said the elder Mendaca! "I think it is time we turn our attentions to what Scylla has brought us regarding the Boss Man's affairs and accounts. I've invited our accountant to sit in and help us work our way through the intricacies of banking"!

For the next few hours, they all sorted through the information that was brought south, with Mendaca's accountant guiding the way. Finally three hours later, he said to the elder Mendaca, "Seems he was not exactly a good record keeper, but most of what he has is in cash. He kept about fifty thousand spread out into four separate bank accounts and as far as I can see, it's still there. In addition he has two safe deposit boxes as what we'll discover, is contained is anybody's guess. Now from what we've determined early, it seemed that he commingled, as he's recently done, about a third of the cash for his transaction with high grade counterfeit currency. As we've discussed with Oscar, we can gradually pass this off in Mexico as the real thing. My guess it that he was going for a final big score by rolling the dice and hoping we'd not notice. As we all know, we noticed"!

"So you're saying we haven't suffered a loss", asked Oscar?

"The only loss, is downstairs as far as I can determine", said the accountant!

"We know the numbers of the two safety deposit boxes, just not the identity code needed to access them"!

"You have all his personal papers. They could be easily duplicated in Tijuana for a price, substituting the Zulu Man's face and with some practice duplicating his signature, gain access to his accounts. Of course there is the fact of the two identity codes that only he has in his head"!

"Then it is time, we placed Scylla in charge of getting that information as she has so many times before", said Jorge Mendaca beaming in anticipation. Senor's y Senorita, we will refresh our drinks and retire to the basement.

Scylla, the first to rise was still in her beach attire, the briefest of bikini tops, barely containing her pendulous breasts, the micro bottom concealing virtually nothing to the imagination, covered by the diaphanous bottom sari, tied in a knot upon her hip shod in low heel sandals. All eyes went to her as she, without a word, made her way towards the basement, eagerly followed by the others. Walking beside the family accountant Oscar said, "Try and contain yourself my friend. For soon your eyes will be treated to one of the wonders of the world. Remember, not a word, nor a whimper, for an artiste' is about to commence work"!

Having just emerged from his drug induced stupor, the Boss Man discovered that he lay, naked, face up and spread eagled on a concrete floor. Each hand and leg, tautly shackled to a metal loop stanchion, cemented to the floor. Across his chest, hips and thighs was a leather strap similar to the others, firmly attached to a cemented stanchion on the floor. He struggled to make sense of his current situation, yet his brain still addled by the heroin was still functioning insufficiently to allow fear to overwhelm him. He could make out the fuzzy forms surrounding him just barely, when the vision of an older Mexican peered down into his eyes. It was the old man Mendaca, flanked by his eldest son Oscar. Then coming into view was Scylla and her brother, each with what looked like a fresh Margarita in their hands. The Boss Man struggled to speak, yet his abilities along with a bone dry throat prevented anything resembling a coherent message from coming out.

"I think I know what's the matter", said the elder Mendaca. "Oscar get him some water, for the moment"! After the Boss Man gulped down some long overdue water, his head started to clear slightly and with that his situation crystallized as a fact, as Mendaca started to speak.

"We been doin' business good together for a long time and then one day you start to try an fuck me. You think me and my people are stupido? We never find out? Well we find out and almost everything you got is now ours. Your Capitan's are all dead. Your house is no more. Your whores are dead. Your money now belongs to us and the shipment of 'Jejo', got all blown up. What is left of the Crips, now belong to Scylla and her brother, the Zulu Man. Just one thing is your two safe deposit boxes. We know where they at, we know the number's, we need you to provide each ones access code. You do that and we promise you a quick and painless death. You don't do that and well, that's why Scylla is here", as he slowly turned around and pointed in her direction.

"We all have seen what she can do, from time to time. Once she involved, everyone talk eventually. You know it and we know it. The decision is up to you now"!

The Boss Man knew exactly what Mendaca meant, yet he tried to buy time and sputtered out, "There ain't nothin' left in the safety deposit boxes. I cashed out everthin' for one final score"!

"Then you wouldn't mind telling us what the security codes are for each box so we can see for ourselves", said Mendaca!

"How you know, I'm givin' you the right security codes", stammered the Boss Man, trying in vain to play his final card of a losing hand?

Mendaca looked at his son, then everyone else each in turn slowly, then back at his prisoner saying, "You know, you're right. How will we know that the codes you give us are the right ones"? He walked around a bit then turned saying, "You will either willingly tell us or you won't. Either way makes no difference. Our precious princess is here and is about to provide our evening's entertainment. Scylla, if you will, while the rest of us will be seated"!

Scylla the stepped forward handing her drink to her brother and brought forward the small table, containing two prepared syringes a small towel and what appeared to the others to be scalpels, as she said, "Guys, tonight's entertainment will be just a little different from what you're normally used to. Tonight's not goin' to be hamburger night at the Roxy, but something different. I hope you'll appreciate the artistry"!

That said, she approached her supine prey and stepped over him, each leg flanking his hips and slowly loosened the knot securing the see through sari that only somewhat shielded her lower extremities from view, as it slid from her hips and was discarded. Then she slowly squatted over his now flaccid member saying, "Boys, please observe the science of animal magnetism as I loosen by top", then slowly she reached behind her neck and undid her bikini top strap, then slowly undid the bottom strap as the twin triangles slid from her frame, displaying the finest set of golden globes anyone had ever seen. Then she slowly undid the side strings one at a time, as the last of her vestments, slid from view, still astride her former boss. The she started to sway back and forth over him, her swollen vulva just an inch above his still flaccid member, she whispered, "Now observe the power of animal magnetism", as she still swaying to a mysterious rhythm that ran through her head, his member slowly began to become engorged in blood, slowly rising to meet its unseen obligation, eventually meeting the vulva, only to discover it eluding its reach as Scylla rose slowly higher and higher, hips still swaying, until she and the object of her intentions stood fully erect. She then turned to all assembled saying, "And that boys is how it's done. The flag pole is open for business"! With that she retrieved one of the syringes, injecting its contents all around the base of the fully erect penis. When she finished, she said, "That should keep Herbie, erect for the duration"!

"Animal magnetism", whispered Oscar in apt wonder. She then reached over to the adjacent table and deftly picked up one of the four razor sharp surgical scalpels by her fingertips, delicately pressing its tip an eighth of an inch into his flesh starting from the base of his neck past his shoulders, down the entire length of his arm, stopping at his fingertips leaving a pencil thin trail of blood in its wake. Then repeating the gesture over and over again, each time approximately a half inch distant from its preceding incision, all the while gently swaying back and forth, her throbbing vulva gently brushing his erection over and over, in a devilish deception.

The accountant sitting next to Oscar whispered, "I'd heard only stories of this sort of thing, quickly dismissing them as more legend that fact, but will she really gain the information your father wants"?

"She's never failed us yet my friend", said Oscar continuing. "Yet the information is but a diversion. Our guest we feel is pretty much tapped out financially, as you have suggested. We have the vast majority of what is needed, so anything in the safety deposit boxes is an afterthought not worthy of much pursuit. Besides, who can trust anything from a man who samples his own product to the point of addiction? No, this is our evening's entertainment and a chance to see whether Scylla is a legend or a fact"!

"She doesn't seem to mind her nakedness in the company of men Oscar"! "In fact she relishes it my friend. Look at her. The supreme goddess of Eros working her will upon a mere man humbled to the point of a nonentity. One day he is a commander, guiding his small army of men in pursuit of wealth, when by the turn of a card here he is in his last hours, overturned by circumstance, our prisoner soon to die utterly alone and broke at the hands of a mere woman"!

"I'm not accustomed, to such a display of this nature"!

"Then savor the moment my friend, for few can even imagine what is before our eyes this evening. Something you can tell your sons and grandsons years from now, or not"!

"So the negrito is going to die, for certain"?

"He was a dead man the very moment Scylla and her brother brought him to us"!

"So how long will it take"?

"Probably the entire evening. When she's finished, the entire front and sides of him will be traversed with deep cuts, both vertical and horizontal, each a half inch apart from the other. He will appear as a checker board, only blood red. The death of a thousand cuts, but with her special twist. Soon she will pause for a bit, her body glistening in sweat from her exertions, while the object of her intentions will be glistening in his own blood. She will have a fresh Margarita; father will wipe her down with a towel. Then she will resume. The interesting part will occur gradually. Take note of her as she teases his erection, eventually it will erupt in a climax, although no insertion has occurred. It is if her pussy had the power to draw a man's inner essence from him by only her close proximity"!

"You've seen this before Oscar"?

"Yes, once only. Father never has. It will be a memorable experience for him"! Just then the Boss Man trying to twist and turn unsuccessfully due to the pain he was feeling from each incision as it occurred bellowed,

"Fuck all ya all jive mutha fucka's", gathering up what scant bravado remained as he tried to gather up a mouthful of saliva and coming up empty. "Especially you Mendaca ya mutha fuckin' Spic. I ain't sayin shit at none of ya"!

Calmly, the elder Mendaca then replied, 'We didn't expect you would. Tonight you are entertainment and nothing more"! Scylla, then sensing a break in her subject's spirit, slowly drug her pulsating vulva up from the base of his shaft to the very tip, repeatedly noting his eyes which now were closed as he struggled to contain himself. "Let it go my love and enjoy the moment since it ain't ever gonna come again", as his erection remained subservient to her charms. Then just at the right moment after repeated teasing's, she slowly rose in triumph as his erection started to erupt, as she neatly swung her leg out of the way of its pale effluence accompanied by the grunting protestations of its host. With a flourish and a look of triumph she turned towards the now small crowd of onlookers raising her arms, who greeted her with applause.

As Oscar's father rose to willingly administer refreshment and personally towel of Scylla's glistening body as he'd predicted, Oscar turned towards the accountant and said, "What do you think my friend? Did I overstate"?

Gape jawed in almost disbelief at what he'd just witnessed he answered, "No Jefe, not in the least. Had I not just witnessed this event I could've never believed this could happen"!

"Oh this shouldn't come as any great surprise. For its said that negrito's will erupt early and often at almost anything that moves. Now the real test for Scylla might be if she can replicate her recent triumph on a eunuch"!

"You mean one who has been emasculated"?

"To see that happen would compel me to have a statue 'Erected' in her honor, pardon the pun. In fact I'm thinking about mentioning that very thing to father. Her life size nude icon done in marble would be a most fitting monument for Fathers portico", mused Oscar!

"What is to happen next"?

"A brief interlude of relaxation and then perhaps a grand finale after she thinks she's shredded every available portion of his body. Then she will start to work on his erection with a fresh scalpel in the very same manner. When she's satisfied with her work she will then and only then separate the Boss Man's erection from the rest of him at the base and present it to father, who will place it in a jar of formaldehyde, along with several others for posterity. The Boss Man will scream in pain most likely, and then bleed out. Scylla will have yet another Margarita, go for a late night swim for us all to enjoy while our deceased guest will be taken far out into the pacific, decapitated then thrown overboard for the fish"!

"The question remains Jefe, how was Scylla able to maintain his erection for so long"?

"And the answer to that is a simple, I don't know. Perhaps it is the injection she administered. Perhaps it is the magic of her considerable persona. It just doesn't rank high in my concerns. After all, a woman of her considerable talents must retain some cherished secrets"!

At just short of eleven in the evening Scylla completed her task, presenting the severed organ of the Boss Man, to the elder Mendaca who nodded his head in acceptance of the gift without touching it then without further word, it was placed in a glass container filled with formaldehyde, as the Boss Man slowly bled out the remained of his life's essential fluids. Then two men attached a hose to a spigot and washed the blood out into the drain and monitored his final moments as everyone looked on.

When his heart beat no longer, each of those present approached, looking into the empty eyes of the departed, as the elder Mendaca announced, "Senor's y Senorita. Our work is done. Let us go out on the beach for additional refreshments and some fresh air. Scylla, you will be kind enough to lead the way"!

As the nude Scylla slowly mounted the stairs, clad in only her sandals, Oscar trailed the procession having picked up her discarded bikini and sari, noting the wisdom of his father's pronouncement. Yet another visual blessing for all that followed. While others released the Boss Man from his restraints and zipped him up in a black body bag and muscled him up the stairs and out onto the waiting boat to carry him seaward.

Oscar approached Scylla standing out on the patio watching the television still blaring the latest remaining snippets of news of events up north, while drinking yet another Margarita.

"I thought I'd bring your suit for you to put on for your swim Scylla"! Finishing the last of her drink in a flourish she took the suit then placed it on the table saying, "Now why would you do that? I'd only have to take it off again wouldn't I"?

Then she slowly walked away towards the roaring surf, for her evening ritual as Oscar turned around to the others saying, "Caballeros, this evening we have all been blessed"!

In the days that followed, Scylla and the Zulu Man went back to Los Angeles, both rounding up the newly minted Lieutenants of the restructured Crips organization eliminating a remaining few of the old guard felt to be untrustworthy. While down south, several competitors, namely the rival 'Bloods' and the Latino 'VVS', (an acronym for the Vato Vikings) tried to quickly encroach upon the 'Crips' territory. The Zulu Man knowing the completion, quickly farmed out a number of hit contracts to competent people, offering twice the going rate, to eliminate the key members of the competition in a very visible way, thus sending a message.

Operating chiefly with much of the Boss Mans money, much of which was the high quality bogus bills, both he and Scylla, quickly spread bonuses around to key people, thus gaining instant loyalty for the time being. One of which was the "Pussy Man", who prided himself of having a posse' of the finest 'Quifs' in southern California. He was quickly recruited and folded into the organization for the price of fifty thousand cash money. With Scylla's help all of his women were interviewed one by one by the trio of Scylla, her brother and their own Pussy Man. For several more problems had to be eliminated before progress could occur unhindered. One was a defense lawyer, long successful in the behalf of the underworld, yet as of late appeared to have lost his MoJo in behalf of the last eight clients convicted and serving time. What made things most offensive, was that his high fee, was all paid in advance regardless of the outcome.

Then there were two judges in the system that we're thought to be long since bought and paid for. For years they had served various purposes well, acting rather liberally in behalf of the accused, much to the chagrin of the prosecution. Yet as late it seemed they'd had an epiphany of sorts, sending various gang members off to prison for very long incarcerations. It just seemed that when someone was bought and paid for, they should stay bought and paid for regardless. It has been said that every man has a weakness, thus it was long known it certain circles that all three objects of the Zulu Man's intentions, had an affinity for the ladies, of spectacular proportions. Thus at the going rate of five thousand dollars each, three of those selected were carefully instructed as precisely how to play their parts in a given scenario of seduction and abduction. Within the space of seventy two hours, each man ended up in a stolen car well north of Interstate 10 somewhere off the beaten path, stark naked, save for his pants gathered about his ankles, with his male member stuffed into his mouth. Of course they'd each gone missing from work without a word of warning, with eventually the police being brought into investigate, a missing person. A month or so after each of their disappearances, a separate video tape of each individual quite suddenly appeared to every Southern California TV station every week for three weeks, showing the subject engaging in a sexual act with a fully nude woman of unknown identity in the passenger seat of a vehicle. Nothing more. Nine months later passing hikers discovered the first of the three bodies located in what later proved to be a stolen car driven deep into the Big Maria Mountains near the California Arizona border. The body had decayed quite a bit during the interim, yet investigators found it interesting that the remnants of his male organ was placed neatly inside his oral cavity. It would be some years before all three of the bodies were discovered in the wilderness.

Within a ten day period all of the designated people had left this mortal plane of existence, to take up their eternal residence in the next. Money well spent, as the elder Mendaca always said. "Dinero and the promise of more, is the tie that binds"!

Days later, Scylla and her brother again joined the Mendaca's at the family compound in Ensenada for dinner. During dinner the elder Mendaca rose to propose a toast to both Scylla and her brother for the masterful way they had eliminated not only the competition, but put to rest a mote in the eyes of the legal system on their side of the border, as he added, "We are all millions to the good with much more to be laid at our feet. And now I once again salute Dona Scylla, in the masterful way she dispatched her former Boss Man. The image of which will last in our minds far beyond our years"!

As he caught sight of his eldest son Oscar he added, "In memory of that moment in time I ask Scylla for one favor for an old man"!

"Ask away Jefe", said Scylla smiling.

"I wish to send away to Madrid for their finest sculptor, at my expense, to come here so he can sculpt you in all of your glory full sized in the finest Sicilian Marble, which will occupy a prominent place in this Casa"!

"So you want me to pose for the guy naked. Are that what you're asking"?

"Yes, Scylla"!

"If it'd make you happy Don Mendaca, then I'd be glad to pose for your sculptor, as long as it doesn't interfere with business"!

"We will see to it that it doesn't", said a beaming Mendaca, noting in his mind that her answer was precisely what he expected. The business at hand always taking priority. As the dinner continued on, the Zulu Man and Scylla exchanged glances and they both exchanged a nod as her brother spoke to the elder Mendaca. "Me and Scylla, we been talkin', an we got something we wanna run past ya"!

"Por favor, continue", nodded Mendaca.

Facing the elder Mendaca squarely, the Zulu Man started, "This is it, Scylla an me got most of the distribution of Jejo in most of LA. What's left of the Bloods got some, the Bikers, the Orientals and an assortment of Latino gangs got the rest. Your people got San Diego. Now Frisco, Portland and Seattle are all split up between the Orientals and the biker gangs. Now we wanna expand east, eventually, sooner not later. Back east they got the Italians, Jamaicans, Russians and Cajuns all makin' money at our expense. Now before, we mention this to the Boss Man and he just didn't wanna hear anything about it, so now we wanna run it past you and get your thoughts along with advice. Of course you would be our only source of supply and to insure that, we'd have to be partners. From what we can see if we don't do this, someone else will sooner or later"!

"Young man the reasons that others stay put are many. To expand into another's territory would mean war amongst ourselves and that would be bad for business under most circumstances"! "But Jefe, you saw how we handled ourselves in our take over and the elimination of the lawyer and the judges", Scylla insisted!

"I'll give you that my dear. You did very well and displayed skill and talent that was quite unexpected, which is why I'm even entertaining your proposal. Yet there is much to consider still. The Juarista's, those in Monterrey and then the Matamoros Cartel, not to mention the Columbians and the Jamaican Posse', each in turn will be greatly disturbed by your encroachment and will strike back hard"!

"Not if you cut off the head as well as the hands before they know what hit em", injected the Zulu Man. We've done it before and we can do it again"!

"Ah yes, the exuberant confidence of youth", said Mendaca rising as he relit his cigar and walked around thinking. Then he stopped, turned as looked at his son Oscar saying, "What do you think Oscar"!

Choosing his next words carefully, "What they say has merit father, for that has also crossed my mind in the past. To tell the truth I'd never given it much thought past the obvious obstacles you've pointed out. To expand would mean a war of sorts, to greater or lesser degrees. Something the authorities on both sides of the border would eagerly want to see, us fighting amongst ourselves, so they could pick us off one by one, infiltrating our ranks with spies eventually. If there was a way to accomplish this and stay below the radar I'd be for a measured expansion. Other than that", his voice trailed off into silence.

The elder Mendaca then resumed his seat and said, "Your plans have merit, yet are fraught with risks. Immeasurable risks for all of us. To the degree, these risks are identified and solutions provided for the good of all of us, then and only then will a prudent plan of expansion be possible. There is still time to consider and plan. Are we agreed"?

Scylla and her brother both nodded their heads in silence, as Mendaca added, "I will always be open to ideas as to how we can enrich ourselves as long as it is well thought out and planned. For my part, Oscar and I will start to investigate the possibilities on our end. Of that you have my assurance. We will talk again of this matter"!

As the evening wore on Mendaca was pleased as he steepled his hands in apparent thought. These two negritos proved highly resourceful and energetic. If their brains matched their cojones, then perhaps things could be accomplished. He and Oscar would stay in the shadows allowing them to apply all of the energy of youthful exuberance to the task at hand. If things didn't work out as planned, then it would be they who would suffer the consequence. His Columbian supplier was after him anyway to expand his horizons, so perhaps if planned well this might be exactly the time to expand. Solidify your base and remove the riff raff. If things went as planned, the only enemy left would be the governments and history proved they could either be brought or killed. Plomo y plata. Better to have ones enemies in front of you than all around you. Yes, things were coming together. Perhaps a new Genesis was in store for all. With two young smart, energetic, fearless and completely ruthless negritos, bound to Mendaca by something almost as good as a blood tie. Gratitude and the knowledge of necessity, plus the element of personal chemistry. They already viewed him as a father figure and he would expand upon that as much as possible from two different peoples from disparate backgrounds. Yes an expansionist union with the negritos would provide a maximum return with minimum risk. He and Oscar would start to make plans, yet as of the moment he wanted to sink the hook of common union and dependence just a little deeper.

But for the moment he just had to secure the services of a master sculptor from the old country. The sooner he had a life sized marble monument of Scylla in his Casa, the better.

24

Time passed and the 'Crips' gradually expanded across America, with an occasional boost from the Mendaca clan. Scylla, her commitment to the elder Mendaca partially completed, with a life sized alabaster Sicilian Marble likeness of her clad in only a wry smile gracing the front vestibule of Mendaca's Hacienda in Ensenada, there to greet one and all.

As they expanded with measured swiftness eastward into cities and towns in the middle and southern part of the nation alliances were quickly forged when necessary and when not an option, key people simply disappeared without a trace. Their operations taken over with the swiftness of a hostile corporate takeover. Plomo y Plata was the by word. Either take the lead in the form of a bullet or take the silver in the form of money and an alliance. As with any cancerous growth the primary expansion went largely unheralded. As key people disappeared, there was always some ready and eager to step up and fill the void. Should they prove incapable or untrustworthy, there was always another waiting in the wings. The world continued to turn and the Crips were ready in the shadows to fulfill America's need for recreational drugs at a price.

Often the competition found itself victim by one of its own having turned on them in a moment of weakness, with several smaller reenactments of the shootout on I-15 taking place, to showcase the effectiveness of the law enforcement community for one and all. Of course in every area of interest, a skilled yet deeply flawed lawyer was discovered to act in their best interests as well as a judge or two to ensure a desired outcome. All were paid handsomely yet discretely. Yet unknown to each were irrefutable records of transactions kept just in case they had a moment of epiphany. In case anyone had a change of heart, there were always the family members to consider. It would be a shame if anything untoward happened to them. Thus once one became part of the team, the unseen 'Sword of Damocles' hung heavy over their heads.

From time to time a certain visceral message had to be sent, to make a visible statement to fall in line quickly or suffer the same fate. Each time the method of dispatch was varied, in order to vary a certain modus operandi for the authorities. The seeming randomness of the various messages we're such that local authorities were unable to connect the dots as to the originators of the isolated killings, rare as they were. In each case great care was taken to avoid collateral damage to any innocent civilians, with the only harm occurring to a known criminal with an extensive rap sheet. Little emphasis was placed upon these killings, with each in time, rolling over unnoticed into the "Unsolved" file, to grow dust awaiting any future developments that never surfaced.

From time to time, the authorities made spectacular arrests, but never of the 'Crips', whose cancerous growth continued unabated. While other organizations sported a very visible persona, with jackets and baseball caps and the plethora of tattoos adorned and illuminated their identity, the Crips operated in the shadows, relentless and making an obscene amount of money.

Yet as with all things concerning expansion came the eventual resultant dissolution of talent and discipline, as the cognomen of the Crips evolved into a visible presence on the streets in the standard form of ball caps and jackets emblazoned with a an oversized skull and instead of crossed bones, were crossed syringes. True, the Crips were the Alphas of the illegal drug world, but certain elements of their organization began to trumpet themselves on the street to others signifying themselves as the masters of all they surveyed, never to be fucked with. Not very smart to make oneself a target for others, yet who would listen? To sport a Crips jacket was to make an unspoken statement the wearer was "One Baaad Son of a Bitch"! Never to be taken lightly. Of course that wasn't always the case, especially regarding those who were badly beaten or killed for their 'Crips' emblazoned clothing. In some cases a given article of clothing changed owners several times in the course of a year, with all of the previous owners either dead, or if they were lucky, hospitalized for an extended stay, only to emerged damaged for life.

In one case, a particular jacket changed ownership seventeen times. All within a twenty block radius of Oakland California within a single year, with only two of the former owners surviving. Each time the jacket in question changed hands, it developed several more bullet holes, which of course were proudly displayed by its new owner for its brief period of ownership. By now, the jacket in question was almost useless as an article of covering, yet highly coveted, by both the criminal and wannabe criminal elements of the various minority communities.

To sport a well weathered 'Crips' jacket was almost akin to those in the know, of a newly minted "Mafiosi" who'd just "made his bones", the implication of which was the wearer obtained the article of clothing by brute force. To sport a bullet riddled 'Crips' jacket implied the wearer was an Alpha Male and one who relished the role as a walking target. One who for certain had a death wish that usually was granted sooner rather than later. Yet in spite of itself or perhaps because of itself, the Crips organization was an elusive entity both above and below the line of visibility.

Thus for the better part of a decade the 'Crips' operated at will, expanding their operations wherever the opportunity presented itself, bringing a dark cohesion to an area that had only knew previous chaos. The simple way of knowing the presence of the Crips close at hand, was after a sudden spate of violence and killings statistically in a given area, suddenly plunging to zero within a short period of time. With the dark cohesion came a certain 'Pax Americana' to a given community. Of course after a brief period, came a rise in robberies and burglaries in the very same area. How else were the addicted, going to be able to afford their drugs, with no visible means of support?

As for those who joined the Crips came a forced discipline not previously known. The discipline of paying ones bills promptly and completely. Justice was swift and permanent, not subject to any negotiation. To go short on a Crips was to risk one's life and that of any family close at hand. They'd take all of the money, along with any real property of value. Rare as it was, entire families were known to vanish from the face of the earth. Of course, they generally weren't of much tangible value to begin with, with the very young almost certain to mature to be a trouble to society at large, sooner or later. Just the Almighty's way of thinning out the herd.

Yet as in all things, change was certain to occur from unknown directions. A hurricane began to drift northward, from deep within the bowels of the Caribbean existence. The hurricane took the form in the "Rastafarians" of the "Jamaican Posse". Dread locked lunatics even more Draconian in their purpose. Plying their deadly trade, spilling out of the poverty ridden ghettos of Kingston Jamaica and Port Au Prince Haiti, like a horde of Brazilian Army ants spreading fear, hate and destruction wherever they surfaced. For those who dreaded doing business with the Columbians, the Jamaican Posse was even worse, as they went where they wanted, took what they wanted. Anything that caught their fancy, regardless, was theirs. In their minds only the weak tried to bargain or negotiate, over a given thing. Through a greater quotient of fear, power and mortal influence, their collective power and authority began to grow in the southern belly of America at a geometric rate. In time few wanted to do business with them and only as a last resort of desperation or as a result of superior intimidation did one risk a transaction and certainly at their designated rate of exchange, counting themselves fortunate to survive the encounter, for they indeed moved an extraordinary mountain of product northward and in spite of the risks involved there was money to be made, by working with them rather than against them or even worse ignoring them. With the Posse', the prudent simply built a mountain of precautions during any transaction and on turf of one's own choosing.

Speaking a bastardized, sing song, barely discernible patois of the Kings English, the Posse' grew to have designs on mainland America as their future domain and therein lay the rub. Gangs were already in place to distribute and sell the Jejo, earning untold millions off the backs of American addictions. Eventually inroads were made through Miami, Jacksonville, New Orleans and Houston as these cities became bloody battlefields for control of the illegal drug business.

For too long a time, the Posse' tolerated the Columbian Carlos Lehder when he operated out of his own bought and paid for private island safe haven in the Bahama Islands. At that point in time, Lehder was their sole source of supply, of Cocaine and Heroin, having invested his money well in the Bahamas', insuring that key politicians, judges and the constabulary were never in need of a single thing of a material nature, thus turning a blind eye on his activities. There was almost as much air traffic out of his small island airstrip, as there was out of Nassau's airport, but mostly after dark.

When the US Government put Carlos Lehder out of business, for a lifetime of Federal incarceration without possibility of parole, the Posse' simply stepped in filling the void and the world kept on turning. Old contacts were renewed and the flow of money to the grateful locals continued unabated. Of course certain cleansings were bound to occur amongst the brethren as the Posse' grew as competent talent was hard to come by. But as long as few innocents weren't caught up in the melee, the authorities, with burdensome workloads of easier to prosecute crimes gave these events a cursory investigation and little more.

Yet a signature of the Posse's involvement in a given locale, was the sudden increase of bodies discovered in vacant fields, washed up on river banks, dead in abandoned vehicles, places of business, or in their residences, victims of home invasions, badly mutilated prior to their demise. Women or children were no exception.

As the Crips and the Posse' began to abrade each other, the casualty count grew to unsustainable proportions for both, eventually the talent pool of competent leaders and shooters began to wane as several years of constant abrasion started to take its toll. Then out of the blue the head of the Posse' sent word out to the Crips leadership, offering a truce. The "Why's" were reasonably clear for it was apparent the Crips source of manpower was endless, given their seemingly endless sources of big city ghetto manpower, while the Rastafarian Posse was not. Being a Rastafarian was a quasi-religious experience and lifestyle common to the underclass of the Caribbean existence, in many cases. Drawing mainly from the Island of Jamaica, namely Kingston in particular and secondarily from Ghettos of Port au Prince in Haiti, the Posse's manpower supply grew thin. The Posse' usually inflicted the greater amount of casualties per incident given their unique protection and greater capacity of sheer firepower, and their willingness to take everything to the limit and beyond.

Going down to the last man standing with all guns blazing till the final bullet.

Young men ever faithful to the 'Ganja weed' and the 'Baron Samedie', the Prince of Darkness, would enter full of hope, bravado and little else, smuggling and distributing the 'Product' into the States, never to return to their homeland, ending up as food for the worms before too many months had passed.

Eventually Zulu Man accepted the truce and set up a meeting with the Posse's leadership, the dread locked "Hoo Doo Chile" on supposedly neutral territory just outside of Santa Fe, New Mexico. In addition to their nationwide struggle for supremacy with the Posse', the Crips were still in a constant state of conflict with the resurgent 'Bloods', as well as an assortment of Mexican, Central American and Biker gangs, all vying for a greater slice of the pie. A dizzying array of temporary alliances came and went between the parties, proving that yesterday's enemy, might be today's friend, reverting back to yesterday's enemy tomorrow.

Thus the fateful decision to partner up with the Hoo Doo Chile, for the time being, he gave them room to breathe once again and rearm. Knowing of their reputation of fearlessness and utter ruthlessness, far beyond even his seemingly limitless capabilities, the Zulu Man committed to a partnership, he vowed to abandon at the earliest opportunity, for he had a deal for them even they would be foolish to refuse. A new form of manufactured chemical dependence that was unknown and at the present not illegal.

Of course, the Mendaca clan could never know of this, for he knew they'd never approve whereas the source of the new "Product" was not from them, thus breaking their long held agreement and inviting both his and Scylla's death. He further knew the Hoo Doo Chile would go after him at his earliest opportunity. It got down to who would strike first and hardest and when. Once he eliminated the Rastafarians he was certain he could make peace with the Mendaca's. An error only encountered by those shortsighted and full of hubris.

Before he could go to Oscar Mendaca for additional firepower, but not now. There was Ortega in Houston that could be brought in to deal with the Rasta's. Besides, it was Ortega that had gotten him interested in 'Crystalline'.

Although initially it was a tough sell, his sister Scylla eventually relented, but not before urging him to consider the Mendaca Clan. Once the involvement with the Posse' was discovered, the relationship with the Mendaca Clan would be finished, which had meant so much to the Crips in time. For a host of reasons the Mexicans and the Rastafarians had a hatred for each other. The Mexicans viewed their Rastafarian Voodoo lifestyle and methods of doing business as an eternal abomination. Scylla argued that one could not be in bed with the Rasta's and the Mendaca Clan simultaneously whereas the Mendaca people were never known to break their word, while the Rastafarians were rarely known to keep theirs.

Yet blood was thicker than water and Scylla vowed she would stick with her brother and brazen things through to the bitter end.

The initial meeting with the Rasta's went reasonably well, held in a ranch house far from the outskirts of Santa Fe. There the fearsome looking Hoo Doo Chile, along with his entourage, that made his appearance and took the measure of both Scylla and her brother. There he was introduced to the viability and profitability of the new Crystalline that was certain to make everyone countless millions. Thus a deal was struck to include Ortega's organization as far as the initial small buy along with a normal Cocaine buy given the DEA had put a temporary crimp in the Rasta's supply line. Scylla would go along to act as an honest broker in the Rastafarian's behalf. She'd done this many times before for the Mendaca's and her brother, given her inexplicable ability to read the buyers intentions during the transaction. Other than that, she was contracted from time to time for her abilities to solve issues of interrogation and execution. She always got the truth out of the most recalcitrant individuals and they always failed to survive her efforts, taking with them to whatever form of afterlife, an eternal memory. She was good at what she did because she enjoyed her work.

During the struggles to obtain dominance in the States, the Posse' discovered a new source of manpower as the Government of Haiti began to crumble with the eventual overthrow of the Duvalier family. First with the death of the Dictator Papa Doc, then later with the removal from power and exile of his son Baby Doc, members of the dictator's secret police, the Ton Ton Macoute', needed work. So they were gradually absorbed into the Posse' where possible. Of course initially there were communication problems, since few of the Ton Ton Macoute' spoke English and few of the Posse' spoke any French at all. Yet when it came to ruthlessness they proved their worth well eventually overcoming the communications problem in fits and starts. The assimilation of the newbies was hastened by their mutual belief in the rituals of the bastardized religion of Santeria and their embrace of the mystical underworld of the 'Baron Samedie', the Prince of Darkness. Longer than shoulder length dreadlocks, clad in long ankle length black, Kevlar lined, leather coats was their trademark wherever they went, seeking confrontation, because their religion stated they were already dead, thus need not fear death.

Under the iron handed control of the "Hoo Doo Chile", the Posse' grew quickly in strength and influence, like a cancer throughout the Southern Gulf Coast States. One of many problems the Federal authorities had was their ability to weed out the weak amongst them making them impervious to internal penetration, for the purpose of prosecution. All of them escaped any possibility of incarceration, for they all went down in a hail of bullets, whenever things came to that. Yet many survived a confrontation thanks to their Kevlar lined coats. Only magnum sized shells, or head shots were certain to bring them down, other than that bring your lunch, for the shoot- out is going to take a while.

In the days to come, the Zulu Man became increasingly uneasy regarding his recent decision to wean himself away from the Mendaca's and do business with the Posse'. He had this feeling that his organization was slowly slipping from his grasp and there was little he could do about it, never mind that he was literally awash in cash. Everyone around him was doing better than ever and had more money than they knew what to do with. Everyone was looking for ways to stash their money. Things had never been better, even for the Mendaca's over the border. Everyone was smiles and yet the paranoia of doom was gradually taking over his life. Still whenever he was in the company of others, he kept up the eminent front, reasoning to himself that paranoia was just nature's way of bringing on "Complete Awareness".

After a few transactions, the Zulu Man promised himself to eliminate the Hoo Doo Chile at the earliest opportunity. "Cut off the head of the snake and the body dies", he reasoned, disregarding all the Voodoo mumbo jumbo he'd heard about from others. In the meanwhile, no matter what happened, it was vitally important the Mendaca Clan never learn of his move with the Rastafarians. For they were not known as a forgiving group and would view his business with the Rasta's as akin to treachery and then he'd be at war with everyone.

Yet in the past year, he'd done some significant deals with this Ortega operating out of Houston. He apparently had a source of the Jejo from South America, independent of the Columbians that the Mendaca's had exclusive dealing with. It was through Ortega that he would cement his relationship with the Rasta's and Scylla would prove the catalyst, as she always had done in the past. After he finished off the Rasta's and their Voodoo business, perhaps he'd sic Scylla on this Ortega and move to Houston. If he could accomplish that then there was little the Mendaca's could do for him or to him. Paulo Sabastiani looked at Lo Phat after disconnecting from the call with Ortega. He related the disturbing news of the apparent alliance of the Crips with the Jamaican Posse. The rumors were now a reality. Sabastiani and Lo Phat represented two powerful entities of organized crime, the Chicago Syndicate and the Seattle branch of the "Golden Dragon" Triad, based out of Tai Pei in the Island of Taiwan. They both agreed the pending deal for the new drug "Crystalline" was far too important to ignore. They'd both seen demonstrations of its effectiveness and came to conclusions as to its profitability. There were only upsides to this product once it was in hand. Easily transportable and currently unknown to the authorities and arriving in a highly concentrated form. But the real killer was that it left no chemical trace or residue in a subject's body. So even if it was eventually declared illegal, good luck to any entity to try and prove ingestion after the fact, for prosecution. The downside was that it couldn't be chemically duplicated, or so they were told.

"Do you trust this Ortega completely", asked Lo Phat of Sabastiani?

"I don't even trust my mother completely. But as of now, I've no reason not to. Done three deals with Ortega's people of sizeable weight in the last two years and they all went off without a problem. He is as advertised and a serious player. Now we never did anything like this before, which is why my people wanted me to bring your people in on this, to spread the risk initially"!

"Paulo, we both go back a long way and have both done much profitable business together. But this deal has both of our 'chops', on the line. Should things go wrong, our profitable past will be immediately forgotten. The fortune cookie's will have no writing on them"!

"Yeah, I know Lo Phat. Ten Atta boys equal one oh shit", said Sebastian! "Same thing with my people"!

"Of course I'll have to make my people in the east aware of the news of the Jamaican's participation", said Lo Phat. After much consternation, my Mandarin's probably still go through with the deal seeing only the upside profits, but expecting further monetary guarantees from the both of us"!

"Seems the Genie has gotten out of the bottle and we're both in it now up to our necks. We'll just have to bring along extra insurance to guarantee delivery, for when one sits down to dinner with a rabid Tiger it's easy to become his dinner. But I'm not going to lose any sleep over this brother, because Ortega's people are all pros and they've convinced me they're in it for the long haul. His quality has always been as expected and his prices in line with others and he's reliable", answered Sabastiani.

"Your point is made Paulo, but I suggest we arrive a little earlier than usual and of course with greater protection than usual, at the drop site, given the possible presence of the Rastafarians. Where is the drop site by the way"?

"Looks good on the map, in the middle of nowhere", said Paulo unfolding a map of Texas. A place called Menard County Texas. Miles away from Bum Fuck Egypt. Good roads according to the map out of the area and nothing but cows and coyotes otherwise. I got a written set of directions as to how to get there. Some long abandoned area on the south bank of this San Saba River. So looks like I'm gonna have to wear my alligator Nocona cowboy boots on this one"! "So your personally going along to Shepard the deal through", said Lo Phat!

"I am now pal. Just to keep the spades in line, besides this is gonna be the biggest deal we've ever done together, so you can tell your people as I'll tell mine if it doesn't happen as advertised, they won't have to bother coming after me, cause I'll be dead right along a whole lotta spooks"!

As they both poured over the map of far central Texas they placed a magnifying glass over Menard County eventually Sabastiani concluding, "A one horse county with apparently good single lane roads in and out in all directions. We'll meet up with some people in Dallas, they'll provide a recently stolen panel Van with all of the right papers and me and my guys'll follow it down to the transfer site. After the deal is done, we'll call you on the cell phone and meet with you at our agreed upon site in north east New Mexico, just west of Raton, for the split"!

"Agreed", said Lo Phat who then asked, "How many men are you going to bring to the party"?

"I'm thinking six men in all, each with a short barreled twelve gauge auto shotgun should keep everyone honest"!

"We have two days to prepare", said Lo Phat emphatically!

25

After Ortega's phone meeting with Sabastiani and Lo Phat, Ortega called Nestor to find out how things were going with the loading of the overly large panel truck with the Crystalline and Scylla's state of health. Scylla's presence was to guarantee things would go smoothly between parties. At least that was the plan.

Things were on track, with the large panel truck being rented in Junction City, by Davalantes, using an easily obtained false driver's license and credit cards, their usage being a one off thing. In addition Davalantes brought along one of the newly acquired young Panamanian thugs to provide extra manpower, since things were stretched pretty thin.

"We gotta big problem here", said Ortega to Magellan, explaining their collective problem with Jaeger.

"So Meyers is in Houston, with the cash expecting the Embraer plans to be delivered. Jaeger has them and is angry that you betrayed him in Sao Paulo and is holding you up for big bucks", Nestor fed back to Ortega over the phone. "Is that the situation"?

"Yeah. The Vato, he cross me up", hissed Ortega!

"Just one question Jefe. Why did you set Jaeger up to be killed? The times I worked with him, he proved himself a valuable and reliable asset"?

"Because he piss me off Nestor"!

"Then why did you ever bring him on board"?

"Cause he piss me off an I decide to bring him in to keep an eye on him. Use him up then throw him away and it's none of your business why I do things. Jus do what I tell you and we all get along"!

"Jefe, as your Segundo, anything that affects you and our operations is my business. Now we have to concentrate on two things at once, when we should be focused on only one. This development could jeopardize all else that we have in the works. Do you want me to come back to Houston to help out"?

"No Nestor", said Ortega wearily. You stay there with the new kid, the Panamanian and send Davalantes back Pronto, so when we meet up with that fuck, we gonna make him into Chorizo"!

"Just as long as it's after the exchange of the Embraer documents with Carlos Meyers. I needn't remind you that if that exchange doesn't occur, there will be nowhere in the world that any of us can hide"!

"You never mind about that. When things over here, I send Davalantes back, quick pronto with enough shooters to help you in Menard County. You got the Jamaican's, the Crips an the Chicago Seattle bunch to deal with. I not leave you hangin'"!

After he hung up with Ortega, Magellan stared out on to the rocky out croppings behind the barn and became deep in thought. Perhaps it was time to sever his relationship with Ortega and even Meyers, after this was concluded. Ortega was becoming increasingly unstable as of late and this unnecessary business with Jaeger was a stupid and senseless interruption. And for what? To satisfy ones ego, at a crucial moment? Clearly Meyers had to be aware of this and to sanction, or even tacitly go along with this was a demonstration of poor judgment, regardless of how brilliant Meyers had been in the past.

He'd stashed enough money and still had his papers. He could go back to Paris. Possibly reconnect with some of his old mates. Hopefully the ghost of Madeleine's memory would have faded and he could make a life for himself. Yet one had to give the devil its due. Carlos Meyers had pulled off some magnificent coups in the past.

The Russian submarine and its subsequent voyage was a masterpiece and as far as he knew, no one was the wiser, for its continual use at a later date. The assemblage of the Bolivian and Peruvian growers into his camp under the very noses of their Columbian keepers was even more formidable. And as far as is known the Columbians and the Mexicans are still unaware of the existence of competition. Now finally the Embraer coup was of even greater brilliance and to allow an act of pure hubris was criminal to the enterprise.

Magellan had been in the business of being, 'on the edge'; to know that it only took one failure, to wipe out years of effort. Ortega had double crossed Jaeger who was out there angry and alert. Somehow he bested Santos and Obregon, real pros of long standing, indicating that everyone had underestimated him. When all of this was finished, he'd simply disappear. He'd have the time and the resources to be selective for the first time in his life.

As Davalantes approached, he said, "You talk to the Jefe, Nestor"?

"Yeah. Got the message. Soon as your people get the last of the selected Crystalline above ground and the rest covered up underground, you gotta drive like hell and get back to Houston for the Jaeger thing. Then soon as you can get out to Menard County before our guests arrive two days from now. We have to get your men well in place before the guests show up"!

"Answer me this Nestor. Why we doin' business with the nappy headed Rastas. It's like we askin' for trouble"!

"The question I asked Ortega exactly and you been with him longer than I have"!

"Why he try an fuck Jaeger? I was just startin' to like the guy. He always hold up his end"!

"Same answer my friend. Ya gotta answer for yourself. Am I better off working for Ortega, as his pistolero, or better off working for those south of the Rio Grande"?

"How you say Nestor? A Hobson's Choice"?

"Just remember when this is all done, everything eventually comes to an end"!

"You gonna be alright here with the other Panamanian and Scylla"?

"We were Ok before you got here and we'll be Ok after you leave. Just handle your business with Jaeger, then get over to the site in Menard County in time"!

An hour later, Davalantes and the others departed for Houston in a cloud of dust, down the single track trail to the main road. Magellan joined the young Panamanian pistolero finishing up loading the large panel van with the remainder of the large plastic barrels containing the Crystalline concentrate.

Still spread-eagled and secure across the hay bales was the partially naked Scylla. The blanket had again slipped off her prostrate body revealing once again her considerable charms. Magellan, in spite of himself, felt a stirring in his loins. It had been quite a while since he'd bedded anyone. Each time a disaster, the memory of Madeleine still lingered like an albatross across his libido. Yet there she was, apparently vulnerable, but when one considered the trail of corpses she'd left behind, common sense took firm hold over any animalistic appeals.

As the newly arrived Panamanian 'Bravo' approached, Magellan wondered whether or not he'd whither in the event they came under fire. He was told that he was a shooter and nothing more. That covered a lot of ground, most of which was swamp. The real test was if he was disciplined enough to be aware of his surroundings and to be one with the others. Most shooters weren't. They never lasted long. All Magellan wanted was for his Panamanian to last long enough. The first signal was the way he stared at Scylla, with undisguised lust.

"Don't even think about it", said Magellan. She's killed far more men than the years you've been alive. She's bartering material only, a hostage to guarantee that nothing goes wrong. She escapes, and then you'll deal with me. Think of it this way. When this is all over, you'll have more money in your pocket than you knew existed and can buy a hundred of the finest whores in Texas"! Seeing that the look of desire had not yet left his face, he grabbed the youngster by his long ponytail and in Spanish said, "Pay close attention for your life and those of others depends upon it"!

"Rule number one. You never shit where you eat". Then he turned his face towards the supine Scylla saying, "See that! She is nothing more than a piece of meat to us. Any thoughts other than that will get us both killed"!

"Rule number two. Never underestimate anyone or anything. Always assume the worst. Anything less than that will get us both killed"!

"The very last rule is, I say, you do, immediately and without question. The answers will make themselves known. Do these things and you may survive and prosper. Do anything else and I will kill you myself, immediately and without explanation. Que Sabe Hombre"?

"Si Senor Magellan", answered the frightened teen, his eyes wide open. "All she's good for is bartering material. She is a very dangerous Mujerita. I do what you say all the time and stay alert"!

"Bueno" said Magellan. "Now go get some food for us all, for mid-day tomorrow we leave for up country"!

After he'd finished talking with Magellan, Ortega got up from his desk and began to pace the room. The pressure of too many events going wrong was finally starting to work its magic on his mind. "Gotta do something about that Magellan", he said to himself. "He getting too big for his pants, tryin' to tell me about my business. He be a good man, but nobody gonna talk to me like that. Gonna have to straighten him out after all this done. Gonna be a busy time the next couple of days"!

Just then, the door to his den opened and in walked a smiling Carlos Meyers, escorted by Rocha, his personal bodyguard and Ochoa one of Ortega's men. Rocha the blade, he was called. Raised in the slums of Mendoza Argentina, he'd no use for firearms, thinking the use of such was for lesser men, trusting his fortune and survival to his mastery of the blade.

Rocha was of medium height, slight of build and sported the pretty boy face of a male model, which usually invited the bravos to make a fatal mistake in challenging his manhood. He usually said little at all times, his eyes constantly shifting everywhere; content to stand in the background unless summoned by events.

"Good Morning my friend", offered Meyers cheerfully offering his hand to Ortega, who clasped it asking, "Your trip was pleasant"?

"Uneventful, yet eager to conclude our Embraer business and return to Buenos Aires. And you"?

'We gotta problem Carlos"! "How so my friend"?

"That fuck Jaeger. He still alive. Killed, Santos, Obrigon an Bujo, in Sao Paulo. He beat us to the Post Boxes an he got all the Embraer plans an my money"!

"Spilt Milk my friend"!

"Que? What is this spilt milk"? "Spilt Milk my friend. This Jaeger takes out some of your best men, thinning out your ranks considerably"!

"Just at the time when the Crystalline deal is close at hand. Does Magellan know of this"? "I just got off the phone with him. Davalantes and the others are on the road back to us and should be here later this afternoon. Soon as we finish Jaeger off I send them back west to help Magellan. Inna mean time he almost set to leave Val Verde and head to the transfer point. He get there early an set up, then Davalantes an the others show up and we prepare for the buyers"!

"So the question remains. Why didn't you wait until after our business was concluded, if this Jaeger was such a bother"!

"Now you startin' to sound like Nestor", shot back Ortega angrily. I got people all over town looking. Either we find him or he find us. Either way we gonna meet, then you get what you want, I get what I want, and that Vato, Jaeger, he get what he deserve"!

"How long has he been back in town"? "Couple of days I think"!

"With several days to prepare, he could've done anything with the Embraer documents. Have you spoken to him yet"?

"We almost had him a few hours ago, but he got away and I just spoke to him again. We got a place to meet later on down at one of my places far out in Jamaica Beach. I'm just waiting for Davalantes to get back, then we go get him"!

"I need not remind you of the equally essential nature of the Embraer documents to the survival of us all, compared to the Crystalline sales to the gangsters. The gangs could always have been put off for days or even weeks, yet you choose to go ahead as scheduled. Should we fail in the deliverance to the Argentines, the future for each and every one of us, will be a bleak one indeed. The resources of the Argentine Military will be dedicated to our destruction", concluded Meyers irritably!

"Yeah, I know. Nestor, he already remind me"!

"Look my friend, I'm just as culpable as you are in this business, from beginning to the end. I went along with your plan to eliminate this fellow Jaeger in Sao Paulo after the business at hand was concluded. Clearly that was a mistake. Somehow Jaeger saw through things. But considering events, just why did you want to eliminate him"?

Clearly agitated at the point of his partners critical questioning, Ortega turned and suddenly started towards Meyers saying loudly, "Cause he piss me off and that's all you need to know"!

As Ortega moved towards Meyers, his bodyguard Rocha moved towards Ortega, the flick knife now operable and ready to intercede in an eye blink, as Ochoa drew his gun. Only Meyer's quick hand stopped Rocha from skewering Ortega, as the standoff froze everyone in place. "Rocha", said Meyers quietly, "Stand down. Senor Ortega means me no harm. Isn't that the case Senor", he said looking Ortega squarely in the eye as Ortega took a step back.

"Listen to what your Jefe say", said Ortega regaining his composure. "I mean him no harm"!

As Rocha folded his blade he turned to see Ochoa slowly putting his gun back into his shoulder holster and winked.

Calmly, Ortega turned and said, "Later on when Davalantes and the others get back, we go down to Jamaica beach and get our stuff back. Jaeger, he be in for a big surprise"!

"I trust this time you will not underestimate him, for apparently he's bested some of your best men. One thing to consider. Will he have any help, down at your beach house"?

"No, I doubt it. When we get him, he's working' for a bail bondsman in Houston. I check him out and find he likes to work alone most of the time.

He doesn't like to split his share with nobody. No, tonight we meet him, he'll be alone, then we surround him an make him feel like Custer at the Big Horn"!

"Then you won't mind if Rocha and I tag along this evening, to enjoy the fun and see things through, observing a master at his work. One never knows"!

"Fuck no Amigo", beamed Ortega. "The more the merrier. We show you exactly how we clean things up"! Then he looked at Ochoa saying, "You might wanna call our friend Jugos and let him know that we'll be needin' him tonight an to be ready when we call"!

Then Ortega turned to Meyers saying, "Lets have a drink, cause we got some time. Tonight you see how we make a problem disappear then tomorrow you fly back down to Buenos Aires, with the Embraer plans and nobody be the wiser. Just a little ripple in the pond. Three days from now, we all gonna be fat and happy. In a little bit we all go to da Galleria have lunch, check out the pussy, then meet with Davalantes an his shooters, then head to the beach, for some unfinished business"!

26

Jaeger leaned against his big Ford, staring out at the vast expanse of the Gulf of Mexico, watching the waves gently lapping at the shoreline. He put his mind in that faraway place as he fished out his harmonica from his trousers and looked at it. It had been quite a while since he'd felt the need for his old friend, as he licked his lips and placed the three notes, over and over. Just like that old movie with Bronson, of the western gunman with no name except 'Harmonica'. He'd done all that he could to plan for the inevitable, now all was in the hands of the eternal. Nothing else mattered except the death of Ortega and as many of his friends as Jaeger could take with him. Now he was summoning the Ferry Man, to carry as many as possible across the river into the depths of Hell itself. There were no illusions as to his survival much past sundown.

In a letter to his lawyer, he outlined as much as he knew about the Embraer Aircraft conspiracy, with names, dates, and bank transfers, with instructions to send copies to the local media, the FBI and the Brazilian Embassy. Rae was instructed to release the real documents to his lawyer for transfer to the Federal authorities. Further in his letter, were instructions as to the final dispositions of all of his assets and to whom. His only regrets were that he'd not be around to enjoy the aftermath of all that he'd wrought. There was a veritable shit storm of almost biblical proportions that would involve two South American nations. But most of all he would dearly miss Melanie. Mel, as she liked to be called. He would never know the warmth of her enduring love.

As the three recurring notes poured out of the harmonica, calling out to the unseen, his mind filled with the arrival of Ortega and his entourage. Ortega would be all smiles and agree to anything to get his hands on the documents. That accomplished, he'd step aside while his shooters filled Jaeger full of lead. No doubt, he'd already given Jugos the heads up that his services would be needed. His remains to be consumed by the citizens of Canal Street within days and the rest consigned to the depths of the Gulf of Mexico, before the sun rose. That may have been Ortega's plan, but Jaeger would see to it that Ortega joined him, regardless of the outcome.

He stopped his playing, lit a cigarette and allowed his thoughts to drift to Melanie, as a wave of sudden remorse and melancholy swept over him, causing his eyes to briefly mist over, a rare event. He really missed that woman. Their six month or so relationship was the high water mark in an eventful life. Even now, months later, he could feel her touch, almost smelling her musk as he allowed his eyes to close momentarily. He went inside the beach house, retrieved another beer from the fridge and went back outside, resuming his location on the rear fender of his car, as he brought back to his consciousness, a moment in time.

As was his custom, almost every afternoon when he wasn't chasing down a runner for Rafferty's Bail Bonding, he'd spend a few hours pumping iron at the Ballys Health Club in Houston's northwest side. From time to time, he'd join Big Randy, the clubs manager and they'd spot for each other. Now there was a specimen harking back to the proverbial missing link. Big Randy was what everyone called him. At six feet seven inches and over three hundred pounds with almost zero body fat, he consumed over ten thousand calories a day and never showed an ounce of fat. Of course he was in the gym every day and a walking breathing testament to what one could aspire to physically given the right commitment. Yet his sheer size was offset by his modest persona. All he had to do was flex, and others would stare in wonder. No one could remember anytime he displayed a scintilla of anger and he was known as the gentle giant.

As big as Jaeger was, he was dwarfed, as was everyone else, by big Randy, who would join him for several sessions, whenever his paperwork was done, every so often, with others looking askance as the bar bent somewhat as the bench press went up then back down, in steady repetition, the grunts echoing amidst the back music in a slow staccato. They chatted amiably as Randy pointed out several of the other of the fit looking instructors preening over their male as well as female charges, with a certain discrete commingling occurring amidst the bevy of women that usually found the surroundings desirable and good hunting.

Then one day his world was turned on its ear as a rather tall and well put together woman he'd never seen before passed before his eyes as he was concluding his final two repetitions on the bench press. There he was Big Randy at the ready coaxing him skyward for just one final rep, his fingers ready as Jaeger struggled to push the bar inch by inch upward, hearing Randy whisper, 'What a pussy you are. C'mon now, just three inches more"! As the bar slid into its resting niche, Jaeger leaned upward into a sitting position, sweat pouring forth from his exertions, as his eyes couldn't help but follow the passing of a goddess to his eyes, as she went to another machine on the far end the mezzanine floor.

Seeing Jaegers distress, Randy bent down and whispered, "Her name is Melanie, and she's been a regular member for the last six months. Last name is O'Bannon. Used to be married to the Oilers football player, before he plunged off the 610 overpass and had that wreck that ended things awhile back. Seems like a real nice lady. Just at let ya know"! "Now why would I need to know her bio", asked Jaeger?

"It's the Jewish in me. My mom was a match maker in Brooklyn when I was a kid. Bon Appetite' sport", he said grabbing his gym towel and leaving! Jaeger got up grabbed his towel and went to the water fountain before doing ten laps around the upstairs track to prepare for a second set on the machines and the weights. As he was slowly jogging, his eyes were drawn to the ground level of the club, at the bevy of walking and stair step machines in use and there she was doing her best on the stair step machine, her eyes fixed on the bank of TV monitors broadcasting the evening news. With each passing lap, her presence made demands upon Jaegers attention, with the subconscious part of his mind shouting to make its presence known.

Afterward, as he showered, the vision of this woman just wouldn't go away, as he unconsciously mouthed her name slowly, over and over. He dressed, then went over to the IHOP restaurant, across the parking lot and ordered a calorie laden meal as he tried to lose himself over the latest edition of the evening newspaper. Normally he found the fare usually satisfying, but on this evening he found the meal tasteless and found that his appetite, somewhere in another star system usually a case of illness of some sort. Yet he wasn't experiencing a fever. An hour later as he paid his bill, the memory of this woman he hadn't even met was still ever present in his mind, leaching away at his insides.

Women had never proved to be a problem with Jaeger, for in his line of work; a lasting liaison was really out of the question. The women he usually encountered earned their daily bread during the evenings by displaying their ample wares. He made it a point to never spend the night, always leaving a significant tip on the nightstand, for services rendered. No point in pissing them off. Later that evening, he went over to the 'Colorado', ordered a drink, parking himself at the end of one of the runways, to perform a quality control check on the new flock of geese, rumored to have arrived, from the Reno and Dallas club circuit.

Normally, he'd discover a new bit of Quif, appealing to his prurient interests, peel of a tenner or a twenty allowing nature to plot a course. Yet over the course of a few hours, the apparent qualities of the new flock of geese notwithstanding, there it was the presence of this Melanie still tattooed on the insides of his eyeballs as none other had ever been. After several hours of drinking, he found himself surprisingly sober and bored, paying his tab and made his way towards the parking lot.

After a restless night where little sleep was to be had, he got up made the coffee, and then jumped into the shower, as the sunlight was just making itself known. After dressing, he watched the early morning local newscast, wondering how many of last night's shootings, would he eventually become part of after the fact. Finishing his coffee, he got into his old Ford, joining the early morning rush hour into the city, wending his way towards the private parking lot owned by Rafferty's Bail Bonding, one block away from the old downtown courthouse. The Central Business District of Houston was a curious mixture of a city in transition, with block after block of gleaming high rise office buildings blending into and around a mélange, of older less well maintained office structures, of prewar vintage. Rafferty's Bonding was safely nestled into the street level of an older two three level brick structure, which long ago exceeded its mortgage lifespan. Jaeger walked up the street and took a window booth at the Copper Kettle for his morning breakfast, just in time to scan the morning papers and follow the conga line of lawyers and assistants making their towards the court house. The Kettle, as it was known, was a wonderful greasy spoon diner, famous for its Chicken Fried Steak and hash brown potatoes, as well as its early morning eclectic regulars.

That completed, he joined all the rest trudging hurriedly towards the Courthouse complex for the business of the day. A myriad of court appearances notwithstanding, he blew into the front door, waving a hello at Wanda, the ample frizzy haired blond bail clerk and receptionist, already busy on the phone. Stopping at the 'Voided Bonds' trey, to see if anything of interest was worth working. He usually restricted himself to the hard cases, where serious crimes had been committed, for they paid far better than the lesser offenses. The larger the Bond written the more serious the crime. The more dangerous and usually resourceful the criminal the higher the risk to the hunter, the higher the fee. High risk, high yield. One of the many constants of reality.

He discovered nothing of interest really worth his time and decided to select a 'Jumper' at random, just to stay busy, when Wanda ambled over and with a raspy, whiskey ravaged voice said, "Hey Bud, heard you were over at the Colorado on a pussy hunt last night and left alone. Wassa mattah you? Got the clap, or sumpthin'"?

"Jesus Wanda, is there nothing in this town you don't know about"?

"Wahl I'll tell ya. I don't have a handle on what goes on in the Mayors or the County Judges bedrooms yet, but give it some time sport, just give it some time", she echoed. "But never mind me. What happened to you last night, stud muffin? Word was you appeared deep in thought. Some of the new dancers in from out west were down right insulted and were pissed off for fair"!

"Wanda, why don't you have a gossip column in the Houston Chronicle? Hell, I can see it now. Your tag line could be, Wanda's Wicked Lowdown. By the way, where's Rafferty? He's usually in here long before this"?

"Probably still at the Colorado, or tryin' to kick some honey outta his digs, so he can get to work? Not my turn to keep watch on him this week"!

"So he was at the Colorado last night? Why didn't he say something"? "Yeah sport, he was there and it was him what ratted you out"! "He purposely laid low in the shadows, just to watch you work. Said for me to tell you that you were mighty sloppy watchin' your six o'clock. Then again he was curious to see if it was true, that you could really lick your eyebrows. But he was really just as happy as a pig in shit, enjoyin' your leavin's. He'll probably wander in sometime this morning', bowlegged, cranky an hung over, but with a smile on his ugly old face, happy to discover that his 'Thang' is still good for something more than passin' water"!

"He got anything on his desk worth a damn"?

"Nope. You seen it all for the moment. But the day is young and I'm sure something will jump up. Hondo's out near Eagle Pass chasin' a skip. But you look a little hang dog. Too young to be goin' through the male change"!

"No just feel restless. Need to stay busy. Do me a favor will ya"? "Speak".

"Make a few calls around and see if any hard cases are available"? "Ya needin' cash sport"?

"Can always use the cash, but to answer your question, I'm OK on cash. Just feelin' restless and need to stay busy"!

"Only thing that can put a man in that condition is another woman"!

"Wanda, just tend to your own business, try and keep me busy an I'll be right as rain"!

"OK sport, I'll call around, but hey, I almost forgot. D'ya remember the Santangelo brothers ya ran down a few years back"? Jaeger thought a moment then said, "Yeah. A couple of rich kids. Raised in River Oaks. Private schools. Low level string of armed robberies. Daddy owned a bunch of car dealerships all over town. Those Santangelo brothers?

"Those Santangelo brothers. Just wanted to give ya a heads up that in a few weeks their gonna be sprung on parole from the Ellis Unit, in Huntsville"!

"A few years early isn't it Wanda? They chopped up their victims up pretty bad on top of jumping bail"!

"Daddy's money apparently works wonders and they been keepin' their nose clean up north and if you'll recall when you delivered then back to the Harris County Jail, they both had to be hospitalized for a month prior to their grand jury appearance"!

"They both got frisky on me and didn't want to come back from Monterrey, so I had to reason with them"!

"Well the word on the ground is that Daddy is gonna finance some people to look ya up and give ya a personal invite to a one way Man Dance"!

"They're just gonna have to get in line Wanda"! "Long line ain't it"?

"Yeah", replied Jaeger slowly. "Just let me know if anything breaks. Gonna Cutta Chogie", he said as he made for the door. He then turned and said, "Hey Wanda, thanks for the heads up"! He wandered aimlessly through the down town area for the next several hours, part of his mind turning to the Santangelo brothers and their father, wondering whether or not to pay their dad a preemptory visit to see how well he could fall down. He decided to leave that lay for the present time. Maybe freedom would bring a change of heart for the brothers, then again probably not. The legal system frowned on the concept of preemption.

As he wandered the downtown canyons, he did all of the things one did to determine if anyone was on his tail. After all, the town had any number of former police detectives skilled in surveillance, all for hire. So he'd put himself out there to see if anyone was building a file on his daily routine. As he walked in and out of buildings and down into the inner city tunnel complex of stores and shops, part of his mind drifted back to that tall beauty he'd seen at Ballys. It just wouldn't go away.

As he wandered up Fannin Street, he went into a shop and bought a pair of sunglasses, and a pack of cigarettes, then went outside with his sunglasses on and went through the procedure of lighting a cigarette, as his eyes scanned the street. As he walked on towards uptown, he rolled over in his mind standard tailing techniques. Hopefully if he had a minder he would be alone. Usually they worked in pairs or more crisscrossing each other if real pros were on his tail, especially government funded. But if it were the Santangelo's father, hopefully he'd try it on the cheap and hire a single investigator. Then there was the possibility that he'd hire two separate minders to tail him, one to watch the other investigators movements and patterns. Tailing a suspect was hard enough, to be concerned with someone tailing you when your attention was focused. As he made his way toward the shops of down town, he entered a Walgreen's Drugstore on Main Street and did some extended browsing, before buying a ball point pen. He'd hoped he'd get some indication prior to the downtown lunch hour when the streets would be a teeming anthill of folks hurrying to feed their face somewhere. As he walked out of the Walgreen's he spotted someone who somehow seemed out of place, reading a magazine in his peripheral vision. Middle aged, short haircut, balding gray hair, sport coat, and tie with a double Windsor knot, slacks and wearing glasses. Something told Jaeger this guy was ex-cop, probably retired, making a living as a PI. He'd wander around a bit more and see if the guy resurfaced.

He hit several more shops as he wandered. Stopping and sometimes entering, eventually coming back on the street with a befuddled look on his face and continuing on. Three blocks over and two more up the street, he spotted the same guy across the street and at the very edge of his field of view. The guy had taken his jacket off and rolled up his sleeves, changing his visual somewhat, but make no mistake it was the very same guy he spotted at the Walgreen's. He was good, but not a great shadow dancer. He should've had a hat of some kind, or a reversible jacket. Now it was time to gently reel him in and see what was going on.

Jaeger looked at his watch and seeing the lunch crowd was about to flood the streets, ducked into a James Coney Island and got three dogs with all the trimmings sitting at a bar, with his back facing the street. Facing a wall length mirror he was able to see the street behind him as he spotted his tail stopping at a sausage street vendor and purchased a sausage on a stick. Hey, he had to eat too. His tail then backed up into the shadows of the street, his eyes on the James Coney Island. Now Jaeger was certain he had his man. The only thing remained, was he working solo or with another. As both kept their eyes on the other, only one was aware of his pursuer.

As Jaeger went back outside he was looking up the street. Now it was time to descend into the downtown tunnel system. Jaeger wished he's brought along some of the things he usually used when he was trailing others, but he didn't. Spilt milk. Yet if he could just string this guy along a little while longer, he knew of a place in the tunnel system where he could turn the tables. He hoped this trailing gumshoe didn't know of the same place. He stopped in a Merle Norman lingerie shop, lingering awhile, talked to a sales woman then made a purchase as his eyes scanned the outside periodically through the large glass window. There he was again across the underground walkway. Soon things would be brought to a conclusion. He then walked out with his purchase, turning right and rounded a corner into another secluded hallway that led to the public rest rooms. He then stood hidden behind a line of upright metal storage bins that contained cleaning supplies, hoping against hope that his minder would be foolish enough to follow him.

Five minutes passed, then five more and here he came. Since no one had entered or exited the men's room it was reasonable to assume it would be empty, as Jaeger peered through the crack between the storage bins, quickly following his minder into the men's room. As the minder looked ahead, Jaeger silently came up from behind and gave him knuckles behind the ear, dropping the man like a stone. He scanned the booths and finding them all empty he dragged the man to the very last one, propping him up on the toilet, went back and retrieved the man's sport coat and his packages, closing the door behind him. He quickly went through the man's pockets finding his wallet, pulling out all that it contained. Then he picked up the micro tape recorder, hitting replay, and listened to several minutes of the playback.

He then went back to the mans' wallet, driver's license, business cards, HPD patrolman's union retirement identification told Jaeger all he needed to know. He flushed the toilet and then reached down between the mans splayed out legs, bringing several hand cups full of water to splash into the man's face, then he stood back. He almost felt sorry for the guy. Probably put in thirty years on the force, then put out to pasture to retire. What did he know how to do with the rest of his life, but be a cop. No doubt he'd have some friends still in the department. Jaeger reckoned he was in his mid- fifties by the look of things, not in the greatest of shape physically, too young for the double Fed X, yet he still had to make a living. His weapon was on the floor, as Jaeger removed the clip, pocketing the bullets.

As the man came around, his eyes focused on Jaeger. "You're all alone sport, or at least I hope you're all alone for your sake. It's time for truth. Speak the truth and you'll walk out of here in one piece and back to whatever family you have. Fuck with me and I'll break you up in little pieces and it'll hurt, a lot. How good is your hospitalization plan"?

"Not good enough", murmured the gumshoe. "Can I rub my head? It hurts"!

"Time for that later and only if you're a good boy. Now your retired HPD with thirty years on the street. You're working as a PI, or so the State License indicates, and you work out of your house, which is why the cell phone number and the PO, Box number on your business card. Now here tis. Who hired you to tail me"?

"Carl Santangelo"!

"Good boy. Now did he give any reason to you for the engagement of your services"?

"He said that you were a former employee and had stolen from him on a business deal"!

"That's it and nothing more"?

"I'm to tail you and build a file on your comings and goings as the first phase of a lawsuit he says he's going to file against you. Then he wants me to dig further into your background"!

"That's it? All of it?

"When and where did you first pick me up"?

"This morning when you had breakfast, then I followed you to Rafferty's Bail Bonding"!

"How long is the first phase to continue"!

"For one week. Then he says he'll pay me for that week before rehiring me for the second phase"! "Good Boy. Now listen up. There's not going to be any second phase of your investigation. Regardless of what he might say. I've never worked for the man. What he says is pure fiction. I work for Rafferty as a hunter. I retrieve those who skip bail. Years ago his two kids jumped bail and went to Mexico. I brought them back. They stood trial, were convicted and sent to a stretch to the Ellis Unit up in Huntsville. Somehow he pulled some strings with the parole board, since his two kids are about to be released on parole soon. I know that he wants to find me so he can have a few guys fuck me up permanently. You don't want to have any part of this do you"?

"No"!

"Good. Now I'm guessing that you've some friend's downtown in the Department that can verify what I've just told you"? The gumshoe nodded his head. "Good" said Jaeger. Now since you gotta complete your contract, you'll do just that only the rest of it'll be pure fiction. I'm never going to see you again, ever. Are we agreed"? Again the head nodded in silence. "If I do, you won't like it"!

"Now, best you watch your back for just maybe our boy Santangelo might just have someone trailing you, to keep proper tabs, on your progress or lack of it. They watch you watching me. See how that works. Now, one other thing. Ya want at work as a PI, then ya just have to be working with someone who has a great connection with a serious law firm. Then you can work as part of a team with greater resources. There's a guy called Randall White in town. He's ex Harris County Sheriff's department. Mention my name and maybe he'll have some work for you. Then again maybe not. Your piece is on the floor and you won't mind if I keep the shells will you"?

Again the head nodded in silence as Jaeger slowly opened the cubicle door saying, "Oh yeah. Take the nightgown back to your old lady this evening. Hope it fits. If not then you can guess what to do with my compliments"! As Jaeger turned around, he saw a teenager at the urinal looking his way and bellowed as he passed him, "What the fuck you looking at"?

He wandered around seemingly aimless, always checking behind him to see if there was yet another minder trailing him. He worked his way back towards Rafferty's, and as he approached his car, decided to check under his Ford in the parking lot to see if any surprise awaited him. Finding nothing, now that it was midafternoon he decided to go to the gym and work off the restlessness he felt. As he drove, the vision of this woman he'd seen at Ballys worked its way back into his consciousness. Her profile was etched into his memory, allowing his mind to reflect on just who she might be. The obvious became readily apparent. Her well paid professional jock husband dead, she was going to get back into fighting shape if for nothing else than to enhance her marketability. Then again, it didn't seem that she had far to travel in that regard, if that really was the case. An example of sentient prurience on the hoof.

After he walked into Ballys, he changed into his gym gear, then climbed the stairs to the mezzanine workout area, jogged ten laps around the indoor track to warm up, then parked himself into the free weight section for the next few hours to grunt through his midweek routine. After an hour of this, he set out on the track to make five circuits, in order to flush the lactic acid buildup from his system, before he hit the machines. As he looked up at the clock on the wall, time was working itself towards five in the afternoon. He'd have to hurry or else he'd find himself awash in the early evening rush of telly tubbies that was certain to invade the place like army ants. Then he hurriedly went to his weight machines, where he sweated through two sets of exertions on each of the selected machines. On his next to last machine, he set the plates to 250 lbs., almost the full rack, then settled under the bar taking several slow deep breaths, focused his eyes on a spot on the ceiling, then pressed upward for the first of two sets of ten repetitions. Upon completion, the sweat was pouring forth as he sat up for a short breather, wiping his brow with his gym towel, and there she was, not ten feet in front of him, starting her set on the abdominal machine.

As she finished her set, she sat up to rest. Their eyes met and held for several moments, far longer than what was considered a casual glance. Jaeger wanted to look away, but was riveted. She met his gaze full on with an apparent puzzled look on her face, then briefly smiled and leaned back into her machine to resume her routine.

Of course it was impolite to stare, but this was beyond him as he leaned back onto the seat of the incline bench press machine staring up towards the ceiling. Her visual profile as well the full on was spectacular, especially since she had only a paucity of make up on as far as he could determine. He reckoned that to gaze upon her face too long would be like looking at the sun for an extended period during its noon day arc. She simply radiated. Then again, perhaps the multi hydra of Medusa would prove a more apt description. Women of that quality usually proved fatal one way or the other. Jaeger made her out to be about five feet ten inches in height, full bosomed, with everything in absolutely perfect proportion, with shoulder length chestnut hued hair, that perfectly framed a perfectly formed face.

Now at long last, Jaeger understood why Paris the Prince of Troy took Helen from Menelaus, plunging that City State into its death knell. Jaeger would've done the very same thing and never looked back. In that, any similarity between the two ended. Her eyes were a light brown in color and of such a natural looking oval shape, that anything more than the slightest cosmetic assistance would detract from the visual effect.

He started once again to press the bar upward, this time to stretch just one additional rep. That accomplished he slowly sat up and looked around only to find her gone from sight. He looked around, from his seated position, if only to verify her departure. She'd vanished from sight like a spectre' in the mist. Suddenly a feeling of overwhelming sadness encompassed him. An interesting paradox existed. Once discovered, her visual presence brought massive discomfort and her departure summoned a feeling of remorse, something foreign to him. Never in his life, had this range of extreme emotions assailed him in simultaneous fashion. When he got back to his place, he went into the bathroom. Looked into the mirror and examined his face and there it was. The answer to her departure. His mug. His demeanor. All of his adult life he always had this perpetual scowl on his face, rarely if ever smiling. As if there was some unseen force field surrounding him, permitting only the lowly underclass to approach at their own risk. He discovered this evident in both genders, especially people of quality, or apparent quality. That was the enduring quality of the anointed Alpha. Then he looked back at his life once again, this time from another prism. His upbringing at the family ranch, his time with the Marines, the solitary time as a student at UT, the sordid nature of the death of his family and the subsequent treachery of his false imprisonment in the Huntsville facility. Then his resurrection back into civilian life thanks to the Machiavellian ministrations of Buffy the Princess of Darkness. His pursuit and subsequent deaths of those responsible for his family's murder. Then his freedom, if that's what one called it? Managing so called Gentlemen's Clubs and now this, a Bounty Hunter. Whatever could he say to a woman of quality if asked the question, "And what is it that you do"? There was that similar hard edge about him that one usually finds in a common whore. That very same edge is apparent in their mannerisms, their voice and their overall appearance. Yet what could he do, to soften the image, yet still retain his abilities. Others had that Chameleon quality. Jaeger did not.

As he looked deeply into the mirror at his ever increasing craggy face, the silent voice from deep within whispered, 'Each man's fate is writ large upon the shifting sands at his moment of birth'…He examined that statement for an instant trying to find a way out of his conundrum. Then the words "Shifting Sands", came to mind. Could it be that his fate was not signed, sealed and preordained? Could this be a celestial loop hole in the laws of nature?

His prescient abilities were of course, not his strong suit. His ability to divine the future accurately we're no better or worse than anyone else's. The way ahead was foggy as far as could be determined. Yet the goal ahead was clear. The restoration as far as possible, of the family estate, was the goal line and above all else that was the only real thing that mattered. Yes, he was making slow progress, but at the current rate, he'd be well past the normal span of time, before that came into fruition, if ever. Time was his ultimate enemy. Yet here it was this goddess, whose image was ever present in his mind. With luck, perhaps she'd go away.

Yet there it was again, the moment when their eyes met and neither one averted. That eternity of time. A gaze held between two people could either attract or repel. Held for too long, could signal a tangible threat, to even the most hardened of criminals much less the average woman. But by the look of it, this woman was in no way average by any measurement.

Then he heard the words of his father saying, "Never spook the livestock", a favorite saying of his. The wisdom of antiquity and what does he do? At least he could've returned the smile. Perhaps another opportunity might surface.

He briefly thought about a return visit to the Colorado, but thought better of it. Somehow its allure had lost its charm. All of a sudden, he could not bear the thought of another woman in is arms. All except one. As the evening wore on, he tried to stay busy, watching the Telly, then when that proved a bore, read several chapters of a novel he'd started, then doing some household chores, left wanting. When next he looked at the clock, it read two in the morning. The image of that woman again came into view. If he never had before, he now had a partial understanding of the power of a formidable woman. Quite apart from her obvious visual qualities, was the way she moved, with grace, apparent certainty and panache'. Every so often one will come along with an aura of inexplicable chemistry so profound; it's capable of monumental movement. He stood silent in the kitchen, thinking, for what seemed like minutes. Then when he glanced at the clock again, it read almost five in the morning. Yet another occasion of epiphany had arrived. Only one of many "Come to Jesus" moments he'd experienced. He wondered how many more of these eye opening events were to come.

Over time, he'd forced himself to repress the normal events he'd missed out on in his life. Falling in love, having a family of his own, growing old gracefully, with the love of your life by your side. As a kid growing up on the family spread outside of Waco Texas, he was surrounded by the normalcy of a loving family. So much that he was, like many others, guilty of taking things for granted. Then one day, all of that vanished and there was nothing he could do about it, except endure. Have the grit, the sand, the abrasive quality to wear all other's down till only you were that last one left standing. Well he had the grit, the sand, enduring prison surrounded by a host of the criminally demented. Miraculously delivered back into society by governmental pardon. Yet, unfit in his eyes to tread the same path of normal society. Now, here by virtue of a silent encounter with a goddess dangled a glimmer of hope, for contentment by the slenderest of threads.

Odds heavily against him, his eyes at long last grew heavy as the sun started its daily journey through the heavens. He lay down on the couch and was soon fast asleep.

At one in the afternoon his eyes flew open, a result of the nearby phones buzzing. It was Rafferty, informing him that he'd contracted him out to another Bonding Agency, for yet another hard case that'd skipped his court appearance. After minimal haggling as to Jaeger's fee, they agreed. Jaeger hurriedly showered, dressed then drove into town eager to see Rafferty and immerse himself back into the bowels of the hunt.

Three days later, he emerged from Rafferty's old military war surplus Humvee, in front of the Harris County Jail. It was shortly after two in the morning as he hauled out Hector Contreras, before Rafferty and one of the Harris County's Deputies to perform the necessary paperwork in remanding him back in jail awaiting trial. Jaeger had to travel to Matamoros Mexico, just across the Rio Grande River from Brownsville Texas. A convicted offender, having done previous time in the Texas Corrections System, for bad check writing, he resumed the only thing he knew how to do well. Write phony checks. A well-meaning Uncle had underwritten his original bail, having placed his modest home as collateral. The home was now in jeopardy of being in default.

After spending the rest of the day wading through his prior alias's and prior contacts, Jaeger discovered the location of one of Contreras's previous girlfriends in Matamoros, Finding the location, he parked Rafferty's Humvee a block away. Taking up a position on a rooftop above the entrance about a hundred yards away from her bodega, on Calle' Montemayor. Taking up residence for what he expected to be a very long wait. Several bottles of water, some over the counter caffeine pills to keep him awake and a few Snickers candy bars would be all that he'd need during the interim. That and a bit of luck that he'd guessed correctly.

Ten hours later, in the early morning hours, his patience and luck was rewarded with the arrival of Contreras and his woman of the moment, clearly lurching drunkenly down the dimly lit street, clearly drunk. As they went through the entrance of her apartment building, Jaeger watched the windows, to see if a light went on in one of the windows. Hopefully, it would be on one the side of the building he had in view, if not his wait would be longer. Then several minutes later, a light luckily came on. Jaeger thought they'd clearly get down to a serious case of 'Slap and Tickle' as they each tore the others clothes off. Most girls preferred to make love with the lights off, but working girls usually performed their services with the lights on, so their customer could see and enjoy what he was getting for his money. Thus by the look of things Contreras's main squeeze of the moment wasn't a candidate for MENSA membership, not during this lifespan.

After an hour and a half, the light went out in the second floor window. He was grateful; they'd had the good sense, to open the window allowing the fresh night air in. As he peered through his small four power binoculars, he saw a way where he could gain entrance straight through the window, rather than risk entry and exit through the front door. He reckoned it was approximately a ten or twelve foot elevation from the ground to the window. He'd wait an hour for the duo to fall into a deep slumber before he went into action. Making his way slowing and quietly down to the street, he hoped all of the dogs in the neighborhood were asleep also. For one barking dog could delay things. He started the well muffled Humvee, and slowly went down the street squeezing into a spot half up on the curb. Hopefully the local cops on the grave yard shift would be at some all-night Cantina, deep in the cups.

A nearby tree, allowed him to gain the height he needed to leap to the open windows ledge and silently pull his body slowly inside. Once inside, he slowly rose, staying very still, listening and allowing his eyes to adjust to the darkness. There they both were, lying all splayed out over the bed coverings, clothes strewn about the room, in the same condition as they entered this world.

The room had the sickly smell of cheap perfume, bodily odors and the smell of scrotal excretions. Jaeger looked at his watch and reckoned that an hour almost had passed since the lights went out. It would be a few hours before dawn and he wanted to be back in Texas before the sun came up. So he removed the covered syringe from his jacket, carefully going around the bed to where Contreras lay and injected three quarters of the syringe into the inert body. Then he went around to the other side and injected the rest into his partner for the moment. After some searching, he found the man's trousers, extracting the wallet. He flicked on his small flashlight and examined the driver's license, to verify he had the right man. That done, he placed the wallet inside his jacket pocket and went about lifting the now completely inert Contreras up and muscling him into the open window in such a way, that when he let him drop he'd land somewhat on his feet, before crumbling to the ground. That completed, he slowly followed after Contreras. Then hoisted him up into a fireman's carry and went to the Humvee. Working very carefully, he opened the welded compartment underneath the vehicle, then secured his wrists behind him as well as his ankles with tie wraps, then slowly crammed Contreras into the undercarriage. He checked the man to make certain he could breathe, fairly comfortably, and then he secured the door. It just wouldn't do to deliver the man back to Harris County dead. He'd return naked as the day he was born, subject no doubt to some Jail House chatter for some time to come, but he had to be returned breathing.

As he drove off, finally he heard the sound of a dog barking relentlessly. As he drove through the heart of Matamoros, Jaeger reckoned that Contreras's girlfriend wouldn't wake up until well after noon. By that time he hoped to be across the river and well into Texas, parked well off the beaten track in some No Tell Motel, for a well-earned rest. He'd been awake well over forty eight hours and Houston was an eight or nine hour drive north.

When he came across the International Bridge Checkpoint, the horizon in the east was starting to slowly brighten. It was a weekday, with almost no traffic for the moment and the border guard was thankfully sleepy. After a cursory glance and walk around the Hum vee, he waved Jaeger on through. At the American side Jaeger received similar express treatment and was off, making his way through the heart of Brownsville till he found the sign indicating US Route 59 and headed north. He drove until he was at the outskirts of Corpus Christi, finding a suitable cheap motel and checked in for the remainder of the day and early evening. He made a short call to Rafferty on his Mobil phone telling him the package was on its way. "I'll call ya when I get to Wharton later on this evening and we can meet up in front of the Harris County Jail. As for now it's 'Lights Out' for me. Talk to ya later"! By mid-afternoon he woke up and went out to Rafferty's Humvee, crawled underneath and examined his prisoner, who was showing signs of coming out of his slumber. With yet another loaded syringe of his magic potion ready to go, he injected yet another quarter syringe of the juice to quiet down into his subject and sealed the container once again. He was able to breathe and that was all that mattered. After all, the guy could afford to miss a meal or two. Let Harris County be responsible for his food intake. Then he went back inside and lay down on the bed tried to get a little more shut eye. As he drifted off, visions of that woman at Ballys flooded back into his mind.

Nothing prurient mind you, simply her face smiling at him. Shortly after five, he showered, dressed and checked out of his room, wandering over to the Golden Kettle, breakfast restaurant that most Motels kept on the premises, ordered a large breakfast, bought the local paper and spent the next hour refueling and planning the drive back to Houston.

True to his word, around one in the morning, he was approaching Wharton Texas; he placed the heads up call to Rafferty. Shortly after two he pulled into the Harris County Jail, as Rafferty and a deputy were waiting. "What took ya so long sport", asked Rafferty smiling as Jaeger slid out of his vehicle. Flanked by Rafferty and the Deputy, Jaeger slid under the Humvee, and seconds later out fell the prisoner naked and unconscious. He cut the plastic tie wraps from his body, only to be replaced by the Deputy's cuffs.

"Damn son. Ya could've at least made certain he had some clothes on", chuckled Rafferty.

"Can the prisoner walk", asked the Deputy?

"Doesn't look like it from here Deputy, drawled Rafferty. "Maybe you need to go back inside and get a wheel chair or a gurney and maybe a few more Deputies. Well keep an eye on him till ya get back"! While the Deputy disappeared inside, he took the Humvee's keys Jaeger offered saying, "Ya done good son and ya done it quick. Looks like the prisoner's uncle is gonna get to keep his house after all. Come by tomorrow when ya can and I'll have your check waiting as we agreed. So tell me how come he comes back to us bare nekkid"?

"Had to wait until after he and this Chula, exchanged bodily fluids and fell asleep. Can't exactly make the apprehension when their doin' the wild and nasty. Then I'd have to knock em both out. There would be noise. Can't have that. Went in through an open second story window, gave him and her shot and dropped him through the window, as I found him"! Then almost as an afterthought he said after reaching into his jacket pocket, "I did get his wallet", as he handed it to Rafferty. "Should make the booking process go better"!

As the deputy returned back with a wheelchair and two other

deputies, Jaeger drifted away, walking back up the street for several blocks to Rafferty's parking lot to his Ford. He checked his traps for signs of penetration, then scooted under his car and scanned the undercarriage, before entering his Ford, for the long drive to the suburbs.

The following day Jaeger showed up to pick up his check and quickly found more work. With only minor skips in Rafferty's bin that paid little, word had gotten around that Jaeger was available to run down the high priced runners. With Rafferty and Wanda there to negotiate for his talents, Jaeger was kept busy almost round the clock. Once in a while he worked with Hondo, the only other Chaser of talents capable to bringing the recalcitrant back to face justice. From time to time it was a messy affair when things didn't go exactly as planned, but they always returned alive, often worse for wear. But mostly things went as planned, given the subtlety of their methods.

After several months of mostly non-stop work, things began to slow down. The local court calendars were full, sullen clients were found guilty by juries of their peers, and were promptly assigned to various facilities in the Texas Department of Corrections, away from the public at large.

Jaeger was tired, after almost seven days a week of returning the bad guys, needing a much earned rest. He'd made a lot of money during the period and it was time he simply chilled out awhile. So he decided to sleep most of the day, then go to the gym and take a steam, then an extended soak in the whirlpool. He'd stay away from the swirl of activity upstairs and the rest of the Hoi Polloi. The clock on the wall indicated almost six PM as he climbed out of the whirlpool and slid into the cool waters of the Olympic sized pool resting his arms on the side of the pool, he stretched out in a prone position, his mind almost emptied, allowing his aching muscles to recuperate; as he watched the others come and go. Then suddenly out from the corner of his eye, there she was. That long limbed beauty, moving from right to left in his field of view, fully clothed in business attire, striding purposefully to exit the palace of sweat, carrying her gym bag, in departure after a session. She moved gracefully in long strides, eyes straight ahead and in about seven seconds she disappeared from view out the glass doors, leaving a permanent visual imprint. In his entire life, Jaeger never avoided anything of consequence as the loudspeaker played the old Brazilian song, "The girl from Ipanima".

But here he was cowering at the sight of a woman. He'd never done that before. What in the world was he afraid of?

Then the answer came to him suddenly. In a word. 'Happiness'. Jaeger tried to search his memory for a time when he was truly happy. Perhaps long ago when he was a child on the ranch, with his mother and younger sisters, or the few times he was hunting with his father in South Texas, particularly one time when a Javelina charged his dad from the rear and Jaeger downed the creature with a single snapped off shot of a single action Colt .45 at thirty yards. As his dad whirled around at the sound of the shot, the Javelina fell lifeless to the ground, just scant yards away. He then looked up and saw his son still in a crouched firing position realizing his life had most likely been saved.

It was then and only then, when he received his very first compliment from his father, who nodded his head saying, "You'll do"! Jaeger holstered his pistol, beaming with joy and the moment quickly passed, with his father barking out, "Well boy, ya gonna stand there with one finger up your ass and the other in the air, swapping off every thirty seconds? Or are ya gonna help me get this critter ready to tote back to the truck"? That was about as good as it ever got from his dad. A formidable task master, yet when he looked back, he had to credit his father's guidance in all things. Never Complain, Never Explain! He quietly exulted as they skinned the critter. They'd gone off with a party of a few other friends to South Texas to hunt wild boar and little 'Jaeger'; the youngest of the bunch was the only one who registered a kill. A heady time for a young boy.

Yet time and circumstance had erected walls around his emotions, strictly enforcing boundaries. Now the mere sight of one certain woman was tearing down those walls that had served him well over the years. He visualized Josuha, making a circuit around the walls of Jericho, blowing a Rams horn, the barriers falling brick by brick, revealing the cowering occupants within. That story ended badly, if Jaeger recalled his bible properly, for Joshua saw to it the occupants all perished by the sword. His eyes closed as the cool water swirled around his body and he wondered if this woman was his Joshua? Somehow he sensed this woman was capable of steering him towards the unknown.

27

Melanie entered her home after her session at the health club. Four days a week, for an hour each visit after work, should do wonders for the cellulite that was beginning to make itself known. She was both tired and surprisingly refreshed, concluding she should've done this long ago. As she climbed the stairs of her town house, she called out to her son Rory announcing her arrival shouting, "Company", only to hear, "Hi Mom, what's for supper"?

"Poop and leftovers", Mel always answered as she entered his bedroom and gave him the maternal hug, and then went to her bedroom to change clothes, then down to the kitchen to put together the evening meal. As she went through her nightly ritual, the disturbing thoughts of that stranger at Ballys, re-entered her head. She didn't quite appreciate his staring at her several months ago in that manner, making her feel quite uncomfortable. The good news was that she hadn't seen him around for a while. The very last thing she needed at this time was another man in her life, for between her work at Enron and raising her son, she had all she could say grace over for the foreseeable future. Yet every time she thought about her son, she just had to smile. A good boy who, just turned eight years old. He did what he was told and got excellent grades. Somehow, she was on the right track as a parent and she supposed that was all anyone could ask for.

Then as she was preparing a salad for the both of them, her thought went back to her former husband, Geoff O'Bannon, heir to the O'Bannon Group of automobile dealerships that spanned Texas as well as the surrounding states. The family had deep pockets and were hell bent to gain custody of Melanie's son and so a two year long custody struggle ensued. Her former in-laws were of a predatory nature in both their business practices and in their private lives. In spite of her well-paying job as an executive secretary at Enron, the legal bills had diminished the paltry inheritance she received upon the death of her husband, as well as relegating her generous salary to little more than chump change on a net basis.

She'd married Geoff only two years out of high school while finishing up her sophomore year at the University of Houston. She was a varsity cheerleader and he was a two time All American Defensive Tackle for the Cougars, in his senior year destined to draft high in the NFL draft. That day on the practice field when he removed his jersey to reveal a rippling physique, only reserved for Greek statuary, she knew full well at the time, he was doing it on purpose to impress the cheerleading squad and that he did. Including her, there wasn't a single girl that wouldn't open her legs willingly to such a man. Every single one of them got moist in their private regions at the very sight of him. On Saturdays they watched in eager anticipation as his speed and strength vanquished offensive linemen, quarterbacks and running backs alike. One didn't even need to see him, but only hear the crack of pads on pads, then the cheer of the crowd, followed by a mournful sigh, then silence to know that Geoff O'Bannon had struck again, breaking bones, rendering others "Hors de Combat", followed by the rush onto the field by the trainers and the subsequent arrival of the ambulance. As he progressed year after year, all knew that he was the supreme meal ticket to a very good life.

Then the fateful day when the Houston Oilers, in dire need of a stopper in their defensive line, leapt at the opportunity presented when miraculously he was available and signed him up to a multi-year contract, replete with a signing bonus that would make a Roman Emperor green with envy. Those were heady days in Mel's life. The whirlwind courtship, during his senior year, the quickie Las Vega wedding during her third month of pregnancy and now married into a family of considerable wealth as well as her newly minted husbands future ahead of him in the arena of combat, insured that she could concentrate on being a superb wife and mother on a grand scale.

Of course he was a drop dead gorgeous man who wore clothes well and by their second date, against her better judgment, she succumbed to his considerable charms. 'What girl wouldn't', she reckoned, wholly unable to help herself. Then every time thereafter, their union always descended inevitably into hot, sweaty monkey love, that held no taboos.

Of course, their marriage made the local society pages. During this period, life was good and Mel was beyond ecstasy, for there wasn't a square inch of either one's body that neither wasn't familiar with. If this was an example of their future together, there would be many children in the O'Bannon family.

Yet things slowly began to turn as his rookie season with the Oilers went as expected, with Geoff garnering "Rookie of the Year" honors for a very mediocre team. The pressures began to build on her husband with expectations running high for even greater benchmarks to be achieved. Money shouldn't have ever been an issue for her family since the massive signing bonus followed by a generous five year contract plus other ancillary contracts and endorsements, indicated on the surface that money would never be a question for the rest of their lives. Yet given the life he led, both during the season and off season, his travel was a single constant with him rarely at home. Their son Rory was born while Geoff was in Los Angeles on a promotional tour, with an additional week in Las Vegas prior to his coming home to see his new-born son. His parents filling in during his absence, whereas Melanie's parents both died the previous year, from an auto accident returning home from their weekly Bingo outing at their church.

After the birth of their son, Melanie resumed her studies at the University of Houston gaining her degree shortly after their second anniversary. By the third year of their marriage, a season ending knee injury sidelined her husband for the duration of the season.

Yet he was still the star player of the team as he worked hard during his rehabilitation after surgery. It was then she started to notice changes in his demeanor. He was now working out almost daily building his body in readiness for the coming season. His normally aggressive personality on the field, transferred to their home life, with their sessions of lovemaking becoming fewer and fewer. The following season, his play on the field was becoming less and less disciplined and his effectiveness began to suffer. Still his off season endorsement obligations continued as before.

The last two seasons of his career were a spotty affair, with Geoff O'Bannon showing brief instances of his old self. Yet gradually their marriage began to deteriorate, with rumors of uncontrolled gambling losses and infidelities while away on business, becoming increasingly common. Then one day, a check Melanie wrote for groceries, was returned for insufficient funds. Upon consulting her bank, she discovered that the vast majority of the money her husband made went to paying off gambling debts. Upon his return when she mentioned this and a host of other rumors to Geoff, he exploded and Melanie ended up in the hospital, with their son temporarily in the care of his grandparents, the O'Bannon's.

While she recovered, she finally reflected upon their whirlwind marriage and time together. In retrospect, she couldn't recall a single time, before, during or at any time of their relationship when her husband ever said, "I love you".

He gave her a good life, while she in turn provided him with a spectacular son, short of that they rarely talked about anything of significance, except for his recent infidelities.

They lived in an expensive home, were supposed to have a great deal of money, but somehow everything indicated they were soon to be broke. Upon her release from the hospital, she said nothing as she retrieved her son from his grandparents, vowing to see what she could do to refurbish their marriage. Yet Geoff became more and more distant.

Entering into the last year of his contract with the Oilers, rumors of a pending trade were rampant given that his level of play was not what it was. Physically he was in top form, yet his level of play diminished. Midway through the final year of his contract, Melanie received a notice of their home in the upscale section of Memorial was about to be repossessed. Repeated calls to their attorney were not returned. Her parents deceased and her in laws providing no apparent help, she went to their lender who held the mortgage, only to find that no payment had been made for well over three months.

Melanie moved out of their home taking nothing with her but her son and their clothes, finding an apartment across town. Fortunately a close personal friend got her an interview with a fast rising company called Enron and with her pluck and perseverance she was brought on board. Of course well-meaning friends that knew the real story of the downfall of her husband gradually began to reveal the litany of his problems. Steroids, Cocaine, heavy gambling debts, and a penchant for women of zero virtue, put clothes on the rampant rumors.

Temporarily resuming her maiden name, Mel started up again for she had a son to raise. She had a good secretarial position with a rapidly growing company and she secured the services of another attorney and filed for divorce. Her soon to be former in laws bankrolled a search for

Melanie in town, for the next six months, while she hid out in plain sight. Her friends were not about to talk. Yet another disappointing season for the local professional football team came and went as no one made an effort to renew Geoff O'Bannon's contract. No one in the league expressed any interest in the man. It was if he had leprosy. His wife had left him, he was almost broke. Almost all of the money he made simply disappeared in every direction, his agent dropped him like a hot stone and no one in the league showed an inkling of interest in him at any price. Now if that wasn't a problem, within a few months his house and all it contained would soon be repossessed. 'Easy come, easy go', he reckoned in his chemical laden mind. He talked to his Dad about coming to work for him, but he dreaded the thought about a regular job, especially selling cars, or working for his father. After time spent being a premier player in the NFL, nothing else was acceptable.

He'd get a shower, get dressed, take a snort or three, then get in his "Vette" and mosey on down to the "Men's Club", or maybe even the "Colorado", drink some booze and find himself some suitable 'Trim' for the night. After all, there was always tomorrow.

The following morning Melanie went through her usual morning routine, getting herself ready for work and her son ready to drop off at day care. Just before pulling into Enron's parking garage, she heard the news of her husband's death over the radio. She parked the car in her slot, continuing to hear the news of his early morning plummet off of the Loop 610 overpass near the Galleria, crashing to the street below, destroying his Corvette and another female passenger in a fiery conflagration. Police accident investigations revealed the "Vette" was traveling at high speed as it broke through the overpass, leaving no skid marks on the roadway. Melanie tried to feel something for her husband, but all that had been driven from her by the remorseless way in which he conducted his affairs, both professionally and personally. The tank was empty with not a thing left. Her task now was to be as good a parent as possible and a good and reliable worker for her employer.

She was on her own. Then upon further reflection as she went up in the elevator, she had been on her own for quite some time. All through the morning the office was abuzz while conduction the business of the day for Enron, which was a tightly run organization, with scant time for personal affairs on company time. At nine AM her boss called her into his office, to give her some instructions as to intra office email instructions he wanted her to dispense. Upon conclusion he asked, "I heard about your husband on the radio coming into the office. Do you need any time to settle your affairs"?

After a few seconds of thought she replied, "No, that won't be necessary. His family is quite capable of settling his affairs. The negotiations our organization and you specifically are entering into are vital to future success and as you mentioned the other day in the meeting, we're going to require all hands on deck for this one. Perhaps sometime next week, I'll ring up Human Relations and put in for a few days' vacation. Thank you for the thought though"!

As Mel left his office, her boss was glad that she was his secretary. She had the right attitude that fit neatly into the Enron Corporate culture. As he rose in the organization she would follow him right up the ladder.

The entire day was spent in media frenzy, in connecting the dots concerning the death of a Houston Oiler. The reporters interviewed everyone they could. The police, current and former players, coaches, team assistants, friends and finally, Geoff O'Bannon's family. Gradually the story began to take shape, as news of the forensic autopsy of not only Geoff's charred remains, but in addition, that of the female passenger were somehow leaked to the public at large.

His charred remains revealed that his male member was missing and the remains of his trousers were unzipped upon impact. This posed quite a mystery since teeth marks around the charred wound were apparent. It wasn't until his female passenger was autopsied, by the County Medical Examiner, that the mystery of his missing member was solved. It lay firmly embedded in her throat, indicative as to cause and effect. That brief conundrum solved, the case was closed, except for every Radio and TV talk show maven, or sports writer and newspaper columnist who just had to put forth their opinion in one manner or the other.

Yet after a week of commentary the news became relegated to the dust bin and the world kept on turning. Mel's lawyer gave her a brief call and they both concluded, divorce proceedings were not necessary. He declined to send he any further billings for his time, forgiving any billing time already in the hopper.

A week later, Mel sat down with her son after dinner and told him a carefully edited version of his father's death. Her son looked at her and said, "Does that mean there's just me and you mommy"?

"Yes Rory perhaps it's just me and you"!

"What about Grandma and Grandpa O'Bannon"?

"I just don't know yet. How do you feel about it"? Her son thought a moment then said, "Member when you and daddy were having trouble and I stayed with them for a few weeks? I overheard them talking about you when you were in the hospital. Can't remember all of it but Mommy, it wasn't very nice"!

"Then tell me whether or not you want to see them again and think about it real good"!

"Daddy treated you real bad and both grandma and grandpa talked bad things about you. You're my mommy and that's it"! Tears flooded into Mel's eyes for a moment then she cringed, wiping her eyes and said, "From this point on it's just you and me sport.

Nobody else is ever going to get between the both of us ever again as god is my witness. I love you as no other"! That said, the tears began to pour forth once again from her eyes, as Rory drew her close saying, "Don't worry Mommy, it's just you and me and I love you Mommy and I'll protect you. You don't worry about me Mommy for I'm gonna be the best little boy ever was"!

Now the flood gate opened full force and Mel and her son embraced tightly solidifying their mutual bond. In the days ahead they would need that unity at full force.

In the coming days, several things occurred all at once. A flurry of lawsuits against the Harris County Medical Examiner's office and each every member of the media that talked about or printed excerpts of the exact reasons of the O'Bannon's son's demise. Eventually the lawsuits came to nothing and were summarily dismissed from lack of evidence. Then a full court search for Melanie and her son was initiated, as an ongoing lawsuit for permanent custody for their grandson grew. This was thwarted by Melanie's employers, the Enron Corporation who closed their ranks shielding a valued hard working employee, who fit like a glove with their corporate culture. Of course her corporate physical appearance, her ongoing demeanor and her top drawer performance at her job cemented their closing of the ranks to any outside scrutiny. She remained hiding in plain sight in a major metropolitan area.

Then again was the question of Geoff O'Bannon's final disposition of assets. Since his death came at such an early age, scant thought or discussion ever broached the subject of a last will and testament, much less a life insurance policy. Since he died "In testate", with no final "Last will and Testament", as to the disposition of his remaining assets. Since his estate or the remainder thereof was subject to the many creditors, he'd amassed. It was given to the local courts to sort things out. His funeral was a closed casket affair attended by only the immediate family of blood ties and two media reporters, standing some distance away. The only thing that was said at the funeral that had any meaning was by the family pastor who intoned, "The candle that burns twice as bright, burns just half as long"! The O'Bannon family wondered about that final remark as they made their way to the limousines, but gave it short shrift in the aftermath. The only thing on their plate was discovering where their son's former wife had gotten off to with their grandson. Their task to gain custody of what they considered their flesh and blood and to that end they'd move heaven and earth if need be.

Their task was monumental, for first they had to find Melanie and her child. Then they had to prove that she was an unfit mother. Throw enough money at a problem and the problem would be resolved eventually. The first ninety days of their search, they spent well over a hundred thousand dollars on detectives. As the second ninety days of their quest to locate her, out of thin air, a report appeared on the evening newscasts, revealing Melanie and her son's whereabouts. Their home, where he went to school and her employer, resurrecting her recent history of her marriage with her former husband. Reporters dogged her for three days trying to get a story. On the third day, a process server hiding amidst a gaggle of news reporters as she appeared at the day care center to pick up her son after work, served he with legal papers summoning her to appear in front of a family court judge, to answer a custody dispute. Up until this moment she had held up rather well, but in front of the news cameras, she finally broke down, looking at each and every one of the reporters with tears in her eyes saying, "When will your entertainment be enough? I'm just trying to live my life and raise my child. Isn't there anything else more newsworthy"?

In his office watching the evening news, sat her former father in law, almost in ecstasy as he intoned, "Gotcha now Bitch"!

The news media, their work completed, settled down to direct their attention elsewhere, while the O'Bannon family went to a full court press, hiring additional detectives and a battery of lawyers to build a custody case against her. Melanie, although paid well by her employers, scarcely had the fiscal resources to effectively combat a legal war against her now mortal enemy, the entire O'Bannon family. Her only resource was the way she lived her life. Her work and her son were the only things that mattered, not necessarily in that order. Yet unlike lesser lights, she refused to allow her personal problem interfere with her performance at work. Soon those who interacted with her on a daily basis marveled at her cheerful demeanor, as she entered the workplace, a model of corporate image, each day. There was time enough, the moment she left the workplace, to shed tears.

Of course, her initial meeting with her attorney was during a weekend and all subsequent meetings were quickly conducted, by phone during her lunch hour at work. Unknown to Mel, was that the O'Bannon family had her home phone illegally tapped a move that yielded them little of any use. Now for the long, costly slog through the courts. Yet this played to their advantage, as the ongoing costs of detectives shadowing Melanie, bore no useable fruit. Her attorney, well-practiced in the intricacies of Texas Family Law, realized quickly what he was up against. A relentless, well-funded attack by those with deep pockets and recommended a Fabian approach of legal delaying tactics. Sympathetic to her cause, unlike many others in his profession, he kept a close watch on his billing time, keeping it to the absolute minimum, yet the flurry of legal briefs and counter briefs presented to the court drove the costs upward.

Three months later, as she went to bed, she knelt down and finally started to pray, for she knew of nothing else to do. Eventually, she reckoned, they would discover something, anything in her past to use against her, to gain custody of her child. They would bleed her dry. In her pajamas, she prayed for the Eternal to send a savior. She hadn't the resources to fight the fight. She prayed for someone to watch over her.

A week later, her eyes reluctantly came across those of a rather rough looking man at Ballys. Her only extravagance. She'd recently joined to shed some weight, but moreover to physically channel her pent up emotions as a form of release. She'd make the appropriate budget adjustments later.

As their eyes met, she felt some discomfort, juxtaposed with a form of flattery, she hadn't felt in quite a while. Yet this individual could simply be a plant by the O'Bannon family to gain an advantage. Yet, on the other hand, if this man was a plant, wouldn't he be a more handsome metro sexual type? Anything was possible she reckoned. Best to keep all thoughts of personal companionship on the far back burner. Better yet, best to shed all thoughts of any sort of companionship off the grid. She'd quickly picked up the corporate patois of Enron rather nicely, she thought. Yet deep in her mind, the ongoing mantra, played over and over. Someone to watch over me. Of course, playing the part of a corporate secretary to a rising star in the Enron heavens, bore many benefits, she had to avoid. Tickets to sporting events, were gratis, yet ignored. Lavish dinners and soirees amongst the corporate Honcho's had to be graciously turned down. During her legal siege, she garnered a hoard of rain checks, for future retrieval, that everyone understood, as she played the part of the stoic widow. After all she had quite enough of that life, as the wife of a local former NFL superstar.

Several days later, she had to take a half days personal leave as she was summoned to court, finally for an appearance in her legal battle. Just five minutes away from the Enron headquarters downtown was the firm of Ledbetter and McHugh, Attorneys at Law, LLC in the Pennzoil Building. The offices were a stark contrast from the gleaming glass and steel building exterior, conveying a somber deliberate message to all that passed its portals. After announcing herself to the receptionist, Mel took a chair and yet another deep breath.

Within minutes a door opened to the inner and a rather severe looking woman of medium vintage entered the reception area announcing to Mel that she was Mr. Ledbetter's personal secretary and to please follow her.

As she entered his corner office overlooking the city and Buffalo Bayou, Charlie Ledbetter was on the phone and bid her to take a seat as he said, "We might have some good news", as he covered the mouthpiece on the phone. Several minutes of silence ensued, before Charlie Ledbetter said smiling at Melanie, "Well Miles, my client just walked in the door ready to go to court, but seeing that your client is feelin' a tad puny at the moment, I'll be a good sport and consult with my client as to whether or not to grant you a continuance. Just a moment while I put you on hold"!

Then he looked at Mel saying, "That Miles Sommerville is one son of a bitch, but a good attorney. As you know we been delaying things as much as possible and now that our options have skinnied up a bit, the heavens have opened up and granted us temporary absolution. He's on his cell phone from Memorial Hospital. Seems his client, Randall O'Bannon has got himself a severe case of gout. A male thing that comes from an overabundance of uric acid in one's diet. Very painful for a man's feet and toes, his carpals and tarsals. Both feet all swelled up and elevated. He's under pain medication to the max. Did all I could to keep from bustin' a gut while I was talkin' to him. Wants to know if you'll be so gracious to grant his client a continuance of say, at least ninety days. Now gout only comes from an overabundance of fine living and when it hits ya, if you're a man, it's a sheer Wholly Booger. He's gonna be laid up awhile in the Hospital, for quite a while. So my good woman should we grant him a continuance or not"?

"It's what we wanted is it not", asked Mel?

"Good. Then I have your answer. Just had to make it official. Gonna make myself a cuppa coffee and have a smoke while that son of a bitch stews awhile. Can we get you anything"? Mel shook her head. Then directly Ledbetter punched the hold button saying, "Miles, you still with us? Good. Had to exert a little moral suasion with my client, but she relented and granted you a ninety day continuance. Now court time is at One O'clock right after lunch. So you're the one who gets to hustle down to the court and file the continuance at your expense. Are we in agreement? Good! It's now just after eleven. I'll expect a fax in my office within the hour affirming our agreement. Goodbye"!

"It's done. Just had to make that little 'Pisher' sweat a little. Seems you have the rest of the afternoon off if ya want. That last little bit on the phone saved you some money. Seems to me that you could use a break in the action. Your boss Herb tells me that you've been hard at it and even a hard charging ass like him says you need a break, to stay in top form. While he's not accustomed to handing out 'Atta boys', he got a nose for talent and a keen mind when he sees it and say's you're the real deal. As you know we both went to Rice University together and I know where all his ancient bones are buried, which is why we're good friends. So go to the house and take the rest of the day off. Think of how much pain Mister O'Bannon is enduring at this very moment.

He set the junkyard Dogs of War upon you and now I've a feelin' the worm has turned"!

Rather than go home, Mel returned to her office fully aware of her boss's workload that lay before him. Just a five minute drive up Smith Street, she sat right down at her desk and plunged right in as if she'd never left. A half hour later her boss, emerged from his office, saw her at her desk and said, "You're supposed to be in court aren't you"?

"Ninety day continuance. The Warlock is in the hospital with gout. Hors de Combat for a while. Now what do you want to do with these acquisition affidavits"?

"Uh, take them up to Murray on twenty three in Legal and tell him to get right on them", said her boss as he rushed off to a meeting smiling, as he said under his breath, "Damn, that girl is a real Hoss"!

As she worked to make up the time lost, she was glad she opted to go back to work rather than lay about back home. There was much to do, made the day go by fast and anyway, when at home her every move was being recorded. While out on the street, her every move was shadowed by someone wherever she went. Early on, Charlie Led-better had someone go through her home and identified every place there was a microphone, pointing them out to both Mel and her son. Taking pictures and identifying the location of each and every one. Then he went through her car with a fine tooth comb, finding a mike and a mini sending unit neatly placed under the dashboard. Then he went to her office, along with Enron's security and examined her workplace and found nothing. Enron's internal security was second to none, such was their corporate culture.

"Go about your business as you normally would, except always be cognizant of your surroundings at all times. Situational awareness is crucial for the duration", said her lawyer!

He then obtained a Court Order, prohibiting any approach or contact by any member of the O'Bannon family or their employees or agents, to the defendant or any member of her immediate family within a radius of one hundred yards, explaining to Mel that in cases such as this, where passions may be inflamed, a legal perimeter must be maintained. "We'll allow the illegal bugs to stay in place and it's vital that we don't let on that we know they are in place, so that I'll have a rather nasty surprise in store for them when we go to trial. The Judge will not be pleased"!

"You don't talk in your sleep do you", asked Ledbetter?

"I don't know", said Mel surprised. "Good. Before you leave I'm going to loan you a small sound activated pocket recorder. For the first ten days I want you to plug it into your wall socket and turn it on every night when you go to bed. It'll only record when a sound is made. If you do talk in your sleep, we'll know what you said. Of course, so will the O'Bannon's. If you don't, we'll know after the next ten days. Each day messenger the nights tape to my office. I'll ring up Herb your boss and clear it with him. After ten days you can return the unit"!

Ten days later ten tapes were collected with a grand total of five minutes of sound recorded, usually the occasional grunt or the sounds of a receptacle flushing. Melanie did not talk in her sleep. She had no visitors. She was for all intensive purposes, "As pure as Caesars wife"! Even armed with the knowledge of the violation of her privacy, Mel was upset by the constant scrutiny. The O'Bannon's knew whenever she bathed or, relieved herself. They knew when she left and when she returned. She had to speak to her own son in hushed tones whenever they wanted to talk, except for the meals they had together, when they both knew that others were listening in. Through it all, her son held up remarkably well, holding to the discipline set forth by the situation at hand. Just one little mistake.

One seemingly innocuous comment could give the O'Bannon's ammunition to gain custody of him. Privately he vowed that would never happen. He would run away and if caught, would run away again and again. Of course he never revealed that to his mother. His mother was now his role model, as she always had been. He would follow her lead.

Later on after work, as she checked into Ballys for her hour long session, she ran into Randy, the manager and as they cheerfully chatted she asked him about the man she'd seen from time to time. "Oh, you must mean Jaeger. He's not bothering you, is he"?

"No, it's nothing like that. It's just that. I don't know how to put this in words, but awhile back, he looked at me and", her voice trailing off. "And you felt uncomfortable", said Randy finishing her sentence.

"Why yes", she answered sheepishly.

"Probably my fault. You see when he first saw you I was spotting for him in the bench press, and your presence drew his attention away from the bar, during the last rep. Anyway, I inadvertently mentioned your name. I know this guy for a long time and he comes here to work out not to chase women like some others do. I apologize, for I've been following your problem in the newspapers and I'll work harder to try and keep your membership here confidential"!

"I appreciate that Randy, but apparently there's detectives trailing me everywhere I go and it's not going to go away any time soon! By the way, what does this Jaeger do"?

"He's an investor of sorts, as far as I know. We don't talk about business too much when working out"!

"An investor you say. He doesn't look the part", offered Mel.

"Yeah, sorta runs against type. Doesn't have the pencil neck and your first reaction to him is typical. Hey people when they first look at me, give me a wide berth, but I'm big as a house. No, I know this guy, five or six years now and I'd call him one of the good guys. Never seen him have a problem in here. But I'll keep an eye out for any strangers if they ask about you, or seem to be hanging out in the parking lot if ya want"!

"I appreciate it Randy", said Mel as she headed for the Woman's locker room to change.

For the next several days, Jaeger reappeared at Ballys daily after a long absence. During their normal workout routine their paths would cross, from time to time and it seemed that he went out of his way to avoid eye contact with her. Could it have been that Big Randy had said something to him about her apparent concern?

A week later as she went up to the mezzanine, she caught sight of the both of them in the free weight area, with Randy hovering over this Jaeger as he was struggling to press upward one final repetition. "One more, ya putz. C'mon man up and get it up there", yelled Randy as the bar, inched upward, with Jaeger bellowing forth a grunt as the bar clanged forth into its resting place. Mel then turned and went to the track for her first of five warm up laps, prior to hitting the machines. This was familiar territory for her, because during her entire marriage to Geoff, she was in the gym many times watching him master the laws of gravity. Grunting, sweating, his body exuding pheromones in massive quantities. Of course, whenever she was around, he always flexed after each session, presumably as a show of his Alpha superiority and of course back then it always worked. It got her horny. That was then. This was now. As she jogged around the track slowly, she glanced into the parking lot below during each lap, through the long glass curtain wall, to see if anyone was hanging around or seemed out of place, holding up a lamp post. Finding nothing out of place as far as she could determine, she thought back to her conversation with Randy, concluding that probably nothing passed between them regarding her, or else they probably wouldn't be working out together. She let it pass from her mind until her fifth lap, when passing the free weight area, she saw Jaeger spotting Randy as he was struggling to press the plate laden bar, bending slightly under the weight, upward bellowing as Jaeger bellowed back, his hands at the ready to provide an assist if needed. The bar settled in as Randy jumped up yelling "Oompah"!

While married to Geoff, she played the part of a celebrity wife. Once the troubles came she downplayed her appearance, knowing full well that she was a head turner. While at Enron, it was vital to be attractive, yet in a subdued, businesslike way, always appearing within the parameters of appropriateness. Yet as much as she hated to admit it, she felt some inking of attraction for this man who went out of his way to avoid her. This had never happened before. The men she encountered previously always made their intentions known up front in a variety of ways, more often than not in a clumsy manner, regardless the venue. Of course, given her current circumstances, this was not the time to entertain any thought of having a man in her life. And yet, the more this man avoided her, the greater was the attraction. Randy, had said that he was one of the "White Hats"! Had the O'Bannon's gotten to him? How could they? Or was it paranoia closing in on her. Then she recalled something Charlie Ledbetter said to her in passing as he outlined the role she must endure during the interim, "Paranoia is simply the flip side of complete awareness. So says that font of wisdom, the comedian George Carlin"!

Of course it was a joke, but deep within, it contained a message worth heeding. She decided to live her life, aware, but in a state of balance. The lawsuit was on hold for the present, the protective court order was in place and she would still be wary of the unseen, but perhaps, just perhaps, she could test the waters and make an acquaintance. Normally a friendly and outgoing sort, she had become one with the enduring false smile, watching the shadows and she didn't like what she was becoming.

From time to time she would sneak a look at the man from across the gym, whose avoidance of her began to prove somewhat a challenge.

She began to form her own opinion of the man from afar, reckoning that he was a highly independent type that as a child was typically in trouble with his betters, who just might have acquired the reputation as, "Not playing well with others", yet had somehow smoothed out during the course of his life. When chance permitted, she sneaked a glance at his ring finger from afar and finding no ring, or the white ring that indicated one was worn, usually and removed whenever the occasion warranted, concluded this man was not a player and whatever he was, he was a serious individual.

Jaeger went through his usual late afternoon ritual whenever time permitted, if he was not off chasing some runner. Since his schedule had diminished somewhat he was now going with greater frequency, taking full advantage of the various services offered other than just the gym. Lately, during each session he kept encountering this Melanie woman as their paths would intersect, providing an uncomfortable moment for each. With each mostly wordless encounter, the tension between them was palpable. Something about her was very familiar, but he couldn't quite put his finger on it. Then he remembered her last name and a light bulb went off in his head. The following day, he went downtown and after finding nothing pressing at Rafferty's, he walked over to, The Houston Chronicle newspaper and spent time in the microfiche files, known as the "catacombs", and poured over a hoard of newspaper articles and pictures, regarding her former husband, his problems, her separation, his death and finally her ongoing problems with retaining custody from the O'Bannon's. That completed, he looked at his watch and decided to eat a late lunch. As he walked around Old Market Square, taking in all of the odors and smells, he sat on a park bench digesting all that he'd learned.

As attractive and appealing as she was, she was trouble wrapped in Christmas packaging. Clearly she was under siege by the O'Bannon family for custody of her son and it seemed they were pulling out all the stops and had the deep pockets to get it done. His life was already complicated, by the news that the Santangelo family was circling the wagons and would be on the warpath as soon as their sons were released from prison. Two wealthy families who made their fortunes selling automobiles. 'What was it with those people', he wondered? They made millions moving metal to the masses. Hard charging types, their people always on the tube, with the allure of the low down and the high take away with the easy monthly payments. They could sell ice to Eskimos and usually got their way in any and everything.

Yet in spite of everything, all he could focus on was the very thing that wouldn't go away, this woman, called Melanie. From the very first time he laid his eyes on her, his appetite, usually quite substantial had withered away. Food held little taste anymore. He had to do something. He reached into his pocket and removed a quarter, flipping it and grabbing it in midair, then slapping it down upon his other hand. As he peered under the covering hand, his decision was made. He was going to lunch.

After work, Mel fought the rush hour traffic, with everyone else, landing in Ballys parking lot. Gym bag in hand, she locked her car and went inside. Minutes later she was upstairs making her initial warm up laps around the track. By the third lap, she caught sight of Jaeger settling into the incline bench press machine, as he set the stop all the way to the bottom she passed him doing a slow jog. By her final lap, she slowed down and made the decision to make his acquaintance at long last, standing right in front of him as he pressed the bar upward, eyes closed, and sweat pouring forth and grunting during his final rep. When the plates fell down with a large bang, Jaeger opened his eyes and there she was a vision from the heavens greeted his eyes, smiling at him.

"Impressive", she said as Jaeger arose to face her, his heart racing either from his exertions or her presence, most probably both. "Hello" she said. "I'm Melanie O'Bannon. Randy says you're one of the good guys", she continued, offering her hand in greeting. "I was wondering if you would be kind enough to give me some pointers on technique. Folks who know me call me Mel"!

Rarely in his life, was Jaeger at a loss for words. This instant was one of those rarities as he took her hand gently into his saying, "My friends call me Jaeger", he stammered, feeling the warmth of her touch, before withdrawing his hand. Then he heard her say as if through a tunnel, the blood rushing to his face, "Jaeger? Good, now what's your first name"?

"That's it. Jaeger. Nothing more. It's all there is on my birth certificate and driver's license. A little lifelong gag my father decided to play on me long ago. NFN, No first name, NMI, No middle initial, Jaeger and that is who I am"!

"A unique cognomen to say the least, but memorable", she said! "Sounds incomplete doesn't it", as they both continued muddling through with the small talk. "But I'm used to it", he mumbled further, now completely under her control, her gaze holding his tightly locked. Her touch brought both discomfort and delight simultaneously.

Then the silence that passed between them in only ten seconds of duration, seemed like an eternity as Jaeger finally said, "I'm sorry, you wanted some pointers on technique"?

"Yes, thank you"! Then wiping the back of the incline machine with his gym towel, he said, "Let's see how you do things, before I comment", he said offering her his place on the machine, as she selected a weight she was comfortable with. When she completed her first set Jaeger then said, "Ok, I can see what you're doing incorrectly. It's your breathing patterns, or lack thereof. Easily corrected. As you push the bar upward, it's referred to as the positive, as the bar returns back downward, it's referred to as the negative. You want to exhale on the positive and inhale on the negative, in every exercise. Sort of counterintuitive, but a great many people either do not breathe during their set, or breathe incorrectly. Your body requires a great deal of oxygen or air when under exertion and proper breathing is vital when exercising"!

"How come you're not a trainer here", asked Mel? "I do other things. This is what keeps me sane"! "So what is it that you do"?

"I, uh, invest"!

"Oh, you're an entrepreneur"!

"No simply an, uh, Investor. They hold and own for a bit. Buy low and sell high, perhaps do some managing of resources along the way"!

"You don't resemble any investor I've ever encountered"!

"No, I suppose I don't do I. A walking paradox, but there we are. Perhaps we should go to the next machine"!

And there it was, the connection made. As they worked their way from machine to machine, he patiently explained the purpose of each machine, and the kinetic purpose it had on each and every portion of her musculature. The time flew by and after they had only completed a third of the machines, she glanced at the clock saying, "Jaeger, my hour's up and I have to hurry and pick up my son. Will you be here tomorrow, same time same station so we can finish with your instruction"?

"Certainly. It would be my pleasure", he said as she turned and rushed off down the stairs. He wandered over to the front of the facility, by the widows facing the parking lot. She had to go through the front entrance to get to her car. Automatically he scanned the lot out of nothing more than habit. Several minutes later, there she was, hurrying towards her car, a late model BMW. Fitting since she was the former wife of an NFL player. She was attired in her work clothes, belaying the fact that she worked for a firm where image was a constant. As she entered her car, he noticed someone in the lot rushing to another car and jumping in it, as she left, the other car was following her. There was nothing he could do, as they both merged into the evening rush hour melee. He said a quick prayer for her safety, promising himself that he'd try and remember the individual and the vehicle the following afternoon. This time, imprinting the O'Bannon tail into his memory. Now some of the dots slowly merged into a reality. She needed help. Furthermore, her presence seemed as a godsend for his very soul. He must tread gently.

If Einstein only knew. As brilliant as he was, he was silent regarding the passage of time as far as it related directly to the human condition. Even the most common of folk, could relate to the glacial pace the passage of time occurred, when in a long line that seemed not to be moving. Or when involved in a task that was completely undesirable, like shoveling manure, or being compelled to attend a meeting or lecture, when the moderator or lecturer droned on and on regarding useless minutiae. Every second seemed like an eternity.

Conversely, Einstein never commented on being in the company of an exciting member of the opposite gender, or when having a grand time in the company of another. Each second apart seeming like an eternity and each second together flew by at warp speed. Of course he couldn't, for his very existence was Uber Mathematics', on a scale hitherto unknown, with no time to be spent on such frivolous affairs.

Yet there it was. The connection made at long last, both Mel and Jaeger, both jointly and severally spent the evening experiencing the very same paradox. The glacial passage of time. At least Mel had her motherly tasks to attend to and the following day, the whirlwind of corporate activity to keep her busy, while Jaeger had little. Read a book, watch the Telly. Usually he could wander downtown and check in with Rafferty, to see if anyone significant had skipped bail. Yet currently he was not of a mind. Once involved, it was all consuming, till recapture. Anything that might keep him away from this Melanie was just not going to happen. Besides, he'd been a busy boy recently, made a bundle of money and could afford, a few weeks of diversions.

Later in the day, he stopped by the nearby Builders Square and made a small purchase. Perhaps later on if Mel's minders made another appearance, he had a low tech way of slowing them down a bit.

Mel appeared at Ballys after work at her usual time. After changing, she went upstairs to the mezzanine and saw Jaeger in the free weight section along with several others of his testosterone laden brethren and a few women in the mix working with the barbells, so she immediately felt right at home. She walked up to Jaeger smiling as he was completing a set on the curl bar; of course he spotted her arrival with the plethora of mirrors surrounding everyone.

As she flashed a smile, she said looking at all of the mirrors, "I just love the smell of Steroids in the late afternoon"! Jaeger smiled and replied, "The movie Apocalypse Now and the line went, "Napalm in the morning", I believe"!

"But we're not at war with anyone are we? Besides its afternoon, isn't it"?

"I suppose your right", chuckled Jaeger. "But before we begin, I need to discuss something with you, if you'll follow me". With that he led her to the front of the mezzanine that looked out upon the front parking lot, positioning themselves near the jogging track that ran the full length of the building. As they both peered out onto the parking lot Jaeger said, "I watched as you left last night and discovered that someone appeared very interested in following you. One man in civvies sitting on the bench in front of the IHOP and another in a nearby car. The guy sitting on the bench signaled his driver as you came out and followed you as you went out onto the street. Now let us see if we can discover who your shadow is"!

Then he pointed out a man, sitting on the park bench in front of the IHOP, reading the paper, and then further scanning revealed a certain model car with someone in the driver's seat. "Same guy different clothes, but the car over there is the same one that followed you out of the parking lot. So I've an idea how to slow em down if you'll stay here in the shadow a few minutes, watch for me to walk out of the door"!

Mel nodded her as Jaeger hurried away. In a few minutes, she saw him emerge from the front door, carrying his gym bag as if he was leaving and walked to an old Ford sedan. He entered the car then emerged again this time without his jacket, sliding down between the cars. She saw him work his way around to the car he indicated, crouching all the way then disappearing for about a minute or so, then caught sight of him again as he went back to his car, crouching between the cars all the way. This time he emerged from his car, without his jacket but with sunglasses on and his gym bag and reentered the facility. Several minutes later he rejoined her in the shadows saying, "That ought a gentle em out a little"!

"I saw you out in the lot but what did you do", asked Mel? "Oh, nothing much. A dozen ten penny nails placed three each in front and behind each of the rear tires, sometimes do wonders, especially during drive time traffic. No matter which way they go, three of the nails will be imbedded in their tires, eventually causing them to run flat. Cars need four good tires to operate well. As they try and tail you home, the tires will flatten causing them to stop. Hopefully in the middle of an intersection behind you as you drive off. I'd hate to be them in about an hour or so"!

"You have a delightfully wicked mind Jaeger"!

"A product of a misspent youth no doubt"! As they walked off to start their workout, Mel asked, "What prompted you to, uh", searching for the correct words to complete her thought, Jaeger spoke up saying, "Stick my nose into your business"?

"That's one way to put it"!

"Old habits. Randy told me your last name that lit a bulb in my head, so I went to the Chronicle and remembered that you were married to a player for the Oilers. Looked up all of the old newspaper articles. Your marriage, your husband's fall from grace, the manner of his death and finally his parents attempt to gain custody of your son. Here, let's start here on the leg lift machine, we can talk between sets"!

After she finished a set Mel said, "So you know everything about me, do you"?

"Hardly, only skimmed the top. The rest is none of my business, unless and only should you decide otherwise. This I do not recommend. We've just met and trust must be earned. Right now you're in a tight spot and if I were you, quite frankly I wouldn't know whom to trust"!

"You make your point well, Jaeger"!

"All I can do is point out the obvious. Your ex was on a downward spiral. It started long before his injury. The injury only accelerated the process. His erratic behavior was due in part to a massive increase of anabolic steroids, along with I suspect cocaine and a brutal gambling habit I'm guessing. The dots connect themselves. You were smart to get out when you did and in the manner you did"!

"Have you been in contact with my lawyer"?

"Don't know who the person is. Besides, I try and keep as much distance between me and lawyers at all costs. Now to your second set. I'll keep you glutes tight and shapely"! As she could hear his constant mantra, "Exhale on the positive and inhale on the negative. Say this over and over each time you perform a set and soon it'll be as automatic as your heartbeat"!

Twenty minutes later while on another machine she asked, "So what do I do when I go out into the parking lot afterwards"?

"Nothing. Put your key in the ignition, start the car, then join the rush hour traffic. Unless they have those very expensive 'Run Flat' tires on their car, they won't be following you long. Just make note of them in your rearview mirror. Unlike the movies, they'll probably be in another lane no more than two cars away, to be less visible. Of course a single tail during rush hour is always a problem, what with all the others cars and the randomness of stop lights. Still, I'll keep an eye out as you leave, just to see what happens"!

"Sounds like you used to work for the CIA or some other agency, not something an investor might know about"!

"I read a lot. And now to the next machine, for you have just ten minutes to go before you have to leave"!

As she worked her pectorals, she saw him standing right before her, watching her go through the motions, seemingly in a professional manner, saying over and over, "Exhale on the positive. Inhale on the negative"! Minutes later, he looked at the clock on the wall and said, "Time. Time to pick up your kid"!

Wiping the sweat from her face she said, "Tomorrow then"?

"Same time, same station"! As she got to the stairway, she glanced back only to see Jaeger watching her, and then went downstairs to change.

Minutes later, Jaeger was in the shadows, by the jogging track watching the guy still on the bench in front of the IHOP, as well as the other one in the car. As Melanie emerged from the front entrance, the guy on the park bench stood up and the car started in his direction, picking him up as Mel started her car and drove towards the Hollister exit and out into traffic and the other car took a parallel exit fifty yards away and neatly slid into the next lane some three cars behind her. Jaeger then saddled up and went downstairs, got his gym bag and jacket and went outside. He went straight away towards the parking spot where the spotter car was. There on the ground, were twelve ten penny nails all facing point forward, which meant, that twelve were firmly imbedded in the wheels of their car. They wouldn't be following Melanie long. Thank goodness for a misspent youth.

The following day Melanie arrived at Ballys and quickly sought out Jaeger beaming with joy. "Well, how did your trip home come out? By the smile on your face and the fact that you're here, must've been OK"!

Breathlessly Melanie said, "It was just as you'd outlined. I saw the other car take another exit and it worked its way up two cars back in the adjoining lane. We went through three intersections and it was still there maintaining its distance, with two people inside. Traffic was thick and we were moving slowly, plus I don't mind telling you I was nervous. Now it was abundantly clear, everything my lawyer was telling me, that I was being followed. Then I had to turn left on West Little York and after a while, the car that was following me was no longer there. Later after I put my son to bed, I was watching the ten PM newscast and there was a report of a crash at the very intersection that I went through at about the same time I went through that intersection. The car was turning left, lost control for some reason and crashed into an oncoming delivery truck. Jaeger, it was the car that was following me. To make matters worse, one of those in the car died when the fuel tank ruptured setting fire to the car and the other is in the hospital with third degree burns"!

"Sounds like the almighty was just thin'in out the herd a bit", said Jaeger arching an eyebrow. My guess is that your minders were retired law enforcement people who got their PI license and were tryin' to make a living the only way they knew. If they had family I'll shed a tear, if not, well", he let his voice trail off to nothing, adding "Whadda ya say we work our bodies? Maximize your time"!

For the next several weeks Jaeger and Mel met each afternoon after her work for an hour of workouts, gradually mixing in free weights and machines, with laps around the track. They each arrived and departed separately. One day they ran into Big Randy while doing their laps around the track and stopped to say hello.

"Damn it Jaeger" he said smiling. "Training the members without a state license. Takin' away income from my trainers"? "Just workout buddies Randy" said Jaeger. "Don't let your shorts get into a twist"! "I'm just messin' with ya. Besides the both of ya look good together. Jaeger, keep an eye on her already"!

"I'll do what I can Randy. Do what I can", he said, as Randy walked away smiling and greeting other people.

"Well, I suppose that makes things at least semi-official", offered Mel! "Semi-official"?

"Randy said we both look good together. I agree. What about you"? Jaeger was surprised by her admission, which of course was Manna from Heaven to his ears, as he stumbled for the appropriate response saying, "I couldn't agree more"!

"Good. Since we're in agreement, I've a question for you"! "Fire away"!

"Do you own a tux"?

"Nope. Never even been in one. Why do you ask"?

"Well, as you know I've been socially inactive for quite a while, for good reason. My boss at Enron, one of the soon to be big wigs, has gotten me an invitation to their annual Christmas Party. Of course, it's not stag, but a drag affair. Must have a suitable escort. Someone who can behave properly in the company of Alpha's. Now of course, there are any number of pencil necks who'd be delighted to escort me. But somehow not a one can pass muster. If I can't have someone suitable to escort me, I'd just as soon stay home. Are you game, sport"?

"Well, it looks like I'm going to have to be fitted for a tuxedo Mel. But since I've never owned one, I'll need someone to help me in the selection. Are ya game sport"?

"The event's a few weeks away and today is Wednesday. What about I give you my number and you call me tonight and we work out a possibility being together shopping this Saturday"!

"What about your son"?

"Well, he'll come along to meet you. Do you mind"?

"Not a bit. In fact I'd enjoy it. Now let's get into our workout"! Later as they finished up they both scanned the parking lot from the shadows of the mezzanine and seeing nothing out of place both went to their lockers and went out together as if it were the most natural thing in the world. As they passed Big Randy at the front desk, he gave them both a knowing nod of approval. Now things were official.

The following Saturday morning Jaeger pulled up to their townhouse and extracted Melanie and her son Rory, for a day of shopping. The rebuilt Ford Galaxie was a point of discussion for both Mel and her son as Jaeger recounted his tale of taking a wreck out of a junkyard and during the period of about a year completely rebuilding it as better than the day it first came off the show room floor. "There were only four hundred fifty of this type ever built and for its day it was state of the art. Of course, I've upgraded it completely, except I decided to keep the bench seats in front rather than convert to the buckets", said Jaeger proudly!

"Cool. That means I can stay up front with the both of you", beamed Rory happily. "Mommy, for lunch, can we go to McDonalds"?

The first two places they went Mel looked over the offerings with a jaundiced eye, finding little of interest, as Jaeger picked up little Rory as if he was his very own son. Finding little, they retired to the nearest McDonalds then made their way further into town. There Melanie went through her paces and selected two tuxedos for Jaeger to try on. She then selected the second one and summoned the tailor, as he took the measurements and made certain adjustments, she made her suggestions known. A little more here, a little less there, until she was satisfied. They both agreed the following Saturday would be a splendid time to pick it up and see if the fitting was proper.

Upon their way back, they stopped at a Toy's R Us store, lest little Rory have a hissy fit. Christmas was near and how was Mom to know what he wanted, unless he told Santa?

As they shopped, Jaeger asked little Rory if he'd been a good boy all year and as Rory answered he kept an eye on Mel. "I've been as good as I can be", to which Mel nodded in agreement saying, "He's been the best", after they waited in line for her son to tell his wish list to Santa, her hand quietly slipped into Jaegers as they both looked straight ahead. As she touched his hand, which gently enveloped hers, Mel felt a brief shiver, summoning a feeling of relief and contentment. Amidst the clamor of the afternoon, the Christmas Carols over the stores PA system gradually evolved into the song, "Someone to watch over Me", as they both listened, their eyes never left her son who was now on Santa's lap, yapping away.

Never in his life has Jaeger felt such peace and contentment. Something mysterious brought him into this woman's life. Something he'd have to earn. Something precious, worth more than gold. Then finished with Santa, Rory ran to his mother and Jaeger saying proudly, "Well Santa has my list, mommy"!

"Will you tell us what you wanted from Santa", asked Mel? When he was finished breathlessly with his wish list, Jaeger said, "I think you left something out"! Rory looked at Jaeger and said, "No sir, I don't think I did"?

"You were born in Texas weren't you"? "Yes sir"!

"You're a Texan aren't you"? "Yes sir. I think so"?

"I think so too. So if the both of you will follow me, I think I've something in mid that will make you smile. An early reward for being a good little soldier and listening to your mommy"!

As they walked to the rear of the store they entered an aisle they never saw before, and Jaeger reached up and pulled down several boxes saying, "A proper Texican boy needs the proper Texican duds and stuff. Boots, hat, six guns and holster and finally a repeater BB air rifle, just like the Red Ryder. Now when I was a little boy just about your age, my daddy got me all this and he taught me how to do the "Road Agent Spin"!

"What's the Road Agent Spin, Jaeger"? Looking at Mel he said, "With your Mommy's permission, we'll walk out of the store right now with all of this as my present to you for being such a good boy and can take it home with you today. Then later on after we've dressed you properly in the hat, boots, chaps, and holster, I'll teach you just like my Daddy did me long ago, 'The Spin' move that few people know."!

"Please Mommy, can I have this, so Jaeger can teach me the spin", pleaded little Rory!

"Only on the condition that he allows me to cook supper for him, this very night"! Jaeger looked at Mel and said, "How can I say no"?

"You can't pardner. Now let's get these to the register before the crowd gets the better of us"!

For the next several weeks, Jaeger and Mel were almost a daily fixture, after working hours. They'd meet every day after her work for a session, then Jaeger would follow her to pick up her son and then to her home, sometimes staying for dinner. Each time he stayed, little Rory would dress up in his Red Ryder outfit, then Jaeger would spend time with him while Mel was preparing dinner, going over and over the basics of, the "Spin", breaking it down slowly again and again.

"Now buckaroo, it's going to take a lot of practice, before you get it right. You'll drop your gun over and over, but don't get discouraged. Took me almost six months of trying before I finally got it right, the first time. Then it was almost a year, until I could do it over and over in my dominate hand without giving it a single thought. Then ya know what my Daddy then said"?

"No", said the eager young face looking at him!

"Well son, then my Daddy said, 'Good, now do it with the other hand. When ya get good with both hands then maybe you'll be of some use', is what he said"!

"Golly, that's gonna take a long time", said Rory!

"Son right now at your age, you got all the time in the world. But ya can't waste it. What'll happen if one of the bad guys gets the drop on you and your mommy some day and he says, "Gimme your gun or I'll shoot ya", huh? "Well the guy is most likely to shoot the both of you anyway, so giving him your gun is a bad move, for you have to protect your mother above all else. So if you master this with either hand as I know you will, you can turn the tables on the bad guy and pump a few rounds in him before he can even blink"!

"Did ya ever have to do this", asked Rory? "Yup once, awhile back"!

"Did you save your Mommy and Daddy"? "Nope, did it to save myself"!

"Is your Mommy and Daddy still alive"?

"Nope their both in heaven, with my two sisters and I'll bet their all looking down on us now and smiling. Now let's both go into the kitchen and see what kind of grub, your mommy has rustled up for us"!

The tuxedo picked up and examined and fitted to Jaeger, to Melanie's satisfaction, they emerged with the proper shoes, tie and shirt replete with cufflinks. As Rory tagged along beside them, they all looked the proper family as Jaeger said, "I've an idea how we can spend the afternoon together. Something that might prove useful and fun"!

"You're not going to tell us, you're going to surprise us aren't you", said Mel!

"That's the plan", said Jaeger. So just after lunch, they pulled into the Shooting range far out in the northwest portion of the county. As they pulled into the parking lot, the din of gunfire ceased, as they heard over the loudspeakers, "All ranges cease fire and everyone secure their weapons"!

Once a target was selected, they secured a bench and Jaeger removed a .22 rifle from its scabbard along with two sets of ear protectors and ear plugs for little Rory saying, "Today Rory I'm going to teach your mom how to shoot. So today you get to watch and learn. Once this is over if it's OK with your Mom, you and I will come back here and then I'll teach you personally, firearms safety and how to shoot like a pro"! Jaeger had placed them at the fifty yard range, loading and placing the rifle in its rest on the bench saying, "Soon, the range master will announce for everyone to take positions.

Once that's accomplished to his satisfaction, then he'll announce to all the signal to commence firing. Here, everything is about safety"! Soon thereafter the Range Master announced over the loudspeaker, "Ready on the left. Ready on the right. Ready on the firing line. Commence Firing"! Standing next to Jaeger as the staccato firing began, was little Rory, who winced at first, but then settled down as he saw his mother take aim at the target down range and do what Jaeger told her to do. He concentrated on Jaeger and tried to listen to what he was saying through the earplugs and the din of the other firearms.

After fifteen minutes of firing, all heard the message of, "Cease Fire. Secure your weapons and step back from your benches"! As they stepped back, Jaeger said, "Someone is now going to go down range and remove and replace the targets for those who are finished. When they return, then we can look down range through the spotter scope to see where our shots landed and make what corrections are needed"!

Little Rory was now in a state of excitement, by this time as his mother knelt down to calm him down. Jaeger lit a cigarette and somehow began to feel uneasy as he slowly glanced around, from behind his sunglasses. Ever since he'd taken care of Mel's minders, suspected to be in the employ of the O'Bannon's, he'd almost forgotten about the Santangelo family. 'Sloppy. Very sloppy', he told himself.

Out of the corner of his eye he saw a man, standing off in the distance, under a tree looking down range with no rifle or firearms bag nearby. Quite out of place for a firing range. Then he looked in the other direction as others milled about and there standing right under another tree enjoying the shade was another man, looking bored and playing with his finger nails. Both men had sunglasses on wearing distinctive shirts. If these two were hired by the cheapskate Santangelo like the retired cop, then Carl Santangelo was wasting his money. The question Jaeger had was, 'Where did they pick him up at'? 'Did they know where he lived'? 'We're they replacements for the former shadow, or were they part of a hit squad'? Jaeger had no way of knowing. He just had to play this out. But now it wasn't just about him, there were two others in the mix of even greater importance.

As Jaeger joined Mel and Rory at the bench he peered into the spotting scope, then invited Mel, then Rory to peer into the scope to see where the rounds hit. "High and to the right Mel, which means your tending to jerk the trigger, just a bit. A smooth and gradual squeeze", he said after going over once again, the firing ritual, the controlled breathing and the squeeze. "Always the squeeze".

After the second sequence of firing, Jaeger decided to buy some time and directed the range to secure and replace the target for a third round saying, "Mel, what say we let your son have a go at this"! Mel looked at her son, whose eyes pleaded with her then said, "OK. But only if you do exactly what Jaeger says"!

When the target came back, Jaeger congratulated Mel on her improvement with several hits right inside the target ring saying, "Rory, I think your mom just might have the makings of a shooter", looking at Mel who was smiling at her accomplishment, as she replied, "The first time I've ever even touched a firearm and look what I've done"!

After the third session, Rory stepped back eagerly awaiting the "All Clear" to approach the bench. Then Jaeger signaled for him to approach smiling as he said, Fifteen rounds fired, two Bulls. Look here Rory at what you've done"!

After the fourth session, he signaled the range employee to bring back their target for inspection. As he glanced around, the very same two men were still there flanking them.

Rory was ecstatic as he showed his mother what he'd done, as Jaeger said, "Mel, I think this target just might be suitable for framing and hanging in his bedroom. You're little critter is only going to get better with practice, as will you. In fact I think both are worth framing if you'll allow me to have this honor"!

"Stay put a few minutes, while I put away the rifle and the bag, so I can get a few pistols and we can walk up to the pistol range"! While Jaeger went to the trunk of his car to exchange weapons, Mel took her son inside for a few soft drinks. Keeping an eye out for his minders as he exchanged weapons, he knelt down and examined the tires, finding nothing surprising, he then extracted another bag and closed the trunk, joining Mel and her son inside the office while he paid for the pistol range slot.

As he set up for the pistol range, he took out an old single action Colt .45 and a small Beretta .25 automatic. Placing each one in a separate firing platform, saying to Rory, "Your Mom is going to fire the small automatic, while I fire this relic. Then he instructed Mel how to fire the Beretta as he loaded the weapon, noting that one of his watchers had joined briefly the other then walked over behind them still flanking Jaeger. Then Jaeger turned to Rory prior to loading his Colt and demonstrated the "shift", smiled and loaded the weapon stepping back, joining Mel and her son awaiting instructions from the range master.

Each of his minders was about twenty yards away, trying not to look interested in Jaeger, which was ridiculous, for at a firing range, no one just stood around watching. Everyone participated in one fashion or another. They were going past their third hour at the range and still the duo stood holding up trees.

Mel had three clips prepared to fire plus one in the weapon, when the signal to "Commence Firing" was given. Jaeger approached and picked up the old Colt and assumed the dueling stance, firing off the first six rounds one by one, then quickly reloading and firing six rounds as before. Quickly reloading he then fired from the hip, fanning off six rounds in quick succession, the reloading again and fired off six more, fanning the weapon, in rapid fire, with each digit singly as if by a machine pistol. Finally he, finished his session by assuming the dueling stance, one shot at a time.

Rory's full attention was on Jaeger, as his eyes filled with wonder. Jaegers minders also exchanged brief glances, after the exhibition. When the signal to "Cease Firing" was given all waited for the targets to be retrieved. Of course Mel's rounds were all over the place, given the pistol range targets were fifteen yards away, still she had a few rounds that made the kill zone, while Jaegers first rounds, were all well in the O ring, while his rapid fire were close enough to be considerable, his final rounds were centered enough to vaporize anyone's midsection. They folded up Mel's target for a souvenir and made their way to his car, while he left his target on the ground for others to ponder.

As they casually walked to the Ford, Jaeger noted that one of the minders went to another car, while the second walked over and picked up Jaegers target folding it up as he went inside the Range office.

Passing the office as the Ford made its way out of the gravel parking lot, Jaeger noticed in his rear view mirror a man hurriedly exit the range office into a waiting car. If there was any doubt before of the game at hand, all doubt was replaced by certainty as Jaeger made note of the car and its color.

The sun was going down as they drove back into town on the Northwest Freeway as Jaeger said, "I'm hungry and I think it's time for the best and largest Burgers and fries in town.

I know just the place on the Katy Freeway"! All signaling their agreement, Jaeger leisurely drove towards town at the posted limit, noting the vehicle trailing a, eighth of a mile in its wake. Soon it would be nightfall and the worm would turn.

Pulling into the restaurant's parking lot, he found a spot near the side of the facility. As they entered the front door, Jaeger noted their minders pulling around the other side into a parking spot away from sight. "Welcome to Chili's", said Jaeger palming a ten spot into the greeters hand saying, "Need a booth for three darlin' and I see a spot right over there. How's about it"?

"Come right this way sir", said the greeter looking over her shoulder. "It hasn't been cleaned yet from the last patrons, but I'll have a bus boy get right on it"! Less than thirty seconds later a harried bus boy appeared and cleared the table, with Jaeger on one side facing the front of the establishment and Mel and her son on the other. The waitress soon arrived with the menus as Jaeger kept his eyes on the front door. In entered one of the minders from the firing range, bending his head down to the greeter who directed him to a seat at the bar, which gave him a good view of Jaeger and his entourage.

While Mel scanned the menu, Jaeger's eyes scanned back and forth between the front entrance and the bar as the waitress arrived and took their order. When she left, Jaeger gave out a groan and a visible grimace saying, "While we're waiting I think I need to go to the Men's room and examine a horse. Be right back", as he slowly rose and made his way gingerly towards the restrooms. When out of sight of the dining room, he quickly made his way through the entrance to the kitchen and without drawing attention from the busy staff through the metal exit door and into the parking lot, behind the facility.

Reckoning correctly the side the minders car was on, he dove into the tall grass and made his way around the lot and slowly found the other car, parked face outward for a quick getaway, its rear tires only an arms-length away. Quickly scanning the gravel that lay before him in the dim light of the lot, he selected two likely pebbles, then stretched his arms out and unscrewed the rubber cap to the tire's nipple. Then he carefully inserted one of the pebbles, hearing an ever so slight whisper of escaping air, then carefully placed the cap back on the air nipple, yet only screwing it half way. He repeated the action on the other tire to his satisfaction then withdrew back into the weeds, grateful that it hadn't rained for a while and made his way back to the rear kitchen door, through the kitchen and back out to his guests, smiling with a relived look on his face.

"Everything come out all right", said Mel with a mirthful look on her face!

"So far so good. Darn Mexican grub. Gonna have to start watching my diet"! Just then their order arrived, as Jaeger glanced at the bar, his minder still in place nursing a drink.

Everything was in place, as they went through the dinner making small talk enjoying the youthful jabbering of little Rory who clearly had a grand day with the grownups. At some point soon, Jaeger would have to tell Mel about their minders as a heads up. He'd wait until they were in the car and on their way, he decided. During the meal, he had to agree with little Rory, this was indeed a grand and exciting day, for in the entire world, he was with the two very best people that he'd ever hoped to meet.

Yet now his concern was about a different level of excitement. Things were soon to come to a head, as he paid the bill and they rose to leave. Looking straight ahead, he saw the other minder hurriedly paying his bill, both cognizant of the other without direct scrutiny.

As they drove off the lot, Jaeger buckled up his seat belt, reminding Mel to buckle up her's and Rory's seat belts tightly.

As they headed eastward back on the Interstate, towards town Jaeger asked Mel to reach into the glove compartment and hand him the revolver inside, glancing into his rearview mirror. "Why? What's the matter"?

"Just please do as I ask. It may not come to anything", he said as he placed the revolver under his left leg as he drove continuing, "You recall a few weeks back those who were following you in the parking lot"!

"You mean the O'Bannon people"?

"Yes. Well, this afternoon, I saw two men that arrived at the gun range after we did. They did no shooting at all, but seemed has an apparent interest in the three of us. Most people go to firing ranges to shoot, not to watch people. After we were done those two followed us out of the parking lot all the way across town to Chili's. One came inside sat at the bar, while the other sat in the car, not exactly normal behavior. Now my trip to the restroom was not as it seemed, I found the other car with the guy still inside and fiddled with his tires. They are about an eighth of a mile behind us. Don't look back. Now if I've done my work well, we'll soon be rid of them. If not, then a wild ride is in store for all of us"!

"Are bad people coming for my Mommy," asked Rory? "Whoever these people are, they will not get to either you or your Mommy Rory. I guarantee it"! Then Rory grabbed his mother's hand as Jaeger drove at the posted limit towards town. All of a sudden he said, "Ah, there it is", as he down shifted and the big Ford leapt forward, changing lanes then back again to the right lane ahead of two other cars. As he saw the Campbell Road exit sign ahead, he was traveling at ninety miles an hour; he quickly down shifted into third gear, then further down into second, the car slowing down quickly from ninety to forty as the ill- conceived exit dropped sharply toward the access road some twenty feet below. Even at forty miles an hour, the quick exit drop was dangerous, but at freeway speed, with two rear tires just about to go flat it was suicide.

As the Ford, reached the bottom of the grade, Jaeger power shifted into third, then into forth gear as the beast roared forward. Coming hard, their minders ignored the posted exit sign indicating 35 MPH. Jaegers downshift slowing the Ford quickly meant that he didn't use his brakes and thus the brake lights didn't light up, as the minders discovered too late, the sudden exit drop off, the driver slamming on the brakes and the vehicle's road adhesion vanishing as it went airborne, turning slightly on its side as it slammed onto the roadway below, into a delivery truck. Traveling behind the delivery truck some six car lengths was an HPD patrol car that slammed on its brakes to avoid collision.

As Jaeger drove off at speed, he saw the explosion in his rearview mirror, causing both Rory and his mother to turn around as Jaeger down shifted, slowing the Fords momentum.

Then he took the U turn under the freeway and drove back to the preceding intersection and took yet another U turn joining the other cars that slowly passed the wreckage as the patrolman waved them past. With the windows rolled down, they could see where the other car had caromed off the delivery truck, sliding into a shopping center parking lot, its fuel tank ruptured and the car inflames, incinerating those trapped within. The driver of the delivery truck emerged from his truck was in the process of sitting on the curb, while the air was filled with the sounds of sirens, as the Ford slowly passed the scene.

Up shifting into forth gear, Jaeger was without expression as they continued their journey. "We're those the bad guys who were following us", asked Rory?

"Yes son, it appears that they were. But not anymore"! "Never seen a dead person before", said Rory meekly!

"And I hope you never do again", said Jaeger as they drove on! "Might want to look at it this way as my Grand Dad, would tell me on the ranch when I was about your age. Whenever we would see that one of our livestock had become a meal for the wolves, he'd always say, "That's just God's way of thinnin' out the herd", that's what he would say. Then we'd go on."!

"You save my bacon once again", said Mel as Jaeger reached under his leg and handed the pistol to Mel saying, "I won't be needing this anymore", nodding towards the glove compartment!

"You think they were part of the O'Bannon group", asked Mel? Jaeger thought a second then said, "Who else could it be"? Then little Rory added, "I hate my grandparents", as his mother hugged him tightly saying, "They never are going to be your family, not after this. Especially after this as God is my judge"! Just then Jaeger turned on the radio, as a commercial was just finished playing, the DJ announced, "Miss Carmen McRae, singing "Someone to watch over me", listen to the music on Houston after Dark"! As the song played on, Rory unfastened his seat belt and climbed on his mother's lap, both of them looking at Jaeger as the car made its way through the city.

"How can I ever thank you", she asked?

"You already have, more than you know"! Still the song played on working its magic in a serendipitous manner, as Miss McRae massaged the lyrics, into a special message that hit home for two people.

The following day, Rafferty called Jaeger offering him a significant bounty on a runner. One of Rafferty's more sizeable clients failed to appear in court not an hour ago and it Quarter million dollar bail they were talking about Jaegers presence was a must. When Rafferty was finished outlining the problem Jaeger said, "I'm going to jump in the shower now. See if Hondo's available? Gonna need him and call me back"!

As he was dressing, the phone rang and Rafferty told him that Hondo was on his way into the office. Then Jaeger got back on the phone and called Duke Vultee, in Dallas.

"Hey Pal. Long time no see, no hear", said Vultee! "Whadda ya know? Whadda ya say"?

"Need some eyes and ears on a project and a favor. Normally I'd handle it myself, but in a few minutes, I gotta hook up with Hondo down at Rafferty's and chase a big time runner. With luck we'll be back Friday and I can't be two places at once"!

"Talk to me big guy", said Vultee! "Whadda ya need"? "You familiar with the Santangelo family"?

"Car dealerships? About a dozen all over Texas? Yeah I'm familiar. They even got a few of em here in the Metroplex. Lemme guess. Word from the Ellis Unit is that his two sons are about get sprung early on

Parole, by the TDC. Apparently Daddy greased a few palms of the righteous. Further word is that when the get out they've got a score to settle with you for runnin' them down and getting' them back in jail. That what's vexing ya pardner"!

"Yes it is. Need to know there and their Daddy's whereabouts' when I get back so I don't get any surprises. Whadda ya say"?

"Hmmm, lemmeseeheah", said Vultee. Dance card seems to be empty for the moment, the club's take care of themselves, so looks like I'll have to get right on it. Just info is what you need right"!

"Info only. I'll handle the rest"!

Jaeger then called Mel at her office and told her that he had to go out of town for several days on business and that he'd call her, upon his return later in the week. She wanted to ask him if he was going to be delayed for the Christmas Party, but something inside said that he'd be there. He was thoughtful enough to call her after all and she didn't want to be the typical woman that pried into one's affairs.

It had been a hectic three days, with Jaeger and Hondo having to go all the way to Gallup New Mexico, to run down the elusive runner. In order to make it back to Houston in time for Melanie's party, he rented a small two engine aircraft and pilot and loaded his unconscious quarry into the rear, tossing the keys of his Ford Bronco to Hondo saying, "Call Rafferty and let him know when to expect us. We'll be landing at Andrau Air Park. Be nice if he was there"!

Once they were in the air, he quickly calculated the cost of the private flight back to Houston reckoning that most of his share of the bounty would be eaten up by the extravagance. But he had made the commitment and it just wouldn't do to let a lady down. 'What a man wouldn't do for love', he wondered silently as the aircraft reached its cruising altitude.

Upon landing back in West Houston, Rafferty emerged from his car as the aircraft came to a rest and Jaeger wrestled his prisoner out from the rear of the plane as he was just starting to revive. "Damn good to see ya back Jaeger. At least you brought the runner back this time with his clothes on"!

"We bring em back as we find em", winked Jaeger! After they booked the prisoner into the Harris County Jail complex, Jaeger and Rafferty went back to Rafferty's office and then went to dinner. Rafferty wanted to ride him home or wherever he hung his hat, but knew better. Jaeger didn't want anyone to know where he lived. Rafferty guessed that he probably had two or more residences around town and he knew of two of his identities, supposing many more. In their line of work, especially those hip deep in the chase, things got very personal very quickly. Just a part of covering one's ass at all times. The grave yards were full of chasers, whose luck ran out. They were always replaced eventually and rarely missed.

Jaeger hailed a cab that drove him to a location a half mile from his apartment. It was a cool evening and he could walk the rest of the way. When he got inside, he checked his messages on his recorder. The lone caller was Duke Vultee. Jaeger returned the call.

"Ya get your man", asked Vultee?

"He's behind bars as we speak. I suppose you have something for me"? "Enough sport. So here tis. Next Tuesday Santangelo's kids are to be released from the Ellis unit and Daddy himself is gonna pick em up. Now he's already rented them an apartment on lower Westheimer Road, near Montrose. They intend to hire some shooters imported from Mexico to stake out Rafferty's until you arrive, then make a very messy rub out. Of course the shooters figure they wouldn't be caught and Santangelo and his sons plan have an iron clad alibi with scads of witness's. Tapped all of Santangelo's known phones and took scads of pictures of his office, home, his mistress's place and the place where he's gonna stash his sons in Montrose. Now I'm in College Station visiting a friend and headin' back to Dallas in the morning. Sometime around noon tomorrow, a skinny looking' guy who answers to the name of Kenny is going to appear at Rafferty's, with a sealed manila envelope, with tapes and pictures and some rough drawn maps of Santangelo's home, main office and the pad in Montrose, with your name on the envelope, "Eyes Only". He's got a complete description of what you look like. He will hand you the envelope and in return you will hand him an envelope with a thousand dollars in twenties.

His plane fare back to the big D plus a little Lagniappe. Are we good"? "We're good Duke and thanks I owe ya"!

"Quid Pro Quo sport, Quid Pro Quo"! Then he rang up Mel to let her know, of his return and to confirm the time tomorrow to pick her up. The following day he took a cab to the Houston Chronicle building downtown and walked the rest of the way to Rafferty's.

"I got your check waiting for you in your box", said Wanda hardly looking up from her typewriter. "Oh and Hondo called from Columbus, he's filling your Bronco up with motion lotion and should be showin' up here in about an hour"!

Fifty minutes later in walked Hondo, tossing the keys to Jaegers Ford Bronco to him then grabbing the envelope that Wanda offered saying, "Cash money on the barrelhead"?

"Now you know better than that. It's always check money on the barrelhead, she replied sardonically. "Well, de well, think I'll head by the bank then go to the house fer some well-earned snooze time", drawled Hondo as he gave both Jaeger and Wanda a nod and walked out the door. As he left, in walked a rather tall skinny type, attired in a loud sports jacket, jeans, well weathered cowboy hat and boots carrying a smallish weathered briefcase. He looked around allowing his eyes to adjust from the outside then walked towards Jaeger saying, "You Jaeger"?

"You Kenny", he asked? The head nodded and reached into the briefcase retrieving a sealed and bulging manila envelope and offering it to Jaeger, in exchange for a smaller envelope. Both men opened their envelopes, giving the contents a cursory inspection, looked at each other and with a mutual nod of their heads, Kenney turned and walked out into the street.

Jaeger returned to the contents of the envelope, seeing several cassette tapes, some three dozen itemized Polaroid pictures and some hand drawn maps along with some additional papers. Satisfied, he put them all back in the envelope and said by to Wanda, who was now interviewing some Mexican woman, no doubt wanting bail for someone. These were now the times to be especially vigilant, as he walked around the Bronco then unlocked the door and started the engine. Hondo's car was missing from the lot which meant that he was gone as Jaeger worked his way along Preston Street, then doing the usual, four left hand turns in sequence, then four right hand turns, each time mindful who was in your rearview mirror. Seeing that no one was apparently following, he then drove uptown turning right on lower Westheimer Road. Four blocks later he came upon the old four plex group of residences and parked his Bronco. Ten minutes later he now had square in his sights, where the Santangelo kids were going to hang out, when they got sprung.

Then he drove up I-45 to the headquarters auto dealership of

Santangelo, Enterprises Inc., parking the Bronco on one of the side streets and donning a snap brimmed hat and sunglasses. Bringing with him an empty briefcase, the went to the dealership and walked around for the better part of an hour, looking like one of those suits from a district office making an inspection of sorts. It must've worked, for not even one of the salesmen standing about approached him for an inquiry, with the standard lame, "What can I do you for"?

Continuing north on the freeway, he turned west on FM 1960 and drove onward, till seeing the entrance to the North Ridge Country Club, one of the several upscale developments built around a thirty six hole golf course. After about a half an hour of driving around the circuitous streets, he came upon the home of the Santangelo family. Surprisingly there was no perimeter fence. Thick chest high hedges that would no doubt grow in time but no fence. By Jaegers reckoning the house sat astride two acres of ground, three stories tall with a six car parking garage adjoining. He now had the image in place and drove back to his place to pour over the pictures and the report Jaeger received. You want a job done right, then you have to have the right people get it done. When it came to casing a joint, who better than a master bank robber? While doing his time in Huntsville, he was fortunate to make friends with Duke Vultee. Even he lost count of the number of banks he robbed, like Casanova lost count of the legions of women he seduced so did Vultee of the banks purloined. Yet no one he knew of could detail a facility the way Vultee did revealing the weakness's, moreover and knowing just how to exploit them to his advantage with minimal effort.

An hour after he got home, Jaeger knew exactly how to gain access to Santangelo's business office, home and the digs his sons would hang their hats in.

By seven in the evening he pulled up to Mel's townhouse and was greeted at the door by Rory attired in his Red Ryder outfit, holding one of his six guns on Jaeger saying, "Reach for the sky's"! Of course as he entered his hands went up, just as he saw Mel, descending the stairs, attired in the standard little black dress, designed to reveal as well as conceal. As she moved the stairs, Jaeger jaw dropped in awe as she approached the first level reaching around him and closing the front door which still was open.

With her son standing guard, his cap pistol at the ready holding a deadly bead in the visitor. Mel took two steps into the vestibule, turned saying "Well"? Jaeger was till speechless and searching for the appropriate response, when Mel looked at little Rory saying, "And son, that's the response I was hoping for"!

"And you got it Mommy, didn't you"?

"That she did little cowboy, that she did", said Jaeger weakly. "Why, my Mommy is the bestest looking woman in the whole wide world", said Rory proudly!

"And Texas", added Jaeger smiling!

Gathering up a prepared bag, Melanie looked at her son saying, "Holster that hog leg cowboy we're going over to your pal Nathan's so you two can spend the night with a sleepover"! As they walked out the door, Mel secured the alarm system saying, "Nathan's mother was good enough to watch my little heathen as they are both thick as thieves at school and at their day care center. I've done the same for her quite often. I'll pick him up tomorrow, if I can tear him away from his cartoons"!

Once, Rory was deposited with Nathan, Mel came down the walkway towards the big Ford and slid into the front seat saying, "Lead on Lochinvar"!

"Sounds like something in a Shakespearian play", mused Jaeger as he put the car into gear! "Probably and then again who knows or cares. This evening is going to be a wonderful evening. I can feel the electricity all around me. And you", asked Mel sliding her knees upwards and pivoting towards the driver showing a generous expanse of her legs?

"I'm feeling like getting to the party in one piece and to do that I've gotta concentrate on driving, which is hard to do when my eyes are drawn to what they're drawn to", said Jaeger shifting gears.

"No self-discipline", asked Mel?

"Some things are beyond self-discipline Mel, so try and be a good girl OK? Believe me when I say, I am impressed. The way you look tonight, soon everyone will be impressed"!

Mel straightened herself in the seat, buckling up her seat belt and faced forward without a word, smiling inwardly. Yet she wondered whether or not she'd gone too far in her choice of her little black dress. At the office, she was the model of corporate decorum, mostly slacks and pant suits, with a minimum of makeup. This evening all of the Honcho's and their wives would be in attendance. She could handle the husbands handily enough it was their women which was a concern. For the better part of a decade, she'd been the good wife and mother and something inside wanted to let it out somewhat.

But this evening, her visuals what they were, she would continue to play her part as the corporate image woman. As Jaeger pulled into the Enron parking garage, he borrowed her card for the entrance swipe and slowly drove upwards following her directions until he came to her parking spot. As he went around the car to open her door, she emerged demurely then stopped saying, "You know, I was wondering why you've never kissed me"? Before he could form a response, she reached up, pulling his head towards her and drew him forward, enveloping his lips to hers. Time passed slowly, as more than one part of their bodies drew close in unity, their hips mutually exploring and discovering common ground. As they drew apart, she reached up wiping a small smudge of lipstick from his lips saying with a wink, "You'll do", then turned on a dime grabbing his hand saying, "We've a party to attend"!

As the elevator door drew open, they were greeted by the sounds of a big band flown in from New York with that unmistakable Manhattan sound, following several other of the corporate couples into the reception area for the name tags showing the invitation to the attendants and went right in to the cavernous meeting room, filled with Enron management and their wives and specially selected guests. Several large Christmas trees flanked the ballroom, dressed to the nines laden with ornaments flanked by two wet bars on either side of the room, and a buffet table laden with calories suitable for a Roman Orgy.

Tables were set around the dance floor, as Mel guided Jaeger along to where they were to be seated by the table placards, through the crowd. She nodded at some of the people she knew, as in each case the husbands tried their best not to look too long, for nothing could ruin an evening quicker than a sullen wife.

"Ah yes, here we are", said Mel as she put her drink down along with her small purse. Then she grabbed Jaeger by the hand again saying, "The music is lovely so dance with me", as they went out onto the dance floor.

Walking back to their table, they noticed that several people had joined them, some of whom Mel recognized as introductions were exchanged. The next table over she notice her boss and his wife, going over to say hello. Upon her return she saw Jaeger talking to a beautiful woman and her older escort. As she arrived Jaeger turned saying, "Oh yes the sole reason for my presence, is at my side. Melanie O'Bannon may I introduce you to Boyd Parmalee and Elizabeth Beauvior, both attorneys and very good ones I might add. After Boyd quietly made her acquaintance, Buffy took her hand saying, "Jaegers far too modest sometimes, for Boyd and I are great attorneys. We've known Jaeger for a number of years now, and have represented him from time to time", as she turned to both of them noting their nodding heads of agreement! "In a business venue I'm supposing", quipped Mel! Turning back to both men, Buffy nodded and said, "That's one way of putting it Mel. By the way, my friends all call me Buffy and I do hope we shall become friends"!

Smiling genuinely Mel answered, "I don't any reason why we shouldn't"! Just then Mel felt a tap on her shoulder and as she turned, saw her lawyer exclaiming, "Charlie. Charlie Ledbetter. What in the world are you doing here"? The missus and I received an invitation from one of the VP's over there on the rostrum. He's going through a nasty breakup with wife number two and the next prospect, the redhead, is the one sitting next to him"!

"Buffy, Boyd, good to see you both. This lovely woman next to me is my wife, Hazel"! As the introductions went around, Buffy asked, "And how do you know Melanie O'Bannon, Charlie"?

"I'm her counsel of record, in her custody case against her former in laws, Randall and Margot O'Bannon"! "Oh, that O'Bannon. The one who died in the car crash, a few years ago", exclaimed Buffy! "My sincere condolences", said Buffy grasping Mel's hand. "Nasty business that", said Parmalee. "The guy had the angels by both wings and everything in front of him and it all slipped away"! All Melanie could do was say, "Thank You for your concern", as she grabbed Jaegers hand for comfort. Noticing the connection, Charlie Ledbetter turned to Jaeger saying, "I see your with Melanie, I'm Charlie Ledbetter and this is my wife and your name is"?

"Jaeger. How do you do", he said softly, shaking hands with both of them, as Ledbetter looked at him asking "Jaeger"? "Why is that name familiar"?

Then Buffy stepped in saying, "Charlie, think back. Rice Stadium, back when you had more hair. On a chilly fall afternoon. The Longhorns were in town and the bookies had the game dead even. You we're playing defensive safety, until a brick wall ran right over you? This was that brick wall"!

"Oh shit", he exclaimed embarrassingly. "Jaeger", his eyes opening as wide as saucers. "Damn, now I remember", he said shaking Jaegers hand embarrassingly. "I suppose I should be angry with you, since I never played football again competitively, but in a way, you did me a huge favor, for it was while I was in Hermann Hospital recovering from the hit, that I met Hazel my wife and then decided upon a career in law"!

"Ah, Serendipity", chimed in Buffy. "Things always seem to work out somehow"! Then Ledbetter continued on saying, "But that was minor stuff compared to what happened next. "The Cotton Bowl game at the end of that season. A big wind descended upon Dallas and while I was still convalescing I witnessed the greatest game ever played and was glad I wasn't on the field. This man in our midst was the sole instrument of the Long Horns victory"! As Mel's eyes opened wide, Ledbetter pressed, "Just one question please Jaeger"?

Jaeger nodded as Ledbetter pushed the envelope, "Legend has it that Texas was all but beat when they went to the locker room at the half and the only thing that brought them together was that you got tired of the coaches palaver and started to walk out in the middle of his harangue and as he asked where you thought you were going, you just turned and said, "The Eyes of Texas are on all of Us", or words to that effect and walked back on the field"!

"That was long ago", said Jaeger. "And to tell you the truth, lotta water has passed under the bridge since"!

"So what happened", asked Ledbetter? "You were a lock for pro ball"! "Like you, unforeseen circumstances compelled a career change. Ya might want to ask Buffy, but then again maybe not. She handles my legal affairs for me. Maybe someday she'll write a book"!

Then Mel grabbed Jaeger by the arm and put his drink on the table saying, "I feel a dance coming on", and guided Jaeger back out onto the dance floor, just as the band slipped into, "The Lady in Red". As they glided together Mel said "My, my, you're full of surprises, this evening. I had no idea I was escorted by a legend"!

"Thanks for rescuing me and no, I'm not with a legend, just a guy", said Jaeger as he deftly guided her through the crowd. Back at the table, Ledbetter and Buffy gave each other a glance and a knowing nod to say no more and enjoy the evening. An hour later, the band took an intermission, while the upper management held forth taking turns on the dais extolling the company's corporate mission and the profit margins maintained.

As Mel's boss was one of the high fliers mentioned as one of those key people, crucial to corporate success, Mel turned his way as their eyes met briefly, exchanging nods, and then turned away. After an hour of self-promoting backslapping for the corporate good, the Chairman finally said, "In behalf of the entire Enron family, I wish each and every one of you a very Merry Christmas and a Happy New Year", lifting his drink on high. "Now I see that our band has returned, so let the music begin"!

Noticing that Buffy was making a bee line to the restrooms to freshen up, Mel excused herself, following her, prompting Charley Ledbetter's wife to do the same. While the ladies were off, Boyd asked Jaeger, "How ya been son"?

"Just taking each day as it comes, Mr. Parmalee. And you"? "Probably going to retire sometime in the next few years and drift into emeritus status. Father Time is creeping up"!

"So who's going to run things at the firm", asked Jaeger?

"Oh there's probably going to be some fuss amongst the partners, but Buffy will no doubt come out on top. She'll certainly have my support"!

"No one in the entire State has a higher profile", chimed in Ledbetter! "By the way", he continued, turning towards Jaeger, "One can't help noticing the way the both of you are with each other. That is you and Melanie. As you know, she's my client and currently is in a very vulnerable situation."!

"Charley, I'm well aware of Melanie's situation in its entirety and I too share your concerns. She's the finest woman I've ever met, deserving only the best life can offer. I'm certain that legally she's well represented. Should there ever come a day when my presence can't be in her best interests of her or her son, that's the very day when I'll sever the relationship"!

As Ledbetter turned to Parmalee, Boyd looked at him saying, "Charley, I've known this man a considerable time and he takes life as serious as a heart attack. When he give his word its cast in stone. Besides Buffy represents him whenever he asks and he doesn't ask often"!

"Then I take him at his word also", said Ledbetter. "I hope you both know I just had to ask"!

"No harm no foul Charley", replied Jaeger graciously. "By the way, what was it that put you out of action, the last time we met"? The subtle message of long ago, cheerfully delivered with apparent concern, prompted Ledbetter to say, "On cold mornings, my neck along with my left shoulder will take a while to get the cranks out. Fortunately we live in Houston where that doesn't happen often. Good thing my wife is a physiotherapist", he said smiling!

While in the Ladies Room, Buffy emerged from her stall and found a place right next to Melanie as both women made the necessary adjustments to their face and attire. Two beautiful women both in their prime, each highly intelligent, focused on their own appearance as Buffy, applying a modicum of facial powder said, "I'm glad Jaeger finally is in the company of someone of quality. The both of you look good together"! Sensing the Alpha qualities of the other and feeling relived at the compliment, Mel answered, "Why thank you Buffy. I've read about you in the papers from time to time and didn't know that you and Jaeger had some history together"!

"I'm glad you used the past tense, 'Had', although one can infer a certain connotation not entirely accurate. What is accurate is that there were times, when each of us had our proverbial tits in the wringer.

He extracted mine, and I extracted his, Quid pro Quo, or Tit for Tat. We rendered service to each in kind employing certain skills appropriate to the occasion. He's an extremely complicated man on certain levels, but at the heart of things, he's a simple creature. He knows what's right and what's not and he takes care of business. A real Mench. With Ledbetter covering your twelve o'clock and Jaeger covering your six, your family will be good to go for the foreseeable future. Now Mel, what say we go back in there and impress the plebeians"!

Melanie smiled, as they both strode out of the ladies room, the crowd parting before them as if they were leading their unseen flock across the Sea of Reeds.

At half past one, they made their goodbyes wishes of a very Merry Christmas to the others and made their way to Jaegers car. Mel slid across the front bench seat of the ancient Ford and opened the door as Jaeger got in and put his key in the ignition. He felt his head turn as her lips softly enveloped his. As he turned his attention to more important things than a car ignition they embraced in a long probing kiss, eventually leaving both breathless as they parted, prompting Jaeger to whisper, "You taste good, with or without alcohol on your breath. Hard to decide which is better"?

"Start the car and drive us home. We'll have the entire night for you to make up your mind", she whispered into his ear!

As he pulled out of the parking garage, Jaeger turned the car radio on. Driving slowly down Louisiana Street timing each light in a sequence of green, both heard the radio DJ, whisper, "Your listening to Houston after Dark. Now listen up children as we hear the song styling of Miss Carmen McRae sing, 'Someone to watch over me', on KTSU, the dark spot on your dial"!

Settling next to Jaeger as he drove through the night, Mel slid her left arm around his shoulders, folding her legs up tightly and placed her head on his shoulder, listening to the prophetic words, feeling completely at peace with the world.

As he drove back to his place the following afternoon, the preceding nights activities stayed tattooed upon his brain. The minute they entered her town house, she locked the front door and without further word was upon him. In less than a minute their clothes lay strewn upon the stairway and there, half way up, was where she got the best of him, straddling him as one would a horse, as his throbbing member found a home deep within. Both sets of lips above and the remaining below were joined in desperate combat, as Mel slowly moaned, as she took the full measure of his being deep. His hand and lips were found wanting as they could not possibly do justice simultaneously with the array of puellent possibilities before them, shifting back and forth desperate in their final resting place, before being summoned hurriedly to another. Completion on the stairwell, then again on her bed, then later on her bedroom floor, they finally fell asleep just short of five in the morning. By nine Mel came into the bedroom in all her glory unadorned save but for a smile, serving the morning coffee. By ten they decided that two can shower better than one, as they soon gave a lie to the whole save water argument, as Jaeger's member once again rose to the occasion, prompting Mel to climb aboard. In the final analysis, Jaeger could never remember being so thoroughly scrubbed so clean he squeaked in the aftermath.

By one in the afternoon, with both reluctant to part, Mel had to pick up her son from his sleep over, while Jaeger grumbled over some alleged paperwork that needed his attention. There was always Monday afternoon at the Gym. He slept until five in the afternoon, then went to his kitchen to re-examine the Santangelo information and plan his next move.

At six he went to the Bronco and removed all that was gleaned by Hondo on their recent trek into New Mexico. Either the office where Santangelo was known to be working far past closing hours at his flagship dealership or at his home was where Carl Santangelo was to be abducted. He decided upon the home. The following Friday his two sons were to be released from the Ellis Unit in Huntsville, so time was indeed of the essence. The tapes furnished indicated that at two PM both sons were to emerge to their freedom and a black limo would be awaiting them for the trip back into Houston.

Late that Thursday evening Carl Santangelo's car pulled into his garage, as he went into his house. He wondered why his two Dobermans usually set outside at night to prowl the grounds were not there to greet him as they usually were, but they probably were on the other side of the property chasing a nocturnal critter. It had been a long day and he'd had to schmooze with some dealer reps the entire day with regard to his floor planning. Of course, his dogs were fast asleep, a result of two large porterhouse steaks specially prepared by Jaeger earlier in the day. By two thirty in the morning, Jaeger had defeated the security system in the house, gaining access through one of the first floor den windows.

It was of great help that Santangelo and his wife slept in separate bedrooms on the second floor, as Jaeger injected the sedative into Santangelo as he slept covering his mouth just in case. Hoisting him up on his shoulders and straightening the covers as best he could in the dark, Jaeger silently went down the stairs with his parcel upon his shoulder and into the den, where he muscled him out the same window he entered. Then he slowly closed the window, standing there for one moment thinking. Rubber gloves on his hands, he was forgetting something. The maid was to be there in the morning, the landscapers too, to tend to the lawn. Ah yes, foot prints in the bushes. A simple matter to erase and confuse. That done he hoisted the inert, pajama clad Santangelo over his shoulders and made his way towards the Bronco parked away from the road, behind some bushes. As he drove out of the subdivision, he saw one of the Sheriff Deputy patrol cars in his rear view, passing on another street inside the subdivision making its rounds. Thirty seconds either way or their paths might have crossed. As it was, Santangelo was extracted and was his now. Jaeger then drove to a secluded junk yard on the far west side of town. The only security there was a padlock of which he has a key. Hard onto the junk yard was the northwest railroad tracks, as he closed the high metal clad gates. Given this time of year, it would not start to get light until six thirty in the morning. At seven the yards few employees would start arriving. At five in the morning there was usually a very long and noisy freight train that passed by. Donning a new set of rubber gloves Jaeger set about selecting a suitable rusty fifty gallon fuel drum to set beside the fence out of immediate notice along with many others. He poked a dozen holes in the top cover with a screw driver and unscrewed the top metal band. Then he muscled Santangelo out from the Bronco and sat him beside the metal drum. Scanning his watch in the dark he saw that he had plenty of time until the arrival of the morning train. He went to the Bronco and removed two, five gallon containers of acid placing them next to the metal drum, then removed a face mask, a syringe and finally, a twin barreled sawed off shotgun, loaded with double ought buckshot, positioning each nearby, finally he took some twine and secured the hands and legs of his subject securing to the metal fencepost in a sitting position. Lastly a gag for the man's mouth. Passing the time by chain smoking cigarettes, he glanced at his watch, reckoning that it was fifteen minutes until the train came.

He grabbed the syringe and injected Santangelo with a stimulant to bring him awake. Within a few minutes Santangelo came around as he groggily tried to focus his eyes and trying to speak could only muffle. "Carl baby, don't cha remember me? Now think! We've never formally met so I'll intro myself. I'm the son of a bitch that brought your sons back from their bail skip. Really I did ya a favor but you failed to see it that way. That's right Jaeger, now do ya remember? Did ya think I'd not find out that you were gonna hire some Beaner shooters from south of the border to take me out? Well I did. Too bad your kids can't keep their mouths shut, but there we are ain't we"? Now no use tryin' to deny it, for I heard it on tape. So here we sit waiting for the train and here you sit truly fucked for fair"! "Just to your left is old rusty fifty gallon oil drum that's gonna be your final resting place in about fifteen minutes. Now later on this afternoon, your two kids'll be released, but you're not gonna be the one who picks em up. I will. Then they'll soon join you, in separate drums of course. Now I didn't have to tell you these things, but you're a special case. It's rare that any of us knows the exact time of our departure from this mortal coil, much less the fate of our children and their final resting place, but like I said, you are a special case"!

Just then Jaeger heard the sound of the approaching Diesel engine Klaxon a half mile away at another train intersection as it approached. "Damn that noise the train makes is enough to raise the dead, much less more than enough to drown out the blast of a shotgun", continued Jaeger as he brought the twin muzzles to point at Santangelo's chest not six feet away. As the noise of the approaching engines grew louder, Santangelo's eyes grew wide with fear.

"Just has to be a pure tee bitch seeing that your end is near and there's not anything you can do about it. How does it feel to be absolutely powerless, knowing your final resting place is gonna be a junkyard and even worse that your sons will be next to you", taunted Jaeger, his eyes conveying a complete certainty as to the outcome. The separate bedrooms told me that your wife stays with you only for the economic benefit she derives, but as I gaze into my non-existent crystal bowl, I think I can see the future. The auto empire you grew from nothing might soon be absorbed by your mortal business competitors, the O'Bannon family. Christ on a crutch, now wouldn't that be a shame. All you've ever worked for, up in smoke. No one will ever find you or your sons, at least not enough to ever identify, for soon you'll be Mexican Stew"!

As the sound of the Diesel engine approached, Jaeger cocked back the hammer on each barrel, seconds later the Klaxon, not thirty yards away belched forth its ear splitting sound, completely muffling the sounds of the twin barrels firing at the hapless Santangelo's chest. Placing the weapon on the ground. Jaeger put on the gauze face mask as he looked at the sightless eyes of a dead man, the very life crushed out in an instant. The hundred car freight train now slowly and noisily passing by muffled the sounds of Jaeger hoisting the cadaver face down into the oil drum. Then he carefully poured the acid, from the two containers over the inert body and completing that, secured the top metal lid to the barrel, fitted the restraining strap around the top lip, screwing the lid tightly until it would turn no more. By his reckoning it would take about two weeks until all the barrel contained was nothing more than a gelatinous mass, of toxic protoplasm. As he looked outside the gate he could see the end of the train a quarter mile down the track. Cleaning up any sign of his being there, in a place laden with refuse, he drove the Bronco past the gate and closed it after him rescuing the lock as it was.

Then he turned to his left and drove to the rail road street crossing and waited for the train to pass and the gates to rise.

Driving back to his place, he thought one down and two to go. As the sun rose, he drifted off to sleep thinking blissfully of Mel. Awake by ten in the morning, he went to a friend of his who owed him a favor, in fact many favors. The owner of a Limousine company with a gambling habit at the Delta Downs Race Track just across the Louisiana state line exchanged his Bronco for one of his black Limos and a badly fitting uniform, for the rest of the day, no questions asked. When one is in deep and mortal debt, it's best to have the memory of an amoeba about some things. By three thirty in the afternoon, Jaeger sat in the Limo in front of the prison gates, engine idling, its original license plates substituted by ones borrowed from a parked car earlier in the day which was replaced by two plates, again borrowed by yet another. He applied the false moustache and goatee to his face trusting that years and his wraparound sunglasses would sufficiently secure his identity.

At four in the afternoon the gates opened and Santangelos sons emerged to freedom laughing and smiling as Jaeger pressed the horn twice signaling his presence. Both of them ran to the car and flung open the door and finding no passengers there said, "Hey, where's our Dad, to the driver"?

Jaeger rolled down the smoke colored front window half way and said, "Your dad's apologies, but he's in Methodist Hospital and your mother is with him. Don't know what's wrong, but my instructions are to take the both of you to him, as soon as possible"!

"Then shut your hole driver and lets get out of here", said one of the brothers as Jaeger raised the window and put the Limo in gear. Half way into town, he pulled into a truck stop, as he rolled the passenger window down half way saying, "Need to put some gas in the tank so we don't run out. I'll be quick", then he raised the window back up as he went to the farthest of the pumps not laden with any other customers. Then he pressed the button depressing the window to the passenger compartment as one of the brothers complained, "Now what"?

Jaeger turned and quickly brought to bear a twin barreled, compressed air pistol that shot two darts into the each of the brothers chests in quick succession. The he pointed a small caliber Beretta into the window saying, "Uh uh, don't touch em if either of you wants to stay alive", the sight of the pistol pointing right at them was enough to buy time for the massive sedatives to do their work and within thirty seconds, Jaeger saw each of their eyes, roll up and they both slumped down on the seats.

Jaeger then turned around, placing the Limo in gear once again and drove slowly back onto Interstate 45 and headed south towards Houston. Everything he needed to complete the day was in the Limos trunk. The boys should be out at least another twelve hours or so and if all held together, by mid-morning he could return the Limo, washed, detailed, its original plates restored, as if nothing happened.

The next day, the Limo returned in spotless condition, a full tank and the ill-fitting uniform cleaned and pressed, Jaeger retrieved his Bronco driving into town to see if Rafferty had anything of interest that needed Jaegers attention. Finding nothing he quickly left and wondered what he could do next. He briefly toyed with the idea of visiting Randall O'Bannon in the hospital and seeing if he might be able to persuade him to call off his custody suit. 'Bad Idea', he reckoned. Luck had been with him thus far, with most of the Santangelo family cooking away in a junk yard. Eventually the police would be called in, a missing persons report developed, perhaps even an investigation of sorts. Insurance investigators and god only knows who else. An article in the papers would no doubt surface. With the exception of possibly Morty talking to anybody about his loaning of one of his Limos to someone, thus implicating him in a murder, something he really needed to steer clear of for any number of reasons, Jaeger was confident this disappearance would just fade away. Perhaps some mention in the business pages, but little else.

As it turned out each time any mention of the Santangelo disappearances made the media, Morty was busy across the state line in Louisiana trying his luck and as things turned out the goddess Fortuna repeatedly smiled upon him as she'd never done before, thus guaranteeing his repeated visits. After some five weeks of visits, Morty was some sixty five thousand dollars to the good and scheming as how to hide it all from the dreaded tax man.

During the interim, the Santagelo disappearances, faded from public view as other news took precedence locally.

The phone buzzed at Melanie's desk one afternoon as she answered "This is O'Bannon"!

"Mel? It's Charles Ledbetter. Are you sitting down"?

"No I'm standing. Why do you ask"?

"Just take a seat Mel"!

"OK, I'm now sitting. So why am I sitting"?

"Two words. Randall O'Bannon"!

"That's a name not two words, unless spoken in the pejorative"!

"What's your fondest wish in the whole wide world"?

"Oh you mean the wish where a Genie pops out and yells, Randall O'Bannon has croaked! Is that the wish you're talking about"!

"Close enough. Just hung up from his attorney. He called me from the hospital as a courtesy. Seems that O'Bannon had a severe stroke, the very day he was to be discharged from the hospital for his Gout problem. The medication finally worked in diminishing the swelling in his lower extremities. Yet when the nurses arrived to do their morning rituals prior to breakfast, there he was all glassy eyed. He's in a coma and fading fast. Now as you know, Randall was the one driving the custody suit. Should he go belly up, I think I can work out something with Margot, to make this thing go away. What say you"?

"I don't know. My brain is still processing everything. First we have to know he's dead, don't we"?

"Watch the evening newscast at five. He's fading fast. By the way their attorney wants to see this go away also, because he knows he doesn't have a winner on his hands. They were hoping that you'd run out of money for legal fees. Oh they'll settle all right. Might have to grant Grandma occasional visitation rights, worst case, but we'll see"!

An hour later, her boss Herb, called her in his office, to watch a special news bulletin, regarding the recent death of Randall O'Bannon as a result of a massive cranial stroke the very day he was to be released from the hospital for an unrelated illness. The report came on the heels of the disappearance of the Santangelo family's father and two sons, leaving an apparent void in the ownerships of two of Texas's largest auto retailing empires. As she watched the first reports of O'Bannon's death, Mel was called to her phone again. It was Ledbetter asking, "Have you seen the news report Mel"?

"I'm watching it now in my boss's office. Do what you can Charlie"! She hung up and ran back into her boss's office to see the last minutes of the Special Report. When it was concluded Herb said, "Too bad I don't have any Champaign chilled, or else the cork would be popping right now. Congrats Mel. You hung in there and outlasted the bastard"!

Several blocks away, Buffy sat with Boyd Parmalee in the conference room in the aftermath of a strenuous deposition. The drinks were brought out and the late afternoon newscast was turned on, the TV. When it was concluded, they looked at each other as Boyd drawled, "That Charlie Ledbetter is some kind of lawyer ain't he"!

"I'm feeling happy for Melanie", said Buffy continuing. "Now a massive load can come off her shoulders"! "What about Jaeger", mused Parmalee!

"Yeah, there's that. Perhaps now he can settle down, get married, make an honest living, be a good husband and father, shedding the demons that been chasing him", Buffy said!

"Really think that's possible Buffy"? "No, but one can hope can't one"?

Margot O'Bannon dropped the lawsuit without any further reservations, just a verbal promise from Mel that she'd be allowed to visit her grandson from time to time. Her husband was quietly buried the following week with but a half dozen attendees to a rain soaked burial service. Ashes to ashes, mud to mud.

For the next six months Jaeger, Mel and her son had never been happier. He was over several times a week for dinner, teaching Rory all manner of things that young boys must know. They would take long walks together, in the park while mom cooked dinner. Jaeger would help him with his homework, but the best of all was when he took Rory out to the rifle range. Rory would always bring back his targets proudly declaring "Look Mom"!

From time to time, he could see the way Jaeger and his mother looked at each other and wondered what it would be like if…He could see it when they laughed together, he could see the way they were polite to each other, he could see they were happy in each other's company and every once in a while whenever they thought he wasn't looking, he caught them kissing modestly together. Just one thing was missing. Perhaps if he prayed hard enough, that one thing would come to pass.

29

B reaking out of his reverie, Jaeger peered out onto the placid Gulf waters, then towards the sunset in the western skies. The sun hung half exposed over the horizon. Its light filtered through thousands of miles of atmosphere, arrayed in the complete spectrum of light was a beautiful sight to behold. He fixed that image into his memory, for retrieval in the afterlife, certain to arrive in short order as he glanced at his watch.

His thoughts drifted back to Mel and her son and of the hosts of regrets he'd drug about all through his life. His all too brief time with her was not enough, betraying his weakness and his needs for a family life of normalcy, stolen from him by circumstance. She'd been through quite enough and deserved better. For things to have a chance of working out with this wonderful woman and her son, he'd have to rediscover his humanity in full measure, living the life of a normal mensch. The 8 to 5 existence, provide security and become normal. Whatever that was, it was driven from him long ago and he'd little confidence that he'd be able to contribute to her happiness in the long run, yet he certainly wanted to. For her, he wanted to move mountains. For as many women as he'd come to know, he couldn't imagine ever wanting to become as one with another woman. And there it was, her very existence made him vulnerable and weakness in his line of work got one killed. Although Jaeger hated what he did, he was good at it and it paid far better than anything else he could've done. He was a hunter of men. Yet even more telling was the ever present possibility of his relationship with Mel and her son, was certain to provide a danger to their safety and he just couldn't have that.

The very moment he met and subsequently threw in with Ortega, provided the momentum to sever relations with Mel. Yet he took the cowards way out and simply disappeared without a word. Yet he did do one thing right, by meeting with Buffy and having a will drawn up, placing all of his earthly assets in her and her son's name in the event of his death or disappearance for the period of one year. Meant having to every so often checking in with her office formally and leave legal tracks, but there it was. If, when the evening's activities were concluded, should he end up fish food, then in six months or so Mel would be provided for.

He glanced at his watch as the car radio blared the Phil Collins dirge "In the air tonight". 'Great song', thought Jaeger, 'with which to summon the Ferry Man', as he lit yet another cigarette. Then he turned his head, seeing the rapid approach of three cars, speeding along the seaside road, towards Jamaica Beach. As they slowed, the cars veered left off the roadway onto the circular drive, surrounding the seaside house. Two of them veered to the right in the front roundabout leading to the rear, while the third veered left circling around to the rear, stopping any possibility of getaway. As the cars slowed to a stop, Jaeger looked inwardly, silently intoning, 'Into your hands, I offer my spirit'.

Ortega and Meyers slowly emerged from the back seat of the Lincoln, while the knife wielding Rocha emerged from the front seat and Pavina, just out of St. Joseph's Hospital arose painfully from the driver's seat. Behind them in the Grey Mercedes, emerged Davalantes and Sebastian Trevino, fanning out silently without a word. Glancing behind him were two others he'd seen around, getting out of a Thunderbird that parked behind him The arrival of Carlos Meyers put to rest any idea of his survival this night. His presence assured Jaeger, of his part in the betrayal in Sao Paulo. He briefly glanced at Davalantes and by the look in his eyes knew, that this was nothing personal, just doing the job, his Jefe demanded. Maintaining his relaxed posture, leaning on the Fords rear fender, he stared straight ahead at Ortega as he approached, noting each man's position as they fanned out around him. As he approached, Ortega yelled out, "Eh Vato, you got da papers an my money", suddenly stopping ten yards away?

"The Embraer documents are in the briefcases", said Jaeger pointing to the extra-large drug salesman briefcases arrayed before him, "And your money is in the Ford's trunk. Now do you have my money"?

"Why sure I do", said Ortega smiling as he turned to Meyers. "You might want to ask your partner Meyers, why then did he commingle half of the money in my trunk that was supposed to go to you, with counterfeit American currency? Doesn't give me much confidence this deal is on the up and up"!

Ortega's eyes grew wide as he turned towards Meyers, along with everyone else, whose eyes apparently betrayed him sufficiently to Ortega. When Ortega turned back to Jaeger he saw Jaeger smiling, as his hand came up as if to shake Ortega's. Suddenly the empty hand seemed to explode, spinning Ortega around, as Jaeger flew into action, the second blast catching Davalantes square in the chest, the third, catching Rocha in the midsection as a knife flew past Jaegers ear, the forth blast caught Meyers in both knees, driving him towards the ground as bullets flew all around a twisting and spinning Jaeger, several landing in his Kevlar vest stinging but not stopping, never stopping, as the two new shooters behind him fired wildly at Jaeger as he moved swiftly. One of Pavina's bullets catching one of the new arrivals in the gun hand while he in turn caught friendly fire from both of them in return. Trevino fired wildly with each round ending up where Jaeger had been, not where he was, as a blast from Jaeger caught him squarely in the hip spinning him around, while one of Pavina's errant bullets found its mark in the house Spinning around up and off the ground, Jaeger saw one of the newbie's struggling to reach his fallen pistol and sent a blast his way ending his struggle. With two rounds left in his forearm shotguns, he used them to end Rocha's struggle as well as ending Pavina's struggle as his eyes pleaded for mercy. Then Jaeger reached down and retrieved both small Beretta's from his ankle holsters, as he walked up to Carlos Meyers clutching both knees in severe pain, keeping an eye upon Ortega and Davalantes, he knelt down, as he said to the ending strains of Phil Collins song, "Can ya feel it, coming in the air tonight Meyers"? The barrel of the Beretta pressed deep into his nostril, coughing once. The small caliber round exploded into Meyers brain, fragmenting into many parts as it ended all movement. Jaeger then went to the two newbies placing a single round in each of their heads, before heading for Davalantes.

Kneeling down, he glanced into his eyes. Of all those downed, he felt some affinity with Davalantes. The man was a soldier, just doing what he was told, nothing personal. Struggling to breathe, he looked at Jaeger and nodded his understanding of what comes next, as he struggled to position Jaegers automatic under his chin, looked at Jaeger, as his hands came to rest at his waist and nodded his head. The Beretta coughed once more and Davalantes came to his eternal rest. He fully knew what lay ahead for his remains. It was part of the price paid, for a life lived.

While the radio station dove headlong into five minutes of commercials, Jaeger slowly approached Ortega, trying in vain to reach for a gun, with a hand that just wasn't working. For during the melee, seems that several other bullets had found their errant marks.

But apparently Jaegers initial blast did the most damage, catching Ortega in his hip and lower midsection, spinning him around, as what was left of his lower intestines spilled out onto the sand. Ortega's half lidded eyes followed Jaeger around in the aftermath as he made his rounds, administering the 'Coup de Gras', to everyone. Wincing each time the weapon "Popped".

Jaeger picked up the gun and went inside the house, then came back out carrying two cans of cold beer, and sat down Indian style with his legs crossed, just a few short feet away. He pulled the flip top on one of the cans and drained half of the can in one long pull saying, "Thirsty work", to no one in particular, then putting the can down and lit a cigarette.

"And now, we're down to just you and me sport, as he began removing the remnants of his battered shirt with both sleeves charred, revealing a Kevlar vest. He removed the vest, and then the multi tubular devise on his forearms. "A little invention of my own. Worked on it a long time. Wasn't fully sure it would work under combat conditions, but as you can see, it worked very well. Almost hated to surprise you, but we both knew this wouldn't be a fair fight didn't we"!

Giving his watch a brief glance, he took a deep drag on his cigarette, amazed at the calming effect nicotine had in the aftermath. Almost like after great sex, he thought, the image of Melanie flashing into his mind yet again. Love and death both were requiring a cigarette in the aftermath. Then he took another slow drink from the can and reached for his cigarettes offing Ortega one, then suddenly pulling back saying, "Geeze, almost forgot. You don't smoke. You'll eat human flesh and snort a line or two but you don't smoke"!

Ortega's breathing was now coming in shallow rapid pants, as he tried to hurl a mouthful full of spittle in Jaegers general direction, but could only garner up enough strength to blow the bloody spit as afar as his chin"!

"I'll take that as a No", mused Jaeger as he looked at the fading light adding, "I take it you have Jugos on call this evening. Don't worry, I have his number. Looks like he's going to have a far busier night than what he planned for, but don't worry sport, I know the drill, remember"?

"Menudo for the neighborhood as well as the finest deer chorizo north of the Rio Grande. I'm told it's to die for, but I've never developed a taste for the stuff myself. Excuse me a moment", he said as he went to the Lincoln rummaged around and came back with a cell phone, calling Jugos on the speed dial and telling him how many black bags to bring, then hanging up.

"He's on his way and should be here in about an hour or so. Once he sees that you're on the menus I'll tell him that this'll be his last shipment of deer meat from the valley. He never liked doing this y'know, I could tell by his eyes, but as long as you were around, how could he say no? Now he doesn't have that problem ever again. Everything you worked for is gone compadre'. All up in smoke. Soon Embraer'll be made public. Might even cause two nations to go to war, then again maybe not. Of course, I know about the Crystalline, just don't know when or where, but I'll make it my business to find out. After I dump yours and the others bones out in the Gulf tomorrow morning, I'll go through your Clear Lake digs and find out. Even if you'd gotten the best of me, the moment you tried to open any of the briefcases, everything would've gone "BOOM"!

"Now, I wasn't just yanking your chain when I said that the money that your pal Meyers was gonna pay you was mostly bogus. Good quality Bogus, but counterfeit none the less. It should give both of you something to chew about when the both of you meet up in Hell. Some partner eh?

Hey, ain't America great? Life, Liberty, the pursuit of happiness and the opportunity for each of us to screw friends and partners"!

As he talked, he could see the hatred growing in Ortega's eyes, along with the realization there wasn't a thing he could do about it. "Really pisses you off, doesn't it? Made two huge mistakes pal, the first was that day at Ballys and the second, ever trying to screw with me"!

He let that sink in a moment before continuing, "The very last thing you will see is me looking at you with utter contempt"! He then fell silent, savoring Ortega's final moments, for now Ortega was beyond pain. His life's essence fleeing his body, Ortega more felt rather than saw the blurred image of Jaeger looming over him as he struggled to speak, but the words refused to come, It was over and this Cabrone' had won, with all he could do was await release.

The very last thing his conscious mind registered was the sound of a fly, buzzing in his ear as his spirit departed a riddled body. Then he exhaled his final breath slowly, with a grudging audible hiss, fighting the inevitable to its last, his unseeing eyes wide open straining to peer into the eternal emptiness that lay ahead. As Jaeger stood over him unconcerned, he could feel the void in Ortega's eye's and sense palpably the spirit as it left his body. Somewhere in the distance, the car radio made music, while Jaeger envisioned Ortega's destination in that unseen dimension, encountering a large neon sign at the entrance barring his entry reading, "No Vacancy", along with an equally large flashing arrow pointing to the "Down" elevator.

He felt nothing at Ortega's passing, similar to what one would feel at the disposal of a rabid animal. One less predator to feed upon mankind, but Mother Nature had little to fear, for there were many more in the pipeline waiting to take Ortega's place and all Jaeger was doing was "Thinnin' out the herd".

He gathered the bodies under the rear parking canopy and emptied all of the pockets and all the vehicles contained into the trunk of his Ford. Then he policed the area for spent shell casings and gathered all of the weapons placing them also into the trunk. Almost miraculously he saw that each of the other vehicles had suffered several bullet holes, while his precious Ford got nary a scratch. 'Talk about one's luck', he wondered.

A half hour later Jugos pulled his pickup truck into the driveway under the canopy. He reluctantly went over to Jaeger and without a word, inspected each of the bodies laid out before him. Then he looked up at Jaeger in the dim light provided by the kitchen inside the house asking, "Ortega, he Muerte"?

"Si Amigo. Just one final shipment of Menudo to take care of and then no more, forever"!

Jugos fell to his knees, making the sign of the cross, looking up at Jaeger saying, "A lotta work. You will help me, por favor"!

"Gladly"!

Within the hour the bodies were encased in the black Visquene bags and the bloody scene was drenched and scrubbed with bleach and washed off with a hose, the sand raked, and the lights extinguished, the house secured. Then the other vehicles were parked under the rear carport and the keys given to Jugos to do with as he pleased. Jeager then followed him back to his Carnaceria to set about with the final rendering. At five in the morning, he pulled the Ford into Ortega's, Clear Lake residence just as the eastern sky was starting to show a glimmer of light. Safely in the walled compound away from prying eyes, he unloaded the bags of rendered bones and cadaver's heads onto Ortega's Chris Craft motor launch, starting the engine and slowly motored out into the Clear Lake estuary.

The morning mist signaled him to engage the radar ahead and go slow, although he knew the way out onto Galveston Bay and then the deep Gulf waters. The fuel tanks full and the twin diesels idling towards the Bay, he recalled the look of eternal gratitude on Jugos's face as he pulled away from his place of business. Never again.

The running lights on, he then turned on the single side band marine scanner to listen into the traffic that worked its way back and forth along the ship channel. Suddenly he remembered the Loran system turning it on. Just wouldn't do to run aground on anything at this juncture, as he slowly made his way down the estuary through the early morning mist.

Gaining his entrance out into the Bay, he turned toward his starboard side and headed out towards the Gulf, heading south as the eastern horizon brightened. He increased his speed to twenty knots, passing several oil tankers riding high in the water and back out into the Gulf of Mexico, their load of crude delivered and ready to continue the commercial cycle that lubricated the world. Passing the tankers, he constantly monitored the Marine radio traffic, making each vessel aware of his presence as he'd seen on previous trips.

Passing clearly out onto the vast expanse of the Gulf, he nosed the throttles of the twin diesels forward gradually until his vessel ran at a consistent thirty knot mark. Then he dialed the heading and timer into the boats autopilot and pushed "Enter". And there it was. The boat was heading towards a predetermined spot out in the Gulf, a location it had been many times before, some sixty miles from shore. Now nothing to do but stand by, the boat would do everything else. As the boat approached its predetermined location, all on board would be alerted, by the gradual decrease in the boats speed, and the noise level of the twin diesels. The only neighbor being two oil rigs barely visible on the horizon via binoculars.

The two large fishing poles attached to the boat slanting towards the stern, stood as a testament as to the boats stated intentions. A visible canard to its real intention to visit the grave yard once again, hopefull for a final journey to "Davy Jones Locker". With nothing left to do, Jaeger felt a message being sent from his innards, impossible to ignore as he went below to seek out the boats receptacle. That completed and having consumed little except beer since this time yesterday, he made his way towards the boats galley to forage for some victuals and was not disappointed, for Ortega always saw that his boat was fully stocked, fueled and at the ready at all times, with everything required for a prolonged stay at sea.

Belly full, he made his way top side to check the headings and the gauges as the boat continued on in the early morning. The water was like glass as the twin diesels droned on, the noise reminiscent of the constant mega moan of pair of bag pipes on steroids. He then went back to the galley and made a Margarita, pouring it into a Hurricane glass and went astern. He removed his sweat stained shirt and placed it on one of the rear facing seats usually reserved for a fisherman trolling for a big one. Glancing at his watch, he reckoned that he'd slightly more than an hour to go, before the boats autopilot throttled back the engines, signaling his arrival.

As usual his thoughts drifted to Melanie and her son as he'd nothing to do but sit in the other chair watching the boats wake and allow his mind to drift. Somehow he felt her presence, knowing full well it was a mirage never again to be realized. He'd taken the cowards way out just leaving without a word. He knew full well that she loved him every bit as much as he loved her. But he just couldn't risk even a scintilla of a possibility of her and her son becoming cannon fodder for the likes of Ortega. Well, it no longer mattered since he'd gotten word before his trip to Sao Paulo, that she'd gotten an offer to join an Austin think tank as a secretary and was departing Enron. A woman like her, beautiful, erudite and highly intelligent could make a great life for herself and Rory at the seat of power. Of course it was never to be. She would be where clean hands made decisions. Where Jaeger was destined to wallow in the neither regions, burying the dead and here he was a modern day Chiron, ferrying the dead across the mythical river Styx to their eternal destiny. As the Prophet was purported to have said, "Each man's destiny is writ large in the sands at his moment of birth"! Jaeger should know his place in the order of things. Still, it was a grand memory that he'd cherish as long as he drew breath.

Turning his seat, somehow he envisioned her sitting there next to him, attired in the briefest of bikini's soaking up the morning sun, her hair being blown aft by the sea breeze.

He closed his eyes, sensing her presence near, her lips lightly grazing his cheek, her essence invading his nostrils, replacing the salt sea air.

The sound of the engines gradually throttling down brought Jaeger quickly out of his reverie, as he climbed to the upper steering section of the boats bridge, scanning the horizon and waited till the auto pilot brought the engines to idle. He then turned on the boats radio and dialed in one of the local stations, allowing the boat to drift. Jaeger went astern grabbing a large screwdriver on the way and started poking multiple holes into each of the black plastic bags so they would readily sink. Ortega and the rest must visit the bottom of the Gulf quickly. Eventually some predatory creature would get curious enough to get an easy meal.

As he made ready to heave each bag into the Gulf's waters, the radio blared, "This is KILT, the hot spot on your dial. Now well lift our kilt and give y'all a little peek at David Lee Roth while he bemoans his fate, now that he's a solo act belting out "I ain't got no body"!

"Oh, I'm just a gigolo and everywhere I go", came the lyrics true to the original Louie Prima version, as Jaeger one by one tossed each bag of remains over the side. One by one the bags quickly filled with sea water disappearing from view, all except the last bag. It received the same amount of punctures as the rest and was half submerged, but refused somehow to sink further, as the songs refrain blasted forth, "Aye…Ain't got nobody, nobody, nobody, nobody. Aye'm so sad and loanly, won't someone please care for me, cause aye ain't so bad"!

The song eventually loudly concluded amidst an orchestral crescendo, as Jaeger patiently waited for the black plastic bag to join the others. There it floated in the water some ten yards away as Jaeger finished off his drink, still waiting. Then as the floatation seemed to start to edge closer to the boat, Jaeger turned and went up to the bridge, returning with the boats flare gun. He cracked open the break front barrel, to make certain that it was loaded, then closed the barrel, as one name entered his mind.

Cocking the hammer back, Jaeger mouthed, "Geeze Ortega, you just don't know when to give it up do ya"? As he aimed the flare gun at the errant bag, he said, "Maybe this'll help", and shot the phosphorus shell into the bag, puncturing it completely. Now the bag disappeared from view completely. Just as he started to turn towards the bridge, up popped a head, from the waters. It was the head of Ortega still afloat. Clearly frustrated, Jaeger Went back to the bridge, returning with the old Webley breakfront revolver, checking to see it was loaded. Returning to the stern he cocked back the hammer took aim and fired off a single round, spinning the head in the water as it hit home, yet the head still floated mysteriously. Cocking the pistol once again, he fired yet again, then again, each round hitting its target with devastating effect. Finally, Ortega's head split well into several pieces, disappeared from view, causing Jaeger to wonder what mischief his spirit was ready to bring to its final destination? That completed, he turned around to survey the horizon, finding a lone seagull circling about overhead, searching for an easy breakfast, as the radio completed its commercial break and dove right into the original Louie Prima band's version of, "I ain't got nobody"!

Sure coincidences happen from time to time, but given the entirety of the current circumstances, Jaeger sensed something inexplicable happening. By all that was holy, he shouldn't have survived last night's, Big To Do. Yet here he was with just a few painful bruises and scratches, with all of his antagonists dead. Ones talents and motivation only carried one so far, from that point on, the unspoken "Help Wanted", sign was lit. He remembered his last visit at Mass, sometime back and that part of the ceremony where the Apostle's Creed was intoned, especially the part that said, "And all that is seen and unseen"!

He quickly gave a silent thanks to the "Unseen" and went back to the bridge. He gradually throttled up the big diesels and turned the craft towards the starboard, setting its direction back towards Galveston bay. Soon he would see the commercial traffic, and fall right in with its comings and goings.

A few hours later, as the boat motored back up the Clear Lake estuary, it passed the "Turtle Club", with its hoard of boats docked close at hand in its marina, swarming with afternoon revelers, getting a head start on the weekend. This was the local place to see and be seen during the long summer months, where every day was in early preparation of the weekend. When one bellied up the bar, one gave a perfunctory glance at ones watch, which was usually absent saying, "It must be after five in Moscow, ain't it"? The signs plastered everywhere said, "Bikini's Mandatory", or "No shirt, no shoes,…OK", portended its prime attraction, being the plethora of femininity arrayed everywhere, scantily attired, working very hard on their tans and working the crowd of eager men hungry for their attention.

As Jaegers boat passed, several cabin crafts moored dockside; he saw and heard the remnants of a party ramping up from the previous night, as the sounds of Peter Frampton blared out across the waters, "Do you feel like I do? That's true"! A bevy of blonde Scandinavian looking milkmaids, proudly displaying their thongs and pendulous breasts, called out to Jaeger to join the party, which apparently required new blood, since their hosts were still rendered 'Hors de Combat' by booze, or drugs, or perhaps by the well-seasoned lionesses. Never was there a better opportunity for one man to 'Whet one's prurient appetite, yet Jaeger yelled back a reluctant apology to his would be companions, continuing onward up the estuary. He had more important things on his plate than merely, 'Dipping his Wick'. One of Ortega's drug deals was to go down and from the bits and pieces he'd placed together it proved to be huge.

He knew that Magellan headed this thing up, but when or where was the question. When he got back to Ortega's digs, he'd tear the place apart looking for something that indicated time and place, failing that, he'd visit Ortega's Teal Stone Condo. Surely somewhere between the two he'd find what he sought. Yet somewhere in the back of his mind was a little voice that said, "Let it go"! Yet he just couldn't. Of course he might have to if he couldn't find any information as to when or where. He'd been running a long string of good luck lately, especially in the 'Man Dance' of last night, with Ortega and his crew. Something drove him onward through the fog, for he'd chosen to deal himself into this hand and was determined to play things out to the bitter end and piss on the rest.

Fifteen minutes later he slowly backed the Cabin Cruiser into its mooring in what was Ortega's hacienda. The boats clock indicated noon straight up, as he secured the boat and entered the homes rear entrance, turning off the security system within the allotted twenty seconds.

He then went to the panel behind the wall in the laundry room and completely disconnected the rest of the security system. It just wouldn't do to have the home visited by the local police, because he'd tripped off some motion sensor in the house. Now able to move freely within, he began his search starting with Ortega's den. Ortega was infamous for keeping hand written notes in his scrawl, with a cryptic script that few understood outside of Ortega. Davalantes and perhaps Magellan, no more he thought. After two hours he'd quickly sorted through a hoard of notes that proved promising, setting aside the rest in a large pile. He was looking for names, dates, time and location. He ran across an old hand written map that indicated Maynard County and a location just south of the San Saba River, but somehow it didn't reveal anything of importance.

Then the phone rang, startling causing him to freeze in place. On the third ring Ortega's voice came on saying, "I'm busy Cabrone'. Talk to the recorder then hang up"! Then Magellan's voice came on. He was angry that no one had gotten back to him, with just thirty hours to go till the deal went down in Menard. He then repeated that he was angry that Ortega had pulled off his help to deal with Jaeger and that with just him and the Panamanian, to pull off the deal with the others, if things went bad it would be Orgetas fault. Then the line went dead.

Jaeger went to the kitchen his mind reeling as he removed a beer from the refrigerator and went back towards the den. He then retrieved the old, barely visible hand written map indicating Menard County, and then rummaged through the rest of the den eventually coming up with a Rand McNally fold up map of Texas, searching for Menard County. Even though he was born and raised in Texas, it was a pretty big place and Jaeger never even knew that Menard County existed. As far as he knew, it was west of Cut'n Shoot, east of Dead Man's Fang and south of Bum Fuck Egypt. Eventually finding it on the map he found a magnifying glass and a yellow highlighter and began to get his bearings. He quickly redrew the old hand written map very carefully reconciling it with the published map. He studied his findings over and over then replayed Magellan's message several times until things became somewhat clearer.

In less than thirty hours, Magellan was to go through a massive drug deal, with this new drug he'd heard rumors about. This Crystalline. 'He was expecting Ortega's people to join him after dealing with me', thought Jaeger. Apparently several parties were to be part of this bang, bang deal. Just Magellan and one other. Not good for him for neither Ortega nor anyone else was available. A great deal of money was about to change hands in West Texas. Somehow Jaeger had to be the first to arrive and set things up. Soon he'd find out all about Nestor Magellan one way or the other.

He gathered up the map and his notes and left. Next stop his place to prepare, then the long drive to Menard County Texas. It would be at least three hours from now before he could assemble what he needed and leave, then a three hour plus drive to San Antonio, then another three plus hours to Menard County. It would be after dark that he arrived, which offered good and bad possibilities. No use fiddle fuckin' around. Time he got hat and got gone.

The last thing he needed now was a traffic jam, as he raced up I-45 through the center of town and connecting to the Northwest Freeway. Miraculously he made it back to his place, took a quick shower, changed into camo clothes, grabbing energy bars, bottled water, an assortment of weapons and the ammo to feed the beast, along with an assortment of ancillary items, throwing them all into the Ford Bronco. In less than forty minutes he was backing the Bronco out onto the street and was off. Taking every single back road shortcut he knew, it took a half hour to race up the on ramp of I-10, just ahead of the afternoon rush hour traffic, as he turned on his CB radio and his radar detector, heading west.

Ten minutes later he hooked up with a small four rig convoy heading towards San Antonio and parts west, sliding right into the 'Rocking Chair' as they gained speed heading towards the afternoon sun.

He departed the convoy just after it passed through Seguin, racing along through a road that ran in a more westward direction, planning to skirt the northern part of the city and not get held up by rush hour traffic. On the other side of San Antonio, his fuel tank running low, he filled up the main and auxiliary tanks and was back on I-10 in side of ten minutes, heading northwest into the Texas Hill Country. As he raced along the Interstate, he recalled the many stories his father had told him about an ancestor, Heinrich (Henry) Jaeger that was here roaming the plains, with John Coffee Hays and others as poorly paid Rangers during the days of the Texas Republic. In those days, they were trying to keep the settlers alive, often with mixed results, against the Comanche and the

Kiowa natives. Old grand pappy Henry was the one who started it all. Times had changed, technology had too, but the same old struggles of good versus evil still were in play.

He had a plan, he was well armed and had a full tank of gas, now all he had to do was find the exact rendezvous point, be the first one there and prepare the area. All, he needed was time and luck. Pressing his luck he pushed the accelerator down as the Bronco passed the ninety mile an hour mark, hoping that the CB radio would alert him to any speed traps up ahead as the summer sun was heading south. He reckoned that he had ninety minutes until the sun disappeared below the horizon and perhaps a half hour of visibility after that. Passing through Kerrville, on the interstate he reckoned that he was somehow ahead of the game as Junction was now fifty miles away, then turn north on State Route Eighty Three for another spell then if the hand written map was right, find a two lane county road, in the dim light of dusk. If he got as far as Menard, he went too far and had to turn around.

Later, having left the interstate at Junction, he raced north on the State route, peering intently in the dimming light, looking for any sign that indicated a county road heading east. He passed a barely visible sign, worn out through the passage of time and slowed down just in time to see what passed for a two lane blacktop road heading east, as he made the turn.

Accelerating now, he felt he was close as he drove for several miles, looking to his left for a worn metal gate to an abandoned farm property Ortega used any number of times to make large drug transfers. He was hoping that no one had removed a simple red plastic strip that supposed to indicate the exact turn in. Going slower now, he passed a farm house on his right, several hundred yards up a gradual hill. Driving slower now, in the dim light he saw a red marker hanging limply on an old metal gate to his left, thinking, 'This must be it'.

Grateful, that no chain or lock was on the gate, all he had to do was unlatch the gate and dive on through the old worn gravel single lane path, latching the gate behind him, moving forward in first gear slowly for about a mile and a half. Somehow instinct told him to move off the gravel path, as something loomed large ahead, perhaps a hill of some sort, visible in the moon light. Seeing a thick copse of trees ahead, he drove towards it, finding an entrance way that shielded his vehicle from view.

As he got out of the Bronco, he inspected the copse of trees walking around it and found it suitable. As he looked upward, he noticed the bright moon in all of its pregnant fullness. The moon would provide all the light he would need for his purposes. Now it that big hill ahead was the semi- circular horseshoed shaped clearing, then the San Saba River would be close by and he was in the right place.

Two solid hours of careful recon work familiarized him with the ground. A half mooned shaped hill laden with trees and overgrowth, shielded a secluded clearing where once, long ago a home stood. Now the only thing to mark the memory of its existence was a single stone chimney and fireplace. The clearing occupied the high ground sloping down towards a slow moving river, some thirty yards away, which must be the San Saba. Now filled with controlled excitement he made his way back to the Bronco.

He then went back to the place where he'd gone off the gravel path carefully straightening as best he could the tall grass flattened by the Bronco as it went off the trail. He was grateful that it hadn't rained in quite a while, or else he'd have left deep ruts, that would be impossible to eradicate in the short time he had left. Satisfied with his work he then went back to the secluded Bronco and set about unloading his surprises for the company that was soon to arrive, trundling his load up the hill and depositing it for later.

He went back to the Bronco, then picked up the few remaining items then went to the small single lane gravel pathway. As the pathway approached the clearing, it curved to its right around the horseshoed shaped hill. He was seeking secluded locations at chest height to insert his electronic claymores. He'd bought a dozen of the mines, truly nasty business they were, capable of shredding a horse in an instant, or an ordinary vehicle as it passed. By midnight, he'd installed four of the mines flanking the entrance and the remaining eight all around the inner cup up the hill enclosure. Thinking like those he was to encounter, treachery was a way of life to these people and he expected some early arrivals.

Going back to the Bronco, he brought some of the other equipment especially the miniature control module, where he programmed each set of electronic mines, to a single button on the, battery powered, three by five inch console. Now all of them were in fully armed mode. Push a button and two mines would be set off, push yet another button and two more would reach out.

One last trip to the Bronco retrieved everything else he'd need for his stay, bringing it all up the back side of the U shaped hill, then looking for a suitable tree that provided sufficient cover from below, yet gave a full view of the clearing. Finding a suitable candidate, he brought all to the base of the tree, then attached tree climbing spikes to his boots, wrapping a length of rope around the base of the tree and made his way upward through the branches. It took two trips to bring all he'd need, some thirty feet up the tree, but as he looked around and especially below him he was secure in the knowledge he'd chosen the spot well. Cutting the two hundred foot length of rope, into a variety of lengths, he secured all of his gear to nearby branches, all at arms-reach. His arms and legs ached from the exertions as he tried to find a reasonably comfortable position amongst the limbs. Finally all was at the ready. He then assembled the short range, .32 caliber semi auto carbine, with a fifteen inch barrel, encompassed by a noise and flash suppressor. It was fed by a thirty round clip that held the subsonic fragmentation rounds. Then he mounted a four power scope with night vision capabilities. When fired, the weapon made a muffled sound no louder than a rats sneeze. Sufficient for close range headshots no farther than fifty yards. It was something he came up with a year ago when tinkering around with a local gunsmith he knew. Strictly a one off thing, he'd play around with from time to time, never thinking he'd ever have an occasion to use it.

Next, he secured the .12 gauge Street Sweeper on another branch. Ten rounds and drum fed, the all metal assault weapon held double ought buck shot. Anything it hit, it brought down, regardless. Lastly was the .357 Magnum Ruger revolver, tightly slung under his arm-pit, with four speed loaders holding Teflon penetration rounds. Yet another branch held five quart plastic containers of energy drink, along with a dozen caffeine laden energy bars.

He adjusted his position in the branches, as he glanced up towards the full moon that lit up the area nicely. No doubt, by this time tomorrow, it would all be over, one way or another. He wondered why all this flurry was happening all within a compressure of time? Now as he gazed at the moon, it all became clear. The full moon was always a driver of events for as long as anyone could recall. No one could explain why, with any reasonableness. Great minds always tried and failed to make sense of it. More murders, more births, more people found each other in the throes of infatuation, with either great things, or terrible things happening for good or for ill, within the period of the full moon. Then the echo of those words he'd heard a thousand times, echoed in his mind, "And of all is seen and unseen"! Yet again he silently intoned, "Into your hands I commend my spirit"!

Still uncomfortable, he fashioned a web of a sort where he could sit upon from the remaining rope he'd brought, weaving it between nearby branches then removed a number of other branches laden with leaves and weaved them between the ropes underneath, providing shielding from view beneath.

Now the waiting would begin as he glanced at the luminous dials of his watch, reading 04:30 hours in the morning. Reaching into his rucksack, he retrieved the small radio he'd brought and inserted the earpiece. He needed some music in the early morning hours to relax, for he'd a long wait ahead. Slowly working the dial, he somehow got an all-night station from Austin that's signal was intermittent. In all the time he lived in Texas, Jaeger never did exactly bond with country western music, his tastes evolving into the more esoteric, running from R&B, to the classics, to jazz and several of its permutations, to R&R. But on this night, from the jump, the music of Miles Davis poured its rhythmic muted wail out into his single earpiece, "Killer Joe"!

"You're listening to KNOP, in Austin, by God Texas, this early moon lit morning", crooned the DJ. "Put all your guns and grenades on the shelf boys and girls and grab your honey and do what come natural. If your honey ain't close at hand, the roll a joint and take a deep toke.

You just listened to Miles Davis, playing "Killer Joe", on KNOP. Now as a change of pace, we're going to play a slightly different version of the same song, by the Manhattan Transfer. Give us a ring and tell us which version you like the best, those of you that can see your hands before your face. If ya can't do what's natural then there's always the alternative, as long as you stay away from the livestock. The latter message was meant for all the Aggies out at College Station", crooned the DJ, with the Transfer taking up the banner as a vocal counterpoint.

As the second song ended, he had to chuckle at the verbal jab by the early morning DJ at members of the student body of another Texas college, long an adversary of the University of Texas in almost all things. All agreed, the unofficial School Motto should be, "Where men are men and the sheep are nervous"! Jaeger decided not to press his luck and turned off the small radio and removed his earpiece, placing it carefully back in the rucksack. 'A fitting song', he thought as he closed his eyes and tried to relax.

Apparently a mild weather front was moving through the area, when he felt a gathering breeze upon his face, the trees finally stirring to life.

Then he heard a crackling of underbrush below him and a muffled voice crying out "What da fuck"? He instantly came awake, glancing at his watch, reading 05:15 in the morning. There was movement below him as he froze in place, slowly moving his eyes from side to side and seeing nothing in view, gradually moved his head. It was darker now, as the moon hung just on the horizon awaiting the arrival of the sun. All of his senses on full alert, he began to see movement of two men below him fanning out as they converged on the clearing, with two more walking down the single lane gravel road that wrapped around the U shaped hill and two more that worked their way down from behind Jaegers location as they all finally converged upon the clearing.

One of the men spoke in what appeared to be a small portable, radio receiver. All of which were wearing the long leather black coats, Jaeger had seen before. Apparently they were satisfied as the one holding the radio spoke into it, in the Caribbean patois, "Yeah Boss, nobody home. We be the first ones heah"!

He then said, "OK Boss, we leave two men heah", as he handed the radio to one of the men saying, "Hoo Doo Chile want you two to stay and keep eyes open. We gonna join him up top. Anybody arrive, you let him know. Fock ting's up, it gonna be bad, ya follow"!

"But what we gonna do for food", asked one of the two selected to remain? The rest handed over some candy bars and chewing gum as the leader said, "Ya want water, there be the ribbah ober dere", handing the portable radio to one of those as the others turned their back and walked back up the road.

As Jaeger looked at the remaining two, he was relieved for clearly they hadn't come across his hidden Bronco and even more telling these were city boys, pure and simple, quite unaccustomed to the country. They were down there for the duration, just like Jaeger was up here.

During the day, the long leather bullet resistant coats would prove a hindrance. Then what would they do at night when the skeeter's came to feed? He'd heard stories about the Jamaican Posse from Davalantes when he was alive. Then again he'd run up against them, just before he'd headed out to Sao Paulo. Overhearing that there leader, the legendary Hoo Doo Chile was close at hand, told Jaeger that this deal was even more important than he imagined. The Posse was clearly here to High Jack the deal. The next to arrive would be Magellan and his lone helper. Later would arrive the Chicago group, then the Crips or whoever else Ortega decided to invite to the party. As the sky started to gradually brighten in the east, his vantage point was due north across the San Saba river. Ortega and Davalantes or whoever, had picked this spot well. A Horse Shoed shaped enclosure, heavily wooded, a long way from the nearest county road, surrounded him. As he looked northward across the river, at least a three quarters of a mile of grassland sloping upward towards a line of trees, guaranteed to suppress any sound that came forth short of a massive ordinance explosion. Magellan was walking into a trap. Either way things went down, a great deal of money was about to change hands and Jaeger had the rest of the day and part of the night to plan which way he was to go.

He drifted off again, as the sun came up. In his mind, he sensed the presence of his father, so real yet so far away, as an image came into view, through his closed eyelids. For the next several hours, an intensely personal monolog entered his subconscious, by the formless spirit, assuring him that all was well with his family and they were united in that other dimension. As Jaeger listened, tears came to his eyes, as his father said all of the things that should've been said long ago, explaining the inexplicable. Then as if expecting it, Jaegers paternal spirit explained to him that it wasn't possible that his mother and his little sisters could be present, yet it assured him that their collective message of eternal love and affection, would be ever present, saying that they'd be in touch at another time, reminding him that time in his reality was not like that of the Eternal.

In his mind, Jaeger reached out, as if trying to touch the image of his father, passing right through formless specter. "Think of this as a long distance phone call, that we used to get when I was in Nam", his father said. "A rare event of limited duration", said his father indicating that the time was soon to be up. "One thing though", said his father continuing. "I can feel your concern that your time is close at hand. All I can tell ya is that I've got it on pretty good authority that the time of our joining is not yet at hand. It's gonna be awhile, from your frame of reference. So we can wait awhile. You've planned well and be not afraid. It's gonna be a close run thing, but you'll come out on top. As far as that other goal you're trying for, remember the Cotton Bowl game. It was my proudest hour"!

Then the image disappeared, as Jaegers eyes came open. His nasal passages were all clogged up with mucous, as he looked at his watch. It was just short of noon; as he cleared his sinuses as silently as he could; lay still high up in his hide. It was as if a heavy weight had been lifted from his shoulders. They were all together. No regrets. No cries for revenge, just harmony and unity, for he'd just received the word from an unimpeachable source. He still had much to do and many miles to travel.

oo Doo Chile, gathered his scouts up into the large white panel van they rented along with the three others and closed the gate the way they found it, then turned the small contingent around and drove back down the county road, then turned left onto the entrance of the Culligan Ranch they'd seen driving by. As they went up the single lane gravel road, the sky was just starting to brighten in the east. Arriving at the rear of the main house, they noted that the lights were on in the kitchen, as all of the vehicle doors came open at once and the Posse' poured forth.

An ominous group they were, all clad in the full length, black leather coats, each man sporting the long snake like weaved locks as if a small herd of Medusa like creatures descended upon the land. Each carried a noise suppressed Mac-10 machine pistol in his hand as they made way for their leader, the massive dread locked Hoo Doo Chile, the last to emerge, from his Van, weapon at the ready.

Rance Culligan and his son came out of the kitchen door and onto the rear porch, interrupted from their breakfast by the arrival of these intruders. As he saw the intruders spread out he whispered to his son, "Get back into the house and bring the shotgun"! Then he thought to himself, 'What in Sam Hill is this, an NAACP convention, with all these niggers here'?

Hoo Doo Chile approached the Culligan back porch at a slow walk, stopping at the bottom step of the rear porch, just as Culligans son emerged from the kitchen with the double barreled goose gun, handing it to his father. Just then the manner of dress of these invaders, registered a mortal fear in the heart of Rance Culligan as he noticed that his shotgun was no match for twenty some men carrying guns.

"Companeee"! Bellowed Hoo Doo Chile as he continued in his deep baritone Jamaican patois, "So ya be wantin' ta know what a bunch of nappy headed niggers be doin' here, at your back porch, now wouldn't ya? Well, we here ta jine ya for breakfast, then when our bellies be full, we gonna take your souls. Dat's what we be doin' here at your back porch. Now lay dat thing down before ya get hurt."! As he finished his statement his Mac- 10 was pointed at Culligan's chest, as well as the weapons of all of the others.

"Inside da house", yelled Bunny as he noted movement in the kitchen. Seeing the outside phone line connection near the back porch, Hoo Doo Chile signaled one of his men to destroy the connection box and cut the line, as three others forced their way into the kitchen, tearing the kitchen phone from Culligan's wife's hands as the phone was ripped from the wall. Then the wife and her two young daughters were herded outside to join the others as they sat down on the ground surrounded by the Rastafarians.

"There now", whispered Hoo Doo Chile, "We gonna be visitin' ya for the resta the day. My men are hungry, so yer wife is gonna cook em all a right proper breakfast, lunch an supper. Other than that, you gonna go about your chores as if it were any odder day. Milk da cows, shovel shit or any other ting ya do. Da onliest ting ya not gonna do is talk to anyone aboud any ting. Now ya behave yer self an jus mebbe I leave you in one piece when we leave tonight. Of course ya gonna be tied up tight, but with some luck maybe somebody come by in a few days an cut ya loose. We be long gone by den, so mebbe you have some stories to tell, or mebbe not. So now we down to it. Have ya milked de cows yet"?

"NN no sir not yet", stammered a frightened Rance Culligan! "Who be milkin' de cows den"?

"Well it all depends", answered Culligan. "Usually my son and me and maybe one or both of my daughters"! "Den I gonna be makin' an executive decision heah", said Hoo Doo Chile! "You an yer son an one daughter gonna be milkin' da cows inna da barn ober dere. Yer wife, she gonna be takin' da odder daughter an makin' us all breakfast, with lotza coffee, da very same as you be eatin'. Now 'Mister Bunny' way inna back, he gonna take some men wid him at watch ya an help tote da milk to da house, while I come inna house, wid somma my folks and watch your wife an chile'. Dat picnic table ober dere be a good spot to feed my men. Some of the odders'll be set up around da place as lookouts, ya follow"?

"Now da next part ya gotta pay close attention to. Jus one little fuck up by anybody, just one'll go hard onna da rest of ya. Ya do what I say, or what 'Mister Bunny tell ya an ya just might come outta dis in one piece. Jus one ting an nobody gonna see da next sunrise, in one piece, ya follow"!

Culligan nodded as Bunny signaled for him and his son to rise along with one of the daughters and lead the way into the barn, while his boss dispatched four of his men to disperse into lookout positions around the front and sides of the main house.

Now quite apart from Hoo Doo Chile, who's massive presence was enough to turn even the bravest of men into quivering creatures, there was Bunny, his Haitian second in command. Recruited from the slums of Port au Prince as an operative of the dreaded Ton Ton Ma Coute', the Haitian secret police during the days of the Duvalier dictatorships, here was a man whose presence gave nightmares. An Albino Negro, completely devoid of any skin pigment, sported the long dreadlocks of the others except the hair was as blonde as any Scandinavian, while his ocular pigment was pink and thus the term Bunny, for the Bunny Eyes that greeted others. Were it not for the overly broad nose and the multiple scars his face sported, along with the perpetual scowl, he might just be considered just another run of the mill albino. Yet just one glance into those eyes, told of an unrelenting evil that ran hard and deep, that matched every bit that of his master, Hoo Doo Chile. His commands were by sign language and a series of grunts and snorts, that eventually his people sorted out and the reason for his silence, was that someone long ago in the service of Papa Doc, removed his tongue during a session of interrogation. Later recruited into the Ton Ton Macoute' he served under the very same commander that was responsible for his life long silence. That service lasted only a year, for the commander disappeared one moonless night, his remains never discovered. Some speculated that he became dinner for the sharks, but without the remains, that would be a mystery unsolved. Since no one was available to take his job it was awarded to Bunny, the only name he was ever known by.

During a visit to Haiti, Hoo Doo Chile, persuaded Bunny and several of his key men to join him in New Orleans as his ranks had been depleted by his ongoing conflict with the Crips and the Zulu Man. A conflict soon to be resolved with eternal finality, if Hoo Doo Chile had anything to say about it.

There was no way in measuring, even the approximate level of terror the entire Culligan family endured as the day wore on. Silently everyone intoned repeated prayers to the eternal God almighty to allow this cup to pass them by. The 'Chile' sat at the kitchen table all day long going over plans of his insertion, at the rendezvous site a scant mile up the road, with several of the others. Once an hour he checked in with those left at the site to see if anything was happening. If anyone had arrived yet. Then by four in the afternoon one of his lookouts alerted him that a very large rental van had passed the Culligan farm. A half hour later, the portable radio crackled alive. It was the men left behind at the site, letting the 'Chile' know that Magellan had arrived with only one other and with Scylla the hostage, in tow. The 'Chile' rose from the table saying, "Time to supper we get now and make it good", as the Culligans scurried around to prepare the evening meal. Then as an afterthought he said, "Ya need at make some extra so we can take it along after we leave. Sandwich's be good"!

An hour later after his men were fed, Hoo Doo Chile rose up from the kitchen table saying, "Dat was good, now you be cleanin' up now, cause we gonna be leavin' soon"! Leaving three men in the kitchen to supervise the mother and her daughters during the cleanup, he ushered the father and his son into the barn saying, "We gonna need rope. Lot'sa rope"! As they scurried around looking for rope, Hoo Doo Chile and Bunny looked about the barn, with Hoo Doo Chile eventually pointing up at the barns rafters and asking, "Bunny now. What do ya tink about da rafters for hanging da family"?

Bunny looked upward, examining the rafters, turned around with a big smile, grunting his assent and nodding.

"Good. You gonna be in charge of calling the Baron for his blessing"! Of course this simple command meant that the Culligan family was not ever going to see another sunrise. For given the Voo Doo rituals of Santeria, whenever an important undertaking was to be attempted, the Baron Samedie, Lord of the Underworld, must be summoned and a sacrifice must be offered and accepted. The greater the task the greater the offering. Seemingly five innocent humans should do the trick. As the two Culligans returned with rope they found, offering it to Hoo Doo Chile for his approval, he nodded as Bunny stepped forward and placed a single muffled round in each of their knees. Immediately as they dropped to the ground writhing in pain, they were set upon by others, who bound and gagged them, tying their ankles together and throwing the remainder of rope over the low hanging support beams and hoisted them upwards hanging upside down, with their hands securely bound behind them. As both of the Culligans screamed, their cries of pain muffled, Hoo Doo Chile, turned to Bunny saying, "Bunny, send em over to the Baron", stepping aside and watching the well-worn Voo Doo sacrifice to the Prince of the Underworld. At its conclusion, the final act was to sever the vein in the neck the blood back to the lungs for more oxygen. That way was the least messy. Soon the subject would bleed out and simply go to sleep, rather than have blood pumping out like crazy in all directions. Took a little while longer, but was considered far more civilized.

As they both hung inverted, empty eyes staring but not seeing any longer, the 'Chile' told Bunny to bring the women out to join the rest of the family. The kitchen finally cleaned, Culligans wife followed Bunny and the others into the barn, where their worst fears were realized. Seeing the inverted, lifeless bodies of the elder Culligan and his son brought forth a unified scream of terror, prompting those Rasta's close by to hit each of them, simultaneously rendering them unconscious. The rest fell upon them securing each of them in the same way as the others and hung them upside down from the support beam, next to the others.

A frowning Hoo Doo Chile walked around them saying, "A family dat hang together stay together. But it woulda been better Juju if they'd be happy in serving da Baron. Still, he gets what he gets"!

Then turning to Bunny again he said, "Bunny, it be show time", as he stepped aside observing the ritual with a keen eye to detail. When it was concluded, and the blood dripped slowly onto the barn floor, the "Chile" walked around the swaying bodies, looking intently into each of the eyes. The male's eyes were open, but the females eyes were all closed, a minor detail in the ritual, overlooked. He hoped the Baron would not feel insulted, for when they arrived at their final resting place, the Baron required their spirit be able to see him in all of his glory. A minor detail, he was certain the Baron would overlook given his recent generous gift. As he looked at his men all assembled around he said, "Ah know what ya be thinkin'. Why didn't we get to sample da women's goodies before dey met the Baron? Simple reason is because of time. Our main guest has arrived just up de road, now we gotsta go get into position to welcome the rest later on tonight. Everybody know their job an we got da Barons blessing. When we be done, everybody gonna get a shit load of money and can buy what dey want when we be back in New Orleans. Kitche kitche ya ya mama," he said prompting all to laugh in anticipation.

"We done heah, so let's move out"!

Magellan's arrival brought Jaeger instantly alert high up in his tree hide. He saw the large rental Cargo Van lumber around the bend into the clearing, jockey back and forth, finally backing up facing the entrance. Both he and the young Panamanian carried out a drugged Scylla carrying her out onto the main clearing, sitting her down facing the Cargo Van and securing her hands behind her to a large tree root that made an appearance out of the ground, then going right back into the ground. Attired in the same shorts, Tee top and jacket that she'd worn that fateful day back in Houston, she still, while somewhat worse for wear, was an appealing female. She'd come around in a few hours, but then as now she wasn't going anywhere.

Now all he had to do was wait, as he looked at his watch. Sometime soon after the sun went down, the Chicago and Oriental groups would arrive, do the deal and depart. A few hours later Zulu Man and his Crips buddies would show up, do the deal, get Scylla and leave with their share of the Crystalline. That is if everything went as planned. Yet, no sign of Ortega. Did the cops arrive when he met Jaeger? If so there would be a shootout, which would explain why Ortega and the others were absent. All day long he was having misgivings. People would have to be on their best behavior for things to go as planned. People were never on their best behavior, ever, unless compelled to be. Yet, with all that money at stake, more than he could ever even count, he just had to risk it. If Ortega was really out of the picture and the deal was done, then his only problem was how to get all of that money out of the country. A problem many in the game had, but never at this level. He'd cross that bridge when the time came.

As he walked around the clearing, a place that only once before he came to, he marveled at Davalantes ability to select secluded places where drug deals occurred. The last time he'd been here, Ortega had a half dozen of his men up around the horse shoe looking down at the goings on weapons at the ready. Fortunately things went as planned. The last time, he, one other and Davalantes were the only ones showing. Perhaps this time things would go along similar lines. If so, perhaps he could go back to France, linger awhile at Madeleine's grave, and then find something useful to do with the rest of his life. If things went badly, then perhaps Madeleine would be waiting, for his arrival.

High up in his hide, Jaeger peered down into the clearing between the leaves seeing what appeared to be a worried look on Magellan's face, yet he was here regardless. Surly he must know that Ortega and his crew would not be joining the party. He had his mobile phone. He'd heard the sound of his voice on the recorded message at Ortega's Clear Lake home. And yet he was here. Only money, in massive quantities could bring someone to this party. High risk, high yield, was the only thing that could attract like a black hole.

Perhaps, Nestor wondered, or hoped, that Ortega would suddenly appear just in the nick of time ahead of the others, yet Jaeger knew better.

As he looked down, he saw Scylla, secured to the large tree root, looking a little worse for wear, attired in the remnants of the same clothes as when he saw her last. What must be going through her mind? Clearly an Alpha for a very long time, now just a pawn in the game of life and death. Then he glanced around and finally saw the Rasta minders lying low in the brush half way up the hill once again. They hadn't moved from their position since Magellan arrived, with one of them appearing to whisper into a small portable radio. Soon Jaeger expected company to surround him below. He'd no doubt as to who it would be, the only question would be, how many would come to the dance? The hours ahead, would prove to be eventful and confusing.

A half an hour later, the sun entering its downward slide, he felt more than saw initially, movement below him. Sitting high up in the branches, he began to see movement below him in the thick brush that enveloped the enclosure. It was the Rasta's, the Posse arriving in force as an avenging demon, bent upon righting the wrong of the overturn of their ambush in Houston, almost a month ago. In a few hours the sun would be down and he would see just how much discipline they could muster with those hot protective coats surrounding them, while the skeeters had their way. Would the Hoo Doo Chile make an appearance? He hadn't the last time out. But here right below him was a reason for him to lend his special touch.

It took some thirty minutes for them all to settle into place, with two of them planting themselves right below him at the base of his tree. They would have to be the very first to depart this world.

The heat of the day still evident, Jaeger heard whispering coming from below as one of the Rasta's complained, "Dis fuckin' leather coat gonna be the death of me yet. Looka heah, it's too fuckin' hot. I'm soaked with sweat through to da bone. Gonna take hours ta dry out"!

The other answered back in an angry whisper, "Shut da fuck up niggah. Hoo Doo Chile find out you take off da coat, you be a dead man. Soon it be night and it'll cool us some. After all, da coat, she stop da bullets, doan she now? An we gonna need da Baron's protection once the bullets start flyin' after dark. So settle down an do like I do"!

As Jaeger sat up top listening keenly gathering only bits and pieces of their discontent below, he now knew two things. Hoo Doo Chile was here and his men were not going to be ready for prime time.

He slowly scanned the wooded hillside, peering into the gloom. Eventually he made out the forms of twenty men, but which one was their leader. There was one over to his far right that looked promising, with long white looking dread locked hair and as he turned his head slightly he made out the colorless face. An albino, who then turned around and motioned to another to move to another position. This wouldn't be the Hoo Doo Chile, but he was a leader of sorts.

No known pictures existed of the Rasta leader, just a vague description. Large of frame, with skin blacker than a gorilla, with black dreadlocks and a small silver streak in his hair running horizontally along the side of his head. In his haste to leave Houston, Jaeger had left behind a miniature directional microphone, capable of picking up a whisper at seventy five yards. Spilt milk. He'd have to do without.

High up in his hide, he sensed a change in the direction of the wind and within the last hour an increase in humidity. Must be cooler weather front coming through, he'd heard over the radio earlier this morning. Moving very slowly, he reached into his rucksack and donned his Kevlar vest, putting his Kevlar, Camo designed field shirt back on. Then he slowly removed the knee length green plastic poncho, slipping it slowly on and putting on the hood.

A half an hour later the rain shower arrived. Nothing major. A gentle rain lasting only for twenty minutes or so in duration, yet dropping the temperature considerably in its wake. Soon the mosquitos would make their appearance. No doubt Magellan and his helper found shelter, but poor Scylla, secured as she was to a tree root, would be a tad wet along with the patiently waiting Rasta's down below.

When the rain stopped, Magellan and his helper brought some wood gathered before the rain shower placed under their Van and put it in the abandoned fire place, and set it ablaze.

Once the initial blaze was roaring they then placed some of the wet wood on top of the fire producing a significant quantity of smoke.

'Must be his Legionnaire training', thought Jaeger. 'Skeeter's and smoke do not get along well. When one has no mosquito repellant handy, make smoke to keep the critters away'. Alternating dry wood, to keep the fire going and wet wood to make smoke, no doubt he was making life difficult for those Rasta's hunkered down behind the fire place, for the gentle breeze was blowing the smoke right at them. No doubt they'd not considered the dense smoke's benefits, only the immediate liabilities. Those Rasta's hidden in the brush in front of the fireplace, soon would feel the presence of their winged visitors, as Jaeger discovered hearing the slap upon one of those below. "Damn Skeeter's", came the stage whisper from below.

Eventually the breeze died down to nothing, as the entire clearing filled with the acrid smell of wet wood, with Magellan's helper adding wood to the fire every twenty minutes or so. Jaeger then saw Magellan go back to the Van and come back with his mobile phone, pressing preprogrammed numbers into the speed dial. With each and every number he pressed into the phone, he became more visibly agitated, finally putting the phone away in disgust. Clearly it looked like one final attempt to contact the dead, who were not coming. But how was he to know? "What will happen now", asked the young Panamanian shooter?

"Choices are fairly simple", said Magellan looking at his watch. "Either we leave now with five tons of the most potent drug known to man, skipping an enormous payday and leave fairly soon for our first buyer is to arrive within the hour, or we stay and brazen things out. Something must have happened to not only Ortega, but Davalantes and all the rest, for they wouldn't have missed this for the world"!

"I'll stay if you will Patron'," said the young shooter bravely. "If they ain't here, it be more for us, no"? "Seems that greed is going to get the best of us, this night my friend", mused Magellan. "Check your weapons.

It would be a shame if they malfunctioned"! Magellan then walked over to Scylla, kneeled down and gave her another drink of the Gatorade he carried saying, "If all goes to plan a group will arrive within the hour. We'll conduct business and they will leave followed by your brother an hour later. Money and goods will be exchanged and you will be set free. Just one question though if you will. Why on earth, were you ever involved with the Posse'?"

For the first time Scylla looked directly at Magellan saying, "It was my brother's idea. We fought about it. Should our Padron', the Mendaca's ever find out, we'd have a big problem. Then again we'd been fightin' with the Posse' for about two years over turf. We seemed to be winnin' the war, when he decided to throw in with them for this thing only. Then Jump em later. Lemme have another drink of that stuff OK"?

After she'd finished, she continued, "But when all is said and done, blood's thicker than water ain't it"?

"I'm not certain that it is", answered Magellan.

"I've never had any brothers and sisters myself and over the years I've discovered that blood kin more often than not, lead to the destruction of the family as often as they help the family prosper. So pardon me if I'm not sold on familial unity"! At that he rose up and walked back to the Van to await coming events. He looked at the young Panamanian shooter, barely out of his teens, by the look of it. Literate, but barely so. Ortega plucked him out of the bodegas of Panama City, just as he came up through the ranks. Just as his father was pulled from obscurity by the elder Quiniones long ago only to become the finest breeder of bulls for the Corrida, on the entire Iberian Peninsula. Time would soon reveal whether or not the young boy would or could stand and deliver. He reached into the Van and handed the Panamanian two tablets saying, "It will be a long night, swallow these. They'll keep us both awake, during the coming hour"! Then Magellan followed suit, washing the tablets down with Gatorade.

His thoughts then went to Jaeger. Could by some chance he been a police operative, or informant? Quickly recounting each involvement they'd both been in on, Jaeger had broken just as many laws as everyone else. He'd taken lives in Magellan's presence without hesitation, which fit in very well with the verifiable fact that he was a convicted murderer.

No, Jaegers hands were just as soiled as everyone else's. He'd have made an excellent Legionnaire, for his manner belied some fashion of military training in the past. Just a soldier of fortune, who somehow, got the better of Ortega, not only once but twice apparently.

He then turned his attention to the rear of the Cargo Van, seeing thirty, 50 gallon plastic drums full of the Crystalline concentrate. In highly diluted quantities, he'd seen just what it could do, to an unsuspecting consumer and its variability depending upon the mixing agent. Fifteen drums to the Chicago/Seattle people, Ten to the Crips and the rest to the Rastas.

High up in his hide, Jaeger kept turning over and over in his mind, what he would do if he was Hoo Doo Chile? He saw the manner of which he deployed his people around the well wooded cupola surrounding the clearing. If his people were reasonably disciplined a sudden cross fire of quick duration would be sufficient to obliterate everyone in the clearing. Once again he made a head count of those around him, this time with his silenced, assault rifle and its night scope. The clouds overhead darkened the light of the full moon significantly, leaving the clearing illuminated by the fire. He counted twenty one people, more or less, laying low in the brush. Had he missed anyone? Perhaps. Then a thought occurred. He had communicated with his people by a hand held portable radio. He'd joined with the people. Wouldn't he like to know when the others arrived? Of course he would. It would be essential. It would be something Jaeger would do. Which meant one or more Rasta's was left behind back near the entrance gate, with a radio. No matter what went down, he'd have to remember the possibility of one more out there Magellan turned and looked out at the hillside surrounding the clearing. Had he known he was going to be alone, he'd have taken precautions. Surrounding the cupola with tripwires attached to bushes at just above ankle height, attached to grenades at key places around the hill. Of course there always was the possibility of some animal setting off an explosion in a serendipitous manner. He then went to the fire and tossed on some more damp wood, creating an acrid smoke that drifted up into the surrounding hill. No mosquito's were felt to be on the hunt thus far so it must be working. Then he called the Panamanian over and they went over any and all possibilities he could think of in case of treachery, what moves they would make and when. Hand and head signals, rather than vocal.

Repeating the possibilities over and over. Perhaps there was a small chance of success after all. High up in the tree, Jaeger was struggling with his own quandary. Two groups were to arrive at different times to transact their deals. Clearly the Posse' was going to try and take down everything. They'd show their hand just after the first group arrived, probably killing them straight out, stash the bodies, then allow the second group to arrive and do the same thing.

But at what point should Jaeger intervene? He'd have to think about that. Of course the river would claim all of the bodies. Focusing on the one he thought might be the Hoo Doo Chile, through his night vision scope, Jaeger saw him speak into what looked like a short range portable radio to his ear. Then he swung his scope back to the albino across the way, who listened in return while nodding his head. Was it instructions he was receiving, or was it an indication from someone else that company was coming? Jaeger opted for the latter as he glanced at his watch.

High as he was in his perch, he could barely see over the top of the ridge behind him, through the foliage, yet he could make out the glow and movement of headlights coming slowly towards the clearing as the sounds of multiple vehicles worked their way laboriously over the gravel pathway came to his ears. Then he looked down at the clearing as he saw Magellan perk up and say something to his Panamanian shooter. Several minutes later, three dark colored, heavy duty panel vans rounded the corner passing the locations where concealed shape charges had been placed and entered the clearing, as Magellan greeted the arrivals, directing them which way to park next to his much larger panel van. His attention swung back and forth between the Rasta commander and Magellan and his new arrivals, who by the look of it was the Chicago buyers, a leader and five others, who seemed to be transacting well enough, but that rarely told the complete story, as he and others were known to pull the trigger while still smiling. They must've wondered why Magellan was all by himself. Did he tell them that others were monitoring the deal hidden from view? Purely a bad bluff, but a probability. Jaeger knew the Panamanian was secreted in the bushes near the entrance they passed into the clearing, but so did the Rasta's nearby. Almost too bad he selected that spot, for in the event Jaeger had to activate the Claymore's, Magellan's shooter was in a direct line for a teeth full from one of the mines pointing towards the river.

As the Chicago boys were struggling to load and secure the second of their plastic barrels into their vans, Magellan was randomly counting currency from the first of two suitcases, signaling the deal was close to conclusion and that soon they were to depart.

Somehow Jaeger just couldn't see the Rasta's letting any of it go, they'd want the entire thing, which meant they'd soon make their initial move, then wait for the Crips to bring the entire gift to them on a silver platter.

As his night scope swung back to the main Rasta leader, he saw him speaking once again into his hand held radio, then his vision swung over again across the clearing to the albino who appeared to just be listening. A little early to start their attack he thought. At least wait until the Chicago boys had loaded their vans. Jaeger then slowly rose up and looked over his shoulder and saw multiple sets of headlights moving down the bumpy gravel path towards the clearing. It was either the cops, or the Crips chose to arrive early. As he tried to peer over the top of the hill, he ruled out the law, for they would've come with a whole host of vehicles and choppers overhead.

No, it had to be the Crips come early for whatever reason. As Jaeger carefully turned around and sat back down, he clipped the mini console to the collar of his shirt and picked up his silenced .32 caliber carbine, for the show was about to begin.

As the last of the three dark panel vans slowly motored down the gravel pathway, the remaining Rasta followed the intermittent glow of their tail lights as he walked behind them at a distance, his Mac-10 ready to speak. He was thinking about the wisdom of the Hoo Doo Chile, sucking the non- believers into his web of deceit. He'd be fortunate enough to not have to endure the brunt of the shootout, just pick off any stragglers that might try and escape. Tonight the Baron would see to it that no one escaped. 'Tonight we'd have it all', he thought.

As Paulo Sabastiani and Magellan concluded their deal, both were wary, yet smiling at each other as the others still labored to hoist the last of the barrels of Crystalline up into the last of their vans. The unexpected noise of approaching vehicles, rounding the corner and into the clearing, caused everyone to stop what they were doing, as Sabastiani reached for his weapon the same time as Magellan saying, "What the fuck is this"?

"I don't know. No one is to arrive for at least the next two hours.

Assemble your men and we'll see who it is", said Magellan. Sabastiani signaled for his men to fan out into the brush.

"I don't like this one little bit Magellan", said Sabastiani disgustedly! "Our deal was with Ortega and he's not here"!

"You know the big man is never present when a deal goes down", said Magellan!

"This time he assured us he'd be in there with us, so where is he"?

"I don't know", said Magellan weakly as the first Van appeared around the bend and entered the clearing, followed by two more as they quickly found a place around the forty yard wide clearing, headlights pointing everywhere, the last of the Crips vans stopping just short of the entrance, enough to block any of the other vehicles in making a quick departure. The Zulu Man quickly jumped out of the lead panel van, quickly followed by four others in each of his vehicles and we're met by the drawn weapons of Magellan and Sabastiani's people.

"Why the guns and who are these crackers", bellowed the Zulu Man angrily, followed by, "And where is my sistah"? "These are the Sabastiani group and they're on time. It is you that are early", answered Magellan. "You didn't follow instructions. You weren't expected at this particular time and as far as your sister is concerned, she's in good health and is right behind you"! Turning around and seeing his precious Scylla, secured the way she was, her brother turned around towards Magellan yelling, "Turn her loose mutha fucka and right now, or else we'll"! Stopping him in mid-sentence, Magellan yelled back, "Or else what, asshole. Look around, you have guns on you as we speak. As for your sister is concerned, the terms of the agreement were to turn her loose after and only after our deal was satisfactorily concluded mutually and not one second more. She's only here because of your underhanded invitation of the Posse', so have your men gather over by the fire place right now, or else I'll put one right between your Eyes right now"! As Magellan and the Zulu Man were arguing, the Rasta lookout came up behind the van blocking the entrance, sneaking up on the driver.

Jaeger decided to eliminate those at the base of the tree, leaned over and placed a single round, in the nearest of the Rasta's, a head shot traveling straight down into his cranium. As he crumbled into the brush, his nearby companion hearing nothing leaned over to see what was the matter with his partner, then hearing nothing, felt a brief downward pressure in the back of his skull, before everything went dark. Not twenty feet in front of the Panamanian was the van blocking the clearings exit, as he saw, this nappy headed Rasta, quickly come up behind the van and open the driver's side door and pump two quick rounds into the driver from his silenced Mac-10 The only thing that went through the Panamanian's mind when he saw that was two words, 'Oh shit', as he glance briefly at Magellan who apparently was involved in an argument with this negrito he'd never seen before. As all eyes turned at the muffled gunfire, they saw the Rasta, yanking the dead driver out from the van and trying to enter the driver's side. He never made it for the Panamanian pumped multiple blasts from his shotgun into the back and head of the Rasta, forcing him to bounce off of the steering wheel and back to the ground with the other.

At that point, the Hoo Doo Chile jumped up from his concealment and opened fire, quickly followed by the others concealed all around the perimeter.

Jaeger immediately reached for his mini console and one by one set off the six Claymores, previously positioned around the clearings cupola, hoping that they would even up the odds somewhat, putting the mini console in his shirt pocket. Then climbing around behind the tree with bullets flying everywhere, he looked through his night scope and fired off round after round at every Rasta he could find in the brush. A difficult task as each round had to be a head shot at people were on the move. Not counting the two he'd eliminated straight away, he reckoned, he'd brought down another six more out of the rest of the rounds in his clip.

One of the Crips made a mad dash for the van blocking the entranceway, running straight into a hail of bullets from the Panamanian in front of him and several from one of the Rasta's who were descending upon the clearing. Several of the bullets flying everywhere found there mark in the Panamanian's shooting shoulder and his thigh sending him crumbling back into the brush.

Sebastiani was one of the first to fall, in a hail of bullets that descended upon both him and Magellan, with Magellan catching a round piercing his side, as he dove for the undercarriage of his vehicle, reloading as he rolled. No time to feel the pain right now, just catch a target and fire without thinking. Two of the Rasta's made it down to the van blocking the entrance way and tried to start the van. Somehow it started and as the driver motioned to the other to climb on in, he slammed the vehicle in reverse.

Seeing this as he reached the ground, Jaeger reached into his shirt pocket and punched one of the two remaining glowing buttons on his console, exploding one of the remaining pairs of Claymore mines, sending hundreds of metal shards into the vehicle. As it still appeared to be moving backward, he pressed the last button as the final pair of Claymore's exploded, flipping the van over on its side and off the gravel pathway.

Now on the ground carrying only his Street Sweeper shotgun and his Ruger pistol, Jaeger ran towards the sounds of gunfire coming from the clearing. One by one he came upon a Rastafarian, shooting as he went everything seemed like it was in slow motion, with bullets flying everywhere. No time to differentiate friend or not, anything that appeared before you, shoot and move on. He didn't know what effect the Claymores had over on the other side of the clearing, but on the left side where he was, it appeared it had minimal effect, whereas he emptied his shotgun on everything that came in front of him, clubbing several others to death and dropping his shotgun and shooting the ones he clubbed each in turn, with his Ruger.

Seeing and hearing the gunfire coming from the clearing he saw the Hoo Doo Chile, running to join an dread locked Albino as they ran toward the largest of the cargo vans, and ripped off several rounds in their direction, one of which was a Teflon penetrator, catching the Albino, spinning him around as he fired wildly into the sky. Reaching the clearing, Jaeger caught sight of Scylla briefly, her eyes wide with terror, as she saw her brother struggling to reach a weapon on the ground just feet away from the Hoo Doo Chile, who quickly pumped two rounds into him without a single word.

As he ground to a halt, the Rastafarian leader brought his Mac-10 to bear on Jaeger and pumped two rounds his way, each striking him in the chest full on knocking him back, before his Mac jammed.

Feeling the pain of the rounds as they hit his Kevlar vest, Jaeger struggled to keep his feet, as he brought his Ruger to bear on the Rasta, quickly pulling the trigger at close range. Hearing the loud "Click" that came forth, Jaeger quickly brought the empty cylinder out extracting the empty shells as the massive Rasta bull rushed him. In a wink the new rounds from the speed loader hit the empty cylinder as it slammed shut. As the weapon came to bear, Jaeger pulled the trigger twice, the vaunted 'Double Tap', both rounds hitting the dirt as the massive 'Chile' barreled into Jaeger with a force he'd not felt since Dexter Mankiller long ago. As he fell backwards he ripped the hands that tried to envelop him away and rolled to his feet, his weapon knocked from his grasp somewhere out of sight, moving in a clock wise fashion as his antagonist rolled to his feet, shedding his leather coat as a flick knife made an appearance in his hand. "Jus you an me chile an its time you met the Baron. Tonight we gonna make anodder sacrifice to da Lord of de under world an you be it"!

As they continued to circle, the 'Chile' made several exploratory charges to gauge Jaegers reaction time. By the fifth charge, his blade found a home leaving a nice gash through the Kevlar camo undershirt Jaeger wore. "Aye children, my boy in fronta me, he be slowin down", whispered the 'Chile' as the blood on his blade made him smile.

While Jaeger and the 'Chile', circled each other in the 'Man Dance', the Haitian Albino struggled to gain his feet, his life's essences flowing red from under his leather coat. Seeing his master circling around this other stranger he'd not seen before, he looked around for his weapon, any weapon, picking up several and finding them empty, his hand finally found one, with a few rounds left. Never seeing the form that closed in on him from the side, he struggled to aim the Mac-10 at the two circling each other as Nestor Magellan lunged at him with his last vestiges of strength, plunging his knife, deep into the Albino's neck, falling upon him as his finger pulled the trigger firing off a wildly inaccurate three rounds as the bolt locked open.

As the knife twisted in his neck with such an unrelenting force, he felt his extremities go numb and immobile immediately as he tried to look into the eyes of the one who lay whispering into his ear, "Not tonight Kaffir", then all went black as his eyes saw no more.

Still lying on top of the Albino, Magellan saw Jaeger as his only hope, as he eluded another charge stopping the massive Hoo Doo Chile with an elbow straight into his nose, and then twisting around him and with a mighty last ditch grasp of his head, twisting the head around and snapping his neck with an audible crack, as they both crumpled to the ground.

Magellan looked around wearily; he could only see three forms that survived the carnage. Himself, Jaeger and Scylla still bound to the tree root, her eyes staring at the prostrate body of her brother. He still clasped the knife that lay deep in the Albino's head, as his eyes met Jaegers.

"Looks like he's dead to me Nestor", said Jaeger as he rolled off his dead antagonist, wearily rising to his feet. He looked around and caught sight of his Ruger, picking it up and checking the load, then walking over to Magellan saying, "He's dead Nestor. Take back your knife. Seems you caught a few rounds in the dust up. Let me check you"!

Magellan took back his knife and folded it up, putting it back in his pocket as Jaeger went over his body saying, "You got three rounds in you with only one exit wound", as he rose to his feet and went to the Albino, picking up his weapon, checking the load then handing it to him saying, "You got a full load, stay put and I'll be back with some first aid, in a few", then disappeared into the brush.

Magellan gathered his energy, looking over at Scylla, the only one who emerged unscathed. As their eyes met she said, "They ain't dead yet, not completely", nodding towards the Albino and Hoo Doo Chile!

"What do you mean? Their hearts are not beating and their eyes see nothing. Soon their bodies with be stiff with the rigor, like the rest"!

"No, you don't understand. Their only resting and they're not like the rest. If you understood Santeria, then you would know what to do"!

"Then explain it Scylla"!

"Both the 'Chile' and the 'Albino' are Santeria priests. They believe in the living dead, what the rest of us call Voo Doo. They hold ceremonies, not unlike priests, but they pray to African gods. The rest are all soldiers. Instruments to do their bidding. To make sure they don't resurrect again, you must cut off their heads and completely separate it from their bodies. Without the heads, they will wander in the afterlife, thoughtless and blind. This must be done or else none of us will ever know peace ever again"!

"Sounds a bit overdone, nothing more than superstitious mumbo jumbo"!

"Do with me what you must, but let me to do this thing, if none of you has the cojones to get this done"!

"Scylla", said Magellan, "Look around you. If think any talk about us having no balls", he let his voice trail off. "We'll discuss it with Jaeger when he returns", as he tried to rise, then sank back to the ground thinking better of it. Fifteen minutes later Jaeger returned driving an old Ford Bronco. As he approached Magellan he said, "Where's the key's to Scylla's cuffs"? "You're not thinking of cutting her loose are you"?

"That's exactly what I'm thinking Nestor", said Jaeger as he stripped off Magellan's bloody shirt, treating his wounds. "Someone has to get you back to Houston, to the queer nurses. No medical facility here as far as I can see and I don't think you'd want any attention to be drawn to any of us. We have the bucks that the Crips brought as well as the money that Sabastiani and his people brought. I think if we ask Scylla real nice, that she might be willing to help out. You're in no condition to be doing any driving anywhere. It's either Scylla helps the cause or I stop right now"!

"Seems we're both in each other's debt. The keys to her cuffs are in the van on the dash board. Jaeger finished up binding tight the most important of the wounds, stopping the seepage of blood and went to the van, then unlocked Scylla's cuffs saying, "You're gonna be a good girl or else I'll do ya myself, aren't ya"! Taking her nod in the affirmative he went back to Magellan. As he worked, Magellan said, "She wants to cut off the heads of both the Albino and Hoo Doo Chile. Something to do with Voodoo superstition"!

"If that's what she wants to do, we ought to agree, don't ya think", said Jaeger looking at her! "Then its settled Scylla. But what are you going to use", asked Magellan? There's the Chile's own knife sitting over there in the dust"!

Jaeger nodded his head as Scylla rose up retrieving the blade, the set to work severing the Chile's and the Albino's heads one by one, lifting them up by their long locks and carrying them to the river, tossing them in, one by one. Upon her return, she than asked, "What else can I do"?

Jaeger gave Magellan a brief glance then said, "Go to my Bronco, you'll find a large flashlight. Then go all around the hillside and gather up all the weapons you find on the dead along with any identification and bring it back here. Leave those in the hills where they lay, those down here, we'll do the same then toss in the river. That'll include your brother. Do you have a problem with that"?

Scylla shook her head then, went to the Bronco. As Jaeger worked on Magellan's wounds, Magellan looked up the hillside, seeing flickers of light as Scylla made her way around the hillside.

"What's to be done with the Crystalline", asked Magellan?

"It all goes into the river, along with everyone else. In a bit when I'm done with you, I'll stoke that fire over there and we'll burn all of the ID from the bodies, Then Scylla and me, will drag the bodies to the river and see about their swimming lessons. Next, is the fun part dragging the Crystalline barrels to the river opening them up and emptying them into the river. Do you have a problem with that"?

"A great deal of time, money and effort went into bringing this into America and the rest of the world. I'm told the formula cannot be replicated, but seeing that I'm in your debt and it appears to be the right thing to do, I have to agree with you"!

"Good, I was hoping you'd say that. Plus I must admit that were it not for you doing in the Albino, I might not be here working on you right now"!

"Yes there is that now, isn't there"!

"But I'm never gonna know whether or not you did that out of the kindness of your heart, or out of a sense of survival. As it is, things with you are touch and go. If we can get you back to the nurses in time, in Houston you just might make it. You've lost a fair amount of blood. So no sudden moves OK"?

"The last thing we'll do is drive all the vehicles into the river"! "What about the money", asked Magellan?

"It's all coming with us, or shall I say me. I discovered that your friend Meyers has been seeding all of his buys with a mix of fifty, fifty good currency and bogus. So I'm sure you won't mind if a friend of mine examines each bill to sort out which is which. It'd be a shame if any of us was busted for passing bogus currency after all of this, wouldn't it"?

"A shame it would be", agreed Magellan!

"As for Scylla, she'll have to be provided for financially wouldn't you agree? Nothing like a woman scorned to keep one looking over his shoulder, especially with her reputation. She's going to be the one that drives you back to the nurses, as you both follow me, when we're through"! "There now", said Jaeger, "I'm finished. Now take these two pills.

They'll relax you and take away some of the pain while not putting you to sleep"!

For the next five hours, both Jaeger and Scylla worked themselves to and past the level of exhaustion, subsisting on a diet of caffeine pills and Gatorade. Finally with the last vehicle driven into the San Saba River, with the weapons and suitcases of money secured in Jaegers Bronco, he lifted Magellan up and placed him into the passenger's seat of the remaining van, saying to Scylla, "Drive carefully and follow me, your future depends upon it"!

It wasn't till they were well down the county road that something drew Jaegers attention to the farm house on the distant hill they passed to his left, perhaps it was a light in the window during the early morning hours as he glanced at his watch, which read 0400 hours. Always the after action guy wondering what he'd left undone, he racked his mind wondering what was left. While the area wasn't exactly pristine, with a number of the Rasta's lying dead in the deep brush on the hillside, there was no identification left on any one of them.

Everyone else was floating to greater or lesser degrees, in the river. No doubt a large fish kill would result and eventually with the number of bodies, in the river some of them would be discovered. Jugos was no longer an option anymore. As the vehicles made the turn onto the State route that would lead them south to the interstate, a light went off in his head.

The Rasta's had to have some way to get there. What happened to their vehicles? As the possibilities rolled around in his head, he quickly dismissed them, for there was nothing that tied any of them to the Posse'. Not a single thing. With any luck, the critters would eventually discover the bodies all around the hill and perhaps someday, a bunch of abandoned vehicles might be come upon by hunters or others. Thus a dangling detail that held no consequences for Jaeger.

An hour later as they pulled into a service station in Kerrville on the interstate miles northwest of San Antonio, for a fill up. Jaeger checked Magellan as he sat in the front seat asleep. Then he said to Scylla, "After we get Magellan to the nurses in Houston, we'll do a little shopping for you. I'll bet those clothes you're wearing are ripe. Then I'll park you at Ortega's Condo, while I get the money thing sorted out"!

"Won't Ortega mind"?

"No he won't mind. He's dead along with all of his crew save for a few street soldiers and they don't matter"!

"Dead? The ass hole is dead"?

"Yep, a couple of days ago", said Jaeger without emotion! "How'd that happen"?

"Why? Does it matter? All you need to know is that he exists no longer in any form"!

Entering the outskirts of San Antonio, Jaeger speed dialed the nurses in Houston, hoping that he'd find them available. "Well dearie I'm going on duty for a forty eight hour shift at eight this evening"!

"Got an emergency here. It's Magellan and he's hangin' in there, with three bullet holes and one exit wound. Got the wounds cleaned and plugged up, he's no longer leakin' blood, but I'm concerned about internal bleeding. He'd gonna need the both of you at your best and soon", whereupon Jaeger outlined the location of the wounds, whereupon the nurse said, "Magellan you say? Oh he's the one with the French accent. What time can you arrive"?

"I'm entering San Antonio now, figure about four hours from now at current speed limits"!

"That would make it around noonish dearie"? "Sounds about right", said Jaeger!

"Ok then, I've got some sick days accumulated, so it'll cost ya the standard twenty large up front in cash, and another ten on the back side when he's on the mend and out of danger"!

"Done. See ya around noon", said Jaeger hanging up as he glanced at his rearview mirror seeing Scylla, some five car lengths behind him.

At just before noon, Jaeger and Scylla pulled into the driveway at the old two story home in Houston's Heights section of town and around to the rear of the house. Fifteen minutes later Magellan was on the makeshift operating table, with a tube of plasma feeding into his veins as both nurses worked at a feverish pace, to save his life, even pressing Scylla into service to clean up and assist.

He counted out thirty thousand from one of the suitcases, placing it in full view of the women as they operated saying, "There's thirty large here. I'll be back in about three hours.

Backing out of their driveway, he dialed Rae on his mobile, explaining what he needed. See ya in about twenty minutes.

Pulling into the back of the building Rae owned which occupied his printing company, Jaeger muscled out the suitcases full of the drug buy money. In Rae's secure back room he said, "Another project for you Rae.

Need to know which of this money is good and which is bogus. But right now, I need about eighty large in good cash to save a life"!

"Jesus, you're a regular money machine lately, aren't ya. Grab a cuppa and give me a few minutes to square things out front and I'll be back"! Fifteen minutes later Rae returned and without further word set about opening one of the suitcases and one by one examined each hundred dollar bill under the black light. By four thirty he had two piles of money saying, "About eighty thousand in that group of bundles and about thirty thousand in the other. The eighty is the kosher money and the thirty is the bogus. It's very good bogus, but counterfeit none the less"!

"How long will it take to separate the entire bunch", asked Jaeger?

"Holy shit, at least a week or more, depending on my workload out front. I do have a legitimate printing business to run", complained Rae.

"Do what you can. I'll stick my head in tomorrow to see how you're doin"!

Twenty minutes later he went back to the nurses home and went right in the back door, just as they were concluding surgery saying, "How's he doing."?

Marge said, "He ought to be in the hospital, a fair amount of internal bleeding, but I think we've got it all accounted for. Got the two remaining slugs out of him, good thing they were standard issue, not hollow points or he might not have made it here. As it is, plasma will go only so far and he's gonna need some whole blood. Don't know his blood type but a friend at the hospital can tell me for a price, and then if his type is available I can probably get my hands on a few pints, for a price"!

"How much extra"!

"About an extra five ought to do it"! "Where's the money I left behind"?

"Over there on the end table", said Harriet!

"Time for a trade", said Jaeger as he scooped up the questionable money. "As we agreed, forty large on the front side, and another five for the incidentals, up front and twenty on the back side when we know he's gonna survive. Are we agreed"? Of course anything north of the agreed upon price was not going to get an argument, as Marge said; we've a spare bedroom on the first floor where we can put him"!

"You two gonna need Scylla for anything"?

"Nope, she's been a big help, but I think we can handle things from here. If we need ya, we'll call ya. But he's gonna have to be kept under wraps here for at least a week"!

"We'll check in with ya a couple of days from now", said Jaeger as he left with Scylla.

As Jaeger drove down Heights Boulevard, he said, "Whats first, food or clothes"?

"Food first, then clothes", came the answer! "Target or Wal Mart", for the duds?

"Neither. But since your buyin', he what got's the gold gets to pick"! "Just a few things to keep you outta the gutter, then in a few days we can get you something more stylish.

Jaeger returned to his digs just before midnight, took a shower and collapsed in his bed.

As he quickly drifted off to sleep, his mind ticked off the things he'd accomplished other than stay alive. Magellan at the nurses, Scylla with some new clothes and sleeping in Ortega's old bed. Tomorrow, he'd need to intro her to Rae for some new photo ID and help her shop for some better duds. Check in with the nurses, then call Buffy, for there was much to discuss.

He picked up Scylla the next morning at ten, dropping her off at Rae's, a half hour later. Fifteen minutes after that, he pulled into Marge and Harriet's house in the Heights. As he walked into the kitchen door, there they sat looking haggard and worn. "Coffee's just made have a cup", said Harriet!

"How's the patient", asked Jaeger?

"Had a bleeder, nothing major mind you, but something we missed on the initial operation. We got it buttoned up in time. Got a friend out of bed and had him verify a blood sample as to type and put two pints in him. He's all medicated and his vital signs have stabilized. So it seems he'll be out of the woods and on the mend. But he's got to stay put for at least a week here. But we've yet another problem. He'll need constant monitoring during the interim and Harriet just has to be at the Hospital at midnight to pull her shift and a half hour ago, I just got a call from the Chief Nurse to come in at Six PM, seems a shortage of staff is at the Hospital. Say what about that girl you brought in last night, what's her name"?

"Scylla, Marge. Her name is Scylla"!

"Seems she took directions quick enough. If you could get her here later in the afternoon to watch over the patient, for about a day. Then we could be back in time to keep him in the land of the living"! Jaeger picked up his mobil phone and dialed Rae and afterwards, hung up and said, "I can have her here by Four PM"! Then he ran back outside, got into his Ford and drove into town to visit with Buffy.

"Ms. Beauvior knows you're here and is wrapping up a deposition Mr. Jaeger, she'll be available shortly. Can I get you anything", asked the receptionist?

"No thanks, I'll take a seat over here", said Jaeger!

Ten minutes later the receptionist looked up from her desk saying, "Ms. Beauvior is now available. She says that you know the way to her office"! Jaeger nodded his head and arose from his leather chair and walked down the long hall and through the double doors.

"Well well", exclaimed Buffy looking up from her desk as Jaeger entered her office. '

"What's it been? Almost a year since we last laid eyes on each other. Oh yeah, I remember now, the Enron Christmas party, when you had the arm of, uh, what is her name? Oh yes, Melanie, O'Bannon. So how are the both of you two doing", she asked as she came around her desk and gave Jaeger a brief embrace, leading him over to the two corner chairs as they sat down.

"We're not. Seems she's taken a job elsewhere", said Jaeger masking a pained look on his face. "That's not why I'm here. I'm here to ask you a question and perhaps a favor or two"!

"Ask away sport"!

"Are you still my lawyer"? "When have I not been"?

"Good. Now another question. How busy are you"?

"Up to my eyeballs in defending the rich who always seem to need me when they screw up their personal lives. But tell me what you need and I'll point you in the right direction"!

"How would you like some National publicity and get right in the middle of what might be an international incident, between two of South America's largest nations and do some good in the process"?

"I take it you're not a chaser for Rafferty anymore and that you've gotten yourself elevated to Prime Time"!

"Been busy elsewhere"!

"That's obvious. OK pal, give it to me straight. Some details off the top"! Jaeger then spent the next twenty minutes giving Buffy an edited version of his time with Ortega and his visit to Sao Paulo Brazil. When he concluded, he watched Buffy as she rolled the events at hand around in her mind, eventually saying, "You have been a busy boy, hanging with serious people. So where are these two people, this Ortega and this Carlos Meyers"?

"Don't ask", said Jaeger emphatically! "I'm your lawyer. Remember"?

"They're not with us anymore"!

"Which means they're dead? By your hand"?

"In a manner of speaking"! Buffy still rolling the entire series of events around in her mind said, "OK sport I'm in at least part way. What do you have in mind"?

"You have contacts in the local media right"? "Sure do"!

"You contact the media and set up a meeting, between you and the local Brazilian Consulate, then you hand over the boxes of the entire Embraer Aircraft fleets plans and drawings, as well as the name of the director that was going to hand them over to elements of the Argentine Government and Industry. In that group of papers, will be a copy of a monetary transaction, between the Argentines and an Embraer Director that was going to jump ship. Now can that do you any good"?

"When can you get the documents to me for examination"?

"How about day after tomorrow. But is there a safe place for you to keep them"?

"A floor above us is a walk in safe, installed about seven months ago. That OK"? Jaeger nodded his head, then said, "And now to the other things. Ortega has this club across town, or should I say 'Had' the club. It currently has no owner since he bought out his partners a few months ago. Further, he had a house on the Clear Lake estuary with all the trimmings and a high rise Condo hide away in the Teal Stone complex on the west side of town. What can be done to transfer the ownership from him to another"? "There are ways to accomplish this, but nothing that I'd like to involve the firm in. However, there is someone in town that I know of who can accomplish this. His name is Anselm Barthez. A shady son of a bitch if there ever was one. It's a miracle he's still got his law license. I'll give you his number and you can mention my name discreetly, but you better show him the righteous path up front and get his attention. Oh, and pay him well. What next"!

"That little thing, we're working on up north. It's been stalled for a while, for the lack of cash, but now it can go full speed ahead"! "Came into some cash recently, did ya", asked Buffy?

"That's one way to put it"! "Anything else"?

"Yes. I had to sever things with Melanie O'Bannon suddenly and without any goodbyes. It's nagged on me ever since. I need to try and make things right. Last I heard, she's working in either Austin or DC for a lobbying group. Now I want to set up a College fund for her son Rory, something in the six figure range, plus I want to set up a financial fallback position for Mel herself. I'm thinking about a safe annuity or something in the two hundred thousand range. Now it cannot have my name on it in any fashion. Is this doable"?

"Of course it is. That woman really got to you didn't she"? Jaeger nodded his head, sheepishly. When Jaeger didn't take the bait she added, "Clearly your momma raised you right", said Buffy. "OK sport here's how it's gonna lay out. Whereas I'm up to my pits in court work, I'm going to call in Boyd Parmalee to handle your request for the O'Bannon's and the full steam ahead business up in Waco. He's retired now, but still has an office here, with all the trimmings, relishing his position as Boss Emeritus. He'll also be involved in the Embraer documents. One of those, for the good of the firm situations. You'll huddle with Barthez on the property transfer issues, but keep Boyd informed of everything you do unofficially, for this Barthez can be a snake, if not watched"!

Now I've got to be in court in about an hour, so call me tomorrow, so we can make the handoff in the parking garage. I'll have our security on hand"!

"Thanks Buffy", said Jaeger rising. "Call you in the morning"!

By Three PM, Jaeger was back at Rae's Printing Company in Montrose. As he walked into the rear door, he saw Rae and Scylla going over the small mountain of money as he examined each bill, handing the good and the bad to Scylla for sorting. "So how's Scylla's papers"?

"She's got a Texas Driver's License, a voter's registration card and we're working on a birth certificate that should roll around here in a few days. Used the Teal Stone Condo address"! "She's got a new last name she doesn't seem to mind"!

"Good. Now I got to borrow her for a day or so to become a nurse"! As they drove back to the nurse's house in the Heights Jaeger asked, "How'd you feel about going into show business"?

"Been there, done that, got the T-Shirt honey. What you got in mind?

31

The severed head of what formerly was the Hoo Doo Chile', was carried down the San Saba River by the current, eventually surfacing about a mile downstream the following day. Six hours after that, the head of the Haitian Albino followed suit, several hundred yards behind. Both would eventually come to a brief pause as the waterway made its way around the various twists and bends of the river, washing up on the river's edge. Occasionally an animal in search of an easy meal would cautiously approach, always scampering away as the eyes of the Chile' and his Albino acolyte would suddenly jerk open with sufficient impetus to roll each head back into the water continuing their journey. Each time the animal would stop and turn around, watching the easy meal float out of reach. One wonders what feral wisdom took hold as each critter in turn must have thought better of it and turned their attentions elsewhere.

Two days after the event, mother nature's wonders took hold as each of the dead, their bodies in the throes of decay, started one by one to surface, their internal gasses taking hold, bloating the bodies and floating each gently to the surface, as they followed the severed heads on their journey. Each and every one, separated only by chance, some face down, others face up, swirled and floated in the final water dance, into the dark unknown.

The following day, late in the afternoon, a small boy out fishing with his grandfather, tried in vain to awaken him from a deep slumber, while their fishing poles worked to tempt a supper out of the river. The small row boat was anchored in mid river. Grandpa had tippled a bit too much of his home made 'Sneaky Pete', floating nearby in the river secured to the gunwale, cooling in the water and was hard asleep.

As the two heads floated past the boat, the small boy saw them bobbing and butting in the rivers current, while the music of Louie Prima and his band played, "Just a Gigolo", over and over. As they floated away, the music began to recede in volume, until the heads were out of sight.

"Grandpa, Grandpa, wake up", the boy cried as he tried repeatedly to jostle the old man from his hard earned slumber. "Grandpa, please wake up", the boy now screamed, terrified by the floating heads and the music that seemed to arrive and depart with appearance of the floating heads. Finally coming awake, the old man sputtered and jerked his body saying, "Godammit boy, what in Sam Hill are ya doin', screwin' up my nap"?

The boy hurriedly sputtered out what he'd just seen and pointed in the direction the heads floated down stream. Just then a sheen appeared upon the water as one by one fish started to float to the surface. Up river one could make out several of the yellow plastic 50 gallon barrels that had caught up with the bodies, as well as a few bloated corpses staring skyward with their arms out as if balancing.

"Floating heads", questioned the grandfather? "Boy, you been sippin' from my jug"? He then turned his sights upstream watching the fish, one by one bobbing to the surface, as the boy shouted excitedly pointing upstream, "Then grandpa, tell me what's that", as one of the snake headed Rasta soldiers slowly approached the boat face down, his leather coat splayed out on the surface, preceded by his snake like locks swirling in the current.

"Snake men grandpa, snake men and there's another of them right over there"!

"Saddle up boy. The fishin' is screwed. Best we go ashore and call the High Sheriff to get his butt out heah an investigate", said the grandfather as he pulled his jug inside the boat and grabbed the oars, rowing towards the shore. As he rowed, he muttered under his breath, complaining about his hankering for river fish, while someone had to up and ruin his favorite fishing spot muttering, "Dang spookie's. Goin' an dyin' in my fishing spot. Pollutin' the river and killin' the fish"!

Sheriff Donny Vasquez, had an extreme case of the 'slow's' as he drove the Menard county patrol car out on the county road, heading east into the early morning sun. The radio traffic in this county where almost nothing went on to speak of was nonexistent as he listened to the radio station out of San Antonio, where the area weather report was blaring. Nothing but continuing sunshine and clear weather was forecasted for the week ahead. He'd spent the night with the new Chulita at the town's only watering hole, called Chuey's Cantina and she went a long way towards draining him dry in the process. The woman was relentless, a veritable machine where it came to satisfying his physical needs. 'Ay Bendito', he thought as he gingerly scratched his groin. 'This Chula's gonna be the death of me yet', he thought as he recalled the previous evening, ending in a draw as far as he could see. Somehow, he didn't mind the huge wet spot on the bed sheet that looked to be some two feet in diameter. That could always be attended to later.

The word was that she was one of the premier attractions at Papa Guayo's, in Nueva Laredo, until her then boyfriend gunned down one of her customers in a jealous rage. Spirited across the Rio Grande, she ended up at Chuey's to become his star attraction. Clearly she was wet and without papers and he was breaking the law by not turning her over to the Border Patrol, where he'd spent over a decade guarding the Texas border.

Of course, part of his charm was that he was the County Sheriff and who better to charm and protect her from all comers than Donny Vasquez. At almost six feet tall, she was slightly taller than Donny and with high heels on she was an Amazon. God only knows what sexual tricks, in lieu of money she had to employ in order to have the trafficker's scoot her over the river and into Chuey's employ, but when it came to milking the snake, this woman had it down. She had absolutely no scruples about running around naked and to tell the truth, a woman like that should never be permitted to wear clothes except in the winter. She spoke almost no English and he'd have to work on that if she was to stay around. He'd make it a point to have a serious sit down with Chuey the next few days and come to an arrangement of sorts. Heads he wins, tails Chuey loses. Because he knew what that Vato had going on.

As he took another sip of the putrid coffee machine brew, the County Judge approved installing last month as a cost cutting move, Donny tried to jolt himself further awake, as he'd received a 5AM call from the Judge, instructing him to look in on the Culligan family, the very first thing, since their kids hadn't shown up for school for the last few days, with the phone calls placed to their residence, indicated a line busy signal. Even more important, the Culligan wife missed the monthly Ladies Social Club inexplicably.

Even with his dark aviator sunglasses, the early morning glare from the sun was blinding as he squinted his heavily wrinkled eyes, searching for the entrance to the Culligan spread on the right hand side of the road.

'Ah, here tis', he thought, slowing his Patrol Car, turning onto the long gravel driveway that led up a long gradually sloping hill, to the Culligan house. Instinct told him straight away, things weren't right as he emerged from his car. Usually at this time of the morning, at a spread like this, the children were just finishing up the early morning chores and preparing for school, thus a beehive of activity. All that greeted Donny was silence. The patrol car was parked near the rear of the home. Folks in this part of the country Rarely used the front door, preferring the kitchen entrance as more convenient. He peered into the kitchen through the curtains, seeing that all of the lights were on. Odd, since frugal folks never had lights lit when Mother Nature provided all the light they needed during the day. He then went back to the patrol car, sounding the klaxon several times and the piercing double 'Whoop' of the siren, waiting a decent interval, for someone to appear. The only sounds in response, was that of several of the livestock in one of the corrals. He wondered whether or not they'd been fed as he went to the kitchen door, opening it as he yelled, "Hello house. Is anyone home? This is Sheriff Vasquez"? His service revolver now firmly in his hand, he went completely through the house, from room to room, finding all of the beds made as if no one slept there for some time and only silence.

As he went back into the kitchen, he found it almost pristine in its cleanliness. Scratching his head, he went back outside, noticing the barn door partially closed. During any given day at a farm or ranch, the barn door was always open. As he approached the barn, gun in hand, he saw several of the cows and a few of the horses, following him with their eyes. Reaching to pull open one of the two barn doors fully open, his nose began to tingle and as the door opened wide, the stench of the dead inside told him why.

An overseas tour with the Army as a military policeman, added much to his education as well as over ten years as a border patrol officer chasing drug smugglers and illegal entrants, but nothing he'd ever encountered could've prepared him for the sight of the Culligan family, father, mother, oldest son and both of his younger sisters, hands tied behind them hanging upside down, by a rope tied to their ankles, secured to one of the barns cross support beams. The smell of the decomposing corpses, coupled with the sight of them, compelled an uncontrollable retching response, as his machine brewed coffee made a hasty exit. Recovering, he opened the other barn door and stepped back, in shock. Then he turned and went to the patrol car. Now out breathing clean air for the moment, he took a series of deep breaths, to compose himself congratulating himself by avoiding breakfast. He keyed the county radio and talked to the dispatcher, who doubled as the Court House operator, directing her to immediately summon the County Judge and two additional patrol units, having all of them to come to the Culligan place, out on the County road, immediately if not sooner. Then he told her to contact old Doctor Hatch, the County Coroner and have him drop whatever he was doing, and make immediate tracks to the Culligan ranch and to bring five body bags.

Finally he directed her to contact the nearest Texas Department of Public Safety office for additional assistance as soon as possible. "What's goin' on out there Sheriff", asked the dispatcher? "Culligan Ranch? Additional units to the scene? The County Judge? The Coroner and five body bags? Thelma Liz, you do the math. Now keep a lid on this till you hear otherwise from The Judge, ya hear? Call me back when you're done to confirm arrival of everybody"! Inside of the home was pristine, yet as he walked slowly around the area, the house, the barn, and the corrals while awaiting everyone's arrival. Clearly from the tire tracks he determined that a number of vehicles had visited and parked in the rear of the house and by the apparent pathways worn into the tall grass that badly needed mowing on both sides of the house, he concluded that two people were posted as lookouts, from the detria left behind. Finally he saw the cigarette butts, at every location. Clearly not American brands, were the imprints of "Players and Dun Hill", brands. Clearly European, more specifically British.

Donny went back to his patrol unit and drove it further up the driveway, blocking rear access to the home. Then he took the yellow police tape out imprinted with "Crime Scene, Do Not Enter blocking off the rear access and the homes front door. As he sat in his car he removed a set of clear plastic gloves and a number of clear plastic baggies, he'd be needing to collect evidence. No doubt with the County Judge and eventually the County Attorney in attendance, things better be done by the book. One by one he received acknowledgement from two of the patrol units, they were on the way, he prevailed on one of them to stop and pick him up two packs of Camels on the way, that he pay him back upon arrival.

Several minutes later he heard back from the dispatcher, who informed him that the County Judge and Attorney were on the way as well as the Coroner and that two DPS investigators were an hour away. It was certainly going to be one of those two pack days, for Donny Vasquez.

While he was waiting for the Cavalcade of officials to arrive, he reached back into his bag and removed several gauze masks and a jar of mentholated jelly he'd need for his next trip back into the barn. Then his mind started to wander, once again reviewing his life so far. Chiefly this penchant of his for whores. During his first year with the Border Patrol, he took up with an exotic dancer he'd met in Juarez Mexico, across the Rio Grande from El Paso. One could make an effective argument that Donny rescued her from a life of endless prostitution in Northern Mexico, where she was certain to come to a bad end and one would be right as far as that went, yet she was lovely and had all of the household skills necessary to tend to his house, not to mention her skills in the bedroom that were considerable. He never formally married the woman, just simply slid into one of those common law arrangements that seemed to be all the rage these days. Besides, how was her going to explain the she was illegal? Through some contacts, he got her a Texas Drivers photo ID license and for a few years all was pretty good. She posed as his wife and on some of his off days they'd cross the border to shop where things were cheaper. 'Boy could that girl haggle a price right down to the ground', he recalled The only work she did was around the house, never holding a regular job. The house and his clothes were clean; the food she cooked was good and most important she kept his snake well satisfied. Yet his job with the Border Patrol kept him away sometimes for several days on end and absence not always make's the heart grow fonder. One could always make a case of that inexplicable genetic wild seed, that never goes away and have a hoard of adherents in agreement. Yet after several years of what appeared to be connubial bliss, she began a series of careful involvements with a coterie of men who always tipped with generosity, during his absences. She was careful to select married men of substantial means, with much to lose should the discovery of their unfaithfulness ever come to light. Her apparent reasoning was that while Donny took his risks in life, so must she, adding a little spice to an otherwise mundane existence. While part of her wanted children, the other part had scant patience for the responsibilities parenthood required.

All might have gone on well for some time longer, if Donny hadn't had to go, to a doctor for a very personal male problem. After the exam and the attendant blood workup at the clinic across the border, the doctor announced that he suffered from a Gonorrheal infection and gave him the appropriate initial shots, directing him to return every day for the next ten days, until the regimen was completed, then another urinalysis and blood Sample taken to determine if all was successful. As he drove back across the river, the blood rushed into his head, with his repetition of the word, "Puta" whispered over and over. He'd had no relations of any kind with another woman ever since she entered his home several years ago. Upon his return, she'd left a note saying that she'd be gone for several days to Monterrey to see her family. The following day he was called into the field office, to assist in transporting a number of criminal illegal's to San Antonio, to the Federal Attorneys office. Two days later upon his return, he walked into his house to find it bare. Everything gone, only the marks of the dust on the floor remained. The following day after he returned from the clinic, he visited the bank in which she had access to his checking account. It also was bare, with the remaining six hundred dollars cleared out of his account. The only blessing being that the following day was payday and that he'd no credit cards, or he'd really be it the shit.

Where she'd gotten to, he didn't care. It was good that he'd had the button to punch in his head, or else he'd have killed her on sight. A lesson learned, or was it? A year later he gotten transferred to the Tucson district, pouring himself into his work, running up the best apprehension records every month, month in and month out, impressing his supervisors. So what does he do one lonely evening? Visit one of the local Titty bars and take up with yet another, version of his previous experience. Big tits and a flashing smile will do in a lonely man almost every time. Of course, she continued in her career of sorts, while sharing his bed every evening. She couldn't cook and wouldn't clean up the place, but boy could she ever drain the snake of its bodily fluids. Yet after a year, things began to wane as is usually the case, when one evening she didn't return home. The following morning he went down to the local police department to file a missing persons report only to discover that she'd been murdered by a patron of the club where she worked. Seems the refusal of a personal service in the shadows of the recesses of the club was sufficient to incite the wrath of a drunken biker who laid in wait as she exited the club. The biker had pumped two round in her from short range, with a sawed off shotgun and as the club security emerged from the sounds of the gunshots, the biker had reloaded and had gotten off yet another shot hitting the armed bouncer, who in turn emptied a half a clip in the biker who was slain on the spot. It was all caught on video tape, a righteous shoot by club security on club property and the assailant dead. As far as the authorities were concerned, case closed. The following day, he rounded up all of her belongings, giving them to charity.

Transferred back to the El Paso district, he was placed in the hands of a politically, well entrenched supervisor, who gave short shrift to all of his previous accomplishments, sounding a death knell on any possibility of career advancement. Months later an incident along the border, involving the shooting deaths of several drug smugglers, along with the serious wounding of one of their own, prompted Donny and several others to seriously consider self-termination from the Agency. The question of simply who shot first in the dark of night placed the hospitalized agent in a precariously poor legal situation which all involved who knew the wounded agent agreed, amounted to the Federal Government dropping the agent into the hot grease, based solely upon political opportunism.

Then, while wondering what to do, he found out about the death by natural causes, of the Sheriff of Menard County. They needed someone to serve out the remaining three years of his term of office. Making the appropriate inquiries, Vasquez got an interview with the County Judge. Later on in the day, he was rubber stamped by the County Attorney and they all fell in with each other. Sure it was a one horse county in the middle of nowhere, but at least there, criminal activity was pretty much nonexistent. No one shooting at him, with little to do except arrest the occasional drunk and most importantly, suck up to the County Judge and Attorney. Keep them happy and one could have a steady and non-eventful job far into ones retirement. They didn't want any waves made in their county and neither did Donny. The worst things that usually happened were that some young rowdies got drunk on some bootlegged Tequila every once in a while, tying together the udders of a dozen or more cows as a prank. As Sheriff he was in charge of a dozen good old boy officers, driving a half dozen patrol vehicles, in three shifts. Not counting holidays, illness's, or vacations. Unlike his much older predecessor who had one foot in the grave, while the other was on a banana peel for a lot of years, driving a desk during the day, Donny was a working Sheriff, out in the field much of the time, giving direction where needed, but other than that leaving his men to do what they always had done. They didn't want waves and neither did Donny.

Now this. The death of an entire family. This was a wave. Then at his residence was the tall Chulita whore. Yet another wave potentially. He'd tend to that later. Right now he had all he could say grace over.

Upon the arrival of the two other officers, he directed them to complete the outlining of the crime scene, and showed them where all of the foreign cigarette butts and detria was, and to secure the area, for the arrival of the DPS criminal investigators.

Fifteen minutes later the County Judge, with the County Attorney, arrived in his black Lincoln with two other patrol vehicles in tow. After the initial greetings, Donny directed one of the others to set up shop at the foot of the driveway and to allow only the DPS investigators and the County Coroner into the crime scene. Then he turned to the Judge and the County Attorney and issued them both face masks and instructed them to lather the mentholated petrol jelly inside their nostrils. "Hope none of you gentlemen had a big breakfast. I haven't eaten yet today, and the early morning coffee I had on the way over just jumped right out. So if ya have any accidents just don't feel too bad"!

"They been in there a few days at least is my guess. The Rigor has advanced to a degree, to where the bodies are well bloated and the flies are starting to lay their eggs. Roger, go back to your patrol car and get your Polaroid and bring mine while you're at it", he said to the other deputy!

"They're all dead", asked the Attorney?

"When we enter, you will see the entire family, bound and hanging feet first by the support beams. My brief examination before I had to bail was that there was a pool of congealed blood under each and every one of them, meaning they all bled out. No other apparent marks, but I was just there for a few moments. The Coroner will the one capable of determining the approximate time and cause of death, but I'm certain that you'll agree when we enter that the family has been dead for a number of days"!

"Speaking of the good Doctor Hatch, where in the hell is that man? I swear that man would be late to his own funeral", said the County Attorney as the Deputy ran up with the pair of Polaroid cameras.

As the barn doors opened wide, everyone could see the bodies of the Culligan's hanging head down inverted as everyone went into the barn to do their sworn duty. The masks and the menthol jelly did their job, but only for a few minutes. Coupled with the visual impressions of a family done a horrible wrong, plus the intense stench of the decaying corpses, only one who was used to the events at hand by virtue of his daily enterprise could endure the situation for more than five minutes or so. When the Judge and the County Attorney began to back up in horror towards the barns entrance, Donny was busy taking Polaroid shots of the scene, handing each in turn to the deputy, who gave him the second camera to continue with when the primary ran out of film. When they had finished, the Deputy quickly turned and made for the barns entrance, following the Judge and the County Attorney as all three never made it outside, regurgitating in their masks as they tumbled out of the barn, ripping off their soiled masks and dropped to their knees, in painful supplication.

A minute later, Doctor Hatch arrived, walking into view and came upon the retching trio, just as Donny Vasquez emerged from the barn, bending down and retrieving the pictures and other camera from the bent over deputy. The Coroner looked at the sorry trio then into the barn catching the acrid scent of decay even from the distance of forty yards away.

As Vasquez, returned from his patrol car, he joined the Doctor who was preparing to enter the barn, his nose duly swabbed and gauze mask firmly in place, as he looked down at the trio still retching up the remains of breakfast saying, "I'm gonna need some help inside are ya up to it"?

"Nothing in my stomach anymore Doc. This'll be my third trip inside. Ready when you are"! Twenty minutes later he and Vasquez emerged back outside, joining the others on the back porch, some distance away from the barn entrance. As Vasquez took aside the now mostly recovered Deputy, he directed him to join the two others collecting evidence, then joined the others as Doctor Hatch said, "My preliminary exam indicates that each of the subjects had their veins opened from the left ear downward, slowly bleeding to death. Their blood laying congealed below each body. Clearly this is a murder scene, since they couldn't have done this themselves. As to who committed the crime, that's for others to discover. As to why, I can't say"!

Just then, the DPS investigators arrived as introductions were traded, as two more Deputies arrived to assist.

"Before we enter the barn, we need to tell you that we've been getting reports of dead bodies floating down the San Saba River for the last day or so. We've got several boats in the river as of this morning and your report of a slain family here in your county somehow fits right in with the other reports. The San Saba is littered with dead fish all the way down' past where it intersects with the Brady and dead bodies are being discovered in the water as far down as Harkeyville. So somehow this all might tie right in with the other dead bodies. Let's go inside and see what we can see."!

The Judge still worse for wear, was not accustomed to allowing outsiders to come in and run things in his county, but clearly after hearing all of what the DPS investigators had to say, concluded this was beyond him and yet having to exert some semblance of local authority, reluctantly joined them back into the barn. When they emerged from the barn all went back to the porch as one of the DPS investigators said, "Doc, do you mind if we call in some help? I can have some forensic people here in about an hour or so by chopper, to assist you in the autopsy"!

Hatch glanced at the Judge who nodded his head in agreement and said, "Please make the call"! The County Attorney, now mostly recovered joined into the discussion, staying quiet and listening. Vasquez then inserted himself by displaying on the wooden picnic table, the bagged up evidence that was collected.

Discarded soda cans and plastic glasses and as they all walked around the crime scene, he showed them of several places where the grass had been worn down by others, clearly as lookout points for intruders. But the final bit of evidence he displayed was the cigarette butts. "Folks, I smoke Camels, others smoke Marlboros, while still others smoke Pall Mall's, but as we all can see, the discarded butts, fall into two brands not commonly found in the US. Players and Dunhill cigarettes"!

"British cigarettes", said one of the DPS investigators. "Sold in Canada and in the Caribbean, mostly in Jamaica. The Posse'," he exclaimed. The Posse' that explains it. Some of the bodies recovered from the San Saba downstream were dread locked Rastafarian gangsters. Just maybe the Culligan ranch had the misfortune to be a staging area for a drug buy. A drug buy that clearly went wrong for them. But the logistics are all wrong. How did the bodies get from the ranch to the river"? The Agent turned to the Judge asking, "About how far away are we from the river"?

"As the crow flies, about a mile more or less"!

"Then that's it. This was simply a stopover for the night for the Posse'. The deal went down somewhere else and somewhere nearby I'll wager! Judge do ya mind if I call in the Rangers to help us"?

"Hell son looks like y'all are runnin' things, so have at it as long as it doesn't cost the County any money"!

As the DPS men pulled out their mobil phones and started making calls, Vasquez, looked at the Judge saying, "Its eleven in the morning, and we're gonna have a lot of hungry people helping us out, the rest of the day and far into the night it seems"!

"You looking' to toss some feed business Chuey's way", said the Judge wryly?

"Who else around her can set up and feed quicker than he can"? "OK, call him up and tell him to get his Mexican ass out here by One and be ready to feed about fifty people and he better not overcharge the County. Just maybe I can get the State to pick up most, if not all the cost"!

Shortly after noon, two trucks laden with food and supplies were allowed through the cordon surrounding the area, as Chuey and several of his people quickly started to set up the feeding station for the growing Ad Hoc task force that was assembling. Shortly thereafter two helicopters landed in the field next to the corral one of which had the logo of the Texas DPS and the other with that of the Texas Rangers investigative units. As they landed, one of Donny's deputies tugged at the Judges sleeve saying, "Beggin' your pardon Judge. I know we got a lot on our plate, but what about the cows"?

"The cows? Dead people all around and you're talkin' about god damned cattle"!

"No sir, just the cows. We all been busy doin' other important things, but the family's been dead these many days and no one has milked the cows and there's a smooth dozen or more that're so full of milk the udders are dragging the ground. They don't get milked PDQ and it'll hurt em. Why I bet their hurtin' right now"!

"So what do you suggest son"?

"I can probably get a few dozen FFA folks over here within the hour to see to it that they're milked proper, and that it's taken away and distributed amongst the poor, in your name Judge"!

"Then make it so young man, but you're in charge of them. They get out of hand and it's Your ass. Get em here and get it done then get em out and stay out of everyone's way, ya heah"?

An hour later with arrivals of the Forensic people from the State, students milking cows, additional helicopters landing in the adjacent field giving the livestock fits, another helicopter made to land, with the logo indicating "TXCN, superimposed on the background of Texas Cable News". As the engines shut down, several cameramen emerged as well as a well-dressed and coiffed female reporter, with well chiseled classic features who quickly introduced herself to Sheriff Vasquez, as his Boss's niece here at his invitation.

She had everything going for her and she knew it. Drop dead gorgeous, long blonde hair, immaculately attired, in a dark blue pinstriped feminine business suit, that revealed a pair of the sexiest looking dancer's legs he'd ever seen. Her voice was strictly from back east, crisp, low pitched, with a hint of huskiness that belayed too many cigarettes and hard whiskey over time, yet highly articulate with just a taste of an affected Texican twang.

"Well of course he knows I'm coming Sheriff. I'm told he's somewhere around here. Would you be a dear and go get him for me"?

"No, but I'll have one of my people do it", as he looked around and directed one of his Deputies to get the Judge. "But until your story checks out you and your crew will be kind enough to not wander off, or else I'll have to shoot you"!

"Why thank you Sheriff", she replied coolly and with that turned and directed her camera crew to start setting up the location shot. As he gave her his undivided attention he marveled at her, attired thusly as if at the studio, yet shod in an old worn pair of cowboy boots. No doubt she had some high heels stashed somewhere close at hand. Minutes later the Judge made an appearance coming around the corner of the corral as he passed his Sheriff giving him a sly wink catching the eye of his niece who quickly turned away from her producer, confronting her uncle with a well-rehearsed dazzling smile, she clearly used to great advantage as they embraced. They huddled a bit just out of Donny's earshot as he slowly approached. She suddenly said, "Oh I can't darling. My day a far into the night is ahead of me thanks to this scoop I've you to thank. But be a dear and give a girl a rain check on that dinner engagement won't you", she gushed.

"But of course", said the Judge. "How can anyone say no to you", as he gave her the twin cheek faux kiss all the beautiful people in the media gave each other. Then the Judge turned saying to Donny, "Since the rest of us are now but an afterthought and the State boys have taken over, I'd like you to personally escort my niece around, giving her the low down on what has happened for her story"!

Then the Judge turned to his niece saying, "Honey, I want to introduce you to Donny Vasquez, the High Sheriff of Menard County Texas. He's a good man and I'm sure you're gonna give him some good air time, won't you"!

Just then rather than gaze into her inviting eyes, something caught Donny's attention as he looked up. All this while everyone was focused on the ground work and no one had bothered to look up, as he caught sight of a dozen vultures circling the barn overhead. 'Of course', he thought. 'Mother Nature's bounty hunters'. Look for the buzzards overhead and you'll find their next meal beneath them.

Following his eyes, the Judges niece caught sight of the vultures, quickly motioning to her cameraman and producer to get that shot for the story. Circling above the vultures were several Eagles, hoping in vain that everyone below would just go away.

As they all looked skyward with the camera rolling Vasquez simply announced, "Company"! "Oh my god, that's a priceless shot", she exclaimed as the video cameras rolled. When the shot had concluded, she then turned to Vasquez and said, now we need to get an interior shot of the barn where the family, it's the Culligan family isn't it, were murdered. Have the bodies been taken down"!

"Yes they have", said Vasquez obediently.

"Well I suppose we could still get a close up interior shot of the murder site"!

"I'd recommend a distance shot, for it'll be days, if not weeks until the barn has had time to air out properly"!

"Just won't do Sheriff. We need an interior shot while the daylight is with us"!

"You've clearly never been within sniff range of a dead critter after they've head time to ripen up a bit have you"!

"There's a first time for everything Sheriff. Now if you'd be a dear please lead the way"!

As they walked up the pasture and around the corral, Vasquez noted a north breeze taking the stench of the barns interior away from the barns entrance as he said, "I've some gauze masks I can give you and your camera crew prior to entering the barn. Best you prepare, prior to entering"! "Nonsense Sheriff we'll be fine", said the Judges niece willfully as they approached the entrance, the north wind still at their backs. He took out his gauze mask from his hip pocket and put it on as she stood before the barn with the video cameras rolling preparing for her intro. She'd now changed her foot ware from the cowboy boots to the stylish high heel pumps normally worn in the studio. The wind at her back she and her crew entered the barn as she continued with her running commentary, cameras rolling. Gradually the direction of the wind changed, as the full force of the stench of accumulated death, began to make itself known. Troopers as they were, carrying on as if nothing was wrong, the camera man was the first to waver as the camera wobbled a bit, then at last the Judges niece, as hard bitten as she thought she was, stopped in mid-sentence, her bile exploding up past her windpipe and out towards the camera man as she fell forward, retching for dear life. Vasquez and several others gathered at the barns entrance, all ran forward as the reporter repeatedly retched upon her expensive clothing. She was gathered up by Vasquez at the same time her cameraman was gathered up by the others and carried outside to the rear kitchen porch. Fortunately Doctor Hatch and a few others were still on hand to lend aid and comfort to the fallen journalista and her cameraman.

As her uncle joined Vasquez both looking on with some small measure of delight, Vasquez heard him say, "Damn is just like my brother. Smart as a whip, but headstrong. Just won't listen to anybody. Has to learn every lesson the hard way. Wouldn't you say Sheriff"?

"Just as you say Judge. Just as you say"! While the Judge's niece and cameraman were recovering, reports were arriving about more bodies being discovered in the waters of the lower San Saba River, along with a massive fish kill. Floating plastic barrels were pulled from the water, by the gathering legion of local and state authorities gathering en masse. A small flotilla of boats started to back track up the San Saba waterway, to track the source of the fish kill.

Now that the Judges niece and her cameraman appeared to have recovered, she sent her producer back to the chopper to get her a change of clothes, more suitable for the country.

The Judge and his County Attorney now took over the Sheriff's task for a time, as the Judge, implied that he wanted Vasquez to become his niece's minder for the time being, helping her flesh out the story of the Culligan massacre for her scoop. Now back on the rear porch, freshly chastened by her recent experience, she presented a more modest approach, to Donny Vasquez as the video cameras rolled, asking penetrating questions of the Sheriff as to his version of the events at hand.

On the other end of the porch, her uncle huddled with the various State groups, as the middle of the afternoon, rolled on.

Towards the end of his on camera interview, it was interrupted, by the Judge as he turned around from his group saying, "Sheriff Vasquez. Oh Donny! What was that you said a while ago, when you looked up and saw the buzzards flying over the barn"?

"Oh, you mean the part where if you look for the buzzards circling overhead, that's where you'll find their next meal"!

"That's it", exclaimed the Judge loudly! "A passing motorist just passed on his observation to one of your deputies that he saw a group of buzzards circling around the old abandoned Lockhart place near the river"!

"Well Judge, that must be where their next meal is coming from. You want me and a few of the deputies to go down there and nose around"?

"You do that son", said the Judge. "And while you're at it you might as well drag the news crew behind you, for proper documentation"! The Judges niece smiled sweetly as she said, "Seems we have our marching orders Sheriff"!

Fifteen minutes later, three county patrol cars, were slowly working their way down the long gravel pathway, as the cameraman and the crews producer, leaned out of the rear windows of the trailing patrol car, getting a shot of the buzzards circling overhead. Vasquez stopped a moment getting out of his car as he noticed a spot where tire tracks and flattened tall grass led off the pathway to his right, directing the last patrol car to investigate while the rest continued onward. As they came around the corner of the horseshoe shaped hill, they entered the clearing that housed nothing more than the chimney and fireplace of what was an old prairie home. As they all emerged into the clearing an eerie presence of death hung as a pall. The entire clearing was shaded by the overgrowth of the surrounding trees. His eyes trained to see what others might overlook, Vasquez caught a glint of light, from a used shell casing and then another and then another, as his radio came alive, with the news that his deputy discovered several abandoned white panel vans, a hundred yards east of the gravel pathway.

"Call the Judge and tell him that and suggest he might want to get on over here, with some of the State boys, cause I've found some recent shell casings left behind. Been some rockin' and rollin' goin' on here recently"! Then he turned to the camera crew saying, "Everybody watch where you step and keep an eye out for me. This is a crime scene and I'd hate for any of you to piss off the Judge. Your video is going to be an official record so follow my lead and missy, feel free to offer any on camera commentary, but you hear my voice, stop your talkin', until I say otherwise"!

Then he directed, the other Deputy to go up into the hill surrounding the clearing and see if any bodies were around. Finding nothing in the clearing except the charred remains of a recent fire in the old fireplace, Vasquez walked back to the clearing entrance, discovering the appearance of drag marks and flattened brush he overlooked. Following the trail, he summoned the cameraman and they both discovered the half submerged panel van wedged into the river. Then as he looked further he pointed out the barely visible top of another vehicle, in the river. Just then he heard his Deputy yell out from the hillside, "Sheriff, we have a dead body over here on the hillside"! As Vasquez and his followers worked their way carefully along the river bank he stopped them, pointing the camera across the river to the opposite embankment, where the remnants of Paulo Sabastiani lay bloated and tangled in the midst of river roots, his eyes long gone into the innards of a buzzard, while several others struggled to salvage what morsels they could.

"Hold the camera steady troopers", said Vasquez! "You're not likely to get another shot like that in your lifetime", as he nodded to the Judges niece to carry on with her commentary. Fifteen minutes later the rest arrived, with a dozen of the States operatives scouring the area, with the Judge and County Attorney in attendance, since the events lay squarely within their jurisdiction. As Vasquez, led the Judge and one of the Texas Rangers to the river bank he said to the Ranger, "You might want to get the Texas Navy to float on up river and bring some scuba divers along with a lot of ambulances and maybe a tow truck or two"!

Two hours later, a much fuller picture of events began to form, as the lead Texas Ranger said to those assembled. "We have a murdered family not a mile from here and evidence of a massacre here in this clearing. Clearly a drug deal of some sort was to occur here, but things went off track as they often do. We have a seller of unknown origin, several buyers is my guess and some people, my guess is the Jamaican Posse', who murdered the Culligan family just prior to ambushing and high jacking the participants of the transaction. There are indications of a third party, thus far unknown, who apparently prepared the area, witness the Claymore mines strategically placed for maximum damage. My view is that whoever set them in place had extensive military experience and knew precisely what he was doing. There are a host of shell casings up on the hill and we'll be days collecting most all of them as we can. Evidence from the submerged vehicles indicates, that a massive gunfight occurred, yet there is no evidence thus far of any drugs or the money transacted. The plastic barrels downstream are all being collected and will be sent to our facilities in San Antonio for examination. It's difficult to say whether or not they had anything to do with this event or not, but my guess is that they probably did. But that is pure speculation on my part"!

Continuing on the Ranger said with the video cameras rolling, "There are two basic elements of a drug deal, the drugs and the money. Neither of which are in evidence here thus far. Our people at the Culligan place are almost completed with their part of the investigation and after a night's sleep will shift their efforts to this crime scene to see if they can discover anything we missed. There is yet another element to this investigation. The massive fish kill along the San Saba River. As you all know, the river flows into the Colorado, River which flows downstream into Lake Travis, serving as the water supply to Austin and other communities downstream. This may well be a localized event, then again perhaps not, so I've alerted the Governor to call in the EPA, to monitor whatever is in the river water. Yet one thing is apparent. Someone survived this engagement. How do we know this? Someone dumped most of the bodies in the river. Someone burned all of their identification documents of the dead in the fireplace. Someone pushed or drove all of the vehicles into the river and someone had to manually empty each and every one of the plastic barrels into the river. Finally someone cleaned up the area as best they could to leave no trace, of what happened. We probably might have come across this place eventually, but we Can thank the hungry buzzards for accelerating our investigation. I wish to thank the County Judge, Attorney and the Sheriff for their splendid co-operation and we'll be out of your hair as soon as we can. Now to the news crew that's along for the ride. You can keep your video tapes as an empirical source of these events for your story. But on the Chopper ride back to your studio, a Ranger will accompany you, plus a Ranger chopper will be close behind. Upon arrival you will immediately have your people make an unedited copy of those tapes in the presence of one of our men, giving the originals to us, for they are evidence of two crime scenes. Failure to do this will result in the immediate incarceration of your entire crew, are we in agreement? Failure to immediately agree will result in your immediate arrest and the forfeiture of your tapes. So what is it to be"? "Of course they agree Ranger, don't you", said the Judge with conviction, as they all nodded their heads.

Around seven in the evening with the sun setting on the western horizon, Vasquez withdrew the rest of his people as they assisted the news crew and the Ranger on to the news chopper as the other Texas Ranger chopper started its engines on its way escorting the other back to civilization.

As the Judge escorted his niece onto the news helicopter, she gave him another Euro kiss and yelled out to Vasquez, "I owe you dinner Sheriff, your call", with a slow wink, as the rotors gained momentum, the blades grabbing more air as the craft lifted upwards, heading east.

Walking back to their respective cars, the Judge said, "Donny, I just want to say how well you've handled this entire mess and especially the courtesy you showed my niece. Money in the bank as far as I'm concerned and I'm sure I speak for the County Attorney"!

"Thank you Judge for your vote of confidence"! "So what're ya gonna do now, Donny"?

"Think I'll go back to the Station to make sure the rest of the county is settled down, then maybe go back to my place and get some rest. It's a shame all of this had to happen in this county. I can see it happening around the border, cause for years I was up to my neck in all that. But here, in Menard County, this sort of thing is not supposed to happen"!

"All part of life son", said the Judge continuing, "Ya gotta take the bitter with the better. Life is usually a long dark ride and if we're lucky, some of us get to see a few rays of sunshine at certain points along the way. By the way, how're things going with that new Chulita you've taken up with"?

"Is there something in this County you don't know about Judge"? "Not much son, not much"!

"Well she's quite a bunny Judge, a real bunny rabbit"!

"It'll be our little secret son. Just let me know if Chuey presents a problem"!

32

Emerging from his morning shower, Jaeger dried himself with a towel, examining the wound he'd received in the shootout in Menard County. It was almost healed. Those tiny Nano critters that were inserted inside him back while in the Ellis Unit of Huntsville prison, were apparently working as advertised. An errant round found a weakness in his expensive Kevlar, taking a nice chunk out of his side. But now all that was left was a bit of tender skin that had shed its crust and was almost mended. The knife wound but a memory.

Scylla was now sole owner of the Teal Stone condo, thanks to some legal skull drudgery by Anselm Barthez, as well as co-owner of what was Ortega's Gentlemen's Club with its current manager still in place. Ortega's former residence in Clear Lake, now belonged to her also, as well as the Cabin cruiser in the boat dock. For his work, Barthez received a smooth hundred G's in cold hard, under the table cash, plus a free ongoing tab at Scylla's Club, for as long as she could put up with him.

The sum total of all the money was separated into two piles, the Kosher and the quality bogus. The Kosher was neatly wrapped and sorted into ten thousand dollar packets, barely fitting into three large suitcases, while the Bogus, was bundled and stuffed into four large footlockers for a later task. For his efforts, Rae's wife was paid a quarter million, for she never allowed him to touch money, except for the hundred dollars a week in allowance she let him have.

Boyd Parmalee was in the process of taking care of Melanie and her son and the ongoing reacquisition of land formerly a part of Jaegers family estate in greater Waco. Now all he could do was relieve the nurses, of their burden and take Magellan up to the Teal Stone where Scylla would allow him to mend. Anyway, she was spending most of her time at the club, working on several dance routines, allowing the current manager to run the day to day functions of the club, while she was determined to embark on a new career.

News reports indicated, the authorities had discovered the events in Menard County, as well as the massive fish kill and the floating bodies along most of the San Saba River, yet had reached several dead ends. They had bodies galore, a growing water pollution problem as well as suspicions and little else.

Jaeger arrived at the nurses residence around mid-morning to retrieve Magellan, pay the nurses and transport him to the Teal Stone to continue his convalescence. Tossing two packets of hundred dollar bills upon the kitchen table, Jaeger looked at both nurses asking, "Are we squared up"?

Marge and Harriet looked at each other, nodding their heads with Harriet saying, "Anytime ya get the sniffles, just ring us up"! Still in his clothes, now washed and mended, Magellan limped into the kitchen, as Jaeger asked, "Hey Sport, how ya doing"?

"Standard aches and pains, of anyone back from the brink"! Marge quickly interjected saying, "The both of you stop this palavering and listen up. I've assembled the ongoing medications he'll need to continue taking in order to fully recover, in this here box along with written instructions. He is to take them until all gone, regardless of how he feels. Bed rest for the next month. His wounds are stitched up with catgut which should dissolve within the next week. His white blood cell count is down significantly enough to allow him to be transported out of here. Anything out of the ordinary arises, our Mobil and home numbers are written down. Now both of you git, cause the both of us are on duty within the hour"!

Both Magellan and Jaeger were quiet as Jaeger drove west on the interstate to Magellan's new resting place. Finally Jaeger broke the silence saying, "Hope you don't mind sharing your convalescence with Scylla, since she's the new owner of Ortega's condo"!

"How did you work that", asked a surprised Magellan?

"A whole lot of very creating lawyering. She also owns the Clear Lake home plus the boat and is half owner of Ortega's club, along with its manager"!

"Ah yes, Capitalism at its finest", chuckled Magellan wryly! "But why so generous when not too long ago she would have skewered you in a heartbeat"!

"Seems she had her come to Jesus moment recently and anyway it's my way of buying a little insurance! As they drove up into the condos parking garage, Jaeger found Ortega's old parking spot and helped Magellan from his car and into the elevator as they both rode up in silence.

"Upon entering Jaeger helped his charge to sit down on the couch and went over to the bar and fixed them both a drink. As he sat down on the opposite end of the couch, Magellan said, "I suppose I'm long overdue for thanking you for all of this considering"!

"Neither one of us is the gabby type Nestor. Guys like us, always have a tough time saying please, thank you, or offering an apology. Never complain and never explain, so don't worry about it"!

"Yet you killed all of Ortega's people. Wiped them out all by yourself, then went out to Menard and did the very same. Why did you allow me to survive along with Scylla"!

"Well lemmeseeheah", said Jaeger pondering. "I would've except that I intercepted your call to Ortega after he was dead at the Clear Lake house, and figured out that you had nothing to do with the bull shit in Sao Paulo. Now as far as Scylla is concerned, hell's fire, it just seemed a cryin' shame that such fine pussy become fish food. Hope I don't live to regret it. Now if you'll get up and walk into your bedroom, you'll see something on your bed that might make it all worthwhile"!

"What about Ortega's offshore accounts"?

"All taken care of as a result of creative legal work"!

As Jaeger directed him into one of the bedrooms, Magellan spotted two new gym bags sitting on the bed, as Jaeger said, "There yours. Open em up"! Magellan then sat down on at the foot of the bed and slowly unzipped the first bag as his eyes grew wide in astonishment.

"Merry Christmas", said Jaeger smiling. "I've no idea how much is in there, but the money is legal tender and the second bag is the same. Now I don't suggest you let Scylla know about this, what with two ritzy homes, a cabin cruiser and half ownership of a thriving business, she's been sufficiently provided for"!

"And you", asked Magellan?

"Doin' well enough sport, doin' well"!

"So how can I thank you", asked Magellan?

"You already have. Odds are slim that we'll ever run across each other again, but if we do I don't want to see you in my rear view mirror. Ya follow"?

"Completely. You have my word on it", said Magellan offering his hand in friendship as he struggled to stand adding, "I owe you my life and am in your debt, an obligation that can never be completely repaid"! Two proud men. Serious men. Dangerous men, clasped each other's hand and looked into the others eyes, never realizing that a lifelong bond between men of honor was just sealed.

Jaeger nodded his head, then turned and walked out, never turning his head, for the day was growing short and there was still much to do. After Jaeger left, Magellan went back into the living room, picked up his drink and opened the sliding glass door to the patio, gazing out at the downtown skyline, its majestic buildings reaching skyward and marveled at his good fortune. His thoughts briefly turned to Madeleine, her spirit never far away. Then his thoughts turned to his mother, safe within the protective cavity of Holy Mother Church. Then his thoughts drew back to himself and the resurrected future that lay ahead. Soon this city would be crawling with some very angry people, asking questions about the Embraer affair. The news of it in the media of both continents raising a firestorm in international circles. All he could do was lay doggo and allow his wounds to heal further. With luck all trails would end at the disappearance of Ortega and Carlos Meyers, now vanished. Seems Jaeger had Jugos perform one final service. Both he and Jaeger would not appear on anyone's radar screen, with businesses, residences and vehicles all registered in offshore private accounts that if Jaeger's people did their work well have already vanished from sight. Ortega's death was of no consequence, for he was a peasant who clearly had over reached his abilities. But the passing of Carlos Meyers was a bit of a blow. Clearly a man of exquisite talent and intellect. Too bad he chose to tag along with Ortega for his final accounting with Jaeger. Wrong place at the wrong time with the wrong adversary. No one would ever mourn the disappearance of either. Yet the news that Meyers had seeded the buy money with counterfeit bills that was to go to Ortega was a surprise to Magellan, who reasoned that Meyers must've run into some cash flow problems. But he must've known that Ortega would eventually discover his betrayal and seek him out for retribution, an agonizingly slow and painful process. Yet in betraying Ortega, Meyers also put Magellan at risk. Everyone betrays everyone else. Well almost everyone. All except Jaeger.

Magellan was certain that Jaeger was unaware of the existence of the stolen Russian diesel submarine that lay snugly berthed far away in a southern Chilean fjord, for Jaeger was never in the loop. All were retired Argentine Naval personnel along with a few Russians and each had more than sufficient reason to keep their silence.

Finally as far as Jaeger knew, all of the Crystalline had been dumped in the San Saba River. He had not an inkling that five tons remained safely buried in Val Verde' county. For now and the foreseeable future, Magellan decided to let sleeping dogs lay. First to be mended sufficiently to travel and Europe beckoned. He then went back inside, checked the front door and went back into the bedroom, picking up both gym bags full of his future, laying them in his closet, then laid down on the bed to rest, drifting off to sleep.

Duke Vultee sat studying the computerized weather projections for the greater Houston area for the next seven days, in his room at the Weston Galleria Hotel. All in the room were silent, awaiting his comments. Rae, Jaeger, Morgan and Carmichael. All were alumnae of the Ellis Unit of the TDC long ago.

Rae and Jaeger were to set things in motion at the appropriate time, whereas Morgan and Carmichael had worked for Vultee previously in successful bank jobs. All knew of his meticulous planning in a bank robbery and had the utmost of confidence in his ability to plan for the unforeseen.

Morgan and Carmichael were each to be in charge of a team of four, three man teams, of serious men, with each team responsible for hitting four banks each in five minute segments. The trick was to hit each bank when the money was arriving, in the morning from the security firm responsible for delivery. Information was everything along with pinpoint planning with military precision and precise help from Mother Nature. Then of course, they would need a massive diversion. All of the elements would have to come together with exquisite perfection in order to make things work.

Of course Jaeger, Rae and Vultee were at one time close friends while in Huntsville, with all getting out at approximately the same time. Vultee, had served his time and time had passed so as far as previous bank heists were concerned He was currently a successful entrepreneur in the entertainment business a distant memory to the law enforcement community. After his release, he worked as a manager of a Gentlemen's club in Houston and during the ensuing years, became the owner of a string of Gentlemen's clubs throughout northern Texas and Louisiana. He was doing extremely well financially, yet always in the back of his mind was a massive score, of biblical proportions. During a casual conversation with Rae over the phone, he became aware of a gigantic amount of bogus currency that Jaeger had come across in his recent activities. Thus, churned his mind as he began to call around the chosen few.

With two choppers fueled up at a small private airfield in the far northwest portion of Harris County and recently stolen and repainted Vans at the ready and men assembled in several motels on the western side of town, all was in readiness, just waiting for the weather to arrive.

During his fifty one years on this earth Duke Vultee had developed a micro science in the art of "Monetary removal from lending Institutions", by always doing the unexpected. Thus, he looked up from his weather charts and said, "Gentlemen, the great unseen hand once writ hath spoken, so it's down to this. Tomorrow is payday and the selected banks will have to have an extraordinary amount of cash on hand in order to meet the demand at days end. The cash will arrive in the morning in armored vehicles. We know the approximate arrival times of each vehicle at each banking facility and for their duration. We hit each vehicle the very moment the exit door opens, disarming the guards, grabbing the money and leaving with all deliberate speed to the next bank up the street. Timing is everything. Now thanks to Rae and Jaeger who will provide for the diversion, one element is lacking in the plan. We just can't have any cops arriving to spoil our fun now can we"?

As he looked around he saw a nodding of heads as he continued, "At approximately six in the morning, Jaeger and Rae will be gaining access to the roof of a high rise building not two hundred yards from our current location, with the help of a building engineer who will be well compensated, for helping them to the roof and reconfiguring the security cameras.

If Mother Nature, in her divine wisdom cooperates, a nasty weather front will arrive in town around just around seven thirty in the morning. The wind will be blowing at around thirty miles an hour from a north west to south easterly direction and mysteriously right in the heart of

Loop 610 and Westheimer Road, in the middle of early morning rush hour traffic, several million dollars in quality bogus hundred and fifty dollar bills will start raining from the heavens, along with the rest of the rain and hopefully lightening. With any luck at all a traffic jam of monumental proportions will occur right in the middle of the Galleria and in both north and South lanes of Loop 610, hastened by thousands of folks eager to help in the collection of all that bogus cash. Now according to our guy inside the Security Company, the bank deliveries of the cash will start arriving on schedule starting at eight in the morning for each banks opening at nine in the morning. We will carefully monitor all channels of the police scanner for the HPD should be overwhelmed by the number of accidents created by the chaos that will soon arrive. They'll call in the Sheriff's department and the County Constables along with every wrecker available as well as ambulances to fall on the Galleria and West Loop to help out with traffic and crowd control. Plus all of this will be happening right about the time that work shifts change for every one of the law enforcement entities. When I've determined the vast majority of cops are engaged at the Galleria, then I'll give the rest of you the "Go" sign over channel twenty nine on the SSB. The whole thing is hit and scoot to the next bank. Speed and confusion are our allies gentlemen. Are there any questions"?

Everyone shook their heads, for they had rehearsed and planned down to a tee. Everyone knew their part and we're in constant contact with each other over secured channels.

"Oh one final thing", said Vultee. "Once the last bank has been hit by each crew, make certain you don't violate any traffic laws. It'd be a crying shame if one of the crews got pulled over for a traffic beef and missed the chopper. Now everyone knows of the assembly point in Burleson County where the split will occur"! Again all nodded their heads as Morgan and Carmichael rose to leave.

When they departed, Vultee turned to Rae saying, "Now this guy that's the building engineer is reliable isn't he"?

"Oh, he'll get us up on the roof alright and shut down the security cameras. He's gonna get sixty large in bogus money, which he'll never get to spend. As far as he knows, it's all just a huge prank that's being played. Once the cold front arrives, Jaeger'll see to it he gets flying lessons off the back of the building thirty floors up"!

"No qualms"?

"Not a one. He's a distant cousin that's a pain in the ass. He's into some Louisiana bookies for fifty G's and we gave him ten on account day before yesterday to keep the bookies at bay. Anyway with the promise of sixty more he thinks he'll be ahead of the game in a few days. He got paid in bogus cash anyway. No loss to us. Besides, I'm not the one giving flying lessons"!

"There we are then. It's now a little past eight in the evening, the weather front is to be arriving in Dallas around midnight and then if the earth still turns arrive here just in time for rush hour traffic. Pay me a visit when you're done so we can have breakfast together and watch everything on the TV. Seen you both tomorrow.

At six the following morning, they were met by the building engineer at the rear loading dock who asked, "What's with the hats and shades this early in the morning? I disabled the in house security camera's"?

"Just a precaution Ambrose, just a precaution. Here, take one of these suitcases while I take the other one, my friend here will take the other two", said Rae!

"As they all rode up to the buildings penthouse in the freight elevator, all were quiet as the elevator came to a stop at the penthouse. The doors opened on to the roof with Jaeger and company schlepping the heavy suitcases along the rooftop to the front parapet facing Post Oak Boulevard, Westheimer Road and the West Loop overpass intersections. The early morning air was heavy and still. Full of low hanging humidity as the traffic below them was starting to build.

Just then Ambrose stepped back a few steps as the others peered briefly over the parapet saying, "Ah hate to break this to ya fellas at this late date, but there's been a change in the economics of our deal."! As they both turned around, Ambrose pulled out a small caliber automatic and racked a round in the chamber saying, "We got's ta renegotiate the whole deal. The money you're offering just ain't enough and ah need more to git clear"! "But Ambrose, what happened to the ten G's I fronted you to keep the bookies at bay", asked Rae in exasperation?

"Well ah paid em the other day, but they ran up some more vig all on me and now I owes em more. Sorry bout that, but ah gotta clear at least ten large when this is all through and I got a notion that this might not be a simple prank after all but something bigger, much bigger, than a simple prank and so it's worth more. A whole lot more"!

Jaeger silent throughout, finally broke through saying, "Well sport we discussed your needs with others and they all agreed. Now at the last moment seems you got us over a barrel, but we don't have the money to pay you yet. Not on us. What exactly did you have in mind"!

"I'm thinking a hundred large should pay my debts and give me some tide over money for a while"! The moment of betrayal was at hand and it was not wholly unexpected as far as Jaeger was concerned, as he wrinkled his brow for a moment in deep thought, finally kneeling to the ground saying as he opened one of the suitcases, "You're a smart bunny Ambrose; you got things partially figured out. There is a greater purpose in this other than a mere prank"!

"Damn, I just knew it", the engineer exclaimed in glee! As Jaeger opened the suitcase, he revealed, stacks upon stacks of hundred and fifty dollar bank notes. More money than Ambrose ever considered possible to exist, as Jaeger continued; "Now all of these are counterfeit hundred and fifty dollar bank notes. Very good bogus notes, yet bogus none the same. You got ten up front from Rae, I can peel off two hundred thousand right now with no problem to our thing, to sweeten the deal" and as he said that he took several stacks in his hand saying, "Each here stack is ten thousand. Here look for yourself", as he tossed both stacks at the engineer, closing the distance between them as Ambrose's eyes followed the two stacks heading his way. At the same time the stacked landed so did Jaeger as the small automatic coughed twice in Jaegers chest. Quickly wrenching the weapon away from Ambrose, Jaeger punched him twice quickly in the nose, and then spun him around wrapping his head in his arms, twisting his head around until a palpable crack was felt. Jaeger quickly dropped the lifeless stationary engineer to the ground, saying "Ouch" unbuttoning his shirt to see two spent bullets fall into his belt, stopped by the Kevlar vest. As he picked one of them up he said, ".22 caliber. The guy shoots me with a .22. What kind of family you got there Rae"?

"He's from the other branch of the tree. You OK Jaeger"?

"Yeah. Been hit harder before"!

"Great, but now how we gonna get off the roof"?

"I suspected a darkie in the wood pile, so being the last one past the metal door I brought along an aluminum piece of metal with some stickum on one side to slide in to the latch in the door, so we could get back to the elevator"! Then he reached into Ambrose pocket saying, "And here is the swipe access card that will get us onto the elevator and back to the parking garage, then out on the street". He then walked over to the back side of the building's roof looking below then came back and dragged the body to that spot, rearranging the roofing gravel as he returned wiping out the skid marks.

"Now Rae, all we got to do is light one up and wait for the weather to change", said Jaeger fishing out a cigarette from his pack"!

"When were through, I'll toss Ambrose over the side and if he falls right he should hit this Pin Oak Tree at ground level. Perhaps suicide if he hits right, after all some nasty bookies were on his ass ready to break him up. Then the suitcases will go over the back side of the building, just make sure your prints aren't on them. Finally we go down stairs and make our way across the street, park my car in the shopping center lot and go join Vultee for breakfast"!

"Sounds like a plan", said Rae. 'Now all we have to do is wait for the weather to change"!

Being the tallest building in the area at that time, by five floors, Jaeger was satisfied that nothing was seen or heard of the events that had just occurred, with the both of them waiting patiently just below the buildings front waist high parapet, Jaeger at one end and Rae at the other to gain as wide a spread as possible. As Jaeger finished each cigarette, he field stripped it, sprinkling the remaining ashes and what little tobacco remained on the gravel soon to be swept away by the wind and crushing up the filter and putting it in his pocket, leaving nothing to betray his presence there, ever.

Of course, time always passes at a snail's pace when awaiting an event to happen driven by events beyond ones control, as Jaeger checked his watch which indicated a few minutes past seven in the morning. At least he had some cigarettes to keep him company, but Rae wasn't as fortunate, for his main squeeze made him give up the evil weed two years ago, as he looked longingly at Jaeger taking the odd puff at his smoke every so often. Every so often he saw Jaeger look at his watch and finally they both caught a change in the wind. It was coming from the northwest as the both looked at each other, with Jaeger shaking his head as if to say, 'Not Yet'. Five minutes passed, then another five and then another as the breeze started to turn into a proper blow. At a few minutes past seven thirty, both men heard the sound of thunder in the distance, then as their hair started to ruffle from the wind, felt the first drops of rain, as Jaeger looked at Rae and nodded his head. It was now, 'Post Time', as each of them reached into a suitcase and opened a pack of bogus bank notes tossing them over the parapet letting the wind do the rest. One by one the bank notes flew carried by the wind. Five minutes later the first of the suitcases were emptied as they both made to open the second, hearing the first of many auto crashes from down below as people stopped their cars in the middle of the street, pouring out of them at a steady pace to gather the manna from the heavens blowing helter skelter in the wind, not one person looking to see its origin.

Twenty five minutes later, their work done both took their suitcases towards the rear of the rooftop as Jaeger hoisted the dead engineer, taking careful aim and heaved him overboard. As Ambrose landed squarely in the treetop Jaeger saw no evidence that he made it to ground level. With luck it would be days until anyone bothered to look up into the tree. Perhaps the buzzards would give him away, but for now…Then both wiped each suitcase clean, closing each one and heaved it over the rear parapet, landing in the trees far below.

As they approached the metal door to the roof, Jaeger carefully opened it, removing the small metal wedge and carefully closed it behind them. Then entering the freight elevator inserted Ambrose's security card and pressed the garage button. They had some time making their way across Post Oak Boulevard, past the gaggle of wrecked cars and trucks and busses, but finally found a parking spot far from the street and then made their way through the carnage to the Weston Galleria as the deluge of rain finally hit full force.

As the duo struggled to work their way across Post Oak Boulevard, the very epicenter of the Galleria part of uptown Houston, Rae pulled out his Mobil phone as the driving rain increased in its intensity, wending their way through the wreckages of vehicles in every direction, people were everywhere, scrambling for the currency still falling from the overcast skies, with police cars, and fire trucks blowing their sirens and klaxons. When the phone answered Rae hollered, "When you hear a knock at your door in a few minutes, it'll be us, wet and hungry"!

Five minutes later a beaming Vultee opened the door saying, "Breakfast is served, the TV is on" and as the door closed added, "And a in a few minutes, the first take down will be a fact. Seems that every cop in town and in the county has come to the Galleria to help out. What few cops are still in the county and town are well east of here, and busy as hell doing other things. Geeze, could you guys get any wetter"?

"Can't think or tote everything", said Jaeger. "The umbrella just didn't make the cut"!

"Well, get toweled off; get some coffee and everything we need for breakfast is under the hood on the serving table. Let's watch the happenings courtesy of the early morning local news"! Several minutes later Jaeger joined Vultee at the tenth floor window facing almost the entire length of Post Oak Road facing north seeing nothing but an entire traffic jam with vehicles of every sort pointed in every possible direction. Some by virtue of a collision, while others were simply jammed in tightly through circumstances of their own making. The swirling effects of the wind working its way through and around various buildings, took many a bank note on a different journey than was originally intended, tempting even the most virtuous of souls, to brave the inclement weather and rescue the money from the weather.

The entire West Loop traffic, not two hundred yards distant from the hotel, was at a complete standstill, again due to an overwhelming plethora of vehicular wreckages, in both the north and the southbound lanes. As they watched the activity below, news reports came over the airwaves of the Southwest Freeway, in similar straits, with vehicular wreckages in such abundance, that neither ambulances, police vehicles, nor wreckers could approach, with people braving the weather to rescue the money.

Looking out at the carnage, Vultee took another sip of his coffee saying, "A hundred thousand vehicles, more or less each day pass through the intersection of Post Oak and Westheimer Roads, each and every business day. The Loop 610 overpass counts another quarter of a million cars passing over Westheimer each business day and the Southwest Freeway, well son I just can't count that high"!

Repeated announcements from all three local station's, indicated that the normal network viewing schedule, would be temporarily interrupted, to bring them continuing news of this important event. Then since no news trucks could approach the scene, only the news station helicopters, circling above braving the now intermittent rain and the lightening brought life to the events occurring below them. One of the chopper reporters was overheard in saying over the airwaves, "I've reported on a great many things from the vantage point of a helicopter overhead and I've seen a great many accidents in my time, but nothing even beginning to approach this. Must be a record of sorts. A record that only Texas could claim"!

Vultee turned his head away from the scene and glanced at Jaeger saying, "Remember this moment in time, for no matter what comes next for any of us, this one will go into the record books"!

They went back to the TV set and sat down, just as the Porta radio crackled to life, with Carmichael saying quickly, "Team One is away and has done its job, heading for the meeting point"! In the next ten minutes each and every team checked in briefly with the same message, as Vultee glanced at his watch every time and smiled. When the last team was reported away and heading to parts unknown, Vultee again glanced at his watch saying, "Just one more hurdle. When both choppers are in the air, we'll get one last call telling us their airborne. Then we can sit back and breathe easy. That ought to happen, if the creek don't rise too high, in about thirty minutes. So all we can do is sit back and listen to the news"!

Jaeger and Rae then went to the bathroom and shed their sodden clothes and shoes hanging them up to dry by the air conditioning vents, returning in bath robes, to sit out the rest of the morning. Thirty four minutes later Carmichael came on the air briefly saying, "Into the air", meaning the choppers were loaded and airborne, heading for the rendezvous point up country.

"What about the die packets each bank bag will have in them", asked Jaeger?

"Carmichael knows how to overcome them so they don't burst. He's riding with the lead chopper. When everyone else arrives, in the different vehicles other than the ones used in the heist, he'll have all of the money out and be starting to divide it as previously agreed"!

"What about the choppers", asked Rae?

"They'll be flown to another location some fifty miles away, wiped clean and abandoned. The pilot's will meet up with Carmichael somewhere in Austin for dinner tonight"!

"Then there's the guy at the security company that furnished the information", said Jaeger!

"Had lunch with him yesterday. Sometime around noon today, he should start experiencing the effects of something he ate yesterday. By two in the afternoon his body will complete its shutdown and his sprit will join others in the happy hunting grounds"!

"Any idea how big the haul will be", asked Rae?

"Estimated at around six or seven mil, but can't say for certain. To be sure the banks'll lowball the figure and the FBI will be in town nosing around"! Then Vultee took another gander at his watch as Rae asked, "When do you think the news will announce the news of the heist"?

"Don't know, but it should be any time now", said Vultee. Thirty minutes later, they all saw an announcement of a 'Breaking News Report'. Try as he may to have been modulated in his tone, the news reader could not help hiding his excitement as he blurted of reports that a string of banks on the west side of Houston were robbed simultaneously at gunpoint by masked people of unknown origin, who made their getaway in the rain. The authorities were immediately notified, but their slow response time was due to the carnage in the Galleria area of town. It took but a few minutes, for the news anchors to connect the dots of the Galleria incident to the string of bank robberies. As the morning wore on and throughout the rest of the day, none of the network programming ever made it to the viewing public, so wrapped up with incoming news of the events in the Galleria and further reports of yet another bank heist that occurred in the early hours of the morning.

Around eleven thirty, Rae looked at Jaeger and said, "Seems that Duke is still the master planner and has tied up all the loose ends"! Then he looked at Vultee asking, "But Duke what if one of us gets caught and spills the beans? The Feds are awfully good at putting things together"! "Correctamundo Rae. Let's reflect a moment. There's you, and me and Jaeger. Are any of us going to do a single thing out of the ordinary?

We all served together at Huntsville and none of us are rats. Now we come to Carmichael and Morgan, again alumnae of the Huntsville institution. In all the time we knew them were they not always stand up guys? Then we come to the others, all ex-military, that me and Jaeger had reason to trust thanks to a certain General Bollinger. All instrumental in the securing of not only his release but mine also. At every occasion in the past each of them preformed with skill and intelligence again as witnessed this very day. Not a one of us are common criminals, slaves to our inconsistencies. All performed as indicated and the fucking FBI can nose around all they want and they'll be coming up with zip. So drive safely and sleep well tonight Rae"!

As the news reports came in fast and furious, one common thread became apparent, no one was harmed and other than several of the security guards that tried to resist and were pistol whipped, no one was seriously injured. Each and every one of the heists, occurred as the door to the Security Van opened and the guards to a man were surprised, as the Vans tires were immediately shredded and in less than thirty seconds the robbers had gotten away with all of the bank bags inside each vehicle.

Vultee kept count of the banks that were being reported as held up and by mid-afternoon the final accounting was tallied as he said, "Sure enough they got em all"! By the same time, the rain had abated completely and the skies were clear, with helicopters still swirling about overhead as they now peered out of the window overlooking the Galleria area, to see that apparently nothing had apparently changed over the last six hours, the traffic snarled to such a degree, the police had to work their way from the various rearward points of the carnage towards the epicenter right in front of the Neiman Marcus store, right next to the hotel.

"Better call your old lady Rae and tell her where you're at and that you'll not be home until morning the way things are looking", laughed Vultee!

By four in the afternoon Vultee got a brief call from Morgan on his Mobil, asking him if their dinner engagement in Dallas the day after tomorrow was still on and Vultee grunted in the affirmative. Then Vultee asked, "How're thing up your way", getting the response, "Everything's five by five. See ya when I see ya"! As he disconnected, Vultee looked at Jaeger and Rae, smiling broadly and said, "Gentlemen, expectations have been exceeded"!

Smiling Rae settled back once again saying, "Reminds me of the time back in Seventy One I think it was, when me and four others soaped Meacom Fountain on South Main Street as a prank. We went to several grocery stores and loaded up with a whole shit load of the largest boxes of laundry detergent we could find and each of us had two boxes already cut open to dump into the fountain and a third in reserve. Six of us packed into this 56 Chevy Nomad wagon and I was the driver. It was just past one on a Sunday morning and traffic was spotty, when we drove slowly down Sunset Street and I dropped every one off one by one as I slowly drove around the fountain. Took three circuits of that dang fountain before all the detergent was in the fountain and we collected everybody. Well we drove through the Rice University Campus dropping the empty cartons along the way, then went to breakfast. An hour later we all visited the scene of the crime, to find traffic back up and moving slowly through the intersection and soap suds high up into the overhanging tree branches. The news reports in the Houston Post the following morning indicated that soap suds were almost up to the third floor at the Hotel next to the fountain. They were talking about that one for days and weeks later. Of course we couldn't get near the fountain due to the Traffic. And to make matters worse, when they finally found the shut off valve to the fountain, it broke off in their hands, due to accumulated rust over the years. It wasn't until sunup when the fire trucks finally made some headway washing away the soap suds.

They finally reckoned it must've been some of the Rice U students who laundered up the fountain, but never specifically who. It made the national news reports and a five thousand dollar reward was put up by the Meacom family, but nobody collected. Up to that point, that was one of the high points in my life. But this"?.... Rae's voice trailed off in reverie.

The retail shopping center across the street where Jaeger had parked his Ford early on became the staging center for everything in the Galleria area. Around four in the afternoon, scant progress had been made in working their way towards the epicenter as a host of helicopters used the parking lot, now cordoned off by police ferried in by Police helicopters in waves, had spread out to take control of the area.

A half hour later, news reports regarding units of the State Guard being activated, to join the local authorities in bringing order out of chaos. Cameras recorded interviews between the reporters on the scene and the City Mayor as well as the County Judge, trying to look worried and important to the viewing public, but in reality just getting in the way soaking up air time, to politically enhance their reputations come reelection time. By five PM the Mayor was joined by half the members of the City Council who were forceful enough to cadge a chopper ride to ground zero.

As the Mayor was being interviewed by one of the local TV reporters, he was seen to righteously declare this day as, "Black Thursday", the declaration making headlines the following day. As the day wore on into early evening, more and more Guard units were hurriedly called up to reinforce the overwhelmed local authorities, who were in addition busily trying to put out the flames of two partially loaded fuel tanker trucks that overturned earlier in the morning on the Southwest Freeway, a mile away from the epicenter as a result of vehicles suddenly stopping at road speed to gather up the currency that flew by.

As the National evening news droned on about the events in Houston, they were eventually replaced by the unfolding story of the stolen plans for the Embraer aircraft fleet suddenly surfacing in Houston, along with a revelation of how, they came to be stolen in the first place, pointing out an international industrial espionage case, involving highly placed individuals in both the Argentine Military and the Government as well as a highly placed individual in the Brazilian aircraft industry.

After the commercial break, the Evening News continued their reportage of events in Menard County as well as the entire length of the San Saba River and concerns by investigators of the EPA, about the quality of the water in the Colorado River that might affect water quality for the entire City of Austin Texas and the surrounding areas. Subsequent preliminary data traced the identities of those discovered floating in the San Saba River as elements of national and international drug organizations, involved in the murder of a family as well as a drug deal that had gone horribly wrong and that a task force of State and Federal agencies was deeply involved in the case.

33

S aturday morning was usually a quiet time for Mel O'Bannon. Get breakfast made for herself and her son Rory. Then deliver him to whatever activity the school had in store for him. Since she'd gotten the secretarial position with the lobbying firm, in Austin and moved there, she'd undergone quite a change from her past. The position at Enron was challenging to say the least, but in the rarified air of State Government she saw close at hand the deals that were made between supposedly honorable men. Still, it paid well and provided a day to day challenge that wore her out at the end of each day. In the six months she'd been in Austin, she'd adjusted rather well considering. She had full and uncontested custody of her son, thanks to Charlie Ledbetter's efforts and while that left her skinny financially, her job promised to even things out eventually. After all her son was definitely worth all of the struggle she'd expended. Three times a year she was to drive down to Houston to share the holidays with her former mother in law so she could see how well little Rory was doing. In time perhaps memories of the past would fade into a better view.

Only occasionally had she thought about Jaeger, these days. Her trips to Ballys becoming less and less over time. She had no idea whether or not he was alive or not, for he'd simply vanished without a trace. Of course she'd never considered asking where he lived or pried into his business affairs, considering that an affront to both of their dignity. She'd briefly considered hiring a private investigator to see where he'd gotten to, but when confronted with the estimated cost dropped that idea like a hot potato. She'd just got out from under a huge financial drain with her son and she didn't need another just to satisfy her vanity.

In the passage of time, here in Austin, she'd allowed herself to succumb to a few lack luster dinner dates with men who otherwise might prove interesting, yet the memory of her time with that son of a bitch Jaeger still lingered like a bad habit, just like the cigarette smoking she'd recently taken up again. Besides, all of these supposedly eligible males were constantly on the make, lawyers to the man. Deal makers that always considered both sides of the coin rather than what was right. Any significant liaisons would eventually crumble of its own weight and she never forgot what her dearly departed mother once told her, that one's reputation was everything, everything. The only thing that others couldn't take from you, yet the very thing one had to willingly give away. Once lost, was pretty much impossible to regain. Then she smiled as she recalled her very proper mother wink as she said, "And dearie, ya just don't shit where ya eat"!

The phone rang and as she picked up the receiver, saying "Hello", she heard the cultured male voice on the other end ask, "Is this the O'Bannon residence"? Answering in the affirmative, she heard the voice continue, "My name is Boyd Parmalee. You probably don't recall but we met some time ago at the Enron Christmas party"!

"Oh yes, Mister Parmalee. I think I recall now. You were the man escorting Buffy Beauviour. How may I help you"?

"As you may recall, I'm an associate in the Law firm in Houston that Ms. Beauvior heads up. She's agreed to a task that her court calendar will not budge an inch for. So I agreed to perform a fiduciary task in your behalf. Since I'm currently in retirement, I've the time whereupon she does not. So, down to the facts. Do you think you can find time in your schedule next week end to visit our law firm in order complete a legal transaction that will accrue wholly in your favor"?

"What's this all about", asked Melanie? Are the O'Bannon's raising yet another stink regarding the child custody dispute?

I've signed all of the papers in Mister Ledbetter's office that finalized everything. I even turned down a half million dollar settlement by the O'Bannon Estate to share custody", voiced Melanie testily!

That was confirmed the other day in a private conversation between Charlie and myself Melanie. I may call you Melanie can't I"?

"My friends call me Mel"! "Good, then Mel it shall be", offered Parmalee continuing. "Please call me Boyd. "This has nothing to do with your settlement with the O'Bannon Estate, for that bit of business is cast in stone. On the contrary, it has everything to do with your financial welfare and the ongoing welfare of your son. Namely the event of his College education should he so choose to attend an institution of higher learning after his graduation from High School. Or more accurately put, the sufficient funding therewith. Since you are his legal parent and guardian, your written approval will be required to fund an interest bearing account to be set up in his name, from which funds may be withdrawn after his eighteenth birthday for his tuition, books and ongoing sustenance. All this must undergo the rigors of legality in order to become fact, thus requiring both his and your legal documents of origin and then when your bona fides are established, quite similar to what Charlie Ledbetter required to finalize your agreement with the O'Bannon Estate, your written approval of the accounts will be witnessed by duly authorized officers of the court"!

"So you discussed things with Charlie Ledbetter", asked Melanie still suspicious of this man she barely recalled meeting!

"Yes I have, in some detail, so you may feel free to call him to verify our conversation and purpose and to allay any concerns you might have. Now he's sworn not to reveal the details of our conversation only to verify the bona fides of what benefits are before both you and your son"!

After she agreed to meet at Buffy's office the following Saturday, giving her office fax machine number to receive directions to the offices, they said their goodbyes. She quickly called Charlie Ledbetter, tracking him down to his Mobil phone during a round of golf.

"Yup, talked to old Boyd the day before yesterday and yes I know all about what's goin' on and Mel it's got nothing to do with the O'Bannon's. it's a separate matter altogether I know you're gonna like. You met Boyd back at the Enron Party last year and I believe you were escorted by this big guy whose name I'd forgotten. Just show up on time, bring yours and Rory's legal papers and bring Rory. Now can I get back to my game"?

As the elevator doors opened upon the floor that Buffy's firm occupied, she was greeted by the receptionist who called back to confirm her arrival. As she hung up she said, "Ms. Beauvior will be here directly to take you back to the conference room where she'll turn you over to Mister Parmalee"!

Two minutes in walked Buffy to the large reception area, wearing casual clothing, smiling broadly as she said, "Mel. How good of you to come. Let's go back to the main conference room, where I'll turn you over to Boyd. Is this your son", she asked as they walked back through a sea of chest high cubicles, partially staffed on a late Saturday morning, working on other matters. "He certainly favors you in appearance"! I'm sure Boyd explained to you that this task had been committed to my firms undertaking, by your benefactor. But since I'm just up to my pits with clients I can't do it the justice it deserves. Now Boyd is currently retired, but before he retired, he was the Senior Partner and I was his junior. Now he enjoys partner emeritus status around here, with all of the benefits and none of the headaches. So you'll be in as good as hands as one could be"! As they entered the conference room, Boyd stood up at the far end of the conference table, smiling as he went to greet them saying, "So this is your son Rory is it", shaking hands with the youngster, "He bears your resemblance"!

"Well he should, since I was there when he was born"! At that Buffy said, "Boyd, there all yours. Good seeing you again Melanie and it was good meeting your son", as she smiled and swept out of the conference room.

"Please be seated Mel and Rory while I go over what ahead of you. Oh yes, did you bring all of your identifying particulars for you and your son"? Without a word Mel reached into her small briefcase handing out a large sheaf of documents that Parmalee collated into their various piles. When he concluded, he said, "Good. Now that the both of are who you say you are, here is why you are here"!

"The documents that you will initially approve represent several annuities that will be funded by the certified funds that are here on the table. The first is to represent a fund designed to provide for your son's continuing education, commencing with his successful graduation from high school. The amount represented is quite substantial as you can see and should be sufficient to fund his baccalaureate and should he desire a master's degree. The second check is to set up an account, to provide for any extraordinary needs that may arise, during the course of raising your son. As you can see it is a rather substantial amount.

Regarding your son's educational fund, the parameters of the account prohibits you or anyone else from access to that account prior to his eighteenth birthday without a significant access penalty, since it is interest bearing for the duration. Quarterly dividend reports will be tendered to you, during the term of the contract.

The second remuneration will be likewise placed in an annuity selected for its annualized yield content as well as track record for reliability. Its initial duration contract will be for five years and will be automatically be renewable unless otherwise indicated by you. In both cases compounding of accrued interest is a given.

Finally, a certificate of deposit will be placed in your name Mel, in the amount of $50,000 dollars in the Texas Commerce Bank locally, accompanied by a modest savings account of $10,000 dollars, that interest dividends can be transferred into at your discretion. Are you in agreement with the terms and conditions set forth, mindful of the fact that once fully executed our firms responsibilities in this matter are concluded in full to your complete satisfaction"!

As Boyd Parmalee droned on, Mel's jaw dropped further and further and upon his conclusion, she could but answer, "Yes I am Boyd. I certainly am"!

"Good Mel. We shall now proceed in the signing of each document as indicated"! As each document was presented, Boyd explained the legal purpose it served and why it was necessary. When the final document was fully executed he said, "Good Mel. Our business is concluded for the day. We will handle the completion of the funding, by the end of business Monday and send to you by courier the completed documents at your Austin address"!

"So all of this manna from heaven is dropping on me from a source unknown and you're sworn to secrecy as to whom the benefactor is. Is that the situation Boyd"!

"The legal profession does have certain inflexible standards that have survived evolvement over the years that are vital to the success of civilized society, chief of which is the absolute compartmentalization of a client's interests"! Just then little Rory who kept his silence throughout the entire proceedings stood up saying, "Momma, we all know who Santa is. He's the one who made you cry. He's the one who disappeared. It's Jaeger Momma. Jaeger"! Mel's eyes grew wide in the revelation. "Of course", she muttered as the answer had been before her all along as she asked, "Has something happened to him"?

Parmalee shook his head saying, "I can't rightly say"! The best of legal responses that gave away nothing. "But what I can do is to secure these documents and ask the both of you to join me for lunch, for it's about that time of the day"!

As they rode down in the glass walled elevator Parmalee asked Rory, "Son, have you ever sunk your teeth into some genuine Texan prime rib of beef"? Rory looked at his mother then replied, "What's prime rib of beef"?

"You'll see son, you'll see"!

34

It promised to be a wonderful day in Central Texas, with the thermometer heading towards the upper eighties. The sun just cleared the eastern horizon about a few hours ago and the air seemed fresh and sweet. The wind was coming in from the south east at a velocity of a mildly exhaled breath, with white wisps of cotton like clouds high above that seemed to just hang there motionless. The 8:30 sun was slanting down on two elderly men, lifelong friends ever since grade school, who were there since dawn, as they both hunched over their fishing poles in their small row boat, in the middle of the long man made finger of Lake Travis, hard on to the hamlet of Lago Vista. They were hearing over the radio rumors of a vast fish kill in the vicinity of the San Saba River, which flows directly into the Colorado River, which feeds Lake Travis. Yet a few days ago the fishing was good, but this morning there was nary a fish in sight.

Both long retired some fifteen or more years from their respective careers, twice a week, excepting for rain and winter weather, they met to fish and trade stories and bitch about the events of the day, as old men are want to do. Both living across the street from each other in the very same homes in which they'd both raised their families, both men lived in relative solitude, whereas they'd both lost their wives not long ago to a variety of terminal maladies.

Other than their respective families, who alternately proved to both a blessing and a curse, the only other people they cared about, even a little bit were each other. Their bond of friendship so much stronger than any blood relationship and constantly tested over the course of many years by a frank and salty daily exchange of rhetoric that constantly stretched, but never broke the ties that bound them as friends.

Once, after a particularly testy and public exchange with each other, when asked why he was friends with Pete, Althus answered, "He be the onliest mutha fucka in the whole wide world, I'd ever let get away with acallin' me Niggah. That Ofay, cock suckin', sheep fuckin' scumbag sumbitch right ovah there! And his slave name is Pete! Why shit, I won't even let another Niggah to call me a Niggah, but Pete can an ah doan mind"!

Conversely, when asked as to what he attributed his lifelong friendship with Althus, Pete would usually reply, "Well, I'll tell ya why. Cause that there Niggah is the most honest, righteous, sumbitch I ever knowed. Shit, I trust him way more than any of my kin and we know each other goin past sixty some odd years now. When both our wives were alive, they were the best of friends as well as us, god rest their souls. We helped raise each other's children, when they were comin' up. Pulled Althus out of I doan know how many scrapes, with those Piney Woods Klan boys back in the day, whenever they'd head up this way an cause trouble, back in the forties, fifties and sixties. Even got shot once ovah that Niggah an his family"! Then he would quickly add, "Now don't let on to that Niggah that ah said all that, kinda he'd get all big in the head and ah'd nevah heah the end of it"!

Thus were two ancient men on the downside of life, sharing a small boat, out in the middle of Lake Travis, trying in vain to snag some fish for their supper. Armed with their small battery powered radio, near the boats bow, playing Stevie Ray Vaughn and ZZ Top, down home Austin style Rhythm and Blues music, they both sat and waited patiently for the fish to bite. As the little hand laboriously worked its way towards noon, both men remarked as to why boat traffic on this stretch of the lake was sparse this day. Usually the occasional boat passed, either going upstream or down, pulling the occasional water skier and depending on how close the boat came, either a big wave would rock the boat churning up the water scaring the fish or a gentle wave would pass through the boat barely sufficient to disturb the level of a glass of liquid. Yet on this morning, no boats no fish, no waves, just a glassy reflective surface on the water almost good enough to shave in. Out in the middle of the channel of the waterway, both banks a quarter of a mile or so away, both men knew from experience, that if a fish wasn't caught by ten in the morning, the rest of the day would be less than slim picking's indeed. Yet with nothing to do but go home and vegetate, both agreed to stay on the lake or like Pete always joked, "Give Athus a little time to work on his tan"!

As their boat gently drifted down stream Pete said, "Looks like it's gonna be another one of those days Althus", referring to the fact that the fish just weren't biting! "Aw, ya mean where the hound dawgs just ain't gonna hunt"?

"Althus. The god damned dawgs don't hunt in the lake", answered Pete!

"They do if'n their African water dawgs"!

"No such thing as African water dawgs, unless they be sportin' Afro's", Pete chuckled!

"Say, what happened to the music? Stopped right plum in the middle of Stevie Ray"! Just then Pete said, "Never mind the music, what in the Sam Hill is that over there floatin' about fifty yards away"? Althus took a look, rubbed his eyes, then moved to the center of the boat, grabbing the oars and slowly rowed the boat over where Pete was pointing. As the boat closed the distance, the radio suddenly came alive, as the disk jockey announced, "And now a blast from the past, with Louie Prima along with Sam Butera and the witnesses, singing 'Just a Gigolo', on KRON, your pirate rock and roll station on the campus of the beautiful University of Texas, in Austin by gawd Texas. An a big shout out to Althus right in the middle of Lake Travis. I got news for you. No fish today"!

With Altus rowing and Pete at the stern moving the rudder, both men looked at each other in amazement as Altus's name was mentioned on the radio, with Altus removing the oars from the water and the boat slowly drifted closer to what appeared to be the severed heads of two dread locked men staring blindly at the sun, as the radio played the opening rapid fire piano introduction as Louie Prima belted out, "I'm just a gigolo and everywhere I go",................

As the boat progressed drifting near, so did the music as each man discerned that what floated before them not five yards away, was the dread locked head of a Negro and the dread locked head of an Albino with Negroid features, gently bobbing up and down in the water. As the boat drifted closer to the bobbing heads, Louie Prima sang the refrain "Cause, Ayeeee ain't got got no bahhhhdie! No body care for me, nobody cares for me. Ahhhm so sad and lonely, wouldn't somebody please care for me cause Ah ain't so bad"! As the refrain commenced both heads eyes flew open staring at Pete and Athus causing both to rear back and scream in horror, each almost capsizing the boat. Then Althus grabbed the oars as Pete grabbed the rudder and rowed for all they were worth back to the docks, leaving both of their expensive fishing rods trailing behind them in the water.

Once they had put some considerable distance between them and the floating heads, the song ended as Pete said, "Althus, slow down you working' on a heart attack, you don't pace yourself"!

"You wanna row cracker, then step right up", puffed Althus! "We see'd an heard the same damn thing together and Ah'm grabbin' hat and makin' tracks back to dry land. Jus you hold that rudder straight. Doan wanna be rowin' in circles"!

Eventually reaching the boat dock, Pete got out and secured the boat, while Althus just Sat at the oars a few minutes catching his breath.

"We gotta call the High Sheriff", wheezed Althus, his face looking haggard and worn"!

"You thinking what I'm thinking", asked Pete?

"Cracker, ah know you since we was kids an not one time could I ever figure you out. So why do ya think I can now"?

"I was thinking that those two heads might have sumpthin' to do with all that mess up the San Saba river we been hearin' about"!

"Ya think? Of course it has everythin' to do with those nappy headed Voodoo gangster's we been hearin' about. Here, help an old man up outta this boat, I'm almost done in from all dat oar pullin'", as he creakily got out of the boat. "We go on up to da boat house an call the High Sheriff an I'll tell ya all about it"! As they sat down on an old wooden bench, Althus gathered himself up and started, "When the slaves got brought over the waters and sold to whoever, they brings with them da old African gods, for dats all dey know. Now as they get sold a lotta the owners long ago they be Spanish and Catholic. So ovah time a blending of the religions come in and we gots Voodoo, or what lotza folk call 'Santeria. This new religion that come up be a little bit Catholic and a whole lotta da ole West African stuff. Bad Juju stuff, cause instead a prayin' to the God above, they be prayin' to a whole lotta gods down below an specially to da Baron"!

"Who's the Baron", asked Pete?

"The Mutha Fuckin' Baron. Baron Samedie. The head mutha fuckin' Hoo Doo witchdoctor god, that's who"!

"Witch Doctor? What're ya talking about? Sounds like a lotta bunk and superstition to me"!

"You saw the eyes of those two fly open as we come up on em. You heard the song come outta da radio, on a station that nevah play dat kinda music. You evah see the eyes of a cut off head fly open? You evah see a cut off head float. Yo was just as much scared as I was. We gotta go call the law"!

Walking uneasily into the boat masters shack, Althus said, "Harold, lemme at your telephone"!

"Whats got you so riled", asked Harold?

"Just give him the phone so he can call 911, then listen up and you'll find out soon enough", said Pete! Minutes later when he hung up Althus said smiling. The Sheriff's department' is sending a patrol car our way as well as a few boats from the lake boat patrol and a helicopter with pontoons so it can land on the lake. "When I talked to one of the officers on the phone he told me that two of the bodies recovered in the San Saba upstream were without heads. So these must be the heads that we found"!

Althus then went to the soft drink machine, bought three Cokes, set them down and began to hand roll himself a cigarette"!

"State don't allow no smoking' in heah", said Harold!

"After what we been through, the State can shit and fall back in it far as I'm concerned"!

Sitting down on the nearby bench, the hand rolled smoke in his fingers and the soft drink in the other, he sat and blankly looked down at the floor mumbling, "Two nappy headed Nigra heads, just floatin' in the water as easy as you please, while Louie Prima singin' ovah the radio, Ah ain't got no body"! Then he looked straight at the boat dock proprietor saying, "Then the eyes open up all of a sudden an look straight at ya. Now Harold, wouldn't ya say that some kinda shit out there on your lake"? A half hour later a County patrol car rolled up to the Marina and the Deputy came upon the trio waiting outside for him. He commandeered one of the small boats with a motor taking Althus and Pete back with him out onto the lake to relocate the two floating heads and await the arrival of the others. While the boat was on its way he said, "Looks like you two came across something significant. In case you're wondering why the fishing has gone south, I'd suggest you both get your fish somewhere else for the time being for there's a lotta dead fish headin' this way, from the San Saba upstream. The State has boats out tryin' to scoop up as many of the dead fish as they can find, but there's just too many of em, floating into the Colorado and then into Lake Travis. Something about the waters sudden acidity or alkalinity"!

Minutes later they spotted both heads floating face up in the water as if getting their daily dose of sun, eyes closed, as the boat slowed to trolling speed, circling around the heads. Then behind them they heard the klaxons of two of the Lake Patrol boats as they approached in the distance from opposite directions, followed in the distance by a helicopter with pontoons with the markings of the Texas Rangers approaching from the south, followed by yet another helicopter, with the markings of one of Austin's TV Stations. As the boats formed a cordon around the two heads, they made room for the Rangers chopper than landed gently in the water shutting off its engines, all within a thirty yard radius of the floating heads. Suddenly a signal was given to all of the boats to shut down their engines.

As all went quiet on the lake save for the sound distant humming sound of the TV Station chopper some five hundred feet overhead.

Just then one of the Texas Rangers in the Lake Patrol boat said, "Where is that music coming from? Somebody turn off that radio", he yelled!

"Sir", said the boats driver. "Everything is off. Engines, radio's, all electronics. Everything"!

"If that's the case, somebody approach the subjects floating in the water for retrieval"!

Then the Ranger got on the loudspeaker and said, "You there, in the small boat, go over to the floating heads and retrieve them and bring them to the Ranger helicopter, since you're the closest"!

The Sheriffs Deputy commanding the small boat that contained Pete and Althus gave the outboard engine a yank and the engine started up as Althus and Pete looked back in horror. Althus yelled, "Don't you do it god dammit, don't you do it", But it was too late as the idling small boat slowly trolled ever closer to the two floating heads.

'Where's the music coming from", asked the Deputy as Altus and Pete had no idea? Their radio left ashore in the other boat. Now as the boat slowly came up beside the floating heads, video cameras were now rolling from the two Lake Patrol boats as well as the Ranger chopper, as well as the telephoto camera in the TV chopper overhead. The piano introduction was repeating over and over as from out of nowhere everyone heard, Louie Prima sing the staccato opening verse then as the Deputy reached down to grab each head by its dread locks, from the small boats stern, with the other two crouched together at the bow, the heads were lifted from the water, as their eyes once again flew open, staring at the Deputy as he held them up in front of him, the voice sang, "Cause, Ayeeeeeee ain't got nobodieee"! Then as if shot in the chest, the deputy recoiled, throwing the heads back into the water with such force, his inertia carried him over the gunwales and into the water on the starboard side of the craft. As the heads and the Deputy hit the water simultaneously, the music and vocals stopped in an instant, with the only sounds heard were that of the outboard engine idling, Pete and Althus screaming along with the Deputy in the water, being quickly dragged underwater as his boots quickly filled with water. From the two Lake Patrol boats a half dozen men quickly jumped in the water swimming to the Deputy to save him from an untimely death, while the rest swam to retrieve the floating heads. As two pairs of hands again reached for the locks of the Rasta's, the eyes flew open and the music resumed, as Louie continued his eternal plea, "Cause, Ayeeeeee ain't got no bodieee", ending with the same result as each swimmer dropped the head, causing the music to stop as soon as the heads hit the water again.

This time one of the other Patrol boats came along side, with a hand held fishing net swiftly grabbing each head in turn out of the water, amidst of yet another return of the music and throwing it in a metal locker built into the boat. As the Albino's head joined Hoo Doo Chile's in the locker the lid slammed shut and the music finally stopped. As the lid slammed shut, everyone looked around to see Althus and Pete, now speeding away from the scene and back to the Marina, as fast as the five horsepower outboard engine could carry the boat.

In the TV helicopter overhead, Faith Marchand looked through the telephoto lens at the goings on below her as she said to her producer, do we have it all on tape"?

"Down and dirty Faith, still rolling so what's next since the two heads are retrieved"!

"Follow those two old guys to the Marina. They're the ones who initially came across the floating heads. I suspect there's a back story there and I want to make them famous"!

Two hours later, Faith Marchand and her chopper crew took off from the Marina after interviewing Pete and Althus, gently seducing every choice morsel of information out of them, as the two old goats eagerly sang at the sight of a world class 'Morsel' smiling at them and weaving her magic, milking a story from the men eager and willing to share. As her helicopter gained altitude, the pontoons on the Texas Rangers chopper touched ground as several Rangers approached Pete and Althus as they watched Faith Marchand disappear.

Later that evening Faith Marchand finished the sign off at the studio, for her exclusive report to be aired several days later in evening prime time in stations all over Texas. While she worked, her agent was busily working deals to eventually sell the hour long report to CBS or NBC whoever came up with the gold and an intro into nationwide telecasting.

"As a journalist and member of the news media, we are required to be objective and factual in our reporting of events. But whatever is happening before our very eyes and ears defies rational explanation. So I'll just stand by and allow our cameras to be your eyes and ears, so you can sort out for yourselves the inexplicable"!

The camera rolled tape as the events in the water unfolded, with but a brief insertion of Faith Marchand whispering in the background, "We bring you this tape as it was shot, completely unedited and warn you that the audio and visual images might be disturbing to the senses"!

When the events on the lake concluded, she then focused her presentation on her interview with Pete and Althus, the two retired fishermen who originally discovered the floating heads. At the conclusion of that interview, the camera came back to rest on the beautifully bewildered face of Faith Marchand in her studio setting as she addressed the conclusion of her presentation to the audience. "I can't explain the inexplicable and have no interest in even trying. I'll let wiser heads than mine try and wrap their minds around recent Events, except to report the floating heads were confirmed by authorities to belong to the recovered bodies of those involved in the events reported in Menard County several days earlier and also regarding the suspected injected substance that is working its way into the waters of Lake Travis and just may possibly effect the City of Austin"!

"This is a confused Faith Marchand reporting from Austin Texas"!

35

Jaeger hadn't been to Ballys for his workout in quite a while. His wound was long healed the enemies at the gates, now seemingly only a memory had been disbursed. His recent exploits had proven very fruitful to such a degree that his goal of restoration was now able to come in view once again. He'd much to give thanks for and also to regret. Yet as his mother always told him, "The almighty set only the way forward to those who will but see"! It's up to the individual to assess the risk and make it happen. When he reflected upon his life, the reasons for his life's path still eluded him. The only rational sense of it was that he was but a blunt instrument, guided along by the unseen. The unseen and completely irrational manner in which his family had been obliterated by the forces of darkness made no sense at all. And yet when he looked back in the mists of time, did not his ancestor, Heinrich Jaeger travel the same path? What hath been taken had been restored many fold. The long, dark ride was not yet concluded. The pathway led down many a dark corridor and with one fleeting exception, he couldn't recall a time when he'd been happy or fulfilled, except an all too brief time. But why should he bitch, he was still alive and breathing whereas others were not. Further most people in the world were mere cannon fodder, hoping against hope for a better day, with without the will or resources to accomplish.

"Never Complain, Never Explain"! He'd learned that hard lesson from his father early on. Take the hits and keep moving and that he did. Scylla was taken care of, as well as Buffy, Magellan, Rae and Duke Vultee and especially Mel and her son. When he allowed himself to think of it, he'd been involved in some rather interesting adventures as of late. His time in the Corps especially the ending, a singular football game with a painful ending, the death of his family, his time in prison and the revenge that followed. Recently the Sao Paolo incident, then the elimination of Ortega and Carlos Meyers plus all that went with it. The prevention of any dispersion of Crystalline in America and possibly beyond and finally a world class series of simultaneous bank heists that had the authorities running around in circles, chasing their tails. All accomplished in a time compression. Ah, what a story. But a tale that must lay dormant. He had his memories, just as Henry Jaeger had his long ago.

Perhaps he could allow himself a vacation. Time to recreate. Perhaps later. As he turned his car into Ballys parking lot late on a Friday afternoon, he had nothing on his mind other than say hello to big Randy the manager. It had been a long time and he was feeling puny. Well a few weeks pressing iron should bring things back into balance.

As he entered Ballys facility to check in, a long bank of TV monitors in front of a line of treadmills half filled with the Tele Tubbies working off the accumulated table muscle, telecasted an assortment of local as well as sports cable channels, for those before it. Of course with all of the noise background of the gym, the audio was muted with the audio text flashing by in real time subtitles, somewhat in synch with the visual display.

One of the monitors caught Jaegers eye as he stopped to watch. The sight of Faith Marchand, the 'Enfant Terrible', of Texan newscasters, dressed to the nines, giving a brief intro to her hour long report of the recent events along the upper reaches of the San Saba and their burgeoning effect on Lake Travis and possibly on the State Capitol in Austin, to air later on, at nine in the evening. On another local channel was a news update on the dual disasters in the Galleria uptown area as well as the string of bank robberies on the western side of town. Apparently someone suspected of being an inside informant for the Security Company responsible for the cash deliveries, was found dead of apparent natural causes. A promising lead for the authorities now just another dead end. Walking into the locker room to change, Jaeger had kept up with the ongoing developments and one by one those fished out of the San Saba, were eventually identified. The authorities had the 'Who', pretty much in the bag, as well as the 'How', but the 'Why' was still elusive. Of those who knew the 'Why' only three remained and it was in the best interests of all three they remain silent. Climbing the stairs to access the mezzanine jogging track he saw big Randy at the top of the stairs. A mountain of a man as he called out, "Jaeger, you old sumbitch where in the world have you been", as they both embraced?

"Oh just doin' all the good I can and shunnin' all the evil I know! So how's business, sport"!

"Business is good, but the same as always with the pencil necks at corporate nosing around and the people with all the excess flooding in every January with good intentions, only to have them fade by the end of March. But as long as they pay their contracted dues, what do I care. Hey since you're here, why don't we work out together? In a half an hour I'm off the clock and since you disappeared I haven't had a decent spotter"!

"Sounds like a plan Randy. I'll be doin' my laps around the track. Holler when you free up"! As he made his way around the track, it felt good getting back into his old routine and seeing familiar faces as he nodded his head and said hello to the acquaintances, he'd not seen in quite a while. During his absence not much had apparently changed. There were those trying to get into some semblance of shape, those serious about their shape, those who were to fall by the wayside sooner or later, the older crowd just doing what they could to clear the arteries, then there were those who were just there to make the next connection, scanning the crowd, making their selections, then moving in for the kill. Cheaper and healthier somewhat, rather than hanging out at bars. This is why the predators always hung around the places of gathering.

As the laps rolled by, thoughts of Melanie rolled by once again. He thought about their brief relationship, concluding the right path had been taken. She deserved better than he could presently offer and now could have the wherewithal to be on her own, make the right choices, not out of necessity, but out of reason and logic. She would be fine. As he passed by one of the TV monitors, he saw on one of the local channels the words crawl by that, this evening was the night of the harvest moon when the full moon was at its zenith. After his twentieth lap, he wiped the sweat from his brow and headed for the free weight section. After ten minutes or so, he was joined by Randy whose workout regime was not dissimilar from Jaegers with the exception of a lot more plates on the bar. The man consumed around ten thousand calories each and every day, with no visible table muscle on his six foot, seven inch frame sporting a shade more than three hundred pounds.

Both men had worked out with each other long enough to know each other's capacity, without asking, as Randy settled in under a heavily laden bar full of iron 45 pound plates. As Jaeger moved behind Randy to spot, he simply said, "Eight", as Randy nodded grasping the bar, with heavily chalked hands holding slightly in excess of 450 pounds of iron, moving the load off its rest, with a massive grunt as it lowered towards his chest, then with a lout shout exhaling air from his lungs, pressing the slightly sagging bar upwards, then back down grabbing a lung full of air, then another exhalation of air as the bar rose upward. As the bar came down from its seventh repetition, Jaeger moved closer to the bar, as Randy by now, his entire body straining, emitted a loud and long bellow that drew everyone's attention upstairs with his entire body straining to conquer gravity for an eighth and final time, Jaeger hands at the ready as Randy's entire body was shaking from the effort as the bar barely rocked into its resting place as Randy leapt from the bench into the air yelling, "Now that's what I'm talkin' about"!

Then amidst a small round of applause from the crowd that had gathered for the mini floor show, Randy quickly moved around the bar removing plates to the more reasonable weight of 300 lbs., in the range Jaeger usually operated in, as he said to the crowd starting to disburse, "This is what can be done if you're dedicated"! Then he looked at Jaeger saying, "Three about right pal"!

"That was awhile back. Let's go with three and hope I'm not embarrassed", as Jaeger chalked his hands and settled under the bar, stoking in as much air as his lungs could process before commencing. In the crowd out of Jaegers line of sight, was someone of significant size that fit in between Jaegers and Randy's girth. Someone very interested in Jaeger. Assessing his size and strength, wondering whether or not this was the time to make his play. Of course he had help close at hand, with several other followers of his all recently released from the Corcoran Unit of the Texas Department of Corrections. While not as massive as their leader, all had invested their time out in the yard pumping iron, as each individual was festooned with tattoo's, representative of their status while as a compelled guest of the State. With the others on the other side of the mezzanine working on the machines, he watched with keen interest, as he had scores of others in the yard, assessing their level of strength before making the go, no go, decision to advance his rep. Now out in civilized society, it made no difference to him for the lessons learned while in custody were those that stayed with one for the remainder, as far as he was concerned. Fifteen years for manslaughter, was but a small price to pay for an intentional slight by another in a bar long ago and here was a gift laid before him for the death of his brother in a prison riot while incarcerated at the Ellis Unit. His brother's name was Elsasser! Word was that Jaeger had bested him in a closet fight. After that he was never quite the same. The details didn't matter, just that of opportunity. The smuggled snapshot of Jaeger made its way from the Ellis unit to the Corcoran Unit, the age old way contraband always travels through stone walls. By way of the prison staff. He had plenty of time to memorize each aspect of Jaeger, for the time they would meet and the time was at hand.

As Jaeger struggled to press upward his bar for the fifth time, the sweat was jumping out of his pores, his chest heaving, his muscles right at their limit, as Randy loomed large behind Jaeger yelling at him to press just once more. As the bar struggled to find the halfway mark upward, Randy placed his massive hands under the bar giving it just the slight additional help to drive it one last time to its resting place as the veins in Jaegers head bulged to the limit, with Jaeger giving out a shout as the bar clanged to its rest.

"Jeeze buddy", said Randy. "Good that you got back here when you did. Lost just a little during your vacation. But a few months from now you'll be good as before"! They continued on with the barbells, with sets of French Curls, Chest flies, before going back to the seated Incline Bench Press's. While they were engaged, Hassan Elsasser went back to the others and joined them outlining his plans for the coming hour. "Jeezus Hassan. We just been out a month. We pull a few deals, make some money. We just startin' to get on our feet and now this. How much this gonna pay"? "Ain't gonna pay a damn thing. Cept mebbe your dues for bein' with me. I gotta score to settle with that guy what fucked with my brother. Now you either with me or your out right now. What's it gonna be"? They all nodded their heads as Hassan said, "Good. Now Rooster, you go downstairs and clean out the lockers and take everyone's stuff to the car and have it ready for splitsville, just in case. You see us runnin' out you be ready to pick us up on the fly. The rest of you keep to your workouts, but keep an eye on me, so's when I get ready to make my play, y'all back me up. I mean to bust that fucker up but good. For the rest of his life, every time he moves, it's gonna hurt"!

It was a quarter till six in the evening and the after work crowd was just starting to arrive. The public address system came alive interrupting the music that was hard to hear anyway, "Randy, phone call on line three. Randy, phone call on line three", came the message!

"Aw crap. Probably the boss on the line checking up on the in the door traffic count. Be back in a few", he said as he rose to go downstairs! As Jaeger continued with his seated curls, a large overly tatted well-built man took a seat next to him placing his small gym towel over the back rest of the seated incline bench. Jaeger gave him scant notice as he continued with his slow repetitions, looking into the wall of mirrors placed to give the adherents a visual look at their technique, as he curled each of the fifty pound dumbbell's slowly over and over towards completion. Then he rose up and went to the water fountain as he rested between sets. As he returned to his seat, something drew his eyes towards a group of three other heavily tattooed men standing around close by, trying not to pay any attention to Jaeger, but being bad actors at their craft. Something eerily familiar in his past came back to his conscious mind. Something he'd seen all too often back in his time at the Ellis Unit. Gang bangers. But why the interest with him? It had been years since his release? One Black and two Mexican's comprised the group, with little apparent interest in working out just appearing to be talking amongst themselves. Then his thoughts drifted back to this very same place, months ago when he was confronted by Ortega and his crew, with his mind saying, 'Oh Christ, not again'! It was then that six large letters flashed in front of his mind, remnants of his days in the Corps. 'BOHICA, aka, Bend Over Here It Comes Again'.

Even in Gymnasiums a certain etiquette exists, between people and one of the unwritten rules are that one should never block the visuals of another when the other is engaged in their routine. Breaks one's concentration. Yet it happens from time to time amongst those unfamiliar with the rules without incident. Yet when someone who should know better crosses the line intentionally, it cannot pass without comment. As Jaeger began his next set of arm curls, the large man next to him got up and replaced his dumbbells back in the long rack in front of the both of them then stopped in front of Jaeger, his back to him as he seemed to ponder what to select next.

Jaeger stopped after a few reps and waited for the man to move on. After a few minutes he selected two other dumbbells and returned to his seat next to Jaeger, while Jaeger completed his set and went back to the water fountain, more as a ploy rather than thirst to assess the lay of the land. As he slowly walked back for his final set, it became clear to him, the guy next to him was the stalking horse, while the other three were set to move in quickly. This was the hand he had to play. He could but only let things pay out as the hand was dealt. As he sat down to start his final set, the man next to him, once again rose up and took a position right in front of him, thus blocking his visuals. Clearly a goad to action.

"You don't want to do that again", growled Jaeger clearly allowing his irritation to show in his voice! "You talkin' to me", said the other as he turned squarely facing Jaeger with a look of utter contempt in his face. Jaeger rose up calculating the arms span distance between the two taking a large step backwards and to the side thus keeping the hovering trio in view as he replied, "I'm talkin' to you pal"!

"You don't know who I am, do ya? Or else you wouldn't be givin' me the sass, I'm hearin'"!

"Nope, haven't a clue as to who you are and don't much care, except enough to know the look and smell of the TDC is still on you. One thing more, if your friends over there move an inch, none of you are gonna like what comes next"!

"Then you better know who I am Jaeger! I'm Hassan Elsasser! That's right, now do ya see the resemblance. You killed my brother while in the Ellis Unit"!

Jaeger smiled at the revelation as he said, "Now that you mention it I do see a vague resemblance. Must be a younger brother, for the other one was much larger. Since its truth you're after, best you know that your brother was killed in a yard riot at the Ellis Unit. Saw him die not thirty yards in front of me, with two other convicts holding knives in his innards carving him while he broke their necks holding each in the air aloft. They all went out together as he was looking straight at me. I suppose to let me know that he was the better man checking out the way he did like a warrior, without a bit of help from me. Now what is true is that I made him eat his tongue in a closet fight he picked. Somehow he was never quite the same after that. Even the prison bunnies could breathe a sigh of relief, after I finished him. One other thing sport. I saved his life the night we tangled. I could've let him choke on his own vomit, but I didn't. So what's the play pal? You gonna talk me to death"?

"I swore if I ever ran across you I'd be the one what put a hurt on you and here we are. You're a gift from Allah"!

"A white cracker converted to the Woggies in prison? Now ain't that a hoot"! Just as Randy reached the top stair of the mezzanine, he could see Jaeger having a serious confab with a heavily tatted man of larger build, with three others heavily tatted ready to roll as he made quick strides to jump in the middle to prevent the 'Man Dance'. Just as he reached the three knocking them to the ground, he saw the other guy facing Jaeger suddenly lunge, closing the distance between them. He didn't see Jaeger neatly avoid the charge, clipping the guy neatly across the eyebrow causing his eye to swell suddenly as he rolled across the floor struggling to get up while Jaeger stood there ready for what came next. Just then Randy loomed large in front of Jaegers assailant bellowing, "You want some of him sport, then try and get by me first. Now all of you are going to leave immediately and take whatever you got hangin' outside"!

"Including me", asked Jaeger!

"No, not you", bellowed Randy! "Good, said Jaeger stepping forward. "For my converted friend here seems to have a score to settle and he must have that chance. So if you'll allow me to complete my work out and give me oh about a half hour, we can continue this dance outside as Randy suggests. Feel free to wait for me in front of that big shiny, red colored, Ferrari parked right in front of 'Clicks' Pool Hall, and I'll be there after I'm done. I'm certain I can ask Randy not to call the police to interrupt our fun. Just one thing though. The car is brand new and I'd be very unhappy if as much as a scratch appeared anywhere on it. We agreed"!

Elsasser nodded saying, "See ya outside later Jaeger", turning quickly and gathering the others who after experiencing Randy wanted nothing to do with him as they trotted down the stairs and out into the parking lot.

As Jaeger and Randy stood at the top of the stairs looking at Jaegers antagonists leave, Randy said, "You still drivin' that old Ford go fast"?

"Yup. Wouldn't get rid of it for almost anything and then not even that. Lotta history between us"!

"Then what's all that stuff about a brand new red Ferrari. The owner of 'Clicks' is the one who bought that car about a few weeks ago"!

"Came upon me as a sudden inspiration to buy some time. Last night after you guys were closed I dropped into Clicks for a few drinks and a few friendly games of eight ball. Ran across your friend the owner who had to show me what a fine set of Italian horses he recently bought. Now as we talked, it became clear to me that you and he were still not on speaking terms with each other and that he was still the same old son of a bitch you've learned to embrace. The car was there when I arrived and as you can plainly see the car is still parked right in front of his entrance"!

As Jaeger spoke, Randy's eyes opened wide as he waited for the dots to connect, as Jaeger continued, "Now I met Elsassers brother long ago. The guy was almost as big as you, we tangled I won. He died later for other reasons nothing to do with me. Now this guy wasn't very smart and I'm counting on that fact that it's an inherited trait. I planted a thought that the Red Ferrari was mine and I'm hoping he bites. Now we know what a pain the owner is. I'm not in any great hurry to go outside so", at that point Randy interrupted to complete Jaegers thought saying, "So, you're gonna take your sweet time, pissing the guy off hoping that he'll key the car or something worse. The bastard at 'Click's 'calls the cops and we know there's a unit not a minute away writing tickets, who'll get here quick and do our work for us, arresting the whole crew"!

"With any luck that's the way things'll go down"!

"What if they don't take the bait"!

"These guys just ain't long on patience Randy"!

As they stood overlooking the parking lot, they could see that the three acolytes were now four along with Elsasser all changing into their civilian clothes in the far corner of the parking lot, by a single car.

"The last thing I need since business is going good is to have something go down involving the police and connecting it with Ballys. The guys at corporate would go ballistic", said Randy absently.

"Which is why we want this to be your neighbors problem isn't it", said Jaeger. "By the way, you might want to unlock the rear fire exit just in case I have to Didi out of here Mo Hinky Dink"!

One final set and both men went downstairs to the locker room, showered, went in the steam room for twenty minutes, then out into the large whirlpool in order to take the kinks out of their muscles, allowing the swirling heated waters to soothe away the physical stress recently experienced.

As Hassan Elsasser paced slowly back and forth in front of 'Clicks' Billiard parlor, he thought of his confrontation with Jaeger inside Ballys.

He kept close watch of his faux Rolex on his wrist, as his boys ducked into the fast food place across the parking lot for a quick bite. So far they were all with him and now, there'd be no Man Dance but an execution.

He thought of all of the years in prison wasted on a bad move, killing a drunk in a bar fight and spending time in prison. His conversion to Islam while in Corcoran was a god send, providing him a pathway he'd never known. The pathway to his own personal sworn oath to his brother to avenge his death was non-negotiable. On this evening Jaeger would die.

Once again he checked his watch becoming increasingly frustrated with the slow passage of time. All he could see was the look on Jaegers face as he lay dying riddled with bullets, as he whispered to himself, 'It's been forty minutes now and that cock sucker is takin' his sweet time comin' out. Gonna kick in his ribs then put a bullet in his head for insultin' me', he thought.

Just then one of his boys came up to him seeing his increasing agitation saying, "Hassan chill out. He ain't gonna get away. We got Roscoe covering the back across the street in case he try an scoot out the back. All of us got Mac-10's wid full clips. We got our bellies full an we can wait him out. If ya want I can call over a few more home boys who'll come runnin' just for the sport, you give the word. We got the firepower an all he got is himself"!

"No Rooster, we don't need anyone else. Go back to your spot an wait for him to come out. Remember we hear shootin' on Tidwell, we go back and help Roscoe. He hears shootin' from here; he comes quick to the parkin' lot. Now git"! Watching Rooster go back to his position to wait, Hassan resumed his slow pacing, back and forth along the entire front of the pool hall.

Inside of 'Clicks', one of the early evening waitresses' noticed a large man pacing in front of the establishment. Since 'Click's' was a upscale establishment, serving a moderate clientele', the man fronting the establishment and walking around the Boss's brand new red play toy, spelled trouble in big letters. Her first thoughts were that he'd scare away any casual after work customers. Customers meant business and that meant tips, to pay her bills. Anything that interrupted, the flow of business was bad. In addition, her Boss had a hair trigger temper and should any little happen to his new red Ferrari, there'd be hell to pay for everyone for week to come. After she served several more patrons all the while, keeping an eye out front, her concern got the better of her and she walked to the back of the pool hall and knocked on her Boss's office door. "Yeah", came the bellowing sound from within!

She opened the door two feet, stuck her head inside and said, "Sorry, to bother you Boss, but there's this great big scary looking' guy outside pacing back and forth and all around your car an I seen him sit on your hood from time to time. Plus I don't know but he might have a gun on him"!

Angry that he was interrupted in getting together his payroll timesheets for his accountant and even angrier that someone was messing with his brand new Ferrari, he turned on his outside security cameras, that scanned the entire parking lot and the entire premises, front, sides and rear, focusing all three cameras on the front, as he pressed the 'Record' button and sure enough there he was. A very large man walking around his red Ferrari, giving it the once over, looking very agitated for some unknown reason. He searched his memory as to if this behemoth was someone he'd recognized from his sordid past, coming up a blank. Then he saw something front monitor that made his blood boil, as the man out front started to kick large dents in his brand new Ferrari as he walked around the car smashing the headlights, ripping off the side mirrors, smashing the tail lights and kicking in the windows.

The owner screeched at the top of his lungs, reaching into his desk drawer and removed an old 1911 Colt.45 Automatic, checking the load as he jumped up, squeezing his overly large frame around his desk as he yelled at the waitress. "Go to the bar and call 911 and tell them there's a robbery in progress, then have Frank at the bar come out with that sawed off scatter gun to back me up"!

As he burst forth into the main hall, he could see the man outside still trashing his brand new car, as he made no pretense to hide his weapon, running through the happy hour gathering yelling, "Gangway. Get the fuck outta the way", now holding his gun aloft as he approached the entrance doors. As he burst through the front glass doors, knocking down two of his patrons in the process, he held his gun low and out of sight as he yelled, "What the fuck you think you're doing to my brand new car"?

Hassan stopped his assault on the Ferrari momentarily hearing the yelling behind him, as he quickly turned, pulling the snub nosed Smith & Wesson .44 revolved from his trouser waist band, behind him.

While everything moved rapidly, it seemed to move in slow motion, as 'Click's' owner saw the man thirty feet in front of him whirl around bringing a gun to bear as he swiftly brought his Colt to bear on the large frame in front of him, both triggers being pulled simultaneously, the barrels bucking hard and both rounds passing each other with an inch to spare, each finding their mark. Yet the 'Click's' owner squeezed the trigger twice in rapid succession, known as the 'double tap', where Hassan only pulled the trigger once. As Hassan's round found its mark high up in his targets chest, knocking him back against the front wall the owner's second round left the barrel. The first, hitting low breaking one of Hassan's ribs, while the second, follow on round, hit him in the shoulder spinning him around as he lost his footing, hitting the ground.

Seeing the initial bursts of gunfire, Rooster rose up from between parked cars some forty yards away, firing off several quick bursts from his Mac-10 after he saw Hassan hit the deck, none of which found a home save for some broken plate glass widows in front of 'Click's'. Then seeing Hassan struggle to rise, he fired a short burst towards someone coming through the front doors of 'Click's'.

Frank, the bartender, was charging through the front door, firing his short barreled scatter gun at the large man who shot his boss, in which part of the double ought buckshot's initial round, found its mark causing Hassan to hit the ground once again, while the second shot fired wildly over him finding a home in several of the vehicles nearby, because of his avoidance of Rooster's Mac-10 bursts. As Frank quickly scrambled away behind some nearby cars, he saw his boss struggling to rise and aim at Hassan, firing off a round wildly, then another in the direction of the advancing Rooster.

From far away across the parking lot some hundred yards away, Rufe was not about to be left out of the melee, as he advanced on a dead run, firing a few mini bursts, from his Mac to let everyone know he was coming.

Across the boulevard behind Ballys stood Roscoe, his Mac underneath his coat as he heard the first semi muted rounds being fired from across the street. He waited until he heard the third volley of rounds being fired, before pulling out his Mac from underneath his jacket and dodging rush hour traffic, running across the first two lanes, then the esplanade, then eluding traffic as he crossed the remainder, bringing two cars to a screeching halt by pointing his weapon and firing a quick burst into the air as he scampered across the grass and around the Balls facility to join the fray.

Traveling east behind Balls, moving slowly with the traffic, Officer Terry Moran, heard the first reports of a 'robbery in progress', broadcast on his radio as the light flashed in his head the location was just around the corner. Then five cars in front of him he saw someone illegally running across the streets, then stopping in front some moving cars bringing an automatic weapon to bear and fire a short burst into the air stopping them as he continued to run across the street and in between the buildings. As he flipped the switch, turning on his overhead flashers and siren as he turned his unit up and over the curb, across the freshly mowed grass, around trees and through bushes, to get around the rear of the large facility, as he repeated over and over, "Oh shit, Oh shit". As he crashed through and over the landscaping to respond, he knew two things. 'Time was of the essence and there would be one crap load of paperwork in the after action workup. But all his life, he ran 'To' the sound of gunfire, never 'Away'.

Sergeant Lester Mathews, the floating watch commander of the Houston Police Department Northwest substation was across the street as he was out of sight from the eyes in Ballys parking lot. He'd been supervising for the last hour, a small four car task force, snagging those who ran the red lights at the nearby underpass interchange. He'd just paid for his evening meal at the drive through window of the burger joint, when the first reports of the 'Robbery in Progress' at 'Click's' across the street came over the car radio. He put his unit in gear, leaving the food at the window, and quickly drove off, responding back to the dispatcher to notify the nearby task force units to also respond as backup.

Now as he tried to navigate between his unit across the street during rush hour between the closely packed cars, with his overhead lights flashing, he heard the intermittent staccato sounds of automatic gunfire, with the singularity of unconscious words repeating over and over, 'Ohh, shit…Ohh shit'. . In his nearly twenty years on the force, he'd never had an occasion to discharge his weapon at an assailant in the line of duty. From time to time, he'd make this known to a subordinate when the occasion permitted, with pride. He was very hungry and working a double shift filling in for others and hadn't eaten since breakfast, given the busy plethora of events that unfolded, during this day of the Full Moon. Thanks to the budget cutbacks of the City Government, he was compelled to work a double shift as a Watch Commander, every other week, thus no time for a sit down meal, especially given the recent spate of crime activity, it was grab, chomp and run, but not tonight.

As Sergeant Mathew's unit bounced over the speed bump while entering the Ballys lot, he noticed another unit rounding the corner of a Burger King, lights flashing, siren blaring, as well as the sounds of the other nearby traffic units coming hard. Mathews and Moran dove parallel lines through the parking lot with Moran screeching to a halt jus short of Ballys front entrance, while Mathews came to a halt forty yards away from 'Click's' front entrance. Since both arriving patrol units came immediately under fire as they skidded to a halt, both officers rolled out of their respective vehicles returning fire with their service weapons, keying their shoulder mike's yelling, "Patrolman under fire. Repeat, patrolman under fire"!

No matter where one is in the US, the two things that'll get every cop to come quick and "drop his cock and grab his socks", will be a report of a "Robbery in progress, or a "Patrolman under fire". From the corner of his eye, he could see a few Ballys patrons peering down at the firefight from their mezzanine window view from the jogging track. They quickly faded after a few errant bullets shattered the windows, sending them scurrying. Moran, knowing that help was on the way had his own problems, in dealing with Willie and Roscoe, working to flank him with their auto weapons and he only with his service 9mm Glock. His unit was shredded with bullet holes as he made to position himself behind tires, and peer underneath, as he saw a set of knees crouch down some three cars away and fired off a triple tap, knowing that at least one of them would find a home. It did as Willie went down howling in agony, as two rounds shattered his legs.

Then as he turned his attention to the other, he saw the image of a patron in jogging clothes up in the mezzanine widow gesturing wildly to Moran as to the other circling to gain advantage. He took note, nodded his head and did some counter circling, as he came across Willie trying to rise and shot him twice, grabbing the Mac-10 to even things up.

Mathews, on the other hand had his own problems as his unit also was met by a hail of automatic weapon fire as it too skid to a halt, with Mathews, the reluctant combatant bailing out of the car, while drawing his weapon.

Rooster had taken care of the bartender firing a short burst at him as he finished reloading his scatter gun, the first burst of which flew passed Rooster finding a home in Ballys windows, while several shots grazed his shoulder while a short burst of his Mac-10 made short work of the bartender. The next burst from Rooster took out the fat owner of 'Click's', while he was trading fire with Hassan.

Finally he'd had enough. Mathews took aim with his weapon and began trading fire back at both Rooster and Rufe, as he saw the arrival of two more patrol units arrive at the entrance adjacent to the IHOP restaurant completing the perimeter with more on the way. As they too, bailed out of their vehicles, they in turn were greeted with the staccato sound of the Mac- 10, thus employing their service weapons as they moved forward around and in between the cars sprinkled around the lot. As Rooster rose up for a better view, Mathews fired his weapon repeatedly at him advancing all the way. While the other officers recently arrived poured fire at Rufe downing him eventually as he made his way forward.

Finally as Roscoe tried to enter Ballys and exit through their entrance door, Officer Moran coming up from the side, using the captured Mac-10, traded fire with Roscoe right in front of the entrance. The bullets from Roscoe while knocking him down failed to penetrate his Kevlar vest, while Roscoe wasn't so fortunate, dropping like a stone under the fusillade from Moran.

Hassan by this time had propped himself up against the wall next to the pool halls entrance. His weapon empty, his body riddled with bullets and bleeding out, he stared at Lester Mathews, his gun laid across his lap, legs splayed in front of him. As Mathews advanced towards him pointing his weapon square at Hassan's chest, he caught sight of the huge eight ball over the front entrance, with the Neon script superimposed over the eight ball that read, CLICK'S. Just then the neon came on as Hassan kept pulling the trigger of his empty gun as it repeatedly made the sound, "Click, Click, Click"!

Removing the empty gun from Hassan's hand he saw that Hassan while bleeding out was still alive, as he called out, "This one's still alive. Get an ambulance here, fast"!

Emerging with his gym bag from one of the front doors not blocked by Roosters dead body, Jaeger with Randy following in his wake walked out onto the parking lot as well as a host of other patrons, some eager to depart, while others wandered around to kibitz, only to be shooed away by the gathering army of policemen announcing a crime scene. Randy and Jaeger went to their respective cars and finding no discernable damage, met again in the center of the parking lot as Randy said, "Geeze, look at that damage. I'd better get corporate on the phone to get over here with the claims adjuster. Gonna be here all night. As they wandered towards the front of Click's, both men saw the dead body of Randy's nemesis in front of his newly trashed Ferrari. Then both saw the splayed of form of Hassan, apparently still alive but fading fast as a pool of blood surrounded him.

As Jaeger approached, with Randy looming behind him, Hassan's eyes caught sight of the duo, as Jaeger took two steps forward and stopped. Their eyes met for one final time, As Jaeger knelt down briefly and asked, "You ready for the Dark Ride sport"? Hassan Elsasser nodded his head and breathed his last, his eyes staring emptily at the full moon that was starting to rise in the evening sky.

"Hey you two, this is a crime scene. Move away now if ya know what's good for you", bellowed a cranky Sergeant Mathews, officer in charge of the crime scene, until a higher ranker arrived. As they moved on Jaeger said, "Must be something in the genes, with those guys"!

"Since you solved a few problems for me, while creating another one, why don't you buy me dinner at the IHOP", said Randy!

"Sounds like a plan", mused Jaeger!

36

Jorge Mendaca and his son Oscar took their late evening dinner at the elder Mendaca's seaside compound in Ensenada. Their security guards paced back and forth just above the high tide line a hundred yards away as they consumed their meal. After they'd discussed the latest deal with the Columbians to the elders liking, the subject shifted to the disappearance of Scylla and her brother.

"So what have you discovered as to their disappearance", asked Jorge?

"No one in LA is talking about it. It seems that no one knows, for certain. Rumors of a new synthetic drugs arrival have proven to be unsubstantiated by fact. The only thing that bears any substance is what we are hearing from the media, of murders in West Texas, involving elements of the Crips, the Chicago Italians, some unidentified Orientals and The Jamaican Rastafarian's that Zulu Man has been struggling with for the last several years. All of them were dead and dumped into some small Texan river. What money was involved has disappeared and as far as any Jejo involved, it may have been dumped into the river. End of story father", said Oscar!

"So what are you doing to fill the void up north"!

"We're currently talking to the remnants of the Crips and a few seem to show promise, but nothing concrete as of yet. I'm thinking we should let nature take its course and see who survives the struggle for dominance in greater Los Angeles. What are your views father"?

"Perhaps you are correct son. We are not a social organization. We've tried that recently and while successful for a time, it proved to be a problem in the end. Such is the enterprise we are in"!

"Just one question father"? Jorge Mendaca nodded his head, bidding his son to continue. "Why did we ever bring them into our family in the first place"?

"A well calculated gamble son. If you'll recall they served us well for quite some time and they were there to exploit. Finally, every time one walks past the statue of Scylla in the main entrance, one stops to admire the female form and wonder"!

"Ah yes father. Venus with arms. But one question more, muy permisso. Did you ever personally spend a night with Scylla"?

"I wanted to son. However as we all know, other than her brother, no one has ever spent more than one night with the woman and survived the experience. We have other women for that. Then there is my age to consider. As we've all seen, she's was a woman of considerable endurance and demands, certain to make a pleasurable experience into one of extreme regret"!

"Do you think she survived", asked Oscar?

"The authorities identified the remains of her brother, so my guess is that her remains are somewhere at the bottom of some river or lake. Whether she is alive or not is of no consequence to me or our family business. She is but a useful memory"!

Then Jorge Mendaca picked up his usual after dinner aperitif, a small goblet of very expensive Napoleon Brandy that was said to help his digestion. When finished, Oscar watched as the goblet was put carefully back in its place, drained of its contents. As the elder Mendaca rose from his chair saying, "It's late and I'm going to bed son. Why don't you stay over in one of the bedrooms and we can have breakfast together in the morning"?

"Thank you father, I'd like that", as he rose to embrace his father goodnight, then sat Back down as he watched his father climb the stairs to his bedroom. Oscar lit the Cuban cigar slowly as he contemplated the next changing of the guard. The poison his father consumed would take all night to have its effects, slowly shutting down his heart rate. He would simply go to sleep, without any pain. In the morning there would be much to do after he was discovered. All of the arrangements, with the funeral, the mortician, the church, the mourners to be hired and a suitable gravestone. It must be expensive, ornate and wholly appropriate for a man of such substance.

37

As the Air France jetliner made its way eastward, Nestor Magellan put down his day old copy of Le Figaro and gazed out the window. The flight back to France took a long time and for a moment he'd toyed with the idea of flying back on the Concorde', but the extravagant cost drove him opt for first class passage. Besides, that's what first class was for. Not having to cross paths with the proletariat, being crammed in from toe to hair follicle. Plus since first class was only half occupied, one could not have to worry about being impolite with someone who wanted to chat, while he wanted to think and plan ahead.

He'd successfully deposited his earnings from Jaeger into a long dormant Swiss account that he'd opened some years ago while in Argentina, working for the French Embassy. He thought back to his recent convalescence with Scylla. Somehow she seemed at peace with her recent status in life as a small time show business entrepreneur, half owner of one of Houston's premier Gentlemen's Clubs as well as owning two prime residential real estate sites on opposite sides of the city. Of course, he slept with a fully loaded gun under the pillow each evening just in case she decided to revert back to her old ways. Yet she tended to his wounds, with seemingly great care. One evening when she decided to advance her ardor, he had a decision to make. Listen to his lower regions, or allow common sense to override.

All he had to do was allow his mind to drift back to thoughts of Madeleine and the decision became simple. After he told her an edited version of his time with her and her subsequent death, he could tell it had an effect as she simply rose up from the bed, giving him a chaste kiss on the cheek and walked to the door, turning and saying, "Nestor, how I envy you this moment. At least you have her memory"!

Two days before he left, he visited her at her club, taking in her featured act as an entertainer. She would become the establishment's star performer packing the men in from miles around. After all, she had a vested interest. The day he left, he simply left a note saying "Thank You"!

He'd three things to accomplish before anything else after he landed. First, to visit General St. Nathalie and his wife, asking their permission to visit Madeleine's grave, then make the trip down to visit his mother in Madrid.

Upon landing, he made it through customs entry with no problem, grabbing a cab and driving to a hotel on the Champs de Elyse for a few days. The following morning, he called the General to make an appointment for a luncheon.

Of course, the General was living alone, now in retirement from the military as his wife, Madeleine's mother, has succumbed to a broken heart, as all would have it known after her daughter's death.

While in the Generals garden, they were served lunch by his housekeeper who left them to their own devices. "She sees to the basic needs of the house", said the general, "Courtesy of the government for an old soldier! So tell me Nestor, if you can, what have you been up to after you left the government without so much as a by your leave. What's it been now three or four years since you were in Argentina"!

"Nothing General that I can reveal at the present, perhaps save for one thing. The incident with the Brazilian aircraft manufacturer, I had a peripheral role in sir"!

"Oh, so you had something to do with that eh? What a mess! I'm happy things were resolved the way they were", he said smiling! "But you. What are your plans? Are you back in France for good"?

"Well sir, I'm planning to go and visit my mother in Madrid and see how she's doing. Then upon my return, I'd like it if we both went to visit Madeleine"!

"Her mother is buried nearby in the same cemetery. Of course, I'd be delighted to accompany you upon your return. But after that what are your plans"?

"I'd like to start a business, utilizing my experience. I've some funds to invest and perhaps you could point me in the right direction sir"!

"Tomorrow I have to catch a train to Munich. I've got a speech to deliver for a NATO conference. I'll be gone a few days. Upon your return from Madrid, ring me up and we'll pay our respects to the women in our lives"!

The following day he took the train to Madrid, checking into a moderate hotel and the following morning rang up the Cardinals residence for an appointment. He was about to be rebuffed by the Cardinals secretary given the heavy schedule the Cardinal had until he mentioned the name, Appolonia Vega. The secretary paused a moment then said, "Can you be here at ten sharp tomorrow morning? Do that Senor Doziel and I'll see what I can do"!

The following morning, Vermiel Doziel made an appearance at the Chancellery and stood before the Cardinals Secretary saying, "Pedro isn't it? We talked yesterday regarding Appolonia Vega"!

"Ah yes, Mr. Doziel! Yes, I recall. If you'll have a seat, I'll just duck in a moment and see if his eminence is finishing up with his current appointment. Muy permisso", he said arising and disappearing behind the massive old doors to his office. A few minutes later the doors opened again and five men attired in business suits hurried out, as the Cardinals Secretary said, "His eminence will see you now. But he only has five minutes to spare, before he has to be elsewhere for a conference"!

As he escorted Magellan inside he announced, "Your eminence, Senor Doziel as we've discussed"!

"Thank you Pedro. Mister Doziel please come in", said the Cardinal arising and coming around his desk to be greeted. "It's been quite a while since we've seen you last"!

As Magellan genuflected, kissing the proffered ring he rose to his full height and said, "I thank you, your eminence for making a few moments so I can inquire about Senora Vega"!

"Please my son, join me as we may sit down for I've news for you"! As they both took two chairs adjoining, the Cardinal said, "I'm sorry to say, the Lord has taken the good Senora into his bosom last year. She died quietly in her sleep. Of course her passing was a great sorrow to us all, for she was greatly loved and admired, always thinking of others and never of herself. We have seen to it that she was buried next to her husband, in the midst of a small copse of trees you visited last. All of the blessings and sanctities of holy mother church were afforded to her upon her demise"!

Nestor fought back the tears as he heard the news from the prelate, as the Cardinal rose up offering his ring, as Magellan joined him genuflecting once again kissing the ring, as he said, "Thank you, your eminence. May I pay my respects to them now"?

"Of course my son. Here I shall walk with you part way while you spend your time with your parents"! When they arrived at their point of departure, with the Cardinals secretary close at hand, the Cardinal said, "You may feel free to visit them any time you wish, with or without announcement. Further, should you ever desire to visit me and I hope you do, let us bury this canard of Mister Doziel and arrive as you are, Carlos Vega. Your secret goes to the grave with not only me but Pedro. Are we agreed? Now I must depart and you go with God's blessing"! Magellan stood there following the duo with his eyes as they departed, then he made his way down the well-worn path the small copse of trees, where his parents took their eternal rest together. Now, all alone, he could allow the pent up grief to overwhelm him. Once again, he went back over his life with a litany of what ifs.

Had he only allowed things to pass, perhaps his father and mother would still be alive this very day, coddling grandchildren. Once again a litany of possibilities passed before him. In the end through the tears, the will of the eternal surpassed understanding. When he allowed himself to think back over the long parade of people he'd sent to their respective rewards, he could only view that as a positive purging of predators upon mankind. Then he allowed himself to dwell upon his present circumstances and the inexplicable way he survived to this very day, saved by someone he barely knew. Eventually he began to feel the presence of Motale and Appolonia enveloping him, as the tears flowed freely once again. They were both speaking to him in that celestial voice reserved for the truly righteous. Telling him not to concern himself with his past but to concentrate on the future and live his life. They were together at last and happy.

When next he looked up, he glanced at his watch which read a few minutes after four in the afternoon. He rose slowly to his feet and bid his parents a fond goodbye, vowing to from now on, visit them annually.

The trip back to Paris, the following day on the train reminded him of his trek long ago somewhat paralleling the same route. It almost seemed like yesterday. The following morning he called the General to see if he was available to join him in his visit to see Madeleine. The General just returned and agreed to arrive at his hotel the following day in his General's staff car.

As they were driven to the cemetery in Chantilly, Magellan related his visit to the Chancellery in Madrid and his brief visit with the Cardinal and somewhat of his private moments with his parents. "It seems you have some very interesting connections in high places Sergeant", said the General affectionately, still referring to Magellan by the artificial cognomen his step daughter always referred to Nestor as, "My Sergeant"!

When they arrived at the cemetery, Nestor discovered that Madeleine's mother was only five plots away from her daughter, as each man went straight to the site of his beloved. As each man knelt down, by the grave of his beloved, both had reluctantly broken down in tears.

After a half an hour, the General stood erect saluting the site of his beloved, then making the sign of the cross, crisply turning to join Nestor. As he slowly approached he could see the Sergeant, as if in a silent conversation with the unseen. Standing silently behind him at some distance, he saw Nestor nodding his head as if in agreement, hearing the whispered words, 'My beloved', over and over. Finally he joined Nestor as they both knelt in homage. The General closed his eyes and saw an image of mother and daughter standing together smiling and holding hands whispering, 'Live your lives. We'll be together soon enough'!

Finally both men slowly turned and looked at each other, each one's eyes puffed up with emotion as they rose together, each made the sign of the cross and crisply saluted, turning a military about face and walked back to the waiting staff car. As the car drove back into the city the General offered the following, "It seems they have both told me a few things Sergeant. First, that during your stay in Paris, you are to find bivouac in my lodgings, as a favor to an old General more than anything else. Next, that I'm to do whatever I can to see that you are well situated in an endeavor that will yield only good things for one and all and lastly from Madeleine herself, as well as her mother, you are to allow someone deserving into your heart and produce children. While they may not formally be considered part of my estate, I wish to be considered a beloved Uncle. Is that possible Sergeant"?

"Mon General, Madeleine said the very same thing"!

"Good. Then things are settled. Driver, take us back to Paris, so we can dine at the Rive' Gauche"!

www.ingramcontent.com/pod-product-compliance
Lightning Source LLC
Chambersburg PA
CBHW031510010826
48973CB00012B/16